Whom God Hath Sundered

Whom God Hath Sundered

Oliver Onions

MINT EDITIONS

Whom God Hath Sundered was first published in 1910.

This edition published by Mint Editions 2021.

ISBN 9781513282879 | E-ISBN 9781513287898

Published by Mint Editions®

 MINT
EDITIONS

minteditionbooks.com

Publishing Director: Jennifer Newens
Design & Production: Rachel Lopez Metzger
Project Manager: Micaela Clark
Typesetting: Westchester Publishing Services

Contents

IN ACCORDANCE WITH THE EVIDENCE

PART I
HOLBORN

I

It seems strangely like old times to me to be making these jottings in Pitman's shorthand. I was surprised to find I remembered as much of it as I do, for I dropped it suddenly when Archie Merridew died, and Archie's clear, high-pitched voice was the last that ever dictated to me for speed, while I myself have not dictated since Archie took down his last message from my reading. That will be—say a dozen years or more ago next August. It may be a little more, or a little less. Nor, since I do not keep it as an anniversary, does the day of the month matter.

Either in my rooms or his, we had a good deal of this sort of practise together about that time, young Archie and I—reading aloud, taking down and transcribing. I am wrong in speaking of my "rooms" though; I had only one, a third-floor bedroom near the very noisiest corner of King's Cross. It was just opposite one of these running electric advertisements that changed from green to red and from red to green three times every minute; you know them; there are plenty of them now, but they were new then. The street was narrow; this horrible thing was at a rounded corner not more than five and twenty yards away; and even when my lamp was lighted it still tinged my ceiling and the upper part of the wall above my bed, red and green, red and green—for I had only a little muslin half-curtain and no blind, and if I wanted to read in bed I had either to turn my lamp out until I had undressed or else to undress in a corner by the window side of the room, because of being overlooked from across the way. I don't think there were any other lodgers in the house. It was a "pub," the "Coburg," but I could get on to the staircase without going through the bars on the ground floor, and always did so. The rather sour smell of these lower parts of my abode reached me up my three flights of stairs, but I had got used to that. It was the noise that was the worst (except, of course, that red and green fiend of an advertisement)—the noise that greeted me when I woke of a morning, awaited me when I came back from Rixon Tebb & Masters' at night, and often became maddening when, at half-past twelve, they clashed to the iron gates of the public-house and turned the topers out into the street, to fraternise or quarrel for half-an-hour or more beneath my window.

But we worked more in Archie Merridew's rooms than in mine. "Rooms" is correct here. He had the whole top floor of a house near the

Foundling Hospital, a pretty house with a fan-lighted ivy-green door, early Georgian, a brightly twinkling brass knocker and bellpulls, and a white-washed area inside the railings to make the basement lighter. His folks lived at Guildford; his father paid his rent for him, thirty-eight pounds a year; and his pleasant quarters under the roof had everything that mine hadn't—he could sit outside on the coped leads when the weather was hot, draw up cosily to a fireplace shaped something like a Queen Anne teapot when it was cold, and the ceiling, truncated along one side, didn't begin to turn red and green the moment the twilight came.

It gives me a shiver to think how atrociously poor I was in those days. More and more of that too comes back with the half-forgotten shorthand. I don't mean that I've ever forgotten that I used to be poor; it's the depth and degradation I mean and that—this will seem odd to you presently, as it seems suddenly odd to me as I write it—that memory is still more horrible to me than anything else I have ever known. My having got rich since doesn't wipe it out. If I were to become as rich as Rockefeller I should never forget the rages of envy, black and deep and bitter, that used sometimes to take me when I thought of Archie Merridew's circumstances and my own.

I have got riches as I have got everything else—*everything*—I ever wanted, by attention to detail. You'll probably agree with me by-and-by that by "attention to detail" I mean rather more than most men do when they give this advice to young men about to start in life. I remember they used to give us, as it were, the empty form and shell of this maxim at the Business College, the place in Holborn Archie and I attended; but you've got to have been down into the pit and come back again before you realise the terrible force there is in these truisms. And no less in doing things than undoing them afterwards (when that has been necessary) have I planned to the very last *minutiæ*. If I have never seemed a particularly busy man, that has been because I have always disliked being seen in the act of doing a thing. And where I have passed my trail is obliterated.

Archie Merridew and I were only half contemporaries. He was younger than I by a good seven years—was, as a matter of fact, only twenty-three when he died. And in nearly everything else we were as sharply contrasted as we were in our fortunes. Indeed, we were much more so, for while I miserably coveted that thirty-eight pound upper floor of his near the Foundling Hospital, my faith in myself and my ambition would have helped me over that. Physically, we were as different as we could be. My almost gigantic size made me, in my cramped red and green lighted apartment, an enormously overgrown squirrel in the smallest of cages; but to Archie's rather dandified little dapperness his series of roof chambers was spacious as a palace. Mentally we diverged even more. I was taciturn, he lively as one of the crickets that used to chirp behind his little Queen Anne teapot of a fireplace. And as for luck—well, if luck ever so much as nodded to me in those days, it seemed to change its mind and to pass by on the other side, while he seemed to pull things off the more easily the more recklessly he blundered.

And he had his people at Guildford, while I had never a soul in the world.

I don't know how we contrived to hit it off as well as, on the whole, we did. Perhaps that too was part of his lucky disposition—he could get along even with me. He always spread some sort of a weak charm about him, and this charm always disarmed me even, when to all intents and purposes he was merely rubbing in my horrible poverty. He would tell me, as if I wasn't already eating my heart out about it, that it was about time I made an effort—that *he* wasn't going to remain in those stuffy diggings of his all *his* days—and that if he had only half my brains he'd be up somewhere pretty high in a very short time (as he probably would had he lived)—all this, you understand, for my good, the cigarette gummed to his prettily shaped upper lip wagging as he talked, and with the best intentions in the world. He was quite devoted to me; would tell me how he had told other people about those extraordinary brains of mine; and he never dreamed (though it was not long before I began to) that our respective ages were even then making of our companionship a hopeless thing. A lad of seventeen may attach himself for a time to a man whose years number twenty-four of bitterness and exclusion, but they will part company again before the one is twenty-three and the other thirty.

I was only an evening student at the Business College, while Archie spent his days there. Often enough he did not turn up in the evening at all; indeed, he only began to do so with unfailing regularity some time after Evie Soames had put her name down for the social evening course of lectures on Business Method. Evie Soames was a day student too, though only on three days in the week, Mondays, Wednesdays, and Fridays; and the lectures on Method were given in the evening because they were specially addressed to those who, like myself, were employed during the day, and deemed to be ripe for the more advanced instruction. I don't think Archie was very much wiser for Weston's (our lecturer) efforts, but he was genuinely grateful to me for my explanations of them afterwards, and would pat me on the shoulder affectionately, and tell me he couldn't understand why everybody else didn't see what a rare good sort I was. That was his backhanded idea of a compliment.

I think, in those early days of mine, I hated pretty well everything and everybody; and I cannot better show you how little I found to love than by giving you, before I go on with my tale, an account of my day at that period of my life—any day taken at random will do.

I had to be at Rixon Tebb & Masters' by nine, why, I don't know, since nobody else of any account whatever turned up much before half-past ten. But eight of us had to be there by nine o'clock, and I will tell you how our eight had been got together.

You know—or don't you know?—that there are firms that contract for the supply of "office labour" of all grades, from the messenger boy to the beginning of the confidential clerks; holusbolus, in the lump, as much of it or as little as you please. You pay, if you are an employer, a certain number of hundreds a year, and the agency does the rest. One down, t'other up; sack one man, and telephone for another. The agency's supply, at the maximum of a pound a week, is practically unlimited, and the firm escapes all personal responsibility in regard to its staff.

I was one of these consignments of labour—or rather an eighth of one. I don't know now what I did. I know that I addressed envelopes and checked columns of figures and lists of names, quite devoid of meaning to me, and got eighteen shillings a week for it. There was no chance that I should ever get more than eighteen shillings. Ask for nineteen and the telephone rang, the agency was informed of your request, and. . . well, three times I had seen that happen.

One chance of escape, indeed, we had; the firm was clever enough to allow us that. It was by way of what I may call the permanent junior clerkship. The permanent junior clerk was, as it were, breveted with the rank of the real clerks in the inner office; and so was hope dangled over the heads of eight of us. There was the junior clerkship amongst the eight of us. That or nothing.

I need hardly say that jealousy, espionage, and scheming besmirched our souls.

Well (to continue my account of my day), I addressed envelopes or read aloud from interminable lists until one o'clock, and then I lunched. This we were not allowed to do in the office, so that usually I ate from a paper bag in one of the quieter streets, or else had a scone and milk at an A.B.C. shop round the corner in Cheapside. I was alone. My fellow-stuff from the agency, always on the lookout for a pretext of mistrust, found one in my (I admit) uncommon face. I put in the time until two, when I was not smothering up annoyance at those who would turn round to stare at a man who had been made half a head taller than the rest of the world, in wondering whether those about me were as rich or worse off than I, and whether they were able to procure a bath as cheaply and easily; and then I returned to Rixon Tebb & Masters' again. At six-thirty I proceeded home, washed, and went out to dinner. I dined at one of the establishments near the corner of Pentonville Road; you have seen them, there is an arrangement of gas-jets behind a steamy window, and, in galvanised iron trays, sausages and onions and saveloys fry. The proprietor of the "pull-up" fetched my dinner out of the window on the prongs of a toasting fork, and I ate it in a small matchboard compartment, or, when these *cabinets particuliers* happened to be all pre-occupied, at an oilcloth-covered table that ran down the middle of the shop. During and after my meal I read the whole of *The Echo*—I was allowed as a habitué to retain my seat longer than the casual diner. But on the nights on which I took a bath (did I say I sponged on Archie Merridew for this convenience, carrying my clean shirt in a paper that also served for the wrapping-up of the one I had removed?), I added to my obligation by supping with him also, and then we walked on to the Business College together. My clothes I bought in Lamb's Conduit Street, my boots in Red Lion Passage. I had always the greatest difficulty in getting a fit in either. At one time I had the misfortune to make myself very unpopular among the proprietors of a row of barrows not far from Southampton Row. This was over the purchase of a collar, and the cub under the naphtha lamp had made some joke or other about the uncommon size I required, saying that the horse collars were to be had in St Martin's Lane. The blow under the ear I gave him was heavier than I intended; I am afraid I broke his jaw, and I avoided the street for a long time.

After the class, I either continued my studies, as I have said, with young Merridew, or else took a walk. In this again I was always alone. I went far afield. If I went west, I usually turned along Great Russell and Guildford Streets, but the moths, English and foreign, of the half light of this last thoroughfare caused me at one time to take the way of Holborn and Gray's Inn Road. The nickname they gave me, they also gave, I don't doubt, to fifty men besides myself, but it seemed somehow to attach itself more conspicuously to me because of my general conspicuousness. It was that of the mysterious and ubiquitous author of a series of unelucidated crimes as to the nature of which I need not be specific.

Then, when I had walked my fill, I returned to my cage opposite the red and green electric advertisement.

This is a fair sample of my days at that time.

II

There is a showy boot shop now where the Business College used to be; the new place is in Kingsway. There, in Kingsway, I am told they have methods and appliances undreamed of in my time—mechanical calculators, wonderful filing systems, elaborate duplicators, and lectures on Commercial and Political Economy and Mercantile Law—but the old Holborn curriculum included shorthand, typewriting, book-keeping, and lectures on method and not very much besides. When I left, I remember, they were just beginning, as a high novelty, advertisement-writing. Later, I myself took this class, though only for a few weeks.

Even then, I think, the Holborn place was condemned to come down. A second-hand book shop occupied the ground floor; and above the book shop window three columns, each of three bow windows, one for each floor, formed the frontage. The three bow windows of the top floor were ours. Inside, the place was small and inconvenient in the extreme. It had been a dwelling-house once, and the old fixtures still remained— dark cauliflower wallpapers, heavy ornamental gas-brackets, and little porcelain fittings by the fireplaces that still rang, in the second of the two rooms that had been knocked into one to form a lecture-room, a row of bells that resembled a series of interrogation marks.

Only four women attended the classes. The business woman was, comparatively speaking, a rarity then, nor can I quite make up my mind as to how much things have changed in this respect and how much they remain exactly as they were. They have certainly changed if it is all on account of her certificate that a young woman can now walk into an office and be promptly asked at what hour it will be convenient for her to begin her duties on the morrow; and, lacking certificates, three of our four students could hardly have fallen back on any natural diploma of personal charms. I mean, in a word, that Miss Windus, Miss Causton and Miss Levey were, to say the least, not remarkably pretty, though Miss Causton was beautiful as far as her figure and movements went.

But Evie Soames was very different. She was, in actual years, twenty; but she seemed still to stand among the debris of her teens as an opening tree stands over its sprinkling of delicate fallen sheaths in the spring. Both graces and awkwardnesses of an earlier time still clung, as it were, to her stem. She had, as I later learned, been at one school until she was seventeen, at a second school until she was nineteen, and now, after a year of indetermination and arrested development at home, was still further delaying her maturity by beginning again not very differently from the way in which she had begun at fourteen. She had, of course, picked up a number of unimportant acquirements by the way, but had never, in those days when I first knew her, given it a thought that Evie Soames was a person Evie Soames might well have some natural curiosity about. She moved, neither woman nor schoolgirl, among the charts and files and dusty ledgers of the Business College, slender, dark, necked like a birch, and with eyes than which, when she looked suddenly round, the flash of a negro's teeth was not whiter.

I have told you how my days were passed, but not yet said anything about my dreams. As I cannot speak of Evie Soames apart from these I will do so as briefly as I can.

Whatever else in my life I may have been, I have not, even in my dreams, been a sensualist. It might in some respects have been better for me if I had. But so far was I from that that I have even been charged (though the charge is really as wide of the mark as it could well be) with a certain inhumanity; by which I mean, not cruelty, but—how shall I express it?—a certain inaccessibility to the ordinary human relation. And I do not believe the woman lives who, given her choice of these two interpretations of the word, would not prefer the former. Only in the latter does she foresee her final defeat.

Therefore, when at midday in Cheapside, or in Guildford Street as I returned from my lonely rambles, or in Holborn or Oxford Street at the hour when shops and offices turned out their human contents, male and female, after the day's work, I watched the pattering feet on the pavements, I was not stirred as the fleshly stockbrocker or conscienceless "blood" is stirred. (You must allow me this generalisation; you know what I mean.) My eyes did not meet other eyes as seeking acquaintance. I never, in train or tram or 'bus, set off my vacation of my seat for a woman against the bow or thanks I might receive. I never, even at my loneliest, held a waitress or attendant in talk for any satisfaction I had in her nearness. Whatever I have learned from crowds, crowds have had nothing of mine. Nor, my heavy and immobile appearance notwithstanding, was I (I affirm this) a solitary because I was refused acquaintanceship. I was a solitary because I refused it.

But what I refused in the streets by day, I could not sleep for seeking when I lay down at night. What I sought I did not and do not know; I was only conscious of a hunger within myself that, not being satisfiable by the eye-profferings and other partial prettinesses of the crowd, were never offered that sustenance. I have heard this hunger described as a Divine Discontent, but that is to beg a question of some magnitude. It might be a very different thing from that. It might just conceivably be an Infernal Discontent. Or it might, in the case of a man who regarded neither God nor devil—But I wander. This, I say, was my dream, and I shared it with no sensualist.

Of course you have already guessed why I say all this. . . guessed what happened. Between the commonnesses under the street lamps which I spurned, and those dreams that were ever unseizably beyond my most ardent reaching forth, I fell in love with Evie Soames.

There are, I know, men in whom a grim and uncompromising aspect is so richly compensated for by other gifts that, like John Wilkes, they may fairly brag that with fifteen minutes' start they would out-distance in a woman's favours the most regular-featured buck in London. Therefore (if I may use a "therefore" without egregiousness) it troubled me little that Miss Windus, not to speak of her two companions, Miss Causton and Miss Levey, found me unattractive. In that coin I could have repaid her, had I wished, with interest. Since I did not wish, my attitude was one of fully-armed reserve. All three of these women seemed to me to be for ever proclaiming, if not in words, yet in everything but words, that men, *as* men, have worldly opportunities given them by a sort of favouritism, and as a kind of present for their circumspection in getting themselves born men—as if in this world either men or women ever got anything they were not quick enough or strong enough or callous enough to seize for themselves. Miss Windus in especial, a sharp-featured woman of twenty-eight, with apertures like little scalene triangles out of which her eyes peered with an expression quizzical and weak and yet perky and self-confident at the same time (as if she was saying perpetually to herself, "We may as well hear what *this* one has to say for himself!") struck me as being the final word in self-importance and inefficiency.

The top-heavy little Jewess, Miss Levey, was a very broker for gossip and tattle, and the remarks she occasionally made about others to me were quite enough to warn me that she would make equally free with myself to others. Both she and Miss Windus seemed to shout aloud the very sex-difference the existence of which they seemed at the same time to be denying. They "could not think of giving trouble" when one or other of the forty men placed a chair or adjusted a light or carried a

Remington for them; but they would have known how to show their sense of the absence of such attentions all the same.

I do not know that Miss Causton pleased me very much more, but she at any rate moved with a wonderful physical harmonious grace and flow. If one might judge from her hands and wrists (a business certificate on which she ever bestowed the most sedulous care) she did not come from quite the same social level as the other two—was, perhaps, the daughter of a doctor who had married his house-keeper, or of a decent governess whose decency had not prevented her from running off with a groom; but I made no attempt to unravel either this riddle or any other that her rather contemptuous grey eyes might contain. The attitudes she took in reaching down a book from a shelf or passing her arm about the waist of one of the other girls when they assembled for gossip were all I wanted of her, and those began and remained a purely æsthetic satisfaction.

Therefore there could hardly have been a more complete contrast than there was between these apparently a-sexual yet in reality excessively sex-conscious women and my delicate unawakened Evie Soames. She made no more difficulty about giving me a "Good-evening," or "Good-night" than she did with the rest of the world; and though for a long time our speech stopped at that, it was yet as much as I had with any other woman whomsoever. That I should get even thus much of what everybody else in the world seemed to get as a matter of course came so gently and softly over me that I did not dream of a worse misery that might lurk hidden within it, and in those early days of my love a mother would not have fought more wildly for her babe than I would have turned on any who had offered to come between me and even this sparse sweetness that had come for the first time into my life.

III

The events I am now about to relate occurred during those early days, while I was still content to possess my dreams, as if as long as I closed my eyes the world would stand still about me.

One November night, as the series of lectures on Method was drawing to a close, I returned with Archie Merridew to his rooms, silent, but exceedingly happy. The cause of my happiness will not greatly excite you, it had been no more than Evie's "Good-night, Mr. Jeffries," given me as I had waited on the stairs of the college for young Merridew, who had lingered behind to ask Weston something or other.

I had heard them coming down from the landing above, and, looking up, had seen the trail of Miss Causton's long grey coat and Miss Windus's blue and green plaid skirt and her gloved hand on the shaky old rail. I ought to say that the western-most of the three pillars of bow windows I have mentioned as forming the Holborn frontage of the college was the one that lighted the various floors of the staircase, and if parties had ever been given in that old house before it had got quite so old, it is odds that the embrasure in which I had just then been standing, that of the first floor, had held a few palms in pots and a couple of figures on its low window-seat many a time. But that night it had only held myself, waiting in the shadow shaped like a coffin-shoulder that the globeless gas of the landing cast.

I had heard Miss Windus's little smothered exclamation. "*Oh!* . . . That man!" but instantly she had gone on talking in a higher voice. Certainly she had had reasonable colour for the pretence that she had not seen me—had I not happened to hear her exclamation.

And if I had heard it, so, of course, had Evie.

"Good-night, Mr. Jeffries," Evie had said as she had passed me, and Miss Windus also, as if suddenly discovering me, had given me quite a bright "Good-night!" Miss Causton also had given me a languid, almost insolent smile.

I was happy. I should probably have taken myself and my happiness off somewhere had it not been that that evening I had made use of Archie's bath, and had left in his place, besides that paper parcel I have mentioned, a notebook of which I had need. So I had returned with Archie, and, not intending to stay, had yet sat down, overcoated as I was, before his fire.

"Better take your coat off for a bit," Archie said. "I'd like a squint at your notes too, if you're not in a hurry."

The notes were part of our preparation for the examination in Method which was to be held shortly before Christmas. I threw apart, but still did not remove my coat, and Archie took up my notebook and read as he stood. Presently, feeling for a chair with his foot, he sat down, still reading the notes.

He looked up from time to time, but the questions he put barely interrupted my reverie. I stared at the fire in the pretty old-fashioned grate. He had no gas up there; his cardboard lamp-shade, green outside and a little heat-browned inside, stood on a chenille-clothed table; and he had given the shade a tilt for his convenience in reading. Thus the fireplace end of the room lay in a sort of irregular parabola of illumination. There were bright circles on the ceiling above the chimney of the lamp; then came spaces of cosy gloom; and below, in the pleasant light, were his arm-chairs, his small book-shelf, and, the rail of it catching the firelight, his high perforated brass fender. In the middle of a great cam of light that lay over the dimity-papered wall between his sitting and bed rooms, his dressing-gown, hanging from a hook in the bedroom door, made a grotesquely human-shaped shadow.

By-and-by, with the book on his knee and his eyes still fixed on it, Archie began mechanically to unlace his boots. I looked up as he reached for his slippers, and then resumed my reverie.

I was glad that Kitty Windus, whether she realised it or not, had been made the subject of an innocently awkward little snub. I couldn't stand the woman. I couldn't stand it that, ignoring my existence when she could, she spoke to me, when she did speak, with a false vivacity that only enhanced the effect of her passing over at other times. And lest you should think I was wasting my detestation on a rather insignificant object, I must ask you again to remember what my days were. The whole Scheme of Things seemed to be against me; but there is not much relief to be had from taking a blind fling at the Scheme of Things. A man with a grudge against the world will be very likely indeed to take that grudge out of the nearest person. I was not prosperous enough to have much time to waste on human charities. So, in my resentful hours, I took it mercilessly out of one against whom, in my calmer moments, I had no grudge except that she was not a thousand miles away. And if she had been a thousand miles away, I should have vented my bitterness on somebody else. I had to get rid of it somehow.

OLIVER ONIONS

But if my thoughts gave Miss Windus more of this than she fairly deserved, perhaps Evie Soames got more in another sort than she deserved either. There was not one of the few stray graces and sweetnesses I had ever known that did not accrete to and abide about the thought of her. No generous emotion, no human impulse I had ever experienced, but came with adoration and rich gifts with which to exalt her. In my heart I lighted tapers about her image. I did not ask myself whether she had supplanted my dreams, existed side by side with them, or was indeed my dreaming made truth. I did not wonder what she might have been in another man's dreaming, nor whether, apart from the dreaming of some man, she existed spiritually at all. I only knew that the fire inside Archie Merridew's fender was not warmer than that central warmth that seemed to steal (as if there also some bud-sheath had yielded) about my heart as I pictured again her sapling-straight figure, the flash of her turning eyes on the landing, and the tone in which she had bidden me good-night three quarters of an hour before. I leaned back as it were in some longed-for luxurious resting-place of the heart. I do not know the origin of the tears that gathered in my eyes.

Suddenly Archie threw the book on to the table and stretched himself. He gave a yawn and put his feet on the fender.

"Oh, I'm sick of work for today!" he said. "When are you going to start smoking?" he added as he drew out a cigarette-case.

I answered something or other—it didn't matter what, since my lovely moment had gone with the breaking in of his voice.

"Oh, well! . . ." he laughed, lighting up. Then, glancing at the blowing end before throwing his match into the fender, he said: "I say—what a jolly sort of girl that Miss Soames seems to be!"

As the cold of a spring night freezes the newly mounting sap of a tree, so I felt some sweet and vigorous change suddenly arrested in my heart.

"Wh-who?" I said. I had to make two attempts at it.

He laughed.

"Oh, of course—I forgot, girls don't interest you. Like your not smoking, I suppose. Hadn't noticed there were any girls at the college—only see text-books and Remingtons. . . Well, not to spring it on you too suddenly, there *are* four girls there, three of 'em rather sticks, but the fourth a ripper. What a rum chap you are!" he concluded with another laugh.

He had drawn his chair still closer to the fire, and now sat with his feet, not on the fender, but half-way up one of the pilasters that supported the chimneypiece. As he kicked off one slipper and began to warm one small foot on the iron-work just inside the pilaster, his profile was turned to me; but I didn't at first risk stealing a look at it for fear of meeting his eyes. Stealthily, however, and moving my head as little as possible, I did so. It was a pretty profile—fair curly hair thick on the crown, his head rather high at the back and of a long shape to the chin, good nose, pleasantly curved mouth—the head of a decent enough but quite unremarkable youngster of twenty-two. He was neatly dressed in a grey stripe, and wore a black-bound red waistcoat with brass buttons. I say he was decent enough, and so he was: I knew he knew the taste of whiskey, but don't think he drank it very often. "Good wholesome beer," he used to say with an air of experience, "was more his mark"; but even then I think the experience was more that of his companions than his own. You wouldn't have said there was much harm in him, and he would probably have to spend his allowance unwisely once or twice before he learned to spend it wisely.

I made the moving of my chair an excuse for getting him better under observation.

"Oh yes, awfully jolly," he repeated, blowing a plume of smoke through which the firelight shone rustily. "Fun. . . no end of fun. . . rather! . . ."

Then he smiled, and the smile came and went and came again as he smoked.

I don't know why, up to that moment, I had never thought of it—never thought of how it might already be or might presently become. I suppose the reason was that a man cannot hold the commerce I held with dreams without to some extent losing his touch of actuality. But now, at last, I was awake enough. . . As if the room had turned colder I pulled my coat a little more closely about me.

It was not then that that heart of mine, which I have likened to a bud suddenly arrested in the moment of its unfolding, became more likenable to a grenade with its fuse waiting exposed for the spark that should bring destruction. . .

But I was quite calm. For the matter of that, I am never anything else when it comes to the point. My angers have served their purpose when they have brought me to the point. I *use* anger. . . Therefore, though I knew already that three careless words of his had opened an

OLIVER ONIONS

immeasurable abyss between us, I was able to speak to him without a tremor, from my chair at one side of his hearth to him in his own at the other.

"You mean Miss——What's her name?"

"Soames," he informed me. "You know—that young girl—you must have seen her. . . Yes, full of fun. . . I laughed. . . I did laugh!"

From the way in which he still laughed there must have been a specific occasion for his mirth. I knew of none such. I wished to know, however, and I also wished to know what he meant by "fun." Young men mean so many things by "fun," and it—But I stifled something within my breast almost before it was born there. When I spoke, my voice was as steady as it has ever been in my life; but the devil, watching a soul that hesitates on the point of sin, does not watch more closely than I watched that fair boy with the cigarette dangling from his upper lip.

"Ah, yes, I've seen her. . . *Pretty, too*," I hinted.

But he put, if he heard, her prettiness aside. He chuckled again.

"I went last Sunday to the Zoo, you know," he said. "They were spending the week-end in town—my folks. And I saw her there. Or rather, I didn't see her at first, it was Mumsie who saw her. 'I think there's somebody you know,' she says to me, and I looked, and there she was, bowing to me. Then up came pater—he'd dropped behind somewhere—and blest if he didn't know her aunt—she lives with her aunt—they have rooms in Woburn Place. So we all went round together. . . I started the fun by saying how like old Weston the secretary bird was; so we went round looking for likenesses—raked up everybody we knew—" He stopped, suddenly.

He wouldn't, had he been a year or two older, have pulled himself up quite so sharply. It is true he didn't go so far as to colour, stammer, or bite his lip; but his meaning, or his inadvertence, or whatever you like to call it, could hardly have been plainer had he done all these things. An anecdote was related to me not so very long ago by an agent I employ to advise me in my picture-buying. It was of the most sardonic of our caricaturists, and this merciless artist had (so the story ran) refused to caricature a certain person, giving as his reason that, while a vain or over-praised or too consciously handsome face was fair game for his ironic pencil, a face already heavily visited by nature went free. But for Archie Merridew's sudden embarrassed check I might have imagined that *my* own visage might have gone free also. It is, after all, not repellent. I bear quite a strong resemblance to at least one public man whose photographs appear in the illustrated papers—a distinguished scientist. My stature is the most striking thing about me, and if your humour takes that turn you can find remote suggestions of any number of people at the Zoo.

I made, however, no sign, and he, judging his clumsiness to have passed unnoticed, went on:

"Funny the pater knowing her aunt like that, wasn't it? Rather fun though. Mumsie said she must come down to Guildford for a few days and stay with us; if she does I shall go home that week-end—you bet!"

My answer gave me no pain. It came, I think, out of just such an automatic reflex as causes an "opening" in conversation to call forth its own obvious reply. It would have been more marked not to say it than to say it, and as I am telling you, in my state of still tension it didn't hurt.

"Oh!" I said. "And when does one congratulate you?"

"What d'you mean?" he asked.

"Why, on your engagement."

Instantly I knew I had said the right thing. There was nothing either false or forced about the little exclamation he made, half scoff, half laugh. His face was clear as crystal. By "fun" he meant, simply, mere physiological laughter, the bubbling-up of the high spirits of his years. Human resemblances at the Zoo are quite enough to call up this purely functional giggling. She was "fun" (the odds were a thousand to one) as his sister might have been fun; with a certain freshness and sense of discovery perhaps, but otherwise not very differently. In spite of the sequel, I still think I am right in making this statement.

"Don't be an idiot!" he said. . . "I say, Jeff, I couldn't quite make out that about indexing and cross-references tonight. Did he mean that the cross-references are a sort of double entry for when the subjects overlap, or what?"

But there was still something I wished to verify.

"Who?" I asked. "The—secretary bird?"

This time I think he did colour faintly, but as he had swung his legs down from the fireplace and was reaching for my notebook again I could not be quite sure.

"Pass me the book," I said.

For the next quarter of an hour I gave him as collected and lucid an explanation of his difficulties as if I had had no other care in the world.

Then I lifted myself up. I buttoned my coat, put the notebook into my pocket, and briefly recapitulated what I had told him.

"Thanks, awfully," he said gratefully, when I had finished. "You are a brick. *You* ought to give the lectures instead of old Weston. I'm sure if I pass this exam it will be all you. Must you go?"

"Must."

"Well—so long—I think I'll make a few notes myself before I forget again."

And, still master of myself, I left him arranging papers and feeling in his inkstand for a pen.

IV

I do not know but what I might still have retained control of myself when I got out into the street again; I do not know, because I didn't try. Instead, no sooner had I got away from him than I went temporarily all to pieces. I remember I passed up Charlotte Street and turned into Mecklenburgh Square; and there I leaned against the railings of the garden that occupies the middle of the Square. I stood with my shoulder against them, looking stupidly down at my feet. There was a thin and melancholy mist; the lights of the boarding-houses and nursing-homes of the east side of the Square struggled through it with difficulty, and presently I found that my foot was playing absently with a few sodden plane-tree leaves that had drifted against the kerb.

Slowly, as I stood there, my stupidity gave place to a dull anger. I don't think it was anger against anybody in particular; it was as objectless as it was useless and exhausting. But if you have had that gall in your mouth that makes all the world taste bitter, you will understand my miserable rage. This changed presently to a shivering, weeping rage The wide portalled door of a house opposite opened, and a servant-girl came down the shallow steps to post a letter; I daresay she supposed I was unwell or a drunkard; and a passer-by might have concluded that I had an assignation with her, or had just had a quarrel.

Then, when I had had a little ease of my anger, I pulled myself together and banished it again. Now that I had come, tardily enough, out of my fool's paradise of the past weeks, I had other things than purposeless anger to think of. I moved away from the railings; the maid, returning from the posting of her letter, quickened her steps to avoid me; and I walked slowly northeastward through the Square.

Quickly I became calmer still. Soon I was calm enough to recognise that I needed this. "What," I said ironically to myself, thunder-struck at a thing so very surprising! "Did you think that because your head was in the clouds. . . come, come, you'd better look at the thing; you mayn't have any too much time, you know; if I were you I'd take a walk and think it out."

I turned into Grays Inn Road, and began to take my own advice.

While I had no reason to suppose that she had fallen in love with him, I knew almost for a certainty that he had not with her. He was not at that stage yet. Already he was nibbling at other pleasures, and with a youngster of his kind one or two nibbles mean three or four. They may even mean ten or twelve. So far so good. I was still in time. I was, in fact, so far beforehand that, of the three of us, I was probably the only one who knew, not what had happened (which was nothing) but what might happen—which was everything. That I took for the starting-point of my consideration.

And I saw that that, at the outset, was an enormous advantage to me. Not only could I watch events, but I could watch them to infinitely better purpose that I knew what to look for. They, when it came—the "it" I had in my mind—(I ought rather to say did I suffer it to come) would not, in the bewildering wonder of it, know what had overtaken them; while I, by a timely use of care and skill, might even turn to advantage those disadvantages of mine which, huge as a church, might have been deemed to outweigh everything else. No more perfect cover for hidden motion could have been devised than I already possessed. Who suspects, of anything, one whom to suspect would on the face of it be absurd? I could, did I find this necessary, use practically the whole of my conspicuous life and narrow circumstances as a screen.

I reached the top of Gray's Inn Road, crossed to St Pancras Station, and, following the line of coal merchants' offices on the left side of the road, plunged into the shadows of the Somers Town arches. It was there that I thought of another thing that I must interrupt my meditation to acquaint you with.

You may have wondered why, if all young Merridew said about my brains was true, I had still, after some years as an agency clerk at Rixon Tebb & Masters', not been able to get away from the place. Well, the answer to that is involved in a hundred other things that have ended, after fifteen years, in my now being able to write this chapter of my personal history at a great square mahogany and leather writing-table, with two softly-shaded electric standards upon it, and, containing it, a lofty panelled study, rich and quiet, with a carpet soft as thymy turf and my pictures and carvings and cabinets mirrored in floor-borders, brown and deep as the pools of my Irish trout stream. You do not want the whole of that long story. I will tell you as much as is necessary here. The rest I may tell at some other time.

The truth was that I *had* left Rixon Tebb & Masters'—had left the place, and had achieved the seeming miracle of being permitted to return. Such a marvel was without precedent, and I cannot say that it had been accomplished altogether by my own contrivance. I said a little while ago that there were eight of us, had over in a lump from the agency; I also said that only by way of the junior clerkship was any advancement possible from that slavery of addressing envelopes that might have been for company circularisation or might have been sent over in shiploads to the Flushing and Middleburg book-makers for all we knew; and I had had the signal luck—I forgot this when I said that luck had always passed me by on the other side—to present myself for reappointment, without any hope whatever of getting it, at the very moment when Polwhele had succeeded to this post.

How Polwhele had chanced to be occupied as he had been occupied when I had presented myself I understand only too well. Sneaking, prying, slandering, peaching—you didn't become Rixon Tebb & Masters' junior clerk without having been through the mill of all this and more. Poor worm, he had got so used to it that he couldn't help it. Having attained to the junior clerkship, he was going to work up through the seniors by the same means, I suppose, and the means he had been making use of, at the moment of my coming upon him, had been the furtive rummaging of a waste-paper basket that had come—I knew this by the pattern of it—from Mr. Masters' private office.

It had been, of course, the perfect opportunity for me, who was subdued to sneaking and peaching also. I had leaned my elbow on the brass rail of a tall desk and stood looking down on him—such a long way down it seemed—he was on his knees.

"Hallo, Polwhele!" I had suddenly said. "Going to put Samson Evitt out of business?" And then I waited to see how he took it.

I don't suppose you've ever heard of Samson Evitt. He has been a solicitor; at that time he described himself as a waste-paper dealer; and what he really did, and for all I know does still, was to buy up, through a hundred miserable agents, and on the chance of coming upon some private letter or secret draft, the contents of such receptacles as Polwhele's fingers had been deep in at that moment.

"Going to start in Samson's line, are you, Polwhele?"

The colour of his face had changed as swiftly as that of the electric advertisement opposite my bedroom at King's Cross. He had gone as white as chalk. I had known perfectly well that he wasn't going to sell anything to Samson Evitt, but was merely playing his own hand with the firm; but he'd had no business at all with Mr. Masters' waste-paper basket, and knew it. It had been rather horrible, but I had known I was as good as reinstated already.

OLIVER ONIONS

"I'm coming back, Polwhele," I had said.

He had not spoken—only looked at me with eyes full of terror.

"You're going to see that I come back, Polwhele," I had informed him.

"My God, Jeffries, you wouldn't have the heart."

"Oh no—not as long as I come back."

Then swiftly he had seen his years of shifts and meannesses all wasted unless. . .

"Oh my God! How can I do it?" he had groaned.

"I don't know, Polwhele."

I did not know, nor do I know now how he did it. Men do impossible things when they've got to. That had been on a Friday evening, at a quarter to seven (the zeal of a new junior clerk always kept him after the others had gone). I had given him Monday in which to see to it. On the Tuesday morning, at nine o'clock, I had been back at my envelope addressing again. These things have to be done sometimes. And I need hardly add that now Polwhele would have turned up at my funeral with a smile on his lips and a nosegay in his buttonhole.

Of the period between my leaving Rixon Tebb & Masters' and my return thither I will not speak. You may guess at the nature of its experiences from the fact that I was thankful to get back to my lists and addresses again.

It would have surprised my fellow-clerks, who saw in me one as listless as themselves, to learn with what unresting energy I had worked since then. I had resolved that my next leap from that frying-pan should not be into the fire, and the means by which I was making sure of this was the Business College in Holborn. I knew my great natural gifts and the power that smouldered within me, but I had also learned, and in a school where the lessons were well driven home, that power and natural gifts were, for a man in my position, practically worthless unless they were supplemented and guaranteed. I had got to get myself certificated.

I don't know what certificates have come to mean nowadays, sometimes, I fear, very little. They seem to me to have lowered the standard with the utmost recklessness. I would not, in my own business, give a pound a dozen for some of these artificially achieved successes that are offered to me almost every day in the week, and it causes me no surprise whatever when I see the highly certificated also unemployed. . . But it was rather different then. Once more I have forgotten my luck and railed at the goddess. It was my luck to be certificated while certificates still had a value, and for a year and a half I had drifted through my occupation by day but worked with an almost demoniac energy by night in order that I might not miss a single one of these tickets of authenticity that it was possible for me to obtain. A First Honours in Method would now complete my equipment.

And, looking back now, I wonder how much superstition there was in it that I wanted all the changes I was planning to come at once. For I meant that the break, when it did come, should be clean and final. As long as I remained with Rixon Tebb & Masters' my wretched single room at King's Cross was quite good enough for an agency clerk; when I left Rixon Tebb & Masters' I would leave those quarters also. Until then, I don't think you could have dragged me out, so strongly had I this feeling. Superstition or what you like, it had, for me, the force of a large and wise, if not yet fully worked out strategy. They tried, of course, at the Business College in Holborn, just as they are now trying at the new place in Kingsway, to teach us this larger generalship of waiting, withholding, massing, concentration, and then the swift development and advance; but I don't think it was much good. You don't get these things in return for so many guineas a year in fees. But I felt their stirrings then. . . I hope I have made it plain that neither at the place in Kingsway, nor in my sordid lodgings over the public-house, nor under the arches of Somers Town that night, was I wasting my time.

And now, like a match to all that I had prepared and was preparing, had come the kindling thought of Evie Soames.

I remember I walked to Hampstead that night, revolving it all. Walking always steadies me, and by the time I had reached the Lower Heath the mechanical calculators at the new place in Kingsway do not work more coldly and mathematically than my brain had begun to work. The advantages I possessed, which had been the first thing to rush into my head, I allowed for the present to take care of themselves; I now envisaged my disadvantages.

You may imagine that these were terrifying. . . I counted them, and was unable to check my groans when, thinking I had come to the end of them, yet another sprang up, stabbing me as it were from behind. They might almost have been veritable assassins, springing out from behind the dark bushes and copses near the Vale of Health among which I wandered. . . Think of them! Think of them!

They, he and she, were of an age, or nearly; I seven years the senior of the elder of them. They met on three days a week at the college, met doubtless to snigger together over their "fun," only on three evenings could I see her. Her people apparently knew his; she would go down to Guildford, and my fancy might picture them, together there, taking walks, telling stories over the fire, laughing at chance resemblances at the Zoo. And all this time I should not cease for a moment to labour at that garden of my ambition above the brown mould of which not a green shoot yet showed. How (you must remember I was desperately facing the worst that could happen and not the best)—how could they help but fall in love? What would it be possible for me to do but to discover the thing after it had happened? And when it had happened, what was there then to be done?

But I need not force all this upon you. You will see for yourself. Look at it, then, and tell me where you would have conceived the odds to lie—with my possibly large-planning but certainly slow-executing brain, or with them and their opportunities and luck and gifts of circumstance and nature, demolishable singly perhaps, but well-nigh invincible in the sum of them?

I weighed it as I strayed and stubbled about the benighted Heath.

I returned from Hampstead at three o'clock in the morning. My horror of red and green had long since been switched off, and I got into bed during the only quiet interval that noisy and populous corner ever knew. I had now balanced advantages and disadvantages together, and was recapitulating the whole. Examining, setting aside, bringing forward again to re-examine in other aspects, setting aside again, checking, dismissing, estimating—my brain worked like a ticking instrument. Clocks struck, but still I pondered; and I was as free from anger now as if it had been another, not I, who had sought the support of the railings in Mecklenburgh Square.

And there dominated all my machination the single thought, that by no slip or carelessness or overlooked detail must they be made aware that I was watching them as a masked thief watches the uneasy sleeper upon the bed.

V

It was at Rixon Tebb & Masters' that I first began to know jealousy, or at least the image of it. I find I must say a little more about this place in which I spent my days at that time.

I have said that Polwhele hated me; but nobody loved anybody else at Rixon Tebb & Masters'. I have worked in offices that have been not bad fun at all; offices where the fellows formed a sort of family, as they did afterwards at the Freight & Ballast Company, with something not unlike the family bond, the family jokes, and an interchange each morning of the adventures of the night before not unlike the exchange of items of news from letters about a family breakfast-table; but there was nothing like that at Rixon Tebb & Masters'. There, one of us could scarcely glance up over the little brass rail at his desk-head without seeing, across the spaces where the green porcelain cones of the incandescents hung, another furtive pair of eyes meeting his own and looking almost guiltily away again. If the partners despised us for our cringing before them they were right; we were a despicable set. I don't think a friendship was ever struck up in the place. We hated, if for no other reason, than because each of us knew his neighbour to be as contemptible as he knew himself to be.

It was in this atmosphere that I wrapped myself about with the thought of Evie Soames. My routine work taxed my attention little; I could do it as well as it needed to be done and live a whole free inner life at the same time; and I was sometimes actually startled when, looking up after some lapse and interim in which I had seen nothing but the shape of Evie's birch-like neck and the brilliant motion of her eyes, I saw the crafty gaze of a fellow-clerk on my face. Once I met Sutt's eyes in this way; I knew his thought, namely, that he surmised the nature of mine; and he smiled, a mean sort of smile. He didn't smile twice, though, while I was there. I don't mean that I said or did anything, but I think he knew what my look meant. . . All the same there got about the office—or rather about the corners and lavatories and behind screens, for it never came nearer to me than that—the only joke I remember ever to have been born there—the joke that Jeffries had all the appearance of a man in love. I took the hint. Thenceforward, as far as I might, I did not allow the faintest flicker of an emotion to cross my face. And more than ever was I on my guard lest I should do so in a place where it would have mattered more than it did at Rixon Tebb & Masters'.

Then, long before I knew of any valid grounds for them, and before a brain less prospectively active than mine would as much as dreamed of them, came these jealousies. Perhaps, like my occasional angers and like that secret fragrant flame of my love, they were emotions at large, unattached to any person but bound sooner or later to become so attached, and already seeking a quarter in which to alight.

They wrung my heart. Hot flushes and rages sometimes came upon me with no warning whatever. Sometimes in the middle of a column of figures or a twelve-inch-high stack of addresses, a devil would slyly lift its head—the thought that while I sat there polishing my trousers on a tall stool and the wrist of my sleeve on my desk, he and my Evie were—where? . . . I have in a remarkable degree that most precious and most hideous of gifts, the gift of mental visualisation, at these times it would have its way with me. I would see them in those moments where I would and engaged how I would. Well nigh as clearly as I see the page before me, I would see him, long boyish head and fair curly hair, red waistcoat and cigarette, and turned-up trousers and all, now making pretexts that something was wrong with her typewriter, now carrying a specimen ledger for her, now choosing for himself a place from which he could watch her, or even passing on to her the explanations of knots and difficulties he had had the previous evening from myself. My fancy (my reason at these times its helpless slave) would dog them—past the general room into the lecture-room—thence to the back room where the charts and apparatus were kept—thence back again through the lecture room into the shorthand and typewriting and senior class rooms, and so throughout every corner behind our three Holborn bow windows. There were times when I used all my powers of concentration to see one of them without the other, and failed. . . And then the fit would pass and my steady reason would reassert itself. I would tell myself I was a fool to thrust knives into myself thus. She was merely that touchingly opening fair young tree; and as for him, if his young male swaggerings in the pride of his twenty-two years included any knowledge of girls at all, they were probably girls of a very different class from hers.

Then would come the other damnable series again, and the sweat would stand on my brow.

No wonder Sutt looked.

Yet I am not sure that, for the sake of certain purely heavenly hours, I would not go through it all again. Would you suppose that in that five-shilling room of mine, where I had to flatten myself against the wall before I could take my clothes off unseen—or as I dined on sausage and mashed at my reeking "pull-up"—or as I roamed the pavements in search of the physical exhaustion that should bring sleep—would you suppose that in these places and living this life I could have heavenly hours? Ah, but I could, and had! . . . I don't want you to think I am sentimentalising about it. The public-house downstairs had knocked a good many ideas about the sanctity of our common humanity out of my head. I never, in my fourpenny dining-place, looked at the drayman or porter at the next table and wondered whether he also knew the heights and abysses I knew. Doubtless he had or had had his own, but all is *not* comparative. There *are* grades in heaven and hell. I knew I stood out, exceptional, destined, marked for signal honour or for signal dishonour. I had no desire to persuade anybody else of this. These things are beyond proof. Attempt to prove them and you but prove their opposites.

And so literally was this slender dark creature "my life," that often at the college itself my resolution all but failed me. More (but not much more) woman than child, she seemed at these times—what shall I say?—not a wonder shrunk, but a receptacle strangely slight and tender for the mighty things preparing for her. At such moments I found myself looking years ahead—seeing many things over and behind us, and myself, perhaps, turning my power elsewhere. And that moved me more than all the rest. For my strength was ever being used for her. Service of her was the law of it, as I now knew it had been its origin. I sometimes had ado not to sob, when watching her young head bent over the page of a text-book, images of great and brooding protection of enfolding and strong and jealous wakefulness, filled my breast as I looked. I felt in those moments that for every hair of her head I could have killed a man and felt no compunction afterwards.

Evie caused me far more anxiety than Archie did. At all times Archie's vanities, quite as amusing to watch as those of any young girl, would blind him to much that lay an inch or two beyond the end of his nose. He was, moreover, deep in his examination work, and I had no doubt that, once the examinations were over, he would indulge himself in a mild little "burst" and flatter his seraphic self he was rather a devil in his way. But she was more difficult. For one thing, hers was a richer nature. She had, or would presently have, far more to give; and already

I saw that, as surely as Miss Windus was one of Life's takers, Evie Soames was one of Life's givers.

I watched—how I watched!—for the slightest of her unconscious betrayals; and, of course, by dint of watching I was able to find a thousand that presently vanished again. I drew trifling tremendous conclusions from the merest nothings. She could not make a gawky, captivating little movement but I would found something upon it, not a pretty coltish gesture but I had my inference to draw. The smile, perhaps, where lately the laugh would have been—the little check of recollection, even as she was perching herself with a tomboyish swing on the edge of a table, that she "was grown-up now"—slight little ceremoniousnesses, stilted little phrases and momentary forgettings again—I missed not one of these. My lovely, lovely flapper! Did you know that you were twenty different creatures in a week, each beyond words adorable until another swelling nodule yielded and allowed a peep of a yet inner tender and rosy heart?

Of course I see now that I was far too clever in all this. I had, in fact, taken the course that was least of all likely to tell me what I wanted to know. For, as a face seen daily shows no change and yet grows relentlessly older, so, because of my watching, she changed under my eyes and my eyes did not tell me she had changed. I have had in my time various things to say about "woman's intuition." I, like the rest of us, have set half of it down as guessing and the other half (the half that events falsify) as a convenient forgetfulness. Well, I hope I make amends when I admit now that in all this I owed my final enlightenment to a woman, and to the woman to whom I would least of all have been indebted—to Miss Windus.

It was on a Friday evening that this enlightenment came to me. Fridays were ever a pain to me, because of the three whole days that must elapse—five if she failed to appear on the Monday evening—before I could see Evie again. Believe me, the last minutes of those Friday evenings always cost me dearly in emotion; and in order that I might make the most of them I had some time before discontinued a former habit of mine—that of working in the senior students' classroom. By so doing I had forestalled any remarks on the fact that I was frequently to be found in the same room as Evie. And even then I knew I was lucky to escape Miss Levey's Hebrew intensiveness.

But on that Friday night I was restless. An absurd trifle had unsettled me (but I have told you how much such trifles meant to me)—nothing more than an alteration in Evie's way of arranging her hair. Until then it had been drawn back and massed in a thick little clump on her nape, showing beautifully the small round of her head; but now she had parted it (I did not think altogether more becomingly) in the middle, and had evidently been making desperate attempts to "wave" it. Certainly the change gave her at once a more adult air, which I supposed I should get used to, unless, as was likely, she changed it again in the following week. Her blouse also was new. It had a high lace collar up to her ears, and I didn't like it in the least. It was mere concealment, without concealment's charm.

I was restless. I had begun the evening by working, for once, in the senior classroom again; but presently, not happy where I was and not wishing to go straightway into the lecture-room where Evie sat, I had compromised by packing up my things and going into the room adjoining hers—the general room. The reference books were kept in the general room, and, presently, having need of one of these, I had crossed to the shelf and taken it down.

I ought to explain that these books were kept in three projecting bays, such as one sees in libraries, that stood out at right angles from the wall. Thus the books of each projecting wing faced both ways and between the bays there was just room enough for the short library ladder of three or four steps with the vertical staff to steady yourself by as you stood on it. As I could easily reach any book there without the ladder, I had passed the bay that contained it, and had taken up my place on the farther side of the wing nearest the window, where I stood with the open book in my hand. I forget what the book was.

As I stood I heard Miss Windus and Miss Causton come into the adjoining compartment.

I had no great interest in either of these women—I may say none, since I could not see Miss Causton's fluent hand; so, merely noting their arrival, I was continuing my reading when suddenly I heard the name of Evie Soames. It was Miss Windus who was speaking.

". . . Oh, I suppose so; in her way, of course—if that's all men want!" she was saying. "Don't you think?" This with a little acidulous rising inflection.

Then I heard Miss Causton's indolent voice in reply. From the way in which she spoke I fancied she was eating sweets. It had lately struck me that she ate more sweets than both the other girls together, and if it wasn't sweets it was something else.

"Don't ask *me*, my dear," she drawled. "*I* don't know what the creatures want."

"Of course not. They do seem to want such—odd—things. The way I'm looked at sometimes—I declare it makes me feel perfectly ashamed!" said Miss Windus. Why she said it I don't know. It was the purest hypocrisy, and it was not likely to impose on Miss Causton, who had a nonchalant, still humour of her own. . . But on second thoughts I don't know. I was not always sure, afterwards, when I got to know Miss Windus better, that she didn't really labour under some such delusion as this.

"Do they?" Miss Causton asked lazily. "They don't worry me much. So long ago since I've seen one that I've nearly forgotten."

There was a short pause, then:

"Really, they stare so," Miss Windus continued, "look one so out of countenance—one really doesn't know which way to turn!"

"No?" came Miss Causton's ironical dawdle. "Oh. . . with a chance, my dear. . . *I* should!" . . . I suppose she smiled as she said it. While appearing to lay herself perfectly open she had far more to hide than Miss Windus had.

Miss Windus was shocked.

"You *dreadful* girl! . . . But really Louie, you must have noticed it. Why, you can see it the moment she comes into the room!"

"Really?" came the other detached voice. "How quaint! . . . Who do you think she's after? Not the Baboon? . . ."

I imagined the chuckle I didn't hear. I took it that the Baboon was myself.

"Mandrill, my dear," Miss Windus corrected. "You really must take a memory powder! . . ."

"Oh, I call it baboon," Miss Causton remarked with indifference. Then she laughed. . . "How ridiculous you are! He's as big as a man ought to be anyway—"

"Oh, quite!"

"——and I declare you can look at him till he's quite good-looking!"

"Oh! . . ." (I could almost see Miss Windus' quizzical eyes.)

"Really, you are absurd! . . ."

There was another short silence.

"And by the way," Miss Windus next said, "*he's* been rather—different somehow—lately, don't you think?"

Sweets crunched for a moment, then:

"Different? . . . Do you mean *he's* been looking at you in that—ahem!—dreadful way?"

"What, *that* creature! . . ."

"Beg yours, dear—"

"*I* should think so! . . . But I fancied he'd been somehow—not quite the same—"

"Well, anything for a change, as the song says. Myself, if I found I couldn't get along without 'em, I should prefer—"

But a "Sssh!" interrupted Miss Causton. Somebody had come into the farther bay, and the rest for a time was whispering.

When next the conversation became audible its tenor did not seem to have changed.

"Scented soap in a little celluloid box, too!" Miss Windus admired.

"One must keep oneself clean," Miss Causton threw off. "Have some of this, dear. I simply had to have some chocolate nougat tonight! . . ."

There was a rustling of tissue paper.

"Well, it's a sign, and so's her hair-waving and polishing her nails and that lace yoke," Miss Windus resumed.

"Oh yes, the pneumonia blouse—"

"*And* her heels—*and* a scent-sachet! . . ."

You see that I was quite deliberately listening. I am not putting on any airs about it. I might have been Polwhele. I wanted to know, so I listened. I did more than listen too. I watched. I knew that the shelves were only half full on the other side; only a screen of stout wire separated the books facing one way from those facing the other; and by pulling out a book or two on my side I should probably find a peephole. . . Very softly I pulled three or four out, found my opening and looked. Miss Causton appeared to be standing with her back towards me; I couldn't see her; but I could see Miss Windus, sitting on the library ladder holding its short staff, with her plaid skirt pulled tightly about one carrot-shaped thigh.

They began to talk again.

"And another thing that makes me *quite* sure, dear! She's going to young Merridew's next week-end!"

"Oh! . . ."

"Don't be absurd. You know what I mean. To his parents', of course; they live in Guildford. . . Not that *she* told me, oh no! Not her ladyship!"

"Who did, then?"

"Not her, though I gave her *every* chance! Six months ago she'd have told me like a shot, but we're getting so blessed artful these days! . . . He told me."

"Then it doesn't look as if it *was* the Baboon?"

"Oh, I daresay she'll leave you your Baboon if you want him."

"Thanks. I think I should know which way to turn in *that* case," Miss Causton replied evenly. "Coming?"

And they left the bay together.

It was by this admirable piece of Rixon Tebb & Masters' work that I learned what, it appeared, I had been watching too closely to see.

VI

I had intended in any case to spend the remainder of that evening with Archie Merridew. Mingled with my restlessness there had been a tremulous sensitiveness that had culminated half-an-hour before in a fit of satanic pride. Lately (I had decided) it had come to be taken rather too much as a matter of course that our frequent adjournments after the evening class should be always to his quarters and never, or hardly ever, to mine. I had quite enough to bear without further gratuitous rubs of that kind, and I had resolved that I would make myself his host that evening though he had lived in a mansion and I in a sty.

But after what I had so altogether discreditably overheard now I had fifty other reasons for wishing him to come along with me. Almost every sentence that had been spoken on the other side of that bay of books had contained a reason. But I realised that before I could trust myself to face him I must swallow the anger that crowded thickly into my throat. There was nothing to gain and everything to lose by letting him see my rage. So I walked back into the empty senior classroom, there to remain until I should have got the worst of it over.

By half-past nine I had got myself in hand. I gathered my work together. Students were coming to the row of washbowls in the small compartment at the end of the senior classroom to wash their hands, and Evie gave me the smile that was to be my nourishment for three whole days as she passed with her towel and the cake of soap in the new celluloid box. Archie had been working all the evening in the typewriting-room; now was my chance, before he could make (supposing him to want to make) any appointment with her, to secure this myself, and I hurried for my hat and coat and sought him.

"Ready?" I said.

"Right-oh; just a minute," he replied. "I told 'em to keep my fire in—I'm going to swot like blazes tonight."

"Oh no—you're coming along with me this time," I laughed. "I shall be ashamed to show my face at your place much oftener. . . unless," I added lest he should shake me off, "you love me merely for what I have—"

He laughed too. He was at the young and squab-like stage that takes a pride in scorning appearances, and even finds the heart more rather than less honest when the waistcoat over it is shabby. He accepted with quite a good grace, got his hat and coat, and we went out together, I giving Miss Windus an unimpeachable "Good-night" as I passed her, hardly a yard from the spot where I had peeped on her less than an hour before.

The electrograph opposite my abode was an advertisement of "*Sarcey's Fluid*," some sort of a disinfectant; and as we approached it Archie looked up.

"Phew! . . . Needs it rather, tonight, doesn't it?" he laughed.

It did not seem to me to "need it" quite so badly that evening as it had on some other evenings—warm summer evenings, for example—I had known. December had come in rawly, and the chestnut stoves and baked-potato engine were out. The poorer streets have no pleasanter smell than that of baked potatoes, broken up, sprinkled with salt from the big tin caster, and closed together again like a South Sea face with a mealy smiling mouth, and I had slipped a couple of these into my pocket for our supper. I suppose Archie meant the fried fish papers in the gutters and (as we entered by my side door) the acrid smell of the public-house; but it was part of my fiendish pride to rub those things in a little that evening, and I made light of them as we mounted the stairs.

"Oh, you're pampered, Master Archie," said I. "I had thought of asking you round to supper next Saturday evening—not tomorrow, a week tomorrow—but I think I shall save my hospitality."

You see what I was already angling for. Well, I caught my fish. Of course he couldn't take Evie down to his folks at Guildford without my knowing of it, but I wanted to see the fashion in which he would make his avowal. We had left the carpeted corner of the stairs that the great ornamental public-house lamp illuminated brightly and were standing on the bare landing outside my room. He answered without an instant's hesitation.

"Afraid you'll have to, Jeff—twice over," he replied. "I've got to go down home that week-end; beastly nuisance! I was going with some fellows over to Richmond—stag-party; but the mater writes that she's asked Miss Soames, so I suppose I shall have to be there to help out—confound it!"

I opened my door and let him into the red and green.

"Oh?" I remarked casually. "Nice change for you. You'll be all the fitter for the exams. Don't tell *me* about your stag-parties though. I know 'em; you'd take jolly good care not to pick the place with the plainest waitresses for tea, what? *I* know you! . . . But if I were you I'd go steady for a week or two, my boy, that Method paper'll be harder than you think, I warn you!"

"I'm watching it!" he replied cheerfully. "By Jove! Jeff, I'd forgotten what a noisy pitch this of yours is! What on earth makes you stay here?"

"Oh, I don't know," I replied carelessly, applying a match to the wick of my lamp and replacing the chimney. "As I say, you're pampered. The place is all right. I don't do much except sleep here. It's a bit cold, though. I'd keep my coat on if I were you—"

"Wouldn't be much sleep for me here," he remarked, sitting on the edge of my bed. "I should want a good stiff drink before I slept much in this racket!"

As I placed the lamp globe on its brass ring I glanced covertly at him. It was a green interval, and his face looked as if he stood by a chemist's window near the big pear-shaped green globe, while his waistcoat was turned to a black purple, with one brass button gleaming green as a cat's eye. Then the red came again, and the lamp flame crept up. I went to the little cupboard where I kept my few cups and saucers and plates. I filled my kettle at the tap on the landing, put it on the half-crown oil-stove, and began to prepare our feast.

In a quarter of an hour it was ready—tea, the baked potatoes, and a wedge of butter apiece. We ate it, he sitting on my bed, I in my sagging and string-mended old wicker chair. I saw quite plainly that already he wanted to be off, and would stay no longer than the barest decency demanded; but he had got to eat that pauper's meal before I let him go, and there were my forty-nine other reasons for having got him up there.

One of these other reasons had, during the last hour, taken complete shape in my mind. Its consequences would have been impossible to foresee, but as far as it yet went, I thought it crafty enough. I filched another look at him; he was burning the roof of his mouth with hot potato as he lolled against my bed foot; and I judged it time to put my plan into execution.

I pushed my own plate away and sank back into my lifeless old wicker chair. He had turned his coat collar up by this time. My plan kept me warm.

"You're a lucky beggar, you know, Archie," I sighed heavily.

He had moved, to set down his cup of untasted tea on the floor. He looked up.

"How?" he asked.

I settled myself farther back.

"How!" I repeated almost vindictively. "Don't you call it lucky having a house and people and so on?"

"Oh! Everybody has—" he began, but corrected himself. "I mean, I thought you meant some special luck!"

"Oh no—just that," I murmured. "Having a place to ask people down to when you want—that's all."

He seemed surprised. "Do you mean Miss Soames?" he said.

"Miss—?" I shook my head absently. "Oh no, I wasn't thinking of Miss Soames—I was thinking of something quite different."

He meditated for a moment.

"You *have* seemed a bit different lately. . . What's up?" he demanded, looking squarely at me.

My plan, to which his last words gave a new and unexpected fillip, was briefly this:

When, over the case of reference books, I had heard Miss Windus make the very remark he also had just made—namely, that I had been "different"—I had had a swift access of alarm. In what particular I had betrayed myself I didn't know, but I realised very clearly, and doubly clearly now that the same remark had dropped from Archie himself, that love and a light cannot be hid, and that if my extreme former care had not secured me from remark no care I was likely to be able to take for the future would do so. I had laid myself open, and should do so again. How was I to cover myself?

I thought I saw my way. I invite you to consider that way.

Were I to give it out to Archie—or rather, not so much to give it out as allow a surmise to dawn on him—that my heart was already pre-engaged in some carefully unspecified quarter or other, not only would this "difference," both he and Miss Windus had remarked on, be admitted and accounted for, but I should at one stroke set myself free from a hundred other trammels of gossip, past, present and to come. After that avowal nothing I did would be unaccountable. I should have a definite place in the general sex-understanding. I should be classed, out of the running, filed and docketed, totally uninteresting to either Miss Windus or Miss Causton and rid of the attentions of Miss Levey.

And I should also—my heart had thrilled suddenly and poignantly as I thought of this—I should also be admitted at once to privileges. I should have my share in such freedoms and exemptions as the married man knows fully and the attached bachelor at least to a probationary extent. This state of things does by tacit acknowledgment exist. The man who can say all to one woman can say more than other men to all women. And the shining immunity I now saw before me would even include what so far I had had to deny myself—conversation, thus safeguarded, with Evie herself.

"By heaven!" my heart now cried within me, "I will do it!"

And instantly a perfect seething of the cautions and reserves with which I must do it sprang up in my brain.

But here was Archie patiently waiting for me to speak.

"What's up? What the dickens are you talking about?" he asked once more.

I let my head drop, as a man might who discovers he has said too much. "Oh, nothing," I replied.

Archie was just as sharp as—neither more nor less than—I wished him to be.

"A lot of fuss about nothing—if it's really nothing," he said suspiciously.

The next moment he had looked hard into my face, taken a long breath, and, suddenly bringing his hand down on his thigh, broken into loud laughter.

"By Jove! Jeff—I really believe—let's have a look at you—by Jove! I really do—*I believe you're in love!* What a——How ripping, I mean! Best congratulations, old chap—my turn this time—ha ha ha ha!"

I drew myself heavily up. The kind of thing I was doing has to be done rather carefully. "Look here, Archie—" I began, trembling between the wrath I felt and the not-too-much wrath I must appear to display; but he interrupted me:

"Well, that's a knock-out! Who'd have dreamed—"

"Why not?" I demanded sharply.

"Oh, I didn't mean that!" he made such haste to say that it was plain as a pikestaff that he had meant precisely "that."

"I only meant, how surprising—how unexpected. I mean—"

I frowned. "*Should* you find it so—if it *were* so?"

"Should!" he said, puzzled. ". . . Isn't it so, Jeff?"

"No," I replied; but a "No" that so exquisitely contradicted itself that I gave myself nothing less than admiration for the performance.

"No?" he echoed. "You're lying, Jeff—you *are*!" he broke out triumphantly. "I can tell by the way you say it! So *that's* it! Dashed if I didn't think there was something! . . . Who is she, Jeff?"

But that, as you may suppose, it was no part of my plan to tell.

OLIVER ONIONS

Neither was it part of that plan to enjoin either secrecy or the other thing upon him. That, I thought grimly, might quite safely be left to take care of itself. "Mandrill, my dear; you really must take a memory powder! . . ." I seemed to hear Miss Windus' voice again over the bookshelves. Oh yes, if he would give currency to that Zoo nonsense he could be trusted not to keep the richer joke, of Jeffries in love, to himself!

For that he and not Evie had been responsible for this pleasantry at the expense of my appearance I had concluded by a much sounder process of observation and reasoning than that my love-lorn state predisposed me entirely in her favour. My watching, a failure in other respects, had at least succeeded in this respect. And that I had found had not been without its barb for me. You may remember my former pathetic gratitude that, while others singled me out for marked treatment, she alone had not, in the trifling forms and observances that are the gracious outside of intercourse as distinct from its inner truth, differentiated me from the rest of the world. Well, I had made a guess at the reason for that. It was, in a word, her upbringing. The aunt with whom she lived in Woburn Place had taught her to "behave nicely," and so on. I could see that education. Such maxims as that one must not "judge by appearances," that "handsome is that handsome does," and, generally speaking, the unexceptional tradition that the "less fortunately circumstanced" have special claims on superior gentleness and pity, form almost the whole of it. I, it appeared, was one of these "less fortunately circumstanced" . . . Of course nobody was to blame. By-and-by the amiable aunt would probably go a little further, and teach her that it is not enough that these unimpeachable precepts should be merely observed, but that the thought behind them must be concealed as well. When you treat a poor devil just as if he was anybody else you must not let it be seen that you do so from perception that he is not. . . Anyway, there it was, and it rather took the shine out of that "good-night, Mr. Jeffries" that had sent me off happy to Archie's rooms on the evening when I had been so startlingly shaken out of my fool's paradise.

Thus I was persuaded, and as it turned out quite rightly, that it had been young Merridew, and not she, who had allowed his tongue this licence both on Weston's physical characteristics and my own.

His cup of tea was still on the floor, and by this time was cold. He hadn't tasted it, and, his renewed congratulations on what he supposed to be my blissful state of mind over, was once more fidgeting to be off.

But it was quite at my own pleasure whether I released him or not; I had the hateful advantage of my baked potatoes and my poverty; and though he was getting colder moment by moment, being less accustomed to the lack of a fire than I, I did not spare him.

"Yes," I remarked musingly by-and-by, as if I had been thinking over a former remark, "I'd take that Method paper quite seriously if I were you. Save up your little fling till that's over. Stag-parties and work don't go together, my son."

He had a little gleam of perspicacity. "What little fling?" he asked. "Who said I was going to have one?"

("Carefully, Jeffries," I cautioned myself.) Aloud I said cheerfully, "My mistake, Archie—I'm out of the running in these things—I'm rather a Puritan by necessity, you see. Perhaps I was taking it rather for granted—"

He chuckled. "A Puritan by necessity! A Puritan by Miss Whatever-her-name-is, more like! Do at least tell us if it's anybody we know, Jeff!"

But I ignored the latter part of his remark. "Well done, Archie," I applauded. "I'm glad you see that when a man's got one woman he's no need for all the others. Stick to that and you're all right."

And that clinched it. "Well, you've got the pull over me there," he said.

I made no reply.

You need not conclude, unless you wish, that I wanted to start him straight away to the devil. I couldn't have ensured his arrival at that destination if I had. But I was prepared to go half way with him if by so doing I could keep him from getting into paradise by the means I had reserved for myself. I was doing him no conspicuous harm. He would have to rub shoulders with the world before long—was already doing so; and I said no more to him—nay, I said far less—than he would have picked up for himself in almost any gathering of young men of his own age that he was likely to find himself among. . . So presently, when after (how shall I put it?)—after having tapped it home that there *was* the one woman and also the others, I returned to the examination in Method again, I was talking as easily as if, his betrayals to Miss Windus notwithstanding, we had been the best friends in the world.

"By the way, that's another thing you're lucky in, my boy," I said. "The exam's in the daytime. I suppose that doesn't convey anything to you."

"How do you mean?"

"Well, it means something to me. I shall have to get a day off."

"Well?" he inquired.

"Well—it doesn't by any means follow that I shall get it."

He stared. "You don't mean to say they'd be such skunks as not to let you off for a day!" he exclaimed.

I laughed. "Perhaps they won't be such skunks," I remarked.

"Oh!" he cried, outraged. "They *couldn't*!"

He was as ignorant about Rixon Tebb & Masters as he was about everything else in life.

Presently, with a "Brrr!" and a shiver, he got off my bed.

"Well, I'm off," he said. "I didn't intend to come round, and I'm going back to swot."

I heaved myself up from my chair. "Must you? Well, wait a moment—I'll come down with you—"

Before I turned down my lamp, filling the room with the red and green again, I noticed his untouched cup of tea on the floor. I made no remark on it, but as I preceded him down the narrow stairs I found myself suddenly filled with a curiosity as to whether I guessed rightly what was passing in his mind. I had made my shot, and was as interested to know whether it was a true one as if I had had a bet on it.

Where the great public-house lamp shone brightly through the landing window the stairs branched, one flight descending to the side door by which we had entered and the other leading to the back bar of the public-house. It was as we reached this bifurcation that I found I had guessed rightly.

"I say," he said, "I'm beastly cold! Come this way and have a drink!"

I shook my head.

"Not here," I said. "Not on my own premises, so to speak. If you don't mind my having something thin I'll come over the way with you."

"Anywhere," he said, with another shiver.

There was another public-house just beyond the *Sarcey's Fluid* advertisement. We crossed and entered it.

"Rum—hot!" he called familiarly, peering under the frame of pivoted glass panes and flipping on the counter with a florin to attract the barmaid's attention. "Come along, Flossie—hurry up! . . . What's your poison, Jeff?"

He had his rum hot; but I drank nothing stronger than peppermint.

VII

His incredible gaucheries apart, I had no reason for hating him. One does not hate a youngster seven years one's junior merely because he is a mass of inexperience and self-sufficiency. Once again my hate was really a hatred of the whole dreary circumstances of my life, and, when I saw this concentrating stormily over young Merridew's head, I made attempt after attempt to divert it. I swear to you I made these attempts. I made them first of all to save him from a contest so unequal as one with my wrath must be; and if I made them later so that I myself should not be merely the slave of that wrath, I still made them. And all the time, as I say, so long as he did not stand in my way, it was a matter of indifference to me whether he took the upward path or that which led downhill to perdition.

Unfortunately I was in love, and no man in love can stand by the rules that he knows ought to govern his conduct. Those jealousies I have spoken of as torturing me at Rixon Tebb & Masters' shook me in spite of myself. When I felt their approach I took care to give young Merridew a wide berth; and I confess that in sometimes letting these fits have their way with me I found an abominable ease. Away from him, my heart was filled with rage and revilings; but these very outbreaks enabled me at other times to meet him with a smile on my lips and a welcome in my eyes. Once I had got rid of the over-plus of my rage I could almost have persuaded myself of my affection for him.

So I alternated, as the red and green of my apartment alternated; and perhaps the red seemed redder and the green greener by the mere force of the contrast. I continued to walk home frequently with him after the class, to share his supper frequently, and to be obliged to him for my necessary bath.

I very soon learned that in the matter of my reputed being in love he had done exactly what I had intended he should do—had whispered the news about the college. It required no further eavesdropping to tell me that; I felt it in the altered air. I saw the knowledge peering through the little scalene triangles of Miss Windus' eyes, saw it in the looks of sleepy and amused curiosity with which Miss Causton favoured me. The latter lady, indeed, sometimes positively alarmed me, for the glances I suffered when I chanced to enter a room in which she was at work held incalculable things, and I no longer dared to look at her own amused and supercilious eyes, her fascinating hands, or that foot beneath the hem of her dress, fine and slender as a violin. And with the least encouragement Miss Windus would, I knew, have sought my company, and, lacking an admirer of her own, would have eased her breast to somebody else's of all the things about love at large that she ached to say to somebody. I wondered, seeing them both, whether there was no middle way with women. The whole sex seemed to be divided into creatures (or rather a creature, for I set Evie apart) to be enskied by men, and the other kind, that a man might fly as he would fly a wild animal. And I am not sure even now that when these two things are found in one and the same woman they ever really shake down together. They seem to go on existing, independently, unreconciled, side by side.

But Miss Levey was far worse. She always seemed to me to crave information, useful or useless, from a mere acquisitiveness; and I may say now that it was she who, later, first roused in me the uneasy suspicion that unless I was exceedingly careful I should find that I had undertaken more than I could well manage. She began all at once to show quite a liking for my company. She mislaid books in the room where I sat, got into difficulties with copying presses when I was about, and glanced up at open or closed windows too high for her reach, as if she felt a draught or the lack of air, it didn't matter which, and must suffer until somebody came to her help. All this had its rise in the idlest curiosity, unless, as I sometimes suspected, she had made a bet that she would get out of me who this imaginary *fiancée* of mine was, and was determined to win it. One day as I saw her struggling with the blind cords in one of the window bays, and advanced to her assistance, she relinquished the cords, and then, as if to apologise for the trouble she was causing me, said, "Oh, thank you so much—you see I'm going to a dance tonight, and have a slight cold already... You don't go to dances, do you, Mr. Jeffries?" I answered that I did not, whereupon she said gaily, "Oh, you must learn! I'm sure you could find *some*body who would teach you! Then you and your partner could join our set—such fun!"

And another time she actually came to me with tickets for one of her "hops," and pointed out to me that I should be saving a shilling by taking both a pink ticket as well as a blue one.

But while these were the results of my whispered false intelligence on Miss Windus and Miss Causton and Miss Levey, the results on Evie Soames were both foreseen and unforeseen. I had foreseen that it would give me a new liberty with her; but I had not foreseen that she, and not I, would be the first to take advantage of that liberty. It came to me entirely as a surprise that she should see no reason why, if my heart was engaged, she should not speak of it as a matter of course to myself.

This, to my great confusion, she did.

It was in the small back room that we called the library, among the book-shelves and glass-cases of mimeographs and gelatine copiers and patent tills, that she did so. I had seen her talking to Weston in the empty lecture-room as I had passed through to restore a book to its place—a new translation of "Schmoller on the Mercantile System," I remember it was—and she had turned as I had passed. I think she had been a little nervous about the pretty little exhibition she intended. It wouldn't surprise me in the least to learn that she had actually practised the words she was going to use, and I am quite sure she meant to go through it creditably. My lady was even then looking forward to the time when, on a small scale or a large one, she would have to do these things. So she followed me into the library, and, with one slender hand on the iron ball-arm of the copying press under the gas said her little piece.

"Oh, Mr. Jeffries! . . . I hear I have to congratulate you!"

For a moment I did not take her meaning. Then it dawned on me, and I felt a quick constriction of my heart that was both bliss and pain.

"Oh? . . . On—on what?" I asked. I couldn't help stammering a little over it.

She wore a brown cloth tailor-made costume and a thick knitted cap of white wool; and the shadow of this cap over her large eyes was not so deep but that I saw the almost reproachful look in them. It was almost as if she echoed: "'On what?' Can such a wonderful thing have happened to you and you ask 'On what?'"

"On this we hear of your engagement," she replied, looking down at her toes. "It's—it's true, isn't it?"

For the second time I felt my facile invention sitting somewhat less easily on me. I stammered again, while she, I am quite sure, misattributed my embarrassment.

"Who told you that?"

At that she was sweetly arch.

"Oh, a little bird, Mr. Jeffries! Don't tell me it isn't true—it would be almost—almost like bad luck—"

"Bad luck?" I repeated foolishly.

"I mean, like wearing your wedding dress before the day, or something like that—congratulating you too soon, I mean—"

By this time I had collected my thoughts. "It isn't true," I said.

Instantly her face fell adorably. In its expression I fancied I detected both indignation against her misinformant and mortification that her dear little attempt at social competence had failed.

"Oh! . . . I'm *so* sorry!" she murmured, all dejection and shame and rich colour. "Please forgive me!"

"It isn't true," I said, "that—that I am actually engaged to be married."

Like a flash she was all eagerness again. She had a book in her hand, not a college text-book but a novelette; and probably the whole of the novelette was in her glad change of tone. I was not exactly engaged to be married, but I *was* in love, and I daresay her brain was already a jumble of surmises about obstinate parents, secret wills, *marriages de convenance*, and true and severed young hearts.

"Oh!" she said again. "I'm so—I mean I hope I shall soon be able to—I mean I hope I'm not rude if I—" She floundered, already out of her depth.

"Not at all," I said gravely. "I only said I was not formally engaged. There are—other reasons for congratulation after all—"

"Oh, then I *do*!" she cried impulsively, with a grateful look that I had helped her out. "I'm *so* glad!"

Then, her ordeal over, she glanced towards the door.

But a daring impulse seized me. This was on a Friday night, and I knew that on the morrow she was going to Guildford.

"I see you're just leaving," I said. "Would it annoy you if I were to walk a little way with you?"

Again the code of her upbringing banished her momentary hesitation.

"Unless," I said, "you have already—"

"Oh no!" she said, with quick frankness. "I only meant that I nearly always go alone, or else with Miss Windus."

"I'm sure Miss Windus can spare you for once. One doesn't get congratulated like this every day," I pressed.

She laughed merrily. "Some of us don't get it at all," she said. "With pleasure, Mr. Jeffries."

I slapped Schmoller back into his place on the shelf, and went off, drunk with bliss, to get my hat and coat.

That night I walked with Evie for the first time to Woburn Place. Never had the Bloomsbury streets seemed so short, never the east side of the British Museum so few paces in length. I remember very little of what we talked about, I know she spoke of her visit to Guildford. The invitation, she gave me to understand, was really to her aunt, and it was to the subject of her aunt that she quickly returned when I insinuated a mention of Archie's name. I insinuated it again a minute later, but after that, noticing the way in which she came back to the aunt again, I forbore.

"But I'm afraid we can't ask the Merridews back, as we ought," she said, once more socially prescient. "We only have rooms in Woburn Place, you see, and you can't very well ask people all that way just to rooms, can you?"

"No," I replied briefly. I was thinking of my own late hospitality to Archie.

"We used to have a house, of course, before uncle died, and you know how poky rooms seem after that."

"Yes," I replied, compressing my lips.

And so we chatted. I forget what our other subjects were. I left her, with our first hand-shake, at her door.

What that week-end was to me I will not attempt to tell you. I did not belong to this earth at all. The fact that actually, in her person, she was enjoying herself in Archie's company at Guildford was nothing to me; the fact that every fibre of me was rapturously tremulous at the thought of her was everything. I triumphed as if I already had her yielding in my arms. Archie? . . . In my possession I laughed. I even felt kindly to Archie—felt towards him that it would give me pleasure to have him, by-and-by, a quite frequent visitor at my house—our house. . . I spread the mantle of my exaltation over the draymen and porters of the place where I dined. Their heavens were not mine, but if a man is full he is full, and I allowed them sanctities of their own. My heart was soft and generous to them. For the first time in my life I knew what folk mean when they say they love all the world.

The sweet influence had not quite left me when on Monday night I went to the college to see her again.

She did not appear that night. Neither did he.

It was Wednesday before I saw her again.

I do not know what damnable difference in me that absence of the pair of them for a single evening made. It came over me so suddenly that I was in its clutches before I was aware. It was a significant transformation. Let me relate it.

I knocked at the brass knocker of Archie's ivy-green door an hour before the class on the Tuesday night, and found that he intended to work at home that evening. (I only learned this, however, some minutes later.) I had had a double reason for calling on him at that hour, and the blood comes hot again in my cheeks as I recall my second reason. I had recently bought a new suit of clothes, not in Lamb's Conduit Street, but made, though cheaply enough, to measure; and though it was only the beginning of the week one of the payments for this suit had already depleted my pocket almost to the last penny. Since breakfast that day I had not eaten. But I knew the hour at which Archie dined.

So nicely had I hit the moment for my self-invitation that I actually followed his hot dinner half-way up the stairs. It was only on the first landing that the servant stood aside with the tray to allow me to precede her. I knocked at his door and entered, leaving the door open for the dinner of which I intended to partake to follow.

He had brought a fowl back with him from Guildford, with one or two other motherly gifts, and I smelt the white sauce even before Jane put the tray down on a side table. Archie was in his brown dressing-gown, standing before his fire. He had taken the green shade from his lamp, and his low-ceilinged roof-chamber looked exceedingly ruddy and comfortable and home-like.

"Hallo! Good man!" he cried. "You're just in time—I was just funking carving—you'd better be getting your hand in for when you're a family man! . . . Bring another plate, Jane. . . Well, how's things?"

It was then that the thing happened that still has power to bring the blood to my cheeks. It was exquisitely cruel in the moment of its coming.

"Oh, so-so," I replied carelessly. . . "But I've just this minute swallowed my dinner, thanks. You go ahead. I'll watch you."

"Oh, rubbish!" he replied, in a tone that hardened me. "I'll lay you haven't had so much but you can pick a bit of Surrey fowl."

I damned the thickness of his hide, but swallowed my choler.

"Really, thanks," I said, turning away to look at a print on the wall that I had seen a hundred times before.

Jane hesitated. It was a long way up from the kitchen, and the old bell-pull of red rope by his fireplace didn't always ring. "Shall I bring the other plate, Mr. Merridew?" she asked.

"Yes—bring it—he'll change his mind!"

But in my hellish pride I had now no intention whatever of changing my mind. Twice again he pressed me, and twice I declined, the second time curtly; and he fell to himself, while I sat in a chair and watched him.

"Oh, by the way," he said suddenly, with his mouth full of food, "I'm going to work here tonight. . . Sure you won't have some pudding?"

I rose. "Oh, well, if you're not coming I'll sheer off; why didn't you say so? Enjoy your week-end?"

"Oh, first rate. But, dash it all, don't be in such a hurry—you're far too early yet."

"Oh, I've just remembered something," I said, "See you again soon."

And I waved my hand and left.

I did not go to the class either that night. I was raging again, and trying to protect that young fool from the injury of my savage thoughts. I failed completely. Not even the thought that my passionate resentment was a force to be confined as it were in a boiler, and only to be allowed to escape by the way that would prove effective, restrained me from clenching my fists and gritting my teeth as I recalled the image of his pretty and ignorant and conceited face; and I am afraid I "let go" utterly. I walked by way of Chancery Lane and Bouverie Street to the Embankment; I crossed Blackfriars Bridge, and after that I don't quite know where I went, trying to forget my hunger, and trying to shake off my hideous grudge against the world that threatened to crash over the head of the egotistical whipper-snapper I had left.

I have related this at some length because it was the first time, but not the last, that that devil of sensitiveness took me in quite that way.

VIII

I had not exaggerated when I told Archie Merridew that I might find some difficulty in obtaining from Rixon Tebb & Masters' leave of absence for the day of the Method examination. That examination was fixed for a Friday, a fortnight and some days after my refusal to set fork into that fragrantly steaming Surrey fowl of Archie Merridew's, and this falling on a Friday added to my difficulties.

Or rather I should say that it added to Polwhele's difficulties, for it was to Polwhele I looked once more to find a way out for me. For Friday was a wage-day, and since I must have my eighteen shillings in order to live, a mere covering of my absence would not suffice. The cashier would have to be taken into the arrangement.

But Polwhele had by now to some extent got over his dread, if not over his hatred, of me. When I put the matter to him he refused. This was in the street, during the luncheon hour. The louse refused to help me, and turned away.

Exactly fifteen minutes later I had bearded the cashier himself, catching him at the door as he was returning from his meal.

At first he looked at me as much as to say, "Did *I* speak to *you*"? Then, finding it impossible to pretend he didn't know who I was, he said, "What is it?"

I told him what I wanted, concealing only my reason for wanting it; and, after his first astonishment that I had taken the absolutely unprecedented course of addressing a request otherwise than through the usual channel, I found him not unmanageable. As a matter of fact, things were slack, and there was only one kind of labour that Rixon Tebb & Masters' would have preferred to that it had from the agency at eighteen shillings a week—namely, a "floating margin" waiting on the pavement to be taken on for an hour or two as it might be required. Gayns saw a chance of saving a day.

"You don't expect to be paid for that day, do you?" he said.

"No," I replied.

He thought for a moment. "All right," he said. "You can come for your fifteen shillings on Thursday night."

And Polwhele set another mark against me, that I had approached a superior over his head.

As I entered the Business College at half-past ten on the morning of the examination it suddenly struck me that I had never been inside the place in the daytime before. By gaslight it was, as I have said, dingy enough, but by daylight it was shabby in the extreme. I walked round the rooms, noticing for the first time that the shorthand and typewriting rooms, which looked on the side street to the east of the block, were by far the lightest rooms on our top floor, and that the library in which I had received Evie's congratulations was little more than a thick twilight, which the cleaning of the single grimy back window that looked out over yards and chimney-pots would probably not greatly have improved. The room adjoining that, the old ledger-room, was not, except for the small high square of glass that gave on the head of the stairs, lighted at all.

They had made, too, quite extensive arrangements for the occasion itself. We had been warned that we should not be allowed to leave the premises until the examination was over, and as far as possible separate spaces had been provided for each of the twenty-five candidates—compartments of screens hired for the day from some furnisher or shop-fitter, and open at the ends to the gaze of the half-dozen perambulating guardians of the probity of examinations who looked as if they too had been had in for the day on the same terms as the screens. The contrast between the new fittings and the old wallpapers and chandeliers struck me. And I remembered that even now, when I had been debited my three shillings to be present, I did not see the place in its normal daytime aspect at all.

The papers were to be distributed at eleven, and at a few minutes before that hour we were all assembled. A man called Mackie and myself were the only two candidates for the Honours paper, and he and I were kept well apart—I told off to a seat in the middle of the lecture-room, he isolated in the typewriting-room. Evie, timorous about her Elementary, was separated from Archie Merridew (who occupied the box between Miss Windus and a pale student, Richardson) by the whole length of the general room. We took our places; in all the rooms at once voices were heard reading some cautionary form or other (my policeman gave me the most mistrustful of glances as he pronounced the words "expelled from the examination-room and your paper cancelled"); the papers were distributed on the stroke of eleven, and the examination began.

I need not trouble you with what it was all about. The importance of that day to me was quite unconnected with the paper on Method. I ought, however, to say that the paper was in reality two papers, the first in Theory and the second in Practice, with the interval for lunch dividing the two. I mention this only to explain how it was we came to be all talking together when, a little after half-past one, our first papers had been collected and we were free to unsnap our satchels or untie our parcels of lunch.

Despite my reduced income that week I had provided myself with a sumptuous lunch—two kinds of sausage from a *delicatessen* shop in Shaftesbury Avenue, a paper of potato salad, a roll, butter, some sort of chocolate *baba* or *moka*, and a bottle of Schweppes' dry ginger ale. That lunch had cost me nearly three shillings—but I intended to eat only a third of it. The rest was to be my chief sustenance during the two following days. I was not among my porters and drivers now—oh no! I was cutting quite a dash. Archie, passing with Miss Windus as I opened my black satchel, did not forbear to remark, "By Jove! doesn't Jeffries do himself well, what?" and it had been in order that I might be assumed to "do" myself equally well every day of my life that I had made my little display. I ate my exact third in the same compartment I had written my examination paper in, and then, closing my bag on the precious remainder, put it under the seat and mingled with the others.

By a sort of natural selection, I presently found myself in the middle bow window, discussing the questions he had just answered with my only fellow-candidate in Honours, Mackie. Mackie, both at the college and elsewhere, was one of these blatantly popular chaps, and I myself didn't like him. In some respects he was rather of Archie's kind, but he was older, more knowing, and had gone further. He was a singer of comic songs at "smokers," and a frequent looker-in at the shilling dances at the Holburn Town Hall after class. He was jubilant over the ease of the Theory paper, and was already so confident of his pass that he was cracking jokes right and left, as if a weight had been taken off his mind.

"It's going to be like money from home if it's no harder than that!" he exulted (almost prophetically, if what I said about the standard of modern examinations is true). "Kitty Windus says she'll eat her mackintosh, with the accent on the 'tosh,' if she isn't all right for the Advanced, and the Elementaries are as safe as your hand in your pocket! What ho! Come out on the stairs and have a Flor de Cabbagos."

I didn't want the Flor de Cabbagos, but I went out on the top landing with him. One or two others were smoking on the floor below, which was as far as we were allowed to stray. A few steps down Miss

Windus and Miss Causton were sitting on the stairs, as if they were sitting out a dance, and Miss Causton moved lower down still as the fragrance of Mackie's "Flor" reached her, and then a little way back again as she caught the whiff that came up the well. Mackie was talking of the paper again.

"All that mugging for a job you could do on your head!" he said, with regret for the time he had lost. "I wouldn't have dropped out of the billiard handicap if I'd known! Play billiards, Jeffries? I'm a regular John Roberts—in my dreams. Give you fifty in a hundred at the Napier when teacher says we can go."

And he ran on, with dull facetiousness.

But suddenly he stopped his rapid flow. He made a slight movement with his finger, and stood listening. I heard nothing except the voices lower down the stairs and the general hum in the room we had just left. But Mackie did.

"Hear that?" he said.

"What?" I asked.

"Sssh! . . ."

I told you how the wooden partition at the head of the stairs, that with the small window high up, separated the landing on which we stood from the old ledger-room. The window was worked with cords on a horizontal pivot, and was swung partly open. Whether Mackie heard whatever he did hear through this window or through the boards themselves I do not know, but a smile came over his face.

"It's that young devil," he whispered.

"Who?"

"Why, young Merridew. He's in there with somebody. . ."

I invite you to notice that I was improving. I was not eavesdropping this time—I was merely letting Mackie do my eavesdropping for me. He glanced round to see whether the women below were watching, and then set his ear against the partition.

"Yes, it's Merridew," he chuckled. "Nice father's hope and mother's joy *that* young man's getting! I don't suppose he's gone in there to talk to the secretary bird! . . ."

I found myself suddenly reminded of what I had noticed for the first time only an hour or two before—that the room beyond the partition was practically unlighted.

Then Mackie dropped again into the "bright" style affected by the singers of comic songs at smoking concerts.

"Ahem—good-hevening, ladies and gen'lmen! How am I? Very well, thank me! Ahem! I will now, with your kind permission, endeavour to entertain you with a few of my well-known impersonations on a subject that will appeal to all of you, no matter what your age, sex, condition, vaccination marks or the number of your dog licence—*London's Lovers*."

"Oh, Mr. Mackie's going to recite for us!" I heard Miss Windus' cry of juvenile delight from down the stairs. "Please be quick, Mr. Mackie—we shall have to go in in ten minutes!"

And those below pressed up the stairs to hear Mackie.

But I did not stay to hear the "impersonation." I walked back into the general room, and, with a violently throbbing heart, sought the seat where I had written my examination paper.

Do you realise what I had just seen? Do you see what had set my heart so thumping? If Mackie was right, and he had really got the cue for his "impersonation" from something that was going on in the ledger-room, young Merridew and Evie were alone in there together.

All that I had hitherto known of apprehension and despair and jealousy of Archie's luck and chances and juniority was eclipsed by the emotion that now flowed over me like a wave. The revelation swept me entirely off my balance. It seemed to me that once more I awoke as if out of a dream. I seemed to be standing as it were a little way off from my own baseless hopes and illusions of the past weeks and coldly contemplating my own egregiousness. I actually gave out loud a low laugh that harrowed myself. What! To suppose that all, all I could do, would prevent youth from coming together at the last!

So I made myself a spectacle of ridicule for myself.

Then, as the minutes passed, that which at first had seemed a pure and perfect whole of hopelessness changed subtly and began to separate into parts. And that brought such a change in me that I trembled to recognise it. The shock of those first moments had stunned me, but I was now coming out of my stupor. My first swift conclusion had been wrong. These were *not* young lovers whom mountains could not sunder. She, my sleeping beauty, who had but now opened her eyes, no doubt thought I was that; her soul was over-brimming; and I remembered her look of wonder and reproach when, after she had congratulated me on that love-rise that is the most wondrous of earthly dawnings I had given a puzzled "on what?" When hearts can no longer contain that with which they ache to bursting, lucky is the one who stands nearest to hand. His it is to have, for the lifting of his finger, what else would spill.

He may not be athirst for the draught; a muddier liquor might quench his fire as well; but this dew and ichor is his, though another parch for it.

For I needed no pointers from Mackie to know young Archie now. This was his ignored and heaven-high luck, and he did not even want it. If their being together in that unlighted room—their being together even as I sat with my head between my hands staring blankly at the yellow deal screen—if this meant anything at all it meant one thing and one thing only, that she must give because it was her nature to give, and the cub was philandering with her.

At that thought my despair gave place to something else. It was eaten up in the white flame of wrath that flashed like a brand in my brain.

"Oh!" I thought. "So *that's* it, my Archie? . . ."

I need not tell you again how I always have made my angers serviceable to me. Five minutes later—though my will was well-nigh deracinated in the process—I was its master again. It still struggled like a beast in my hold, nor did I know whence the help could come without which it would presently have me in its power again, but I still retained my throttling hold on it. One last wild struggle the beast made; this was when beyond the end of my screen-enclosed compartment, I saw them issue, with an interval of half-a-minute between their coming out of the library doorway. He was pink and triumphant; at her I forbore to look. A minute later Mackie passed and gave an infinitesimally small jerk of his head and a wink; but by that time I was holding my savage beast down again.

Then a bell rang; there was a buzz and movement the candidates were making ready again. Once more attendants read the caution, and then the second paper was distributed. Mechanically I turned over the gelatine-copied leaves that had been handed to me.

But I pushed them away again. A man who is engaged as I still was—a luckless hunter who has missed his shot and is struggling desperately body to body with his intended prey—has little time for anything but the business in hand. True, I did draw the paper to me again and tick off the questions that would be productive of the highest marks, but it was long before I got any further. There would come between me and my page Archie Merridew's pink and boastful face as I had seen him issue from the library door.

I do not know how long I sat thus.

Draggingly at last I settled to work. But it was well-nigh hopeless.

I came to myself after a long interval to find that I was staring blankly before me and muttering softly to myself. I had not written more than half-a-page. Wearily I tried again.

The next external thing that I was fully awake to was that from the typewriting-room there came the single "Ting" of the small clock on the mantelpiece. I started. That single "Ting" always meant one of two things—one o'clock or a half-hour. I had no watch.

I tried for a moment to persuade myself that the clock had just struck half-past two.

Then I heard the attendant's voice: "You have one hour left."

"Good heavens!" I groaned.

I drew my paper to me again.

For a time I was not conscious of anything but the questions that must be answered by half-past four. Indeed, so feverishly did I work that I did not hear the attendants announce that we had only half-an-hour longer. The next announcement I heard was that fifteen minutes only remained.

Swiftly and flurriedly I turned over what I had written. I was just half-way through the paper.

Wildly alarmed, I broke into rapid shorthand—the shorthand in which I am writing this now. I did not know whether the shorthand would be accepted; I only knew that in its larger aspect the object of the examination was to determine whether I was master of my subject. I was master of my subject. Those already diluted tests of capacity, the questions, dictated their own replies: I put on top speed.

"You have five minutes more," sounded the relentless voice.

But I could have sworn that not one minute elapsed before, much louder and more peremptory, came the final call:

"You must now cease writing!"

As I mingled with my fellow-candidates again I heard Mackie crying joyously, "Oh, we got medals for this in Paris!" But I passed him by without a glance. Nor had I any desire to linger about those premises my first sight of which in the daytime had cost me three shillings in cash, and a murderous rage that might indeed have closed the gates of heaven in my face. I went quickly for my hat and coat, almost colliding with Miss Causton as I turned a corner and muttering I know not what as she shrank back and gave me a look that I could hardly reconcile with her usually ironical and ruminating eyes. I merely wanted to get out of the place. . .

But I did not escape so quickly but that I saw Archie and Evie following me down the stairs. No doubt they were going together to her aunt's to tea.

A week later I learned that I had passed with distinction in the Theory part of the paper, but had failed in the Practice portion. The examiners made a joke about "Paper Number Two," saying they had decided to hold it over for next year's shorthand examination. Everybody knew whose paper Number Two was. . .

Mackie had passed in both portions.

PART II
WOBURN PLACE

I

Some time or other during the period of my engagement to Miss Windus (an episode of my history I am now approaching), I happened to remark on the pleasant arrangement that had removed many of the temptations of London from Archie Merridew's path by giving him a "home from home"—the wholesome influence of the Soames' house in Woburn Place. My charmer agreed with me that no arrangement could have been happier. It is of that arrangement that I must now speak. But first I must tell you as much as I can recollect of the party with which the Christmas term closed.

Little as things of that kind appeal to me, I had been to that breaking-up party. Why I had deliberately sought this misery I find it difficult to say. It had been Miss Levey who, the very evening before the result of the Method examination had been announced, had broached the matter to me, and that of itself would doubtless have decided me had it not been for Miss Causton, who had come up just as I was refusing.

"Mr. Jeffries says he won't come!" Miss Levey had said, turning to Miss Causton, "but we want a few of the seniors as guests—you and Mr. Mackie and Mr. Weston—you're the lights of the college, you know."

I had been quite unaware that my mental comment on her "we" had shown in my face (she was quite twenty-five), but apparently it had, for she had added, with a laugh that had struck me as contemptuous even of herself, "Oh, I call myself a junior too!" and had turned away.

Of course I ought not to have gone, and, after I had learned of my failure in Method, I had been on the point of renewing my refusal. But then there had seized me an almost mad desire to see how much I really could endure with a smile (Evie and Archie, of course, had been among the first to accept). So the very thing that ought to have kept me away had driven me there. Of this extreme of perversity I am afraid I must ask you to find what explanation you can. I am merely setting down the thing as it occurred.

So I had gone, though, to Miss Levey's disappointment, *sans* "lady," and had had, moreover, the pleasure, such as it was, of also disappointing those who had expected that my failure in Method would plunge me into gloom. I was far beyond gloom. Mere gloom would not have expressed my feelings; it would have lacked the ecstasy of my misery. So I daresay I had appeared, not less, but more cheerful than my ordinary, and perhaps that was even set down as courage that was merely the numbing of sensibility.

A most extraordinary experience to me that party had been. On the occasion of the Method examination screens and tables had had to be imported, but this time the opposite had been done, and all day half-a-dozen of the students had been busy, stacking desks and tables away in the old ledger-room and clearing the lecture-room for dancing. The senior classroom had been turned into a refreshment-room, and an upright piano had been got in and lifted upon Weston's lecturing dais. Blackboards indicated the way to the ladies' cloak-room (the library) and that of the men (the room with the washbowls), and by the time I had arrived, at half-past eight, everybody had assembled. Nine had been fixed as the hour when dancing was to begin.

Sisters and friends had brought up the number of women to perhaps a dozen, and Miss Levey had not failed to remark on my coming alone. Her short legs had started to bring her to me almost before I had looked about me.

"Oh, Mr. Jeffries—then you *haven't* brought a lady friend!" she had reproached me. "I hope you understood that the invite was for two!" At this, setting my face into a rocky smile that had remained on it thence forward, I had looked at her over her fan.

"Oh?" I had said. "Then it was my 'lady friend,' not me, you wanted to see?"

But she had been equal to me. "Oh no—but there are three times as many gentlemen as ladies, you know. Come and let me introduce you—"

But I had evaded this, preferring, in the words of Mackie, who had passed just then, to "paper the wall."

From my station by the thrown-back folding-doors of the lecture-room, with that carved smile on my face for all the world as if my heart had been temporarily atrophied, I had been able to look even on Evie almost unmoved. The whole scene had been a haggard but quite painless nightmare to me. When, at nine o'clock, the piano had begun to play, I had watched the men in their black sparrow-tails and white gloves, stooping, posturing, offering arms, revolving, as if the picture had been a flat representation, lacking a dimension, the blackboard behind the pianist and the old bells like interrogation-marks above his head quite as important as the moving figures. And I had smiled and smiled. After all, one might as well smile as not. Once you had got the smile into its place it was just as easy. Really it would have been the taking of it off again that would have required the mental effort.

It was as I had stood there that Miss Causton had come up to me and asked me if I did not dance. Her voice, as she had done so, had hardly detached itself in my mind from the noise about us, and even her figure, lending as it were its own life to her dress of oyster-grey, had seemed no less flat and diagrammatic than the rest of the scene. "No," I had said, and "No," she had repeated, with a nod, "getting the piano up and down would be more your style, for it nearly killed those boys this afternoon. . . But won't you let me teach you?"

"I've no gloves."

"Gloves!" she had said softly.

And so, since besides smiling one may as well dance as not, I had taken a dancing lesson from Miss Causton. But we had only gone twice round the room—for which, considering my weight, I could hardly have blamed her, and then, panting a little, she had proposed a rest. And in the very bay from which I had once overheard her conversation with Miss Windus I had talked civilities to her, still smiling. I had asked whether she was coming back after Christmas and had been told "Yes," and when, by-and-by, as being less trouble than thinking of a new one, I had put the same question to Miss Levey, I had got a "Yes" from her also. After that I had worked that question really hard, putting it at least once more to Miss Levey, and once to somebody who was not at the college at all, after which I had found a new one, I forget what, making two quite useful social accomplishments. Once again Miss Causton had come up to me. "——since you don't come to me," I remember her saying; "I should like some coffee." But she had barely tasted the coffee I fetched her—I remember wondering whether I ought to take her to the coffee or fetch the coffee to her—and then, just in the middle of my third brilliant conversational find, she had suddenly got up and left me.

And so on. The last had been similarly phantasmagoric. I had smiled when Evie had come up and said reproachfully: "You can dance with Louie!" and again when she had said: "I should like something to drink—no, you mustn't fetch it—when you're asked for those things in the middle of a dance it means that somebody wants to sit out with you—but, oh dear! I forgotten that this was Archie's, and here he is! . . ." It hadn't hurt much but I had had enough. The last person I distinctly remember speaking to was Miss Levey, who had said that I really must bring "somebody" to the next social. They had still been dancing when I left.

Now that the disaster of my failure had befallen me, a year must elapse before I could make a second attempt; and so it became quite unnecessary that I should return to the college after the Christmas vacation of a month. The faraway autumn would be early enough for that. The fees, small as they were, came fearfully heavy on me, and I could study in the Patent Office Library for nothing.

But I wished to return in January. My many reasons for this are clear to you. To the more obvious of them I will only add, that I seemed now to be doomed to remain at Rixon Tebb & Masters' for another year, and, now that that strange and rather frightening calm of that night of the breaking-up party had passed, I simply could not face the time ahead without the alleviation, or at least the change of pain, that the prospect of seeing Evie afforded.

So I decided to continue my course.

The days until the college should reopen on the 21st of February were—I almost said purgatory to me, but in truth they purged me little. It was the rainiest and muddiest of Christmas weeks; nobody was out of doors who had a fire to sit by and leisure to sit by it, and the streets were a bobbing of umbrellas and a squirting of mud about the turned-up trousers of men and the skirts of women lifted to their wearers cared not where. I tried to make the use of dubbin take the place of the resoling of my boots, and in my chamber, which was warmed only by my oil-stove, my garments never dried. It was a short week at Rixon Tebb & Masters', we were paid short too, and I shall never forget my Christmas dinner of that year. For a fit of desperation and impotent rebellion took me. I went for a change to another "pull-up" than my usual one, and there paid tenpence for a wholly insufficient dinner. I rebelled, I say. I brought my fist down on the table, and out of sheer recklessness ordered the whole lot over again. This proved too much for me. I couldn't eat half of it, but I didn't care. How I was going to recoup myself for the double cost afterwards I didn't know. If I had to have more money, I knew I should have to get it somehow, that was all.

That was a villainous Christmas for me!

And I was alone—Archie at Guildford, Evie and her aunt I didn't know where, perhaps at Guildford too, everybody with homes to go to and faces to talk to over a fire. Archie's absence, too, cost me several sixpences—the price of the hot baths I could not very well ask for at his quarters while he was away. I spent my evenings in the Patent Office Library, where it was warm.

I was glad when Christmas was over. I felt somehow that I was not missing quite so much.

Then those who had been away for a holiday came back; the second and third weeks of January passed; and on the twenty-first, a Monday, I went to the college again, as piteously joyful as if I had been an outcast returning to open and welcoming arms again.

There were changes at the college. New students had come, several of the old ones had left, among them Mackie, whose course was finished, and we had a new "professor," who, it was said, was to start an advertisement-writing class. But the biggest gap seemed to be left by Miss Levey and Miss Causton, neither of whom, in spite of their answers to my question at the breaking-up party, had returned. Miss Levey, indeed was not returning; she had got a job; and I do not conceal that this was a small relief to me. It put an end to the hints and guessings and pertinacities that might still further have embarrassed my not very clearly explained situation. But Miss Causton, I gathered, had merely not come back yet. As it turned out later, she did not come back. But nobody knew yet. So, until she should do so, Evie and Miss Windus remained our only two woman students.

It is plain that I had had to think out a plausible reason for my own return. I neither wished, nor would it have been credible of me, to be regarded as one of those high-and-dry relics (every college and school has them) who wear on to middle age seeing whole generations of juniors out, and become pathetic "institutions" merely because they had not initiative to stop doing what they have once begun. So I had hit on an explanation of my reappearance that, as it subsequently turned out, cut two ways. In one of these ways it proved magnificently sufficient for me; in the other it proved inadequate with an inadequacy that I only partly rectified when I became engaged to Miss Windus. In a word, I had had an idea.

My idea was this:

Starting from the old "Method" course (which, despite my failure, I knew back and forth and inside out), I had begun to evolve for myself a whole new course of private study. Much of this, I anticipated, I should be able to pursue at the college; for the rest the British Museum and the Patent Office Library would serve. The germ of my notion lay (or at least began) in certain questions that bore on the consolidation of

Commercial Distribution; and I fancied, rightly as it turned out, that my idea was in harmony with the broader developments of the day. More than that I need not say. All that concerns this story is that my new inspiration landed me straightway in a dilemma. On the one hand, the newness of the idea proved to be the foundation of my fortune, on the other, because of its very newness, and because it surpassed the terms of the then known, it appeared to those who wanted to know "what Jeffries was about," a subterfuge and a blind for something else. In a small sense, as you are aware, it was that; in a larger one it emphatically was not.

It is odd what difference a New Year makes in such colleges as ours. The influx of new students always drives the older ones more closely together, so that a person with whom the previous term you had little more than a nodding acquaintance becomes, when you meet again, almost an old friend. You have memories and associations in common that the new-comers know nothing about, and quasi-amicable rearrangements are made. I may say at once that it was not this that finally drove me into Miss Windus's arms, but it helped in the early stages by breaking down other resistances, and so made our extraordinary subsequent relation possible.

Evie had told me, on the night when I had first walked home with her to Woburn Place, that she usually went home either alone or else with Miss Windus, who lived in Percy Street, Tottenham Court Road; and while I, of course, had gone no farther than the gate, Miss Windus, I knew, had on more than one occasion gone in to supper. In the new order of things (which included Archie's "home from home") the three of them not infrequently went to Woburn Place together, and I began to see his light near the Foundling Hospital more and more rarely as I passed. Of course it didn't at all follow that because he was not in his own quarters he was at Woburn Place; I knew for a fact that very often he was not; and I learned from Mackie, whom I ran into one evening as I was returning from Rixon Tebb & Masters', and to whom I forced myself to talk, that on at least one recent occasion Master Archie had been seen flying a none-too-steadily-balanced kite in the neighbourhood of Leicester Square. The "home from home" was a capital one from the point of view of Mrs. Merridew, no doubt; but from that of Miss Soames the aunt, into whose house, whether she knew it or not, some whiff at least of another atmosphere was being brought, the thing seemed very open indeed to question.

Evie, I could see now, was lost in love of him; and I sometimes wondered whether I was not becoming hopelessly one-idea-ridden to suppose that it could all possibly end in any but the plain and obvious way—by her marriage to him. Changes that I shall speak of presently were taking place quickly in myself, and perhaps it was the first sign of them that sometimes, when I found myself utterly spent and broken, melodramatic magnanimities rose in my brain. In these moments I was tempted to throw up the struggle, to take myself off somewhere, and to leave them to arrange matters as they would. I wonder—I wonder!—whether I should have had the strength to do it!

And I wonder too whether, had I done it, it would have been "strength" at all! I hardly think it would. I will not generalise about slack young men and blind and innocent girls; I am not concerned with collective morals; but I was concerned with the given case, and already saw how things would almost inevitably turn out. Archie, after the manner of his kind, would sandwich in his visits to Woburn Place with more suspect pleasures; presently there would come some accident of detection, or there would not; if there did he would make a more or less (probably less) clean breast of it, and if there did not it would become a question of how far he would go with Evie. At that also I could make a guess. A "home from home," is not quite what it seems when the home contains a young creature who follows the befriended young man about with soft and adoring eyes; parents and aunts notice these things; one day something would happen; and Archie, who never took any other line, would take the line of least resistance and, seeing that it was expected of him, become formally engaged to her.

And then what? Ah, I foresaw that too!

She would be, as the expression goes, "no worse" for him. For that also he lacked the courage. He would sloven himself and her into a love that would soon prove irksome to him, a bitterness to her, and pure only on a technicality. I knew his breed; To the best of them Woburn Place is Woburn Place, and Leicester Square Leicester Square; and to the worst of them these two things quickly interpenetrate and weld. And what would that mean for her? I looked at my love; I looked about me at other sad and disillusioned women who have survived their fair dreams as examples of the way in which this love-slovening actually works out; and I shuddered.

No, a magnanimous removal of myself would not have been "strength" at all.

Yet if you think I became engaged to Miss Windus merely that I might have a pair of eyes frequently in Woburn Place, there you are wrong again. I became engaged to her because I had no choice. The contributory causes were several. Among the earlier of them had been a conversation I had had with Archie Merridew a week before the examination in Method.

After I had been at pains to give out the information that I was engaged as it were at large and without further particularity, I had begun, as you have already guessed, to be the victim of my own ingenuity. Our committances have this way of taking matters into their own hands. I had quickly found it impossible to be thus unspecifically betrothed. Too many questions had instantly sprung up, and Archie, if not Miss Levey, had known too much about the circumstances of my life.

At first I had tried to fob him off by speaking of "some girl in the City," but that had been useless. If that was so, he had wanted to know (probably having gossipped it all over with Miss Levey), why did I never see her in the evenings, and why was I so often at liberty on Saturday afternoons and Sundays? I had protested, I had made jokes. How, I had demanded, did *he* know where I passed my spare time? . . . Well, he knew (he had retorted) where I spent five evenings out of the seven!

Miss Levey, you see, had started him, and it amused him to go on.

And so his intrusiveness had begun to narrow me down to the college itself.

This had given me the choice of just two *inamorata*—Miss Causton and Miss Windus (for I still supposed that Miss Causton might walk into the college as usual any evening). To the latter lady I was at that time exceedingly averse; and on the night of this conversation of which I speak, after Archie had been almost beyond endurance jestingly importunate, I had all but declared myself point blank for the absent Miss Causton. (The conversation had taken place in his rooms.)

"The question is, Archie," I said gravely, looking at him with sharp doubt in my eyes, "can I trust you? I suspect you've already set something going, you know."

He had coloured a little. A mere honourable understanding was never in the least binding on him, and I was never quite sure to what extent the exaction of a definite promise would be so.

"Oh, dash it all, Jeff!" he had scoffed rather awkwardly, "anybody'd think you were ashamed of it! All I said was quite harmless—really—"

"I know," I had commented, "*meaning* no harm. Nine-tenths of the harm in the world's done that way. I don't know that I don't prefer the man who means harm; at least he knows what he's doing. . . But why are you so curious about it all?"

His curiosity, I knew, was nothing more or less than a slack indulgence of his desire to hear a secret. He had too Miss Levey's racial gift of turning these things to account. But he had put it rather differently.

"Oh, just friendly interest," he had replied, slapping his jacket pocket. "Where did I put my cigarette case? . . . We *are* friends, aren't we?"

"Rather less so when you go chattering about me."

"Sorry, old man," he had replied contritely, though his contrition had been less for his blabbing than that I apparently had taken it amiss. "I didn't think—you didn't tell me not—it slipped out—"

"Well, well—no great harm's done. But if I were you—" if I had hesitated it was merely for a private and subtle relish "—I'd take a memory powder, to use an expression of Miss Windus's."

(You will remember how I had come to overhear that expression, and you may see, by turning back, the precise context of the allusion.)

Archie had been sitting in his favourite attitude, with his stockinged feet against the pilaster of the fireplace. He had twinkled again.

"I don't think it *can* be Miss Windus," he had chuckled again. "Anybody can see you can't stand her."

"Oh? Sorry I've allowed that to appear."

"And the college isn't exactly swarming with girls," he had continued.

I had told him that he was dragging the college in entirely on his own responsibility.

"Oh no!" he had said promptly, with a far too cunning glance at me. "You don't put me off like that, old boy! I've got you down to that, and I'm going to hold you to it! Serve you right for your dashed secretiveness! So if it isn't Miss Windus, and it isn't Miss Soames—"

At that I had been able quite calmly to jest. I had fetched up a laugh.

"Steady a minute," I had said. "If you're really bent on going into the Sherlock Holmes business you'll have to do it properly, you know— give reasons for your eliminations. Accuracy's everything. Let's have your reason for ruling Miss Soames out."

"Good old Jeff," he had remarked, laughing; "accurate even in his jokes! Well, say Evie's a young twenty, and you're a damned experienced old thirty—how will *that* do?"

I believe, taken with all the rest, that it had seemed to him perfectly conclusive.

"That's better," I had approved. "I only meant that if you're going to be methodical you must *be* methodical, that's all. Good mental training for you, my boy."

"So it is," he had agreed, with the forthcoming examination in his mind. "I say—we'll have a shorthand speed-test presently—but first I'm going to drag this out of you. . ."

And by-and-by I had all but made the confession that it was Miss Causton whom I adored from a distance and hesitated to approach.

Another contributory source to this oddest freak of my life was the terms on which I had returned to the college. That wide and unexpected development of my new studies was no explanation to anybody but myself; I had confessed myself, through Archie, to be in love; and the more closely I applied myself to my mysterious work the less mysterious did my whole conduct appear. Yet on the whole, even if Miss Causton had returned at once, I might at the last have feared the hazard with one at once so suspiciously open and problematically deep as she; and there was no allowing matters to remain as they were. There was only Miss Windus for it.

You see the mess I had landed myself in.

Yet my unhappiness in all this was only a part of a general change that was quickly leavening me throughout. It was a change altogether for the better. I was sick, sick of shifts and tricks and meannesses. I was no less sick of them in myself than I was when I encountered them in the Sutts and Polwheles among whom my life was passed. I panted for a clearer air and a more spacious prospect; I panted for these things because Evie had loosened the band that had confined the wings of my own spirit. And with my own spirit thus freed, I would find a way to escape from the cage of my circumstances. Once I had done with that old life I would have done with it for ever. And, strange as it may seem, it was because hope was at last greyly and tardily dawning for me that I entered into my last despicable tortuousness with Kitty Windus.

II

For as I got deeper into my studies I began to see in it nothing less than the finger of Providence that I had failed in the second part of the examination in Method. That frustration altered the whole course of my life. I am, of course, speaking in the light of subsequent events, but I see now what a mere pass would have meant—a sort of success no doubt—but a success in a narrow and short-reaching attempt.

Up to that time my plan had been to qualify myself by means of certificates, to find a billet elsewhere, and then, with Rixon Tebb & Masters' recommendation of steadiness and sobriety, really to begin in some firm where promotion was possible otherwise than by our bottle-neck of a junior clerkship. I had actually had the choice of no less than two such firms, and had been already wondering what I should do with my extra twelve shillings a week—for I should have begun at thirty shillings.

And then I had failed.

Well, heaven be thanked for it. In that failure I sounded, for the last time—but no; for the last time but one—the bass-string of my poverty.

For now, as I saw my new work gradually unfolding, it sometimes so excited me that I could hear my own heart thumping in my breast. Do you know that feeling—that in your brain there is already born, and growing apace, an idea that you do not believe to be guessed at by any creature in the world except yourself? As a matter of fact I now know that my idea was being simultaneously worked upon elsewhere. Sir Julius (then "Judy") Pepper was pegging away at it in his back room in Endsleigh Gardens, hardly a mile from where I brooded over it myself; and if you have never heard of the association of Jeffries and Pepper you know very little about these things. Still, all was in darkness then save for that single ray far ahead that seemed to indicate a way out; and even now I have only just begun my life's work—the keying up to concert pitch of certain branches of commercial distribution that, by the time I and my successors have finished, will make men wonder how such a phenomenon as, say, the railway strike of last year could ever have been possible.

Nor was this deepest peace that the man of action knows—his certainty about what his task in the world must be—the whole of my spirit's unexpected re-birth. This held out the promise of material—and shall I say "ethical?"—well-being; and my eyes were now opened to more than that. I hesitate to call this new thing "religion." I would rather define it as the clear and immutable knowledge that all things *do* work together to an end, good, bad or morally unconnoted. It was a perception of powers and forces, not at variance, but working in harmony towards some cosmic consummation. I don't think that is religion. I don't think it would save a soul. But it not only saved, but made altogether its own, my reason. I believed in the power and divinity of a thing, if not in those of a Being. And I believe that I should have got further even than that.

And if it be true that we treat the world as we are treated by it, this changed my attitude to all with whom I came into contact. I am not thinking now of Kitty Windus, for she, poor soul, was but an episode, though one I have found is hard enough to make away with. I am thinking of Sutt, of Polwhele, of the proprietor of my public-house, of the drivers and porters of my restaurant, of the men and women, seen and to be seen no more, who passed me in the streets. And I am thinking of Evie Soames.

For it was side by side with her sweetness that I conceived all this authority and strength and vision to exist. It was all, I knew not how, hers—hers and mine. I could not successfully resolve a problem nor work out an equation but something within me cried, "That is ours, my love!—something seized from the limbo of things-not-known-yet, for you, dear, and for me!" I could now even bear to work away from her, in another room of the college, among the files of the Patent Office, at my own place. When her face rose, as it ever did, between me and my paper or page, I knew peace now, not jealousy. Had I put into words the thoughts that then filled me those words would have been, "Yes, my own—you see what I'm doing—it is for us, and it won't be long— go away, sweetheart, but not very far." And so I dreamed harder and worked harder than I have ever done in my life, and both came easily to me, because I had at last clearly seen my goal.

Yet you are not to suppose that I was not unwinkingly wakeful too. This was my inner life, and it informed, but did not abate, the vigilance of my outer one. I think that three times out of four I knew (at first at any rate) when Archie had been to Woburn Place, and perhaps twice out of four when he had sought a lower pleasure elsewhere. It would take too long to tell you how I ascertained all this. I did so under a mask of casualness that practice and my new-born hope had now made quite easy.

And so I come to my acceptance by Kitty Windus.

Espionage upon Woburn Place was only a part, and by far the lesser part, of it. I had my impossible position to explain. And not only had I to explain it, but my original lie had left me only one other way of explaining it—the giving up of Evie once for all. That I could have more easily done months back than I could now that hope had brought her so (I speak comparatively) tantalisingly near. I admit that the chance that I might be introduced at Woburn Place as Miss Windus's *fiancée* did weigh, and horribly. I no longer hated her. I pitied her. I do not mean that this pity was in the least degree akin to love in that word's sense as between man and woman; but by salving a little my self-content it did, practically, help me to carry the thing out. But I swear, however much I may appear to put myself upon the defensive in doing so, that of itself the prospect of Woburn Place would not have swayed me.

I have not the heart to remember the earlier stages of my duplicity. Too many crawling things lie beneath that stone of my life for me to wish to turn it over. Let me summarise by saying that, by a slow and nicely calculated relaxing of my stiffness, and a gradual and lingering and gratuitous prolongation ever and again of certain opportunities of intercourse, I had, by the beginning of March, so counterbalanced my former aversion that, in a word, anything might happen, and at any moment.

Poor, lonely, starved spinster heart! I have far more ruth for what I did to you than for what I did to another!

But let me, before I go on, see whether there was anything during the months of January and February that I may not omit. . . No, I think there is little. Miss Causton still remained away; I pursued my new investigations; that segregation of newness of the first-year students relaxed a little, but without affecting that slight unconscious coming together of the older ones that it had brought about; and I think Archie Merridew divided his time between Woburn Place and Leicester Square pretty equally. I think that is all. I pass on.

It was in Lincoln's Inn Fields that I entered into a pledge with Kitty Windus that I had no intention of ever redeeming. I had not thought when I had left the college that night that it would come so quickly. I had planned a long walk, and, passing through Great Turnstile, had come upon Miss Windus looking into the window of an antique shop. I had stopped and gazed with her, and then, presently moving away, we had passed together into the square.

She told me afterwards that she had been merely aimlessly wandering, having been to Woburn Place the evening before and fearing to weary her welcome there by going again the next night; but I did not know this then. Therefore, when presently she stopped at the corner where the street leading to Kingsway now is and said, "Well, I think I'll go back," I was a little surprised. Then I understood and laughed.

"I'm so sorry," I said, "I thought this was your way. I don't know that it's particularly mine—I was only taking a stroll—so if you don't mind I'll walk back with you."

Thereupon we turned back into the Fields.

It was this mutually made discovery that neither of us was pressed for time that brought simultaneously into our minds some slight self-consciousness that for the first time in our lives we should be thus killing an hour in one another's company. Her own embarrassment presently gave expression to this.

"How nice," she said, after we had walked half the length of the central garden railings in silence, "to feel sometimes that you haven't got to talk if you don't want to!"

The remark, commonplace as it was, gave me a new glimpse of her. I knew that she read a better class of novel than my Evie, and with the results you might suppose. I don't seriously believe that Evie's "scions of noble blood" and the rest of her novelette paraphernalia had any point of contact with real life for her, but Miss Windus carried over the triteness she got from her reading into her thought and speech. Therefore, since I myself, though no eloquent speaker, believe that tongues were made to talk with, I again laughed a little.

"Yes," I replied, "provided always that you aren't silent merely because you've nothing to say."

I think this penetration, such as it was, struck her with quite remarkable force; and, as the novels provided no reply to it, she was again silent for a time. We were approaching the corner of Great Turnstile again, but I don't think she noticed it. We turned down by Stone Buildings and began to complete the circuit of the Fields.

"Mr. Merridew said you were very clever," she remarked at last. "What *do* you study all by yourself in the senior classroom, Mr. Jeffries?" she asked, the quizzical little triangles of her eyes turned up to mine in the light of a lamp that hung like a beacon over the garden railings. She wore a plaid Inverness cape and a boat-shaped hat that night, I remember, and would doubtless have worn rubber heels had those articles been invented. Never woman made a slighter physical appeal to man than she.

"I'm not quite sure myself yet," I replied, as truthfully as made no matter. "Part of it at any rate is human nature in business."

"I love human nature," she said.

I knew I had only to speak. In the light of the wrong I was about to do her I freely forgave her all her past pretences towards myself. All grapes had been sour to poor Kitty, and I didn't doubt she had made brave attempts, and still braver concealments of failure. Baboon or anybody else, there she was at his pleasure so her reproach be but taken away. For already I had decided that it might as well be now as later.

"Yes," I answered, as if absently, and we walked on.

The night was slightly frosty, and over the houses to the north of the Fields the glare of Holborn shone rustily. There were few people about. As we walked, by this time almost used to the strangeness of one another's company, I wished that the central garden of the square had not been closed; at least she would have had the association of a tree and a plot of grass to go with her plighting. But I knew that such weaknesses as this were not safe, and shut peremptorily down on them. She seemed so pathetically small and skimpy by my side, and had I yielded even a little I could almost have persuaded myself of a tenderness for her. This I refused to do. I would do nothing to make easy for myself what would by-and-by prove cruel enough for her.

We were half way round the Fields on our second circuit before I spoke again. I moistened my lips and steeled myself.

"Miss Windus," I said.

I think a tremor took her instantly with my change of tone. She looked up, but I did not hear whether she said anything.

Nor did I say anything. Our hands, as we walked, were close together. I took hers.

She made no attempt to draw it away, and we walked so. Presently I took the hand in my other one, and this brought it across my breast. I daresay she felt the beating of my heart.

"Kitty," I whispered.

She pressed against me a little.

I don't think it ever entered her head that I intended anything but just that we should walk, for that one night, round Lincoln's Inn Fields like this. I don't believe she thought of anything. With even that heel and paring of love she was content—just to walk so, tomorrow if it was to be, if not then at any rate tonight, with her hand in a man's and her shoulder pressing lightly against a man's shoulder.

Well, she had it.

"Kitty," I whispered again. This was in a dark shadow on the south side of the Fields. Without prearrangement we had ceased to walk, and were standing together, she with her face turned downwards and away, quite ready to give me all she supposed I wanted of her.

She couldn't murmur my name in return. She didn't know it. It was, for her, merely "Man." But instead she gave me that for which I stooped over her. She gave it with a heartrending impulsiveness throwing back her head suddenly and leaning her bosom on mine. I felt a pair of dry, slightly cracked lips on my own and was conscious of an odour of clothes. . . Then we separated again.

"Oh," she said, with a shaky little exhalation of her breath, "I. . . I didn't think you'd ever look at me—Jeff!"

This last was a quick invention, to cover her ignorance of my Christian name.

She meant that she hadn't thought that anybody would ever look at her. Every shred of the old pretence of the pertinacities and annoyances of strangers had fallen from her. She lifted up her face again—and again—as if by present gluttony to forestall insatiable hungers of the morrow and the morrow after that.

For a minute I was well-nigh resolved out of sheer compassion to keep my word and marry her.

And even then—think of it!—she had no idea that I contemplated what was, indeed, my sole reason for action—an acknowledged engagement. She never dreamed I meant to marry her. It was I who spoke of this, half-an-hour later. By that time we had been to the bottom of Chancery Lane and back, and were in the Fields again, once more in that same shadow where I had kissed her first. She looked at me.

I can hardly write it. There was first a gleam of fear in her eyes, and then a leaping.

"*Jeff!*" she cried in a loud voice that cracked.

I had to catch her as she began slowly to sink at the knees.

So I BECAME ENGAGED. AT the college it was a nine days' wonder, but I let them wonder. So did Kitty Windus, merely pretending that the thing had been for long a secret understanding. Archie, I remember, smirked through some form of congratulation when I told him: "What, *not* Louie after all!" but it was only when Evie Soames flung her arms about Kitty Windus' neck and well-nigh about mine also that I began really to wonder what could possibly come of it all.

III

During those little pauses and lapses of study in which men scribble abstractedly on the margins of paper, idly forming letters or noughts-and-crosses or inexpert attempts at portraiture, I myself had a way of filling my blanks at that time that may serve to explain the change that had more and more come over me. I used to rub with a pencil, as evenly as possible, two little squares of grey, and then to put into the middle of the first of them a spot as black as my pencil could make it, leaving in the second a similar spot, but one of clean white. Unless you have tried it you may not believe the difference in effect. The black spot of the first seems to make denser and darker the whole square; but the white one lightens and relieves it as the sun does when it struggles through a mist. By what law of optics this is to be explained I cannot tell; I can only say that if Kitty Windus, wondering what I studied all by myself in the senior classroom, had come upon me at these times, she would have found me pondering over these marginal trifles as in some way a symbol of my own life.

For had it not been for this gloomy blot of my betrothal to her I would not now have exchanged my life for that of any man I knew. So did hope now irradiate it. I was still an eighteen-shilling Agency clerk; I still lived in a red and green loft over a public-house; but I now believed in myself, longed to be able to respect myself, and had already grimly resolved that others should respect me.

I was in this state of mind when I first set eyes on Angela Soames.

I was taken there, of course—to Woburn Place, I mean—by Kitty Windus. It was within a week of our engagement, so that I had not to wait long for these first-fruits of my extraordinary position. That night was the second time I walked with Evie to her abode, for Archie followed a few yards behind with Kitty Windus. We had dropped into this arrangement on leaving the college, as men tacitly pay each other's partners the courtesy of their attentions.

When I have said that Evie's home was in Woburn Place I have gone a long way towards describing it. She lived in one of those large apartment houses that are full of Japanese, Americans, and Indian law students, with a half-pay officer here and there. She and her aunt had rooms of their own upstairs, but they dined in the large common dining-room downstairs, at a table that would almost have resembled that of a public dinner had it not been for the gaps left by the absent boarders, several of whom were always dining elsewhere. I never saw that table full. I have tried to carry on a conversation with my neighbour across two intervening empty chairs. I have had to accept the highly polished civilities of Indians and Japanese, who have refused to disturb me when I have removed a rolled napkin in a numbered ring and put a flat and freshly ironed one in its place. One met niggers and gouty subjects and antiquated old ladies in the hall and on the stairs; and I was quite prepared to find Miss Soames the aunt one of these last.

But she was not in the least so. There was not very much more difference between her age and my own than there was between mine and Evie's—though of course what difference there was was all on the wrong side. She was, I should say, forty-three or four, and I wondered the moment I saw her how she had got through these forty odd years and remained Miss Angela. Let me say at once that she had no secret sorrow (though Kitty always vowed she had). When, later, she told me, with the greatest self-pluming in the world, that she "could have been married" more than once or twice, she told me nothing I should not have guessed; but merely to have had these opportunities seemed entirely to content her detached and unruffled and rather aimless soul. She had had the refusal of them—and she coquetted with that. She had avoided the pains of marriage—and remained the white-haired *ingenue*. It later became one of Kitty's irritating tricks to "wish she had hair like that"—a beautiful tower of it dressed *à la Marquise*; but in nothing else could Kitty ever have resembled Angela Soames. . . But perhaps I may be wrong in my estimate after all. Perhaps no man can really understand that kind of woman, who cannot lose all herself even when she marries and loses not very much less when she does not. Evie, I concluded, probably had her passion for abandonment from her mother.

I was introduced to the elder Miss Soames in her sitting-room. This apartment, like herself, seemed to trail even into Woburn Place hems and fringes of past prosperity. The room itself was not much more than a cold-blue-papered, corniceless box—but, as the first of a number of odd little contrasts, a shield-shaped embroidered firescreen hung on a slender stem near the fire. The door was painted yellow and grained—but a pair of handsome silver candlesticks stood on the mantelpiece. There was a threadbare lodging-house carpet—and a black bear-skin hearthrug, the head of the animal worn bald by Miss Angela's paste-buckled slipper. And so on. On the round table stood a rosy-shaded lamp (that did *not* change to a corresponding shade of green as you looked). Miss Angela herself wore a soft old grey with a thin Indian silk shawl cast over her shoulders, and I remembered, as I looked at her, certain former angry conclusions I had come to about her. I took them all back. Charmingly unsure of herself in everything, from her love affairs downwards, she might be, but she did not parrot precepts about the "less fortunately circumstanced." We shook hands, and I was told that I might smoke. Archie had come in smoking.

I did not talk very much during this my first call. Indeed, Miss Angela murmured, as if to herself, some half-mischievous, half-tactful remark about an "ordeal"; and my slight nervousness passed as part of Kitty's "showing off" of me. But the others made up for me, and I listened, smiling, but silent except when I was directly addressed.

This I presently was by Miss Angela, and on a point no less interesting than the way in which Archie spent his evenings. It had already appeared that he was to celebrate a birthday two days thence, and Miss Angela had asked him to spend the evening with them.

"You've given us a very cold shoulder lately," she said; "why, your mother's been remarking on it!" She pulled a faded tapestry hassock towards her with her foot, the fire being too hot to allow her to make use of the bear's head, and reached for a paper fan with which to keep the heat from her face. "I hope it's not *you* who take up all his time, Mr. Jeffries?"

I answered that it was not, and Evie, who had removed her hat and coat and was now tidying her hair before the mantelpiece mirror, laughed.

"Mr. Jeffries' time is spoken for now—isn't it, Kitty?" she said.

I saw her look at Archie as she said it. He was astride the hearthrug, allowing the smoke of his cigarette to stream up his nostrils, and she, as she arranged her hair, had to look at herself almost over his shoulder. Her occupation left the whole of her young bosom quite defenceless had there been a pair of arms to pass about it, and the soft look she gave him was a double provocation. But he did not return the look. He moved a little aside, also finding the fire hot, and flipped his cigarette ash into the fender.

"I don't think an engaged girl ought to come between a man and all his old friends," Kitty pronounced. Her look at me was a promise that she would never come between me and Archie.

Miss Angela gave a contented little laugh.

"Ah, you all say that at first! Well. . ." She glanced past Evie at me, and took me into her confidence with a private smile. It was as if we two older ones understood that there was something in process that must not be disturbed. "But if you don't come, Archie," she added, "I shall write straight to your mother! You'll come too, Miss Windus?"

Kitty glanced at me.

"Oh, of course I mean Mr. Jeffries too!" said Miss Angela archly.

"Oh, of course him too!" quoth Archie, from the hearthrug, loosening his scorching trousers. "Two hearts that beat as one—you bet—twopence into a penny show *now*, Jeff!"

And again Miss Angela, with a look this time past him, seemed to invite my attention to something.

You may guess that my attention needed little inviting. So far, my surmise, that she adored him while she took the admiration a little impatiently, seemed to be pretty near the mark; and I was confirmed in this when she presently sat down on the companion hassock beyond the end of the fender, and, with her face a little averted, sank into moroseness. It was merely because her glance as she stood before the mirror had not been returned, but I myself had known too well what it was to be uplifted and cast down again by these nothings not to understand.

And Archie too understood, if the jocular and would-be easy manner in which he tried to drag her into the conversation again meant anything. I suspected that this was not the first incident of the kind that had occurred between them. Presently he had twice addressed her directly without getting more than the shortest of replies; and the third time he did so (he, Kitty and Miss Angela had been talking about some indifferent matter) he added the words, "that is, when Evie's found her tongue again."

My darling had a temper of her own. "I didn't know I'd lost it," she said, with a little perverse snap.

Then she dropped into her sulks again.

"These lovers' quarrels!" Miss Angela's private smile to me seemed to say; but this time I evaded the discreet invitation to participate.

"Well," Archie said presently, looking at his watch, "I must be off; I've a chap to meet. Thanks, Aunt Angela (beg pardon; I know you don't like being called that). I'll come on Thursday, then."

But Miss Angela exclaimed: "A man to meet! At this hour!"

Archie took his hat from a chair. "Yes. About a dog. Why not? Fox terrier," he added facetiously; "must make sure they've got over the distemper, you know. Thursday then. You two are staying a bit, I suppose?" he invited us.

He made his adieux; but almost before the door had closed behind him Evie had risen from her hassock.

"You'll excuse me, won't you?" she said quickly. "I've got a headache. I shall go straight to bed. Good-night."

And she followed him out—whether straight to bed or not I don't know. Kitty and I followed shortly afterwards.

And now that I've got to this Woburn Place portion of my story I may as well, while I am about it, skip the two intervening days and come to the evening of Archie Merridew's birthday.

Thursday was not in any case one of Evie's class evenings, and on that Thursday she must have been very busy indeed. We were to go to supper at eight; and as the routine of the boarding house did not provide for private entertainments the aunt and niece had had all to do themselves. The supper was therefore of necessity cold, with the exception of some hot soup, which I suspect to have been heated over a bedroom fire; and for the furnishing of the round table with the pink-shaded lamp Miss Angela had rummaged in drawers and trunks and bundles, with notable results. White heavy plates with the name of the boarding house contained within an oval garter were set between common knives and delicate and worn old silver forks and spoons, really beautiful glass finger-bowls stood on straw mats with a circular hole in the middle; and a long slender-handled punch-ladle stuck up out of the cheap earthenware jug full of home-made lemonade.

I suspect, too, that Evie had changed her mind a dozen times about the height of her dress at the neck; and probably her aunt's guidance had led her finally, since she had no special dress for the evening, to reject the compromise of altering her blouse to an intermediate V. Her dark hair had been newly washed. A softer lace than Kitty Windus' came quite up to her ears, and Miss Angela had lent her a pearl ring, which seemed to be mutely asking to be transferred to the finger next to the one on which she wore it. She was in white, with a longer skirt than usual; Miss Angela wore the old grey and Indian silk shawl she always wore; and Kitty looked prettier than I have ever seen her in a spotted blue foulard (I think I have that right) with wonderfully crimped sleeves and a cameo brooch at her rather wiry throat.

She and I arrived before Archie, who, indeed, was a full quarter of an hour late. When he did turn up, there mingled with his apologies the bumptious assumption of ease with which he sought to make a joke of his negligence. He came in noisily, as if he intended to make the party a success out of hand; and before he had been in the room half-a-minute a whiff told me what I had instantly surmised from the brightness of his eyes—that he had been drinking sherry and bitters already.

"Thanks, Aunt Angela—but that's not all, I hope!" he cried, as Miss Angela wished him many happy returns of the day.

And he skipped to her, passed his arm about her waist, and kissed her.

"Hope you won't mind for once, Jeff," he went on, dancing to Kitty Windus. Kitty both stiffened rigidly and flushed with excitement as he kissed her also on the cheek-bone.

"Here—I'm going all round now—where's Evie?" he demanded.

But Evie had slipped out of the room.

We sat down to supper.

I found Archie insufferable. He made the whole running with an ignorant egotism that caused my fingers to itch to box his ears. More than once he contradicted Miss Angela flatly, instantly trying to redeem the grossness by laughing loudly and crying, "Excuse my frankness—no offence—only Archie's way!" He made so familiar both with Kitty and myself that, out of mere hostility to him, I came very near to an alliance with her. Evie, I saw, was miserable. How much she knew about his habits I could only guess; I think that already she knew more than a little; but his had been the fortune to reveal her to herself, and I am not sure whether that ever wholly dies. I think it has since died as much as ever it can.

"But," Miss Angela said by-and-by, seeking to quieten him, "I've forgotten to ask you how your father is. Better, I hope?"

"The pater? Oh, he's all right; it's only a bilious attack. Afraid he got poisoned with some *foie gras* he ate—jolly good tack *I* call it—I'll have some more, please. And what's that you've got to drink there, Evie?"

Evie poured him out some lemonade. He looked at it, but made no remark on it.

"Here's your *foie gras*—have some cress with it," said Miss Angela.

And so we fêted his lordship.

After supper there were nuts and almonds, which we ate sitting round the fire. I say "we," but Archie had what was left afterwards.

With a "Half-a-mo," he had gone out, and I myself thought our party much pleasanter without him.

But as he remained away, Miss Angela had no choice but to say presently: "What *can* have become of our young man? I wonder if you'd mind fetching him, Mr. Jeffries!"

I went, and found him.

He had picked up, on the stairs or in the hall, a Japanese with whom he had contracted some sort of acquaintance, and I heard his call as I passed the half-open door of the dining-room.

"Here—Jeff!" he called. "Hold on—I sha'n't be a minute—come and let me introduce you to Mr. Shoto—Mr. Shoto, Mr. Jeffries."

I distrust that too affable little race from the other side of the world, and I gave Mr. Shoto the most perfunctory of nods. Archie was having a very golden whisky and soda with him.

"Come along—you oughtn't to clear off like this," I said curtly. "Miss Soames is asking for you."

"All right—good old Angela—just a minute till I finish this. We were talking about Japan, or rather Mr. Shoto was. Tell him that about the Yoshiwara, Shoto."

But that cunning little alien had evidently summed me up already, and had a different choice of subject for me.

I haled Archie back. I wondered, as he sat down by Evie, whether he would have another man about another dog to see presently, but he hadn't. Magnanimously he gave us the whole of the rest of the evening. This he did in spite of the cold encouragement he got from Evie. Twice, I was certain, while his face did not cease to be animated with the talk he gave the rest of us, his hand sought hers behind the arm of his chair; but she drew away. Nevertheless she drew away discreetly. By doing so openly she could have shown him up, but evidently she did not wish to show him up. There was no irreconcilable difference between them. She was angry, but not to the point of refusing to make it up afterwards. And I knew she was not far from unhappy tears.

Kitty and I were the first to leave. This was at half-past eleven, and I had no desire to outsit Archie. He would either leave in another half-hour, which would leave him time for another golden whisky and soda, or, setting the smoothing over of Evie's ruffled temper before the attractions of the public-house, would linger till after closing-time, when there would be no hurry. To see which alternative he would take didn't on the whole seem to be worth waiting for.

So Kitty and I took our leave; and as I walked with her to Percy Street—where she had two rooms over a modiste's—I—and she too—had to suffer as best we might the kind of thing I will relate in the next chapter.

From the beginning she wanted one thing, I another. She was prepared to "love" me (as if it had been a matter of will, to which, nevertheless, I am quite certain she would faithfully have adhered) on the condition that that heart of hers should be no longer a parched pod; but I wanted no more of her than that my name should be linked with hers as that of her suitor. To me the appearance was the indispensable thing; she wanted the substance. And she was already plaguing me for it.

God knows I gave her what I could give. Afterwards, when all was over, she still had the memory of it. I hope she found comfort in it.

For of course it was precisely over that which was Evie's, and which I was resolved to keep for Evie, that we were locked in a grapple. She lisped and besought and cajoled. Before I began sometimes utterly to forget that we were betrothed at all I could often have groaned aloud at her inexpert playfulness; and I doubt whether the wit of man could have devised a more acute torture than that which I now began to undergo at her unsuspecting hands.

For Archie's birthday was early in March, and already the crocuses were out, and the barrows in the streets were so aflame with daffodils that the flowers almost illuminated the faces of the sellers of them. It was still cold and backward, but the days were long past the turn, and while single twigs were still of a wintry iron hue, in the mass they took a softness, and the vistas of the parks had perceptibly changed. In the streets of the wealthy in which I walked the house-painters were at work, painting doors and railings and window-boxes; and even at my King's Cross corner the railway companies' announcements told of the coming summer. Spring was breaking in London—spring, the merry time of the year—spring, when lovers cannot keep asunder—and when Kitty and myself could not, yet must, keep asunder.

In the streets I knew I was fairly safe. Her hand on my sleeve filled me with no repugnance. Let me, for example, tell you of our walk back to Percy Street on that night of Archie's birthday-party.

As we crossed Tottenham Court Road she slipped her hand into my overcoat pocket, and my own encountered it there. It held it. It retained it along dark Percy Street, and still retained it when we stopped together at the side door next the window with the two fly-blown hats on pedestals that formed the whole of the modiste's display. There I would have left her; but "Don't go just yet, Jeff," she begged; "just eentie walk?"

"Well, a short one," I said.

We turned up Fitzroy Street into the Marylebone Road, but I was wary of the dark empty spaces about Regent's Park. The streets and the crowds for me. Indeed I may say that during this period of our "walking out" no couple in London sought solitude as I sought to avoid it; and I resolutely suppressed the thought of what was going to happen when the warm days should come and she should ask me to take her to Richmond or Epping or Kew. It was no good meeting that horror half way.

Therefore. "Well," I said, as we approached Portland Road Station again, "hadn't we better be turning? It's getting late."

"I suppose so," she sighed reluctantly, with a pressure of my arm. "Let's go this way."

She indicated one of the darker side streets. We took it.

By-and-by we stood by the modiste's window again. That is not a very reputable neighbourhood, and as she stood there, lingering out our talk to the thinnest of excuses, I guessed what was in her mind. But the general environment of laxity only produced a primness in her. In being all that she should be, she was sometimes a good deal more. Still, there was no harm in dallying with a secret thought.

But under all circumstances she ever displayed a sort of tempted prudishness.

"You and Evie and Miss Soames must come in one Sunday and have tea with me," she said resignedly at last, allowing the thought that some day I might go up with her to recede.

"That will be charming," I replied.

Then she sighed. "It has been so lovely tonight!"

"In what way?" I asked, forcing a smile.

"Archie was horrid, and you, Jeff—"

Yes, I remembered that hostility to Archie certainly had resulted in a *rapprochement* between ourselves.

"Well," she said at last, lifting her face, "good-night, dearest—I know who *I* shall dream of!"

I kissed her, heard the sound of her key in the lock, and, turning, saw her little face still looking through the half-closed door after me. I returned to King's Cross by way of Woburn Place, but there was only a glimmer of light within the fanlight of Evie's dwelling as I passed. Perhaps Archie had chosen the whisky and soda after all.

I soon saw that only by means of a studied unemotionalness should I be able for long to head her off from the things she sought; and I set about the creation of this atmosphere without loss of time. In this I found my far-reaching ambition useful to me; I had simply to be preoccupied with business to be spared much. I had not to play this part. I actually was a ferment of new plans. That my absorbing ambition was all for her sake was allowed to pass as understood. And when she began to make touching attempts to be interested in my affairs, I, lest a worse thing should befall me, encouraged her. I talked fully and freely, knowing that I ran no more risk of betrayal than Napoleon did when he laid before a Russian peasant woman unacquainted with French the plan of campaign he feared to trust to his own staff. This I did as the almonds pushed forth their pink, and the plane-trees budded, and the building birds sang loudly. Once she called me her building bird.

I had had to tell her, vaguely, about my employment; and I was also vague about where I lived. Here her own tempted timorousness helped me. It was not difficult for me to be stern about the proprieties, and indeed, as she saw this, and began to feel perfectly safe with me, she even affected a liberality of thought. "Why not?" she would sometimes ask almost defiantly; "why not see one another in our own places—if there was nothing horrid?"

And for that I usually found a surprised stare answer enough.

But the hunger was on her, and I had to give her morsels. That was a haggard horror. It was the more horrible that her vanities always turned on the things of which she had the least reason to be vain. As an affectionate and devoted and dull spinster my heart was often soft to her; but her coquetries would have made an angel groan. For example: her hands were not remarkably pretty; her fingers had almost the pinkness, and a little of the shape, of the smaller claws of a freshly boiled crab; but she gave them no rest from display. I was sometimes commanded, with a vapid imperiousness, to make much of them. And once, on a seat on the Embankment, she yielded to a temptation never far removed from her. It was at night; unnoticed, a portion of her hair had shaken loose; and, suddenly becoming aware of this, and doubtless with some idea of maddening me with the thought of something prohibited, she put up her hands, shook down the short mass on her shoulders, and grimaced at me. The next day she begged, with a shamed face, that I would try to forget this sin in her—for apparently she had intended it as sin; but I had nothing to forget. All that I remembered was the contrast, as she had put the hair up again, between the bosom under her uplifted arms and that other bosom from which Archie Merridew had turned away as Evie had stood before the mantelpiece mirror in Woburn Place.

Her dwelling, which I first visited with Evie and her aunt, was on the first floor of the modiste's at the back. Her sleeping apartment I never saw; and of her sitting-room I have no very clear memory now. There was a penny-in-the-slot gas-meter on the landing, I remember, and the floor of the room into which one walked was covered with a greenish jute "art square," with the wide spaces of bare boarding about it stained with Condy's Fluid. The previous occupant had left on the walls a "French boudoir" paper with a pattern of thin vertical lines and tiny garlands of pink rosebuds (Kitty had cleaned it with dough on taking possession). The furniture was scanty, with a good deal of muslin about it, and a sewing-machine stood in the back window, which looked over a restaurant yard. When she had more than two visitors at once she had to fetch an extra chair from her bedroom, and from the sound her heels made at these times I gathered that that room was uncarpeted.

As by quickening degrees she began to accept her unlooked-for situation more as a matter of course, her thoughts naturally turned to the future and that I found to involve her whole attitude to Life. The things we were to do "when we were married" were dictated by the narrowness of her outlook. She had about a pound a week of her own money, I don't know exactly where from, but I think from some tramways Edgbaston way, and this sum, together with whatever she might be able to earn for herself, was practically the limit of her conception of any income she was ever likely to have. From the stories she told me of her earlier years I gathered that she came from a social stratum in which the men are lords indeed, sometimes "in work," sometimes "out," and apparently content during these last vicissitudes to be dependent on their wives or sisters or mothers. It seemed to me such a pitiful little world, of milliners, lodging-house keepers, music-mistresses, fancy needlewomen and daughters in offices; and I was given the corresponding male standing. As with the men her cousins (her nearest relatives) had married, if I should ever happen to earn money, well and good; if not, so much the worse. She reckoned only on her weekly pound and her own efforts. And as I learned that Cousin Alf and Cousin Frank were boundlessly optimistic, and looked forward to a future no less bright than that of which I felt the certitude within me, I soon discovered that I was merely indulged in what in her heart she set down as vapourings. It was the woman who, in her experience, "kept the home together," and she was prepared to keep me.

"Well," I laughed, "I daresay I shall learn to pare the potatoes as well as Cousin Alf in time."

But she smiled a sad, wise little smile. I might joke, but she knew.

"And it's just possible that some time or other I may make a pound or two," I said, smiling back.

"There'll be your clothes and pocket-money," she replied.

So I was to be kept—kept by virtue of my masculinity, as one keeps a dog to bark. I was to be kept, I divined, somewhere in a suburb, in a house the smallness of the rent of which would be exactly balanced by the increased cost of the season ticket that would take me daily to my work, when I was "in." Even when I was "out" I was to be treated with a nice consideration, for she "never had liked to see Frank washing up—it looked so unmanly," but as she said nothing about cleaning boots or fetching coals, these things apparently were not unmanly. And I wondered whether the Alfs and Franks were more numerous than I had thought, or were becoming so. Small wonder their women treated them with almost contemptuous tolerance, blazing out once in a while into a row. And I now see that in this sense I wronged Kitty when I said she was one of Life's takers. There are always two sides to a thing, and on this side she wanted nothing but to give.

But, willing as she was to do all this in the future, I soon discovered that she wanted her small solatium in the present. In the matter of little treats and outings I did not compare very favourably even with her Franks and Alfs. As you know, I simply had not the necessary shillings. And so I began (I knew) to appear "near" and "close" to her. One Friday evening, as we left the college together, she allowed as much to be seen.

"Jeff," she said suddenly, as we approached the corner by the Oxford together, "do you know, you've never taken me to a theatre yet!"

Personally I have never greatly cared for the theatre; but it happened that I had spoken to her once or twice rather off-handedly that evening, and was not unwilling to make amends. Besides, the theatre might save a walk in Hyde Park. I pumped up a vivacity.

"No more I have," I replied. "Good idea. It's too late to go tonight, but we might have a walk round and see what's on."

She fell in with the suggestion gleefully, and we walked down

Charing Cross Road and Shaftesbury Avenue, looking at theatre announcements as we went. At the Circus we turned along Coventry Street, and presently found ourselves opposite the Prince of Wales'. I think it was *La Poupee* that was running there; if it wasn't it was some other piece that seemed light; and as I like, when I do go to the theatre, to be amused rather than instructed, I plumped for *La Poupee* as against Kitty's suggestion—some stern and ennobling tragedy. I had drawn my week's money that evening. It would be a sorry business if, with all those years of Alfing and Franking before me, I could not once in a while spare five shillings out of my eighteen; and so we elected for *La Poupee* for the following evening.

We went. We waited for perhaps two hours outside the pit door, but, as Kitty said when at last we did get inside, our places were worth it. When we were married, she said, we ought to be able to afford at least one theatre a month—she didn't in the least mind going to the gallery—and it would be something to think about for the next month. She didn't intend, when we were married, to get rusty. We were going to have our little outings like other married people, and if I continued, when we were married, to like light things and she serious pieces, we would choose in turn. And so on. I only half heard. I was spreading my remaining ten shillings over the week to come—ten shillings, mark you, not thirteen, for I had had to buy Kitty a ring, for which I was paying at the rate of three shillings a week.

Nothing happened at that performance of *La Poupee*. I am merely telling you this in order that you may see exactly how we stood, not at the crisis of our lives, but during the intervening stretches. I added to the problem of the coming week by giving a shilling for a box of chocolates, and no extravagance I have ever committed brought me a richer return than Kitty's look of pleasure. I suppose that really this was all that was demanded of Alf and Frank—a trifling, unexpected superfluity once in a while. Lucky fellows! I, however, was neither a Frank nor an Alf, my dreams were not the mere beguilings of an idleness; and neither during my courtship (my real one, I mean) nor thereafter was I going, in any woman's heart, to lord it on so little.

V

I remember the Sunday on which Evie, Miss Angela and I first took tea with Kitty Windus for two reasons. The first was that Miss Angela, who at first had begged to be excused, had come after all (knocking on the head my plan of walking back with Evie alone). And the second was Kitty's asking me to remain behind after the others had taken their departure.

We had gone at four o'clock; and even as the three of us had walked towards Percy Street together (I had picked the others up on my way) I had wondered what had suddenly come over Evie. She had seemed pale and jumpy and morose, and had scarcely spoken a word during the whole of our walk. Nor had she said very much more as we had eaten the hot muffins and drunk the tea Kitty had provided. Indeed, the greater part of the talk had been between Miss Angela and myself, and even that had languished.

Then suddenly Miss Angela had said something that had, I thought, explained matters. Archie's father, whose illness Miss Angela had asked about on the evening of the birthday-party, had taken a sudden turn for the worse, and Archie had been summoned to Guildford the day before.

"Well, we must hope for the best," Miss Angela had concluded. "There's no need to begin moping yet, child—"

Miss Angela also had jumped at my own explanation of Evie's moodiness—that now that Archie was in trouble his misdoings were forgotten.

I was to learn my error half-an-hour later, when Evie and her aunt rose to depart.

I, of course, had intended to leave with them; but as I held the door open for them to pass out Kitty said: "You stay for a few minutes, Jeff; I've something to tell you. . . Good-bye, Evie dear. I do hope your cold will soon be well, Miss Soames—"

And she waved her hand to them as they passed down the stairs.

I swore under my breath, but there was no help for it. I followed Kitty back into her sitting-room. She crossed to the fireplace and sank into a canvas deck-chair with her back to the sewing-machine. I remained standing, with my hat in my hand, at the other corner of the mantelpiece.

She had allowed her head to fall back against the sagging canvas, and had closed her eyes.

"Sit down," she said, without opening her eyes, and, wondering what was wrong, I reached for her bedroom chair and sat down.

"What's the matter?" I asked, a little alarmed already, though I knew not why. I wondered if anything had been discovered about myself. There were, as you know, plenty of such things to discover.

Her eyes still remained closed, but her head fell a little on one side. It was not until I had asked her again what was the matter that she spoke.

"It's—it's dreadful!" she moaned. "I—I can see you haven't heard—"

"What is? Come, come!" I said, with some concern but more impatience. "No, I've not heard anything to take on like this about—unless you mean something about Archie's father? . . ."

"No, it's nothing to do with Archie's father. Oh, I can't possibly tell you, Jeff—"

It was on the tip of my tongue to say that in that case it was of little use my remaining; but she went on.

"Just a minute," she said. "You haven't heard. . . about Louie Causton?"

I was certainly surprised. You will remember that I had not set eyes on Miss Causton since the evening of the breaking-up party, when she had danced twice round the room with me, sought me out again subsequently, and told me what the result had since falsified—that she was returning to the college in the new term.

"No," I said abruptly. "What about her? Nothing wrong, I hope?"

But she only sobbed, "Oh, Jeff!" and with her eyes still closed put out a helpless hand.

I had to approach and take the hand before I learned what the mystery was. I don't know whether you have already guessed it. I hadn't, but for all that my surprise, great as it was, passed even in the moment of Kitty's broken whispering in my ear. I had known Louie Causton for a deep, still pool; I don't think any revelation whatever could have added to my respect for her powers of irony and nonchalance; and yet when I say that my surprise passed it passed only to return. Good gracious! . . . I seemed to hear her carefully lackadaisical voice again as she had munched nougat: "So long since I've seen a man, my dear" . . . and other circumstances, unmarked at the time, flashed on me now.

A child!

"Good gracious!" I breathed again in consternation.

My next thought was of Evie.

I was kneeling by Kitty's chair, holding her hand. I asked quickly: "Does Evie know of this?"

"Yes."

"And does she know you're telling me?"

"Yes."

"And of course Miss Soames does not know?"

"No."

"She thinks as I thought, that it's about Archie's father Evie's so upset?"

"Yes; but perhaps she is about that too a little. I'm horribly upset, Jeff."

This last I took as a hint that the effect of this very startling intelligence on Evie was not the first thing to be considered.

"Yes, yes. . . I see. . ." I murmured.

We were silent, and I felt Kitty's fingers move within my grasp. They pressed mine more closely.

"Don't leave me just yet, Jeff," she begged faintly. She was genuinely prostrated.

"No, no," I said. "Let me think for a minute. . ."

The next moment my brain was buzzing with thought.

I knew that only some such contact with plain raw actuality as this had been lacking in order to make Evie's transition from girlhood to womanhood complete. No longer now was she the fair young tree standing over its sprinkling of delicate discarded sheaths; this puff of Life's east wind had carried away the last of them. She had heard of these things, and so in a sense knew of them; but that somebody she knew. . . that it should have come so near. . . yes, poor shocked heart, that finished it. Archie's insupportable vanities had begun her enlightenment; the menace of his father's condition had touched her with the fringe of its shadow; and now this revelation had come upon her.

Mr. Merridew's illness, moreover, had a plainly seen peril for me. I knew that if anything happened Archie would immediately have enough money to marry on, and my own labours—all that I had planned and done from the first moment of my loving her to this present hour when I sat in Kitty Windus' back room holding Kitty's hand—would go for nothing. They, Evie and Archie, would probably marry, and I—I knew this in that moment for a certainty—I, from sheer yielding, should find myself married to Kitty Windus the moment I could scrape the money together.

I gave a soft groan. I don't know whether Kitty supposed my groan the commiseration for Louie Causton.

Yet what else, if I had chosen a different line, could I have done? Nothing! My shrinking heart cried, Nothing! What was I to have spoken to a young girl of marriage? An Agency clerk—with dazzling hopes! A dweller over a sordid publi-house—and a dreamer of visions! The possessor of a single suit of presentable clothes, the knees of which I was even now deteriorating past remedy—and of a heart tapestried with purple and gold, filled with an almost insensate ambition!

And I saw Evie only at all on the well-nigh insupportable footing that I was the betrothed of Kitty Windus!

Oh, if I had but had two suits of clothes, and thirty-six shillings a week instead of eighteen shillings, I think I would have cut the knot there and then and have sought Evie out that very night and asked her to marry me!

Then after a time I became more practical. Things, even the heart-breaking small things of my life, were after all slowly changing. One of these things was that my slavery at Rixon Tebb & Masters' was already promising to draw to a close. I have not yet spoken of this. Let me do so, briefly, now.

Once more I had been looking for a billet elsewhere, and this time I had excellent hopes of success. The post for which I had applied would not be vacant for six weeks yet, but I had forced a personal interview with one of my prospective employers, and had done what I had intended to do—impressed him strongly with a sense of my mental capacity. He had promised me his interest, and, unless he forgot it again (which, of course, was not impossible), I might have at least enough for one to live on before long. And once more my wider hopes were, I knew in my soul, not illusions. Soon there would remain only the bond that tied me to Kitty, and, with that broken, I would no longer envy even Archie Merridew that luck and weak charm of his that in the past had so often seemed more valuable than all I possessed.

But Kitty, lying back in her deck-chair, had opened her eyes again. They were full of softness and fright. She spoke.

"I wonder, Jeff—whether—" she said timidly and stopped.

"You wonder what, Kitty?" I asked gently.

"I know how strict you are—and if you say no I won't—but if I might go and see her—"

"Miss Causton?"

"Not if you don't wish it, Jeff—"

I considered.

"Has she asked you to go?"

"No—but if you wouldn't mind—very much—"

It mattered little to me, but I had to pretend to ponder deeply.

I really don't know whether I felt sorrow for Miss Causton or not. She was altogether beyond my comprehension. For all I knew my sorrow might be an impertinence. So I must seem to ponder.

"Where is she?" I asked.

"She's taken rooms in Putney."

"Alone?" I asked, with a quick glance at Kitty.

"Oh yes! . . . Until June or July, that is—"

"It is then that she expects—"

"Yes. . . And I thought, Jeff, that perhaps next Saturday—we shall be out that way—"

We had arranged a little excursion for the following Saturday, the four of us—Evie and Archie, and Kitty and myself. We were to wander on Wimbledon Common.

"I never really knew her well, Jeff, understood her, I mean," she went on, "but after all I did see a good deal of her. It's horrible, when I remember the things she used to say. . . And—and—you've made such a difference to me, darling—I wasn't going—to be married—before. . . I should like to go, Jeff—just once," she begged.

"You wouldn't commit yourself to anything?"

"Oh no!"

"Does Evie want to go too?" I asked.

"No. She says she couldn't bear it. She cried half last night as it is."

"Then you'd call on your way next Saturday, and meet the three of us later?"

"Yes."

"Very well," I concluded. "You'd better go."

She threw her arms impulsively about my neck.

Then a change came over her. I think the change began with the failure of the supply of gas from the penny-in-the-slot meter. She had arranged for her little party a pink tissue-paper shade about her milky globe, an idea she had borrowed from Woburn Place; and slowly its colour faded. I had several pennies in my pocket. Quickly I felt for them.

But she moved closer to me. I was still on my knees by her deck-chair.

"Don't bother about it—just for once, Jeff," she murmured.

She could do it with impunity now. After what had passed our situation could hardly be commonplace, and our nearness was as little compromising as nearness ever can be. She luxuriated in her little perilous letting-go—could toy with, and yet be immune from, a danger.

Slowly the gas expired, and the firelight glowed on the blue and white check tablecloth and the disarray of tea-things upon it. On the back wall of the restaurant yard was a square of orange light which the shadow of a waiter's head crossed from time to time. I don't know that with some men—Mackie, for instance—her position would have been all she supposed it to be, but, poor heart, she had had little enough experience from which to surmise that. And I myself could hardly be said to be there at all. She lay in my arms; and in whatever false sweet fancies she lay endrowsed she was not alone. I had my torturing vision too. It was neither of her nor of Louie Causton, that vision. I was trying to persuade myself that she was another than Kitty Windus.

VI

O f our visit to Wimbledon on the following Saturday I intend to
say as little as may be. When you have read it you will not, I know,
ask my reason.

Archie did not appear. This time he had cause enough. The wire
which was handed to me at Rixon Tebb & Masters' a little before
Saturday midday (Polwhele brought it to me with a look that said
plainly, "What next?") announced that his father had died during the
night, and he had despatched it from Victoria Station on his way down
to Guildford. Instantly my heart leaped.

Kitty was going to see Miss Causton. If, this new tidings
notwithstanding, Evie would still keep to the engagement, I should
have an hour with her alone.

I persuaded Evie to come. At first she obstinately refused, but I
had the support of Miss Angela, to whom I privately whispered the
desirability of "taking her mind off it." We left Woburn Place, the two
of us, called for Kitty, and sought the Putney 'bus. Kitty left us at the
corner of a street off the New King's Road, and Evie and I passed on
to the bridge.

That was about four o'clock, and Kitty was to rejoin us near the
Windmill at an hour that would depend upon the length of her stay
with Miss Causton. She expected to be at the Windmill by five.

But at five there was no sign of her, nor had she appeared by half-
past five. At a little before six I said to Evie, "She'll know we've gone on
to the nearest place to tea, and will follow us. Let's go—"

Not far from the Windmill, on the Wimbledon side, there is a sort
of small hamlet, with cottages and alleys and split-oak palings, and a
refreshment house at the end of a garden. There Evie and I had tea, and
there we sat after tea, waiting for Kitty. I talked of this and that, all very
much away from the two subjects uppermost in her heart, and by half-
past six I had given Kitty up.

"She's missed us," I said. "We may happen to run across her, but it's
no good waiting here. Shall we take a turn before we go back?"

We left the refreshment-room, and walked among the gorse and
birches in the direction of Queen's Mere.

It was a green and amber evening, with the shadows already
deepening over Coombe Woods and the calling of homing rooks in

the air. Here and there in the glades family parties still continued to play games with a ball that was quickly becoming difficult to see, and lovers appeared among the coppices. The blackthorn was over, and the may hung in sprays of delicate drooping buds; and in the south-west hung the pale sickle of the new moon. Evie and I, saying little, dropped down a steep over-grown alley that led to the mere, and it was in a sandy bottom at the foot of the alley that I heard a distant rasping call. Another call followed it, and then a throaty thrilling, and then another short series of acrid and moving calls.

It was a nightingale.

By the time we had reached the motionless amber-green water it had broken into full song.

I cannot tell—hitherto I have not attempted to tell—the mystery of that eve and of the song with which it rang. I cannot speak—nor would I if I could—of the responses that eve and that song called up in my heart. It was, I think, for both of us as if that bird's voice cried aloud all that we had left unuttered during the past few hours. Even Louie Causton, even Archie's father, had their part in it. It was as if that voice spoke of the feeble and infinitely moving wonder of birth—of the impinging of that relentless shadow that closes all—and of the griefs and joys and smarts and healings again of the brief passage from that unknowing to this forgetting again. All this crowded upon me in that exquisite agony of notes. And more came, until I could hardly endure it. There was no poignancy, no utter melting and surrender, that those importunate wellings did not give to the falling night. The unattainable greatness of Life and our own puny reachings forth for that greatness—Life's glory and the indignities of the miserable livers of it—Life's majesty and the nosings and burrowings of the fallen heirs to that majesty—all these shortcomings were reconciled in the song; and what man would be, that for an hour he was. I fail in expressing this; Evie, I am sure, did not seek to express it; but in that loud and lost and anguished outpouring, raptures and torments were folded together as in an Amen. . . For one moment only I shuddered; I had remembered that but for an accident I might have stood by that water, listening to that song, with Kitty Windus, but the physical convulsion passed, and the bird sang on.

I had not looked at Evie. I do not think she knew she had drawn a little closer to me. Other listeners had been attracted by the melody, but we stood in a shadow, near a rill that fell into the mere. The water was nacre; the moon's sickle in it was a thin blade of amethyst; and I thrilled unspeakably as the bird's song changed without warning to long, low, caressing notes that drew the heart out of me as the nectar-bag of a floret is drawn from a flower. I heard Evie's slow sob.

Oh, might I but have crushed out that other nectar, to transmute into honey of our own!

Suddenly Evie flung herself on my breast, sobbing and strangling. Her fingers worked at the lapel of my collar; by bending my head I could have touched her small white knuckles with my lips. I was conscious that in my efforts not to do this I bared my teeth like a dog, but I remembered in time that to snatch was to lose. It was not my bosom against which her bosom heaved—it was the nearest sentient resting-place on which she could lay it. Her unhappiness and her happiness, her dream and her disillusion, her knowledge and her already failing hopes, rushed together in her sobs. Her love of a wastrel and her love for all he was a wastrel, and that hidden and sacred nook from which Louie Causton had ruthlessly ripped the curtain—for the pure strangeness of these things her tears gushed forth. I felt the long heave of her body.

"Come, come, my dear!" I said, with an infinitude of tender encouragement, close to her ear.

"Oh—oh—oh!" she sobbed.

"Dear, dear girl!" I murmured, passing my arm about her to support her.

But at that moment I could no more have said or done more than this than I could have sued for a favour by the bier of a scarce-cold lover.

"Hush, poor child!" I whispered, patting her shoulder. "Come, let's go. Let's leave that dreadful bird."

"Just a—mi—mi—minute—" she quavered. "I—I—love it—and I can't bear it—"

Even so did I love, and yet could scarce bear to hold the tender form in my arms.

Presently we left the mere, mounted the dark lane, and began to cross the common. Her hand was now on my sleeve, and it did not leave it again. Once her fingers made an impulsive little pressure on it, which, I cried sternly to my heart, I must not regard. But God knows the war there was between the sweetness of it and my fortitude.

"Jeff," she said more quietly by-and-by, using that name for the first time. "I—I couldn't have borne it if it hadn't been for you. It was too—too—"

"Never mind, dear," I soothed her. "Let's walk a little more quickly—your aunt will be wondering what's become of you—"

She laughed tremulously. "Kitty will be wondering what's become of *you*," she said. Then she added timidly, "She's a lucky girl!"

"Oh? Why?" I asked.

"You're so—so—"

But she did not say what.

We turned down Putney Hill.

I SAID I SHOULD SAY little of this, and I shall say no more. I took her home, but did not go in with her, neither, though I ought to have done so, did I seek Kitty. I went home, but all that I knew of my getting there was that I found myself sitting, with my hat and coat still on, on the edge of the bed in my red-and-green-lighted apartment.

They were turning out from the public-house below when at last I rose sluggishly and began to prepare for bed.

For half the following week I was outside and beyond myself.

But exactly a week, less a day, from that Saturday on which I had held Evie in my arms there dropped a thunderbolt into my life. On that Friday evening I had gone as usual to the cashier for my wages, and he had paid me; but as I had turned away again with my eighteen shillings he had said, as if giving utterance to an afterthought, "Oh—Jeffries—we find we shall not require your services after this week. You can have your notice in writing if you would prefer it."

And he had turned to pay Sutt, the next man in the queue.

PART III
THE GARRET

I

Poor, fussy, well-meaning Kitty had done it—had done it all unwittingly. In telling her vaguely where I lived I had left the number of my house unspecified, and when a letter had come for me to the Business College on an evening when I had announced my intention of being away, she, inspired by the urgency of my affairs, had got a directory and readdressed the letter to me at Rixon Tebb & Masters'. It was a letter from the firm into whose service I hoped soon to enter, and I examined the flap of the envelope carefully when finally it did come into my hands. Polwhele (I have little doubt it was he) had steamed it open, read it and closed it again.

This time all I could get out of Gayns, whom I once more approached, was that Rixon Tebb & Masters' had no use for an employee whose mind was already elsewhere.

It was true that the sack from Rixon Tebb & Masters' was not now a matter of the first importance. That was not the thunderbolt. Scanty as my wages were I had still saved up nearly three pounds out of them; and, as the letter that Polwhele had tampered with contained the news that I might hold myself in readiness to begin my new work a month from that date, the sum was enough to tide me over. But the letter had a postscript. This was a merely formal intimation that it was assumed that I could produce the usual references of steadiness, reliability and so forth. I myself never dreamed that I should be denied them.

I was denied them, however, by Polwhele.

"But—but," I stammered, aghast.

Polwhele referred me to my real employers, the Agency. I gave him a long and gradually lowering stare.

"Do you mean—" I began slowly.

"I mean what I say," he snapped; and as he turned away he added in a lower voice, "You ain't surprised, are you?"

And, remembering how I had seen him with his fingers in Mr. Masters' waste-paper basket, I could not say I was.

Again I sought Gayns. This time the cashier flew into a passion.

"Confound you!" he cried. "You're more trouble than all the rest of them put together! What is it now? A character? Oh yes, you can have a character! I'd advise you not to show it to anybody, though! First leaving us—then coming back—then days off—then dickering with other firms! Go to Polwhele—go to the Agency—go to hell!"

I left Rixon Tebb & Masters' without references.

Without references my new firm refused to have anything whatever to do with me.

I come now to the deepest slough of my poverty.

It was early in the month of June that I was thrown out of work, with thirty-five shillings in my pocket. The drizzling winter had given place to a glorious early summer, and the days increased in heat until they became torrid. Men walked Piccadilly at night in evening dress, with their light dust-coats thrown over their arms; and ragged urchins hailed the appearance of watercarts with whoops of joy and danced barelegged in the refreshing puddles behind them. Horses wore straw bonnets, out of which their ears stuck ludicrously up; in whole districts the water supply began to be cut off at certain hours of the day; the pitiless sun gave every street the appearance of a hard, hot snapshot; and, as the heat got on people's nerves, the cries of children at play became intolerably strident.

My corner at King's Cross was well-nigh insupportable. Why the quantity of torn paper in the gutters should redouble the moment the sun begins to glare on London I do not know, unless it be that the fried fish and ready-cooked provision businesses suddenly boom; and certainly the refuse in which I frequently walked ankle-deep was mostly heavy with grease. Even had I been able to afford it, my "pull-up" had now become such a stove that I do not think I could have entered it. I dined, or rather supped, late at night, at one of the coffee-stalls where the electric trams now sweep round from Gray's Inn Road to St Pancras Station; and I breakfasted (my only other meal) on bread and the water I drew from my tap on the landing before it was cut off. The council didn't save much in my case by cutting the supply off. I filled every vessel I could lay my hands on early in the morning. As Miss Causton had once said, one must be clean, and Archie, whose bath I could now have passed my days in, was seldom to be found in his rooms near the Foundling Hospital now.

For three weeks I trudged the streets looking for work; and then a bit of luck befell me. The new "professor" at the college broke down under the heat; it was not desired to give up the Friday evening advertisement-writing class; and I daresay my anomalous standing at the place, something between student and pathetic high-and-dry "institution," was the cause of its being offered to me. I got five shillings for the evening, and that five shillings kept me for five days. I discovered that I need not pay my rent. The first week I missed doing this I made a shamefaced apology to my landlord, the publican, and discovered that he was not a bad sort. It was too hot to worry about trifles, he said, and so set himself a precedent that cost him pretty dearly until, long afterwards, I saw to it that he was not the loser for having harboured me during that time.

Wherever I sought work my inability to produce a character damned me; and on the other hand I was not a Discharged Prisoner. Two or three times I was taken on casually, once as a packer at a large furniture emporium, once at a stocktaking for bankruptcy purposes, and once (I forget how I tumbled into this) I spent a whole day locked in an upper room of a town hall, counting the voting-papers in some borough or vestry election—a lucrative ten-shilling job. This was before I got, and retained for some weeks (until I had the Corps of Commissionaires down on me), the post of hall porter at the offices of a sporting paper. I will tell you about that presently. You will see that I am making all the haste I can to have done with this horrible time.

Among other things, the general deterioration in my appearance had forced me to tell Kitty Windus that I was out of work. But I had made light of it, saying that, on the whole, it was rather a good thing, as I needed some sort of a spur; but I daresay Alf and Frank had said the same thing many a time. Presently my former boastings, about the great things I was shortly going to do, had committed me to the lie that I had at last found employment. It was my week's stocktaking that I told this particular lie about, and Kitty never knew when that temporary job came to an end. Nor, poor girl, did I tell her what she had done when she had forwarded that letter to Rixon Tebb & Masters'. It would become me ill to say that she stuck to me because it was myself or nothing for her; already I had begun to dread that it would be no easy matter to get rid of her when I might find it necessary to do so: and many a time, as my despair grew upon me, sweeping all personal reluctances and physical repugnances aside, I threw pride to the winds, and ate, in her sitting-room in Percy Street, the only food I had tasted during the day—becoming an Alf or a Frank in very fact.

For—perhaps this was partly the effect of the unrelenting heat— her insipid coquetries had begun to exasperate me more and more. I became increasingly petulant when I was commanded to "tiss eentie finger" and to look into the little scalene triangles of her eyes and say that I loved her. Presently, I am afraid, I began to cause her many tears. We wrangled frequently. I was "near," I was "close," I did not treat her as other engaged girls were treated, I never took her anywhere except for a bus ride, or to a cheap theatre once in a blue moon.

Then one day, without warning, she brought it up against me that I had "given her the slip" that afternoon on Wimbledon Common.

Of this I was technically so innocent, but morally so entirely guilty, that I broke out into anger, and there was a scene.

"I know some girls are younger and prettier than I am," she broke out, with unbridled temper, "but you *did* ask me to marry you after all."

"So I did," I admitted, in a tone that made her flame.

"Yes," she cried shrilly. "And not only that—I've seen you looking at Louie Causton too."

"Oh?" I said, noting with relief that her jealousy was not specially of Evie. "Well, there are one or two pleasing points about her."

"And she was the only one you danced with at the party."

"Before I asked you to marry me?"

"And me—you've never *once* taken me to a dance, though I've *seen* Rachel Levey offer you tickets."

"Perhaps you've seen me look at Miss Levey too?"

"And you never spoke to me, and sat behind the books with Louie."

"Well, there only remains one other suggestion for you to make."

And so on. It was degrading in the extreme. But I was sufficiently punished for it later, when she lay with her head on my breast, sobbing out phrases of contrition for her vindictive temper and supplication for pardon.

All, all gone now was the hour of exaltation in which I had heard the nightingale sing and had felt my glowing girl's breast heaving against my own. I was a hungry, desperate man, living a life against which I knew I should not be able to bear up indefinitely, and already glancing into the public-house as I entered by my side door and beginning to wonder whether they were not wiser than I who made use of the anodyne of drink. Why not drink, and forget for at least an hour? And one night, meeting Mackie again, and having eaten little, I did succumb, and for the first time in my life got drunk. I got drunk at his expense. He had heard the news of Louie Causton, and wanted to talk about it. I, like a cur, let him. . . I broke away from him at last, but not until my loosened tongue had said I know not what.

My relation with Evie during this time is difficult to define. She never quite put me back again into the place I had occupied before that Saturday when we had heard the nightingale together, but newer preoccupations overlay this relation. Archie now had money (I never knew quite how much) at his command; but he still showed no sign of putting it to the use Miss Angela, if not I, had expected—that of entering into a formal engagement with Evie. Miss Angela found excuses for this out of her own imagination—that his father had only lately died, and so on; but I could have set her right even then. I knew how things were drifting. From the little I remembered of my talk with Mackie, Archie had found in his coming into money quite another opportunity. What might have facilitated his marriage with Evie actually delayed it. He was getting rid of his money in Leicester Square again.

So Evie's name was associated with his, and yet there was no plighting between them, and Evie swayed, now happy but with a fear, now despairing, but not hopelessly so. There was no trouble she could have brought openly to me even had she wished, but nevertheless she often turned to me significantly full of silence. She, Kitty and I often walked homewards together through the sweltering streets, and when Evie had left us Kitty would speak her mind freely about Archie Merridew.

"He's one of the Jewness Dorey now!" she exclaimed one evening, taking the phrase, I don't doubt, from one of her "better class" novels. "And it's no good saying it's got nothing to do with us! I think *you* ought to give him a talking-to!"

This was in the typewriting-room of the college, within ten minutes of the close of an advertisement-writing evening.

"What can I say to him?" I asked. "It's no business of mine." She little knew how much I had made it my business.

"Oh, that's just like a man!" she said impatiently, all aglow with the *esprit de sexe*. "The poor child's moping and fretting, and you say it's no business of yours! Of course it's the business of *all* her friends!"

"Of all her women friends, maybe," I answered. "Well, if that's so, why don't you and Miss Angela have a talk about it?"

"As if we hadn't—twenty!" she cried. "You and your bright ideas. It isn't fair—it *isn't* fair to Evie!"

"But what is it you hope for?" I asked.

She stared. "Why, that he'll marry her, of course!"

"Quite so. But I don't mean that. I mean, do you and Miss Angela think you can bring any pressure to bear?"

"Yes, I do—young idiot!" she broke out. "He ought to be ashamed of himself!"

And I didn't doubt that a certain amount of pressure might be brought to bear. If it was made less trouble for Archie to marry than not to marry, he would probably marry. He had not manhood enough, if it was clearly shown that marriage was expected of him, to hold out. And I knew how those marriages turned out. . . I meditated.

"But," I objected, "why meddle? You know what a marriage of that kind would be! You see what he is anyway!"

But here I had touched Kitty's limitation. For her, as for her novels, marriage was the end of the story. If joybells closed it nothing after that mattered, and the look she gave me was a personal confirmation.

"But," she went on presently, "you could help, Jeff. We women can't talk to him—though he's not getting very many smiles from *me* just now!"

I smiled. "You're an unscrupulous crew," I remarked.

"Will you see him?"

"Well—I won't say I won't."

"But *will* you?"

"Perhaps—if I see a fitting opportunity."

"A fitting. Look!" Her voice dropped. Evie had just come into the typewriting-room on her way to wash her hands before leaving. "I'll tell you what," Kitty said quickly; "you go along with her now. See if it isn't as I say. Then tell me whether you won't give that little idiot a dressing-down at once."

She had quite forgotten that twinge of jealousy that had been the cause of our recent scene. If she hadn't, the more honour to her sense of sex comradeship. It was about this time that I was beginning quite frequently to forget that our relation was that of lovers, and as long as I could forget that, she had pathetic little magnanimities that I even admired.

"All right, if you wish it," I said.

So for once Evie's society was absolutely thrust upon me.

That night she was all that Kitty had said—plunged in despondency. She was, of course, "in love with" Archie, but that after all is only a generic expression. Even love comes down to cases, and I think that in her case, even then, she was wondering whether, had things happened a little differently, she might not have been equally "in love" with somebody else. Of that I myself had never a doubt. With Archie's money, or even a decent job, I would have flouted the whole world in my triumphant security that I could make her mine. And I should do so yet. Though for the present my power might go a-begging, I vowed that it should yet be taken and richly paid for. The dark and solid houses were less solid than that something I knew to be within myself, that makes and unmakes houses and streets and towns and lands. . . But gently, gently; I was not out of the mire yet; by-and-by would be time enough for these boastings; things must go on as they were for a little while longer.

So though I did not speak a word to her that night that bore directly on the case as Kitty understood it, I did more. I did—I know this now—make her feel that, glooms and delights apart, she had in me an affectionate friend to whom she would not come with troubles in vain. I have been told, and am inclined to believe it, that I have this power with women.

And her eyes were soft with friendship as I left her.

"Good night, Jeff," she said fondly, as I took her hand. "I do like being with you sometimes."

And that night, as I lay half suffocated in the room I did not even pay rent for, the words rang like a chime in my head until the morning noises marked the beginning of another torrid day.

THE COMMISSIONAIRE'S JOB I SPOKE of I got in an odd way. I got it through the combination of my unusual size with unusual strength. I was walking along Fleet Street that day when a horse fell, and I, with others, helped to raise it again. When we had finished, a man at my elbow spoke both casually and penetratingly.

"That was as good as anything I've seen for weeks," he said. "Have you had much practice in holding a whole horse up while the others fasten the buckles?"

I laughed. I had certainly had the heavy end of the job, but "Not quite that," I said.

He gave me a scrutinising look. "Out o' work?" it seemed to say; but he did not speak the words.

"Here, come and have a drink," he said.

His name was Pettinger. He was a sporting journalist, and so a judge of "form" and "condition." I was not in the best of either, but I must have struck him as having "the makings" of I don't quite know what. He gave me a drink, which I didn't want, and a plate of sandwiches, which I did want rather badly; and he also gave me, as I say, this commissionaire's job. Pettinger is a friend of mine to this day; and since he is a simple and lovable animal of a fellow (he fully concurs in this description of himself) he is the only man I can bear to speak much to about that time when, clad in a sky-blue uniform, I kept the door of his newspaper office, touching my cap to proprietors, and being jocularly prodded by sportsmen and journalists, as if I had been an ox at Smithfield Show.

II

I t was about this time that Archie Merridew's light was once more beginning to show regularly, evening after evening, over the leads of his top floor near the Foundling Hospital. This was after a period of months during which his abode had been in complete darkness. But as his visits to the college had become infrequent, and as I did not know what he might be up to, I had kept away.

When, some little after my commission from Kitty, I did look him up again, it was by no means that I might deliver Kitty's message. I went, rather, as a matter of attention to detail. There were certain things I could not afford not to know, and, more important, there were certain appearances I could not afford not to keep up. Nevertheless I did not dream with what consequences my visit of that evening would presently be fraught.

I was in a state of great nervous irritability before I went. The weather still continued almost insupportably hot, and to my other discomforts had been added a new perturbation that worked on me none the less that in all probability it was quite groundless. The evening papers had started a scare about "low-flash oil"; my red and green room was little cooler than a furnace; and I had lately begun to glance at my cheap lamp from time to time as if it had been a bomb. I mention this merely as an indication of the state to which I was becoming reduced. I thought of that lamp, I remember, as I walked from the college to Archie's rooms that night and half hoped in my peevishness that the thing had exploded in my absence.

It was only ten o'clock, but Archie was already in bed. He wore blue silk pyjamas and on a small table by the side of his bed stood a medicine bottle and a siphon; but when I asked him whether he was ill that he had need of these last he made light of them. It was this beastly weather, he said, and perhaps the beastly weather also accounted for his drinking the milk that Jane presently brought up in a sealed bottle. When Jane had gone, Archie, with an attempt at his old disarming impertinence, turned to me and said, "Well—how's the blue uniform, Jeff?"

Ah! He knew of that!

"Didn't think I'd heard, did you?" he grinned. "Well, I only did hear yesterday. Nothing to be ashamed of, old chap. I know one of your fellows, you know—"

I too knew the sub-editor whose name he mentioned. He was something of a bird of the night too. Already the fact that Archie knew of my occupation had set me swiftly revolving the new dispositions I should certainly have to make in my relation to Kitty and Evie.

"Ah, yes," I said. "I shouldn't attempt to drink with the sub-editor of a sporting paper if I were you. You've been trying, I expect," I added, looking suspiciously at him. He seemed drawn and ill. He never had any stamina.

"Sha'n't tell tales out of school," he replied, with another weak attempt at his old facetiousness. "Well, how's the fair Kitty?"

Ill as he was, I could have boxed his ears for the tone of it, but I answered his question, and he grinned again.

"Rare good sort," he said appreciatively. "Give us a splash of that soda, and pass those cigarettes, Jeff. . ." Then, lighting a cigarette, "Look here, you old scoundrel," he said, "I've got a crow to pluck with you! Guess what it is?"

I could not.

"Well," he leered. "I saw Mackie the other night."

You will remember what had happened the last time I myself had seen Mackie.

"So there!" he triumphed, after some recital or other that had for its point my single fit of intoxication. "*Now* what about it, you old humbug?" he demanded.

I knew I must keep my face and smile. I did not know why I must do these things, but I did them, looking at him and noticing again how sallow and changed he was. Then I looked about the room, mentally commenting on the evidences of the patrimony that had done him so little good—his new dressing-gown, his silver-topped bottles, and a new travelling-case, these things thrown anyhow among his older belongings. One of the newer objects I held in my hand; it was the gold cigarette case I had passed him; and I gazed smiling at it as he went on.

"Yes," he told me, with humorous accusation; "Mackie told me all about it—ha ha ha! What price the old puritan Jeff now? Eh? Sad dog, sad dog!"

I replied, quite calmly, that the dissipations of commissionaires were limited by their circumstances.

"And what the devil are you doing being a commissionaire?" he demanded. "I'll tell you what it was, Jeff," he continued familiarly, "that failure in Method seems to me to have broken you all up. What the dickens made you fail?"

I was conscious of an interior stirring of hate. What, indeed, had made me fail!

"Oh, over-confidence, I suppose," I answered lightly.

And he continued to talk.

At last I rose and said good-night. He raised himself on one elbow in order to shake hands.

"Come in again and see a chap soon," he said. "It's hellish slow up here all alone."

I was already at the door, but I turned abruptly.

"What do you mean?" I said. "Do you mean you're laid up? You said you weren't."

But he only gave a confused little laugh. "Eh? Laid up? Of course not! Can't a chap turn in early once in a while?"

"'Once in a while'? . . . But you said—"

"That you might come in and see me? Well, do. No harm in that, is there? Say I'm going slow for a bit, that's all," he added.

I agreed with him that to "go slow" for a bit was a course he might with advantage have adopted some time ago, and, though considerably puzzled, I turned slowly away.

My lamp, I discovered when I reached my dwelling again, had not exploded in my absence; but I did not light it. This was not, of course, through any actual fear; it was merely part of my general nervous condition. I remember, as still further explaining that condition, that I had passed a Board School that day as the children had poured out for their morning recess of a quarter of an hour; I have said how more than commonly strident the heat seemed to make all noises; and at the sudden outburst of the children I had broken into a copious flood of perspiration. I was not much steadier now. Pushing the lamp aside I flung up my window as high as it would go, drew out my old string-mended chair, and, sitting down, began to stare at the "*Sarcey's Fluid*" advertisement across the way.

The rippling of its incandescents had a trick that always fascinated and irritated me intensely. Before the last letter of the first word was an apostrophe, but its single bright spot always appeared out of its proper order. S—A—R—, and so on, the thing ran, but the whole legend was complete before that apostrophe started into its place. I used sometimes to watch as if I hoped the whole mechanism might suddenly alter, but, of course, it never did. I began to watch it again that night, while my ceiling and the wall above my bed became red and green, red and green, red and green. . .

I am afraid that what I am now about to say I shall have to ask you to take on trust. I have no evidence to offer of a phenomenon that, I am told, is shared by madness and genius alike. Nor will I trouble you either with any talk of prevision or of inner certitude, nor with the gradually deepening brooding that led up to this phenomenon—the brooding over the countless slights and slurs and rubs I had suffered from Archie Merridew's reckless and ignorant tongue ever since I have known him—my appearance, my private affairs, the side-splitting joke of Jeffries being in love. I will pass straight to the sudden and complete illumination that, as I sat there, so irradiated my intelligence that I wondered why it had come to me now, an hour later, and not then, the moment I had seen him lying at that extraordinarily early hour in bed.

It came, this flash of illumination, in exactly the same manner as the changing of the electrograph before my eyes—and, as you will see in a moment, with the same bloody apostrophe. And with its coming my room was not more suffused with the crimson glare than my mind suddenly was with the same morbid and flaming and dangerous hue.

I had suddenly realised what was really the matter with Archie.

Let me now tell you the kind of man I have sometimes, though possibly mistakenly, supposed myself to be.

He has aspired, that man, I have sometimes supposed myself to be, to the stars; but his feet have also known the burning bottom of the pit. His heart has been lifted up until sometimes, through eyes drowned with tears, he has had his poor and fragmentary glimpse of a larger Fatherhood than earth knows; but he has also exchanged intelligence with the devil. His heart has flowered with loves and charities; but that same heart has also been a rock with a toad in it. He was born in heaven, but has lodged in hell. So in him, according as he has been used, have opposites met.

And yet, as I say, I may be wrong in supposing that I am this man.

Yet the man who, in my red and green room that night, leaped up from his chair, and with a bursting, ringing cry shook his hand on high, was not the James Herbert Jeffries who now writes this feverish shorthand. He who writes the shorthand was not the same James

Herbert Jeffries who stood, with those violent dyes flooding his face, vowing that if that sick young buyer of infected merchandise dreamed for one instant of doing that which it was sought to make him do, and which apparently he was ready to do, he should pay for it with the last thing he had to give. That James Herbert Jeffries was plunged in that hour into a place of stench and infernal brightness that God forbid was ever his destined abode.

I cried aloud, shaking my fist up at my cracked and blackened ceiling:

"*Though Christ died for man in vain. . . let him but think of it. . . let him. . . let him. . . and I. . .*"

After that I passed into a curious state of mind. You have heard how I make, when I can, anger serviceable to me, but here was an anger past my bringing into control. Yet, as ordinarily I plan calmly, so was I calm up to a certain point now. The result of these two things was that my brain worked like a worn and cranky machine, sometimes doing more than it ought, sometimes less; sometimes jerking startlingly ahead, sometimes refusing to work at all. And as there was thus no continuity in my thought, and as my recollections are curiously associated with that changing red and green that now for the first time seems to me to have run through my story like a fateful burden of jealousy and blood, I will set down such isolated reflections as rise of themselves out of the jumble of my mind.

CRIME (I REALISE THAT THE word leaps with some suddenness into these pages) has suffered more at the hands of criminals than it has at the hands of justice. There are few perfect crimes. Most of them are accidental, the mere explosion of momentary passion. And that is well, for the world wants few masterpieces in that sort. I have not read De Quincey's essay on the subject, nor ever shall now; but if crime is to be considered as an artistic medium, it is the only medium in which bungling is better worth to the world than competence. Other arts one prefers to see superlatively practised or not at all; but it is only of the bungled crime that man can endure to think.

THE ORDINARY CRIMINAL BEGINS AT the wrong end. Dull fellow that he is he does not recognise that his first task must be the creation of an attitude of mind. Or if a glimmering of this does cross his inflamed consciousness, he thinks that it is the attitude of his own mind that is of the first consequence. That is why he suffers either the retribution of justice or the visitings of his own conscience. In either of these cases his act is unsuccessfully committed. He pays in common with his victim.

IT IS NOT THE INJURED man who knows the full quality of hate. It is the one who injures. The injurer has no refuge from his own transgression; he has him whom he has injured constantly upon his mind—perhaps upon his soul. Another is the lord of his peace of mind. Thus it is peculiarly the wronged man's part to pardon, but when the wronged man would not pardon, but would avenge for another's sake?

COULD ARCHIE BE GIVEN A mind more sensitive than a stone? Could his weak and spongy nature be hardened to a point of view? Could such an attitude be created in him that what otherwise would have been an assault would take on the stern justice of a punishment? Can any dull or egotistical mind be either punished or rewarded? Ultimately, can the God who created it do anything save quench it again? Wickedness may be vanquished at the last, but Ignorance—? And Conceit—?

BUT BAH! PROBABLY HE WAS not even thinking of it. Perhaps he was even now seeking a way out. Well, I would help him. Ten words to him in private. . . Faugh!

So *that* was it. . . And the world allows it! Could he be proved to be merely insane at the time of his marriage the world would not allow it; a mental insufficiency beyond his control would be a bar; but this other, that he had deliberately sought, would be allowed. And Evie. . .

THAT BLOODY APOSTROPHE AGAIN! . . .

THE CRIMINAL FORGETS TOO MUCH in the moment of action. It is a sort of stage fright. Rehearsed perfectly, however. . . Not that the thing is not admittedly difficult. A button, a fingerprint, a drop of blood, the resources of the laboratory, the microscope, the spectroscope—oh yes, it cannot be said that there is not a deal to watch. And a memory, a chance association years afterwards, an attack of debility rendering the eyes subject to deceits—any one of these things may at any moment throw him into the hands of the law as a fate more merciful than that which he has not been clever enough to forestall within himself. Yes, there is much to consider; but then, as all the world knows, masterpieces of crime or what not, are difficult of accomplishment.

Ten words, then, on the morrow, and he would never dare. . .

BUT BAH! I WAS NOT even sure! He *could* not be contemplating it, and I was vile to think it. . . Still, prudence. I must make sure. Till then, nothing—not even these thoughts that ticked as if out of a tape-machine from my brain. Tomorrow. . .

YET, AH! I WAS SURE for all that!

THIS RED AND GREEN, THIS red and green!

THESE ARE SUCH FRAGMENTS OF it all as I can remember. I don't know how long they occupied me. I had begun to trace with my fingers little patterns on the deal top of my table, patterns that sometimes had a meaning for me, sometimes not, but that always had a meaning for Archie Merridew if he thought. . . if he as much as thought. . .

Then the red and green advertisement was switched off suddenly. Only a rhomb of dim gaslight on my ceiling remained. . .

But I still sat in the darkness, my brain taking those backward and forward jerks, and my lips muttering, though without sound, that if he dreamed. . . if he as much as dreamed. . .

III

I t was a "record" even for myself to get the sack twice in one week, but that now befell me. They gave me no notice at the newspaper office, but they were decent, and I had a fortnight's wages in lieu of it. Pettinger especially showed himself my friend.

"It's rough on you," he said, "but I really don't see that anybody's to blame. . . Look here, I'll tell you what we'll do. Go down to my place at Bedford; I'll telephone them you're coming; and you can do what there is to do in my garden for a week or two until something turns up. You won't mind working under the old chap I've got there? Right. Off you go. You've got your money, haven't you?"

"I shall have to come up for Friday evening; I've a class," I said.

"Well, have a change till then. You look as if you need it. Catch the twelve-fifty, and I'll telephone them now."

So I took off my sky-blue uniform and wondered, as I folded it neatly and laid it aside, where they were going to find the next man it would fit.

This was at half-past ten in the morning, so that I had some hours to spare. Ten minutes, if I could catch him, would suffice for all I had to say to Archie Merridew, and, as he was not an early riser, and had told me that he was not spending his days in bed, I hoped to find him before he went out. But as the Business College lay on the way I determined to call there first. I walked up Chancery Lane into Holborn.

But he had not arrived at the college when I got there, and I did not wait for him. I had walked home with him often enough to know his unvarying route, and I set off for his place half expecting to meet him on the way. But I did not meet him, so I knocked at the brass knocker of his ivy-green door.

Jane told me he had only that moment gone out.

"To the college?" I asked.

Jane thought so, but was not sure.

"If I don't see him I'll call again," I said. "Tell him, will you?"

I returned to the Business College, and there waited, talking to Kitty, who had just arrived.

Kitty seemed extremely embarrassed that morning, and of course I guessed the reason. She had heard of the sky-blue uniform, doubtless through Archie. (For two nights I had not seen her.) I was none the less sure of this that she did not mention the circumstance directly; nor did she comment on my being at liberty at that unusual hour of the morning. Presently she said:

"I don't think he'll come this morning now. He may this afternoon."

"I can't wait till the afternoon," I said, glancing at the little clock on the mantelpiece of the type-writing-room—the little clock that had given the "Ting" that had startled me so on the day of the examination in Method.

"Is it anything I can tell him?"

That, of course, was quite out of the question. "I'll see if he's back home yet," I replied.

Then Kitty's uneasiness and curiosity got the better of her delicacy about the sky-blue uniform. She looked fixedly at her thin wrists and her fingers gave little touches to the lace about them as she spoke.

"Jeff," she said timorously, "I don't know whether you know what—what they're saying about you—I'm sure it's a hideous lie, but—but it's upset me frightfully—" She stopped abruptly, and seemed even then to wish she had not spoken.

"You seem very easily upset nowadays," I said shortly, quite ready to quarrel if needs be.

But she ignored my tone. "You know they're saying—everybody's saying—all the people here, I mean."

"What?" I demanded.

But her courage failed her. She stopped the fiddling at her wrists, and, giving me a long look said, "You know I love you, Jeff, whatever happens—"

It was what I had begun to fear—that there would be no shaking her off. She was far, far too faithful.

"I see," I said slowly. "I know what you mean. . . Well, it was quite true. I *was* a commissionaire—until an hour ago. They've sacked me. . . I suppose Archie told you?"

"Girl-faced little wretch! But, Jeff—"

I took her up. "Well, it's that that I want to see him about. But as regards you and me—if you want it to make a difference—"

It was a plain offer to release her, but I don't think she understood it as that. Indeed, her manner puzzled me entirely. It was eager, shrinking, wistful and apprehensive all at once, and she appeared to be trying to shake off something—something preposterous. Well, that sky-blue uniform had been preposterous enough.

"It shall make a difference—if you wish," I offered again proudly.

"No," she murmured, apparently understanding this time, and busy with her lace again.

Then I entered into I know not what fantastic explanation of the curious fact that a man with the world in his grasp should have chosen to touch his cap to editors and proprietors. She tried to look as if she believed me, but it was plain that she didn't in the least. Once or twice she tried to interrupt me, but my patience was quickly running out.

"So you see how it was," I said at last, dropping my voice as Weston, the secretary-bird passed. "It was no business of his, and I want to know what he's got to say about it. You can tell him so if you like."

Again that inexplicable look of timorousness came into her small eyes.

"You *mean* the commissionaire's job, of course?" she said.

"I mean the commissionaire's job," I replied.

That, I thought with satisfaction, would cover my real reason for wishing to see Archie as well as anything else.

Weston passed again, and gave me a look. That look struck me. It was just such a look as a policeman might give a loiterer whom he suspects, yet against whom he has no charge; and I felt my colour mount a little. That tattling little animal! Little he cared, as long as he had his joke, that my five shillings was put in jeopardy. For a business college that styles itself advertisement writer "professor" naturally doesn't want commissionaires on its staff, and I saw my second dismissal looming ahead.

Then, with a new and cautious idea in my head, I turned to Kitty again.

"On second thoughts," I said, "*don't* say anything to Archie about my wanting an explanation. I'll settle with him. After all, it was bound to come sooner or later. It doesn't much matter. I'll see to it... Well, I'm off. Good-bye, dear. I don't think I shall be able to see you again till Friday."

And I left her, nodded to Weston, and passed out.

I daresay you guess what my new and cautious idea was. I had something of the last privacy to say to Archie; it was just as well that I should have the cloak of comparatively trivial personal remonstrance to cover it; but this was only part of it. The truth was that my brain had suddenly taken another of those startling leaps forward. In some conceivable last event (I was not planning one, you understand; it was merely that my mind was working somewhere ahead, independently and beyond my control) it might be necessary that I should have *no* personal quarrel with him. In such an event none must suppose that our relation had been other than amicable. Yet I should be overdoing this (purely anticipatory) prudence to pass over the episode of the sky-blue uniform entirely. The thing was, or might become, a matter of nicely measured proportions. Already I was making the slight private affront serve my turn; presently I might want to make the pardon of that affront serve my turn also. This kind of thing is what I mean by the creation of an attitude of mind and "attention to detail."

I made one more attempt to find Archie as I walked to St Pancras, but he was still not at home. Then I had to run for my train.

I worked in Pettinger's garden that week, carrying water, wheeling barrows, and filling baskets with fruit as I passed between the canes. Pettinger was away for two nights, but on the third evening he came up to me as I was pushing a heavy roller over the lawn and began to talk. I think he began for the sake of a pleasant word or two, but something I said seemed to engage his interest, an hour or more passed, and then, as the phlox and canterbury bells began to glimmer in the twilight, he suddenly said, "Leave this and come inside—we can talk comfortably there."

We went in. I shall never forget that night. It was made memorable by the fact that master and gardener talked till two o'clock in the morning.

"Well, Jeffries," he said at last, with a sleepy yawn, "you're an extraordinary chap. I'm afraid you've made rather a lot of work for me this last hour or two."

"How so?" I asked.

"Well, I was going to try to get you a job something like your last, but you're a difficult man to find a job for. I won't ask you whether you know you're extraordinary; of course you know you are; and I'm going, if I can, to give you a chance—a real chance—not like that other—those cut-throats—what's their name."

I had told him about Rixon Tebb & Masters' and the rest of it.

"I've a bit of a pull here and there," he went on sleepily. "There's the 'Freight and Ballast Company'—I know a couple of their men—but we'll talk about that in the morning. I'm off to bed. Hope they've made you comfortable?"

It does not come within the scope of my present tale to speak of my later rapid rise; but I may say now that I owed my chance to Pettinger and to the berth he got me, with the coming of winter, in the offices of the "F. B. C."

I remained in his house all that week; then, on the Friday evening, I took a return ticket to town in order to attend my class.

I had not been half-an-hour in the college that evening before I was aware that something had happened. Archie Merridew was not there, but Evie was, and so was Kitty Windus. I went through my work as usual, and then, at half-past nine, sought Kitty. It was she who told me the news.

"You've not heard, have you?" she asked, with a glance towards the senior students' room, through which Evie had just passed. Again she was, in some manner I could not understand, eager, reserved, apprehensive and fidgety all at once.

"Heard what?" I asked.

"About Evie. It's come off. She and Archie are properly engaged."

From that moment dated a division of me into two separate men, of which I shall have more to say presently.

"Oh?" I replied, with complete calm. "That's good news indeed! Wait here a minute—I'll speak to her—don't go, for I want to see you."

I met Evie returning with her towel and celluloid box of soap. She too was excited, so excited that she would have passed me, but I thought I understood that. I stopped her.

"Well, Evie?" I said, smiling.

She waited, painfully full, I couldn't help thinking, of emotion.

"It was you who congratulated me before," I said. "It's my turn now, I hear."

She looked at me and away again, and again at me and away.

"Thank you, Mr. Jeffries," she said, beginning to make little pointings of her foot this way and that on the floor.

I spoke very gently. "Jeff—or Mr. Jeffries if you prefer it—wishes you nothing but happiness, Evie," I said.

"Oh, thank you," she said, with increasing perturbation, "thank you very much indeed—thank you really—Jeff."

It was odd in the extreme. She gave me the reluctant "Jeff," and somehow I wished she hadn't, it came with such difficulty. Something, I was convinced, lay behind it. I did not expect her in the circumstances to be quite collected, but her manner was—I don't know how else to describe it—almost that of a child who has pleaded with authority for permission to bestow one final charity on an undesirable associate. . . What! I thought, she also ashamed to know a commissionaire!

"When are you going to be married?" I asked, after an awkward pause.

"Quite soon," she replied, equally awkward. "As soon as I can get my things ready." She stopped.

"I suppose Archie's coming here for you—tonight, I mean?"

"No—he's got a man to see—a friend—in Store Street, I think."

"Then may I walk along with you?"

She seemed to have feared the question. "Oh," she said quickly, "if you don't mind—I've something awfully private to say to Kitty—she and I have arranged to go on together."

("Not wanted," I said to myself.) Aloud, "Well, I hope you'll be happy, Evie," I added.

"Thank you," she said again, lifting curiously appealing eyes for a moment.

I turned abruptly from her, and sought Kitty, who was still waiting. I had picked up a sudden suspicion, and wished to confirm it.

"Ready?" I said, in a tone as matter of fact as I could assume.

Again she began to flutter. I couldn't understand what had come over the whole college.

"I'm sorry, Jeff," she began, with rapid effusiveness. "If I'd only known you wanted—but I've got to go somewhere."

I knew that, Evie had just told me.

"Woburn Place, you mean?"

"No, dear—somewhere else—quite different."

"Really?" I said, incredulously smiling and frowning both at once.

"Of course! How funny you are!"

I looked searchingly down into her eyes.

"I think *you're* funny," I said slowly.

"You really must excuse me, Jeff—if you'd only let me know."

But I had had enough of this. Gently but irresistibly I took her arm.

"Come along, Kitty," I said quietly. "I particularly want to talk to you."

She quailed, but still hung back.

"Very well," I said. "Will you tell me where you're going?"

She was obstinately silent.

"You're going with Evie, of course?"

I knew by the little rush with which she spoke that she was telling the truth and was relieved to be able to do so. "Oh no!" she said. "I'm going quite alone, quite alone—honour, Jeff!"

"Evie's not going with you—to Store Street or wherever it is?"

She stiffened. "I don't know what you mean by Store Street, and I think you've got Evie on the brain," she said.

What the devil ailed them all?

And why had Evie said she was going with Kitty?

As abruptly as I turned away from the one I now turned away from the other.

The next moment: "Er—Jeffries!" I Heard.

It was Weston with my five shillings. I turned.

"Oh, Jeffries! I'm sorry to say—glad in one sense of course—that Professor Hitchcock will be taking the class again next Friday. The college wishes—wishes to thank you for stopping the gap as you have done. It's been most obliging of you."

I said something—I was glad Hitchcock was better, I said.

"Yes—er—he's quite well again now—quite on his feet again," said the secretary-bird. "And—er—Jeffries—I'm exceedingly sorry, but I've a rather unpleasant duty to perform."

I was utterly mystified. "What is it now?" I demanded almost roughly.

"It's that the Board is of opinion—has come to the conclusion—that consisting as we do of younger students than yourself—it would be of advantage—perhaps of advantage to you too if—if—"

I helped him out. "If I don't come again?"

"I wished to break it gently to you—but that *is* the substance of it," he stammered.

Curious. . .

"Thank you, Weston," I said. "I quite understand. Will you please tell them that I didn't ask for any explanation?"

Exceedingly curious. . .

"Yes, yes, yes," he murmured sympathetically.

"Now," I said to myself some minutes later, as I descended the stairs, "it only requires Miss Angela to turn me down."

I walked to Woburn Place, and there asked a Swiss boy if I might see Miss Angela. Archie's friend Mr. Shoto passed me as I waited in the hall, but I did not speak to him. After some minutes the Swiss boy returned. His answer was what I expected. Miss Soames had a nervous headache, and asked to be excused from seeing me.

And all, I thought with amazement as I turned away, because for a week or two I had worn a sky-blue uniform!

IV

That division of me into two men that I have said dated from the time when Kitty told me of Evie's engagement to Archie Merridew was, in a sense, no new thing. I had felt it in some measure before, when I had deliberately avoided Archie that I might give my anger its head and had smiled in his face again when the fit had worked itself out. I had striven, too, to stand between him and the black rages he and my general circumstances had provoked.

But no sooner had the words, that Evie was now definitely engaged, come from Kitty's lips than I knew this division to be complete and irrevocable. Even did he withdraw in time he had still contemplated it; and in my soul I did not now believe he would withdraw. "The Devil was sick, the Devil a Saint would be." And I knew at last who his friend in Store Street was. A name, seen on a medicine bottle in his room, had leaped into my memory. His "friend" was some obscure practitioner of a doctor.

So I now became as the Giant in the story, who was so exquisitely cloven from head to middle by the magic blade that he did not feel the wound that was his death. "Cut, then!" he laughed. "Shake yourself," he was told. And he fell in twain.

A shake, and I too should fall in twain.

I will now tell you how I got that shake.

Thinking over my sudden ostracism in Pettinger's house that night I only became more and more mystified. That the Business College should no longer require me I could understand—for snobbery plays a terrible part in business. That Kitty had reproached me for my lack of trust in her about my commissionaire's post was also easily to be accounted for. Miss Angela might in truth have had a headache and have begged to be excused from receiving me. But that Evie should turn against me was inexplicable. It contradicted every tradition of her upbringing. My being forced into a humble, but not ignoble, occupation could never have made this difference in her. If anything in the whole business could be taken as a certainty, that could. And so the more I thought about it the more sure I became that, though I myself might conceal my real reason for wishing to see Archie Merridew by giving out that I merely wanted to remonstrate with him about his chattering, others were using that very giving-out as a screen for something I was in total ignorance of. Kitty's timorousness returned to me; I believed now that she had actually been trying to tell me something else, whatever it was; and so I tossed and turned on my pillow, vainly racking my brain.

I finally decided to have it out with both Kitty and Archie on the morrow.

I went up to town the next morning, and walked straight to the Business College. I did not wish, after what I had been told the night before, to go up, so I found an office boy on one of the lower floors and sent him up with word that somebody would like to see Miss Windus. Then I waited, just inside the Holburn entrance.

In a few minutes she came down, hatted and gloved. Her face looked old; her eyes were dull, and almost closed—with weeping, I was instantly sure; and she touched my sleeve almost as if she feared I might shake her hand off again.

"I thought it would be you," she said, in a dull voice. "Let's have a walk. I've something to say."

We walked without speaking along Holborn, and presently turned into the little courtyard of Staple's Inn. We sat down on the bench that surrounds the tree in the middle.

She had broken into speech almost before we sat down. It was as if she feared that if she did not get it out at once she would not speak at all. She was intensely agitated.

"Jeff," she said, "I've wronged you—cruelly and basely."

I did not smile at the melodramatic little phrase. I had not the ghost of an idea what she meant, but that something was impending I was already aware.

"I saw you didn't know last night," she went on. "This morning?"

It was a question. "I'm no wiser this morning," I said.

"You asked me where I was going last night."

"I did."

"Can you guess why when—when I tell you it was to Louie Causton's?"

I shook my head.

"Even then I cannot guess."

Then she began to tremble. She grasped the edge of the seat with her hand so that I should not see how she shook.

"Jeff," she said, in a low voice, "if you never want to see me again—I can't blame you if you don't—not after this."

I waited.

"Not that I shouldn't always, always love you. It will be my punishment—I shall have to bear it."

Still I waited.

"Yesterday it was you who offered it—now it's me—it will serve me right."

I thought she would never go on. "You mean our engagement, of course?" I said.

"Yes," she gulped.

"Why?" I asked suddenly.

"Because—because of what I've been beast enough to believe of you, Jeff."

"And that is—"

As I again waited for her to speak I looked round the courtyard. A clerk was at work in a first-floor window, and he caught my eye and looked away again. In another window an office boy stood with a pen in his mouth, turning the pages of a ledger. Then, after a while, and very disjointedly, Kitty went on:

"They said you said it yourself, and I—at first I didn't—but then I believed it. I know I was beastly about it once before—then we quarrelled—but I didn't mean what I said then—believe me, I didn't. . . And," she went on, "I didn't know who—who—it was. . . She never told me—you know what I mean. . . I hate myself—now. I suppose I'm jealous—the green-eyed monster, Jeff—but they did say it—said you'd as much as said so yourself—and—"

I was beginning to get impatient with her rambling.

I said "And what?" but I don't think she heard me.

"So that's why I went to Louie herself—to ask her—right out—"

All at once I felt it coming.

"Well?"

But suddenly she buried her face in her hands, and her thin shoulders shook. Again I saw the clerk watching. . .

"Oh!" she moaned. "Can you ever, *ever* forgive me?"

"For—"

"For ever thinking that you and Louie—that you and Louie—"

She lifted her piteous eyes to mine.

I THINK IT WAS THEN that the Giant shook himself and fell in twain. He has been more or less roughly cobbled together since, and the halves rub on somehow side by side, but to this day the one man in me faints for the great sweet things of Life, while the other has the devil ever at his elbow.

THE WHOLE COURTYARD HAD SWUNG round; I actually seemed, with my physical eye, to see it for some moments out of the vertical. Then it righted again, and the whole mystery of the previous evening dissolved in light.

"You and Louie—you and Louie—"

Yet again the courtyard seemed to lean and slide sideways for a moment; then I flung a blazing searchlight back across my memory.

Louie Causton's super-subtle mask. "So long since I saw a man, my dear—the Baboon?—oh, I should know which way to turn *then*!"

My half-admissions to Archie when he had tried with such persistency to get out of me who it was I was in love with.

Her failure to return to the college, that alone had thrown me into Kitty's arms rather than into her own.

That something, God knows what, that I might have said to Mackie when, after having eaten nothing, I had drunk with him.

Kitty's own desperate possessiveness and jealousy.

All these things fell into place as the coloured granules fall when the kaleidoscope is given a turn. I had been accused of being Miss Causton's lover!

As I remain that divided Giant henceforward until the end of my tale, I will divide my name also, and tell you of a colloquy that began within me between these two men—the honest, human, enraged Jeffries, and that other, whom I will call James Herbert, at whose elbow stood the devil.

"Ah!" choked Jeffries, flaming red.

"Quietly, quietly!" whispered his interlocutor.

"That's Merridew again!" choked the other.

"Quietly—keep your face—there's a clerk in that window watching you!"

"The whole world may see me—let me go and find him!" It was as if this Jeffries struggled to break away there and then.

"No, no—sit still—leave it to me, and keep your face before this weeping woman—*I* was born where they understand these things!"

And after a hellish minute—the voice of that one prevailed.

I turned to Kitty.

"Good gracious!" I remember I said, with an air almost of amused incredulity. "Why, who on earth told you that ridiculous tale?"

The one who came from the place where they understand these things was right. Kitty looked up. At first she seemed unable to believe her ears—unable to believe that I could treat the monstrous thing with amused disdain. Then, as she slowly realised, her face shone. She gave a quick glad cry.

"Jeff!"

"What, dear?" I said, smiling.

She choked. "Oh. . . my good, big man!"

("Laugh now," the wicked one prompted; and I laughed.)

"Good heavens, what a tale! . . . Who told you? Archie? Just you see if I don't tweak that young man's ears!"

In her infinite relief the poor woman broke down utterly. She shook with the mingled gratitude and humiliation of my pardon.

"Louie Causton!" I scoffed. "You actually asked her that? Why, how she must have laughed!"

"Oh—you're wonderful, Jeff!" Kitty adored me.

"Oh," I replied, quickly recollecting myself, "don't think I'm not angry! I'll give that young man a jacket-dusting! He shall have a wedding present from me he'll remember, I promise you! Why, of all the mean tricks! . . ."

I went on. Presently Kitty had found me so wonderful that once more she could even toy a little with a peril.

"Louie wouldn't tell me. . . who. . . she said she'd die first. . ." she half sobbed by-and-by.

I looked into her little puffed eyes. "Then," I said, smiling, "you've only the word of a not very trustworthy woman for it that after all. . . eh?"

A saint could hardly have cheapened the worshipping look she gave me.

"So," I resumed presently, "that was what ailed you all last night, when I was thinking all the time it was my uniform?"

"Yes—I tried hard to tell you, Jeff—"

"And does Archie really believe this tale himself, or is it just one of his little pleasantries?"

She didn't know.

"Is he at the college this morning?"

"Yes."

"Good. Will you send him down to me if I walk back with you? I think we won't lose any time over this."

"And you'll give him a really severe talking-to?" she asked eagerly.

"I will," I promised. "Come—"

Twenty minutes later I was again in the doorway of the Business College, waiting for Archie to descend.

And as I waited I reflected how well-nigh irrevocably I had tied myself up with Kitty now. I think that up to then she would have stuck to me even had this of Miss Causton been true; but now she would never, never let me go. Perhaps I may here mention the plan I had at first had for getting rid of her when I should require her no longer. I had based that plan on the fascination the "compromising situation" of her favourite novels always had for her. I never knew anyone so self-conscious about her defencelessness, and I had worked it out that I had only to propose my own chamber for an assignation and she would conceive herself to be looking into the bright face of danger indeed. All peril and all romance would lie for her in her setting foot on the lowest of my stairs. . . And doubtless one glance at that naked room of mine (I had pawned even my oil-stove) would, I had estimated, drive her away in instant and horrified fright. . . I had not been above planning this.

But now she would never, never leave her big, wonderful man.

Yes. I had fettered myself fairly completely.

Holborn was noisy that morning, and between the sound of passing vehicles and Archie's own light tread I was not aware of his presence until he spoke. Instantly I saw that he thought he knew why I had come and had resolved to take one bull at least by the horns.

"I say, Jeff," he began at once, with embarrassed sincerity—a sincere desire, that is, to be out of the mess he had landed himself in, "Kitty's just told me. I know—I know you must be beastly angry with me— quite right too—I'm awfully sorry and—and ashamed. It was caddish. But I really didn't mean anything, and—and—and I thought you as much as said it yourself, you know—"

I judged it best not to speak just yet. I stood looking at him.

"You're an awfully good sort," he went on, conciliatingly, "but— but—I really thought you *were* a bit sweet on her (that was all I meant)— that time—you know—before I knew it was really Kitty. I simply said to Mackie—he watched you too at the party—I admit I was 'on' a bit, and never thought it would end like this—"

Then I spoke. "You mean you didn't think it would end in my getting the sack and being cut by everybody I know except yourself and Mackie? How did you think it would end, then?"

He jumped eagerly at a chance, ready to promise anything.

"I'll see that's all right, old boy—and Hitchcock *was* coming back anyway, you know—you only had the job while he was away—"

"Oh!" I said, with a nasty laugh. "And in your opinion that's all? . . . What about my character?" I demanded suddenly. "Eh?"

"I know," he said, with hanging head. "It was rotten of me—but I was 'on'—I really was. And your character's all right, Jeff, with anybody who knows you—they know what a first-rate sort you are—"

"Thank you," I said stiffly. "And what about—the partner in my guilt?"

"Oh, *her*!" the little animal said, as if *she* could be left quite out of the question. Then apparently he felt the stirring of returning rectitude. "Well, Jeff, I have apologised. . . I don't see what more I can do, except of course to see you all right. . ."

I noted the birth of the attitude I wished to create. I began to appear to let him down by gradual degrees.

Exactly how much of it was appearance you see. I abhorred the little wretch. And his renewed apologies, promises, explanations! . . . He had been "on" he had "simply said" to Mackie; I "should have lost my job soon in any case"; and "he'd see I was all right!" . . . That was all his sense of a hideous slander! And his almost rebellious "Well, I have apologised." Good heavens, he would be putting *me* in the wrong presently! . . . Every muscle in my body was straining to be at him.

But that, I knew, would never, never do.

Presently I turned once more to him. All this, after all, was not in the least what I had come to talk to him about. It was only a screen.

"Very, well," I said at last. "What's done's done. We'll leave that for the present. Now there's something else I want to say to you. Do you know what it is?"

"How should I know?" he said, relieved that the subject was turned.

"Think. . ."

When Kitty had come down to see me an hour before she had done so in her hat and coat. She had had her confession to make, and had, I fancied, done me even in her attire the courtesy of hinting humbly that she was entirely at my disposal. But Archie evidently thought that our difference could be arranged in a five minutes' talk sandwiched in between two lessons. He had not even put his hat on. He stood, a small fair figure, red-waistcoated, brass-buttoned, hands in his pockets, leaning against the name-board of the tenants of the various floors of the building, while I, with one hand against the board, hung over him like a huge angel of good and evil, bidding him think.

"Think," I said again.

He suddenly realised what I meant. I could no more hold his eyes than I could have held those of a chidden dog. They cringed, evaded, even dared short defiances.

"Think," I said once more.

All at once he said, "I don't know what you mean."

"Then," I said, "I shall have to tell you."

"So," I concluded some minutes later, "do you think you are—doing right—to marry?"

We still stood, he with his back to the name-board, I with my hand against it, almost enveloping him with my physical presence. And now, no detail of my arraignment spared, I had at last caught his eye. Even before he spoke my heart gave a savage leap. Already his soft and spongy nature had begun to be hardened to that attitude I needed.

"Oh!" he said. . . Then, proudly, "But this is interference."

"You think," I repeated slowly, "that you have the right to get married?"

His very admission was a defiance of me. "I know I've been rather a rotter," he blustered.

Once more I repeated monotonously:

"You still think, after what I've just said, that you have the right—"

"I think," he broke out, "that if you looked after your own girl and left me to look after mine it would be better. I'm frightfully sorry about the other thing, of course, but—dash it all!—"

Our long exchange of looks said the rest, and it was not my fault if he didn't understand what his refusal to heed me would involve. Some people never understand, and cry afterwards, "You never told me that!" as if one man had the right to demand of another that he should speak the uttermost word. I cannot see that there is any such right. For such as these there is no uttermost word. Elias and the Prophets cannot make them understand. Though one rose from the dead to tell them they would not believe. The God who made them as they are cannot make Himself known to them—He can only destroy them again. They go out into the night in their ignorance, and for them there is no resurrection in knowledge. . . Therefore if the uttermost word will not enlighten them, why speak it? Weakness lies in that word. Because it is weak.

Art leaves it unspoken, and the Seer, having spoken it, comes down from Sinai no more. Only by a withholding from it does man achieve. Making three parts greater than the whole, he does not put forth to the last. He will not return bankrupt to heaven. The unuttered utterance is his credential, to be restored to the Bestower of it.

Therefore I did not, at that time, tell Archie Merridew that if he married I should slay him. But all, all else was in my eyes for his taking.

Then our gaze severed.

As I dropped my hand from the wall the devil frisked in me again. I had warned him, and had my own safety to consider now. Without attention to detail you can accomplish nothing in this world, and a thing is bunglingly done when you yourself suffer the consequences of it. Whatever I might do, I intended to suffer no consequences.

"Well, Archie," I said, as a man speaks who washes his hands of something, "I've told you what I think about it. There's no doubt it is, as you say, an interference, but I think it's justified, and so I'll say no more. . . And now, about that other: I need hardly say that I expect you to make things all right for me again."

"I will—I really will, Jeff," he promised at once.

"You see," I amplified, while the devil in me frisked, "leaving my reputation out of the question, it's beastly inconvenient. For instance, I'm badly in need of some shorthand practice, and I certainly don't intend to go up these stairs again until I'm rehabilitated."

He leaped at the chance of a reparation that would cost him little. "Oh, that's easy," he said. "Of course your own place—I mean, why not use mine, as you used to?"

"Oh," I objected, "I can't very well use your place when you're not there."

"I'm going to be there most of the time now," he replied. "Perhaps you think I'm off on the skite again, but I'm not." ("The Devil was sick," thought I again.) "I'm dead off all that now—straight. I do wish you'd come!"

"But," I said (while that imp in me positively capered), "you'll be awfully busy—with other things. I hear you're to be married at once—"

"Not too busy for that, old man," he assured me. "Do come!"

"Well, I'll see," I promised.

Half-an-hour later I was sitting in the British Museum reading-room with a stock of books on Medical Jurisprudence before me. Those two spirits within me were whispering again—plotting, machinating, discussing common ground of action. I had not yet resolved to take any action; but I had resolved, and firmly, that if action was to be taken I myself was not going to be caught unawares.

V

I t was true that Archie was busy. His "skite" had cost him a good deal of money, and he intended to make good some of the loss by economising on his marriage. With this end in view he had determined that his honeymoon and his summer holiday should be run into one, and had fixed, or Evie had fixed for him, a day towards the end of August for his wedding. He was going to Jersey, for the sake of the breath of the sea (I fancy that in this he was following Store Street advice); and he intended on his return to go into rooms until he should have had time to look round for a house.

His personal preparations were extensive. Ten porters and carmen a day called at the house near the Foundling Hospital, delivering purchases, and his upper floor was heaped up with bags, boxes, drawers taken from their cases and laid upon the floor, brown paper, cardboard boxes, new clothing. And one day—I won't set down the date—he lost his latchkey in the muddle. He did not know that he lost it as a result of my own close studies in the reading-room of the British Museum.

"Can't find the blessed thing anywhere!" he grumbled. "I took it off the bunch to slip into the pocket of my evening waistcoat—you can't carry a bunch of keys about in your evening clothes—and I can't think where the devil I put it! . . . Well, I shall have to ask Jane for another."

It was also a consequence of my deeply private studies that about the same time I had an accident with the hook of his bedroom door. The night being sultry, I had removed my coat, and hung it on his hook, over one of his, and, somehow, in going through the pockets of the undermost coat in search of the key, he had several times twisted the collar-tab by which my own garment hung. In taking my coat down again a little later I used some force; I used so much force that I fetched the whole hook down, leaving a small piece out of the wood of the door, and, Archie, busy emptying a drawer, remarked that to put it up again would be something for the next tenant to do.

"Oh no—better leave the place as you found it," I said. "You go on—I'll attend to it."

"Well, I don't know where you're going to find the screw-drivers—with my latchkey, I suppose," he remarked.

But I knew where the screw-driver was. I found it, and put the hook up securely again, a couple of inches below its old place.

I also carried constantly in my pocket, ready for use at any moment, a written page of notepaper, the compilation of which had cost me a good deal of thought in the reading-room.

Yet I must make perfectly clear to you that these and twenty other things that had the appearance of preparations committed me to nothing. They were merely part of the prudent course of making ready, not for the best that might happen, but for the worst; and that the worst might be avoided I plotted at the same time with almost extravagant care. For all this last, however, the effective human mind works as it were in separate compartments of the job to be done, and there was no denying that this was or might become a job. I treated it as a job. And as a job it cost me no more qualms and tremors than the cool preparation for an examination in Method might have done. I did not turn pale when I read in a book of forensic medicine that when one man slays another he commonly uses far too much violence; I merely noted the fact, and reminded myself of it from time to time, to be perfect in my (I still hoped superfluous) lesson. I did not blench when I learned that, judicial executions apart, ninety-nine per cent. of hangings were suicidal, so that, certain other precautions being observed, a presumption could be made preponderatingly probable. I merely turned my attention to the qualifying precautions. And as for that sheet of paper I carried— well, young men have killed themselves for less reason, and seldom for greater. Indeed, to die by his own hand might be the final virtuous act in which he took his farewell of the world. I would—still in the last event, you understand—allow him that empty semblance of virtue. Whether he needed it in heaven or not, I needed it on earth.

And (I am still talking purely hypothetically) I now recognise that I had prepared our respective mental attitudes with instinctive skill. That clever fiend within me had seen to that before I had become awake to that fiend's existence. By about the—till say a fortnight before the day fixed for his wedding—none could have told that I had the shadow of a grudge against him. He had made, for his slander of myself, a sort of semi-public apology—that is to say, he had mumbled a few words in the presence of Weston and the Principal of the College; but by that time the question of slander had been already so far from me that I had hardly had to affect an equanimity of manner. Without any effort whatever I had hit the necessary degree of magnanimity to a nicety, and there had been an end of that. I was free to return to the college again. This now mattered little since we were within a few days of the end of the summer term, and it was proposed to have, not a breaking-up party on the premises, but a boating-picnic at Richmond.

That I was in love with Evie Soames none knew. Did they? Could they? She was engaged to Archie, I to Kitty Windus; but I examined it again, to make sure. . . No, no suspicion of jealousy could attach to me; none would think of a *crime passionel* . . . And was it jealousy? Was it a *crime passionel*? I do not think you can say it was. True, I intended in the teeth of all the world to marry Evie Soames, just as I intended one day to be rich and to make my inherent power felt; but there would have been other ways than murder of accomplishing that. I should have found a way. . . No; he had the best reason in the world for what I was so carefully planning for him. To me none whatever could be attributed. My preparations (for the worst, of course) would be complete when I had made use of that paper I carried in my pocket.

It was one evening less than a week before the day of his wedding that I chose for the completion of these preparations, and I had walked with him as far as his home. There, with a good-night, I was artfully passing on when he himself detained me.

"Aren't you coming up for a bit?" he said. He had been monstrously hospitable since I had taken him to task about the slander. I had reckoned on this.

"No," I replied, "I must get some shorthand practice—I'm off home."

"Oh, come in," he urged, taking my arm. "I sha'n't get much either this few weeks—come in, and we'll have an hour together at speed. Come on—I've got some books you may as well have—I sha'n't want two sets."

He meant he wouldn't want Evie's text-books as well as his own. I had not been able to afford books for my studies, and so had had to make use of those belonging to the college. This was the nearest he had come since my accusation to speaking about Evie and himself together.

I went up to his rooms for a speed practice in Pitman's Shorthand.

"Here are the books," he said, when he got in. "Better put 'em where you'll have your hand on 'em—once you lose sight of a thing in this mess you can say good-bye to it. That blessed latchkey of mine hasn't turned up yet. Well, shall we get work over first and then talk a bit?"

He swept aside with his arm a heap of new shirts and collars and tissue-paper, took a writing-pad from the drawer of his table, and then looked round for something from which to read aloud. I produced from my pocket a newspaper, which I tossed over to him. I also had cleared a portion of the table for myself and was sharpening a pencil. My pad lay before me. He was taking his watch from the guard.

"Do I read first?" he asked, opening the newspaper. "Right-oh. Say when you're ready."

I drew up my chair. "Right," I said.

And in his rapid, clear, high-pitched voice he began to read.

It was the speech of some politician or other he read, and my pencil flew over the paper, swiftly taking down. Page after page I wrote, and I had almost forgotten that I was engaged on anything more than an ordinary exercise when suddenly he called "Time!" I stopped, and took a long breath.

"Now transcribe," he said. "You'll find paper under those gloves."

"No," I said. "You take down now. Saves time. Transcribing's the slow part, and we can both be doing that together."

"All right," he said, passing over the paper and making ready.

"Right? Go," I said.

And I began in my turn to read.

He had given me a continuous speech, but I gave him the Police Column. "Big Blaze in Bermondsey: Suspected Arson," I gave him. ("That chap'll get a couple of years for that," he interdicted). And then I passed to "Alleged Bucket-shop Frauds." I had already got my paper from my breast-pocket, that paper I had compiled in the reading-room of the British Museum. . .

"—bail being granted in two sums of £500," I concluded the bucket-shop paragraph and went on without pause:—

"Pathetic Confession"

"At Marlborough Street yesterday Rose Baxter, 24, seamstress, living in Osnaburgh Street, was charged before Mr. Siddeley with a determined attempt to commit suicide by hanging herself in a shed adjoining her dwelling, the property of Messrs Wright, Knapton & Co. The beginning of the case was reported in *The Argus* of 24th June. Inspector Woodhead read aloud a letter purporting to be in the prisoner's handwriting, from which we take the following."

("Cheerful subjects you choose, I must say," commented Archie, *sotto voce*.)

"'Dearest mother, I cannot face the disgrace. I hope you will forgive me for the trouble I am bringing on you. I have put it off as long as possible, hoping things would get better, but there is only one end to it.'"

("Kid, eh?" murmured Archie, writing.)

"'I trust God will forgive me. I am not afraid to die, I am afraid to live and face it. I cannot do E. this wrong. Please, dear mother, think of me as I used to be. I have tried and tried, but it is all no good, and I am better out of the world. Give my love to everybody, and try, dear mother, to forgive me.'"

"Time!"

Archie leaned back in his chair.

"Phew! Was that five minutes? Seemed short," he said. "Just a breather before we transcribe." He lighted a cigarette. "I say, Jeff: do you know any dealer who gives a decent price for second-hand clothes? I've heaps here I sha'n't want any more."

I had small use for such a dealer. "You might try Lamb's Conduit Street," I said. "I've bought clothes there."

"Silly ass——I didn't mean that!" He was now monstrously careful of my feelings.

"Say when you're ready to transcribe," I said, pushing across a wad of paper.

"All right, let's get it over. I'll race you! Ready?"

We plunged into our longhand transcription.

"Ah!" I said, twenty minutes later. "Beat you, Archie!"

He was racing through his last paragraph. "Not by much, you haven't," he said, and then, following our practice with exercises at the college, "No you haven't—you haven't signed—hooray!" he cried, dashing in his signature and looking at his watch. "Thirty-two minutes—pretty smart, what?"

An hour later I left, with his exercise as well as my own slipped between the leaves of Smillie's "Balance of Trade"—one of the text-books he had given me.

My hypothetical case was now completely prepared.

AND NOW I SPARED NO effort to save him. When it is yours to slay or to spare, you have in a sense slain even in sparing, for a life has been yours, even as Archie Merridew's life lay in the folds of that signed sheet of paper.

I carried that signed paper in my breast pocket on the day of the breaking-up party to Richmond. It had not been my intention to go to this picnic, for the sufficient reason that I was penniless *pas le sou*—but once more Kitty, to whom I had told some tale or other about pressing work, had broken out upon me.

"Oh yes—of course—I might have known!" she had cried, doubtless knowing that "pressure of work" tale of old from Frank and Alf. "Oh yes—it was quite enough that I should set my heart on it and I might have known you'd be busy or something! Busy!"

Her scornful little laugh had set me tingling: I—busy! But I had already seen that I should have to go. It had only remained for me to climb down to the level of Frank and Alf in the easiest possible way.

"Don't carry on like that, Kitty," I had said shortly. "It isn't so much the work; the fact is I'd like to go; but I can't very well ask them to pay me for the work before it's done, and the fact is I've rather miscalculated this week. It will be all right next week, of course."

"Oh, if that's it," she had said, her hand going as naturally to her pocket as if she had inherited the gesture as she had inherited her features or her name.

So I had accepted her purse, having accepted only meals before, and Alf and Frank and I were of a marrow.

The paper was in my breast pocket as we walked down to the stages to hire our boats. We were a largish party, but except for those in the boat in which I presently found myself—Evie, Kitty and Archie Merridew—I have no very clear recollection of who was there. I took one oar, Evie the other, Archie was not exercising himself physically; and he lay back in the steering seat with Kitty. It was hot; I should have liked to remove my coat; but I dreaded to part myself even by a yard from that paper. As it was my movements caused it to work up a little in my inside pocket; I saw a corner of it at the opening of the coat; it had the appearance of wishing to take a peep at Archie; and by-and-by Archie asked me why I didn't take my coat off.

"Not clean shirt day, eh, Jeff?" he laughed, with the recollection of numerous brown-paper parcels in his eyes.

He himself was taking extreme care of a pair of spotless flannels, and at one stage of the afternoon, I forget when, that suddenly struck me as almost funny enough to shriek aloud at—his care for his flannel bags and carelessness about everything else. It struck me as—I use the words quite literally—devilishly funny. It fascinated me, so that I could not keep from watching him. My eyes wandered from time to time to the other boats of our party and of other parties, moving on the shining river, but they always returned in less than a minute to him, irresistibly drawn. This *galgenhumor* almost mastered me as the paper again crept up to take another peep at him as he lolled, this time with Evie by his side, for Kitty had taken the other oar. It needed so little, so little imagination to look forward and see, strung out into the future, the results of that irrefutable Evidence in my pocket—the inquest at which I should not even be called as a witness—the funeral I need attend only as a mourner—the shock—the hushing up—and the certainty of everybody that they knew all about it! It was all horribly, horribly perfect. . .

A picnic? Oh yes, this was a picnic. . .

"*Do* take your coat off, Jeff—you'll be so much more comfortable— why, you're streaming!" This came from Kitty, who had the air of publicly possessing me, though only partly by reason of having paid for me, I think.

"Oh, I'm quite all right—really quite comfortable," I replied.

And then I thought of Evie, and that horrible humour rolled away from me. Evie. What about her? She spoke even then.

"Jeff's doing *all* the work," she said. "I'm sure Kitty and I could manage the boat quite well."

"Better stay as we are," I replied. "Archie and I wouldn't trim."

Yes, what about Evie?

Well, for her it was only a choice of sacrifices. The choice was not of my determining; I put that responsibility on him. There was still time; I would save him if I could; that was settled; but further than that I would not go. Should she fail to survive the shock it would be he, not I who had killed her. Better that, however. . .

If you can see what else I could have done, tell me. I am willing to learn.

And so we went up the river, and drew in under a bank for tea, and then went ashore for a walk, I with Kitty, he with Evie, and so back to the boat again. I do not remember quite how the time went. I know that the sun went down in a flush of rose, and that Japanese lanterns appeared on the water and in the water in long smooth reflections, and that parties were singing and playing banjos in the twilight. I could not have sat by Evie—it really would have put the boat out of trim—and so I had not to sit by Kitty either. She and I pulled again; Archie and Evie in the stern seat were hardly distinguishable; and Archie, who had been singing, was quiet again.

And I must have succeeded in keeping that dreadful mirth of mine to myself, for Kitty had noticed nothing. She stood by my side in the crowded station afterwards, murmuring to me how lovely it had been.

That is all I remember about that picnic.

Nor have I any reason for not telling you the truth about this. I am concealing neither the man nor the devil in me. For many years I have been almost entirely untroubled by it all, and I make even this slight qualification only because during the last month I have had feelings, not of remorse, but of something that is better described as a sort of backward curiosity. Perhaps it is a little more even than that, for a certain measure of admiration is not entirely absent from it. Don't misunderstand me, however. That tincture of admiration is not so strong that I cannot rest unless somebody admires my cleverness with me. Nothing irresistibly urges me to give myself away. But I have felt a little that backward pull of a man's own acts. I do not know, though practically it has not come near me, why men revisit places. I do not revisit that house near the Foundling Hospital—yet I do write this shorthand carefully locking my door before I begin and committing it to the most private recess of my cabinet as I complete each instalment. . . Yet other compunction, if this be compunction, have I none. I am rich, I am serving my age by a more arduous grappling with its economic problems than any of my contemporaries, I could have had Pepper's knighthood had I wished for it, and I have been married this long time to Evie Soames. . . No, on the whole I do not believe in melodramatic retributions. No shadowy shape of a fair-haired and red-waistcoated figure glides at my elbow or steps with me into my brougham, and when I close my eyes at night I do not see as on a painted curtain that dimity-papered, lamp-lighted upper chamber of his. I do not start at sudden sounds, nor fear to be left alone in my library when it grows late. I play with my clean-born children. Evie is happy with me. And I even have Miss Angela in a cleft stick—for, when things go well, she is my gentle and much-loved maiden aunt by marriage, but when they go across she is my mother-in-law, who would stare incredulously at any who might hint that my brain could plot a horror and my two hands execute it.

And yet I write this, and sometimes waste an hour in wondering why, all of a sudden, Kitty Windus threw me over without giving a reason, and, when I went for one, had left her rooms in Percy Street and gone goodness knows where.

But bah! They are wrong who say that for every crime somebody has to pay. They speak from hearsay. I do not speak from hearsay. To my own knowledge one crime has been committed for which nobody has paid and nobody ever will.

Well, things are as they are. . . and so I will make an end.

My desperate struggles to save Archie Merridew included an interview that I had positively to force from Miss Angela. I had to force it for the reason that, though I was now theoretically exculpated from the charge under which I had lain, slander always sticks, and some of it still stuck with Miss Soames in spite of her efforts to forget it. That, I think, was the reason why she saw me in the dining-room at Woburn Place instead of in her own sitting-room, where, I knew, Evie was. There, among the empty chairs, toying with Mr. Shoto's napkin-ring and putting it down again as I remembered whose it was, and then unconsciously taking it up again, I told her in such terms as I could find how matters stood. She nodded from time to time.

Again it was not my fault if she failed to understand. She did, I now know, fail, and failed the more hopelessly that she thought she did understand. Many, many thick wrappings lie between placid Aunt Angela and the stark realities of Life.

"I see perfectly," she said, when I had made that statement that would have appalled any but herself. "It was exactly the same with George. (I was once—engaged—to a man called George.) George put a precisely similar case quite plainly before me. *He* was consumptive, or rather his poor father was, and they do say it skips a generation—poor George!"

I shook my head, but she only sighed with gentle content. She did not really miss George.

"But," she went on, while my eyes wandered to the corner by the

OLIVER ONIONS

sideboard where Archie had had his conversation with Mr. Shoto about the Yoshiwara, "I shouldn't have refused him for that. (I did refuse him, and I heard afterwards that for weeks he ate scarcely anything at all.) It was something quite different that came between us—I've never told even Evie what the real reason was."

I interrupted her. "Are you sure, Miss Soames, that you've quite understood my real reason?" (More plainly I dared not speak, lest later there should be a chink in my own armour.)

"Oh yes!" she purred lightly. "Old woman as I am, I *quite* understand! As you say. . . 'the children.' . . ." Then, forgetting her attitude for a moment, she became playfully roguish. "Of course, it isn't as if you weren't in love with Miss Windus, and so in a sense feel it more nearly. You know how *you* would feel about it. I only say this that you may see that I *quite* understand these things do make a difference—eh?"

"But when I solemnly assure you that that has nothing whatever to do with it."

She adjusted the Indian shawl coquettishly about her shoulders.

"Ah, that's what you think! Come, Mr. Jeffries you're positively ungallant! As if I was so old that I'd forgotten! And not only George either! I hope you won't be offended, Mr. Jeffries, if I tell you that I suspect—I suspect—that in this I know you better than you know yourself!"

Against that phrase there is no argument. Some people do not and cannot see. And again I did not think Miss Angela had the right to extract from me the uttermost word. I was aware that the very possession of that awful weapon of mine was dangerous; merely to have it might be to use it; but the question is one of your resolve, and I was fully resolved. My job had to be done, or (as I still dared in certain moments to hope) not to be done; but if it was to be done, it was going to be done thoroughly. My neck was not going into a noose because of other people's blindness. It was of no use talking to Miss Angela.

And that being so, I abandoned my attempt with her. I smiled.

"Well, perhaps you're right," I said. "When one is in love oneself, and looking forward—well, perhaps it does bring it home to one. Perhaps it makes one a little of a busybody. So," I concluded, "I hope you won't exaggerate what I've been saying."

And a few minutes' further talk of things she had actually seen for herself in Archie—such things as his slight intemperance on the night of the birthday-party—made me quite safe with Miss Angela also.

To Kitty I was able to say even less than this. Indeed, she now detested Archie so thoroughly that I was scarcely able to say anything at all. And, looking back with all the care I am master of, I cannot see that anything I did say could have been the cause of that extraordinary breaking off with me without a word.

To Evie I said nothing at all.

There remained one more attempt with himself.

The time I chose for this was fixed by the exigencies of all the circumstances. I would have wrestled with him for the whole of the two days that remained before his wedding, but his own absence for a day precluded this. And as during that day I sought him in vain, I thought, very wearily, that he must now take his chance. Therefore, when it came to the very last day, the day before his wedding, I recognised that that also gave a perfect touch to the Evidence. The *very* eve of his wedding.

Several evenings before would somehow have been less plausible.

As I walked to his rooms that night I carried with me three things. Under my arm was my old brown-paper parcel—for to make a final use of his bath had seemed to me the most natural excuse for my calling on him. In my breast pocket I carried that piece of paper that was to be the Evidence to the world. And in another pocket I had his latch-key, for which I foresaw a use later in the evening.

I knocked at his door a little after eight, and Jane admitted me. She gave a familiar look at the parcel that contained my shirt, and also said something about a box Mr. Merridew was leaving behind for the care of which he wanted me to be responsible. I passed this box on the first landing. It was locked, but only half addressed—Archie had not yet secured the rooms to which he would return with Evie. But he had not yet said anything about the box to me.

I found him walking about his rooms, taking last peeps into empty drawers to see whether there was anything he had forgotten. His packing was finished, and he kept stopping in his prowl to throw another handful of old letters on to the smouldering heap in his old Queen Anne teapot of a grate. A little pile of these condemned letters still remained by the side of his perforated brass fender.

"Hallo!" he cried as I entered. "Just give a squint round, will you, and tell me if there's anything so big I can't see it. And I say: I've left a box downstairs; I wonder if you'd look after it for me? I've told Jane."

"Right!" I said. "Bath ready?"

"All ready. By Jove! how letters do accumulate! You go and scrub yourself, while I polish this lot off."

I went into his bathroom.

But I did not make use of his bath. Somehow I could not bring myself to it. I only wanted the bath to be known as my motive for calling. So I filled it, stood by it for a number of minutes, and then ran the water off again. I took the same brown-paper parcel with me into his sitting-room that I had brought out.

I did not stay long after that. I was coming back. At nine I rose.

"What, are you off?" he said. "I must say you take what you want and clear off pretty quick! Supper'll be up presently."

"A last stag-party?" I said. "I'm afraid you'll have to have it without me. I've got to get to Bedford yet. So," I added, "I shall have to wish you—you know—get it over now."

"Oh, don't put on so much blessed ceremony!" he said. "It isn't as if you weren't going to see me again!"

It wasn't.

"Oh, about that box," I said. "Better call Jane, and tell me in her presence."

"Well, if you *will* leave me to eat my last bachelor supper alone. But I should have had to clear out myself just after. Got to have a word with Aunt Angela—she let's me call her that now."

He moved towards the door.

"Where are you going?" I asked.

"To call Jane," he replied. "Bell's busted now—time I cleared out of here—whole place is coming to pieces. . . Jane! Ja—ne!" he shouted down the well of the stairs.

Then as Jane didn't hear he descended to the floor below.

His old red woollen bell-rope lay in a heap on the floor. That also had happened as a result of my studies in the British Museum. I busied myself with it. . . By the time he had returned I had made it quite ready and was gazing thoughtfully into his fireplace.

I went downstairs with Jane, who herself closed the door behind me. I gave her a very express good-night.

THE REMAINDER OF THAT EVENING I can divide into four distinct stages, and I will adopt that course, taking them numerically.

The first stage was one of an almost overwhelming lassitude. I had an hour and a half and more to kill, and this lassitude came upon me suddenly as I walked slowly in the direction of Cheapside. I was in its power before I recognised its dangers. The man of action had suddenly sunk into abeyance with me, and, now that all was ready, all interest in my job had departed from me. The drudgery of actual performance was all at once beyond my powers. I could have gone on planning—I wished there had been more to plan—but now to carry out. . .

I collapsed suddenly.

Why (I asked myself wearily) trouble after all! Why trouble about anything? Life was short, yet already too long; its activities overlauded, its glories contemptibly little; why waste it in striving—nay, why live it all? Thirty years of it had brought me nothing; whatever another thirty years might bring me I should have to leave, and what would it matter after that whether I left much or little? Nay, were there really an Infinite Mercy to be "squared," it was perhaps better to cast myself before it helpless, naked, and without profit of my life. Why not end it all now? Why not kill, not Archie, but myself?

I turned with bowed head down the Minories, and something within me—I think it was that honest and beaten and bloody-minded Jeffries—whispered "The River!"

Presently I stood not far from the Tower, looking over a parapet into the dark water.

Yes, the river would settle it, that was the real way out. No more Agency clerkships and red-and-green-lighted apartments and sham betrothals on the other side of that parapet. And no more heartrending strivings to be free of the circumstances into which the world malignantly thrust me back the moment I raised my head. Striving? I realised all my striving in the past—Rixon Tebb & Masters', the Method examination, my commissionaireship, the wanton slander, my late perfected plan—and the thought that the years to come might be but repetitions of all this hit me like a hammer. I could not face it.

Then a detached sentence from one of the books I had read in the museum sprang up in my mind, and I started a little. The sentence was to the effect that a man who leaps into water always removes his hat before doing so. I did not remember that I had taken my own hat off, but there it lay, on the parapet, at my elbow.

Then, "Well, it will do to cover some other poor devil's head," murmured that tired Jeffries, "Get it over, and send that conscienceless young scamp to hell with *your* blood on his head. Somebody always pays, you know."

I removed my coat.

But that tired Jeffries never spoke unanswered, and these words were answerable. To make a hole in the water from sheer weariness was one thing, but to destroy myself to compass another's damnation was quite a different one. The other Jeffries spoke.

"Why should you kill yourself for his sin? Each man must bear his own. Nay, it is not committed yet and will not be if you are strong and play the man. Are you going to fold your hands and allow Evie. . ."

And at the thought of Evie I felt my sluggish blood creep again.

"You live in a practical world—be practical," continued that satanic James Herbert. "Prevention is better than cure. Even could he be punished afterwards, how much better off would *she* be. . . *then*? What right have you to bring this horror on her? He's selfish, ignorant, cruel— it would be dreadful at the best; but. . . oh, think, man! Think of her now. . . and tomorrow!"

"You only want her yourself," growled the other.

"You do—but that's not your motive!" cried the first. "You've overlooked all he's done to you—but this isn't to you! Coward—if you allow it! You won't allow it—to kill him would be better than to allow it. . . Come; what time is it? She'll be preparing for bed by the time you get there."

I put on my hat and coat again.

This was my first stage.

The second began with my approach to Woburn Place.

The sitting-room with the pink-shaded lamp lay at the front of the house, but Evie and her aunt slept at the back. The sitting-room was in darkness as I passed. I took a side street, and then a back cartway used by tradesmen. A high wall was in front of me, but by stepping back I could see the hinder part of the row—landing windows, bathroom windows, tiny conservatories, bedrooms—various oblongs at different levels, some blinded, some with lamps, many in darkness. Behind me was a mews, with horses that moved their feet in their litter and dragged at chains from time to time.

The tradesmen's entrances were unnumbered, and I do not know whether I hit on the right house; but that did not matter. I have mentioned my uncommon powers of mental visualisation, and these sufficed me. I fixed my eyes on a window; it might or might not have been Evie's; but to all intents and purposes it was. Somebody was retiring there, and the blind was lowered.

I saw no hand, no shadow on the blind. Only the light went out suddenly, and from the sound the blind made as it went up I judged it to be a spring blind. A piano had begun to play somewhere, but save for that all was silent.

It was the last of her single days.

Tomorrow.

My heart was hideously alive again. What! Fold my hands— drown—and Evie as she still was up there.

Soft and terrible exclamations began to break from my lips.

"Ah, would he? Would he? He would, would he?"

A clock struck half-past eleven.

This was my second stage.

I will begin the third at the moment when I pushed gently at the gate over the whitewashed area near the Foundling Hospital.

His light still showed over the leads, but the basement was in darkness. Evidently Jane had gone to bed. I felt in my pocket for his latchkey, mounted the three steps, and with infinite softness put the key into the lock and turned it. The door opened noiselessly, and I prevented the click as I closed it again by letting the little brass knob gently back with my thumb. Then silently I began to mount his stairs, passing on the way the locked box that had been put into my charge. I reached the top. The first sound I had made since entering the house was my tap at Archie's door.

"Come in!" his tenor voice called from behind the door.

I entered.

At first he did not seem more than ordinarily surprised to see me; it was only after a moment that the oddness struck him.

"Hallo!" he began, in natural though not altogether cordial tones. . . Then, "Hallo! I thought you were in Bedford by this time."

"Missed my train," I said.

He stared mistrustfully. . .

He had been preparing for bed. He had removed his collar and tie, and his red waistcoat was unbuttoned. Through the chink of his bedroom door I saw the light of his second lamp.

In his surprise at seeing me back again, he had half risen from his arm-chair. He remained, his hands on the arms of it, neither sitting nor standing, as he asked suddenly, "Who let you in?"

"Myself," I answered, in an even tone. "A little unceremonious, perhaps, but I knew Jane had gone to bed and didn't want to fetch you down. The fact is, I've found your latchkey."

"You've found my latchkey!"

"In my coat pocket. Don't ask me how it got there. Our two coats were hanging together one night, but even then I don't quite see... Here it is anyway."

I put it on the table.

"That's a rum 'un," he said, slowly sitting down in his chair again, but keeping his eyes on mine. "So you came back to give it me?"

"I came back to give it you. Besides," my eyes were on his slender bare neck, "since I was coming back—I thought I'd like another word with you before—" I paused.

For a moment I could not understand the readiness with which he took up the thing I had not said. His lips had compressed a little.

"Ah! Again?" he said, with a little kindling in his eyes.

"'Again'?" Then I saw. He had seen Miss Angela during the last hour, and she had doubtless spoken of my own call on her. "Yes, again," I answered.

That third stage had a curious close. That close was nothing less than the reunification of those two halves of the Giant to the fabulous splitting into two of whom I have likened my mental state. They came together again, these two halves, as the two forces come together that make the thunder clap... but of this in a moment.

After several moments of increasingly rapid talk, we were both standing, he defiantly with one hand on the edge of the mantelpiece, I at the other end of the hearth. He had risen a moment before at certain words of mine, as if to inform me that our interview was over. Once I had seen his eyes move towards the place where the bell-rope should have been, but that lay, a red woollen heap, on the floor behind me, and he would have had to pass me in order to get into his bedroom. He had found an appearance of forcefulness in the use of violent words.

"Why, damn your impudence!" he blustered. "Look here, my good man! If you suppose I'm going to be talked to like this by you or anybody else—"

"Then deny the fact," I said for the fifth time.

"I'll not deny or anything else till I know what right—"

"I know it comes late, but I've spoken of it before."

"Yes—sneaking behind my back!" he said hotly, probably again remembering his recent conversation with Miss Angela.

"To your face."

"Yes—and if it hadn't been for something else I should have told you then what an interfering devil you were!"

"Merridew," I said slowly, "it's the last time."

He sneered.

"I'm glad of that—and confound you for a meddler!" he cried. "If that's all you came for, get out, and I'll get somebody else to look after my trunk!"

We were silent for a space, and in that space I heard the voice of that human Jeffries, almost pitifully seeking still to save him. "Give him every chance," sobbed that Jeffries, "he's only a weakling—you could crush him mentally as you could physically—it would be little better than infanticide—try him again—show him that red thing on the floor—and that carved thing on the door."

But now Archie in his turn seemed to have become divided. He had suddenly turned white. But an habitual pertness still persisted in his tongue. I don't think this had any relation whatever to the physical peril he seemed at last to have realised he was in. I stood over him huge and black as Fate. . . "Spare him if you can," that generous bloodthirsty devil in me muttered quickly.

"Merridew," I said heavily, "you'll disappear tomorrow morning. . . *or*—"

"Shall I?" he bragged falteringly. . .

"And you won't come back. I shall stay here tonight and put you into the train myself."

"Then you'll have to sleep in the bath—and you should know by this time how small that is," came from his lips.

And yet it came only from his lips. His terrified heart had no part in it. His only chance now was to have screamed aloud.

But he did not scream. Instead, he stooped swiftly, caught up the poker, and struck at my head with it.

It was then that the thunder-clap came, and that I was James Herbert Jeffries, whole, and a murderer. Swiftly as Archie and I came together the halves of that Giant came together. Instinctively I had guarded my head, perhaps realising—I cannot say—that a single drop of blood might mean for me precisely what I intended to do to him; but it mattered little whether blood blinded my eyes or not. Another redness gorged me, and then, my mind became whitely blind. As colours are lost on a disc that revolves, so all my plans and preparations spun and mingled. All was there, yet nothing was there. For an instant my visual memories of that pleasant, dimity-papered apartment stood separate; my own old experiences and new divinations also stood separate; I saw ahead, three or four minutes ahead, his struggles in my great arms, my left arm about his ankles, my right hand over his mouth, the red of the woollen bell-rope against his white neck. . . and then all wheeled hideously together. . .

I was upon him, smothering him with my bulk, and wondering even as I bore him backwards to the door whether I myself was bleeding. . .

THE FOURTH STAGE WAS CHARACTERISED throughout by an extraordinary quietness. There was the light sound of the turning of paper in it, for I had to search in a pile of old books and papers for his shorthand pad and to make sure I had the right one—I had to take from my breast pocket another sheet of paper and to glance at that also to make sure that it also was the right one—and then I had to approach the bedroom door and to drop this into his pocket. . .

But before I did any of these things I tiptoed to the mirror over the mantelpiece in order to see whether I bled.

I did not. My left eye was of a dull red, but not with blood, and I could deal with that. As a preparation for dealing with it I emptied at a draught the brandy flask he had prepared for his journey on the morrow.

Softly as a cat I continued to move about.

Then I had to remember which of his stairs creaked to the tread. They were the fourth and the tenth from the first landing; I knew that as well as I knew my own name; and yet for a time I really could not remember the numbers.

The room was quiet as a grave as I gave a final glance round at the displayed Evidence. . .

Then behind his Queen Anne grate a cricket began to sing.

Nobody saw me leave the house. I had to bring his latchkey away. Without it the latch would have clicked as I closed the door from the outside.

Then I crossed Mecklenburgh Square and walked towards King's Cross.

A quarter of an hour later an apparently very drunken man of uncommon stature lurched heavily through the swing doors of my public-house and fell full length on the floor in the middle of a knot of drinkers. A barman dived quickly under the flap of the counter, with an "Outside!" rushed towards me. I was hauled to my feet. I had a hand over one eye.

"'*E's* copped the brewer all right!" a cheerful voice sounded in my ear. "Just smell 'im! Must ha' been drinking it straight out o' the cask."

"'Ere—'old 'ard—ain't it your lodger?" somebody else said suddenly.

"Is it? Lumme, so it is! Look at 'is eye!"

"Ain't 'alf a mouse!"

"'Ere, 'elp me up with 'im the back way, Jim—Lord! 'e weighs a ton! I've never known 'im 'ave a drink 'ere, but there, they get it at one place if they don't at another."

Then somebody bawled to me:

"Look out—don't blow your nose—you'll 'ave your eye up if you do!"

But I wanted my eye "up." Up it came instantly, large as an egg, and there was a laugh.

"Well, 'e won't brag much about where 'e got *that*!" somebody said.

And they helped me up to my red-and-green-lighted room.

THEY SAY SOMEBODY ALWAYS PAYS. Well, this my story. It is a long time ago, and nobody has paid yet. Nor, as far as I can see, is it likely that anybody ever will. There is only one detail that I have not been able properly to attend to, and even that has attended to itself—for of course Kitty Windus fled because she realised that I was in love with Evie. I could hardly expect her to stay after that.

No: nobody has paid. Nobody ever will.

THE END

THE DEBIT ACCOUNT

PART I
THE COBDEN CORNER

I

One day in the early June of the year 1900 I was taking a walk on Hampstead Heath and found myself in the neighbourhood of the Vale of Health. About that time my eyes were very much open for such things as house-agents' notice-boards and placards in windows that announced that houses or portions of houses were to let. I was going to be married, and wanted a place in which to live.

My salary was one hundred and fifty pounds a year. I figured on the wages-book of the Freight and Ballast Company as "Jeffries, J. H., Int. Ex. Con.," which meant that I was an intermediate clerk of the Confidential Exchange Department, and to this description of myself I affixed each week my signature across a penny stamp in formal receipt of my three pounds. I could have been paid in gold had I wished, but I had preferred a weekly cheque, and I took care never to cash this cheque at our own offices in Waterloo Place. I did not wish it to be known that I had no banking account. As a matter of fact, I now had one, though I should not have liked to disclose it to the Income Tax Commissioners. The reason for this reticence lay in the smallness, not in the largeness, of my balance. I had learned that in certain circumstances it pays you to appear better off than you are.

It was a Sunday, a Whit-Sunday, on which I took my walk, and on my way up from Camden Town across the Lower Heath I had passed among the canvas and tent-pegs and staked-out "pitches" that were the preparation for the Bank Holiday on the morrow. Tall *chevaux de frises* of swings were locked back with long bars; about the caravans picked out with red and green, the proprietors of cocoanut-shies and roundabouts smoked their pipes; and up the East Heath Road there rumbled from time to time, shaking the ground, a traction-engine with its string of waggons and gaudy tumbrils.

I was alone. Both my *fiancée* and the aunt with whom she lived in a boarding-house in Woburn Place had gone down to Guildford to attend the funeral of a friend of the family—a Mrs. Merridew; and as I had known the deceased lady by name only, my own attendance had not been considered necessary. So until lunch-time, when I had an engagement, I was taking my stroll, with a particular eye to the smaller of the houses I passed, and many conjectures about the rent of them.

You will remember, if you happen to know that north-western part of London, that away across the Heath, on the Highgate side, there stands up among the trees a lordly turreted place, the abode (I believe it then was) of some merchant prince or other. My eyes had wandered frequently to this great house, but I had lost it again as I had descended to the pond with the swans upon it, and approached the tea-garden that, with its swings and automatic machines, makes a sort of miniature standing Bank Holiday all the year round. During the whole of a youth and early manhood of extraordinary hardship (I was now nearing thirty-five) I had been consumed with a violent but ineffectual ambition, of which those distant turrets now reminded me. . . I had been hideously poor, but, heaven be thanked, I had managed to get my head above water at last. Those horrible days were over, or nearly so. I had now, for example, a banking account; and though I seldom risked drawing a cheque for more than two pounds without first performing quite an intricate little sum, the data for which were furnished by my cheque, pass and paying-in books respectively, still—I had a banking account. I had also good boots, two fairish suits of clothes (though no evening clothes), an umbrella, a watch, and other possessions that, three or four years before, had seemed beyond dreams unattainable.

And when I say that I had for long been ragingly ambitious, I do not merely mean that I had constantly thought how fine it would be could I wake up one morning and find myself rich and powerful and respected. Had that been the whole of it, I don't think I should have differed greatly from the costers and showmen who dotted the Heath that Whit-Sunday morning. No; the point rather was, that I saw in the main how I was going to get what I wanted. I, or rather my coadjutor "Judy" Pepper and I between us, had ideas that we intended to "play" as one plays a hand at cards. Therefore, as I walked, I dare say I thought as much about that distant castellated house as I did about the far humbler abode I intended to take the moment I could find a suitable one.

I wandered among the alleys and windings of the Vale of Health, noting the villas with peeling plaster and the weather-boarded and half-dilapidated cottages that make the place peculiar; and I was ascending a steep hillock with willows at the foot of it and the level ridge of the Spaniards Road running like a railway embankment past the pines at the top, when, chancing to turn my head, I saw what appeared to be the very place for me.

It could not have been very long empty, for I had passed its door, an ivy-green one with lace curtains behind its upper panels of glass, without noticing the usual signs of uninhabitation. Then I remembered the approaching Quarter Day and smiled. The chances were that somebody had done a "moonlight flit" and had left the lace curtains up in order that his going might not be observed. There was no doubt, as I could see from where I stood, about the place being untenanted now, nor that it would not remain so for very long. I stood for a moment examining it from half-way up the hillock.

There was not much of it to examine. It was very small, fronted with stucco, and had a little square verandah built out on wooden posts over its tiny garden. More than that I could hardly see of it, but it adjoined a much larger house, and to this I turned my eyes. This larger house was a low, French-windowed dwelling, with a pleasantly eaved and flat-pitched roof, very refreshing to think of in these days of Garden City roofs and diminutive dormers; and its garden was well kept, and gay with virginia stock borders and delphinium and Canterbury bells in the beds behind. It seemed likely that formerly the two houses had been one.

I was descending the hillock for a closer view when I remembered that I could hardly expect to be shown round that day. I looked at my watch. It was half-past twelve, and my appointment, which was with Pepper, was not for another hour. There would be plenty of time for me to walk round by my turreted place and back by Hampstead Lane. I left the Vale of Health, crossed the Viaduct, and continued my saunter.

But I walked slowly, and in a deepening abstraction. The sight of that little house had set my thoughts running on my *fiancée* again. And as I presently took that little house, and married my *fiancée* not long afterwards, and as, moreover, my meditation of that morning has a good deal to do with my tale, I had better state at the beginning what the trouble was, and have done with it.

I had known Evie Soames for close on five years; and though I had loved her ever since the days when, with her skirt neither short nor long, and her hair neither loose nor yet properly revealing the shape of her slender and birch-like nape, she and I had attended the same Business College in Holborn, it had been only during the last six months that we had become engaged. On either of our parts a former engagement had ended abruptly; and this, for her sake at least, was the reason why

I would gladly have had her anywhere but at Guildford that Sunday morning.

For it had been to the late Mrs. Merridew's son that she had been engaged, and the affair had terminated with tragical suddenness indeed. You cannot but call it tragical when a young man is discovered, on his wedding morning, hanging by the neck from a hook in his bedroom door, with a letter in his pocket that only partly sets forth his reason for taking his life, leaving the rest for the medical evidence to determine—and then to be kept for very pity from his womenfolk. Yet this had happened four years before; and it was because I dreaded to revive the memory of it, and especially to revive the memories of those subsequent days when Evie must have tormented herself with vain and fruitless guessings at what a coroner and a jury-panel and a doctor in Store Street had smothered up among themselves, that I walked brooding and with downhung head.

And about women generally I had better confess myself at once as, past praying for, a Philistine. I subscribe to nothing whatever that this New Man so strangely risen in our midst nowadays appears to hold about the ancient and changeless feminine. And I take it that most men not profligates or fools will understand me when I say that I think there are some things that it is worse than useless that women should know, and that this sordid four-year-old business was one of them. To those born to knowledge, knowledge will come; the others will never know, no matter what the facts of their experience may be. Oh, I had seen these weak and vainglorious vessels go to Life's Niagara before, thinking to fill themselves at it—and had seen the flinders into which they had been dashed. Therefore I had deliberately resolved to stand between Evie Soames and many things. I ever thought of her as a flower, a flower of dewy flesh, joining its fragrance to that of the morning of her mind; and though I knew that that too lovely stage must quickly pass, perhaps into something better, I could never think of that passing unmoved. I was prepared to fight for a last—and perhaps impossible—protection of it. There was much knowledge that I would take on myself for the pair of us; a few more of life's weals and scars would make no difference to me. . . And if you tell me that this was merely a foredoomed attempt to keep from her the knowledge of the world into which she had been born, very well: I accept the responsibility of that. At any rate, she might find what fantastic explanations she would of the mystery that I and the jury and a doctor in Store Street could have explained. I would open no door to admit her to horrors which would haunt her for ever though I closed it again in a flash.

I hope you see why I cursed that funeral, for bringing even the fringe of that old shadow back over us again.

So absorbed was I in my meditation, that I passed my turreted house without noticing it. It was as I was approaching Waterlow Park that a clock striking one woke me out of my reverie. I shook off the weight of my thoughts. If this shadow had claimed Evie again, I must put something in its place when I met her and her aunt at Victoria that evening, that was all. I had now my coming interview with Pepper to think of.

I faced about and began to descend Hampstead Lane, suddenly occupied with business, to the exclusion even of Evie.

"Judy" (now Sir Julius) Pepper and I have been partners for ten years now; and while he is sometimes a little inclined to overrate what he calls my "imaginative qualities," I on the other hand have never been able sufficiently to admire his own hard, gay, polished efficiency. I still think of him, as I thought of him then, as of a diamond, that could encounter steel and come off with never an angle blunted nor a facet scratched; and if he in turn likens me to the handle in which that graver is set, and even to some extent to the guiding power, I pass that, thinking it as graceful to accept a compliment as to pay one. Exactly how our combination works is nobody else's concern; the important thing is, that between us we undoubtedly have made our mark since those days when he kept up appearances in Alfred Place, W., and I poked about the Vale of Health in search of a house that should come within the limits of my three pounds a week.

II

I was leaving the road at the Spaniards and striking across the West Heath when I came upon him. He also appeared to have been early, and to have been taking a walk to put away the time.

"Hallo!" I called, and he turned.

He was a short, rosy man of thirty-eight, with an inclination to plumpness that he only defeated by assiduous exercise; and his silk hat, "frocker" and grey cashmere trousers might have served some high tailor for an advertisement plate of perfect clothes. Perhaps they did, for I don't think that at that time he paid for them otherwise. His shirts and undergarments, of which he spoke with interest and readiness, were also perfect; and he not only made me feel in this respect like some rough bear of a Balzac, always in a dressing-gown, but even gave me, though quite without offensiveness, that and similar names. He gave me, in fact, this one now.

"Well, my dear Balzac!" he said, his rosy face breaking as suddenly into a smile as if a hundred invisible gravers had magically altered its whole clean modelling. "Out seeking an appetite?"

I laughed. "You're walking last night's supper off, I suppose?"

"N-o," he said, as if impartially looking back on whatever the excellent meal had been. "No—I'm scaling fairly low just now—just over the eleven stone. What are you, by the way?"

"Sixteen and a half—but then look at my size!"

He had the neatest and smallest and most resolute mouth, from which came speech so finished that I never heard a slurred word fall from it. He made it a little bud now, and whistled.

"Sixteen and a—! I say, you'd better sign on at one of those shows I saw over there!"

"Well, with you as showman I dare say we should make it pay," I answered, falling in with this conception of our respective rôles.

His smile vanished as magically as it had come.

"Well, that's what we're going to talk about," he said; "but after lunch will do. . . What sort of a tree do you call that, now?"

That was one of Judy's little affectations. He knew as well as I did that the tree at which he pointed was a birch, and I had thought, the first time I had exposed this dissimulation in him, that he would not try it on again. Fond hope! Though you knew that Pepper was laughing in his sleeve at you, and let him see you knew it, his face remained translucent and impenetrable as adamant. . . So he took it as a piece of new and interesting information that the tree was a birch, and we walked on. . .

I had first met Pepper, or rather he had first spotted me, at the F.B.C., and we were both still at the offices in Waterloo Place. But while Pepper still moved his little wooden blocks (representing trains and ships) about vast box-enclosed maps with glass lids that shut down and locked, solving for the Company intricate problems of transport and the distribution of produce and manufactured stuff, he had already crossed the line that divides the Mercantile from the Political, or at least from the Administrative. Already that highly tempered cutting-point of manner had made a way for him into circles where I have never been at my ease; and dining once a month or oftener with the President and a Permanent Official of the Board of Trade, he was a valuable channel of information in such matters as Arbitration and the settlement of Trade Disputes. And he had been quicker than I to see the Achilles' heel of our complicated mercantile economy. Hitherto this vulnerable spot had been conceived to lie in Production, as in the last resort it certainly does; but short of that and actual industrial war, there was the equally effective and less perilous paralysis, the secret of which lay in Distribution. Shipping lines, railways and the postal organisation were the real nervous system; and Judy Pepper, strike-preventer rather than strike-breaker, was getting the ju-jitsu of it at his finger ends long before Syndicalism became aware of one of its most potent weapons.

You will see the manifold bearings of this on a Democratic Age.

And it was no less bold a move than our secession together from the F.B.C. and setting up on our own account that we were to discuss at lunch at the Bull and Bush that day.

We walked along a short street with cottages on one side and a high wall on the other, passed under the fairy-lamps of the Bull and Bush arch, and sought one of the little trellised bowers at the edge of the lawn.

Waiters always bestirred themselves to attend to Pepper, and the two who approached us at once neglected earlier comers to do so. Pepper gave his order, and we went through the Sunday "ordinary." Then he ordered coffee and liqueurs, bidding the waiter leave the bottle of *crème de menthe* on the table and not disturb us again. He lighted a cigar; I, not yet a practised smoker, fumbled with a cigarette, at the pasteboard packet of which I saw my ally's glance; and then, spreading a number of papers before him, he plunged into business.

It was highly technical, and I will not trouble you with more of it than bore on our immediate secession from the F.B.C.—a step to which I was strongly averse.

"You see," Pepper urged presently, "this Campbell Line award precipitates matters rather." (I shook my head, but he went on.) "As a precedent it's going to make an enormous difference. I'll show you the Trinity Master's statement presently. . . No, no, wait till I've finished. . . It means among other things a revision of the whole Campbell scale, and the other lines will have to follow. Then that'll make trouble with Labour, and Robson and the Board of Trade come in. Here's Robson's letter; better make a note of it. You don't write shorthand, do you?"

"N-o."

"Hm! You hardly seem quite sure whether you do or not! . . . Well, I'll get Miss Levey to make an abstract for you. Here's what he says. . ."

And he began to read from the letter.

As he did so I was wondering what on earth had made me tell him I didn't write shorthand. I do write shorthand. I keep, as a matter of fact, much of my private journal in shorthand, and I had not the slightest objection to Pepper or anybody else knowing of my accomplishment. . . And yet, as if Pepper had somehow taken me off my guard, that doubtful "N-o" had come out. I bit my lip.

"Well," he concluded, folding the letter again, "there you have it. Of course I see what you mean about our using the F.B.C. for the present, merely as a going machine; but this seems to me to outweigh that. . . You still don't think so?"

I still did not. Laboriously, for I never could make a speech in my life, I set my reasons before him. He nodded from time to time, opening and shutting his slender silver pencil.

"So you still think wait?" he mused by-and-by. It was evident that I had not spoken in vain.

"You can be going ahead with all you want to do as we are, and for the rest I'd wait and see what happened."

"Of course there's this war—" he admitted reluctantly.

"It's not the war. It's what'll happen after the war."

"Well," he said, with a shrug, "you know you're my heaven-sent find, and that I'm going to keep you to myself. . . So we wait? That's decided?"

"Wait," I repeated doggedly.

Then, as if he had sufficiently tested my belief in myself, that smile broke over his agate of a face again. He leaned back to look at me.

"You're an extraordinary chap!" he positively sparkled fondness at me. "What are you getting now at the F.B.C.—three pounds?"

"Still I say wait," I said, nodding once or twice.

"And getting married on it!" he marvelled.

"Almost immediately."

Then Pepper laughed outright. "Well, I won't say you're like the chap who asked for a rise to get married on. 'You get married—you'll get the rise then!' his boss told him." Then, the smile going out again, he added, "And suppose we're forestalled on this new scale of rates?"

I spoke with strongly suppressed energy. "They can't forestall you and me. Don't you see? Don't you see we're *hors concours*—in a class by ourselves? We are what they can only make a bluff at being—ever! 'There is a tide'—but it hasn't got to be taken before the flood!"

He took the whole of me in in one shining look, as a camera might have seen me. He was openly admiring me.

"By Jove," he burst out, "but you don't lack confidence! . . . Of course you see the joke?"

"You mean—'Jeffries, J. H., Int. Ex. Con., £3'—two-ten for his suits—eighteenpence for his dinners—getting married—and still hanging back from this because it's going to pay fifty times better twelve months from now?" That, I took it, was the joke.

"And you're quite—quite—sure?" he dared me for the last time, his face radiant.

I brought my hand softly down on the table. "Yes!" I cried. "I'm talking what I *know*—you're only talking what you *think*!"

His small manicured hand flew out to my great one.

"Oh—bravo!" he cried. "Wait it is, then. By Jove, when it does come, you'll have deserved it! . . . Here, shove your glass over—I believe you're entirely right—but if it was only for your consummate cheek we should have to drink to it!"

And he filled up the two glasses with the vivid green liqueur again, touching his against mine.

I left him shortly after, or rather he left me in order to keep one of his urgent and mysterious appointments; and I wandered slowly down towards my own abode.

This was a large upper room near the Cobden Statue—a proximity that for some reason or other always afforded my partner-to-be private mirth. I had taken it because its size fitted it both for living purposes and for the storing of the things I had got against my marriage as well. It was the fourth of the five floors of a new, terra-cotta-fronted, retail drapery establishment (experience had taught me that the biggest rooms are always over shops); and from its plate-glass windows below to its sham gables held up like pieces of stage scenery by iron braces above, it was a mass of ridiculous ornament—coats of arms, swags of fruit and flowers, and feeble grotesques with horns and tails and grins, the whole looking as if it had been squeezed on from some gigantic pink icing-tube such as they use for the modelling of wedding-cakes. But I lived inside it, not outside, and I had made the place exceedingly comfortable. I had no fewer than four large windows, two looking over the High Street, one diagonally from a rounded corner, and the fourth over the little railing-enclosed garden of a neighbouring crescent. As I was high enough up to dispense with blinds and curtains, these four windows admitted a flood of admirable light on an interior that, large as it was, was over-furnished; and there was no frippery to prevent my throwing up my sashes and looking down among the terra-cotta gargoyles on the walking hats below.

Evie and I had done much of our six months' courting in second-hand dealers' shops. Resolving that our engagement should be a short one, and knowing that those who have little either of money or time have, in furnishing as in everything else, to pay through the nose for their purchases, we had started at once. What had remained of a sum of money Evie's aunt had long had in trust for her against her one day setting up housekeeping on her own account had enabled us to do this. At first the sum had been one hundred and fifty pounds; a former purchase of clothing, of which only the black garments had ever been worn, had reduced it by more than a third; and of what had become of more than half the balance my light, lofty room now bore witness.

It improved my spirits to be among our joint belongings, and by the time I had made tea for myself, much of my despondency of earlier in the day had gone. I looked round, and began to tell myself over again the story of our acquisitions. There was not a piece that did not contribute its chapter. That bow-fronted chest of drawers with the old mirror on it we had first seen on a pavement in Upper Street, Islington; and we had had a long debate in Miss Angela Soames' sitting-room in Woburn Place before deciding to buy it—a debate much interrupted by less practical matters, with Miss Angela's pink-shaded lamp turned economically low, and Miss Angela herself intelligently off to bed. I had only to look at our odd assortment of chairs in order to see Evie again as she had stood in the dim back parts of this shop or that—to see again the whites of her eyes, brilliant as if her skin had been a Moor's, her hair dark as a black sweet-pea, the round neck with the little pulse in it, and the slender, just-grown lines of bosom or back or hips as she stooped or straightened. Over one extravagance her voice had broken out in shocked and delicious reproach; over another happy find she had had to turn away lest the dealer should see her eagerness and increase the price; and there had been laughs and bickerings and confusions and byplays without number. . . I have become something of a connoisseur since then; but nothing I have acquired at Spink's or Christie's means to me what those coppery old Sheffield cream-jugs and caddies and those now-valuable sketches of Billy Izzard's meant. . .

Then, at seven o'clock, I washed, put on my hat, and went out. Evie and her aunt were due to arrive at Victoria at a quarter to eight.

I picked them out by their attire far down the platform, and advanced to meet them. With a leap of relief I noted Evie's little quickening as she saw me. Black "suited" Miss Angela Soames—suited her tower of white yet young-looking hair, as it also suited her habits of rather aimless retrospect and toying with stingless memories; but I hoped that Evie's present wearing of her four-year-old mourning would be her last. Naturally, she had not passed the day without tears. Her eyes were large, sombre patches; she held in her hand a little hard ball of damp handkerchief; and I noticed that a little graveside clay still adhered to the toes of her boots. But I judged that a night's rest would set her up again, and as we rumbled in a bus past the Houses of Parliament and up Whitehall, I bespoke her time for the afternoon of the morrow. I asked her, could she guess why? and, putting the screwed-up handkerchief away, she said something about the F.B.C.

"No," I replied,—"not directly, that is."

"Mr. Pepper?"

"No."

Then, the decorum of her sorrow notwithstanding, she gave my sleeve a quick, light touch.

"*Not* a house, Jeff—you don't mean that you've found a *house*!"

But I refused to tell her. It was better that her mind should be occupied with guessing.

III

As I have said, I took that house in the Vale of Health. It wanted only three weeks of the June Quarter, so that I had to take it or leave it without overmuch delay. Evie and I went up to see it on the following day, and a scramble indeed we had to force our way through the Bank Holiday crowds. It took me nearly half-an-hour to get the key at the neighbouring tea-garden, where I had been told I must apply; on that day, they said, they couldn't be bothered; but I got it, and at the mere sight of the outside of the little house Evie gave a soft "Oh!" of pleasure.

"*What* a little darling!" she said. "Look—a separate tradesmen's entrance—and a little garden—and the Heath at our very door! I wonder what it's like inside!" she added, much as she still scans the handwriting and postmark of a letter for a minute for information she could have at once by opening it.

"I don't know yet," I replied.

"You dear, not to have seen it before me!"

I put the key into the glass-panelled door, and we entered.

Later I came to hate that little house; but that day, with Evie's spirits still a little tremulous, I did not dwell on drawbacks. It had only four rooms, two on each floor, and we walked straight from the street into the room that later became our dining-room. Behind this lay the kitchen, completing our ground-plan. Facing the door by which we had entered, and with a triangular cupboard underneath it, rose a carved and worn wooden staircase, that turned on itself after three or four steps and gave access to the floor above. Here the drawing-room exactly repeated the dining-room, as did the single bedroom the kitchen. But the drawing-room, besides having an extra window over the street door, had also the feature I had seen from the hillock on the previous day—the platform or verandah built out on wooden posts over the garden. This was gained by two steps and a glass door at the end of the room, and it provided me with my first disappointment. For, when I stepped out on to it, I found that we had *no* garden. The garden belonged to the adjoining house, the tenant of which had, moreover, secured his privacy by building in our little platform with a screen of boards and trellis. There would be just room enough on our little quarter-deck for a tea-table and a couple of chairs; but of prospect, save for the side of the hillock, had we none. For the rest, ceilings sagged, the worn old floor creaked and did not seem over-safe, the panelling (the whole place was wood-lined) was badly cracked, and the late tenants had turned the bath into a dustbin and general receptacle for rubbish.

I saw Evie warm to the drawing-room, our best room, at once. Already in her mind she was arranging our furniture. I, for my part, content to see her kindling interest, began to poke my nose into corners, making notes of such things as waterpipes, locks, window fastenings and the like. I squeezed into the narrow bathroom again; I am a little squeamish about baths, and, not much liking the pattern of this one, was wondering whether it could be altered; but the room was little more than a prolongation of a bedroom cupboard out over the staircase, and there would have been no changing the bath without pulling half the interior down. I bumped my head against its floor as I descended the stairs again, and passed into the diminutive yard that had the verandah for a roof. There I inspected a coal-house, and peeped through a knot-hole into my neighbour's garden. Then I sought Evie in the drawing-room again.

"Well?" I said, smiling, as she advanced to meet me. . .

Outside, the air was jocund with the incessant sounds of singing, calling, penny trumpets, the steam organs of the distant roundabouts, and all the bustle of the holiday. From our little verandah we could see the sides of the hillock dotted with picnic parties and coster lads in their bright neckerchiefs and girls in feathers and black lamb's-wool coats, making love after their own fashion. A party came round the house, singing and playing on mouth organs a dragging sentimental song—arms linked about necks, feet breaking into little step-dances, and feathers shaking from time to time to kisses that resembled assaults; and I was glad of it all. It was precisely what I would have chosen for Evie that day. She was dressed in brown again; a brown jacket, brown velvet skirt, close brown toque of pheasants' feathers, and brown shoes that showed their newness under their slender arches as she walked; no more black! For Life, after all, was made for joy. We had youth, she and I, in a truer sense than that of fewness of years—we had the youth which is Hope. Oh, I thought, let us then meet the years to come singingly—if a little stridently no matter—believing in our luck—full and spilling over—and taking as it came, like these outside, all the fun and dust and heat and perspiration of the fair! So I thought, and Evie too took the contagion. We were standing by the glass door of the verandah when suddenly she crushed herself hard and impulsively against me. I knew what she meant. It did not need the little tight grip of her hand to tell me that all was now "all right." I drank those tidings from the deep wells of her eyes. And because the flesh had little part in this promise, but must for once give place to other things, I did not seek her lips. Instead, my own moved for a moment about her hair. . .

Then a burst of catcalling caused us to fly from the verandah doorway. We had been seen from the hillside by the party with the mouth organs. Evie, adorably red, gave a low laugh. . . and this time I did kiss her, to fresh cheers and calls of "Wot cher!" The lads and lasses outside did not see the caress, but perhaps, after all, it was not very wonderful thought-reading.

Then, after another delighted tour, we locked the house up and came out on to the Heath again.

And now that the scales of preoccupation were removed from our eyes, we could look on all the life and colour and movement spread before us and feel ourselves part of it. It was well worth looking at. There is a long ravine near the Viaduct; we looked across it through a bright stipple of sunny birches; and to close the eyes for a second or two only was to see, on reopening them, a new picture. Purple and lavender and the black lamb's-wool coats pervaded that picture; the colours were sown over the hillside like confetti. They moved slowly, as coloured granules might have moved in some half-fluid suspension; and spaces that one moment were spangled with them, the next were unexpectedly empty patches of green. I am speaking of the thing in the mass, as of a panorama. Doubtless the sprinkling of white that lay everywhere would resolve itself on the morrow into torn paper, to be laboriously impaled on spiked sticks and carried away in baskets; doubtless today much of it on a nearer view would consist of impure complexions and rank odour; but it was strong and piping-hot Life, inspiring, infinitely analysable, and irresistibly setting private griefs and joys and over-emphasised sensations into place and proportion. . . And as we left the Viaduct road and approached a great show in a hollow, the increasing din of a steam organ became as if we waded deeper and deeper into a sea, not of water, but of sound.

I only remembered that I still had the key of the little house in my pocket as we pushed and jostled through the crowded town of striped canvas that covered the Lower Heath. My fingers encountered it as we took a back way behind a long fluttering sheet against which cocoanut balls smacked every moment. It was necessary to return with it; and, as men behind the lace-curtained caravans began to make ready the naphtha lights for the evening, we turned into another thoroughfare down which the purple and lamb's-wool and lavender and bright neckerchiefs poured as if down a river-bed. In twenty minutes we had reached the tea-garden again; I spied a couple in the act of leaving a leafy arbour that held a table awash with spilt beer; and I put Evie into a still warm seat and bade her hold it against all comers. I left her, and presently returned with two glasses, of which I had managed to retain the greater part of the contents; and I sat down by her.

"Did you give them the key?" she asked, seizing my arm.

"Yes, I gave them 'the' key. I'm going to see the agent tomorrow."

"Oh, Jeff!" She said it as if there was something miraculous in it that an agent might actually consent to be seen about that little house on the morrow.

"That is, unless tomorrow's a holiday too."

"Oh, you *must* go!" she broke out. "It would be *too* awful if we were to miss it!"

Then, as a waiter came with a sopping cloth to wipe down the table, we ceased to talk.

Already they were beginning to light up everywhere. The crowded garden became a complexity of ceaselessly moving shadows with a hundred little accidents of light—the flames of sudden matches, yellow shafts as people moved aside from windows, the twinkling festoons of the arbours, the gleam of liquid spilt on tables. A glow like that of a furnace rose behind the trees in front of us, and over the tree-tops rose swinging boats, sometimes one, sometimes two or three at a time, with lads standing with bent knees on the seats and the girls' feathers tossing and boas flying in the golden haze. The noise became a ceaseless twanging everywhere, and I watched with amusement a half-drunk but wholly happy sailor at the next table, who nodded sleepily from time to time, then looked with wideawake and amiable defiance about him, and had quite forgotten that he wore his companion's hat hearsed with black feathers.

"Do you want to change hats?" I said to Evie, with a glance at her pheasants' feather toque.

"No—but—" I saw her own glance at the sailor's thick wrist, which had appeared on our side of his companion.

The next moment, though with protests, she was leaning farther back in the shadow.

Then, close and in murmurs, we began to talk.

I am not going to claim for Evie that she ever had any very remarkable gift of tongues. I don't mean that on occasion she couldn't talk for half a day on end; but I do mean that beyond a certain point she displayed a diffidence, talk became something of an adventure to her, and she had a way of advancing upon a silence as if it was a fortified place, to be carried by assault, and not to be won by beleaguering. Therefore, seeing her now sensible of a new liberation and joy, I was not unprepared for little excesses, things said out of mere fulness, and perhaps even to be slightly regretted on the morrow.

Yet I didn't want fulness on the subjects of which she now began to ease her breast. I didn't want to hear of the events of the day before, nor of the people who had been there, nor of whether these people had or had not "thought it odd" that she should have become re-engaged. I didn't want to hear about the late Mrs. Merridew's lingering and comatose illness. And when, in a burst of almost passionate candour, she spoke of the relief it was to be able at last to unburden herself thus, I would gladly have stopped her had I known how. But I lacked the courage to tell her, when she asked me whether I did not think it a good idea that she should keep nothing secret from me, that I thought it the worst of ideas.

"You see, Jeff," she murmured, out of a beautiful sense of rest and surrender, "I do so want ours to be a friendship as well as a marriage!"

Already the nearness and warmth of her had set me trembling. I don't know that I wanted more "friendship" than needs be; I wanted something, oh, far deeper and rarer. I wanted that full treasury of her warm blood and odorous hair and large and mobile eyes. Friendship? I laughed softly, and gathered these beauties closer. . . Understand, I don't for a moment mean that she was unaware of these possessions of hers; I call that oval mirror that later we set up in our bedroom to witness that; but she merely wanted something else, being human, and wanted it the more, being feminine. And as she told me now what she wanted our marriage to be, she put me away a little, with her hands on my breast.

"Don't you, too, darling?" she appealed, with a look that put "friendship" quite out of existence. . .

"Don't I what, rogue?"

"Want it to be like that."

"No," I bantered, adoring her. . .

"Oh! Then there's something you won't tell *me*! . . . Very well," she pouted, "keep your old secrets, but I shall tell you everything for all that, just to shame you. . ."

With a laugh I was drawing her towards me again, when I was arrested by a circumstance so oddly trivial that I really hesitate to set it down. The first I knew of it was that with an involuntary and nervous start I had checked the movement, and had put her slowly away again, looking into her face as a moment before she had looked into mine. To explain what I saw there I must mention that, a few minutes before, the sailor and his girl had risen from the next table and lurched away, their heads together making an apex that wobbled over its base of purple skirt and wide trousers; but I had been only dimly conscious of the noise with which a fresh party had pounced upon their empty places. Now suddenly our alcove was filled with a raw crimson shine. Evie's face, as I held it away, was as if a stage fire glared upon it. And scarcely had the bloodshot light died away when it came again, another violent flood. . .

I had looked round in less time than it has taken me to explain this. It was only one of the newcomers playing with a penny box of Bengal matches. He struck another. This was a green one, and as he waved the spluttering thing about the shadows of leaves ran to and fro in our little interior.

Then as the match went out, all became an ashy darkness again.

WHY, AT THE MERE STRIKING of those fusees, had all the life and joy suddenly gone out of me? I did not know. . . But stay; I am not sure that in this I do not lie. Perhaps it would be nearer the truth to say that I would not know, and yet again that is not all. . . Perhaps I had better pass on; you may know soon enough, if you care, what was the matter. Red and gold would now have been better suited to those two mainsprings of my life, my Love and my Ambition; but suddenly to change the gold into green, the hated hue of my past Jealousy. . .

Let me pass on. The thing will soon be clear.

FOR A MINUTE AND MORE I had hardly heard Evie's chatter, but presently I became conscious that she was repeating a phrase, as if a little surprised that she got no answer. I roused myself.

"Eh? . . . What were you saying, dear?" I apologised.

As if the striking of those matches had made an alteration in her too, her playfulness had vanished. Apparently another little access of candour had taken its place. Evidently I had missed some necessary link, for she was now murmuring, "Poor dear—I haven't been able to get her out of my head—it seems wrong somehow that I should be so happy and she—"

"She? . . . Who?" I asked in surprise, now fully awake again.

Evie mentioned a name. At the next table another crimson match went off, leaving, as it died down fumily, the yellow twinklings of the garden a bilious green. I spoke slowly. The name she had mentioned had been that of my own former *fiancée*.

"Kitty Windus?" I said. "What about her?"

Evie made no answer, but only stroked her cheek against the cloth of my shoulder—a familiar gesture of hers.

"I'm afraid I don't quite understand," I said.

Nor did I quite. I could not believe she was jealous. If Evie was jealous, never, never woman had had less cause. Except as the bitterest of mockeries, I had never been engaged to any woman but herself, for only that old horrible poverty and despair of mine had been the cause of my playing a trick with more of the falsely theatrical about it than of real life—the deliberate engaging of myself to one woman as a means to getting another. The impossible situation had lasted for a few months only, and had then ended in the abrupt vanishing, without explanation, of Kitty Windus from that part of London in which she had lived. From that day to this I had not set eyes on her.

I leaned over Evie. "Dearest," I said gently, "do you mean that there's something you would like to know about Kitty?"

Then, with a little shock, she seemed to realise that I might think what in fact had for the moment crossed my mind—that she was jealous of Kitty.

"Oh, Jeff. . . no, no—really no!" she assured me in tones of which there was no mistaking the sincerity. "I didn't mean that—poor thing!—I was only joking when I said there was something you wouldn't tell me! Oh, do see what I mean, dear! It's only because *I'm* so happy that I want everybody else to be—Kitty too—everybody! Really that's all, Jeff!"

It was not quite all, though it was enough to make my heart a little lighter. Mingled with it was something very human that only endeared her to me the more. Her glow and vitality had always put poor Kitty's skimpiness completely into the shade, and what ailed her now was that wistful longing of the victress to be magnanimous that is the uneasy aftercrop of triumph. On herself it had all the effect of a generosity, but that, and not jealousy, was really it. . .

"Well, after all, we don't know that she isn't happy," I said cheerfully. "Anyway, she pleased herself, and—it's four years ago. . . Just listen to the row!"

I was glad of the diversion that came just then. Led by a Jew's harp, the party at the next table had broken into "Soldiers of the Queen," and for the five hundredth time that day the song had "caught on" instantly. The whole garden was now vociferating it, standing on seats, dancing between the tables, their rising and falling heads a dark and bizarre tumult in the conflicting lights. At the gate of the garden a barrel-organ stopped and took up the same song in another key, but they drowned it:—

> *"Who've b—ee—een—my lads!*
> *And s—ee—een—my lads!"*

Talk in that uproar was impossible, and again there enwrapped us that strong sense of rich and rough and abundant life. As we leaned over our little table to watch, Evie's finger was moving in time to the song, and even the thought of the little house a few hundred yards away disappeared for a moment from my own mind. A chair with a couple of girls upon it broke, and there were shrieks and applause and whistles and laughter; and then the song began to die away. Cheers followed it, and cheers again, for throats cheered readily then; and then our neighbours of the next table formed themselves into single file, and, with a last shrill

> *"Who've b—ee—een—my lads!*
> *And s—ee—een—my lads!"*

marched round the garden and out into the crowds beyond. I seized my opportunity. Evie and I followed them, I with her tucked safely away under my arm; and we joined the dense stream that was already pouring southwards. And as I struggled for places on a bus at Hampstead Heath Station, my heart was grateful for that illusion of the day that had banished, first, the remnant of Evie's sorrow, and had afterwards cut short that impossible course of unmeasured confidences to which that moodiness had given rise.

I began to foresee those inconveniences that afterwards made me hate that house in the Vale of Health as soon as I had signed my contract and got the key. The contract was for a year only, and as for any period less than three years the agents had refused to "do up" the place for me, I became plasterer, painter and plumber myself. I suppose that from the strictly conventional point of view Evie ought to have had no hand in this; indeed, she read me, from the "Etiquette" column of one of her weekly papers, a passage that informed me that between her choice of a house and her going into it as its mistress in the eyes of all the world a bride-elect ought to betray no knowledge of that house's existence; but as she delivered this from over the bib of an enormous apron, holding the journal in one hand, while the fingers of the other rubbed the lumps out of a bucket of whitewash, the knowledge came too late to be of much use. Anyway, there we were, with Miss Angela or an old charwoman or else nobody at all for chaperon, scraping walls, mixing paint, puttying cracks, fixing shelves, dragging at obstinate old nails; and seeing that from the point of view of Etiquette we were already numbered with the lost, we made no bones about walking into a shop in Tottenham Court Road together and brazenly asking to be shown the bedstead department. After that we took tea, with never a human eye upon us, in my lofty room near the Cobden Statue. Doubtless this cut us off finally from that dim eschatological hope when even the devil shall have his respite of a thousand years. Our only solace was that we found ourselves in the company of a good many others who have to square their Etiquette with their opportunities as best they can.

But about those inconveniences. Why, with the whole Heath before them, the children on their way to or from school should make our doorstep their playground I didn't know; but they did, and it needed no gift of prophecy to see that when the schools closed later in the summer they would be an almost hourly nuisance. That was the first thing that struck me. Next, the crown of my head was like to be sore from many bumpings before I had learned to avoid the bathroom floor as I mounted our creaking, turning stairs. Next, ready as I should have been to secure my own garden from overlooking had I had one, I resented that screen of trellis that limited the view from our little balcony to the slope of hillside opposite. Add to these that not a window-sash fitted within half or three-quarters of an inch, that not a door was truly hung, that, wherever I wanted to make good a hinge or fastening, the woodwork was soft as a mushroom with old screwholes, and that I should have ruined a whole shopful of tools had I even attempted to level our splintery old floor, and you will see why I rejoiced to think that our tenancy might not be a very long one. But I need hardly add that, after all, these things weighed but a trifle against my impatience, and that I was careful not to let Evie suppose that I did not think our little nook the most delightful spot imaginable.

As a matter of fact I was compelled to leave a large part of the work to Evie; and capitally she did it. She had forgotten her old smattering of business training so completely that she always found it easier to go through her day's duties than she did to balance her expenditure afterwards in the highly ornamental "Housekeeper's Book" I bought for her; and while I was allowed my way in such unimportant things as where we should put our old-fashioned chests of drawers and Sheffield caddies and those sketches of Billy Izzard's, the department that began with the frying-pan and ended with general cleaning was hers. I had given her a second key, not only of the new house, but also of my own quarters in Camden Town; and sometimes at the F.B.C. I would look up from my work, gaze past the Duke of York's Column with its circling pigeons and away over the Mall, and wonder what she was doing now— taking our new dinner-service from its crates and washing it, peeping down the long cylinder of kitchen linoleum and wishing I was there to cut it to the floor, lighting fires to get rid of the damp, or (strictly against orders) scrubbing out the bath which, later, strive as I would, I could never successfully re-enamel. Then in the evening I would hasten for the Hampstead bus, stride up from the Heath Station, and, arrived at home, throw off my coat, put up shelves, fit carpets, see how my new paint (an ivory white) was drying, and only knock off when, not Etiquette, but the lateness of the hour and the distance I had to take Evie home compelled me.

I liked the daily life at the F.B.C. Our various departments were to a great extent isolated, so that the intermediate clerks like myself could only guess at the relation of their own portion of the work to the whole intricate business; but I have told you how I myself was privately "let in on the ground floor" by Pepper. I had three "Juns. Ex. Con." as my immediate subordinates, and they were first-rate fellows, and amusing company into the bargain. All three, Whitlock, Stonor and Peddie, were younger than I by some years; and as they were all bachelors, and there was plenty of time yet for them to begin to take their work very seriously, they showed not a trace of envy of me. Indeed, being rather "doggish" in their dress, and reckoning the work of the day as little more than a killing of time until the pleasures of the evening should begin, they even made something of a pet of their "Balzac in a dressing-gown"; and as if the nearness of our offices to Piccadilly put on them some responsibility that the character for gaiety of that gay part of London should not suffer through their negligence, they had an air of owning the quarter. They furnished drinks at Epitaux's as a man might in his own house, and introduced their companions at Stone's as if they had been veritable guests. True, funds did not often run to the old Continental over the way; but they knew by sight many of the loungers who entered its portals from four o'clock in the afternoon on, and would exchange intelligent glances over their filing or posting as suède boots, or picture hat, or something that looked as if it had stepped out of Stagg & Mantle's window tripped seductively by.

Pepper, of course, was my own immediate superior, as I was of my three boys; and while our private arrangement put me after office hours straightway on a level with the mandarins of the concern, we strictly kept our respective positions at Waterloo Place. I prepared drafts for him of such matters as Paying Ballast, Railway Digests, the daily postings at Lloyd's and the fluctuations of Insurance Rates; and these he changed into factors of policy in high council with the lords of other departments. His private office was immediately above ours; and twenty times a day his secretary, Miss Levey, descended the broad mosaic staircase or came down in the gilt and upholstered lift, either commanding my attendance, or bringing me instructions. It was a "wheeze" among my three boys to pose as her admirers, but I never thought she was quite so unconscious of their real thoughts as they supposed.

I was going to pass on; but while I am about it I may as well say a little more about this Miss Levey, and my reasons for regarding her as a person to be rather carefully watched. She was short, and a victim to her race's tendency to early stoutness; and as she had no neck, and always wore hats far too large for her, her appearance was top-heavy. Of her too large and prominent features her pot-hook nose was the most prominent. Her manner towards myself was that of one who would have liked to be familiar, but lacked the confidence; and doubtless her perpetual hovering on the confines of a liberty arose out of some slight acquaintance she had had with Evie in the days of her business training. As if Evie's health was as liable to fluctuations as the Export charts and Trade returns on our walls, Miss Levey never omitted to inquire after it each morning, becoming daily more *empressée* as our engagement proceeded; but so far she had not succeeded in what I divined to be her object, an invitation to renew the old acquaintance. And though I could keep the greater part of our intercourse strictly to business, I could hardly avoid occasional meetings on the stairs, in the lift, or sometimes a walk up Lower Regent Street with her as far as the Circus.

It was during the course of one of these short walks, one lunch-time, that, having obtained from me her daily bulletin, Miss Levey rather put me in a hole by asking me what I thought Evie would like for a wedding present. Secretly I neither wanted a wedding present from Miss Levey nor wished Evie to receive one, but I could hardly give her the slap on the face of telling her so. Instead I answered, a little abruptly, that I really didn't know—that it was awfully kind of her—and that she wasn't to think of it; but she did not take the hint. So, knowing her capacity for swallowing, but not forgetting snubs, and really feeling that perhaps I had gone a little too far, I hastened to repair a possible rudeness. We were approaching the tea-shop near the Circus at which I usually lunched; we reached it, and paused together on the kerb; and then, on the spur of the moment, I suggested that she should lunch with me. With a little demonstration of pleasure she accepted, and we entered and took our places at a small round table in the shadow of the pay-desk.

I knew, of course, that I had been cornered, and that she knew it too; but in these cases the thick-skinned person always has the advantage. I resolved that that advantage should be as slight as possible. And for a time—though probably not for one moment longer than she wished—I succeeded. As she ate her rissole and sipped her chocolate she talked with animation of this and that—the morning's business, the people in the crowded shop, the theatres, and so on; and then she returned to the subject of the wedding present, the date of my marriage, where we were going to live, and the rest of it. I was as reserved as my unwillingly given invitation allowed me to be, but presently I had to promise to ask Evie what form she would like the present to take. With that, Miss Levey went off at score, speaking of Evie as she had known her.

"I suppose she's prettier than ever?" she said. "Such a lovely girl I used to think her! I'm sure you're very lucky, Mr. Jeffries, if you don't mind my saying so!"

I did rather mind her saying anything about it at all, but I answered quite conventionally that I considered myself very lucky indeed.

"Those were jolly days!" she passed on into reminiscence. "I loved that poky little old place in Holborn! . . . Do you remember the Secretary Bird, Mr. Jeffries?"

I did remember Weston, the wan, middle-aged "professor."

"Poor old soul! I wonder if he's going with them to the new place? Of course you know they're pulling the old one down?"

"Yes."

"Such a huge one, that one in Kingsway! All the latest improvements—everything! But it won't ever be the same to me. . . 'Not room to turn round'? . . . No, I suppose there wasn't, but I suppose I'm rather faithful to old places and old faces. You aren't, Mr. Jeffries?"

"Not just because they're old," I fancied.

"Oh, I think I am, just because they're old!" she replied brightly.

From faces and places she passed to names, though—this was quite marked—only to certain ones; and I became rather obstinately silent except when she actually paused for a remark. For far more significant were the names she omitted than those she pronounced. These, indeed, she positively had the effect of shouting at me, and I suppose it was some heavy-handed delicacy that led her to speak of Weston but not of Archie Merridew, of Evie, but not of Kitty Windus and others she had known far better. I supposed her to be merely gratifying her racial greed for general (including personal) information, on the chance, so to speak, of turning up in the dustheap something she might later sell for twopence; and, noting one of her marked omissions, it occurred to me to wonder whether she might not have seen Kitty Windus, and, failing to get anything out of her, was now pumping myself and looking for an opening to pump Evie also. My eyes rested from time to time on her prominent-featured face and wide, high shoulders; and she did not know that I was wondering whether she was so deeply in Pepper's secrets that we should not be able to dispense with her services when he and I cleared out of the F.B.C. together.

I maintained my silence while she went on with her *Hamlet* without the Prince, that is to say, while she talked of the now demolished Business College without mentioning Archie Merridew, Kitty Windus,

Louie Causton and the rest; and then, pleading an engagement, I rose. She rose too. With her purse in her hand, she made quite an ado about refusing to allow me to pay for the lunch to which I had invited her. "Please—or I shall feel as if we can't lunch together again!" she said; "let me see; sevenpence, that's right, isn't it? There! You will remember me to Evie, won't you?"

And she scrupulously put the sevenpence into one of my hands while with the other I held the door open for her to pass out.

I did not give Evie Miss Levey's message that evening, for when, at a little after seven, I reached the Vale of Health, I found Miss Angela there. The elder Miss Soames, I ought to say, regarded our wedding as so exclusively Evie's (myself sometimes appearing to have no part whatever in it) that I was constantly invited to share her own detached delight. Giving up Evie's bedroom only, she intended to stay on at Woburn Place; but from the number of offerings she brought us her own sitting-room was like to be sadly denuded. She brought, and if possible hid in a corner for us to discover after she had left, heavy old silver tablespoons, her shield-shaped embroidered fire-screen, her Colport dressing-table set with the little coral-like trees for rings, and other gifts; and it was in vain that Evie laughingly protested.

"But if you go on like this we shall have to have you come and live with us!" she said. "Make you up a bed on the verandah—but perhaps that's what she's really after, Jeff—"

But Miss Angela shook her head demurely, ignoring the joke. "No, no—young people ought to be alone; they don't want old things like me interfering. I shall be just as happy thinking of you both as if it was my own wedding."

And I really believe she was.

For the Etiquette of our preparations, Aunt Angela threw herself pathetically on my mercy.

Her sitting-room in Woburn Place, however, was not the only one that was rapidly becoming denuded. My own place with the terra-cotta festoons and hobgoblins was now more than half empty. But I was not relinquishing it yet. I knew I was committing a sentimental extravagance in thus being lord of two domiciles, but (Etiquette having to be considered) I did not wish to go into the new place until I should go there with Evie. So already two cartloads of my belongings had been fetched away, and that very day Miss Angela had been assisting in a task that more than any other seemed the beginning of the end—the removal of my carpet. They did not tell me of this removal. They allowed me to discover it for myself when I went, without light, upstairs into the drawing-room. They had already laid it down; my foot struck its softness in the dark; and I experienced a sudden little thrill of pleasure. It seemed to bring all so suddenly near. . .

They had crept up after me with a lamp to enjoy my surprise. The room really looked delightful, and all my sense of drawbacks vanished. Four glass candle-sconces with musical little drops—I had picked them up cheap in the street that runs from the Britannia to Regent's Park—were fastened to the walls, two between the window-bays over my breast-high mahogany bookshelves, the other two at the sides of the fireplace in the opposite wall; and across the windows themselves the long chintz curtains were drawn. Evie set the lamp down on the little table that folded almost to nothing against the wall, and tripped round with a taper, lighting up. All my chairs were there, and the couch for which I had ransacked half the catacombs of the Tottenham Court Road, and I can't tell you how pretty it all was, with its ivory woodwork, its dark blue and crimson blotted carpet, and the candle flames turning the polished glass lustres to soft sprinklings of gems. Miss Angela, delicate Pandar, seeing Evie's hand steal towards mine, affected to be very busy at the mantelpiece. . .

"So," I grumbled presently, "this is your idea of the cheapest way of lighting a room—candles at goodness knows how much a pound?"

"Well, there's no electric light," retorted Evie.

"And what have you left me at the other place? A bed and a broken chair, I suppose, to make shift with for three weeks and more!"

"*And* a jampot for your shaving-water. Quite enough for a bachelor."

"And I'm to get my meals out, I suppose, and pay twice as much for them."

But they only begged me to look where they had put Billy Izzard's two sketches—one on either side of the verandah door.

I had, in truth, begun to feel the least bit alarmed at the rate at which the money was going. Kitchens, I learned, cost like the dickens; but, as Evie frugally extinguished the candles again and led me down into her special province, I could not deny that that looked pretty too, with its bright tins, hanging jugs, overlapping rows of plates and saucers and the new linoleum of its floor. The dining-room, into which (as Evie said) "all the dirt was brought," had been left until the last, and was knee-deep in straw, torn packing-paper, split box-lids and cut string, and of course I grumbled again that good brown paper had been torn and useful string spoiled, until I was brought into good temper again by being allowed another peep at the lighted drawing-room—this time without Aunt Angela.

V

We were to be married at half-past ten on the following Saturday morning but one, at St. George's, Hart Street, Bloomsbury. We had chosen a Saturday because of our honeymoon, which was to be a steamboat trip either down the river to Greenwich or up the river to Hampton Court—we had not decided which. A good friend of mine, Sydney Pettinger, who had given me my start with F.B.C., had promised to give Evie away. Pepper would have done so, but Pepper always dazzled Evie a little. He was almost inhumanly never at a loss for a word.

Our little house was now quite ready. They had left me not so much as a chair in my room near the Cobden Statue. My pallet bed and my shaving-tackle were about all that remained within its walls, and I was on the point of disposing of the bed as it stood to a dealer in Queen's Crescent, when Billy Izzard proposed to me that he should take over the place.

Let me describe Billy Izzard as he was then—as he still to a great extent is for the matter of that, for his innumerable quarrels with dealers and intransigence on hanging committees have resulted in his being less well known than the high quality of his painting warrants. He was a tall, double-jointed, monkey-up-a-stick of a lad of twenty-four, with well-shaped features that always seemed a little larger than the ordinary (as if you saw them through a very weak lens), and two or three distinct voices, the most startling of which was the sudden, imperious tone into which he broke when he "saw" something—saw it absolute, in the flat, and as if it had never been seen before—but possibly you know his painting. He had exquisite manners, which he never used; he dressed in tweeds that made my own shaggy garments look like the finest broadcloth—they always seemed stuck over with fishing-flies; and, a sufficiently large studio being beyond his means until he should cease to quarrel with his bread and butter, he too had discovered the advantages of the large rooms that are to be found over shops.

He came up with his wedding present, yet another painting, just as I was contemplating the sale of my bed. The picture, wrapped in newspaper, was under his arm. He scratched his head under his porringer of a "sports" cap, looked round the big four-windowed room, and said, "Good light—south and east though—what?"

"South and east," I replied; and added, knowing Billy, "Rent paid monthly, in advance."

"How much?" he demanded.

"Twelve bob a week."

"Hm! Rather a lot for me," said the man whose practice (for his theory never amounted to much) has since been made the foundation of a whole school of modern painting. "Wish I hadn't brought you this now—I was offered three pounds for it—that would have paid for the first month—"

I hastened to grab the painting, to make sure of getting it. It was only a small flower group, a straggle of violets, a few white ones among them, in a lustre bowl, but the other day I refused sixty pounds for it.

"Too late, Billy," I said; "you know you can't fight me for it. . . I'll throw you in my bed if you want the place, but you're not to give my name as a reference for your solvency."

"I think it might do," he said. "I could shut off some of the light, and I don't suppose they'd mind my making it an un-Drapery Establishment sometimes."

Billy was just beginning to paint flesh as truly and seeingly as he painted flowers.

With the exception of Aunt Angela's constant trickle, Billy's was our first wedding-present; but others followed quickly. Pepper, of course, contrived to get his joke out of his own very handsome offering. One day, at the end of one of our morning interviews in his office, he said: "Oh, by the way—I sent a small parcel off to you yesterday. I suppose 'Jeffries, Verandah Cottage, Vale of Health' finds you?"

"Yes."

"It brings all good wishes, of course. Being a bachelor I've had to rely on my own unaided taste. If the things don't seem very useful just at present, they will be."

In spite of his twinkle, I did not fear that his present would not be in the best of taste, and I thanked him for it, whatever it was. Then, when I returned to my own office, I found another surprise. A square, shop-packed, registered parcel lay on my desk. This, when I opened it, I found to contain a large silver cigarette-box with my name upon it, the offering of my three "Juns. Ex. Con." It was full of cigarettes of a far finer quality than any for which I had yet acquired the taste; and though only the mandarins of the F.B.C. were supposed to smoke on the premises, "Whitlock—Peddie—," I said, "have a cigarette?"

All of them appeared to come with a start out of a quite unusual absorption in their work.

"This is very good of you fellows," I said awkwardly.

So we lighted up, the four of us, and with the coming of lunch-time I had to stand whiskies and soda at Stone's. I learned later that on my wedding evening all three of them got quite disinterestedly drunk in honour of the occasion.

I found on reaching home that evening that Pepper's "small parcel" was really two, the larger one about the size of an ordinary bureau, the smaller one perhaps no bigger than a tea-chest. As both were addressed to me, neither had been opened; but I really feared that this severe continence had done both Evie and her aunt an injury—so much so that I mercifully cut short my affectation of not noticing the huge packages.

"If he's not going to sit down without opening them!" cried Evie, revolted. "And a hammer and chisel put ready to his hand—!"

"Oh, these things," I said. "They're from Pepper, I suppose. Do you want them opened at once?"

"Do we want—! Open them instantly!"

"Well, I can't in here—"

I carried the boxes out into our tiny verandah-roofed yard, and there prised the lids off. Then I fell back before the onslaught they made on the straw with which the cases were filled. The smaller one contained a silver-mounted champagne-cooler; the larger one two enormous branched silver candlesticks, big enough to have furnished the table that stood before the Ark of the Covenant. So splendid were they that Evie, seeing them, did not dare to touch them; and I remember how Pepper had said that they would be useful by-and-by—which, I may say, they were.

"Hm!" I said. "Well, we'd better pawn 'em at once. We've certainly nowhere to put them."

And indeed, the objects, the cases they came in, and ourselves, almost cubically filled the little yard. Besides taking the shine completely out of the rest of the house, they cost me getting on towards a pound of candles that night, for of course we had to have another grand illumination in their honour; but Pepper only laughed when I told him.

"I'm setting you a scale of living, my boy," he said. "If you spend a lot you've got to make a lot—that's all about it."

"Well, I'll be even with you," I replied, "for your champagne-cooler's going to be my waste-paper basket."

And so it was, for long enough.

In this "setting me a scale of living" Pepper was aided and abetted by Pettinger, for if the candlesticks of the one meant the extravagance of candles, so did the two great china bowls of the other a constant expenditure of money on flowers. The only immediate profit I had of any of these magnificences was a plentiful supply of firewood. The cases they all came in, when knocked to pieces, made quite a respectable stack of timber.

There were only a couple more wedding presents that I need particularise. The first of these puzzled us for a long time. It came by letter post, a small, soft parcel addressed to Evie, containing a crochet-bordered teacloth; and except for an "L." written on a blank card, there was no indication of who the sender might be. Then I remembered Miss Levey.

"Of course—how stupid not to think of it!" said Evie. "I'll write her a note at once, and you can give it to her tomorrow."

"Oh—we'll spend a penny on it," I said.

But that very evening, before the note was posted, Miss Levey's present came, a pair of chimney ornaments—bronzed Arabs taming mettlesome steeds—brought by a young man who might have been either a cousin or a pawnbroker's assistant.

And as an explicit note accompanied the Arabs, the crochet teacloth remained unaccounted for.

AND SO THE DAYS SLIPPED by. I was now unfit for anything until I should be married, and Evie was as restless as myself. A great shyness now began to come over her at times, leaving her, perhaps in the middle of a conversation, with never a word to say; and I understood, and secretly exulted. She bloomed indeed at those moments. . .

Let me, without losing any more time, come to the eve of my wedding and the last night I spent in my bachelor rooms.

I paced for long up and down my empty room that night. I had put on a pair of soft slippers, for the room was immediately above a dormitory where a number of shop-girls who "lived in" slept; and the light of my single candle was reflected in one or other of the squares of my naked windows as I walked. Then I threw up one of the sashes, and looked out among my terra-cotta Satans and festoons.

It was a marbled night of velvet black and iron grey, the two hues so mysteriously counterchanged that you could have fancied either to be the cloud and the other the abyss beyond until a star peeped out to tell you of your mistake. It was very still, and must have been very late, for down the road a mechanical sweeper was dragging along with a hiss of bristles. I watched it, but not out of sight, for before it had disappeared my eyes had wandered from it and were not looking at anything in particular.

I was thinking of Life—not only of that stormy share of it that up to the present had been my own, but also of that other portion of it that lay, unknown and unknowable until it should arrive, still before me. And so all my thoughts turned on the morrow as on a pivot. In nine hours or less I should be a married man, and a new time would have begun for me.

It was on the nearness of that new beginning that I brooded restlessly and passionately. For just as my Ambition had set itself the aim of that large house over Highgate way, so my Love also was going to be a thing of brightness and terraces and spires—nothing meaner, such as men shake down to out of their failure and disillusion. Ah, if care could compass it, mine was going to be a marriage! I believed that, and looking out over the Cobden Statue, I appointed that moment of our union for an expunging of all—all, all—that had gone before.

For what man old enough to have heaped up his sins does not, out of that very ache for a new beginning, seek to bespeak one of heaven by appointing a time and a season for it? Not one. Poor pathetic things of the fancy though his decrees may be, he cannot live without their expediencies. In his mind at least he sets an hour for his release.

And on that night of all nights I could not but remember all. Sins I had committed; and though some might have called that a sin which I should have proclaimed in the face of heaven to have been a righteous act, that also I remembered. . . It seemed, that night, to matter little that I was acquitted of one guilt when I had incurred a wrath by other guilts innumerable; it was from the whole body of an ancient death that I fainted to be delivered. My worldly ambition I knew to be not an empty boast; oh, might but this other rebirth of mine prove to be equally well founded! A rebirth—a white page for Evie and myself to write the story of our love upon—and even that spectre of her own life, of the dreadful coming of which this was in a sense the anniversary, would not have been an agony endured for nothing! Not all in vain would have been the grim discovery of that which, four years before, had hung from a hook in a bedroom door! Not all lost, not all lost, might but the morrow prove my second natal day!

So, passionate and unresting, I prayed among my swags and emblems and gargoyles. The street-sweeper had long since gone; soon would come a lamplighter extinguishing the street lamps; now all was quiet. I dropped my head on my arms for a moment. . .

Then, looking up at the marbled clouds behind which the stars seemed to drift, I muttered, to Whomsoever might be up there to hear:

"Oh, let it all but sink and die away—let it all but sink and die away—and my life shall be—it shall be—"

I do not know whether my lips framed the promise of what my life should be, could I but strike my bargain.

PART II
VERANDAH COTTAGE

I

In speaking of the early days of my married life I must throw myself largely on your consideration. I have not guarded through the years that sharp impatience that I presently came to feel with that tiny house in the Vale of Health. Lately I have thought more kindly of it, as if at some stage of my journey through Life (though I cannot tell when) I had heard a call behind me, turned my head, and, forgetting to turn it back again, had continued to advance backwards, recognising things in proportion as they receded. I live now in a mansion in Iddesleigh Gate; that ambition of mine, my spur in the past, is becoming a mere desire that when I go my successor shall find all in working order to his hand; and so the shabby brown earth I once trod has taken the lightsome blue of distance, and many things are seen through a sheen that, perhaps, never was there. Therefore if you would see that sheen it must be by your own favour and through whatever of glamour time and distance have given to your own young years.

For, when all allowances are made, I still think that that relation which is more than friendship was ours. Male and female (the New Man notwithstanding) we were created, and to a lower conception than that I have never in all my life declined. I have seen that declension in others, and know how it sinks ultimately to the mere comfortable security of a banking account. Whatever else I have known I have escaped that. By what wide circuit of the spirit I know not, I have returned to find the divine where others have not stirred from grossness. And I have even had glimpses of that shadowy apocalypse that finds its images, not in thrones and sceptres, but in the flesh-hooks and seething-pots of the kitchen. . . But to Verandah Cottage and the Vale of Health.

I was happy with Evie, she with me. From my daily leaving her at nine o'clock in the morning until my return at half-past seven at night, she had almost, if not quite, enough to occupy her; and though I could have wished she had more friends, so that when she had finished her work the summer afternoons might not have appeared quite so long, yet I exercised a care that almost amounted to a jealousy in this regard. Understand me, however. It was against no person that I protected her with this jealous care. It was always with pleasure that I learned that Billy Izzard had looked in and talked to her for an hour at tea, or that Aunt Angela had been up to take the air or to fetch her out for a couple of hours' shopping. I merely mean that I saw no reason for her identifying herself with a set of circumstances that before long would probably have changed completely. It was part of my Ambition that, until I should have attained it, we should be a little solitary. Nor was it that I thought that the people we might by-and-by be able to meet on equal terms would be any better than those we might have known at once. It was a question of the place we were ultimately to occupy. And I begged Evie, if at times she did feel a little lonely, to be patient for my sake. So for quite a long time Billy and her aunt remained her only visitors.

The house next door might have been untenanted for all we saw of its inmates, and that, I confess, made me a little angry. I did not know the niceties of the matter, nor whether the difference between a thirty-five pound rental and one of perhaps eighty pounds outweighed those confident dicta of Evie's penny journals about "cards," "calls," and the rest; nor yet did I deem it a reason for taking anybody to my bosom that only a wall separated our dwellings; but the fact that they, whoever they were, never called stiffened me. An eighty-pound house! To put on airs about a matter of eighty pounds! . . . But I saw the humour of it too, and laughed.

"I'm sorry if it's rather slow, little woman," I used to say, "but wait just a bit. Let's stick it out on our own for just a little while. You'd rather be with me, now, than have waited for a year or two till we were better off, wouldn't you?"

"How absurd you are!" she would reply, nestling up to me.

"Well, keep going for a bit longer, and see what happens. I'm not deliberately hanging back from Pepper's offer for nothing, I promise you. . . And at any rate the Vicar will be calling."

You see, we had agreed on the imprudence of having children at once.

But the Vicar never came, which was a fair enough hit back if he meant it for one, since we only attended his church once, and after that, I am afraid, went to churches here and there, attracted by good singing, a beautiful fabric, a man with brains preaching, and other things that perhaps mitigated the quality of our worship. And very frequently we did not go to church at all, but explored the Heath instead. And often, on Saturdays and Sundays, we went still farther afield. Greenwich had been hallowed to us by our half-day's honeymoon, and as if in this Hampton Court had suffered a slight, we made amends by going to the latter place quite often. We must have gone four or five times that summer, so that we got to know the Lelys and the Holbeins and the tea-shops, and the long drag home again from Waterloo in the old horse-bus, quite well. And one week-end we spent with Pettinger, at his place at Bedford, with two cattle-show men, an actor and an International footballer, all on their best behaviour until Evie had gone to bed. Then, when I joined her, she accused me of having had more than one glass of whisky, and wanted to know what we had been talking about all that time. I tried to tell her "the bubonic plague," but my tongue betrayed me, and I came a cropper.

So, as I had done before during our engagement, I could look up from my work during the day, past the Duke of York's Column and over the Mall, and wonder what she was doing at that moment—changing our pillow-cases, popping the pared potatoes into the saucepan of cold water, dusting, washing up, polishing, or pottering about the flower-boxes I had set on our little balcony.

Miss Levey had still not been asked to come up and see Evie, but so quietly tenacious of her purpose did I divine her to be, that I was sorry I had not invited her at once and got it over. The thing was beginning to look almost like an unacknowledged contest between us. At times I forgot my original reason for keeping her at arm's-length—her forwardness, pertinacity, and racial hunger for the rags and bones and old bottles of gossip; and that she "spelt" to be asked was in itself reason enough for ignoring her hints. I may say that by doing so I cut myself from quite a distinguished circle of acquaintances, and on this point had sometimes to check my three clerks. For never a notability called on Pepper but Miss Levey, on the strength of being called in to take down in shorthand a conversation, claimed him for a close acquaintance. And as far as I can make out, she must actually have believed it, for she kept up the fiction even to us, who knew perfectly well all about it. Goodness knows what she told outsiders. . . So with Whitlock, Stonor and Peddie it became a byword to say, when speaking of somebody exalted: "You know who I mean—that pal of Miss Levey's—Lord Ernest," or "Miss Levey's friend—what's his name—the President of the Board of Trade."

After the present of the silver cigarette-box, not to speak of the handsome compliment of their intoxication on my wedding night, I had thought it the least I could do to ask Whitlock and Stonor (Peddie lived out Croydon way, too far to come) to come up one Sunday and have tea with us. So they had been, and for two hours had displayed manners as highly starched as their collars. They had been, I fancy, a little surprised that, if I was a Balzac in a dressing-gown, my wife at any rate was no Sand in a flannelette peignoir. (For that matter, nothing was ever neater than Evie's skirts and blouses, and when by-and-by she began to make her own things there could hardly have been anything more becoming than her clear, sweet-pea-coloured muslins, that really would have been too rippling and Tanagra-like altogether had it not been for the stiffer petticoats beneath.) I surmised later that Stonor had taken, so to speak, a mental pattern of Evie, for matching purposes when he should come upon another girl like her; and Whitlock, whose pose it was that he would never marry, could on that very account admire the more openly.

The visit of the two clerks, of course, made my attitude towards Miss Levey all the more pointed; but I still preferred not to have her at the Vale of Health. And seeing this, Evie vowed that she did not want her either. The two Arab horse-tamers stood on our drawing-room mantelpiece, not because I admired them, but simply because we had nowhere else to put them; and they were all of Miss Levey that was absolutely needful to our happiness.

Yet I recognised that the lack, not of Miss Levey, but of company in general, was far harder on Evie than it was on me. I knew exactly why I didn't want overmuch company; Evie, who had the deprivation actually to bear, had to take the reason on trust. All my interests lay ahead; she knew only the tedium of the present. It was her part, if I may so express it, to keep bright those ridiculous empty candlesticks of Pepper's without my own certainty that candles were coming to fill them—to polish those rose bowls of Pettinger's without knowing where the roses were coming from. And I could hardly blame her if sometimes she seemed to be a little in doubt whether, after all, the things I prophesied so confidently were not merely fancy pictures of what I should like the future to be.

So, more to occupy her than anything else, I bought her out of my small earnings a hand sewing-machine, and paid for a lesson for her once a week at a skirt-maker's. And that made things rather easier. She could now pick not only her blouses to pieces, but her skirts also; and from a fear lest my interest in these occupations of hers might appear simulated when she showed me the results on my return at night, I actually did cast an eye on a costumier's or modiste's window now and then, relating to her, though goodness only knows in what masculine terms of my own, what I had seen. And during the day I could gaze past the Duke of York's Column with its wheeling pigeons and think of her, unpicking, pinning tissue-paper patterns, basting, threading the eye of her sewing-machine needle, or, with some garment or other tucked under her crumpled chin, trying to see the whole of herself at once in the narrow strip of mirror she had fetched from the bedroom.

Between Evie's happiness and my important affairs with Pepper, I do not know which was my major and which my minor preoccupation. If my Love and my Ambition were really one, that only meant that often I had to do half a thing at a time. Since Judy and I did not discuss our private affairs at the offices in Waterloo Place, it followed that we had to do so after the day's work was over; and, having been away from home all day, this sometimes caused me to absent myself for the greater part of the evening also. At first, unwilling to do this, I had brought Pepper home with me; but as he always seemed altogether too bright a jewel for our little cottage, and as Evie, moreover, besides getting flurried about what she was to give him to eat, always drew in her horns in his presence, reproaching herself afterwards that she had seemed stupid to my friend, that had not so far proved a great success. The only alternative was, that I should dine with him, getting away afterwards as soon as I could. I did not like this, but it was unavoidable.

From my observation of some at least of the hotels Pepper took me to, I judged that he had some sort of a running account, balanced afterwards, whether in cash or consideration, I knew not how; for often enough, barring the tip to the waiter, no money seemed to change hands. At other times and other places he paid what seemed to me extravagant sums. Sometimes he was in evening dress, sometimes not; I, of course, never was; and so, places where the plastron was *de rigueur* being closed to us, I did not at first see Judy in the full blaze of his splendour. On the whole, we dined most frequently at Simpson's, where morning dress is not conspicuous; and it was one night at Simpson's that Judy mentioned this very matter to me.

"By the way," he said suddenly, over his coffee, as if he had been on the point of forgetting something, "better keep a week next Wednesday free. I want you to meet Robson."

I was conscious of a sudden slight constriction somewhere inside me. Robson was not royalty, but as far as I was concerned he might almost as well have been.

"The Berkeley, at eight," Judy continued. "You'll dress, of course!"

I wondered what in. His champagne-cooler and candlesticks, perhaps. . .

"You needn't be afraid of Robson," Pepper continued, perhaps noticing my dismay. "As a matter of fact, he's rather afraid of me, so *you* ought to be able to pulverize him."

I saw that I must take my stand at once.

"You can bring Robson to Verandah Cottage if you like," I said shortly, "but I'm not going to the Berkeley."

"Rubbish," Pepper remarked lightly. "The table's booked. Robson's coming down from Scotland specially, and Campbell will be there too, and George Hastie. Hastie's put off a visit to Norway on purpose. You've got to tell 'em what you told me that Sunday at the Bull and Bush."

"Then if they want to hear that, they'll have to have it from you."

Pepper showed not a trace of impatience. "My dear chap, don't I just wish I *could* put it as you did!" he flattered me. . . "No, no; I've told them all about you, and it's you, not me, they're coming to see. . . What's the difficulty?" he asked, with a little scintillation of amusement.

"The difficulty is that if you'd told me this a week ago, I should have stopped it."

"So I thought," he replied dryly. . . "Do you know West's, in Bond Street?"

"No."

"Well, you'd better go there tomorrow." Then he patted my arm. "Can't be helped, Jeff. The plunge has to be taken. You won't find 'em snobs. It's the waiters you dress for—I expect that's why you dress like 'em. Good Lord, these chaps have got far too much on their minds to bother about *that*! . . . Go to West's and take my card; I'll 'phone 'em. I gave way to you before; if you don't give way to me now, you'll wreck us. I'd have had it at Alfred Place if I could, but I don't want Hastie and Robson there. So you go to West's tomorrow, and remember, a week on Wednesday, at eight."

I did go to West's on the morrow, and my brow grows moist yet when I think of it. It appeared that before West's could dress me they had to undress me, and my wild and half-formed thoughts that I might pass as a bushranger or miner or wealthy and eccentric antipodean vanished. Miners' flannel shirts are not patched as neatly as Evie had patched mine; bushrangers do not wear loose cuffs with gold-washed links at eighteenpence a pair; and the respectful "Sirs" to which my two acolytes treated me made my hands itch dangerously to knock their heads together. . . So they ran their fingers over my burning body; and because Pepper had let me in for this, I partly, but only partly, got back at him by ordering an admirable lounge suit also, which, for all I know, he owes for to this day. Then I left that place of torture, almost prepared to think twice of my Ambition if it was going to involve very much of this kind of thing.

Evie had received the news of my approaching introduction to exalted personages with a certain wistfulness, which she had tried to cover with an extreme brightness of manner. Of course my position was altogether anomalous; that "scale of living" of Pepper's, coming far too early for my circumstances, was a white elephant; but I don't think it was that that made Evie at the same time brightly fussy and secretly shrinking. Rather, I imagine, it was that for the first time she began to fear my Ambition a little. I don't mean that hitherto she had been hoping that my great plans were baseless imaginings, but I do mean that she was settled and happy as she was, and that a Verandah Cottage twice as big would have contented her to the end of her days. When I brought that really splendid dress suit home (for I had had it sent to the F.B.C., not wishing those ducal tailors to know the poverty of my address), I think her mind suddenly enlarged to strange disturbing vistas, and she examined the stitching of the garments thoughtfully.

"They're beautifully made," she said softly. "I never saw anything finished like that. But I wish Mr. Pepper had not had to pay for them."

"Pepper pay?" I laughed. "Pepper'll pay when the cows come home. It isn't that that's troubling me."

"What then?" she asked.

"I want to see you dressed like that too. . . But don't you want to see me with them on?"

"Yes," she said, but as it were obediently, because I had suggested it.

I went upstairs and got into those costly garments. I had ordered shirts, and ties too, and, not being in the habit of wearing undergarments, I had to consider what to do with the small tab beneath the plastron that should have anchored me forrard. With my penknife I finally performed the operation for appendicitis upon it. Then, looking bigger even than usual, I descended, black, white and majestical.

"Your tie won't do," said Evie. "Come here."

But suddenly, as she was refashioning my bow, she flung her arms about my neck and burst into tears on my breast. Then, when I asked her gently what was the matter, she only withdrew herself, wiped her eyes, and said that she was silly. Queer creatures. It was only the newness and unfamiliarity of the prospect. It was as if she was quite happy in her poverty, merely thinking of riches. . .

I myself had the trifling care on my mind of who was going to sit with Evie while I lorded it at the Berkeley. Ordinarily I should have counted on her aunt, but Miss Angela had announced that she must go to Guildford that day on some business or other connected with the late Mrs. Merridew's will. There was, of course, Miss Levey, but I still considered Verandah Cottage too humble for the friend of Lord Ernest and the confidante of the President of the Board of Trade. Evie protested that she would be quite all right alone, but that I would not hear of.

"I'll tell you what," I said. "Give Billy Izzard dinner that evening. I'll go round and ask him to sit with you. That'll be the best thing."

"I should be quite, quite all right, dear," she said again.

"No," I replied, "I'll get Billy. I'll write a note to him now. Then I'll show you the other suit."

The other suit did not flutter her quite so much. It was just as exquisite in its way, an iron-grey hopsack, with trousers for which I had had to peel three times, but it did not speak quite so plainly of functions and high assemblages. I really did not know where I was going to keep these two suits, as I had no trousers press, and our wardrobe accommodation was exceedingly limited; and I discovered, on arriving home early on the evening of the Berkeley dinner, that I had no summer overcoat fit for my *grande tenue*. As the choice lay between taking a cab the whole of the way and wearing my heavy winter ulster, I chose the latter alternative; and Evie tied my bow and turned up the bottoms of those trousers that pre-supposed broughams and wicker wheel-guards and alightings on red druggets under awnings built out over pavements.

"Billy'll be here in an hour," I said. "I'll look in on him as I pass. You'll be quite all right till then, and I'll be back as soon as I can. Good-bye, darling."

She stood in skirt and delaine blouse at the ivy-green, glass-panelled door, and waved her hand as I turned the corner. I sought the bus terminus in the High Street, treading carefully, for it had been raining, and there were puddles to avoid. The bus started. Twenty minutes later I got down opposite my old place with the gargoyles and terra-cotta ornaments. I mounted the stairs and tapped at Billy's door, entering as I tapped.

"Time you were starting for Verandah Cottage, Billy," I said. . .

The next moment I was staring open-mouthed at what was before me.

II

All right, Louie—thanks," said Billy Izzard. "Right-o, Jeffries—I didn't think it was so late—"

But the model on the throne did not get down.

I had parted my ulster in coming up the stairs, and my dress beneath showed. The contrast struck me as brutal. For one moment I was conscious of it; I don't think that she was, even for one moment. I don't think she saw anything of me but my eyes. I did not of her.

Billy had turned his back on his work, but still she did not move. More even than my own ceremonial dress the bit of crochet woolwork that lay on the edge of the throne seemed to accentuate the drama that was all sight, with never a word spoken. As if my eyes had moved from hers, which they did not, I seemed to see the whole of that room that had been my own—the imps beyond the sills, Billy's traps, his arrangements of curtains about the four windows, the bed behind the screen where I divined her clothing to lie. I say I saw all these things without once looking at them. . .

The exquisite study was on the easel, and I saw that too—the thing as it was, east-lighted, admirably cool, the work of an unrepeatable two hours. Billy, I knew, would look on that canvas on the morrow as an athlete afterwards measures with astonishment his effortless jump. It was the eye's flawless understanding. . .

"It isn't a picture," Billy grunted over his shoulder, his fingers rattling the tubes in his box. "Where the deuce did I put that palette-knife?—Just a study—I had it in my hand not two minutes ago—"

Still she and I stood as motionless as a couple of stones.

"Dashed if I won't be methodical yet! I never—ah, here it is. . . Right, Louie; I've finished. Chuck my coat over the screen, will you? Sorry, Jeff—I'd forgotten the time—but I must wash these brushes."

My eyes parted from Louie Causton's as reluctantly as a piece of soft iron parts from the end of the magnet. She moved, became alive, stepped down from the throne; and as she passed without noise to the screen I saw again, by what legerdemain of visual memory I cannot tell you, the soft flow of draperies that had always drawn my eyes as she had moved about the old Business College in Holborn.

Not until she had disappeared did I myself move from the spot I had occupied since I had taken my first two strides into the room.

"Just turn that thing with its face to the wall; I don't want to see it till morning," said Billy, bustling about. "Sha'n't be a minute—"

He dashed out with a cake of soap and a handful of brushes. The tap was on the landing below. From behind the screen came soft sounds as Miss Causton dressed. . .

I have wasted paper in trying to set down what my thoughts and sensations were. Not to waste any more, I will tell you instead what I did. It was some minutes later, and already the running of the tap at which Billy was washing his brushes below had ceased. Time pressed. Without quite knowing how I got there, I was standing by the screen. I spoke in a low and very hurried voice.

"Miss Causton—"

The moving of clothes stopped.

"I can't see you now—I'm late already," I said.

Miss Causton's voice had formerly been drawlingly slow, but it came back quickly enough now, and altogether without surprise.

"Yes, yes—I want to see you too—quick—how late shall you be?"

"I don't know—eleven—I can't ask you to wait—"

"I'll wait—I'll have my dinner here—"

"Where, then?"

"Where are you going?"

"Piccadilly way—"

Then, breathlessly, "Swan & Edgar's, at eleven—"

"No, no—"

"Sssh—there's no time to talk—there, at eleven—"

"Half-past ten—"

"Yes—"

Billy came in again, but I was away from the screen by then. "Better hurry, unless you want a cold dinner," I said, moving towards the door; and "Better hurry yourself," I heard him say as I left. . .

I dashed across the road for a bus that was just starting; but it was not for some minutes after I had settled myself inside it that I began to realise what I had just done.

Then as bit by bit I grew calmer, it struck me as in the last degree remarkable. What had so suddenly impelled me to say, "I can't see you now?" And why had she replied that she too wished to see me? Why should I have wished to see her at all? Or she me? And why that long, long stare of eyes into eyes?

Robson, the Berkeley, my painfully marshalled statement, Pepper and Hastie and Campbell and all—these things had gone as completely out of my mind as if they had had no bearing at all on my life and fortunes.

I had squeezed into a corner of the bus farthest from the door, and the vehicle had glass panels forward. These were blurred with a fresh shower, orange squares, with now the halo of a lamp moving slowly past, now a muffled or umbrella-ed figure. We pulled up for a moment before the pear-shaped globes of a chemist's window, ruby and emerald, and then went forward again, and I seemed once more to hear that breathless "Swan & Edgar's—eleven," and my own "No, no!" . . .

I had not wanted that. I had not wanted to keep her at *that* corner, draggle-skirted, searching faces for the face she wanted, looked at in her turn, perhaps moved along by the police. For whatever I had thought before, if I had thought anything, that long union of our eyes had held no meanings of commonness. . .

But why the appointment at all?

"Well," I thought within myself as the bus drew up for a moment at the Adam and Eve, and then started forward again down Tottenham Court Road, "at least this explains the 'L' on the teacloth." . . .

After a lapse of time of which I was hardly conscious, I became aware of the glow of the Palace and the lights of Shaftesbury Avenue. By sheer force of will I dragged myself back to the present. Inexplicable as it all was, it must wait. My other business could not wait. Now for the Berkeley. . .

Perhaps the strange incident helped me rather than otherwise in a thing I had had quite heavily on my mind. This was the stepping out of the hansom I had picked up in the Circus and my entry into the hotel. Concerned with so much else, I had now no unconcern to rehearse. I threw my hat and coat into a pair of hands that for all I knew might not have been attached to any human body, and grunted out Pepper's name as if I had been a preoccupied monarch. I was one of twenty others who lounged or waited in the softly lighted hall, but I think the only conspicuous thing about me was my size. . . Then I was aware of Pepper himself, beckoning to me across intervening heads and shoulders.

"Here he is—late as usual," he said, as if a nightly unpunctuality at such places as the Berkeley was a weakness without which I should have been an excellent fellow.

To my abstracted apology I added that not only was I late, but must leave fairly early also.

"Not unless it's for a woman," Pepper laughed. "We'll let him go then, eh, Robson? This is Jeffries—Sir Peregrine Campbell—Mr. Robson. Well, let's go up. *Seniores priores*, Campbell."

We sought the private room Pepper had engaged.

Even had the deep disturbance of my meeting Louie Causton face to face (if I may call it that) not banished things of less consequence, I still do not think that, socially speaking, I should have let Pepper down too badly. It was less formidable than I had feared. Robson, whom I need not describe, since you know his face from his countless photographs, had evidently, from the look of his shoulders, brushed his hair after putting his coat on; and Sir Peregrine Campbell made his vast silver beard a reason for not wearing a tie beneath it. A watch-chain or a ring apart, Hastie's and Pepper's clothes were no better than those I wore. The table was round. I was put between Pepper and Robson, and Pepper's command to a waiter, "Just take that thing away, will you?"—the thing being a centrepiece of flowers—enabled me to see Hastie and Campbell on the other side.

Pepper's tact on my behalf that night was matchless. Especially during the early part of the meal, when Robson was talking about Scotch moors, Hastie of tarpon-fishing in Florida, and Sir Peregrine (in a Scotch accent harsh as a macadam plough) of places half over the globe, he protected me (who had seen the sea only at Brighton and Southend) with such unscrupulousness and mendacity and charm that I really believe I passed as one who could have given them tale for tale had I chosen; and I gathered that he had carefully concealed my connection with the F.B.C. . . . "Has Jeffries shot bear?" he interrupted Hastie once, intercepting a direct question. "Look at him—he doesn't shoot 'em—he *wrestles* 'em—Siberian fashion, with a knife and a dog! . . . I beg pardon, Robson, I interrupted you—" And so on. He told me afterwards that my hugeness and my taciturnity had created exactly the impression he had wished. You would have rubbed your eyes had you been told, seeing me in those evening clothes, that less than four years before I had worn a commissionaire's uniform in Fleet Street and touched my cap to the proprietors of Pettinger's paper.

But until our real business should begin I took leave to drop out of the conversation more and more. That low, urgent whispering over Billy

Izzard's screen ran in my head again, with the thought that I had made an inconvenient and apparently purposeless appointment for half-past ten. *Why* had that quick exchange of whispers been as it were torn out of us, and *what* had she to say to me, I to her?

Again I remembered her and her story. I remembered her cynical concealment of depth under the ruffled shallows of lazy speech, the dust it had pleased her to throw into eyes by her affectations of perverseness or indifference, her munching of sweets, her exquisite hands, her violin-like foot, her soaps and pettings of a person that even then I had divined to be ill-matched with her not strikingly pretty face. I remembered the vivid contrast between her and Kitty Windus—Kitty's ridiculous fears of non-existent dangers from men in omnibuses or under gas-lamps, and Louie Causton's nonchalant, "Men, my dear? So long since I've spoken to one I really forget what they're like!" And I remembered the event that had unstrung poor Kitty and shocked Evie once for all out of her unthinking girlhood—the news that, however it had come about, Miss Causton had one day given birth to a son. That son must be between four and five years old now. . .

Yet it was hardly likely she had wished to speak to me about her little boy. . .

And why had she sent Evie that piece of crochet as a wedding present? That too became the odder the more I thought of it. Had the teacloth been, not primarily a present to Evie, but a message to myself? The teacloth—that long, long stare—that breathless conversation over the screen—were these, all of them, calls of some sort to me?

Yet to appoint Swan & Edgar's, at half-past ten! I disliked that intensely. Not every lonely woman who has taken to herself a lover would willingly court what, were I but five minutes late, she would have to endure at that rendezvous. And the more I thought of it the more convinced I was that, not anything base, but austerity, command and a glassy clearness had lain in that long regard I had met on pushing at Billy's studio door and seeing her standing there. . .

Then it crossed my mind that Evie was probably thinking of me that moment and wondering how I was getting along in my high company. . .

I could not have told you that night what the Berkeley dinners were like. I ate and spoke mechanically, and plates were taken away from me of which I had barely tasted, yet of which I had had enough. Then there came an interval without plate, or rather with a plate, doyley and finger-bowl all stacked together, and I heard Pepper say: "Let's have coffee now and then see we aren't disturbed. . . Well, what about business?"

Five minutes later we were deep in the matters that were the reason of my being there.

These again Judy handled exquisitely, making of my own statement especially the most skilful of examinations-in-chief. Ostensibly laying down lines of policy himself, he contrived that these should be a drawing of me out; and it was only afterwards that I recognised how frequently he set up a falsity for me, coming heavily in, to demolish. Though ordinarily I can concentrate my thoughts when necessary for a day and a night together, I have no power of sustained speech; and so Pepper "fed" me with opportunities for destruction or approbation or comment. No large occurrence in any part of the world is immaterial to our business; as we have to look forward, reasonably probable occurrences and developments are more important still; and so our talk ranged from current events, such as Hunter's recent loss, Rundle's operations, or Loubet's plans for a *rapprochement* of the municipalities, to the coming American elections, the state of the labour world, and the health of the Queen. To the test of these general conditions, particular proposals were submitted; and though I had long known Pepper's private "hand," the skill with which he now played it was a revelation to me. At one and the same time he was laying the foundations of a dividend-paying business and of an administrative programme of which he and I were to be an indispensable part; and so, knowing more of some things than Robson, and more of others than Campbell, he set them one at another, coming in himself from time to time with an idea born of themselves five minutes before, but given back so cut and polished that it had the appearance of a new thing. I prudently said little save on an overwhelming certitude, but I think I encompassed it all and made my presence felt, now sweepingly, now as a mere deflection. I was now oblivious of all, save our conference. I seem to remember that at one juncture I must have spoken for getting on for five minutes, a feat unparalleled for me; but I knew my ground. It was of the academic Socialism and the newer kind, then just showing over the horizon, and perhaps better understood by those who like myself had gone through the fire than by any official. I was only interrupted once, by Pepper, when I mentioned Schmerveloff's name, the Russian social doctrinaire. "Ah yes, your neighbour," he murmured, and I went on. . .

Then suddenly I looked at my watch. It was ten minutes past ten. I still had some minutes, and I used them for a sort of cadenza to whatever my performance might have been. Then, rising abruptly, I said I must be off.

"I must be getting along myself presently," said Pepper.

He came downstairs with me and saw me into my hat and coat. I saw his glance at my new topper, but he said nothing either about my appearance or my recent demeanour. Instead it was I who said suddenly, as we walked to the door, "By the way—you didn't tell me that that neighbour of mine was Schmerveloff."

He laughed. "Didn't I? Well, you ought to know who your neighbour is better than I do!" It was only then that he added, "Well, I think we've done the trick, Jeffries!"

I left him, and turned towards Swan & Edgar's. I had another trick to do now, though of what its nature might prove to be I had not the faintest conception.

III

As they had done three hours before, again our eyes met simultaneously. She had been sheltering in a doorway, but she advanced immediately, and without hesitation took my arm. I suppose she must have chosen our direction, for we had crossed to the corner of Lower Regent Street before I had as much as wondered where, at that hour of the night, we were to go. It was still raining; the flimsy umbrella she carried protected her soft grey hat, but not her skirts; and I did not wish to take her to any of the brightly lighted establishments of the Circus for two reasons—first, because I had only four shillings in my pocket, and secondly, because I wanted—well, say to distinguish. The west-bound buses start from the corner to which we had crossed, and it looked as if we should have to talk in whichever of them took her homewards.

"This one?" I said laconically, as a West Kensington bus drew up.

But she drew me away. "Let's go this way," she said.

I took her umbrella, and with her hand still on my arm she led me down Lower Regent Street.

If we had anything important to say to one another, it was extraordinary how we delayed to say it. We reached the offices of the F.B.C. without having spoken, and turned along Pall Mall East and into Trafalgar Square still without a word. And when presently she did speak, at the top of Parliament Street, it was merely to tell me that my hat would be spoiled if I didn't take my share of the umbrella.

"Then you might at least turn your trousers up," she added, as I made no reply; and I stooped and did so. We resumed our walk, stopped at the Horse Guards, and made our way slowly towards the Mall.

"Are you warm?" I asked some minutes later.

"Quite," she replied; and the silence fell on us again.

At last, somewhere near the spot where the Artillery Memorial now is, she did speak. It was a curious question she put, her fingers working slightly on my sleeve as she did so. During the past minutes a sense—I hardly know how to describe it except as a sense of protection—had begun to grow on me, the odd thing being that it was not I who protected her, but she me. Perhaps the perfect calm with which she had claimed my arm had begun it; it certainly now informed the very curious question she suddenly put.

"Are you happy?" she asked.

You may imagine I was a little surprised. Quite apart from the nameless reassurance that thrilled in her tone, some queer gage of fidelity, though fidelity to what I could not make out, the question itself was a long way out of the ordinary. Was I happy! Ought I not, from any point of view she could possibly have, to be happy? Newly married—sure of myself—wearing clothes the luxury of which was only an anticipation—fresh from a conference with the great ones of the land (though to be sure she could hardly know all this)—what else should I be but happy? It looked as if for some reason or other she had supposed I would *not* be happy. . . I spoke slowly.

"I wish you would tell me," I said, "what makes you ask that?"

She looked straight before her through the rain. "Why I ask that? It's just that that I wanted to ask you," she replied.

"It's just that that you—" I repeated after her, stopping, however, half-way.

Yet I felt somehow that that she had just uttered was no banal compliment. She was not thinking of the kind of felicitation that had been implied when she had sent Evie the teacloth. She had not asked after Evie, and was not, I knew already, thinking of Evie. And again I had that odd sense that she was protecting me, and would continue to protect me.

"Well, it's an odd question—the whole thing's odd, of course—but since you ask, I don't mind telling you. I am happy."

She turned under the umbrella eagerly, almost (I thought) joyously. "You *are*?"

"*I* am," I emphasised slightly.

But still she did not mention Evie. Again we walked. Then:

"You are? After all—that?"

Softly from the background of my memory there came forward what I conceived to be her meaning. It was a humiliating one, and I hung my head humbly.

"You mean after—poor Kitty?"

But it seemed I was quite wrong. "No, I don't mean that," she said. "Or at any rate only partly that."

"Then," I asked quickly, "will you tell me what you *do* mean?"

In Billy's studio we had been positively straining at one another to speak; since then, free any time this last half-hour to say what we would, we had hung just as desperately back; but now came a sudden enough end both to straining and to reluctance. She turned to me; my eyes would have fallen before the gaze she gave me, but were compelled to endure it; and the lightning is not more instantaneous and direct than were the words that now burst from her.

"Tell me—you killed that boy, didn't you?"

I SAID YOU SHOULD HAVE it soon. It has been a little longer than I thought. At any rate you have it now.

THE REMAINING EVENTS OF THAT evening are easier to set down than to account for. My difficulty perhaps is that I am trying to tell an extraordinary thing in terms that are inappropriately plain. Nothing, for example, would be simpler than to say how we stopped in our walk, presently resumed it, slowly passed the Palace and the Royal Mews, and in course of time found ourselves walking up Grosvenor Place. It is true that we did these things, but it is also true that they are all more or less beside the mark. I need not urge my point, how beside the mark they are, by comparison with the remarkable results of being asked by a woman whom you have known only slightly and whom you have almost forgotten all about whether you have killed a certain young man. Therefore if, as may very well be the case, you yourself have no experience on such a point, that is all the more reason why you should trust me to give, in my own way, the essence of an hour without parallel in my experience, and, I imagine, to be matched in that of few others.

As she had spoken I had stepped back, without haste, a pace from her, taking her umbrella with me. I was stepping back another pace, when my back encountered the iron railings, stopping me. Until then her hand had not left my sleeve. Now perhaps three yards separated us, she standing in the rain, I with her gimcrack of an umbrella. There was a lamp not far away; the veil of falling rain held and diffused the light of it, so that I actually saw her with more evenness of detail than I should have done had she stood directly in the light, one side of her face illumined, and the other dark; and probably my own face was not entirely lost in the shadow of the umbrella. Our eyes had met again, exactly as they had met in the studio. . .

On her soft floppy hat and over the shoulders of her three-quarters grey coat I saw the rime of fine rain gather. It became a sort of soft moss of rain, that gave her figure a faintly discerned outline of light. Though her wrists were damp and dark, and her skirts straight and heavy, I still did not think of passing her the umbrella; it is wonderful how many small things escape you when you have just been asked whether you have put an end to a young man's life. The rain came on still more sharply. I saw it gleam on the backs of her kid gloves. . .

It never occurred to me to wonder how she knew. I suppose I ought to have wondered this, but I gave it no thought. Instead, I was wondering why I had never noticed before what her eyes were like—why, indeed, I had thought them to be quite different. Had you asked me that morning what Louie Causton's eyes were like I should first have rummaged in my memory for who Louie Causton was, then have dismissed them as ordinary and a sort of grey, and so have missed a wonder. Grey? Yes, they were grey, but that is not saying anything. And perhaps after all it was not the eyes that held me. Perhaps the eyes were no more than rounds of crystal between us, pure crystal, hiding nothing. Better still, perhaps they were of that substance which, placed across itself, allows no light to pass, but, turned parallel, ceases to intercept. Formerly I had seen those tourmaline rounds of Louie Causton's grey eyes as it were transversely placed, opaque, riddling, mocking, impenetrable; now, quicker than the flicker of a camera-shutter, they had changed, and, for me, would never again change back. I had seen down into her soul. Her physical form, three hours before, had not been more openly offered to my gazing than was that measureless deep interior she showed me now. . .

And that she too had plunged to the bottom of my own soul, her question was sufficient evidence.

And now, as that vision of her spirit, stark and piercing as Billy Izzard's of her body had been, must abide with me for ever, there was no special need for hurrying matters. Though I had known it not, it was for that last stripping look that I had whispered so breathlessly to her over the screen; and she, unlike me, had known why she had whispered back. So, the thing being now done, our time was our own. As slowly as I had retreated to the railings, I advanced from them again. Once more I held the umbrella over her.

"Come," I said. "You're getting wet."

Again, without a moment's hesitation, she passed her hand under my arm, and we moved towards the Palace.

There are some supreme moments—they say the moment of violent death is one of them—in which all Life's obscurations are made instantaneously clear; but if my own supreme moment ought to have taken that form, I can only say that it did not. No sudden explanations of the hitherto inexplicable flashed through my mind. Afterwards, when a certain amount of imperfection had supervened between me and that perfect look, these explanations did present themselves, yes, in crowds, but not then. I did not ask why, knowing me for a murderer, she should still take my arm. I did not wonder how she regarded the matter from Merridew's point of view. I did not trouble myself about how she knew, nor, for the matter of that, whether she did know—for she had made no charge, had only put a question. I cared for nothing but that sweet yet terrible depth and stillness I had seen beyond the tourmalines of her eyes. Indeed, somewhere near the Palace, I suddenly found myself irresistibly longing to look into those eyes again. We were approaching another lamp. I stopped. Again I did not notice that I did so under a dripping plane-tree. I looked. They were still the same—flawless transmitters, accesses to the ether of her soul. . .

Again she put her question.

"You did kill that boy, didn't you?"

"Yes." (I could not have dared to lie to her.)

"Ah!" . . .

We walked on again.

And I know not what rest, akin to the longing of a weary spirit for death, I found in it all. Nor do I know whence came the special and unimaginable peace that filled me. For that peace was special. My marriage had been a different rapture; the dreams of the first days of my love had not been the same; and it was perhaps this that I had implored in vain that night when, stretching out among my swags and gargoyles, I had cried to Whatever lay beyond the marbled sky that, might I but be delivered from this body of an ancient death, my life should be a dedicated thing. And now, when I least expected it, I had it. Between me, a man who had committed murder, and her, the mother of a nameless child, something I knew not—something still and splendid and awful—had come into being. Do you wonder that, in the stillness and splendour and awe of it, my brain slumbered within me, so that though those grey abysses full of answers waited for me, not a question did I put? . . .

"Yes," I said. "You know I killed him."

And "Ah!" she said again.

You will not find it difficult to believe that when you have been asked the question I had been asked, you and your questioner are not on ordinary terms. Indeed—believe me—you are hardly flesh and blood at all. You become eyes and voices, and yet not exactly that either—you are parts of an immanent vision and speech. You will also see that to dare such a question is to dare to be questioned in your turn. Therefore, less as wanting the information than as doing her the reciprocal honour of putting her on the same stark footing as myself, I again sought those marvellous eyes.

"You asked me," I said, "whether I was happy. I told you. . . Are you?"

You have learned what she was; to what you already know I will add one or two things I picked up later. I wish to show you what elements she had to make happiness out of. She did fairly well out of her sittings. Ordinarily she made as much as two pounds a week, and she made more still when she was engaged for an evening class. To this were to be added the small sums she made by her crochet-work during her short rests. (Evie's teacloth had been made during the rests.) When she did not crochet, she made garments for her boy. She rose daily at seven, dressed her boy, breakfasted with him, and at nine o'clock brought him out with her. They walked a quarter of a mile together to her bus, where the child was met each day by a guardian, an old governess she trusted. She kissed him, and blew him another kiss as the bus turned the corner. He always waited with the old governess for this, but sometimes other buses intervened, so that she went without her last glimpse of him. Then she sought the studio where she happened to be engaged. There she posed, crocheted, posed again, lunched, and once more posed. She usually reached home again at eight o'clock, but when she secured evening sittings it was eleven before she got back. By that time her boy was in bed. She dressed him well, fed him well, told him tales, and bought him tops and toy soldiers. She paid the governess ten shillings a week. Sundays were her heavenly days. If they were cold or wet, she spent them in playing with the tops and soldiers on the floor; if they were fine she took him out on to the commons of Clapham or Wandsworth, or to the Zoo, for which her employers gave her Sunday tickets. She had saved a few pounds, and was adding to this sum by shillings and half-crowns, against the day when she would have to send him to school and start him in the world. This was her life.

And when I asked her if she was happy, she said, in a voice little above a whisper, "Yes—now."

Then, with another deep, clear look, she added, "I think I have all the best of Life."

It did not occur to me just then to wonder what she meant by that "now." I was pondering her last words. All at once, on a sudden impulse (though I was pretty sure beforehand what her answer would be), I said:

"He left you?"

Her answer was supremely tranquil and unaffected.

"Yes—as far as he was ever there to leave. It meant nothing—a folly—merely stupid—it had no significance whatever. I've no grudge against him. He didn't really wrong me. It hardly mattered, ever—it doesn't matter—now—"

A question must have shown in my eyes even as I decided not to put it, for all at once she laughed a little.

"Oh, I'd tell you if you wished to know, but you'd be no wiser. It's a name you've never heard. But one thing I should like—" For one moment she hesitated.

"I ask you nothing."

"No; but I should like you to know one thing—oh, quite for my own sake! If ever you *should* hear a name—three names—four—you needn't believe them. I lied perfectly recklessly. It seemed to me—stupidly perhaps—that I owed him that. So I blackened myself. You see, they tried to find out—my friends—"

"You mean—?"

"Oh, one lover was enough," she answered, with another laugh, rich, low, and without bitterness. "And it doesn't matter—*now*."

It was then that I knew what she meant by that reiterated "now." The thing that beat suddenly in on me explained in a flash that curious attitude of protection towards myself. That kiss blown from the top of the morning bus—the shillings she earned by sitting to morose and impatient artists—those heavenly Sundays—that desertion which also she ranked as a happiness—her self-slanders rather than betray her betrayer—all these things together had not, somehow, seemed to me to make up that "best part of Life" of which she spoke. Beyond even her beautiful devotion to her boy must lie some other deep sustaining dream. Without such a dream, her life would not have been what patently it was—full. . .

But now it was all in the eyes she turned on me. . .

And I knew that the look that told me she loved *me*, had long loved me, and must now go on loving me to the end, put love between us high out of our reach for ever.

"You can't prevent it," she almost triumphed, shining it all out on me. "It's mine, whether you want me to have it or not. And of course it makes no difference to you—"

"None," I murmured mechanically. . .

"Then *haven't* I all the best of Life?" she exulted, smiling up at me.

And before that strange tension that for so long had held us had quite left us, I had muttered, with a little choke, "God bless your little chap, anyway!"

It was all I could say. The other thing she had told me could make no difference to me.

THEN CAME THE SWIFT CHANGE. It came as we reached the top of Grosvenor Place, turned, and descended again. It came as a torrent of rapid speech, sometimes both of us speaking at once, both stopping and waiting, and then both breaking out simultaneously as before. They were short, half sentences, taken and given back with bewildering quickness.

"And now you want to know—" she said.

"Yes—?"

"—how I knew?"

"How did you?"

"I didn't—quite—I knew in myself—not otherwise."

"In yourself—how?"

"Oh, how does one know these things? One sees this—hears that—"

I clutched at her hand.

"Not so quickly. What 'this'? What 'that'?"

"Well, for one thing, Kitty Windus—"

"Does she know?"

"No—"

"You hesitate."

"She doesn't know. She helped me to knowledge. She doesn't know she did."

Again I snatched at her hand.

"That's not the same thing. She may know of—that other—but not know she's let you know."

"That's just possible. That's why I—"

"Oh, anything's possible!" I broke out. "Let's be plain. Does she know that I killed—?"

"I don't think so. Indeed I'll say no."

"But you hesitate again. (Come this way—it's quieter.)"

As if a fusillade had been suspended there came a thrilling silence. We were passing St. Peter's Church at the east end of Eaton Square. We were in the Square before she replied.

"Very well. Don't interrupt unless I ask you questions. I'll be as plain as I can. It's extraordinarily difficult. . ."

I waited.

"You see," she began carefully, "Kitty's so—queer. You couldn't expect that insane arrangement with her to go on indefinitely—I mean that incredible engagement of yours. She was bound to find out something. She—"

"Yes—that's it—what *did* she find out?" broke once more from me.

"Sssh! . . . Of course she found out—about Evie—that it was Evie you were in love with. Naturally she did. What woman wouldn't? *I* saw it, with far less reason than Kitty had. We won't waste time over that. So after she left you, she expected week by week to hear of the next thing—your becoming engaged to Evie. Week by week, I say. How many weeks was it?"

"Four years."

"Week by week, for four years. All those weeks. If it didn't come one week it would be the next—you see. She prophesied it. It became an *idée fixe*. You never saw her during that time?"

"I never as much as—"

"Nor heard of her?"

"No."

"You didn't hear of her breakdown?"

"No; but all this doesn't—"

"Doesn't go beyond you and Evie. I know. Don't interrupt. And Evie didn't hear of her breakdown either?"

"No—I think I can say that."

"What did Evie think of—let us say Archie Merridew's suicide?"

I hesitated. "What should she think? She thought what everybody thought—more or less."

"As something inexplicable?"

"I assume so—but of course I've never—"

"What does she think now?"

"I hope she doesn't think of it at all. As far as I've been able—"

"Yes, yes, yes. . . Plainly, then, have you told her? Told her what you did?"

"Told her? No!"

"Have you *thought* of telling her?"

"Have I thought. . . do you mean have I thought of killing her too?"

Louie was suddenly silent. A hansom slipped swiftly through the deserted Square, its wheels making no sound and the slap of the horse's hoofs dying gradually away in the distance. The rain had stopped, but the trees still dripped sadly, and something vague and far away had approached, resolved itself into a policeman's shining cape, and passed again before Louie spoke.

"Well," she said slowly, "after all, that's not the immediate point. That comes later. The first thing's Kitty's condition. That condition, as far as I can make it out, is this. You showed yourself clever and unscrupulous almost beyond belief in one thing, and she found you out in that; now, I fancy, she thinks there's no end to your cleverness and unscrupulousness. Positively no end. You're *capable de tout* . . . So she broods. Of course she ought never to have been allowed to live alone. . . And she knows she has these—fancies—about you—and so when she's all right she's quite persuaded they *are* fancies. And most of the time she *is* all right. Then the fits come, and—she's off."

A quick shiver took me. "Do you mean—?" I faltered.

"Violently? Oh no. At the best she's just as she used to be; at the worst she's merely helpless, a child. Otherwise I should never dare to have her come and live with me."

"What, you're—?"

"Well, somebody's got to look after her."

"And so you—?"

"She's coming to me next week."

"I see," I said slowly. . .

Again such a silence fell on us as, after prolonged sound, has an importunate quality that even sound has not. As if in a dream, I strove to realise that Evie and Billy Izzard were away over in the Vale of Health, dozing probably, awaiting my return from the Berkeley. I tried to understand the plain fact that I was walking the wet streets in the company of a woman who, judged by ordinary standards, bore a smirched reputation, and that I had permitted that woman to make, though without words, a declaration of her love for me. As this last grew on me a little, I let my mind take that particular bypath of speculation. I almost forgot her presence by my side in my odds and ends of memories of her. Once, at a breaking-up party at the old Business College, she had said to me: "As you don't come to me, I come to you," and at the same party she had asked me for a cup of coffee, which I had brought to her in the crowded room instead of giving it to her in some sequestered corner where we could "sit out." Then other memories came. Memory adding itself to memory until I had all the leading facts of her story—that fatal, insignificant, desperate accident—then, mockingly too late, her love for myself—her so strangely happy life, its fulness now to be turned into a superabundance by her voluntary taking up the care of a weak-minded woman—all, all her happy-unhappy story. And now for us to be thrown together like this! Extraordinary, extraordinary! I fancy we were somewhere in the neighbourhood of Sloane Square by this time—Sloane Square, with Evie and Billy waiting for me in the Vale of Health, and her boy asleep many hours ago! . . . I smiled, though grimly enough, as my eyes encountered my own trousers. Those expensive garments were soaked to the knees. Louie, broken by her day's arduous sitting, now hung heavily on my arm. Her sleeves lay flat to her arms, and her skirt held pounds' weight of water. And we were still walking down Lower Sloane Street, and approaching the Barracks. . .

It was in Lower Sloane Street—there is a little naturalist's shop thereabouts—that I stopped, once more facing her. It seemed to me that there was something which, if she didn't know it, she ought to know.

"Louie," I said slowly, putting a hand on her shoulder to turn her face towards mine, "I don't know whether you know what you ought to do?"

I saw that she did know. For the first time I saw a return of her old ironical smile. But "What's that?" she asked.

"What, unless you do to me, I can now equally do to you."

"And what's that?" she smiled.

"There are no accessories in this business. You're a principal too."

She laughed outright. "All right, Jim," she said. "I'll trust you not to give me away."

"But listen to me—"

That was exactly what she would not do. She cut in brusquely.

"Oh, my good man, be quiet! Anybody'd think you thought I was going to blackmail you!" Then, leaning heavily on me once more, "I suppose all you men take that view of it," she went on, with an energy that triumphed momentarily over her fatigue, "but here's *my* view if you must have it—that men deserve rewards who stamp out creatures like that! Oh, you needn't look at me—*I'm* experienced if anybody is, and *I* know why young men hang themselves just before their weddings! And that, Jim—come along, it's no good standing here—that's why I asked you whether you'd told Evie. You know your own business best, but I'll tell you this—that if women were on juries not a jury in the land would convict you! *Oh!*—" She shuddered the more strongly that she earned her daily bread in the way she did. "*I* can face these things. I've learned—I've had to. Am I the same woman you once knew? I think not. And I tell you plainly, that if you'd done what you have done for me I'd kiss your feet and ask you to bless me! But of course there's Evie. I don't know why you haven't told her: I don't know her very well, you see. My own opinion is that you'll find you've got to tell her. I'm sure that sooner or later you'll find that. And that reminds me of something else. What do you suppose you ought to do about Kitty?"

I smothered a groan. "Oh, I'm past supposing," I answered dully.

"Poor man! . . . Well, this is how it is. Kitty's unreliable. She has these outbreaks. I hope she'll be better with me, but I can't answer for that. So—I'm only preparing you, Jim, but it *may* come to this, that before she gets it fixed in her head once for all that young Merridew *didn't* hang himself she's got to be made quite certain that he *did*. Even if she's got to be told so she must be made certain of that. And I shall be greatly surprised if you haven't to tell Evie exactly the opposite. *Voilà!*"

I scarcely heard her now. An overwhelming weariness had come over me. It was a weariness of the mind no less than of the body. My mind too seemed to be making an endless pilgrimage through wet and benighted streets, far from its rest; and even that strange hallucination of Louie's protection had left me now. After leaving Lower Sloane Street I suppose we must have turned still farther west, for I seem to remember that we passed the Chelsea Hospital, but in this I may be wrong, unless they have since pulled down a row of old houses I distinctly remember seeing across the road. It must have been not very far from there that I went for a time, physically and mentally, all to pieces. Probably the net result of all this talk had just begun to sink into me—that, the intervening years notwithstanding—my well-nigh flawless planning notwithstanding[1]—my cares and prayers and vigils notwithstanding—all was not yet over. I have boasted in my time that I have been untroubled by what I had done, and that is also no lie; but the consequences are another matter. Suppose even that Louie were right, and that I had done nothing but a worthy act; there are still worthy acts

---

1. See "In Accordance with the Evidence."

that overwhelm the doer of them. So the prophets were hounded to their death—and I was no prophet, but, for a space of time of which I took no account, a broken man, who, in a doorway somewhere near Swan Walk (it was an old doorway, with a porter's grille and an antique bell-rod), gave out utterly, began to double at the knees, and would have fallen but for the two arms of a woman as spent as himself—a woman who murmured, with unthinkable selflessness and a charity and encouragement and comfort past telling: "Oh, come, come—come, come!" . . .

By-and-by—it could not have lasted very long, for a clock somewhere was striking one, and the public-houses had been closing as we had left Sloane Square—I was better. I was well enough to walk, still supported by her, to a bench on the Embankment, where we sat down. Her umbrella was still in my hands; how I had come to break it I didn't know; but I had broken it, and I remember thinking dully, as if it had been a great matter, that I ought to get her another. . . or get that one mended. . . It was only right that I should pay for it. Somebody would have to pay for it, and in common fairness it ought not to be she. . . And, I thought, while I was about it, I might as well get her a cab also. She must be unspeakably tired, and I had four shillings in my pocket. . .

"Thanks," I said. She had taken off my ruined silk hat and unfastened my white bow and collar, and was bending over me solicitously, fanning my face ineffectually, now with my own hat, now with her hand. "Thanks. That was absurd of me. I'm not—not in the habit of giving out like this—but we'll finish—another time, if you don't mind. Where do you live?"

She lived near Clapham Junction. "But what about you?" she said, as we rose.

"Oh, I'll take a cab too. I'll walk a little way though. Up here—this seems a likely place for cabs—"

We took one of the minor streets that led to the King's Road. There I hailed a hansom that was returning eastwards. I had put her into it when a thought struck me.

"By the way," I said, "what is your name—your business name, I mean?"

She smiled, as if at a wasted care. "Oh, the same," she said.

"Does Billy Izzard know you know me?"

"No. That is, he didn't."

"Well, he does by this time probably. If Evie and he have been talking—"

("'Urry up, gov'nor!" growled the cabman.)

"He'll think it odd I didn't speak to you. Never mind. Where can I hear from you?"

"Your office—?"

"Yes—no, I mean, not there." I had suddenly remembered Miss Levey. "Give me your address."

She gave it to me, and I gave it to the cabman. "You really will take a cab?" she said, looking anxiously at me as the vehicle pivoted round.

"Yes, yes."

And she was off.

I was in the King's Road, without a penny. It was a quarter to two when I passed the Post Office near Sloane Square, and it was twenty past by the time I reached Park Lane. After Park Lane I lost count of the time. I came out of the doze in which I walked to find myself at various times in Upper Baker Street, near Lords, and, I don't know how long after that, on the point of missing the turning into Fitzjohns Avenue. The day began to break greyly. I still walked, sleeping as I went. It was only as I ascended Heath Street, hardly a quarter of a mile from home, that I came sufficiently out of my torpor to begin to wonder what account I should give of my absence to Evie.

IV

Three weeks or a month after that night on which I had reopened, so to speak, a bottle containing a grim and familiar genie, an incident happened that riled me exceedingly. This was nothing less than an unexpected meeting, on one of our Sunday visits to Hampton Court, with Miss Levey.

Under other circumstances this meeting would have been too ludicrous for annoyance. It happened in the Maze, of all places, where, in some moment of physiological high spirits, I had taken Evie, threatening to lose her and leave her there. As a matter of fact, I had lost both her and myself. Perhaps you know the Maze. Its baffling windings of eight-foot hedges have their single legitimate way out, which you may find if you can; but, for the release of burrowers at turning-out time, there is also a locked iron gate, as impossible to miss as the true exit is to find. Half-a-dozen times, believing ourselves to be at last in the proper alley of green, we had been brought up by this gate; and it was at the gate that we met Miss Levey.

At certain points, where the high mattress-like hedges are a little thin, you can almost see through them; and several times we had caught sight of a scarlet shadow, accompanied by a young man in checks. Now, at the gate, we came full tilt upon this scarlet. Her wide hat and buttons only were black, and from her bosom projected an enormous frill, very white against the red cloth, that gave her the appearance of a pouter pigeon. She had lost Lord Ernest or the President of the Board of Trade or whoever her companion was, and of course there was no avoiding her.

"*You* here!" she cried, seizing both Evie's hands and setting her head so far back and on one side that it was half lost behind the frill. "Vell!" (I write it so, though her accent was in reality less marked.) "This *is* delightful!—You see, Mr. Jeffries—!"

I was mortified, but couldn't very well show it. I laughed. "Oh! What do I see?"

"Dear Evie and I do meet after all!" she half jested.

"Oh!" I laughed again. "Well, if that's all, you could have met long ago. I assumed that you didn't come up to see us because you didn't want to."

It was, of course, lame in the extreme, but Miss Levey saw fit to affect to believe it. Again she put her head back like an inquisitive bird, dandling Evie's hands up and down.

"Oh, *I* thought I wasn't wanted! So of course I stayed away. . . Vell, Evie, I *am* glad!"

So Evie said she was glad, and I said that I was glad too, with something about the ridiculousness of such old acquaintances standing on ceremony, and Miss Levey, I knew, was the only glad one of the three.

"Isn't it annoying, the way we always find ourselves at this gate!" she said, when at last she had dropped Evie's hands. "Aschael and I have been here at least ten times! You ought to know the way out, Mr. Jeffries, a clever man like you!"

"I'm afraid I don't, but there's the man up the perch there—he'll always point out the way."

"Oh, but one doesn't like to be beaten!" she said, with a covert look at me. "Dear me, I'm quite hot! I think Aschael must have given me the slip. Perhaps you wouldn't mind finding him for me, Mr. Jeffries?"

My polite "With pleasure" didn't in the least represent my feelings, but as I thought I should recognise the pawnbroker's assistant who had brought our Arab horse-tamers, I bade them stay where they were, and left them.

After I had found the ringleted Aschael it took us half-an-hour to escape from the pair of them, and even then it was done only at the cost of the invitation I had so obstinately withheld. Miss Levey was to come up with me from the F.B.C. on the following Wednesday evening, and Aschael was to fetch her away again at ten o'clock. It seemed quite a nicely balanced point whether she would kiss Evie or not when she left, but she did not, and for some minutes after we had lost sight of them I saw the man up the perch pointing out turnings and heard his calling to them.

"Deuce take her!" I muttered, twenty minutes later, when Evie and I had also been shown the way out. We had passed the glowing parterre, and were just turning into the cool Fountain Court.

"It couldn't be helped, dear," said Evie. "It was all there was to do. We needn't get into the habit of asking her if you don't want her."

"Oh, it doesn't matter," I answered absently. I was once more wondering whether Pepper intended to take Miss Levey over presently from the F.B.C. Already I was pretty well resolved that he should not.

And I was quite resolved on this point when Evie next spoke. We had stopped by one of the arches, and were looking over the grass plot and fountain in the middle. The Court was deliciously cool, and I should have liked Billy Izzard to make a sketch of Evie as she leaned against the pillar, dressed in soft pink muslin, her hand touching her cheek, and only her dark eyes darker than that Black Knight sweet-pea of her hair. Those eyes were full of grave thought.

"Jeff," she said diffidently by-and-by.

"What, dear?"

"You know where you left us just now—"

"Left you and Miss Levey?"

"Yes. . . She told me something I think I ought to tell you."

"Oh? She didn't lose much time," I could not forbear remarking.

"It was something I know you'd far rather I told you—it was something about poor Kitty," Evie went awkwardly on.

"Oh?" . . .

You may guess from this "Oh?" that I had told Evie no more than I had thought fit about my meeting with Louie. Indeed, of that extraordinary walk that had begun at Swan & Edgar's corner and ended in the King's Road, Chelsea, I had told her nothing at all. When I had reached home again, at four o'clock in the morning, Evie had been in bed, Billy asleep by the ashes of the dining-room fire. He had yawned hugely and stiffly: "A-a-a-h! . . . I like your idea of a couple of hours in the evening, my friend! I say, you look rather done up; what have you been doing with yourself? . . . Evie? She went to bed at two; she would sit up till then. What time is it? Nice goings-on at the Berkeley!"

And Billy and I had lighted the fire and breakfasted, moving about quietly so as not to wake Evie. Evie did not know the exact hour of my return, and had made no remark about the condition of my hat and trousers.

It seems an odd thing to say, but I simply had not dared to tell her. When I say that she would never, never have understood I am not belittling her either; she simply would not have understood. It would have been different had I been able to tell her all, but better nothing than half. Nay, what she already knew was in its way almost too much, for of course Billy, taking studio mysteries for granted, had told her, rather as a joke against myself, of my coming upon Louie Causton. Seeing Evie's almost painful blush, he had been a little sorry he had spoken. For while Evie liked Billy, she could never get used to the idea of his models. It was a little as if some outwardly very charming person should be in reality a known dynamiter. And even when she had grasped the model (so to speak) in theory, it had only to be made a personal matter for the blood to rise into her cheeks. Suppose I had come upon Aunt Angela thus! . . . So, unable to tell her all, of the later events I had told her nothing.

But now she said again, looking over the quiet Fountain Court, "It's about poor Kitty. Louie didn't tell you, I suppose?" (I had admitted having had a few words with Louie.)

"In Billy's studio, do you mean?"

"Yes."

"No," I answered, with what strictness of veracity you will observe.

I saw, by the way she dropped her great eyes and pushed a bit of gravel about with her toe, what had come over her again. Just as, on that Bank Holiday evening in the tea-garden in the Vale of Health, she had had Kitty, if not on her conscience, at any rate on her magnanimity, so she had her now. By reason of that slight emptiness and waiting state of her life (in spite of all that I could do), her thoughts still flew back. Between my departures in the mornings and returns again o' nights, reminiscences, the freer in their play that her work was merely mechanical, still occupied her. These reminiscences welled up again in her now, and, added to them, filling her breast completely, was that half-compunctious desire of the victress for the squaring of accounts that is to be found in the exercise of compassion.

And as I saw her perturbation, something welled up in me too. She did not know I was looking at her, but I was, and already I had begun to see the only thing that would be more than temporarily efficacious against these strayings. There was only one thing. A picture came into my mind of a woman who blew a kiss from the top of a bus, played on the floor on Sundays with her boy, and found her life full and happy. . .

"Oh, my darling," I thought as I looked at her, "is it so very, very long—so very long and empty? . . . Very well. . . It will modify a good many plans, but better that. . . Your life too shall be full—and your arms—"

When next she looked up there was, about her eyes, a tiny bright edging of tears that did not fall.

"Jeff," she said, unusually quickly, "Kitty's ill. She has attacks of some kind. I couldn't quite make it out. I suppose Miriam Levey'll tell us all about it on Wednesday. I know you don't like Miriam, but she's awfully troubled about Kitty, and thinks she ought to be looked after. Somebody told her—told Miriam—that poor Kitty'd been found one night walking round and round Lincolns Inn Fields, and when the policeman asked her, she couldn't remember at first where she lived. Oh, Jeff, it does seem so sad!"

Privately I found that horrible. It had been in Lincolns Inn Fields that Kitty and I had walked together, and to think of her still haunting the place, alone, I found very horrible. But if that horror was mine, it was not going to be Evie's if I could help it. I nodded gravely, and took her arm.

"Well," I said (although I was again cudgelling my brains to see how Miss Levey's visit could be frustrated), "no doubt you will hear all about it next Wednesday. I wouldn't worry till then. . . What about tea?"

We left the Palace, and sought the teashop near the Bridge. Miss Levey and Aschael passed the door of the shop as we sat, and Miss Levey waved her hand and gave us an artificially bright smile. But her goose was cooked with Jeffries & Pepper. I had far too much respect for her inquisitiveness and persistence to admit her to our new enterprise. Between her and myself Pepper would not hesitate for long, and I intended, if necessary, to put the matter in precisely that form. . .

After tea, Evie and I took another turn in the Palace. It was a golden evening, with a wonderful bloom on the old walls, windows flashing yellow, and the forests of twisted chimney-stacks brightly gilded. Her arm was in mine, and her hand made little delicious pressures from time to time, and ever and again her cheek seemed to be on the point of falling against my shoulder. Louie Causton's touch had not thrilled me thus. Some high forbiddance would ever have said Louie Causton and myself Nay, but here was flesh of my flesh, and the promise of sweet and rosy flesh between us—for we had spoken of it, and the west that bathed all in golden light was not more tranquil than that other heaven in our hearts. . .

I remember very well our journey back from Waterloo in the old horse-bus that night. I remember it because of that whispered new pact between Evie and myself. She, tired out no less by that gentle vista than by the fatigues of the day, slept for the greater part of the way with her head on my shoulder and her hat in my lap; and I had to wake her to change buses. In the new bus she settled down again; and I was left free to consider whether the promise I had passed would or would not necessitate a hastening of matters with Pepper. If it should turn out so, so much the worse. In any case it had to be done. For fear of the seven devils, Evie's mind was no longer going to be left as it now was, swept and garnished.

As it happened, I was spared the trouble, though not the subsequent responsibility, of putting Miss Levey off for the following Wednesday evening. On the morning of that very day, as I took Judy a number of drafts, he said, in Miss Levey's hearing, "Are you doing anything tonight?"

"Tonight? I'm afraid I am," I replied, though solely for Miss Levey's benefit. "Tomorrow I'm not."

"Tomorrow won't do. You're a dashed difficult man to get, Jeffries!"

"You should have given me a little notice," I said, though foreseeing already that Pepper would eat Miss Levey's supper that night.

"Well, we'll talk about it presently; if you can possibly put your engagement off, do. . . Now, Miss Levey—"

He began to give instructions to Miss Levey.

Later in the morning Miss Levey sought me.

"Oh, Mr. Jeffries," she began, very *empressée*, "I think we won't come tonight. Mr. Pepper—"

"It is rather awkward," I admitted. "I'm awfully sorry—"

"Please don't apologise. It really doesn't matter. I can come up any evening, you know."

"Well, in that case—"

"We'll fix another evening. I know you and Mr. Pepper have private affairs."

"Yes," I thought, not very graciously, "and to be in at 'em's the only thing you want more than to pry into my domestic ones." But aloud I said, "It's awfully good of you—do tell Mr. Aschael how sorry I am."

So it was Judy Pepper, and not Miriam Levey and Aschael, who dined at Verandah Cottage that night.

Were it for no other reason than to let you know a little of these Schmerveloff neighbours of mine I should have to tell you of Judy's visit that evening. This sounds a little portentous, as if my tale were about to take a sensational turn, with bombs and secret agents in it. Be calm, it is not; I only mention these Schmerveloffs as standing, in a way, for certain forces of which Pepper and I intended to make use. A very few words will explain what I mean.

We are not social theorists, Pepper and I; we have to handle social problems practically, as they come; and so in the wider humanitarian sense we may be all wrong. But even then this Schmerveloff school of thought had its importance for us. It was very useful to us, for instance, when the Aliens' Act was drafting; and with the outbreak of

Syndicalism, with all the bearings that has had on Trades Disputes, it became very important indeed. Perhaps, after all, the only hint I need give you as to the way in which we handled it is this: that, the rate of progress of this International Socialism being necessarily that of the slowest-moving and most backward partner in the alliance—Russia—we have used that fact either as a drag on Syndicalism or as an apparent encouragement of it, as the needs of the moment dictated. And when I say "apparent encouragement," I mean that we have winked at all this translation from the Russian pessimists that has harnessed art to purposes of social propaganda. That, since racial development is of far greater lasting weight than economic theory, has seemed to us the readiest way of letting folk see that Russia's problems are not necessarily ours; and if we can only keep Syndicalism in check, they may Russianise our literature completely for all Pepper and I care.

So we talked of Russia that night. Evie, as soon as she had seen Pepper instead of Miss Levey, had worked herself into a flurry in changing preparations at the last moment, and had had to run out for candles for our guest's candlesticks. But when dinner was at last served, half-an-hour late, nowhere could have been found a prettier waitress than we had—Evie herself. Indeed, she seemed to prefer waiting to dining. As long as she was doing things she felt herself on safe ground; it was the folding hands afterwards to talk to our terribly engaging visitor that she dreaded. She strove to attain by little formalisms what he achieved by the mere ease of nature, and, as she stuck tenaciously to it, I admired what was neither more nor less than a kind of courage in her. We finished dinner, and ascended to the drawing-room, I carrying those cumbersome candlesticks.

Pepper worked really hard that night to put Evie at her ease, but alas! through no fault of anybody's, but by the sheer decreeing of the stars, his labours were not a success. The first accident he had was when he asked her how she found her neighbours, compelling her to say that she didn't find them at all—didn't know them. And when he said, "Ah, Russians are like that," and related an anecdote, she perturbed me a little by asking him whether he had been in Russia—for I did not know that the extraordinary man had, and fancied the question not very kindly put. But Pepper surprised me by saying "Oh yes," and went on to tell more stories. . .

With these stories he was safe for a time, but presently he again had bad luck. He was speaking, as if he had come for no other purpose than to tell us travellers' tales, of the difficulty of the Russian language, which I gathered to be great; and suddenly he said, "But it's an exceedingly valuable asset from a commercial point of view. Should you have a boy to put into business, Mrs. Jeffries, let him learn Russian."

It was, of course, hyper-sensitive of Evie, but not unnatural in the circumstances. She coloured deeply; she rose; she said good-night; and even then Pepper was not at the end of his troubles, for, advancing punctiliously to open the bedroom door for her, that insecure old door, that always opened at a touch, flew back, displaying the unmade bed on which Evie had lain that afternoon, and the general disorder of the interior. Pepper was already in the midst of a deep bow, but he must have seen. . . After that I got him whisky; we settled down to our talk, and, ordinary speech being plainly audible from the bedroom, he dropped his voice to match my own tones—and was, I dare say, heartily glad when the evening was over.

This mention of our cramped quarters reminds me that I may as well get those inconveniences of which I told you over at once. To save time, I will tell you both what they were then, and what they afterwards became.

I had begun well-nigh to hate children. The schools, you see, had not yet reopened, and urchins played under our windows till half-past nine or ten o'clock at night. I frequently had work in the evenings that demanded close concentration, and it mostly happened that, when I sat down to it, as if by appointment the noise began. I do not know which howl or thump or bump was the most hideous. Iron hoops, driven with a hooked iron rod, were bad, but the shouts and whoops and calls, all in a blood-curdling Cockney accent, were worse; for while by great resolution you can nerve yourself to endure an iron hoop, you never know which yell or shout a child is going to emit next. These had all the horror of unexpectedness. I used to make mental bets on it, and I was always wrong. . . And then sometimes there would come an endless racket that resembled nothing so much as a fire-engine in full career, which, on descending, I should discover to come from a diminutive cart at the end of a string, pulled by a toddler of four.

Sometimes these noises drove me half frantic. I carried my papers from the dining-room to the drawing-room—thence to the bedroom—I even tried the kitchen; and this, mark you, was important work, work that has since, I may say without boasting, become of national value. I spoke to policemen—I even used the power of beauty, and got Evie to speak to policemen—but only to be told that they were as helpless as I: "Children is eddicated now, and not as afraid of bobbies as they used to be." And on a fatal evening I was so unthinking as to distribute a number of pennies in order to buy an hour's peace for a calculation that seriously involved the interests of three shipping lines. That settled it. Thenceforward I was never without children. One Sunday afternoon I forgot myself and boxed the ears of the biggest of them. That brought round a parent—not a father, but a mother. . . Ugh!—

And the house itself was far too small. Billy Izzard's sketches on our walls shook to my tread, and passing vans made the very foundations tremble. In order to get even our small belongings into the place Evie had to put boxes inside boxes, and boxes inside these again, so that in the finding of a garment she had not worn for some time the whole tiny bedroom floor was choked with boxes. Save for the little recess in the kitchen, the triangular cupboard under the stairs was the only storage accommodation we had. With the greatest care, Evie could not always avoid hanging an old skirt over my best hopsack (West's, Bond Street), or mislaying some article of which I had need in the very moment of bolting for my bus. And worst of all was that screen on the verandah that gave us nothing to look at but a short slope of parched green. Verandah Cottage! By Jove, yes! . . .

One other thing I will mention, though this did not come till the winter. The neighbouring house, which hitherto had been a tomb, became alive. I never knew the reason for this sudden awakening, nor whether Schmerveloff had suddenly found himself reduced to taking in lodgers, or whether he was merely holding out a helping hand to co-revolutionaries in the hour of their need; but I do know that presently he began to have a succession of extraordinary visitors. Hairy, uncouth-looking men, with soft hats, came for a week or a month, and brought their women, fat, spare, astrakhan-capped or bare-headed. They wore smocks and embroidered *portières*, and worked at peasant industries. One of them had a child, the sweetest of little girls—but oh, her sweetness vanished from me when she began to play at all hours in the garden, shouting, crowing, and impossible to turn away! I went so far as to wait on Schmerveloff himself about this dreadful child, and was told that, inconvenient as these things might be to me, the question was not a private one at all. It was a Social Question. Society oppressed them, they oppressed me; it was Society that was wrong. . . I told our fellows this afterwards, when the Aliens' Act was drafting; Robson was immensely amused. "What did you say?" he asked. . . Of course there was nothing to say. . .

And then, about Christmas, the Social Question became acute indeed. For the development of the peasant industries the most Asiatic barber-robber of the lot set up a furnace, a lathe and an anvil. . .

No wooden walls (save Nelson's) could have kept that racket out. . .

Had the sum of the world's beautiful things been added to, I could have grinned and borne it, but it was beaten copper-work the Asiatic made.

And I could do nothing.

I pass on.

Weeks before this invasion of beards and embroidered casement-cloth, I earnestly hoped that my firstborn, when I should have one, would never remember that little house with the glass-panelled door and the verandah. But the prospect of our "domestic event," as Miss Levey called it, hardly weighed on me yet. I gave little heed to Louie Causton's prophecy, that I might sooner or later find myself driven to take the desperate course of telling Evie what, so far, only Louie and myself knew; and I did not see, as Louie seemed to see, where the peril lay. If it was only a question of keeping Evie busy and amused for a little while longer, I thought I should be able to manage that. Only later did I see myself as a man who pours water constantly into a vessel and tells himself that because the level remains the same there is no leak. I still intended to stand between Evie and Life. In effect, if necessary, I would live much of her life for her. And now let me, before I leave this part of my tale, tell you briefly what that life was at its loveliest.

V

Had there ever been any shadow of a division between Evie and myself, which there had not, it must have vanished now. I did not attempt to conceal from myself that her gifts did not extend in all directions equally. Socially expert in Pepper's sense, for example, she could hardly yet be expected to be, and I should have been unreasonable to have reproached her for not grasping the intricate problems that, if the truth must be told, frequently filled Pepper and myself with perplexity. But these things are independent of deep humanity, and by as much as she fell short in them she was richly dowered in other ways. It was still the love of a woman I wanted, not the semblance of a masculine friendship; and I had it, and was glad at the thought of my rich possession. Often, for pure emotion, I caught her in my arms when I saw her, rejoicing yet timorous before that which was presently to come to pass; and whether it was a pallor that sometimes crossed her face, or a sudden glow as of some warm and Venetian underpainting or else a smiling, happy lassitude infinitely moving in its appeal, all spoke of the pledge that had been given and taken between us.

Quite past telling was the peace this pledge brought to me. I was, after all, to begin anew. Despite Life's mauling of my hapless self, here was a tiny white leaf preparing for the writing of a record that should supersede and obliterate my own. Deeper things than men know were seeing to that ushering, and by nothing less miraculous than a birth was I going to be delivered from the body of that haggard death. Often, as I seemed to be busily writing at our small folding table, I quite lost myself in the contemplation of this coming manumission; and day by day, looking out over Waterloo Place and the Mall, I conjured up her image—resting while Aunt Angela (who now came up from Woburn Place almost daily) dusted or swept or washed up, taking her easy walks on the Heath, sewing (though not now for herself), or doing such light work as would not tire her. Fortunately, the Social Question next door had reached the crisis of over-production in the beaten-copper market; a glut had supervened; and the making of the wooden bowls and carved porridge-sticks that are designed for oppressed serfs and sold at a high price to the amateurs of the Difficult Life, caused less disturbance to our panels and pictures. The whooping child too had gone.

Aunt Angela had bought Evie a deep wicker basket lined with pale blue, and with the greatest circumspection I delayed to fill this basket too quickly. We talked for a week before making a purchase, and, in one case, for quite three weeks. This was when I bought, at a shop near Great Turnstile, what Evie called a "jangle"—a beautiful Jacobean coral mounted in silver, with many silver bells and a faint piping whistle at one end. Both as I entered the shop and left it again a grey nightmare tried to fasten itself upon me, of a woman who had forgotten where she lived, walking the Fields round the corner, alone at night; but I shook the horror off. . . Even down to such details did I keep Evie from fancies—for she had fancies, the ousting of which was a matter for diversion rather than argument. One of these fancies was that she now wanted to see Miriam Levey. Another was that she did not want, just then at any rate, to see Louie Causton.

For as it chanced, Louie came the nearest (though with a nearness sad enough) to a married woman of anybody she happened at present to know; this, of course, largely as a result of my own exclusive attitude. Aunt Angela, by virtue of George and her other experiences, knew as much as ten married women, and that was frequently precisely the difficulty. Certain charwomen, I gathered, inured to immoderate families, gave Evie the benefit of their advice now and then, but that was about all. And it was one evening as I cast about for an opening to introduce Louie's name that Evie herself said once more that she would like to see Miss Levey.

"Certainly," I said, with a readiness that was only the result of seeing no way out of it this time. "As long as she won't tire you."

"I won't let her do that," Evie promised.

"All right," I said. . . "And by the way"—I put this as if it had just occurred to me—"should you care to have Louie Causton up if Billy knows where to find her?"

"Yes, I should some time—but not just now, dear. You'll tell Miriam, then?"

"Yes."

I had promised it before I remembered something that might have made me less ready to promise it. It was now the beginning of October. We had to take our holidays in rotation at the F.B.C.; for a fortnight I had been working late in order that Whitlock might take his; and next on the list in our department was Miss Levey. Grumbling that it was almost too late to take a holiday at all, she was going away for a week-end only. Instantly, I saw what that meant. . .

The next day I capitulated to her as gracefully as I could.

"You'll be able to have a really satisfactory visit now, a whole day," I said. "It would only have been a couple of hours before."

"I'll take *such* good care of her!" she purred.

"I am sure you will," I said conciliatingly. . .

Three days later Miss Levey was up at Verandah Cottage. She was up there the next day also. Although she had always gone by the time I returned at night, she was up several times after that.

Well, it couldn't be helped. . . and I was going to tell you, not about Miriam Levey, but about my happiness and Evie's.

Today, in my house in Iddesleigh Gate, there are many things thrust into dark corners that will ever occupy odd corners of my heart. They are the pieces of furniture from that poky old place in the Vale of Health. The people of my household tell me they are shabby, but as I never see them divorced from a hundred gentle associations, their shabbiness matters nothing to me. In the children's day-nursery there is the old shop-damaged couch from the Tottenham Court Road cellar. Its pegamoid is frayed and its springs broken, but Evie lay on it before those destructive little hands came into being. She lay on it with her legs wrapped in an old, faded, mignonette-coloured Paisley shawl—for presently the days were shortening, we had started fires, and Verandah Cottage was a Cave of the Winds for draughts; and my housekeeper had a bad five minutes only the other day when that shawl nearly went out of the house with the bottles and crates and old rags. The bookshelves Evie used to dust and polish still serve me; and quite a number of smaller things, including that first wicker basket into which the "jangle" was put (Evie keeps that) carry my mind back in a twinkling to that early time.

Evie had her little jokes about our unborn mite. Still further to repair the slight on Hampton Court of our Greenwich honeymoon, the infant at one time was to be called "Hampton," but as she had ten different names for it each week, a name more or less didn't matter. Its eyes were to be so-and-so—the colour also varied day by day. If a boy, it was to be of my own bone and stature; if a girl, less. I used to joke with her when, seeing her brooding and gently smiling, I pretended to discover these and a hundred other patterns and specifications in her eyes; but, however lovely these imaginings were, they were no lovelier than herself. Though the days now seemed less long, the little *élans* with which she ran to me when she heard my step at night were a passionate rendering of herself far greater than before; and I will end this part of my tale with the first time, the very first, I heard her sing.

She had gone into the bedroom that night, and I had heard her moving about; and then there had stolen out low contralto notes that might have belonged to somebody else, so new were they to me... She was happy. She was so happy that she was learning to sing. I stood listening, with tears gathering in my eyes and suddenly rolling down my cheeks...

She was happy...

She did not know why, a few moments later, with the face of one who hears joyful news, I pushed at the bedroom door and took her, half ready for bed as she was, into my arms.

Oh, to hear her, of her own accord, sing—and to know that soon her song would not more gently rock those feeble limbs and close those unknowing eyes than it now brought rest to my own weary frame and sleep to my own heavy eyes, weary with watching for the day that at last, at last was coming!

OLIVER ONIONS

PART III

WELL WALK

I

As far as my worldly position is concerned, two leaps have sufficed to place me where I stand today—the first from the Vale of Health to the Well Walk, not a quarter of a mile away, and the second from Well Walk to Iddesleigh Gate. I am omitting such interludes as furnished rooms for short periods and odd times in which I have packed Evie off with the children to the seaside. We were in the Vale of Health for exactly a year, and in Well Walk for three. I took the Iddesleigh Gate House, wonderful ceilings and Amaranth Room and all, from the late Baron Stillhausen.

But this is a very summary statement of what my real advance has been. Those who have called me a lucky man—which on the whole I also am persuaded I am—know nothing of my hidden labour. Of this, since it is just beginning to show in the contemporary history of my country, I cannot say very much; and so, picking out a fact here and an incident there, I shall take leave for the rest of my tale to keep as closely as may be to my increasingly intricate personal story.

The incident with which I will resume—the incident which resulted in Louie Causton's appointment to the post still held by Miss Levey—came about as follows.

In taking the Well Walk house—(here I am skipping six months; my infant son was born; I still had seven or eight weeks to run with the F.B.C., but already our plans were perfected, and the new Consolidation had already secured its premises in Pall Mall)—in taking the Well Walk house I had made a woeful miscalculation of how far the Verandah Cottage furniture would go. Indeed I had so over-estimated its quantity that our new abode was almost as bare as a barracks, and, occupied as I was with important business, I had almost got used to its barrenness. But as Evie had to live in the place, I had found that I really must raise a sum of money for carpets, curtains, and other things indispensable to married folk who find themselves three; and I had decided that part of the one hundred pounds I got as an advance from Pepper was going to be spent on a dining-room table that I had not always to remember I must not sit down on. Well, on a Saturday afternoon in October this table came. I saw it into the dining-room, and then, feeling the need of air, I put on my hat and coat and took a walk as far as the Whitestone Pond. There I met Billy Izzard, in the dickens of a temper.

"Well, how goes it, Billy?" I asked cheerfully, seeing that he was put out. Billy's grumblings always have the effect of cheering me up.

He looked up, scowled, and then resumed his gazing across the Pond. Then he watched the passage of a horse and cart through the water, looked up again, and broke out.

"It goes rottenly—that's how it goes!" he growled. "Do you remember coming into my place one evening when I had a girl sitting for me—tallish girl, with a perfectly exquisite figure—Louie Causton her name was?"

I said that I did remember it.

"Well, she's the trouble. I want her—must have her—and I can't get her. She says she isn't sitting any more; her doctor's forbidden it. Her doctor! . . . The jade's as sound as a bell; she never had a doctor in her life, I'll swear; she just won't sit, doesn't want to. She wheedled that sketch out of me too, the one I was doing that day—walked off with it under her arm—stole it, practically—and now I can't get her for love or money."

This interested me. It interested me so much that to conceal my interest, I made a joke. "Oh? Tried both?" I said; but Billy went on.

"Perhaps she'll change her mind when she finds she's nothing to live on. She'll sit in costume, it appears; some cock and bull story about chills; and she said, Couldn't I paint her in some old supers' duds that she can hire at the Models' Club for sixpence a day?—me painting theatrical wardrobes à la Coleman, Roma? . . . And her crochet!"

"What about her crochet?"

"Her crochet? Why, when I told her she wouldn't make fifteen shillings a week as Marguerite with the jewel-casket—she's not pretty—I told her so—she said she could fall back on her crochet! A goddess, I tell you. . . and she pitches me a tale about a doctor that she can't help laughing at herself!"

He ran on, to Louie's detriment from his special point of view, but already I was wondering what her own point of view might be.

That I had not heard from Louie since that night of the Berkeley dinner had been, as far as it went, reassuring. Had she needed me, or I her, whichever in the tangled circumstances it might be, I should have heard from her; and I had had no reason for seeking her out. When Evie had told me that Louie now had charge of Kitty Windus she had told me nothing that I had not already known; and as Evie had had this from Miriam Levey, I find I must break off for a moment to speak of my relation with that lady.

Since she had got her fat, high-heeled foot inside my door, Miss Levey's devotion to Evie had been as unremitting as if, lacking her attentions, my little son would never have got himself born at all. Not a week had passed but she had dropped in once or twice, mostly alone, but not infrequently with the ringleted Aschael. It annoyed me that Evie should like her as much as apparently she did, and my annoyance was the greater that I could give no reason for it. One night I had given way rather petulantly to this annoyance. It had been just before we had left Verandah Cottage. Billy Izzard had come in and had made some remark about our Arab horsemen, and, more that I might relish its artistic vulgarity than for any other reason, I had taken one of these objects down from the mantelpiece. I had not known that I had held the thing in a rather vindictive grip until suddenly the plaster had broken in my hand. My other hand had made an instinctive movement by no means prompted by presence of mind. I had saved the body of the ornament from total smash, but the heads both of tamer and steed were in fragments. I had been on the point of throwing the ridiculous thing away, but had changed my mind, and put it back on the mantelpiece. Later I had expressed bland sorrow to Miss Levey, and had assured her that I was going to have it mended; but I had not done so during the remainder of our stay at Verandah Cottage. I did not know what had become either of it or of its companion statue.

During the last anxious days before the birth of our child, Miss Levey had triumphed over me completely. There had been no withstanding her. She had bidden me fetch hot-water bottles, had informed me when it was time for Evie to go to bed, and, conspiring with Aunt Angela, had, in a word, taken things out of my hands entirely. Once or twice she had overdone this even in Evie's eyes, but I had been dull enough not to see at first that her ascendancy over Evie was not direct, but mediate. Only lately had I discovered that Evie's real interest was, not in Miriam Levey, but in Kitty Windus.

For those talks I had dreaded yet had been powerless to prevent had already borne fruit. I don't think it was so much that Evie experienced again those compassions and magnanimities that had given her that gentle heartache in the tea-gardens on that Bank Holiday evening, as that she remembered the wish into which they had solidified—the wish to have Kitty completely off her mind. Miss Levey, I was pretty sure, had seen to it that this wish should become firmly fixed. She had evidently assumed, for example, that I should be adverse to a meeting between

Kitty and Evie. "Your husband wouldn't like it," I could imagine her as having said; "quite naturally, my dear; one can't blame him; and so I suppose that ends it." And to the last words I could imagine her as having given the meaning, "We do seem to be dependent on the will of this dull opinionative sex for some reason or other—why I can't make out." Miss Levey, you see, was an economically emancipated woman.

So, though not a word had been said, Kitty had come, by reason of I knew not what sympathy Miriam Levey had worked up on her behalf, to be between Evie and myself. That poor Kitty deserved all the sympathy we could give her I had never a doubt, but you see the two things that stood in the way—the lesser thing that Miss Levey assumed I "should not like," and that other huge and fatal thing that was the truth. To the multitudinous harassings of my business these two things made a dense background of private harassings. . . But I did not intend that another long and dogged duel should begin between Miriam Levey and myself. She was not going to be taken over by Pepper, Jeffries and the Consolidation. If this enterprise did anything at all it would do something very big indeed; soon I should be placed high above the wretched little Jewess's power to hurt; and after all, there is no man who attains to great power but leaves in his train a score of these carpers, wishful yet impotent to harm.

But the offering of the new post to Louie Causton was another matter. I hesitated and wavered. Plainly, I doubted whether I had the right to find Louie a job. In the close-packed fulness of her life, struggles and anxieties and all, her happiness consisted; and though she might need the money, as matters stood she had a peace that money could not give, and might take away. Let her, I thought at first, toil and keep her heaven.

But that, I thought presently, might be all very high and fine, but practically not very much to the point. Billy had been perfectly right when he had said that by costume-sitting and crochet she would hardly make fifteen shillings a week. I knew of old what heaven in those circumstances meant, and I had had no boy to look after, and no woman intermittently infirm. One can have too much even of heaven on those terms. . .

And yet it would be impossible to attach her to my own office. What I had seen in those grey eyes on the night of the Berkeley dinner would not brook daily meetings, dictation of letters, and the other duties I had already cast Whitlock for. Myself left out of the question, she, I was quite sure, would never accept it. Turn her over to Pepper, then? That would hardly be fair to Pepper, who might wish to choose for himself. . .

And one other thing, of which I will speak presently, had already caused my cheeks to burn.

Well, I should have to see what I could do.

It did not surprise me much that when I reached Well Walk again, Miss Levey was there. That echoing, half-furnished house of ours, I ought to say, was on the south side of the Walk, and my own study was on the ground floor at the back, with Evie's drawing-room immediately overhead. I heard this drawing-room door open as I entered, and it was on the bare half-landing, against the red and blue window, with cut-glass stars round its border, that I saw Miss Levey's flamingo-coloured costume with the black satin buttons.

"Oh, here he is," Evie was saying; "he'll take you on to your bus. Good-bye, Miriam, dear—remember me to Aschael—"

"Good-bye, darling—don't forget, will you?"

"Good-bye."

I remember that it was as I took Miss Levey to her bus that afternoon that she asked me to call her by her Christian name. Instantly I did so—and forgot her request again with a promptitude even greater. To tell the truth, that "Remember me to Aschael" of Evie's stuck a little in my throat. A little more ceremony, it seemed to me, would have fitted the relation better, and I differed from Miss Levey if she thought that in asking me to call her "Miriam," she, and not I, was conferring the favour. Therefore as I saw her off I again addressed her as "Miss Levey" and let her take it as an inadvertence or not as she list. Then, with that "Remember me to Aschael" again uppermost in my mind, I returned to Evie.

In hoping to see her alone, however, I was again disappointed. This time Aunt Angela was there. She was standing by the new dining-table, and apparently deploring my purchase.

"*What* a pity!" she was saying. "Just when I'd arranged for you to have that one of mine! I meant it as a surprise—oh, why didn't I tell you sooner!"

I have referred, I hope not unkindly, to a certain laxity in this dear and harmless spinster's hold on life. Since the birth of our child this laxity had become intensified, if such a word can be used of laxity, and very rarely had she come up to see us empty-handed. From some mysterious hoard of belongings that seemed ever on the point of exhaustion and yet ever stood the strain of another gift, she had brought, now a tiny pair of knitted woollen socks, now a shawl, now a bit of silver, and even the mite's cradle was that in which Evie herself had been rocked. She found a pleasure quite paradisal in these continual givings. I think they were her spiritual boasts of how little she required for herself.

"*What* a pity!" she purred again. "But I dare say they'd take it back—"

"Hallo!" I said, shaking hands. "Take what back? What's that you're saying?"

"This table. I'm sure they'd let you off your bargain for ten shillings or so. The money would be so much more useful."

I laughed. "Oh, money's no object," I said.

This, of course, was mere mischief. The truth was that Angela Soames, like Evie, had begun to hold my ambition a good deal in dread. It had been good fun to think about in the early stages; they had enjoyed that part as much as anybody; but to take the plunge as I was taking it was—in Miss Angela's case I might almost say "impious"; certainly it was a storming of destiny that was bound to bring a crop of consequences they were sure I had not sufficiently weighed. So it had become my habit to hold their timidity over them as a joke, talking sometimes in sums that might have staggered even the Consolidation. "Oh, money's no object!" I said, laughing.

"Well!" Aunt Angela retorted, "even you can't afford to throw it away till you've got it. So, Evie, I thought my round table in place of this one—send this back—and the tea-urn I promised you in the middle of the sideboard, with Mr. Pepper's candlesticks on each side of it—just here—and you could buy a quite nice pair of curtains with the pound Jeff turns up his nose at."

I interrupted. "Your tea-urn? Oh, come, come! We're not going to accept that!"

But she only dropped her eyes. "My wants are few," she said, "and I've more than enough for them. You young people come first. How do you know I haven't had a legacy? . . . And of course I shall have the table repolished, Evie, and if Jeff *will* be stupid, you can have it in the drawing-room, in that corner by the bureau—"

I was about to laugh again at the artless mixture in her of expansive unworldliness and quite astute machination when suddenly I thought better of it, and turned away. Aunt Angela was taking off her hat and giving coquettish touches to her tall, snowy hair. As that meant that she proposed to spend the evening with us, I had to postpone what I wished to say to Evie until she should have departed.

II

This was no more than that I thought the Christian name business was being a little overdone; but the more I thought of it, the less easy did it become to put. Perhaps you see my difficulty. It was, in a word, this: that a man on whom circumstances have pressed with such unique urgency that he has had, or conceived himself to have, no choice but to effect the removal of a fellow-being from the world, cannot take even so small a matter as this precisely as another man can. The quick of his soul is perpetually exposed. There are no trifles in his world. What is another man's slight annoyance is to him the menace of an assassination; another's nothings are his doom. A single unconscious touch and the toucher starts back with an amazed "What's this?"

Yet I have said that it was not remorse that bred this sensitiveness in me, and I hasten to maintain that. Remorse is a damage, in which a man is penally mulcted; but this of mine was no more than a price, fairly and squarely agreed upon, which I was prepared to pay. It was a heavy one; you may take my word for it that there is no more costly purchase in the whole market of human happenings than a righteous murder; but it still remained a price, in the fixing of which I had concurred. More than this: men have been known, from remorse, to give themselves up; but at the thought of such a surrender I grew hot and vehement. I appreciated the point of view of the very revolutionaries against whom my life's work has been directed. What! Suffer an outside judgment when I was acquitted in my own! . . . I laughed, and in my laughter found courage. Not I! . . .

And a man is not in the grip of remorse who, asked whether he would do his deed again, can reply with a deep "By heaven—yes!"

Nevertheless, I was perilously open. I alone among men could not rebuff the freedom of a Christian name without bringing my soul into the transaction; nay, I could not even buy a dining-table without having (as I had just had) to check an utterance and to turn away. For at Aunt Angela's words, "How do you know I haven't had a legacy?" I had become vigilant again. She had had no legacy; I knew that; but she *had* been twice or thrice to Guildford, and, if she wished to indulge herself in the luxury of giving, would be likely to make the most rather than the least of whatever mementoes of the late Mrs. Merridew she might have chanced to come by. You see how, on an afternoon taken at random, two nothings had made still denser by a fraction that background of which I was every moment conscious. I was beginning to realise that I was the man who was denied the luxury of carelessness. I might not jest or laugh or move a finger without first looking around the corner. I went hampered among free men. I tell you it is a hard thing to live in a world that has no trifles. . .

Still, exposed or guarded, I had my life to live, and I was no longer disposed in the matter of this intimacy with Miss Levey to do nothing at all. Therefore, when I returned from seeing Aunt Angela away and found Evie still in the dining-room, I took my risk.

She ought to have been in bed; but instead she had drawn up a chair to an old bureau, and was quite unnecessarily fiddling with old papers and letters and nondescript objects put away in the nest of drawers. She looked up as I entered, and the vivacity with which she spoke seemed a little forced.

"Fancy, Jeff!" she exclaimed, her fingers in the leaves of some old twopenny notebook or other, "I can actually read my old shorthand yet! I should have thought I'd forgotten all about it, after all this time! I'll bet I could read as quickly as you!"

I stirred the dying fire. "Isn't it time you were in bed?" I said.

"Oh, just let me tidy this—I sha'n't be many minutes."

And while I picked up an evening paper she went on with her pottering about the bureau.

But the light sound of the moving paper began to get a little on my nerves. It does that sometimes. I suppose it's like some people fidgeting if there is a cat in the room. And presently I noticed that when she supposed me to be busily reading the rustling stopped. It was no good going on like this; the sooner I came to the point and said what I had to say, the better. I thought for a moment, and then put down my newspaper.

"Evie—" I said.

"Yes, dear?" she said brightly. . .

I put it with perfect gentleness. Suddenness and sharpness also are among the trifles of life I had had to forego. When I had finished, she did not seem surprised. She only nodded once or twice.

"I see," she said slowly. "Well, Miriam—I mean Miss Levey, if you wish it, dear—"

"No, darling; I don't know that I go as far as that. I was only speaking of these broadcast intimacies."

OLIVER ONIONS

"Miriam, then—Miriam said you would object—"

"Well, I never denied Miriam a certain acuteness."

But she shook her head. For a minute or two I had been sure that I was not the only one who had something to say. When she did go on, it was at first haltingly, and then with just such a little setting of her resolution as she had used when, years ago, a sweet and awkward flapper, she had complimented me on my spurious engagement to the lady whose name she now suddenly mentioned.

"I don't mean to object to—to what you've been saying, Jeff. I mean—I mean object to this about poor Kitty. I know," she quickened, as if to forestall a remark, "that we haven't said anything about it—you and I—for a long time—but"—once more the rush—"I've felt you've known what I've been thinking, Jeff—"

I gained a little time. "But I wasn't speaking of Kitty Windus, dear," I said. "It was something quite different."

Then, before her look of trouble and appeal, I ceased my pretence.

"Very well, dearest," I sighed. "But tell me one thing. If I hadn't said anything tonight, *you* wanted to say something."

"Yes," she mumbled in a low voice to the twopenny notebook.

"Is that what Miss Levey meant when she said 'Don't forget' an hour or two ago?"

"Yes."

"You hadn't to forget to—to bring something, whatever it is, up about Kitty?"

Her silence told me that that was so. Then, slowly:

"And why should she think I should object to that?" I asked.

Evie's manner changed with almost electrical suddenness. She thrust her hands into her lap, straightened her back, and spoke almost victoriously.

"*There!* I *knew*! I told her so!" she triumphed. "'Miriam,' I said, 'you're *quite* wrong in thinking that—that—'"

"In thinking there's something to be ashamed of in an old engagement you've changed your mind about?" I suggested gently.

"Yes!" she exulted. "I said to her, 'Jeff wouldn't in the *least* mind my going to see her if I wanted'—and you wouldn't, would you, Jeff?"

"No," I said quickly. I said it quickly lest I should not say it at all. Then I qualified. "No. . . One shrinks from pain, that's all, either enduring it or giving it."

"Giving Kitty pain?"

"Well, does Miss Levey think it would be pleasant to her—or is she merely willing to hurt her if she can hurt me too?"

"But—but—Miriam says she would really be awfully pleased—Kitty would—and I'm sure you're wrong, Jeff, about things like that lasting for years and years! They don't. I—" She checked herself.

But whether it was the check or what not that made the difference, all at once she started forward from the bureau and sank on her knees at my side. She herself put one of my hands about her waist, as if to compel it to a caress, and stroked her cheek against the other. The words she murmured were disjointed enough, but her tone was, oh, so eloquent. . .

"Dear, dear!" she besought me. "Miriam *was* wrong, wasn't she? Not that I care in the very least, only I've been, oh, so wretched, thinking there was something between us! I don't want to see her—Miriam— nor Kitty—very much—but it was so lonely—till Jack came—and there isn't anything now, is there, Jeff? I know there has been—but it's gone now, hasn't it? . . . Great strong hand!" She moistened it with her breathing. . . "But it *is* all right now, isn't it, Jeff?"

I did not know why, all in a moment, I found myself remembering that curious prophecy of Louie Causton's: "I think you'll find that sooner or later you've got to tell her." Perhaps it was that in that moment I had my first glimpse of what Louie had really meant. Already it was useless to say there had been no slight shadow between us; Evie, who knew few things, at least knew that; but I had not dared to acknowledge it for fear of worse. . . Yes, I began to see; and with my seeing I again grew hot and rebellious.

Why, since the act I had committed had had at least as much of good as of evil in it, should I be hounded thus? Why should trifles accrete to an ancient and hideous memory until it became a corporeal, living, malignant thing? Why should that commonest of experiences, an old rescinded engagement, not, in my case also, be what Evie thought it was—a wound made whole again, or at any rate so hardened over that it could be touched without provoking a sharp scream of pain? It was intolerable. . .

Oh, never, if you can help it, live in a world without trifles!

Evie, at my knee, continued to supplicate. "Oh, darling, I've so, *so* wanted it to be like it was at first! Do you remember—in Kensington Gardens, sweetheart?"

And she turned up those loveliest eyes I ever looked into. . .

IT HAD BEEN IN KENSINGTON Gardens, early on a September evening, that I had asked her to marry me. Our chairs had been so drawn back into the clump of laurels that the man with the tickets had not noticed us, and we ourselves had seen little but a distant corner of the Palace, and, forty yards away across the grass, a dead ash gilded by the setting sun. At the F.B.C. Pepper had just begun to single out his new Jun. Ex. Con. for special jobs, and as a matter of fact I had had a small rise of salary that very week. Little enough it had been; certainly not enough to warrant me in exchanging our footing—one of increasingly frequent calls at Woburn Place and goodness knows how much lingering in likely streets on the chance of a sight of her—for a more explicit relation; but—well, as I say, I had thrust all else recklessly aside, and that evening had asked her to marry me.

There are some things that one must needs exaggerate if one is to speak of them at all; so if I say that at first it had seemed to her that my proposal was merely that two bruised spirits should thenceforward make the best of things together, I must leave you to discount that. I don't think she had known clearly what she had felt. The hand I had taken had trembled a little, and in the great dark eyes that had looked steadfastly away to the dead ash I had fancied I had discerned the beginnings of a refusal—a refusal out of mere customariness and a settled acceptance of our former relation. I had fancied that—

But even to the trembler a tremble may speak truer than words, and she had trembled and become conscious of it. For the first time it had occurred to her, sweet soul, that we had been all unconsciously passing from friendship to love, and were now making the discovery together. She had not known that I had never had anything but love from which to pass; and another access of trembling had taken her. . .

"The last evening you and I had a walk together," she had whispered at last, her eyes still gravely on the pale ash, "we—we didn't think of—this."

(Did I mention that during all the time I had known her we had only spent one other evening out of doors alone together? It had been more than four years before, and we had heard a nightingale sing on Wimbledon Common.)

I had not answered. To allow the memory of that other evening to repossess her had seemed the best answer to make. For though we pack our hearts daily with the stuff of life, only time shows us which is the tinsel we have coveted, and which the lump we have not known to be gold. More than four years had passed; presently those four years would have opened her eyes to differences too; and so I had waited. . .

And, if not yet discovered, at any rate sudden and troubling new questions had crowded into her eyes as I had watched. Another silence of many minutes, then:

"We've been such friends up to now," she had faltered, as much to the darkening evening as to myself.

"Need that mean 'No,' Evie?" . . .

"I don't know—it's so—strange—I never—"

I had drawn a little nearer.

"Never? Never once? You never once thought that perhaps—?"

Then once more had come the memories of that other evening, with the unhappiness of another's bringing, and the comfort of my own. Night had begun to creep under the trees, but the shadows but made zenith the purer. On such evenings lovers vie with one another in looking for the first star, but we were not lovers yet, and could see nothing save the ash, now become grey, and away to the north the faint yellow haze of the Bayswater Road. Evie's own figure had become dim until little of it had showed but the handkerchief in her lap, the narrow white stripe of her black and white blouse where her little black jacket parted, and, as at last she had turned, the motion of her eyes.

"You don't want an answer now, Jeff," she had said quickly, immediately dropping the eyes again.

But I had wanted my answer there and then.

"Now," I had replied as quickly as she, with I know not what grimness and resolution mingled with my tenderness.

"Not now, Jeff—I'm fonder of you than of anybody—you know that—but—but—"

But if her "buts" had included the vanished Kitty Windus, Archie Merridew, or anything else from that four-year-old dustheap, I had allowed them to avail her little. Over my heart too had come that nightingale's song, heard by a still mere, and her hapless sobbing on my breast because Life was harsh, and my own desperate struggle not to clasp her there and then. Repression so powerful as that had been is not given twice to a man, at any rate not to such a man as I; nor had I thought that she, whose tremors were more eloquent than her speech, had desired it either. . . "Not now, Jeff—please—soon—" she had half sobbed, shrinking as it were from the wonder of her own enlightenment; and her handkerchief had fallen to the grass. . .

The next moment, in returning it to her, I had had her in my arms.

Those truer tidings than any words of hers could give expression to had come from the lips that had not even sought to avoid mine. Sought to avoid them? I call the first star that peeped through the laurels to witness the handful of dust that friendship of ours had become. Speech? Language? She used neither; to me in that moment she *was* both speech and language—vocal flesh, her very hair and eyes an utterance. You will not ask me an utterance of what; I take my chance of being understood in the light of what Woman is to you. Make her what you will: a riddle herself—or the answer to the deepest enigma of the soul; as much earth as a man's hard hands must needs be filled with—or as much spirit as he can bear until he himself is all spirit; a lovely casket—yet not too lovely for the scroll of the Freedom it contains. Have it your own way. I only know that if she spoke thus I heard as if my whole body had been one attuned and exquisite nerve. We had drawn a little deeper into the laurels. . . Again we kissed. . .

And in my heart there had been jealousy of no man, dead or living. That dead young man had awakened her from sleep, but I had made her mine with her eyes wide open. He had taken her by surprise, but me she had chosen. And as our lips had met once more, I had known that she loved even the pain I caused her in straining her in my arms.

"You never once—never once thought of it?" I had said huskily at last.

"Dear—dear! How *was* I to?"

"Kiss me—kiss me—"

And now, on her knees at my knee by our dying dining-room fire, she asked me if I remembered that evening in Kensington Gardens.

All at once I vowed that I wouldn't stand it—wouldn't stand the intervention of anything on earth, whether of my own making or another's, between us and that first joy. And again, as I held her, I thought of Louie's words. Louie was right—or at least half right. For the present the shadow had passed, but unless I did something now, it would return. Again we should drift apart, and Miss Levey would keep us so. If I did not partly explain, circumstances might do so entirely. Yes, Louie was so far right. If I was to keep the dearest thing on earth to me, I must make a half-truth seem to guarantee the false remainder, and tell Evie of that cruel Kitty Windus episode.

And so I come to my first, though not to my last, attempt to tell without telling, and, as they say, to make my omelette without breaking my eggs.

Her cheek was still against my hand; I looked mournfully down on her. With such a goal it didn't much matter where I began.

"What do you suppose, darling," I began, "Miss Levey's object is in all this?"

Evie's eyes moved to the mantelpiece. It was a bare entablature of black marble, with nothing on it but a small Swiss clock and one or two cabinet photographs—no Arab horsemen. Shyly she glanced from the mantelpiece corner, where the horsemen should have been, to me.

"Yes, she asked today whether you'd got it mended," she murmured.

"Do you really like her?"

"I was so lonely, Jeff," she pleaded.

"Poor child! . . . Evie—"

She looked quickly up at my change of tone.

"What?"

"I want to tell you what her object is. I don't find it easy."

"What do you mean, Jeff?" she asked, strangely abruptly.

"And I'm afraid you won't find it easy either."

She had dropped my hand. "Jeff, what do you mean?"

"I mean that she thinks she's found out—is finding out—something discreditable about me."

At first I did not understand the change, almost to horror, that came into Evie's eyes. Only after a moment almost of fear of what I saw there did I fathom her thought. I don't know how men speak who have an unfaithfulness to confess to their wives, but it flashed on me that Evie actually thought it might be that—so can pure innocence and worldly experience be pierced by the same fear.

"Jeff," she said faintly, her colour all gone, "don't you—haven't you—loved me?"

"Loved you?" I laughed for the irony of it. "Yes, dearest," I said quietly, "I've loved you. Never fear for that. That was the beginning of it all."

"The beginning?"

"Of what Miss Levey thinks. Dear, could you bear to think she's right, and that I've been a blackguard?"

So great was her suspense that the little sound she made was one almost of irritation. "Oh, Jeff, say what you've got to say—"

"It's why I spoke of causing pain to Kitty Windus—"

"Oh, you're cruel—!"

I moistened my lips. "Very well. . ."

Locked up in my private desk, written in Pitman's shorthand, there lies a full statement of that curious affair of mine with Kitty Windus; but I am not going to quote from that statement here. So long as it is understood that that heartless thing had existed side by side with a love for Evie that had never for a moment wavered, that is all that matters. I had now no longer a thought for the undesirableness, the danger even, of a meeting between Evie and Kitty; risky though that would be, I now saw nothing save that we were reunited, and that we could only remain so by passing on to her a portion of my shame. If you don't see this you are lucky. Your life has trifles in it. You can buy dining-tables, and use or reject the familiarity of Christian names. You have not had to carry upon your shoulders a weight greater than a man can support, nor to choose which portion you are to leave on the road behind you unless your back is to break. You have not known the conclusion to which—but you shall hear the conclusion to which I have been driven all in good time.

In the meantime, sparing myself in her eyes no more than I am sparing myself in yours now, I told her how little she had ever had to fear from Kitty Windus.

The hands of the tiny Swiss clock on the mantelpiece pointed to half-past ten by the time I had finished. I gazed at the clock dully, thinking for a moment how little time my recital had occupied. Then I remembered that the hands had pointed to half-past ten before I had begun. . . Mechanically I took the clock down and wound it up. To wind up a clock was something to do until Evie should speak.

She had not once interrupted me. At one point of my story she had merely got up from my knee and seated herself in a low rocking-chair, in which she now rocked softly. As I still sat with the clock in my hands I tried idly to remember at which point of my story she had got up; it might be an indication of her state of mind; but I forgot this again, and found myself examining the back of the clock almost with curiosity. I did not look at her. I put the clock back on the mantelpiece again and once more sat down, still without looking at her. Glancing presently at the clock again I saw that its hands pointed to five and twenty minutes to eleven. I had wound it up, but had forgotten to set it right. That again was something to do. I adjusted it by my watch, and again sat down.

Then she spoke, and my heart sank. There was nothing in her tone but wonderment—wonderment, not at the story I had told her, but that I should have found it worth telling at all.

After all that portentous preparation—only that!

Odd enough, of course—sad enough, if you liked—but—

"Well, but, Jeff," she said, puzzled, "what about it?"

"Don't you see?" I asked, in a lower voice.

"Of course I see—how do you mean, 'see'? And I think you were awfully stupid. She was *bound* to find out, and she did find out, and left you, poor dear. It was absurd from beginning to end. Really I shall begin to think myself clever and you a simpleton, if that's all you've been moping about."

As you see, I had not advanced matters by one single inch.

"It *is* all, isn't it, Jeff?" she asked anxiously, suddenly sitting forward in the rocking-chair. "I don't mean," she went on more anxiously still, "that the whole thing wasn't awfully queer—not quite nice, dear, to speak the truth—but—but"—again there returned that quick look of fear with which she had asked me whether I had not loved her—"but—there wasn't—anything—Jeff?"

I sank back in my chair.

"No, there wasn't—anything," I said wearily.

"Then, Jeff—" she cried gladly.

And the next moment she was at my knee again, overflowing with comfort and compassion.

"You poor boy—you poor darling boy!" she crooned, so melted by my contrition that my offence went uncondemned. "Poor love! . . . And," she looked adorably up, "how *could* Evie reproach you, Jeff, when it was all for her? Darling!" she broke out, "*you* ought to reproach *me*, for thinking. . . But you were so fearfully solemn. . . I thought perhaps you hadn't loved Evie. . . *Has* always loved Evie, hasn't he? And *will* always love her, yes? Great strong hand!"

And as she murmured thus, again I thought of Louie. It was with something like awe that I did so. "I think you'll find that sooner or later you've got to tell her." How did she know that? Did she know it? Had she foreseen how half-attempts would end, and known them beforehand to be wasted breath?

Then there came upon me the great need to see Louie again. I must see her, and quickly. With Evie still unenlightened, the actual perils of a meeting between herself and Kitty stood forward again, exactly as before. Evie herself might not now wish for such a meeting, but that would be on my account, and not that, if Kitty didn't mind, or positively wished it, she saw any reason against it. Why should she, if

Kitty didn't? . . . Yes, I must see Louie again, at once. Tomorrow was Sunday. I must see her on the Monday. I must write—telephone—do something—

"And tomorrow, Jeff," Evie was saying, with decision, "you really must have a walk. You're working yourself ill—you look worried to death. I can't come, of course, but I wish you'd go to Amersham or Chalfont or somewhere, just for a blow. Leave horrid business just for one day, and I'll have a nice supper ready for you when you come back. I shall be all right. . . Hush! Listen!"

From upstairs had come a low, reedy cry.

"That's Jackie—I must fly! Don't sit down here, dear—come now—"

And she was off.

I followed her; and as I stood looking down on the boy, who had gone to sleep again of himself, I remembered my former dream, that by the wonder of an innocent birth atonement was to have come. I sighed. Apparently it hadn't.

Well, I must see Louie on the Monday, that was all.

I did see her on the Monday. I saw her at the models' Club, to which place I telephoned early on the Monday morning. I had the luck to get on to her immediately. "Yes? . . . This is Miss Causton," came the diminished voice over the wire; and she said she would see me that evening at seven. I sent Evie a message that I should be late.

Perhaps you know those premises in the Chelsea Square. Two houses have been thrown into one, but all I know of the establishment is the two rooms of the ground floor, which, barring a narrow passage with a rustling bead curtain across it, communicate. The room on the left of the curtain is a large bare apartment that is used for parties, tableaux, dancing and such like entertainments; that on the right is the tea-room, sewing and wardrobe room, and room for general purposes. At one end of it is a kitchener; placed near the kitchener is a small service counter, brass foot-rail and all, that has done duty in some saloon bar or other—it was probably picked up in the York Road, N.; and the furniture has been given piecemeal by artists and is characterised by great variety. The members can get tea for threepence halfpenny and dinner for eightpence; and of course I was Louie Causton's guest. She was looking out of the window as I approached the house; she herself opened the door to me; and we walked through the bead portière and entered the party-room on the left. We sat down by a yellow upright piano at the farther end of this room. I heard the frying of chops across the passage. They wouldn't be long, Louie said, and then added that I was looking pretty well.

A long walk round Chalfont Woods the previous day had, in fact, done me good. She herself appeared to be in excellent health and spirits. She asked me whether I had seen Billy Izzard lately, and then, without waiting for an answer, laughed as two girls, in waltzing attitude, balanced in the doorway for a moment, and then, seeing us, went out again. "The girls dance in here," Louie explained. "Oh, do you?" I remarked. "Oh, I don't," was her reply; and she went on to ask what was new with me. It was all refreshingly ordinary and matter-of-fact, and there was no indication that she had any serious care on her mind.

A stout woman in an apron appeared in the doorway and announced that our chops were ready. We passed into the other room. I said that the furniture of the Club had been given by artists; the table at which we sat down had been a card-table. As I could not get my legs under it I had to sit sideways at it, and our plates, cups and saucers were edge to edge, with the salt and pepper in the interstices. Louie smiled and said something about our interview being literally a tête-à-tête, and we attacked our chops.

From where I sat I could see the vista of the party-room across the passage, and Louie's eyes, as they met mine from time to time, had something of the same soft sheen of the polished floor of that apartment. She wore a navy blue skirt and plain white mercerised blouse without collar or any other finish at the neck; and as we ate and talked of this and that there rose in my mind again that surmise I had had when Billy had told me, by the Whitestone Pond, that she had stopped sitting. Nothing that I can describe happened to confirm that surmise, and yet somehow I was conscious of the growing confirmation. It had begun when she had twinkled and said, "How's Billy?" and a moment or two later, when the two girls had stood poised in the doorway for dancing, she had smiled and said, "Oh, *I* don't dance." The twinkle about Billy had not been lost on me; and when I tell you that the single dance of my own life had been with her, years before, at a breaking-up party at the old Business College, perhaps you can make a guess at the nature of my surmise.

For I had read in those eyes of hers, on that night of the Berkeley dinner, that she loved me and must go on loving me; and she herself had said, in so many words, "It's nothing to do with you—you can't help that." And now she had taken this fantastic resolution not to sit any more. Whether I would have it so or not, she had a right in me, in which, quite calmly and ordinarily, she now exulted. Yet had ever before mortal woman exulted over anything less substantial? The whole thing seemed to me both preposterously lovely and quite movingly absurd. She had wheedled out of Billy that perfect sketch that had stood on his easel that evening I had walked, unannounced, into his room opposite the Cobden Statue. Why? What ridiculous and sacred tapers did she burn about it? Billy must now paint her in costume or not at all. Why? Of what beautiful and empty union was this a consummation? Did she seriously intend that thenceforward no eye but mine—But I waste words. You see it or you don't see it. That, as near as makes no matter, appeared to be how things stood between us, and there was nothing to tell me that she was not happy in this beautiful lunacy. As for myself, I supposed I must be content to be owned almost to the point of insult in possession.

"I'm just beginning to get used to it," I remember she said to me at one stage of that evening—the thing she was just beginning to get used to being sitting under the new conditions. "Did you know it was really harder? Your clothes tingle on you, you know."

I mention this only to show that, since she might speak at her pleasure of a thing of which I might not even recognise the existence, her tyranny over me was pretty complete.

We had finished our chops, and I was wondering what she supposed my reason for having sought her to be, when she herself put the direct question. She put her plate on the floor so as to make room for her elbows on the table.

"Give me a cigarette if you have one," she said. "I'm afraid I've picked up that habit here. All the girls do it: there's a cigarette-case in their bags if there's nothing else."

And when I had given her a light, she put her elbows on the table again, her wrists and forearms fell into an attitude that really made me sorrow for Billy, and she said: "Well, what is it?"

With no more waste of words than she herself had used, I told her of Miss Levey's voracious curiosity, of Evie's perplexed sense of something unexplained, and of my own unsuccessful attempt to have my eggs and my omelette too.

She listened attentively: the change of which I shall speak in a moment did not come all at once. Other girls had now come into the Club, and two or three of them were gathered about a brown-paper parcel, some purchase of dress material or other which they were discussing with animation. Others fetched cups of tea from the saloon bar counter, eating and drinking, perched carelessly on the ends of tables, the spiral twist of the work of their stockings telling how readily they got into and out of their clothes.

Before I had finished my story Louie interrupted me with the first of a little series of detached remarks.

"One moment," she said. "When do you start—this Consolidation, I mean?"

"In a few weeks. We shall send some of the men on in advance in about a fortnight. Why?"

"You don't intend to take Miriam Levey over with you?"

"I do not."

"You don't suppose she doesn't know that?"

"Well?"

"Well—but go on." She made a little gesture. "I interrupted you."

I went on.

"Half-a-minute," she came in again presently. "All this was quite—I mean, there was no quarrel?"

"With Evie? No—oh, no, no."

"Well—"

And the next time she interrupted me was merely to ask me whether I had another cigarette.

I admit that there had come over me as I had talked an increasing sense of the burden I had placed upon her. Nor do I mean that I had not had this sense before. I had, indeed, thought of little else during my walk to Chalfont the previous day. But it is yet another coin added to the price of a righteous but unlicenced slaying that a man's selfishness becomes merely inordinate. I had known more or less what she must bear; exactly what she had to bear it with I had taken for granted. She had perhaps herself to thank for that, and that tense and incredible calm she had shown on the night I had dined at the Berkeley. I had known the depths of her womanliness that other night; soon I was to learn the shallows of her femininity.

"Well," she said, when at last I had finished, "I really don't see what else you expected. And," she went on, but more slowly, and somehow as if she didn't quite trust herself, "I don't see either what you expect of me. I told you what I thought before."

"You mean that I should have to tell her?"

"Yes."

"Well, tell me why."

"You've just told me why."

"Well, put it another way. You see the frightful risk—to her. The question is, ought it to be taken?"

For a moment those tourmalines of her eyes seemed to flicker, as if she would have shown me again the abysses beyond them; but they remained shut as she spoke more slowly still.

"That's not quite the question. Can you—go on—as you are doing? And if you can't, what's the alternative?"

To that I had no answer to make.

Her cigarette had gone out, and her beautiful fingers were holding it listlessly. All at once I found myself noticing the contrast between her and the chattering group of models down the room. The girl with the brown-paper parcel had approached a cupboard and taken out some second-hand property or other of frayed velvet and torn gold: "It's hardly worth re-making: I vote we cut it up," I heard her say. And I wondered whether Louie had sat in the torn and tawdry thing—now that she had been warned against chills. The giggling and the skiddle of teacups went on, but Louie pressed her fingers on her eyeballs for a moment. Perhaps it was this pressure that made them, when she looked up again, seem dull and tired.

"At any rate, that's how it strikes me," she said.

She looked suddenly older—much older—so much older that it gave me a pang. During my walk on the previous day I had told myself over and over again that I must have made of her life also exactly what I had made of my own—a fearful thing without trifles; but I had *had* to tell myself, if you appreciate what I mean. Now, to see it with my own eyes was another matter. There was that other quantity, the quantity unknown to me but drearily familiar enough to her, I didn't doubt—Kitty. . . A word of advice to those who contemplate the putting out of a life on their own responsibility: When a woman, on a rainy night in St. James's Park, or wherever and whenever, lets you look down into her soul, and drops a plummet into your own, and asks you whether you are not a murderer, and you no more dare to lie than you would dare a foulness in the face of majesty, then do anything you like—fly from her, bite out your tongue, kill her also—but for mere pity of her don't answer "Yes." Don't, that is, unless you are sure that she will betray you. If you do, depend on it she'll ask you to a Models' Club or somewhere, and the horror of a life without trifles will come over you, and you'll see her press her fingers on her eyeballs and then look up again, five years older in as many minutes.

"What about Kitty?" I asked abruptly.

She answered quickly—too quickly: "Oh, Kitty's all right; you needn't bother about Kitty; leave her to me. As a matter of fact she's been awfully useful to me."

"How useful?"

"Oh, in quite the most material way," she said, with a short and mirthless laugh. "That's not been pure philanthropy, I assure you. I dare say you know—"

I did know that Kitty had perhaps a pound a week of her own money, from some tramways out Edgbaston way.

"And she types at home, too—authors' manuscript—when she can get it—and I save the ten shillings I had to pay somebody to look after the boy."

"And you yourself?" I ventured meaningly.

"Oh," she answered evasively, "we've not stuck fast yet."

"In spite of your chills," thought I; and then, as another burst of laughter broke from the girls down the room, I said aloud: "Tell me—I've never asked you—how did you drop into this kind of thing? You used to be at a business college."

Again she smiled. "Did I? Sometimes I can hardly believe that was I. It's precious little I learned there, anyway. And this other—I could explain to Billy—I'm not pretty, I know, not my face, but—well, it seemed a fairly obvious thing to do. There wasn't much else, anyhow, and remember I did fairly well out of it—better than most girls in offices."

She had grown faintly pink, and again the tourmalines had given, as it were, a half turn. I dropped my voice and looked earnestly at her.

"And these—chills—aren't they anything you could ever grow out of?"

The soft irradiation deepened as she looked as earnestly back at me.

"No," she said.

"I see. And what you learned at the College—have you forgotten all that?"

Then, looking almost challengingly at one another, we began to speak rather quickly, and a little elliptically.

"I think I can guess what you mean," she said, dropping her gaze again.

"I think you do."

"That's why I asked you just now when the Consolidation was starting. . . You don't suppose she'll love you any more for throwing her out of a job, do you?"

"She can't hate me much more than she does."

"Well, you may depend upon it, she knows she's going."

"Well, that saves trouble."

"Oh, no, it doesn't."

"Ah!—You think not?"

"I'm sure not."

A pause.

"I gather you've seen her?"

"Oh, often."

"At your place?"

"Yes."

"I don't suppose you love her much. Why do you have her there?"

"You don't love her either. Why do you?"

"Well, there's Evie."

"And there's Kitty."

Another pause, and then: "I see."

Then suddenly I spoke a little more to the point.

"Well, would you accept the job if I could arrange it?"

She hesitated. "It's very necessary, of course, that I should do something."

"You'd take it?"

"I almost think—there's my boy, you see—but we'll talk about that in a minute. You were asking me about Kitty. I don't think you need worry about her. I keep her in hand. I don't think it would matter very much if she and your wife did meet, and, on the whole, you'd be doing more harm by objecting beyond a certain point than you would by allowing it. So, as far as she's concerned, things had better drift. The worst of it is"—again the fingers on the eyeballs—"they don't drift."

"Don't drift?"

"You know what Miriam Levey is."

I caught my breath. "You don't mean *she's* any idea—" I said quickly.

"Oh, none whatever," Louie said hurriedly. "I don't mean that at all. But I *do* mean she'd thoroughly enjoy seeing you made uncomfortable—got at—scored off—get her own back—you know what I mean."

"That's noth—" I began absently, but checked myself. "That's nothing," I had been on the point of saying, but there were no nothings for us. Louie's vigils must be as unremitting as my own.

Suddenly I found myself without the heart to ask her in detail what these were. We now had the tea-room to ourselves; the bevy of models had scurried off to the party-room, and two of them appeared to be playing an elementary duet on the piano, with wrong notes loudly and laboriously corrected, amid laughter and general high spirits. Again the contrast was cruel. *They* hadn't to look before, behind and about them for the dread of a ruinous inadvertence. . . You will find it difficult to reconcile with remorse, by the way, that, stealing another glance at Louie's drawn and anxious face, I cursed a heedless young cub who had gone to his account nearly six years before.

"Anyway," she said, after a long silence, "I'll see to that as far as I can. Plan as we like, we've got to take some risks. Don't look at me like that. It isn't more than I can bear. There's joy in it too. The only thing I don't quite understand is why *I* should want to throw that joy away by—by giving you the advice I did."

"The advice you did?"

"To tell your wife."

"But—" It broke agitatedly from me. Again the tourmalines seemed to move.

"The risk; just so; don't think I don't see it. Oh, I see it—far more plainly than you do! Haven't you thought that perhaps it's that that—" She stopped abruptly, ending in a little twanging murmur.

And I had at last become conscious of something that hitherto I had only half consciously noticed—namely, that she spoke of Evie repeatedly as "your wife." Obstinately she refused to use her name. I think that I felt even then our approach to what I have called the shallows of her femininity. Can you wonder at it? Is it so very surprising that, with the tremors of those shut transmitters of her eyes, the whole fantastic and exhausting fabric of my interpretation of her feeling for myself tottered? He has to be a greater painter than Billy Izzard whose fiction can fill the life of a woman already past thirty, whom you have so heaped with cares that her face takes on age as you look at it! Her voice shook as she strove to hide all this from me.

"But you see the disadvantage you have me at," she said. "*You* know what you really want, though you haven't put it quite plainly yet; but even if I were to try it you wouldn't let me say what *I* mean."

"Oh, say it, say it: we're in the mess, and it's no good keeping things back."

"No, no—you've no right to expect that of me. I'll do everything else, but I'm only a mortal woman, with limbs and hungers, after all."

"You're a very wondrous one."

"Tch!" The exclamation broke from her as if I had blundered on a nerve with an instrument. "You're making big demands of my wondrousness, Jim!"

I gave a low groan. "Poor woman! Is it more than—"

But she broke out into quite a loud cry.

"Not that, Jim," she commanded, "not—that! That's the only thing I will *not* bear! If you're going to make me out noble, or disinterested, or self-sacrificing, or anything of that sort I—I can't bear it. I'm not. I hate Evie. I hate myself. I almost hate you when I see how stupid and clumsy you can be. Oh, *you* know what *you* want! You want just one thing—to be happy with her; but do you think I scheme and contrive for you because *I* want you to be happy with her? Oh no! I do it because I can't help myself, and because it's that or nothing between you and me, and that's all there is splendid about it! I won't be called 'Poor woman.' And you needn't shake your head either. If I could get you, I would; but there it is, I can't, and that's all the loyalty I have for *her*! And you ask me," she broke out anew, almost furiously, "you ask me whether I 'don't see' things! It's you who don't see, and never will! You get a fixed idea into your head, and everything else—" She snapped her fingers. "What do you suppose your wife would say if she knew you were here with me now? *I* shouldn't care a straw about her knowing, but have you told *her*? *Will* you tell her? You know you won't! You daren't—you daren't trust her! Oh, I know what you're going to say—that you can't discuss her with me—but in that case you shouldn't take my position quite so much for granted. I'm the last person to put on a pedestal. You ask me whether I see things: don't I! Don't I see what they might have been—yes, even in spite of the mess I made of them! With half a chance I could have—"

"Louie!"

"Sssh—it's got to come out now! I was happy till that night—you know the night I mean—and that night I was fool enough to think it was possible to stop up there—away up in the air. I gave you and got from you that night what no other woman on earth could have done, and I thought we could stop at that. I thought I could go on living at that. I thought that would be enough for me; and when I found it wasn't, I began to—bolster it up. You've seen Billy—you know what I mean. And I still have something of you that nobody else has, and—I want to give it away! I want you to give her that too! I advise you to tell her and leave me with nothing! I must be mad! Jim!"—her voice dropped with startling effect—"you once said that to tell her would be to kill her: *if I could only think that*! . . . But there, you'll tell her, and take away the last thing I have of you. . . But she won't get that thing. It's beyond her. That's yours and mine whether you wish it or not. If you don't believe me, try it. Tell her. Tell her her husband made away with her sweetheart; tell her why; tell her what you've told me, and if she takes it as I did, I haven't another word to say. I hate her; I'm not running away from that; so perhaps I'm not just. Perhaps there is a chance: if so, it's your only one. I've had no luck. I'm out of it, and there's no more to say. Give me a match."

She took up and relighted her half-smoked cigarette.

I have merely set down what she said, and the way she said it; for the rest, I leave you to draw your own conclusions. Perhaps it is unusual to allow these freedoms to be taken with your wife, but I think you will admit that the occasion was unusual. She had told me, in effect, that murderers ought to be careful whom they marry, and that I had married the wrong woman: but she had left out of the account one thing that made all the difference. You know as well as I what she had left out—the supreme sanctification of the flesh: "With my body I thee worship." . . . It was Evie, not Louie Causton, with whom I had heard that nightingale sing on Wimbledon Common. They had been Evie's lips, not Louie's, that had not sought to escape my own on that September evening in Kensington Gardens. It was Evie whom I had married. . . It was natural that Louie should see how things might conceivably have been different; you can say that however they turn out; and perhaps that was where the fatality came in. Circumstance, propinquity, accident, a step rightly or wrongly taken, and the rest is predicated with a terrible inevitability. Louie had had no luck; and now, not because I had placed a crushing weight upon her, but because I had given her the pity while another got the love, she had broken out upon me.

At any rate, I saw her own position sadly clearly now.

And, there being no more to say, she rose.

In the hall, however, she did find one more word to say. They were playing Sir Roger in the party-room as I held aside the bead *portière* for Louie to pass, and the couples, seen through the gauzy hanging, seemed spectrally charming. Louie stood on the other side of the curtain, mortal, unspectral enough under a cheap square hall lamp with tesseræ of coloured glass. With head downhung, she moved spiritlessly towards the outer door, where she stood meditatively with her hand on the letter-box. At last she looked up.

"About what you were saying about Miriam Levey," she said, without preface. "I don't think it would do—not now."

I knew she meant her own acceptance of Miriam's place. I asked her why not.

"Oh, I've said too much for that to be possible now. We've been too near. We mustn't come so near again."

"But surely," I said dispiritedly, "a job—"

She shook her head. "I should be seeing you," she said. "It wouldn't do. Good-night."

And I lost the strains of Sir Roger as the door closed between us.

IV

Looking back over what I have written, I find it will hasten my tale if I take events with rather a free hand in point of time, sequence and so forth; and I shall do so. For example, the setting up of the Consolidation in Pall Mall did not actually take place until the following spring, but our arrangements were complete long before that time, and, as my tale is about myself rather than about the Consolidation, I will say as much as is necessary about that enterprise now, and have done with it.

We have to all intents and purposes absorbed the old F.B.C., and this has been greatly to the advantage of both concerns. The Company's mercantile position is the firmer, and we are left the freer for things both larger and more special. In the handling of these Pepper has been brilliant. True, he has taken chances, sometimes more than I have liked; but he is a born taker of chances, and it is astonishing, on the whole, how seldom things have failed to come off. In his own line I have never met his equal. I think I mentioned that he had been in Russia: I never knew exactly what his errand was there; but I can make a guess at the kind of thing. Last summer, for instance, he was out in the West Indies—with a few tin specimen-boxes and a butterfly net (this is the man who doesn't know a butterfly from a bumble-bee, and once asked me what a birch was). Out in the West Indies he met Magnay, of Astbury, Phillips—a valetudinarian after tarpon. Sichel was there too; I forget whether he was playing golf, or healing a lung, or merely yawning his head off in deck-chairs. And of course (a nod being as good as a wink to a blind horse) there could be no possible connection between these innocent pursuits and the Panama Canal, trans-shipment stations and the South American coasting trade. . . So maybe Pepper had had no thought of hides or timber or tallow when he had learned the Siberian method of hunting bear. . . Anyway, all I want you to understand, without making it too plain, is that we leave these things to Pepper. He dines geologists and botanists and explorers and concessionaires: he does them well, and is perfectly charming; and it may quite well be that, before he has finished with them, a little inconspicuous piece of paper that not one in a thousand as much as glances at is posted up in Whitehall one day, Britain has proclaimed a new Protectorate somewhere or other, and the Consolidation is at the bottom of it. It pays us that Pepper keeps his nails manicured and knows his way about a wine-list. It may not be noble or altruistic or anything of that kind, but it's the way things get done in this world, and be hanged to Schmerveloff and the humanitarians.

So, while we were still with the F.B.C., Pepper was playing every ball straight back to the inquisitive folk who wanted to know what was in the wind, we were ready to go over at a month's notice to that great new cathedral of a place with the mosaic floors and the bronze statues in the niches, and I was free to rub my rosy prospects into Aunt Angela to my heart's content. It had come off, or, thanks to Pepper and Robson and the rest of them, could hardly now fail to do so. But Aunt Angela, when I twinkled at her, and mentioned this, only gave me back my smiles thrice spiritualised. She never failed to rejoice, for our sakes, whenever a new piece of furniture came into the house in Well Walk, but for herself, her attitude was piously and amusingly penitential. I never knew austerity so resemble luxuriousness—or the other way about, whichever it was. And of this new furniture we presently began to have quite a lot. Collecting, as I have since come to understand the word, was as yet, of course, far beyond my means; but I used a bronze copy of a lioness by Barye on my desk as a paper-weight, I had good autotypes of Méryon on my study walls, I had bought Evie a dinner service, quite good enough for most occasions even today, and I had sales' catalogues and auctioneers' circulars, a dozen a week. Oh, yes, we were getting on, and Pepper winked, remembering his candlesticks, but said nothing.

But let me return to Aunt Angela for a moment. The effect on her of these evidences of our increasing prosperity was curious. Without the loss of a jot of her amiability, but rather to the increase of it, she set herself apart from our modest splendours. If I use the word "religiosity" I mean it only in its most innocent sense: but something of the sort had been incipient in her for a long time, and now merely became declared. Perhaps I cannot do better than tell here of the evening in which I first discovered how far this had gone. If at this point my narrative seems a little diffuse, it is merely because the longest way round is often the shortest way home, and also because Aunt Angela's attitude was not the only thing I learned that night.

I think it would be a little before Christmas, on a Tuesday or Wednesday; I know the day, if not the week, because it was what Evie, who corrected some of my own recklessnesses by still clinging to small economies, called an "eating-up night." On those nights I was expressly forbidden to bring anybody home to dinner—I except Aunt Angela and Billy Izzard, who came when they pleased. As it happened, they had both turned up on that very evening, and had partaken of a rather scratch supper; and I, who had had an exceptionally heavy day, hoped that nobody would come in afterwards—not that anybody was very likely to. As Jackie had gone to bed, Billy had been allowed to play Evie's new piano only with the soft pedal down (Evie herself, I may say, did not play, but was resolved to learn); and Aunt Angela had several skeins of wool to wind into balls. From the arm-chair in which I half dozed I could see Evie, still in the waterproof apron in which she had given Jackie his bath, setting the child's basket to rights. Our only maid was taking her "evening out" and was probably up on the Spaniards Road.

I was not too sleepy to see that Aunt Angela needed somebody to hold her wool, and I volunteered drowsily for the service. But, "No, thanks, Jeff," she replied; "you have a nap; besides, I must be getting used to doing things for myself." I did not insist, and the last thing I remember before I dropped off for forty winks was seeing her reach for Pepper's candlesticks, place them on the hearthrug, and, passing a hank of wool about them, begin to wind.

It seemed to me that several sounds awoke me simultaneously—the stopping of a hansom at the front door, the ringing of a bell downstairs, and a quick exclamation from Evie. It was not impossible, of course, that any one of a number of visitors might have called in a hansom at half-past nine at night, but Evie had concluded, and rightly as it happened, that this was the one with whom she was least of all at home—Pepper. I heard her suppressed exclamation of "Bother!" The next moment she had whisked off the waterproof apron, thrust it under the piano lid, then, seeing Aunt Angela still placidly winding, had said, "Quick—in case—hide them, Auntie," and had flown to answer the bell.

But Aunt Angela, in her flurry, had only succeeded in making the candlesticks a hopeless cat's-cradle of wool before Evie's voice of vivacious welcome was heard, and Pepper himself entered.

He had Whitlock and a stranger with him, the latter a bearded and taciturn provincial who was introduced as Mr. Toothill. Mr. Toothill, indeed, I gathered to be the reason of the visit. Pepper has to be charming to a great variety of men, and is not often beaten, but occasionally there does fall to him ("for his virtues," he says) a man he can neither dine, wine nor take to a show, and I know the signs in him when he is at his most affable and most intensely bored. I may say at once that Mr. Toothill has no connection with my tale other than as having been the cause of this visit.

Now Pepper has the gift of being able to make all manner of things (especially men) invisible when he chooses; and although Aunt Angela, in making out of sight with the wool and the candlesticks of Pepper's own giving, had only succeeded in putting them on the table and making them the most conspicuous objects in the room, for Pepper they did not exist. That bright photographic eye of his took in every other object in the room, but no candlesticks.

But not so Mr. Toothill. He came, Whitlock told me afterwards, from the West Riding of Yorkshire, where he was a power; but so little of a power was he in London that, had Pepper not rashly burdened himself with him, he would probably have waited in King's Cross Station for the next train back to his own parts. Anyway, here he was in my house, and as his eyes fell on the wool-winding, they lighted up (so Whitlock said) with the first spark of interest they had shown that evening.

"This is like ho-o-ome, at all events," he said, giving the word I don't know how many "o's." "But you've got it felted, haven't you? If the ladies will excuse me—"

And without more ceremony, and in spite of Aunt Angela's protestations, he drew the candlesticks towards himself, began to unravel the ridiculous tangle, and became for purposes of conversation a piece of furniture with a beard.

Of course Mr. Toothill had been foisted on us merely because Pepper had not known what else in the world to do with him; but Pepper's beautiful candour rarely confessed much of what was really passing in his mind, and I awaited with relish the reason he would give for his call. By this time I was quite wide awake again; and Mr. Toothill had refused the whisky I had got out.

Well, Judy had several reasons, all sufficient, all perfect; but alas! he and Evie ever hit it off with deplorable lucklessness. He and Whitlock were Jackie's godfathers; but, as against the rather loud way in which he had rung the bell, his urbanities about the spiritual relationship availed him little with Evie. Her looks said plainly, to me at all events, that if Pepper intended her to believe that he had called on an eating-up night merely to ask how Jackie was getting on, he mistook her. Driven from this outpost, Pepper proudly refused to urge the commonplace excuse of private business with myself. Instead, he delicately adjusted his trousers, produced his cigar-case, besought Evie's permission with a glance, and then, lighting up with deliberation, astonished myself hardly less than Evie by saying: "Well—unless Whitlock's already told you—I've come for your congratulations, Mrs. Jeffries."

"Oh? What on, Mr. Pepper?" said Evie. She had summoned up a ready, glad look.

"Ah, I see he hasn't told you. Stupid of me—of course he couldn't have, as I only heard myself about four hours ago. Dear Mrs. Jeffries, you may congratulate me on my impending knighthood."

Evie jumped up. "*Really?*" I myself was not so much surprised at the fact as at the moment of its coming, though my surprise at that also passed instantly. Of course it would be so much prestige for the Consolidation.

Yes, Judy was down among the approaching New Year's Honours. And so he ought to have been. If there is official recognition for a man who can merely advise in a party's interest which provincial mayors can be given the accolade without being made the laughing-stock of their neighbours, Judy's services to the Administration had been far greater. To the man on 'change this would doubtless seem a feather in the cap of the F.B.C.; only a few knew that before long it would prove a thorn in their sides. Yes, it was distinctly good preparation for the coming Consolidation, and, in the meantime, there was the knight-elect's health to drink, and I had only got the whisky out. I myself fetched up the claret for Aunt Angela and Evie. Both the announcement and the manner of it had been a huge success, and Billy Izzard, remarking "I won't say 'may I,'—" reached for Pepper's cigar-case.

"Well, I *am* glad!" said Evie, maybe, wife-like, casting ahead in a wonder as to what my own chances might be. "And are we really the first to know?"

"Except Whitlock and Mr. Toothill, yes. But of course I needn't say—"

"Oh, of course we wouldn't breathe a word! Isn't it splendid, auntie?"

Indeed, Evie seemed quite won over. I think she came nearer that evening to liking Pepper than she has done either before or since.

As I said, I have an object in relating all this—several objects. The next thing happened perhaps half-an-hour later, when Mr. Toothill had almost freed one candlestick of wool, but otherwise had not greatly added to our sociability. For that half hour Pepper had reigned among us, but then, bit by bit, he had begun slowly to slip back again. We had guardedly discussed the prospects of the Consolidation; and then, as a preliminary to his coming down presently with a run, Pepper made a perfectly innocent but altogether luckless remark. It was about Miss Levey.

"It was understood she wasn't to come over," he grumbled; "I agreed to that; but I don't see why she should be taken away from me just now." (I had got rid of Miss Levey that very week.) "Hang her private convictions! What do I care about her private convictions as long as she does her work?"

I laughed, though a little lamely. "My dear Judy, we don't want a woman whose job interferes with her propaganda, and she's been incubating 'rights' of one sort and another for a long time. Send her to Schmerveloff: he receives that sort with open arms. Let him make a case of persecution out of it. We want efficiency."

"But, dash it all, she *was* efficient."

"She wasn't. You had to pull her up last week, and I had twice the week before. She'd been warned."

Judy, who really didn't care a button about the loss of Miss Levey, laughed. "The red rag again, Jeffries! You have here, Mr. Toothill, quite the most insular man in this realm, *and* the most obstinate. I can make him do anything he's a mind to—and not much else. Well, well, if you won't have a suffragette, perhaps you'll find me a member of the Women's Primrose League?"

But here Whitlock struck in. "By the way, I'd an applicant this morning."

"From the Women's Primrose League?" Pepper tossed over his shoulder.

"I don't mean for the private work, but as general amanuensis," Whitlock went on. "I asked her how she heard we wanted anybody, and she said she hadn't—had just looked in on the chance."

"Go to Jeffries, since he's made it his affair," Pepper grumbled.

"Well, Miss Day *is* getting married," Whitlock went on, "so that we shall want somebody in the outer office. Then promote Miss Lingard—"

"What was she like?"

Billy Izzard's eyes were dreamily on the smoke of Pepper's expensive cigar, but I saw a change come into them. Whitlock has a passable gift of description. He began to describe the woman who had looked in on the chance of a job: before he had finished I had no doubt, and Billy (I gathered) not much, of who the female out-o'-work had been. "Hallo, my model!" I guessed to be in his mind; but it was no business of his, and he appeared to be relishing his cigar as before.

"I've forgotten her name, but I have it in the book," Whitlock concluded. "Clouston or Christian or something like that."

"Well, see she isn't anti-suffrage either," quoth Pepper; "as far as I can see, that would be just as bad."

And he selected a fresh cigar.

My first thought had shaped itself in the very words for which Louie herself had pulled me up so sharply: "Poor woman!" For it was pathetically clear what had happened—what must have happened. Once more she had taken a resolution too heroic to be held to, and whether she had caved in because of myself or because of the necessity for feeding and clothing her boy made no practical difference. I could only hope it was the last. Poverty leaves little room for heroics. Later, as I think I told you, Louie got Miss Day's post, and after that Miss Lingard's, which she has still.

And my second thought was that, as she had applied of herself for Miss Levey's place, there would now be no more love lost between her and Miss Levey than there was between Miss Levey and myself. I began to muse on this. . .

But let me go on with that curiously broken evening.

Ever since Pepper had told us about his knighthood Aunt Angela had sat, her slender fingers folded in her lap, smiling from time to time into the fire. Now knighthood is a temporal distinction, and, as such (I am putting this bluntly), another nut for that new and dainty humility of hers to crack. For worldliness, it was my own promised wealth in another form; and against such things she seemed to have taken up some sort of a position. I think the less practicable human charities had given her a tenderness even for Miss Levey, for I had not escaped a soft look of reproach when I had made my observations on that lady; and altogether she appeared to be wrapped in a little private veil of dissociation from the rest of us and our doings.

So—again to anticipate what became plain a little later—she also was nursing her little surprise for us. Several times during the last month or two she had spoken vaguely of leaving her rooms in Woburn Place, the rooms she had shared with Evie before our marriage; but I had not taken her very seriously; she was welcome to come to us (as she afterwards did) whenever she chose, and she knew it. But she had got it into her head that she would like to take a single room—oh, quite a large, airy, cheerful one—and, as it turned out presently, she had actually done so that very day.

Some chance remark of Pepper's—I think it was something about how pleasant it was to see us thus in our little family circle—gave her the opportunity for her announcement. There had been a little byplay between Pepper and Evie, who had wanted to know why in that case he didn't get married himself; and to that Pepper, abolishing (as it were) the candlesticks under his nose by an act equal in potency to that of creation itself, had answered gallantly (and, in the presence of those candlesticks, rather naughtily) that our own ménage set him a standard which he would rather cherish in thought than fall from in miserable actuality. It was then that his look embraced Aunt Angela, and my maiden aunt by marriage smiled.

"I suppose Mr. Pepper thinks I live here because he always finds me here," she said. "But that's only because I've no conscience about inflicting myself on other people. *My* dwelling's a much more modest one than this, Mr. Pepper."

I think Pepper was insincere enough to reply that that it might quite well be and yet almost everything that could be desired.

"I forgot to tell you that, Jeff," Aunt Angela continued, turning to me. "As a matter of fact I only settled the matter today—so you're not the only one for whom today's been *quite* important, Mr. Pepper." She preened herself.

"Oh!" I said shortly. I thought the whole idea rather stupid. But she continued:

"I go in in exactly ten days, as soon as the paint's dry. And as I don't begin to pay till Christmas, I actually get a week for nothing. That might not be much to some people," she purred, dropping her eyes, "but it's quite a lot to me. So, Jeff, I shall want you to bring a hammer and a foot-rule—or whatever it is. He's *so* clever at putting up things, Mr. Pepper."

She ran amiably on, describing her proposed arrangements.

I could hardly blame Pepper that, to save himself from talking, he drew her out. He was bored to death with the drowsy banality of the evening. So Aunt Angela told us how cosy she was going to be in her new quarters. With her bed screened off in one corner, and the day's fire still burning, she would be able (she said) to lie happily awake and watch the firelight on the ceiling and indulge "an old woman's fancies"; there would be no stairs except when she came out of doors; and she wouldn't have to cook in the same room, for there was a little landing with a stove left by the last tenant—and so on. Pepper was the picture of polite interest.

"And I shall give a little housewarming, I think," she said, as one who knew that hospitality consisted in the hostship and not in the entertainment provided. "Really I should like to ask you all, Mr. Toothill too."

Toothill, who had now finished the "unfelting," had struck a match and was experimenting to find out how much of the worsted was cotton and how much wool. He looked up for a moment, but resumed his occupation. Pepper hoped that *he* would not be left out of Aunt Angela's housewarming.

Aunt Angela murmured that that was very sweet of him.

And the smallest of small talk went on.

I don't know that I need give any more of it. Indeed, I don't remember any more of it. Toothill found the wool to be "sixty Botany" or something of the kind, and we sat on, everybody wanting to break the party up, but nobody (not even Pepper) knowing quite how to do so without an open reference to a watch. I omit the details of Pepper's complete downfall in Evie's eyes. I know that by some accident or other the piano lid was opened, displaying the waterproof apron, and that poor Evie, flurried until she hardly knew what she was saying, committed the solecism of calling Pepper "Sir Julius," grew pink (poor dear), and hated, not herself, but Pepper. Also her frugality received a shock when it was discovered that the hansom had been kept waiting all this time. Then the maid, returning from the Spaniards Road, filled my poor wife's cup by bringing in I know not what homely provision for Jackie's comfort during the night. Then they went.

Now, except when the flattery of personal attention is of the highest importance, Pepper turns all provincials over to Whitlock; and I myself, if ever Mr. Toothill turns up at my house again, shall take the precaution of having a whole barrow-load of worsted for his entertainment, and if possible a kitten to "felt" it for him.

V

I have now to tell how Aunt Angela was as good as her word about the housewarming of her new abode. I hope that in these last pages I have not seemed harsh in thought to the kind and aimless soul. She did not meditate the mischief that came of that evening, and it was not for lack of anything she was able to do to remedy it afterwards that partial, if not total shipwreck came. But that helped little. Malevolence, in my experience, is not the worst of dangers a man as exposed as I has to fear. It is the mischief hat grows as it were of itself, inherent in persons and their diverse characters and manifold relations that is the deadly thing. That is not mere bad luck; it is fatality, and there is no defeating it. I myself was so specially open to it that to all intents and purposes I might as well have gone skinless through the world. . . Well, I grinned and bore it. Only one other person knew that I was skinless, and she, alas, was skinless too. Oh, take it on my authority if you cannot take it otherwise, that you will do wisely to keep out of my predicament unless you are of a different temper from mine, have skins to spare, or are prepared to endure the shock I was presently to endure.

I made no attempt to see that other skinless person. If she had found herself driven, from need or any other consideration, to seek a job with the Consolidation, so much the worse; I did not see that that released me from anything she had laid upon me. In any case, as Miss Day's successor, I should rarely see her; even did she pass to the place lately held by Miss Lingard I should, no doubt, be able to avoid her; and for the rest, as she herself had said, things must drift. Sometimes, if I must confess the truth, I found myself getting quite childishly petulant about her. Why had she given me to suppose she was something she wasn't? Why had she let me see her all caught-up and wise and able to bear, as she had shown herself on that first memorable night, and then gone to pieces like this? *I* couldn't have known her private feelings, but *she* must have known them. . .

And what kind of impossible situation was going to be created if, even avoiding other intercourse, I had to encounter those tourmalines of her eyes every time I passed through the busy office to Pepper's room?

So sometimes I forgot what I had laid upon her, and was callous enough and harassed enough to entertain almost a weak resentment against her.

Aunt Angela's new dwelling was in one of those curiously secluded little squares or "circuses" that lie immediately east of King's Cross Road in the neighbourhood of Mount Pleasant. You turn up from the squalid shops and public-houses and trams, and the length of a short steep street brings you into a space with well-built houses about it, trees and birds in the middle, and long narrow gardens with apple and plum and pear at the back. Away to the north the heights of Hampstead seem positively precipitous, and, looking the other way, the multitude of turrets and towers and spires, with St Paul's reigning over them all, is singularly inspiring. Aunt Angela's rooms were very advantageously placed for both these prospects. The first time I went she took me up a breakneck ladder, through a square trapdoor in which I almost stuck fast, and out on to the leads. The sky, torn in primrose-coloured rents and all smoke-browned, was very stormy and fine; and Aunt Angela was looking forward to taking tea out on the roof when the summer came.

"And I shall be able to look away to where my dear ones are," she said, looking north again.

Her room was immediately under this flat roof. It had two windows which looked on the trees in front, and, at the half turn of the stairs, a third which gave on the grimy back garden. In this garden poultry scratched; but there really was a plum-tree, and also a fig that had been known to bear. Her bed, being convertible into a couch by day, did not require to be screened off after all, and the tiny fireplace had brown tiles and a blackleaded iron kerb. One peculiarity the apartment had which I ought to mention: this was a large enclosed cistern, which by rights ought to have been on the roof outside. It held the water supply for the whole house, and as the ball inside it rose and sank, its sounds varied from a gentle tinkling to a soft whispering; the sounds never quite ceased. A stout post some feet from the wall supported one corner of this cistern, and this Aunt Angela, or rather I for her, converted into a hatstand.

It was as she handed me the four black hooks and the paper of screws for this purpose one evening that the sound of the cistern sank to a hissing. "Oh, do give a look to it," she said; "perhaps it wants a washer or something: you can reach it from the window-ledge. And oh, dear, I've got the screws but no screwdriver! There have been hooks in before, haven't there? You'll have to put these higher up then. I'll see if I can borrow a screwdriver downstairs; but see to the cistern first."

But there was nothing to be done with the cistern; if she stayed there she would have to get used to it, that was all. I went up from Pall Mall several evenings to see to her installation, but I never imagined she would stay there very long. The place looked too suddenly cosy when the fire was lighted and the tea-table brightly set.

And so I put her the hooks and a shelf or two up, and made her as comfortable as I could.

Then one night, just as she was settling down, I went in about something or other and found Miss Levey and Aschael there. They seemed to have come for the evening, for their hats were on the hooks on the cistern post. Miss Levey appeared to have forgotten that I had virtually forbidden her my house and turned her out of her job as well; as we shook hands anybody might have supposed that we were the best of friends. She and Aunt Angela appeared to be on quite affectionate terms; and I gathered that Miss Levey was giving lessons by post in secretarial work and doing quite well out of it. Her passing over by the Consolidation she spoke of as a resignation. She was planning to link up her Commercial Correspondence Class with some Guild or other for the Economic Emancipation of Women, and wanted to tell me all about it. I did not stay long.

And of course I couldn't choose Aunt Angela's associates for her.

AT FIRST I HAD REFUSED to go to that party of Aunt Angela's. I had grounds enough for my refusal, for we live half our lives two or three years ahead at the Consolidation, and there were clouds on the economic horizon. Men who live what I may call "short-date" lives can provide for contingencies as they arise, but the surveyor of the future, though he may know things to be inevitable, must be prepared, not for one way in which they may come about, nor even for the most probable way, but for all possible ways. Any one of a thousand symptomatic occurrences may make the Consolidation's most elaborate plans of yesterday of no avail, and work is ten times work when this happens. It had happened several times lately, and but for Pepper's marvellous resilience, my own capacity for long spells of forced labour, and the invaluable inertia of administrative departments, it would have proved too much for us.

I can honestly say that, full of these preoccupations, I had not been influenced by the fact that in all probability Aschael and Miss Levey would be there. I had forgotten all about them.

But Evie's look of resignation when I had told her that I was not going had touched me. We now knew quite a number of people, some of them quite charming people too; and while Evie made less use of this advantage than I could sometimes have wished, I couldn't reproach her for being faithful to her older friends. For a long time we had not been anywhere together. Therefore, seeing her patient yet fallen face, I had promised to make an effort at least to fetch her away, and to arrive earlier if possible. Her instant brightening had amply repaid me.

The party was given on a sharp night towards the end of January, and, try as I would, I had been unable to leave Pall Mall before half-past nine. I should have liked to walk, but that would have taken nearly three-quarters of an hour, and so, near the old F.B.C., I had hailed a hansom. "King's Cross, and then I'll tell you," I had said to the driver; and as I had sped along Holborn and up Judd Street I had relapsed into consideration of the affairs of the day again. The stopping of the hansom and the lifting of the trap aroused me. I gave the man the name of a chapel, and bade him then take a turning to the left; and we went forward again. We passed up a short, steep street at a walk, and stopped in the little "circus."

Aunt Angela's two front windows were lighted and open at the top, and as I paid off my cabman sounds of a nasal singing floated out. I ascended the steps and rang twice—Aunt Angela's signal; but I had to give the double ring again, so merry were they making upstairs. Then I heard steps descending. They were a man's steps, and I gave a sort of mental nod when Aschael opened the door. I had thought he would be there.

"Ve'd about given you up," he said familiarly. "Come in, von't you?"

I followed Aschael upstairs.

It would not greatly have surprised me had Miss Levey taken it upon herself to receive me, as her *fiancé* (if he was her *fiancé*; I never knew) had made me welcome downstairs; but Aunt Angela, trying to appear calm, but really one flutter of pleasure at the success of her little party, met me at the door.

"How late you are," she said gaily. "Yes, yes—I know you'd have come sooner if you could. I'm not scolding you. Now I expect you're hungry; you must have some supper first, and then you shall be introduced to anybody you don't know. Mr. Aschael, you'll get him all he wants, won't you?"

"Vith pleasure, Miss Angela," said Aschael, bustling about, all hands and smiles and ringlets.

Along the wall to my right, as I entered, ran a table, spread with the disarray of a quite elaborate supper. Plates were littered with banana skins, grape-twigs with the tiny morsels of pulp still on them, broken biscuits and remnants of jelly; and beyond this table, under the cistern in the corner, was a smaller one, with half a frilled ham, the wreckage of a tongue and a severely mutilated cold pie. Several flasks of colonial Burgundy had been opened; syphons stood among these; and from that secret and inexhaustible hoard of her belongings Aunt Angela had unearthed quite a large number of wineglasses, red ones, green ones, and some of clear glass. Nay, the entertainment had even run into a large box of Christmas crackers; the coloured paper and bright gelatine of these lay scattered among the plates; and my first impression of the number of people who made the room very warm was that half of them had flimsy tissue-paper caps and bonnets on their heads.

But, as I happened to be more than a little hungry, I merely sketched a sort of general and inclusive bow, sat down, and allowed Aschael to wait on me.

Then, my hunger appeased, I began to look about me.

That the gathering was too large for Aunt Angela's not very large room I instinctively set down to Miss Levey's account, for several of those present appeared to be her friends. There must have been ten or a dozen people there. Miss Levey herself had already given me several welcoming nods across the room from where she sat, cross-legged and resolutely youthful, on the floor at Evie's feet; and on her black hair was a tissue-paper cap of Liberty, with a red spot on one side of it. I had already discovered that the sounds of nasal singing I had heard came from the metal corolla of a gramophone. This, I surmised, belonged to the gentleman who was operating it, a little Japanese named Kato, whom I had seen once or twice at Aunt Angela's old boarding-house in Woburn Place. He wore a dairymaid's bonnet of pale blue, with torn strings. Two other of Aunt Angela's old fellow-boarders also were there, one of them a delicate little man with white spats, a Mr. Trimble, the other an attenuated little lady, with the red marks of a pince-nez across the bridge of her nose, and very thin hair, silver save for a few strands of a yellowish hue. Sitting on Aunt Angela's couch-bed was a younger couple, not very obviously engaged, yet nevertheless carrying on what I gathered to be a courtship by means of quick glad exchanges of the more paradoxical sayings of Schmerveloff. "Oh, rather!" the lady gasped from time to time; "And do you remember that passage?" . . . "Remember it! *I* should say so—about the 'man-made law' you mean?" These at any rate bore all the marks of being friends of Miss Levey's, and members of the Emancipation Guild. Aunt Angela herself, Evie, and Billy Izzard completed the party.

As I was pushing back my chair, having supped, the gramophone broke out again. Not to interrupt it, I sat where I was, watching the little Japanese who operated it. Mr. Kato seemed to have neither eyebrows nor lashes, and the slits of his eyes with their little bitumen dots held, as he looked slyly up from time to time, that indulgent, insulting expression that I distrust in his race over here. He had the appearance of trying the air of the "Intermezzo" from *Cavalleria Rusticana* upon us, as if he contemptuously thought to gauge our taste; and his small hands touched screws and lifted little metal arms with a negligent intelligence. He, too, had nodded to me, though our acquaintance was of the slightest; and with him on the one hand, and Miss Levey on the other, I hoped Evie would not want me to stay very long.

The tune had finished, and I had made another motion to rise when suddenly a few words of Miss Levey's caused me to start, and then to sink slowly back into my chair again. She was speaking to Mr. Kato.

"Oh, *do* let's have 'Ora pro Nobis' again, Mr. Kato—Miss Windus loves it so—don't you, Kitty?"

The next moment the lady whose silver hair was intermixed with brownish strands, the lady whom I had taken to be an old fellow-boarder from Woburn Place, had given a little nod and said "Please." As if to hear the better, she set her pince-nez on her nose.

I saw the little scalene triangles of her eyes. . .

Like so much obliterating smoke, the past six or seven years rolled away. . .

Only six or seven years, and I had failed to recognise her!

Not quite knowing what I did, I found myself crossing to the table under the cistern and returning again with a great hacked-off piece of tongue. I sat down to supper again.

There were candles on the table, and little bright refractions of light came darting through the angles of flower-stands and glasses. I watched these as I made pretence to eat. Presently I found myself quite curious about which fleck of light came from which angle, and my eyes sought to trace each sparkle to its origin. A few moments before I had been drinking Burgundy from a green glass; another glass, a red one, stood close to it; but as the candles were placed neither dyed the cloth with the little spot of its own hue. Perhaps—I am trying to tell you quite literally, and as nearly as I can remember, the infantile occupation that had suddenly engrossed me—perhaps if I moved the candle I should get the little spots. I moved the candle this way and that. Presently each of the glasses stood over its own little jewel of light, this one red as a ruby, the other green as grass. . .

And I cannot better tell you how curiously stunned even my sense of hearing seemed to be than by saying that I heard not one note of "Ora pro Nobis," but only the soft hissing of the cistern overhead in the corner.

But, after I know not what space of time in which I had become half hypnotised by those two tiny refractions of coloured light, I suddenly put the glasses away from me. Also I heard the gramophone once more, and felt the returnings of methodical thought. There came to me, after all this time, the very ordinary reflection that Kitty must have recognised me—had probably known I was coming—and had not been able to endure my presence in the room. . . I remembered Evie's words: "I think you are wrong if you think that things like that go on for years and years." Looking covertly up, I saw that Evie had moved, and was now on the other side of Kitty from that occupied by Miss Levey. As I watched, she picked up Kitty's handkerchief, and Kitty smiled. Kitty's eyes even met mine, but whether they saw me or were merely full of "Ora pro Nobis," which was being played for the second or third time, I could not tell. They moved away again without having given any sign of recognition.

Then the tune ended, and Miss Levey jumped up.

"Now, let's have something jolly!" she cried. "And Mr. Jeffries has finished his supper—make room for him in the circle—move up, Aschael."

It came suddenly upon me that there was one place, and one place only in that room for me to take. I had risen. I strode over the box of records in which Mr. Kato was rummaging, sat down next to Kitty Windus, and held out my hand.

"How do you do, Kitty?" I said.

So far was she from starting or trembling that she merely turned, blinked a little, and, taking my hand, said, in the thin little voice I used to know so well, "Ah! I *thought* you'd come and speak to me, by-and-by."

So if Miss Levey had deliberately planned this for my confusion, I triumphed over her.

FOR A QUARTER OF AN hour Evie and I sat one on either side of Kitty Windus. There was no difficulty whatever. Kitty, though she spoke little, showed no more restraint than it had been her wont to show, and there was nothing to bring up even the ghost of our past relation. And if I triumphed over Miriam Levey, so Evie triumphed over me in the private glances she gave me past the back of Kitty's head. She had been right, and I wrong. Those stories of how Kitty had been found walking round and round Lincoln's Inn Fields at night, unable, when confronted by a policeman, to remember her own name, or where she lived—I strongly doubted them. I even found Louie's account of her mental state difficult to believe. . . She spoke of her neuralgias. She had been a martyr to them, she said, but they had been better lately. Somebody's Tic Mixture had done them more good than anything else. I ought to try it—she'd write the name of it down for me on a piece of paper in case I forgot—she hadn't been remembering things very well lately herself. Louie had advised her to try Somebody Else's Tincture, but she didn't believe in that at all; it was one of these imitations that the shopmen were always trying to palm off on people. . . At this point, seeing she had mentioned Louie, I thought it safe to venture an offhand, "Oh, how's Louie, by the way?" But Kitty, apparently forgetting that she herself had introduced the name, pursed her lips. Louie, she mumbled, hadn't behaved very well. She didn't mean to herself; she wouldn't in the least have minded that; but one had friends, and liked to see them treated as friends, which some people—She stopped as Billy Izzard came up, perhaps hearing Louie's name.

So great was my relief at all this, that I suddenly found myself quite carelessly gay. But for Miss Levey's presence I might have been positively happy. But that lady's fussy attentions to myself did not cause me to drop my guarded attitude towards her. I smiled when she put a paper cap on my head also (she had kept a cracker specially for me, she said); and I made a joke when she read some amatory motto or other; that, I said, would be more in her friends' line—indicating with a glance the couple who conducted the intellectual courtship on the couch. But Miss Levey wagged her short finger at me; she wasn't going to have fun made of the members of her League, she said; and she even went so far as to slap the back of my hand with a paper fan she carried and to tell me I was naughty. Mr. Kato, the dotted almonds of his eyes blinkingly comprehending us all, ran through the remaining records and then asked if there were no more; and Aunt Angela herself said that if he wanted more she was afraid he'd have to fetch them from the landing. It was only then that I learned that the gramophone was Aunt Angela's. I had supposed it to belong to Mr. Kato.

So we sat and laughed and enjoyed ourselves. Billy Izzard had taken an old letter from his pocket and was making a jotting of the scene. I suppose that mixture of littered supper-table, grotesque tissue-paper caps, and Aunt Angela's miscellaneous furniture must have appealed to his always keen sense of the incongruous. They had got fresh records; I had seen Mr. Kato come in with an old soap-box, and had heard Miss Levey's cry of juvenile delight: "Oh, they're all comics!" They were entreating Aschael to sing, who liked being entreated, but said, No, Miriam was the singer. Miriam replied merrily that unless they were careful she *would* sing, and then they would know all about it. Aunt Angela laughed heartily at this: and in the end Aschael sang, not very appropriately, "The Boys of the Bulldog Breed." Mr. Kato "Hurrahed" and Miss Levey "Banzaied," and Aunt Angela, who had slipped out during the song to wash glasses in her little pantry, called the little nonentity from Woburn Place to help her in giving us all claret-cup.

"What a pity Mr. Aschael's voice isn't properly trained!" Kitty remarked, turning to me.

"An awful pity!" Evie struck vivaciously in from the other side of her. "I'm sure he'd have a splendid voice!"

It was odd, the way in which the pair of us took Kitty under our wing.

"You don't sing, do you, Kitty?" Evie next asked.

Kitty didn't. Evie admitted that she didn't either. "But," she said, "we aren't going to let Mr. Aschael off with one song, are we? Come, Mr. Kato—you're Master of the Ceremonies—"

"I'm just finding one he knows." Mr. Kato grinned over his shoulder.

"A comic, mind," warned Miss Levey, "and then Kitty can have 'Ora pro Nobis' again before we go."

And in token that the song was going to be comic, Aschael got up on his feet and set himself in a gesture he had doubtless picked up at the Middlesex Music Hall.

"Now, Mr. Aschael," said Kato.

Aschael cleared his throat.

At the first notes of a curiously thin piano accompaniment, I felt Kitty shrink and close as a daisy closes at the approach of night. . .

You will tell me that I ought to have stopped the machine—smashed it—fallen on it—done something, anything; but put yourself in my place; nay, put yourself in the place of the three of us who sat together, and who had sat together the last time we had heard the song Aschael sang. Did I tell you when that had been, or didn't I? I had better tell you now. . . It had been up the River, with a summer twilight falling, and distant banjos sounding, and the Japanese lanterns making long, wavy reflections in the water. Our party had been four, not three, then, and the fourth of us had sung this song Aschael was singing now. He had sung it, lolling in the stern, beating time with one hand, and very careful about the spotting of a new pair of white flannel trousers.

Oh yes, I daresay I ought to have done something rather than let those two other poor things hear *that* song again. . .

But a hideous fear, of which they knew nothing, kept me fascinated and still. So long as they *only* remembered the song and that other occasion they were the lucky ones. I envied them their luck. No let-off so merciful was mine. . . And my horror was enhanced, not so much by those two faces at which I dared not glance, as by our atmosphere of tawdry festivity—the sprinkling of coloured gelatine on the floor, the mocking caps of tissue paper on our heads, and the florid antics of Aschael, turning and grimacing, now this way, now that.

That I might keep this added horror of mine from them, there was even yet a chance. . .

For the song, you understand, was being sung *twice*, once by the unknown maker of the record in the machine, and the second time, as it were over it, by Aschael. As the two voices did not perfectly coincide, the result was a sort of palimpsest of sound, with, as sometimes happens in palimpsests, the old and almost erased message the more significant one. Aschael kept irregular pace with a far-off amateur voice and the faint tinkling of a piano. . . Like a bolt into my brain had come the knowledge of *whose* that horrible instrument had been, and how it had come into Aunt Angela's possession. I remembered her visits to Guildford; I remembered Mrs. Merridew's funeral; I remembered her old kindnesses in providing a certain young man in London with a "home from home." The machine had come from Guildford, a legacy, a memento, a giggle from the tomb. . .

But they, those two poor stricken souls, could yet be spared that knowledge. It was dreadfully too much that they knew the song, and that he had known it, and that he had sung it that summer's evening up the River. The rest of the horror might still be kept from them.

"All together—chorus," cried Aschael jubilantly:

> *"Why—don't—you marry the girl?*
> *D'you want—the poor thing—to die?*
> *You can see—she's gone—upon—you*
> *By the twin—kle in—her eye!*
> *Do—the trick—for se—ven-and-six,*
> *Take—the tip—of a pal—*
> *I've—been—watching your game—*
> *Why don't you marry the gal?"*

Then I felt that last desperate hope of mine slipping away—Aschael was beginning to forget the words, and to make out with gestures and grimaces, leaving gaps through which there started up thin and tinkling and facetious horrors. . . I saw that Kato had realised; I had once come upon him and Archie drinking whisky and soda together; his eyes met mine curiously, and I fancied his lips shaped the name:

"Merridew?"

This next I have from Billy Izzard. He tells me that all at once I sprang to my feet and cried, in a huge and boisterous voice that drowned everything else, "Never mind, Aschael—chorus—all together!—"

> *"Why—don't—you marry the girl?*
> *D'you want—the poor thing to die?*
> *You can see—she's gone—upon you*
> *By the twin-kle in—her eye!*
> *La—la la—sing up!*
> *Take the tip—go on, Aschael!—*
> *I've been—watching your game—*
> *Why don't you marry the gal?"*

Clapping my hands, Billy says, I fell back into a chair.

But I was out of it again in an instant. I was not to escape so easily as all that. Kato had his finger on the lever; I cannot say how, nor whether, he guessed what was to come, nor whether he tried to avert it; if he did, he was too late. From that damnable box there came a long catarrhal wheeze—high-pitched and tenor the words came:

"Now, Evie—Evie's turn—make her sing, mother—bosh—of course she's going to sing!—"

I was neither at Aunt Angela's party nor yet in a boat on a summer's evening up the River. How can I tell you where I was? In what drawing-room? Sitting on what chair? Surrounded by what company? . . . I swear to you that I have seen a place I have never seen, been in a place I never in my life was in. I can describe to you a family gathering with Mrs. Merridew there, and her son there, and Evie there, and myself never, never there. I have seen, whether they ever existed or not, French windows opening on a lawn, and a slackened tennis-net beyond, and an evening flush in the sky, and the air dark with homing rooks. . . Nothing will persuade me that these eyes are in fact ignorant of that quiet home of Archie Merridew's—and yet Guildford is a place in which I have never been.

THEN A SOUND LIKE THE hissing of a thousand cisterns filled my ears. Through it I heard Kitty Windus's scream of terror, but it sounded an infinite distance away. From Evie I had heard nothing. For one moment I saw everything reel and aslant—Kato, the Schmerveloffians on the sofa, the cistern-post with its hats and coats and one hook empty, steeving up towards a tilted ceiling. . .

Then came the blow on the back of my head, and the sounds of the cistern ceased. I had fallen across Aunt Angela's tiled hearth, and lay in a cloud of steam from the kettle I had overturned in my fall.

PART IV

IDDESLEIGH GATE

I

It is against the advice of my doctors that I have written these last pages—these last chapters in fact—at all. But I wrote them only a very little at a time, after I came back from Hastie's place in Scotland. And I went to Scotland only after I came back from Egypt. But I am back at the Consolidation now, having missed nearly a year, and I really don't think that this private writing tires me too much.

I admit that it seems odd that I should wish to do it at all, and doubly odd that I should have kept, not one private record, but two.[2] I thought I had finished when the first one came to an end. Then I found I hadn't. Let me say quite plainly, however, that the second one is no retractation of the first. There is not a single statement in that first writing from which I recede. I stand by every word of it. I wrote there, for example, that I did not fear to be left alone in my library at night; and that is true. I wrote that there glided no shadowy shape by my side when I stepped into my brougham or passed between the saluting commissionaires in Pall Mall; and that also is true. It is true that I play with my clean-born children, both of them, and still do not pardon even the meditation of that old crime that would have made the life of her I love an abhorrence worse than death. These things are as true now as when I first wrote them, and I shall die without regret for them.

But the impulse that drives a man to write about himself at all still remains a curious thing. I don't find it an inexplicable one—but as I shall return to this by-and-by, I will leave it for the present. Let me say this, however, now; that whatever cares may or may not weigh on me, I neither consider myself on my defence nor yet join hands with Schmerveloff and his crew in their sweeping and futile denunciations of the whole Scheme of Things as they are. If I cannot stand alone I can at least fall alone, and I haven't fallen yet.

Nevertheless, this writing will have to be less frequently indulged (if that is the word); there is little sense in paying doctors if you don't take their advice. There have been few physically stronger men than I; especially my strength of finger and forearm and wrist have been remarkable; and I can still bend a half-crown and make a dog's leg out of a thick poker. But I don't pretend that I am the man I was. Separately,

---

2. See "In Accordance with the Evidence."

my brain and body work as well as ever they did, but they do not always jump together. I don't know whether this is due to the hole Aunt Angela's blackleaded fender made in my skull. It was a bad hole, and I cracked three of Aunt Angela's brown tiles. Perhaps that is the reason why my doctor advised me to get to bed early, and cautioned me about the use of stimulating drinks and heating foods. . . Let me see, let me see. . .

Ah, yes, I was going to speak of that evening. Mercifully, Evie was spared the worst of that shock. So gently and easily that for quite a time nobody discovered it, she had slid off into a faint at the very beginning of that song of Aschael's, and so had not seen my own headlong fall. This saved us from a disaster, for otherwise our little girl would probably not have been born in the following July, not to be welcomed by her father until October came. Indeed, I had to wait till October before I learned a good many things; but such was my state of lassitude that I was able to do so without impatience, and even without much interest, content to be free from pain and to be looked after by those people of Hastie's party. After a time they began to allow me to do little things—superintend the packing of the luncheon-baskets and, as I grew better, to join the guns in the clearing when the whistle went; and Evie, away at Broadstairs with Aunt Angela (who had given up her room in the little "circus"), sometimes seemed part of a charming but not very moving dream to me. You see from this how bad I was. . . Then I returned, and the winter in Egypt and Hastie's house in Scotland began in their turn to fade.

Apart from my work at the Consolidation, I began to be full of a curiously single preoccupation. I had not brooded on this while I had been away: as I have said, I had not brooded on anything; it merely came back to me as the most natural thing to do, a matter of course. It was the thing that Louie Causton, against what she conceived to be her own interests, had advised that night when I had dined with her at the Models' Club. There was something I must now tell Evie.

I think I let it go, vaguely, as "something." It was not that I did not know perfectly well what it was; but those lazy days free from pain among the heather had made that also somehow unreal; I suppose I had worn smooth the thought of it; and it seemed nothing to make a fuss about. It did not even require resolution. It was merely something that ought to have been done long ago. This was my attitude of mind then. I don't say that it is now.

That long separation had altered our relation in more ways than one. With such joy did I rejoin Evie that for both of us it was as if we were newly, and yet both more strongly and more peacefully, married again. My lovely little Phyllis had put even poor Jackie's nose out of joint. On the other hand, a year is a year, and if my own time had been one of vacancy and healing, Evie's had not. I had only to listen to her and Aunt Angela to become aware of this. They had made quite a circle of acquaintances in Broadstairs; several of these had since been kept up in London; and there were things I was at least temporarily out of. I mention this not because I wanted to be in at them; indeed it all seemed to me a little casual; but I could hardly have expected Evie to sit moping in a boarding-house parlour all that time, and certainly she looked a picture of blooming health. I say "looked," because it was only later that I learned what the first question of the doctor who had attended her had been: "Has she ever had a severe shock?"

I am unable to explain how it was that at first I was quite incurious to know what people had thought of that extraordinary collapse of mine, and why the effect of that song on Kitty Windus, for example, should have been less marked than its effect on myself. For Kitty, though she had screamed, and babbled incoherent things that probably I have never been told about, had sustained no lasting injury. An icy breath had passed over everybody there, and nobody, I thought, would be so morbid as to push their inquiries into the varying degrees of iciness. I may say at once that I thought quite rightly. Nobody has, not even (so far as I am aware) Miriam Levey.

It was from Aunt Angela, of course, that I learned what that first question of the Broadstairs doctor had been; and it brought me face to face with that so easily assumed resolution of mine rather sharply. By mere luck Evie had escaped that shock of the party, but the original one, the seven or eight years' old one, remained. That I might know exactly to what extent this might affect my determination, I had the Broadstairs doctor to meet my own more distinguished one. I told this one of the tragedy of Evie's former engagement, and related the affair of the gramophone. He looked grave.

"You must see that she doesn't get another shock," he said.

Evie herself was not made aware that the visit had more than an ordinary significance.

But Louie's advice now seemed rather beside the mark.

I saw Louie daily now; and whether it was that she had been able to entrench herself behind her work in my absence, or had found some *modus vivendi* midway between that ecstasy of the night when she had supported me in a Chelsea doorway and the anguished outbreak of that other evening in the Models' Club, or however it was, my fears for the impossibility of the situation now appeared to have been groundless. Whitlock, indeed, saw more of her than I. He spoke exceedingly favourably of her. She used quickness and common-sense in her work, he said, and, when he had half-a-dozen things to do at once, did not take down a remark interpolated to somebody else as part of the letter he was dictating. I was not surprised to learn that she "flashed" intelligently at unexplained meanings. She converted Whitlock's rapid mumbled instructions into (commercial) English with ease, and had already attracted Pepper's notice.

I don't know whether it has struck you that Evie, who had given it as a sufficient reason for renewing her intimacy with Miriam Levey and Kitty Windus that they had been at the old Business College in Holborn together, had never once urged the same thing on behalf of Louie Causton. It was not that I wanted her to do so; as a matter of fact I very much preferred them apart. And I thought I saw the reason for Evie's silence. Louie trailed an unhappy story behind her. Louie had been a model. Aunt Angela had not asked her to her party. If there was any coolness between Miriam Levey and Louie, which now might well be, Evie would naturally be disposed to take the part of the former. I don't mean to say that she looked down on Louie. It was only later that I learned that she wasted a thought on Louie. I only mean that their paths lay in different directions, and that Evie had hitherto appeared content that they should do so.

It was in a roundabout way that I discovered that Louie had a place in Evie's thoughts. Acting under my doctor's orders, I had begun to come home early in the afternoon, seldom working after tea; and I entered the drawing-room one afternoon to find a couple of her Broadstairs acquaintances, a Mr. and Mrs. Smithson, with her. Smithson was, I think, a cycle agent; she was an openwork-stockinged, flirtatious little woman, for ever making eyes, and apparently under the impression that all conversation would languish unless she took the greater part of it upon herself. I imagine it had been she who had sent Evie one or two vulgar seaside post cards that, had they been addressed to me, would have gone straight into the fire. It appeared that they knew Peddie slightly, my old Jun. Ex. Con. of the F.B.C., and now Whitlock's abstract clerk; and I was not disposed to congratulate Peddie on the acquaintance.

They were just leaving as I arrived, so that we only exchanged a few words; indeed, the ringing of the telephone I had had fixed up in my study gave me an excuse to cut our leave-taking short. I went to the instrument; it was Louie Causton with a message from Whitlock; and I gave my instructions and returned to Evie.

Now Jackie, who was just beginning to babble and notice things, was greatly interested in the telephone, and I entered the drawing-room just in time to hear him make some remark about "plitty typies." As I took no notice, Jackie repeated the unchildlike expression. Evie was pouring me out more tea.

"Plitty typies, farzer," Jackie clamoured, imperious for notice.

I turned to Evie.

"Where did he pick that up?" I asked.

Evie said: "Oh, it was some silly joke of Florrie's."

"Florrie is Mrs. Smithson?"

"Yes."

I was not pleased. I suppose that, like Charles Lamb, I am squeamish about my women and children, and I remembered Mrs. Smithson's post cards. One of them had borne the legend, "Detained at office—very pressing business," and if you have seen these things you will not want it described. But I was loth to raise again the question I had formerly raised about Miss Levey and Aschael, and so I merely asked whether it was not possible for her to give Mrs. Smithson tea without having Jackie there. She said, "Very well," though in a tone a little subdued. She knew what I meant.

It was ten minutes later that, returning of her own accord to the subject, she said a little poutingly: "I don't see much to make a fuss about. He doesn't know what it means."

"That doesn't improve matters very much," I said. "It seems to me to make them worse."

"Oh, very well," she answered.

But she returned to the subject yet again. She spoke defensively.

"I had to have him at Broadstairs with me. You couldn't have him in Scotland with you."

"Jackie, you mean?"

"Yes."

She gave a slightly marked shade of meaning to the words "in Scotland." To tell the truth, it was a little on my mind that I had had the more desirable summer of the two of us. I am no snob, but I do prefer some people to others, and if people do run in strata, well, nobody can tell me much I don't know about the clerk and cycle-agent class, and they don't charm me. I spoke with a little compunction.

"I wish it could have been helped, darling. Anyway, we sha'n't be separated again."

(I may say that I don't think Evie had thought it very remarkable that I should have had that accident at Aunt Angela's party. She had fainted herself, and knew little of the later events; and we have lived too long together for her not to be aware that, rugged as I may appear to the rest of the world, I am a sensitive man.)

After a moment's silence: "Mrs. Smithson has asked me down to Broadstairs for a week," she said. "She—of course she hadn't met you."

"You mean she's asked you without me?"

"She hadn't met you," Evie excused Mrs. Smithson.

"And—shall you go?"

She answered quite readily: "Of course not—not without you."

I got up and kissed her. I had expected no less of her.

But I knew that she would have liked to go to Broadstairs, and was only staying away out of her duty to me, it was not for me to deny her her sex's equivalent of a grumble—a sigh. Then we began to talk.

We talked quite equably: I never in my life wrangled with Evie. I said, quite gently, that I did not wish the boy to acquire precocious chatter about pressing business and pretty typists, and Evie made no opposition; indeed, she laughed when I suggested how unlikely it was that any pretty typist would have pressing business with myself. By-and-by she asked me who had rung me up, and I told her. "Oh, yes, I forgot; she's with you now," she said; "Mr. Whitlock engaged her, didn't he?"

"Yes," I answered. Then, after a little further talk, we kissed again, and she went out to give Phyllis her bath.

Oddly enough, very soon after speaking thus of Louie after that long silence, she saw Louie herself. One morning she announced that she was going shopping that day, and would call for me at Pall Mall and bring me home to tea. She finished her shopping earlier than she had thought she would, and, not wishing to disturb me before the appointed time, had come upon Louie in the counting-house. She told me this when we got home. She had asked Louie to show her round, and was full of the wonders of the place—the lifts, the telephone exchange, the series of waiting-rooms, the advice-board from Lloyd's, the acre-wide office full of busy clerks. "What a change from Holborn!" she said she had said to Louie, and then Louie had brought her to my own private room.

The next day Louie made a mistake in a rather important draft. It was not like her, and Whitlock blamed himself for having left too much to her intuition. The error necessitated a consultation between Louie, Whitlock and myself. It was set right, and Louie was going out again when I glanced at Whitlock. He looked inquiringly, nodded, and left us. There was something I wanted to say to Louie; perhaps it was rather something that it would not be very graceful not to say; perhaps it was both.

I think this was the first time I spoke to her at the Consolidation except on business.

"Well, that will be all right," I said, dismissing the error in the draft. . . "By the way, you saw my wife yesterday, didn't you?"

She gave a little nod.

"And showed her round? It was very good of you. She enjoyed it very much. She told me all about it."

Louie said something about it being no trouble, and then appeared to be going. But I stopped her. Then, when I had stopped her, I didn't quite know what to say.

"Oh—er—" I said awkwardly, looking at her and then looking away again. "Without opening matters up—you know what I mean—going into things—I want to say just one thing. It's about—a piece of advice you once gave me."

She had half opened the inner door, and stood, as it were, on the threshold of the box-like space between the inner one and the outer one of baize. The look she gave me was almost hostile, and the tourmalines were shut. I don't think, by the way, that she ever heard of that incident at Aunt Angela's party. I neither asked her whether she had, nor ever told her about it.

"If you feel that you must—" she said, not very invitingly.

"It's merely this," I said rather hurriedly, "that what you suggested is impossible now."

"Yes," she said; "I suppose it is."

"Her doctor's forbidden it—I mean, he says she mustn't have another shock."

Instantly I saw, by the way in which she said, "Oh!" that she had had something else in her mind. "Oh! . . . I see," she said, and I pondered.

"Ah!" I said at last. "You mean you've just seen—just this moment?"

She made no reply.

"You've just seen, just this moment. Then why did you say yes, you supposed so?"

Her answer was impatient. "Oh, *must* you?"

"Must I what?"

"Must you do this?"

"Ask you why you assented when I said something was impossible now?"

"Ask me anything at all!" she almost snapped.

I gave her a long look. "Shut the door," I said. . . "Now tell me why you agreed with me when I said that it was impossible to take your advice now."

The tourmalines flickered almost scornfully. "Don't you know?"

"I do not."

"What! You can't guess?"

"Will you tell me?"

For a moment she looked as if she was going to sit down for something that would require time; but she changed her mind, and stood, a crumple of skirt grasped in either hand.

"Ask me again and I will," she said, in a slightly raised voice.

"I do ask you."

Then, with a harsh little laugh, Louie made her second mistake of that day.

"Because she's jealous," she said. "Evidently that wasn't *your* reason; I don't know what yours was; but that's mine."

"Oh!" I said. In the face of a statement so preposterous I really could think of nothing else to say.

"What else did she come here yesterday for?" Louie demanded.

I smiled. That was too absurd. "Well—shall we say to keep an appointment with her husband?" I suggested.

"Oh, if you like! . . . Then why does she want to come and see me at my house?" she demanded.

It was news to me that Evie did want to go and see Louie at her house, but I was careful not to let Louie see that.

"Oh!" I said, still smiling. "And you think these grounds enough for your statement?"

"My good—" she broke out. "I'm not asking you to accept them. I know better than to try to persuade *you*! You asked me, and I've told you; that's all."

"And if I say once for all that it is not so, and that nothing could make it so?"

"Make it so!" she broke out. "Really, Jeff, you talk like—a man! 'Make it so!' . . . If you can't see your little definite reason for everything, you deny the fact! If I could say that Kitty Windus and Miriam Levey had been chattering—I'm not aware that they have, but if I *could* say that—I suppose you'd call that a reason, and listen to it; but anything else—pshaw! I don't care a button for your reason! Your reason may have made this business, but it won't persuade a woman against something she knows—myself *or* Evie. It just is so, and there's an end of it. And of course you see the beautiful new fix it puts you in." She gave a little stamp that made her garments quiver.

"Louie, I can't—"

"Oh, a perfect fix! Really, I'm curious to know what you're going to do about it! Try to persuade her that there's nothing between you and me! Try it, try it! Why, how shouldn't she be jealous when I am? Do you think she doesn't see that? Oh, I don't know why I waste words with you! . . . But you see your fix. It was Kitty before, and you tried half telling then; now it's me; but it isn't either of us really; oh, if it only could be! . . . It's the secret, Jim. You've got to tell her—and you can't. I don't know what this is about a shock, but it's too late now. Try it if you like—I don't care what you say about me. Try the half truth again—give her reason—the reason's yours whenever you want it."

Of course I couldn't listen to this nonsense and immodesty and worse. Who should know better whether Evie was jealous or not, Louie or I? Evie jealous! . . . Of course, if it were so, the position *would* be precisely as Louie had stated it. I *should* have to choose between Evie's love and the risk the doctor had so gravely foreshadowed. Our very existence together *would* hang on precisely that last desperate chance. And from the bottom of my heart I blessed my Maker that, tossed and buffeted as my life had been, at least that perfected anguish of body and spirit was to be spared me. . .

I had risen. Smiling rather sadly, I turned to Louie.

"Well—as I said—I don't want to re-open things," I said.

With the door already half open, she turned.

"Do you think they're closed?" she said.

And she did not wait for my reply.

II

It is as I feared: this writing, as a continuous record, will have to stop. My life is getting too full. I daresay its crowded outward happenings are a good thing for me; it is better, as the saying is, to wear out than to rust out; and I am beginning almost to enjoy change for change's sake.

My newest change is a removal. Pepper's latest cosmopolitan, Baron Stillhausen, wants to be rid of that Iddesleigh Gate house as it stands, and already I have taken Evie round to see it. It almost took away her breath: I didn't know how near delight could come to timidity—I almost said to dismay. When I said, "Well, darling, am I to take it?" she looked at me as much as to say "*Dare* you?" . . . I think I dare—though I have only to remember my own beginnings to be a little intimidated myself. I walked over to Verandah Cottage the other evening; a sign-writer has the place now; and it seems either very much more or very much less than four years since I lived there—sometimes hardly four months, sometimes half-a-lifetime. . . But Evie will very quickly be turning up her nose at Well Walk. Already she had begun to shop quite freely. For getting to and from Pall Mall (I told you I was to spare myself physically for the present) I have bought a small runabout of a car. Really it is only an ordinary taxi, with a rather superior shell placed on it, and I have an agreement with a young fellow who has just taken his driving certificate; but Evie was talking about a livery for him the other night, and I was pleased. That is as it should be. It will be a joy to me to see her take her proper place. . .

So this record will have to be more and more a diary, jotted down as I can find opportunity for it. I need not say that the change to Iddesleigh Gate will be a larger undertaking than, say, Aunt Angela's installation in the little "circus" near King's Cross was. And there is the Consolidation. That is heavy work, and the heavier that at present we are working very much in the dark. In these present industrial troubles, for example, we do not quite know where we shall come out; we can only throw in our weight with the big natural forces that, in history as in dynamics, balance themselves in the end. The air is thick with dust of Schmerveloff's raising; and though all this dust may turn out presently to be like the comet's tail, packable into a portmanteau, for the present it certainly obscures our vision. We have to take into account, too, that even dust is not raised without a cause; and so in public we sit, Radicals all, in solemn inquiry into things, with plenty of Westminster stage thunder, while behind the scenes we get in good old Tory heavy work, not necessarily because we are Tories, but because Toryism serves a useful purpose just at present. Once or twice lately I have disobeyed my doctor, and stayed at the office for tea, so closely in touch have I had to keep with various Committees and Conferences; and we have had to keep our staff late too, which is rather hard on them, since they get none of the kudos. But the days when I could burn the candle at both ends all the time are over for me, I'm afraid.

Louie Causton rarely gets away early now; in that respect she was better off when she sat for the evening classes at the Art Schools; but she gravitates more and more to Pepper's side of the business. That bee she has in her bonnet about Evie's being jealous of her does not, I am glad to say, impair her business efficiency. The other day Pepper remarked on her distinguished carriage, and, as he never neglects appearances, he chooses her, when an amanuensis is necessary, for his more important consultations. The other night he took her and Whitlock to dinner before going to Sir Peregrine Campbell's. I can picture his dismay had it ever been suggested that he should take Miss Levey out to dinner. And Stonor and Peddie do not crack the old jokes they did at the F.B.C., about "Miss Causton's pal—Sir Peregrine," or "You know who I mean—that friend of Miss Causton's—the Under Secretary for Foreign Affairs." Indeed there seem to be fewer jokes going about than there used to be. We are all getting older—Louie (save for those slender yacht-like lines of hers), Aunt Angela (whose self-satisfied humilities have rather lost their resilience since that night of her housewarming in the little "circus"), Evie (who now takes the prospect of a day and a night nursery as a matter of course, and has bills sent in to me quite naturally) and the rest of us. Even Billy Izzard, clean painter as he is, seems to be forcing his jokes. He has lately found an artificial amusement in balls and pageants, rather to the neglect of his work; and all this, slight as it seems—I mean the spread of the love of amusement—has actually more to do with Consolidation than you would guess. . . But I must stop. I get Consolidation enough during the day without bringing it home with me at night. Evie has just knocked at the door. That is her signal that I have "consolidated" enough—as she calls this journal of which she has never heard.

For the first time I make this frankly a diary. According to my agreement, we go into Iddesleigh Gate on Lady Day; as a matter of fact we are there now. My lease is for ten years. I got as many of Stillhausen's effects as I wanted at forced-sale rates; a good deal I didn't want. Evie went half wild with joy about a certain crystal bath; I about the Amaranth Room. It is extraordinary how few pieces it takes to furnish this last splendid apartment: a settee, a few chairs, a few cabinets, a bust or two, and the vast turfy carpet. . . A smaller room would look half empty with twice the furniture. Billy says it's the proportions, and is puzzling about them, seeking what he calls "the unit," and taking now the length of a gilt Empire settee, now the height of a lacquered cabinet, now his own height, etc., etc. It is Evie's music room; she has begun her lessons; but it will be some time, I am afraid, before she makes very much of it. Billy threatens to quarter himself on us while he makes paintings of the whole house. Aunt Angela has two rooms on the second floor, with distempered walls; and she began her furnishing with a crucifix. My library is stately. The heavy, slow-moving doors scarcely make a click when they close, and a bell-connection down the passage warns me of the approach of anybody. I suppose Stillhausen found this useful; he was in the Diplomatic Service; and perhaps it is well that these stamped leather walls do not whisper secrets. There is a secret of my own that I keep in the bureau by the heat-regulator there. I am not sure that the fire would not be the best place for it. It is odd, by the way, that this impulse to burn these papers should lately have become almost as strong as the impulse to write them formerly was.

I have a telephone switchboard to half the rooms in the house, and the line to Pall Mall is doubled, the second wire not passing through the Company's Exchange. A switch turns on the masked lights behind the cornice, and what with one device and another, it would pay me to have a private electrician. Aunt Angela, I may say, who has managed to reconcile herself to heavier expenditures, is harrowed at the waste of electric power, and wanders about the house turning off switches. On a Jacobean table at the far end of the library are two small bright things with branches—that is to say, they seem small until you take a walk to them. They are Pepper's candlesticks. I have attained the scale.

That impulse to destroy these papers has reminded me of a little thing that happened while I was away in Scotland. One of Hastie's boys, Ronald, aged fourteen, has a little den of his own in the back part of the house, and during my convalescence he was so good as to make me welcome there. The paraphernalia of I don't know how many hobbies littered the place; his latest had been chemistry; and he stank of chemicals, and had his clothes red-spotted with acids. His greatest success, at which I was privileged to assist, was to fill ginger-beer bottles with hydrogen and explode them. One day he invited me to witness a really superior explosion. It was lucky he did invite me. He had charged an earthenware jar, as big as a bucket, with the gas and would probably have blown the wall out. He said he didn't funk it, but I did, and we opened the window and allowed the gas to be lost.

I feel rather like that about this writing. Last night I almost made away with the dangerous stuff. But I hung back. It has cost so hideously dear. This may be a sentimentalism, and obscure, but there it is, and as it puzzles me I shall try to get to the bottom of it. . .

N.B.—Evie says she will soon "begin to feel that she lives here." She is getting used to having things; soon she will be getting used to having people. Soon she'll have to be thinking about her first dinner-party. Must stop now. The more sleep I get before midnight the better. I shall think about the destroying, though.

29th April

(A month since I made an entry.) A rather curious conversation with Evie last night. You will remember that Louie Causton, trying to justify that ridiculous attitude of hers about Evie's jealousy, had exclaimed, as if that clinched something, "Why does she want to come to my house, then?" Well, she has been. Apparently she went some little time ago, but she only spoke of it last night. I shall not ask Louie for her account of it; this is Evie's:

She went on a Saturday afternoon, taking the train from Clapham Junction. Louie was just setting out with her boy to the South Kensington Museum, but she turned back. Since Kitty left her she has got another governess for the lad, but she still devotes her Saturdays and Sundays to him. There are several things about Evie's account I am not quite clear about, but I admit that she has no great gift for picking out the essentials of a conversation, and perhaps unconsciously she has emphasised the wrong things. She told me, for example, a good deal about Master Jim, but said very little about Kitty's reason for going over to Miriam Levey. She wandered off into old recollections of the

Business College in Holborn that I had forgotten all about, and allowed these things to divert her from the visit itself. I had to ask her whether Louie seemed comfortable in her rooms, whether they were decently furnished or not, and so on; and she said, "Oh, of course, you've never seen them," and described them to me in excellent detail. Then suddenly she asked me whether Miss Lingard (who had been away out of sorts), was back at the Consolidation yet. Miss Lingard was my own private amanuensis, and during her absence Louie had had to help with her work. . . And so we talked. This was in our own bedroom, while Evie was making ready for the night.

"Well," I said, yawning, "and what did you talk about besides the Holborn days?"

"Oh, lots of things," she answered brightly, busily brushing. "She's got to look older since then—but I daresay you wouldn't notice that, seeing her every day."

"Louie Causton, you mean?"

"Yes."

"Did she say anything about Miss Levey?"

"Oh, yes. Her correspondence class is a great success. Schmerveloff's taken her up, and she's no end of pupils. Wasn't it funny, our living next door to Schmerveloff and not knowing it? They little thought that in a few years we should be living here!"

I laughed a little. She glows prettily when she shows her pride in my achievement. Then I yawned again. "Well," I said sleepily, "I hope Kitty's changed friends for the better."

"Oh, she thinks so," Evie replied promptly. "You see, it wasn't very nice for her, when she'd had the boy all days, and Louie didn't come in till ten or eleven or twelve at night, or later, to be snapped at and spoken crossly to."

Here I checked a yawn. "What's that?" I said. "Miss Causton didn't tell you that, did she?"

"Eh?" said Evie. "Oh, no, of course she didn't. Didn't I tell you I looked in at their offices in Gray's Inn one day—Kitty's and Miriam's? Oh, that was a fortnight and more ago! I'm sure I told you, Jeff! . . . And Miriam took me to the New College in Kingsway. It's nothing like the Consolidation, of course, but it's such an improvement on that poky old Holborn place! How we ever gave a dance there I can't imagine. You remember that dance, Jeff?"

And she was back at the old College once more.

I said this conversation was curious, but perhaps that was not quite the word. Slightly distasteful would be nearer, for of course you see what it all implied. It implied that Evie might easily be dragged into some trumpery quarrel between Louie Causton and Miriam Levey. For Miriam would not be at all above concluding that Louie had schemed to get her place, and that I had thrown my influence into the balance; and anybody could always make poor Kitty agree with them. I didn't want Evie mixed up in anything of that kind. I was even a little sorry she had been to see Louie. How little, for my own part, there existed in the way of affection between Louie and myself you already know; and, if the thing was not quite the same from Louie's point of view, I did not see that any useful end would be served by their being much together. On that morning when Louie had first made her ridiculous suggestion about jealousy, her whole manner had been rather that of one who throws up the sponge, ceases to exercise care, I don't know what; and there is no sense in deliberately manufacturing something that doesn't exist. And about that other visit to Gray's Inn. I am quite sure that Miriam Levey would not scruple to hurt me in any way she could. . . There's the telephone; Whitlock, I expect.

10th May

In a week Evie is to give her first dinner-party. Naturally she is a little timorous about it. The fact that Pepper, with whom, I am sorry to say, she gets on no better, will be there to watch her, would be quite enough to flurry her; but there will also be other people there whom she hasn't seen yet—the Hasties, the Campbells, Sichel, a Mrs. Richmond (a very smart little woman, a friend of Pepper's) and others. Poor dear, it will be rather an ordeal for her, and no wonder she spoke to me the other night a little crossly. It hurt a little at the time, but I have forgotten it. I will put it down, however.

Among all these "Hons. and Sirs," as she calls them, plain familiar Whitlock and Billy Izzard (I am dragging Billy in because these people may be useful to him when he has got over his pageant craze) were her chief comforts; but the question of the final chair, a lady's, had arisen. There being nobody else I particularly wanted, I had been disposed to call on Pepper, who can always produce a prettily frocked woman or a well-turned-out young man at a moment's notice; but Evie had managed to get a dig in at Pepper, at which I laughed heartily. "He might bring Mrs. Toothill for all we know," she had said. "No, Jeff, it's our party," she had demurred, and had then ruminated. . .

"All right, anybody you like," I had agreed cheerfully.

"You don't like Mrs. Smithson," she had then said doubtfully.

Of course, having just given her full liberty, I ought not to have qualified it, even by a look; but I confess my face fell. It was only for an instant, and I hoped my darling hadn't noticed it.

"Have Mrs. Smithson if you like," I said a little shortly, I am afraid.

But she had noticed. She spoke shortly too.

"No, thank you, not to have her thrown in my face afterwards. I know you don't think the Smithsons are good enough."

I was shocked. "Dearest," I said slowly, "when have I 'thrown things in your face afterwards,' as you call it?"

She must indeed have been tried, otherwise she would never have said the absurd thing she did.

"Well, if you don't say it, you think it. Better have your friend, Miss Causton. She can go out to dinner with Sir Julius, it seems."

"Evie!" I exclaimed, for the moment deeply wounded.

"Well, you told me she did, and if she can dine with him she can with you, I suppose."

I turned away. "I shall leave it entirely to you," I said. I reproach myself now for my impatience.

But instantly her generous little heart was itself again. She ran after me and threw her arms about my neck.

"Forgive me, Jeff," she pleaded tearfully. "I didn't mean anything, and I am *so* afraid of it all! I'm *not* used to it, you know, but I am doing my best. Do ask Mr. Pepper to bring somebody."

And we kissed and said no more about it. Perhaps I am foolish to write it down.

14th May

Evie has made the acquaintance of most of her guests for the seventeenth beforehand. The Hasties have called on her, and Lady Campbell, and Pepper has brought Mrs. Richmond (who, I confess, strikes me as rather a superfine Mrs. Smithson), and half her fears are gone. She didn't much care for Mrs. Richmond, she says; "toney" was the adjective she used; but she quite took dear homely Lady Campbell under her wing. She likes receiving, she says, and remarked, rather acutely, that what makes these little afternoon functions the occasion for bickering they are, is that people seem to rattle off what they have to say without an interval for breath, and then to take their departure. She had Jackie down, and Phyllis was brought down for a moment by her nurse; and Jackie showed Lady Campbell his ship. Lady Campbell married her husband when he was master and a fifth-part owner of a coasting boat; and when Jackie lifted the hatch of his model to show her the "cabin" she laughed, and said it was a far more comfortable cabin than that in which she spent her honeymoon. Then Jackie, of course, wanted to know what a honeymoon was, and when told made some remark about a honeymoon that set everybody laughing except Evie, who blushed. I hope she will not forget how to blush among all her smart ladies. I find her blushing adorable.

17th May, 4 P.M.

Without warning, a thing that I had thought impossible has come upon me. For nearly twenty hours—since nine o'clock last night—my thoughts have been such a series of jerks, stoppings, leapings forward and dead stops again as only once before in my life I have known. I have paced my private room at the Consolidation for half the day, and have done no work since I looked over and signed the papers that were brought to me here last night. Were I able to speak of "mere nothings" I should say that a mere nothing has brought all this about. Let me tell it. I have come home for the purpose of telling it.

Since I began to leave the Consolidation early, papers have often been brought to me here. Usually Stonor brings them, and is shown straight into the library. You may judge of their urgency when I tell you that last night there was nobody to bring them but Louie Causton.

Evie, Aunt Angela and I were just finishing dinner when the servant whispered to me. I think he said "Somebody from Pall Mall, sir," for if he had said "A lady" I should have wondered who the lady was, which I didn't do. I was expecting the papers; they would not keep me long; so, telling Evie that I should be back in a few minutes, I followed the servant out.

Louie was standing by my desk. She had not lifted her veil, and I do not know what it was about her attitude that struck me. Something did; I suppose it was some proportion or relation; something that Billy would perhaps have called the "beautiful unit" of the room; some purely æsthetic quality, I don't doubt, which it is odd I should remember now. . .

She was looking towards me as I entered; she had heard that discreet bell of Stillhausen's; and only when I advanced did she push her veil back.

"Here are these," she said, with a twisted, pained sort of little smile. "The others had all gone home, and I understood they were to come at once. No, thanks, I won't sit down."

Even when it appeared that, after all, the papers would need a few minutes' looking into, she still refused to sit down. She stood as close to the papers she had brought as if, without them, her sole reason for being there, she might have been ejected; and as she still persisted in her refusal to sit, I sat down myself.

It took me perhaps a quarter of an hour to go through the papers. It was as I was pushing back my chair that Stillhausen's bell purred again. A moment later there was a tap at the door. "Come in!" I called.

Evie entered.

I was not embarrassed. It humiliates me to have to write that word now, so many hours later. There was nothing to be embarrassed at. Indeed, as Evie advanced from the door, I barely explained the reason for Miss Causton's call. Louie touched the hand Evie extended. Evie was not, as she was with Miriam Levey and Kitty Windus, on kissing terms with Louie.

"I think you'll find these all right now," I said, giving Louie back the papers. "I don't know whether Miss Causton has had supper, Evie?"

Evie smiled graciously. "Yes, won't you have something, Miss Causton? Let me have them lay a tray for you—it will be really no trouble."

But Louie would take nothing. She had drawn down her veil again, and was extending her fingers to Evie. "Don't trouble to come, Mr. Jeffries," she said, moving towards the door, while Evie prattled polite phrases.

But I took her to the door. Four words—a "Good-night" on either side—were all that passed between us. Then I returned to the library.

Evie was standing where Louie had been standing, but no sooner did I enter than she passed me. Taking into account the warning of Stillhausen's bell, she must have waited for the purpose of so passing me. But this did not strike me until a little later. Only when she reached the door did she turn and speak.

"Did Miss Causton ask for me?" she said.

"Eh?" I asked, surprised. . . "No. Why?"

"Oh, nothing. Only that I thought that when one called one asked for the lady of the house."

I smiled as I set my writing-table to rights. "'Called?' It was hardly a call, my dear."

"Evidently not."

I looked quickly up. Evie's tone was new to me.

"Come, come, darling—a necessary matter of business," I expostulated.

"I'm sorry I interrupted."

"'Interrupted!' . . . Good gracious, Evie!"

"But of course I didn't; you can't be interrupted here."

I was astonished.

"Why, what—what do you mean?"

She looked coldly at me, without replying.

I frowned. I am ashamed to say that it cost me a little effort to master an impatience that had suddenly arisen in me. I spoke slowly for that purpose.

"If by your last remark you mean that bell, Evie, it was here before we came, and I fancy you knew it was. At any rate it shall be taken away tomorrow."

Very irritatingly (I have told you how I am not quite the man of phlegm I was) she took me up at my last word.

"Oh, yes, about tomorrow," she said. "You don't happen to be going out tonight, do you?"

"No. Why?" This was stranger than ever. She knew I never went out at night now.

"Because Mrs. Hastie telephoned me today. Joan isn't well, and can't come. So perhaps you'd like Sir Julius to ask somebody else—unless, of course—"

"Unless what?"

"Unless—there's somebody you'd rather ask yourself."

For a moment I was silent; then, "Evie," I said slowly, "do you—I don't see how you can, but do you—mean Louie Causton?"

She laughed tremulously. "Oh, very well; if I can't, I can't, I suppose, so that ends it."

And the next moment she was gone.

Half-an-hour later I met her on the stairs.

"Oh," she announced, without preface, "Phyllis isn't very well, and I think I shall spend the night in the nursery with her."

She has done so.

I have had a wretched night. I turned and turned, but found no sleep. By dint of turning, I found something else, though—a new meaning in those words Louie Causton had said to me: "If I could say that Miriam Levey and Kitty Windus had been chattering, which I can't—" I tossed and tossed.

At half-past ten this morning I went round to the offices of the Women's Emancipation League in Gray's Inn. I can't say, even when I found myself there, asking for Miss Levey, that I was very clear in my own mind as to why I had gone, but if anybody *had* been tampering with Evie, it was as likely to be the Jewess as anybody else.

She kept me waiting: a thing, I may say, that few people do nowadays. I waited in a matchboarded anteroom, among emancipated flappers and middle-aged disciples of Schmerveloff. Then Miss Levey herself came in as if by accident, and gushed out into apologies. She had had no idea it was I, she said; she did so beg my pardon. . . She showed me into an inner room in which a hairy man, the single male-bird of the run, was expounding from a Blue Book to three or four more women; one of them was the lady who had participated in the intellectual courtship on the night of Aunt Angela's party. I turned to Miss Levey.

"I should like, if I may, to speak to you in private," I said.

She asked if Mr. Boris's room was empty. The hairy man, looking up from his Blue Book for a moment, said that he thought so. She led the way into Mr. Boris's room.

At the sight of her all my old dislike revived, and I found myself able to go straight to the point. I did so, without wasting a word.

"I've called to ask you, Miss Levey, whether you've given my wife the impression that I was the cause of your leaving the Freight and Ballast Company in order that room might he made for Miss Causton?"

She gave a shocked "Mis-ter Jeffries!" but I held up my hand.

"I know I'm putting it bluntly. You can be as blunt as you like also. Will you tell me whether that is so?"

"May I die, Mr. Jeffries—but *surely* you know I'd arranged with Mr. Schmerveloff long before!"

"I see. You dismissed us. Very well. Then let me put it in another form. Have you, in my wife's hearing, associated my name with Miss Causton's in any way whatever?"

This time her answer was not quite so ready. When it came, it was a question.

"Do you mean lately, Mr. Jeffries?"

"At any time, but especially lately."

Then she broke into glib speech, and all her "w's" became "v's."

"There, now I *knew* there vould be mischief before it was all over! 'Vot *is* the good of going into it?' I said; 'vot *is* the good, ven nobody even believed it at the time? Evie was there,'I said, 'and knew it was not true, so vy rake it all up now, Kitty?' I said. 'Ve all knew all about poor Louie,' I said, 'and vot's done's done anyway, and Evie doesn't vant to hear about it.'"

Here, suddenly tingling curiously all over, I interrupted Miss Levey. I spoke with a steadiness that astonished myself.

"One moment. You seem to be speaking of a definite occasion. Was this lately?"

Miss Levey was all pouting bosom, thick lips and fluent hands.

"Vy, *yes*! Ven Evie came here. Evie and Kitty and me, though vy I have Kitty here at all I don't know, seeing she makes slips in her work, and Mr. Schmerveloff grumbles, and the other girls has it all to do over again—"

And the torrent continued.

I don't know what else she said; the rest didn't matter. Why it didn't matter you will see when I tell you that the tongue of a dead young libertine once, years before, had made free with Louie Causton's name and my own, and that the abominable slander, which had lasted for some days, had turned on nothing less than the paternity of Louie's child. All at the Business College, including Evie, had known of it; they had known, too, of the public apology I had been prompt to exact; but that mattered nothing, nothing, nothing now. This wretched little Israelite, revelling in her "v's," and even touching my sleeve from time to time, had seen to that. What the filthy rest was I do not know. Doubtless, beginning with that, and with the feeble Kitty to support her, she had made a complete history of jealousy. . . And she did not even triumph openly. She lisped and protested, and put all on Kitty. . . I left her, and almost fled from Louie also when, returning to Pall Mall, I encountered her coming out of Whitlock's room.

And now I have sat since lunch wondering what is to be done next. The afternoon hours have brought me no more light then those of the night did. Dully, I liken my life to that Maze at Hampton Court in which, one happy Sunday I don't know how long ago, Evie and I spent an hour. As then I seem to see Miss Levey's flamingo red behind the green hedges; she seems to lurk in my life, too wary to confront me, too malicious not to scratch. I am lost in winding intricacies. True, there is a door, even as there is a door at Hampton Court that is opened when the labyrinth is to be emptied. I find myself brought up against this door time after time, but I do not know what lies beyond it. You see what the door is: it is to tell Evie everything—everything. . . Too wonderful Louie! Why, if you foresaw all this, did you not *make* me tell her—thrust me into a closet with her and keep the door until it was done—instead of letting me grope in my blindness and slip ever further and further away from her? . . . Oh, I am tired, tired.

I am too tired even to be angry for my poor practised-upon darling. For they have sprung this horrible thing upon her. Half the time she does not, cannot, believe it; of the other half of her life they have made a torment. Poor lamb! Of course if they are cruel enough they can make it seem plausible to her; I only wonder that, harrowed as she must have been for all these weeks, she has borne up at all. *I* know the horror she must have wrestled with! . . . That *that* wicked old story should crop up again! . . . But I must stop. Perhaps an hour's sleep will do me good.

5.30 P.M.

That was a reckless thing to do, to go to sleep with these papers spread out on the table and my door unlocked. Not that my household is a staff of commercial collegiates, able to read this out-of-date old shorthand; but it was foolish for all that. Anyhow I am rather better, and think I can face the dinner tonight. After that I don't know what I shall do. I have not seen Evie all day.

I never felt less up to a dinner. But a little champagne will keep me going. They will be here in two hours and a half. It will take Evie an hour and a half to dress; I wonder what she is doing for the final hour! Dear heart, if she only knew how I ache to go up to her; but I must not do that until I have made up my mind what course to take. I shall have come to a resolution before I sleep tonight that will settle things one way or the other. We cannot stop at this *impasse*. I don't think Evie's is a real jealousy. Tomorrow she will be sobbing on my shoulder that she has harboured it. But at present it has the venomous effect of the real thing, and if I do not put an end to it, it will recur. Let me think. . .

Again it comes upon me—why do I write this at all, that I shall most certainly be destroying? I have hardly the heart to think it out, but as it may have some bearing on what I shall have to say to Evie presently I must. I don't think it's that I'm urged to set myself right with anybody, even with myself. At first, when I began, I thought it was that—the need for self-justification—but now I don't think it's a question of justification or condemnation at all. It is a far more essential question. Suppose we call it the question of the personal standard. . .

I dare say my standards pass for low. That physical basis of marriage, for example, may pass for low—I'm sure it must to that ardent young couple who pant for intellectual companionship and Schmerveloff. And I confess that several of the Beatitudes are beyond me. To tell the truth I am not really at home with anything much higher than the best of human intelligence; and when I hear people speaking glibly of "man-made laws," I recognise that some folk are on terms of affability with Omnipotence that are denied to me. I suppose I am temperamentally reluctant to alter as much as a regulation once it is established, and I am certainly not ready with divine amendments to everything of man's offhand. Man's law I hold to be a necessarily imperfect, but roughly sufficient measure of man's conduct, and in the light of that law I may presently have a murder to confess.

I say *a* murder, not murder. Is there a difference? I do not know, and I am too weary to split hairs about it. Call them, if you like, one and the same thing. Still, if the one command be absolute, for the other a case may be stated. Do I, then, write to state a case?

But state it to whom? There is one Addressee to whom I have not lifted up my eyes. I, proud and conquering whom among my fellow-worms, have found the lesser law press hard on me, but I have not straightway invoked the greater. Man's decrees I have found strong and wise and admirable; the other is too wonderful for me. And this is the conclusion I promised you. To man, man's law is of more consequence than God's. Perhaps the damned are not utterly damned, so long as they do not add presumptuousness to their error. To have appealed and to have had that appeal rejected *were* damnation. . . I do not appeal.

Nor can I see that I state my case to man. Nay, for I confess man's authority, lest it should appear that I do not, I shall destroy these papers. Tonight or tomorrow I shall destroy them. Man shall not say that I have shirked the human issue. I refuse to plead at all. Let any who take it upon themselves to accuse or defend me plead or charge what they will. I am mute. I burn this. . .

I am tired. . .

And yet one boon I do crave. Perhaps those standards of mine, by their very lowness, may be the evidence, not of a smaller, but of a larger conception of Him Who Reigneth than might at first glance appear. . .

I am tired. . .

But all this advances me little with my resolution. Indeed, a fresh glare has just broken in on my brain. I was looking back a few moments ago on that long chain of circumstances with which my darling has been torturing herself—that old slander, innocencies between Louie and myself possible to have been misconstrued, my coming upon her that night in Billy's top room, Evie's own temperamental bias against Louie's profession, her silences, her belief of the calumny. Had Miriam Levey but known of my visit to the Models' Club and that strange walk of ours on the night of the Berkeley dinner, her case had indeed been complete! I had been reviewing all this, I say; and suddenly it struck me, suppose I do tell her? *What then?* . . .

Do you see—as the terrible Louie had seen—what then? I am supposing that the revelation did not kill her; do you see what then?

At last I saw it, and groaned. What then? Why, what but that I had put another before herself? What but that, while she had shared my board and bed, that fatal burden of my honour and confidence and trust had gone to another? What but that Louie, after all, *had* had the key and password of my life that I had denied to herself? What could I answer did she live to say, "What, you married me without telling me this? You tell me *now*, after having concealed it until concealment is no longer possible? You give me, *now*, something she's had the use of and has passed on to me? What is she to you, then, that *I* am not? Where do I fall short as a wife that *I* couldn't have borne this for my husband or died trying to bear it? Take it. Give it to her. She can have it. Fool, that I couldn't see this for myself, but must have Miriam Levey to point it out to me!"

Oh, my dear, my dear, my dear! We had never a fair start. . .

I do not know whether she intends to spend the night in the nursery again. . .

Seven o'clock. I must dress. And I must drink something now, or I shall never get through the evening. . .

And even yet I have not come to my decision.

11.30 P.M.

This page at least it will be almost superfluous to destroy. My hand shakes like dodder-grass. That is the liquor I have drunk, but I had to do it.

They have gone. As I thought would be the case, I have had to play Evie's part too. That's twice Billy Izzard has seen me do that, for tonight was to all intents and purposes a repetition of that other night, when I tried to silence the voice of a gramophone by jumping up and bawling out an overstrained merriment. I don't mean that I jumped up and bawled tonight, of course. I merely had a number of flowers removed from the table, so that my eyes had a straight lane to Evie's at the other end, and sent down smiles and encouragement and support to her. And I allowed the men a bare ten minutes afterwards before I hurried off to her aid again. That and plenty of champagne; and I think I pulled it off. Billy, who lingered behind until I turned him out, says everything went splendidly. He didn't know I'd such gaiety in me, he said.

And Evie has gone to the nursery, but is not going to stay there. She told me that, with a hot little kiss, and a grip of her moist hand. . . This was on the stairs, and she whispered (*words illegible*), and she had to run away so that the gratitude in her eyes would not run quite over—but that she whispered (*words illegible*) . . .

I shall do it tonight, unless my tongue is as shaky as my hand. There is a perfect stillness in my brain. I can see the whole thing spread out in my mind like a map; never have I been so triumphantly the master of a thing. . . (*words illegible*) . . . The map is as steady as a rock, too; I turn my attention from it for a moment, choosing the form in which I shall present this aspect of the case or that, and when I return to the map it hasn't moved. Words, whole phrases, rise up in my mind, all so perfect that there will hardly be any shock at all. Evie cannot help but see it as I see it, and then I shall beg her pardon that I didn't tell her long ago. I have never loved her as I love her tonight, and those lovely pools of her eyes on the stairs (*words illegible*).

At last we are going to have a fair start. We hadn't that, you know. I still think I was right to stand between her and much of life, but this other thing was really too huge to be hidden. And she will not be jealous any of Louie when I tell her that though Louie dragged all this out of me—she's no idea really how clever Louie is—my pulse has never quickened at Louie's touch nor my eyes brightened when they have met hers. "With my body" I have worshipped Evie, and shall (*words illegible*) . . . And so tomorrow will be a new beginning for us. I am rich; I have power; my only desire is now almost within my grasp. It was nonsense I wrote an hour or two ago—or perhaps it was the other day—about this only being the beginning of a deathless jealousy between those two. Evie will see. I shall make it all perfectly plain. I could almost do impossibilities tonight, with the words running like quicksilver in my mind and that chart I have in my brain steady as a rock. And if the anticipation of peace is such bliss, what will the peace itself be? . . .

I suppose she will be ready about twelve. I mustn't let this wondrous stillness of my brain slip from me. I was clever enough to foresee that it might, and so had the tray of liqueurs sent down here. But it doesn't do for an abstemious man to mix his liqueurs; the brandy again, I think. (*Several lines undecipherable*). I have only been drunk once in my life; I forget when that was; and once I shammed drunk; I don't suppose I shall ever be drunk again. A moment ago I felt a twinge where I made that dent in my head on the corner of Aunt Angela's fender, but it has passed. . . It was a good dinner-party; I saw to that. . . Evie, sweetheart—she'll be ready about twelve. . .

It is a quarter to now. I must be getting up. But first I must put these papers away. One of them slipped away somewhere a few minutes ago; I stumbled and upset a pile of them, but gathered them all up again, all but that one; never mind, I will look for it in the morning. It was my foot that slipped, not my brain. My brain is all right. . .

Well, it will be all right tomorrow. . .

END OF JEFFRIES' JOURNAL

Envoi

Sir Julius Pepper Dictates

E r—Miss Causton—can you stay for an hour or so? No, a private affair; I hope it's not inconvenient; thanks, and if I might give you supper afterwards? . . .

"Fact is, it's about poor old Jeffries. Better date it, and keep it safe. They've asked me to write something about him, and I'm no writer; but Izzard's found me a man who'll lick it into shape if I supply the material. 'Just talk it anyhow,' he said. Easily enough said, about a chap like Jeffries. . .

"You've seen this cutting, of course? No, not the first one; this from this morning's paper, about Mrs. Jeffries. By Jove! it has followed quickly; awful! (By the way, you once met her, didn't you?) No, I want this copy; you can get another tomorrow; I'll read it out:

Tragic Death of a Lady

We have to report a melancholy sequel to the death of Mr. James Herbert Jeffries, of the Exploration and Mercantile Consolidation, Pall Mall, which was announced in our issue of the 10th ult. The circumstances of Mr. Jeffries' sudden demise are still fresh in the public mind. The deceased gentleman, it will be remembered, succumbed to an attack of cerebral hæmorrhage brought on by strain and overwork and culminating on the night of a dinner-party given by him at his mansion in Iddesleigh Gate. It is with the deepest regret that we now announce that his widow has survived him only a few weeks.

We understand that during the intervening time the bereaved lady had occupied herself by going through the private papers of her late husband, sitting up late at night in order to render this last devout service. At about three o'clock yesterday morning Ann Madeley, a housemaid in Mrs. Jeffries' employ, suffering from insomnia, had recourse to a medicine closet, situated where the servants' quarters adjoin the dwelling parts of the house. Her attention was attracted to a strong smell of escaping gas. She woke James Baines, a butler, and the two, wisely refraining from striking a light, made their way in the direction from which the smell of gas seemed to come. This brought them to their mistress' room. Obtaining no answer to their knocks, an entrance was forced, and in a small dressing-room lately used by Mr. Jeffries—

"I hope this doesn't distress you too much, Miss Causton—

—Mrs. Jeffries was found, fully dressed, stretched on a couch. The doors and windows had been closed, and a gas-fire turned on. We understand from Baines that Mrs. Jeffries had remained as usual downstairs in the library until a late hour; and a page of notes in her husband's shorthand which has been found under one of the pillars of the writing-table—

"I've got that page of notes, by the way.—

—is sufficiently eloquent testimony as to what her sad duty had been. Dr. McKechnie, who was at once summoned, certified that life had been extinct for some hours. The deceased lady, who was a great favourite in society, leaves two children in the care of a maiden aunt, Miss Angela Soames. The inquest is fixed for Tuesday next.

"Sad business, sad business. . . Afraid they'll have to bring it in suicide—through grief, probably. . .

"Well, let's put it down as it comes. Of course he was a big man; lived an intense crowded life too. I should say at a guess there weren't many things he hadn't done at one time and another, short of committing a murder or a matrimonial infidelity. Don't think he could have been tempted to do that. One woman could do anything she liked with him, but the others wouldn't have much chance. Oh yes, a full life. Did you know, Miss Causton, that the man who first passed him over to me found him helping to pick a fallen horse up in Fleet Street, when he hadn't a penny to his name? He was a commissionaire once. . . As you know, he was the steam of this concern; it was the chance of my lifetime finding him, poor chap. Extraordinary man! He used to go at things by a sort of intuition; he tried to explain it to me, but I never could understand it. Once I said something about 'scientific method';

but he said it wasn't scientific method at all. Scientific method, he said, was something purely empirical, concerned with investigation, and not practically constructive in the least. Constructiveness came after. His method, he said, was based on the truths of art, 'the only truths we know anything about,' he said, whatever he meant. I never could follow him at all. . . Well, if that's so, it rather explains a lot of these business giants going in for collecting—I mean it isn't that they just have the money to gratify their artistic tastes. But, as I say, I could never make head nor tail of it. . . Which reminds me; that paper that got wafted under his desk; that was a dabbling in art in its way; fiction; did you know he tried his hand at fiction, Miss Causton? Here it is—an odd page—Whitlock knows a bit of shorthand, and he transcribed it for me:

'—show him that red thing on the floor, and that curved thing on the door.'

But now Archie in his turn seemed to have become divided. He had suddenly turned white. But an habitual pertness still persisted in his tongue. I don't think this had any relation whatever to the physical peril he seemed at last to have realised he was in. I stood over him huge and black as Fate. . .'Spare him if you can,' that generous bloodthirsty devil in me muttered quickly. . .

'Merridew,' I said heavily, 'you'll disappear tomorrow morning—or—'

'Shall I?' he bragged falteringly. . .

"And so on—

His only chance now was to have screamed aloud; but he did not scream. Instead he stooped quickly, caught up the poker, and struck at my head with it.

"And that's the end of the page. Sort of grim tale he would write. Queer hobby for a mercantile and political giant, wasn't it? But I'd go in for fiction myself if I thought it would make me like him.

"Verandah Cottage—that was no place for a chap like him. I hated to see him there. He could always go anywhere, meet anybody, was on equal terms with the best—and he without antecedents that I ever heard of, standing out solitary against a black background, just genius. . .

I wonder who his people were! Something uncommon, or else he was just a gigantic 'sport'—

"Of course—*de mortuis* and so on—but he did marry the wrong woman. To tell the truth, she was as ordinary as they make 'em; would have looked her best in the lights of the Holborn Restaurant at half-past six, waiting with the rest of the shop-girls for her bus home. He was a mass of contradictions, and one of 'em was that he merely idealised her. Pretty, of course, but poor Jeffries could have done better for himself than that. She never could bear me. . . Well, there's nothing to be said now, poor creatures. . . But sometimes it made me almost angry that he hadn't married the woman he ought. . .

"Well, let's begin with the day he first came to the F.B.C.—"

And Louie's pencil flew on.

THE STORY OF LOUIE

PROLOGUE

In an old number of *Punch*, under the heading "Society's New Pet: The Artist's Model," is to be found a drawing by Du Maurier, of which the descriptive text runs:

> "And how did you and Mr. Sopley come to quarrel, dear Miss Dragon?"
>
> "Well, your Grace, it was like this: I was sitting to him in a cestus for 'The Judgment of Paris,' when someone called as wished to see him most particular; so he said: 'Don't move, Miss Dragon, or you'll disturb the cestus.' 'Very good, sir,' I said, and off he went; and when he come back in an hour and a 'alf or so he said: 'You've moved, Miss Dragon!' 'I 'aven't!' I said. 'You *'ave!*' he said. 'I 'Aven't!' I said—and no more I 'adn't, your Grace. And with that I off with his cestus an' wished him good-morning, an' I never been near him since!"

Du Maurier may or may not have been wrong about the newness of this craze of "Society's." If he was right, the Honourable Emily Scarisbrick becomes at once a pioneer. Let there be set down, here in the beginning, the plain facts of how, a good ten years before the indignant Miss Dragon "offed with" Mr. Sopley's cestus, the Honourable Emily found a way to bridge the gulf that lies between Bohemia and Mayfair.

Except in the case of one person not yet born into these pages, the report that the lady had engaged herself, early in the year 1869, to "Mr. Buckley, her drawing-master," had only a short currency. It was probably devised by the Honourable Emily herself in order to soften the blow for her brother, Lord Moone. The real name of the man to whom she engaged herself was James Buckley Causton. Under this name he appears on the rolls of the 4th Dragoon Guards as a trooper in the years 1862–1867; and as "Buck" Causton he attained some celebrity when, in the last-named year, he vanquished one Piker Betteridge in the prize ring, in a battle which, beginning with gloves and ending with bare knuckles, lasted for nearly nine hours.

For all we know, it may have been Miss Dragon's Mr. Sopley who, seeing the magnificent Buck in the ring, first put it into the ex-trooper's head to become an artists' model. However it was, an artists' model he did become, and, as such, the rage. No doubt Sopley, if it were he, would gladly have kept his discovery to himself; but a neck like a sycamore and a thorax capable of containing nine-hours-contest lungs cannot be hid when Academy time comes round. Sopley's measure was known. If Sopley painted an heroic picture it was certain he had had a hero as model. The Academy opens in May; before June was out Sopley's find was no longer his own. Sir Frederick Henson, the artist who moved so in the world that in him the tradition of the monarch who picked up the painter's brush for him might almost have been said to live again, saw Buck, marked Buck down as his own, and presently had sole possession of Buck.

The Honourable Emily Scarisbrick already had possession of Sir Frederick. To be sure, it neither needed a Sir Frederick Henson to teach her the stippling of birds' eggs and the copying of castles for the albums of her friends, nor was the great Academician accustomed to stooping to the office of salaried drawing-master; but—the Honourable Emily was a Scarisbrick, of Mallard Bois.

In Henson's studio the Honourable Emily first saw Buck Causton.

To say that she fell in love with him would demand a definition of the term. Certainly she fell in something with him. Perhaps that something was the something that at the last thrusts baronies and Mallard Boises aside as hindrances to a design even larger than that in which they play so important a part; but we have nothing to do with large designs here. Call it what you will: something proper enough to legend, but of little enough propriety in a modern lady's life; a feeble echo of Romance, perhaps, but never itself to become Romance unless, of it or present scandal, it should prove the stronger. At any rate, it was a very different thing from anything she felt, or ever had felt, for Captain Cecil Chaffinger, of the White Hussars, her brother's nominee for her hand.

It was a word dropped by the gallant Captain, himself a follower of the fancy, that led her to the discovery that the hero of some feat or other of extraordinary skill and endurance, and the young Ajax, all chest and grey eyes and brown curls, who did odd jobs about the studio in the intervals of posing for Henson's demigodlike canvases, were one and the same person. Her already throbbing pulse bounded. She herself was twenty-eight, a small, dark, febrile woman, given over to discontents based on nothing save on an irremediably spoiled childhood, and perhaps hankering after an indiscretion in the conviction that indiscretions were of two kinds—indiscretions, and the indiscretions of the Scarisbricks. Naturally she became conscious of a quickened interest in her art.

The first indication that this interest passed beyond birds eggs and castles was that she began "Lessons in Drapery." If here for a few moments her story becomes a little technical, it may be none the less interesting on that account.

The study of Drapery *as* Drapery has not much interest for anybody unless perhaps for a student of mechanics. For all that, it is, or then was, regarded by drawing-masters as a self-contained subject, to be tackled, ticked off, and thenceforward possessed. To the study of Drapery in this unrelated sense the Honourable Emily apparently inclined. Seeing her therefore, in this fundamental error, Sir Frederick, a master of Drapery, took from her the "copies" which had already supplanted the "copies" of castles in her portfolio, and good-humouredly began to tell her what she really wanted. What she really wanted, he said, was to rid her mind of the idea that folds existed for their own sake, and to endeavour to realise that their real significance lay in the thing enfolded. Miss Scarisbrick thanked him.

So, at first from the lay figure, and then from Henson's model, she began to draw Drapery with special reference to the thing draped.

About this time she gave Captain Chaffinger for an answer a "No" which he refused to take. His devotion, he said, forbade him. If by his devotion he meant his devotion to his creditors, his constancy remained at their service. In the meantime he was still able to pay his old debts by contracting new ones.

The Honourable Emily's studies became diligent.

There is little to be said about these things except that they do happen. A word now about Buck's attitude.

Had the Honourable Emily's maid thrown herself at his head he would have known what to do. His sense of the holiness of social degrees would have received no shock. But the Honourable Emily, who could command her maid, could not command what in all probability her maid would not have had to ask twice for. The most she got (when after much that is omitted here, it did at last dawn on the bashful Buck that she had any will in the matter at all) was a blush so sudden and violent that it compelled an embarrassed reddening of her own cheeks also. Buck was not personally outraged. It was his sense of Order that was outraged. He remembered the lady's station for her, and, stammeringly but reverentially, put her back into it.

Now to be merely reverential to a woman who is in love with you is to provoke impatience, anger and tears. On the other hand, to see a woman in tears because you will not permit her to humiliate herself is to have the other half of an impossible situation. It was one luncheon-time (the Honourable Emily now lunched frequently at the studio) that the tears came.

"Oh, you don't care for me—you don't care for me!" she sobbed.

Buck could not truthfully have said that he did care for her; but there she was before him, in tears.

"If it were that Dragon girl, now—"

Buck, while not failing to see the force of this, could only make imploring movements for the Honourable Emily to calm herself. Presently she did calm herself, sufficiently to change her tone to one of irony.

"Do you read your Bible?" she shot over her shoulder.

"Yes, miss," said Buck—"that is—I mean—"

The reason for Buck's hesitation was that he had suddenly doubted whether the Honourable Emily would know a Racing Calendar by the name she had just used.

"Do you mean *The* Bible, miss?" he said, fidgeting.

She snapped: "Yes—the one with the story of Joseph in it—"

She burst into tears anew.

"Oh, that I should have to beg a man to marry me! I hate myself—I hate you!"

Her hatred, however, did not prevent repetitions of the scene. At the last repetition that need trouble us here her tears conquered. The helpless Buck comforted her after the only fashion he knew anything about—the fashion he would have used towards her maid—on his knee.

He still, however, called her "Miss."

They were privately married in the June of 1869.

"Don't call me 'Miss'!" she broke out petulantly one day in the middle of the honeymoon. "And you are *not* to have your meals with the servants! I shall lunch in my room today, and you are to be ready to take me out at three o'clock."

"Yes, m'm," said Buck.

Probably Lord Moone had less to do than he supposed with the separation that took place in the September of the same year. We may assume that a much more potent factor was the Honourable Mrs. Causton's remembrance of her own words, "That I should have to beg a man to marry me! I hate myself—I hate you!" She did very soon hate both herself and him. Poor Buck merely hated the whole subversive anomaly.

He accepted the proposal that they should separate with perfect docility. It seemed to him entirely right. Indeed the only thing he had not accepted with docility had been his introduction to Lord Moone, on the only occasion on which the two men ever met, as "Mr. Buckley, the drawing-master." Buck hadn't liked that much. He had made himself Buck Causton in nine hours of terrific combat, and as Buck Causton he preferred to be known. But all else he suffered with touching obedience, and at the proposal that they should go their several ways his finger flew to his forehead.

"Yes, miss," he said; and his heart, if not his lips, murmured the prayer that begins: "God bless the Squire and his relations—"

They parted.

They only met once more. This was in the January of the following year, in the great antlered hall at Mallard Bois, that was as regularly used on all occasions as if there had not been salons and galleries and drawing-rooms in a dozen other parts of the great place. The Honourable Mrs. Causton lay on a couch drawn up to the fire-dogs; her husband looked submissively down on her, dwarfing the suit of armour of Big Hugo by which he stood.

She made a new proposal. It was that he should put it into her hands to set herself free once for all.

"Yes, miss," said Buck.

"Then," said the Honourable Mrs. Causton a quarter of an hour later, "there's the question of cruelty."

Buck's thoughts wandered slowly back to the Piker.

"Yes, miss," he said.

"I need hardly tell you that as far as—er—procedure—can be stretched it will be stretched."

"Yes, miss. Thank you, miss."

Then wistfully Buck's eyes wandered from Big Hugo's suit of armour to his wife's face again.

"Beg your pardon, about that cruelty, miss," he said unhappily. "Couldn't I go down—just for once, Miss—as Mr. Buckley?"

"No; but I can assure you that *I* don't want this talked about more than must be either. Perhaps I ought to tell you that I shall probably marry again."

Buck's finger went to his forehead again, this time in a duty to his successor. Then his eyes grew grave. His wife had made a slight movement.

"If I might make so bold, miss—there's another thing—"

She knew what he meant.

"You've nothing to do with that," she said quickly.

Buck would have thought that he had, but if a lady said he hadn't, well, he hadn't, that was all.

"Yes, miss. . . And asking your pardon again—about that cruelty?"

"Oh, that's over," said Mrs. Causton, closing her eyes. "Six months ago."

"I—I don't remember," said Buck; but once more, if a lady said it was so, so it was. Again the grave look came into his eyes, and again she understood.

"I can have it looked after better than you can," she said.

"And—please—you will?" he dared to supplicate.

She nodded.

Still he hesitated.

"If it's a little boy, miss—I might be opening a Sparring Academy—strictly for the gentry—I wouldn't charge him nothing—"

And after a little further discussion the shameful piece of collusion came to an end.

They were divorced in the March of 1870. On the 15th of April the child was born—a girl. Fifteen months later the Honourable Emily married Captain Cecil Chaffinger, of the White Hussars.

II

The child never got on well with her mother. Mrs. Chaffinger never forgave her her paternity. The gallant Captain, on the other hand, treated her as he would have treated his own child—that is to say, he bought her extravagant toys if the proximity of a toyshop put it into his head to do so, pinched her arms and cheeks and neck jocularly whenever he found her head at the level of his waistcoat, and then departed, as likely as not to pinch maturer arms and necks, not Mrs. Chaffinger's, elsewhere. He took his wife's former *mésalliance* with perfect serenity. She had paid his debts and enabled him to spend a day or two in his father's house when he cared to do so, and the Captain, who was a gentleman and not very much else to boast of, held faithfully to his part of the bargain. He even dropped in once or twice at Buck Causton's new *Salle d'Armes* in Bruton Street. The child was called by his name—Louise Chaffinger; he called her Mops, because of her quantities of thick brown hair. The Honourable Emily became querulous and an invalid; took to falling into dozes no matter who was present, and waking up again with alarming cries; and she busied herself with charitable works performed in an uncharitable temper.

Louie was not pretty; but the jocular Captain pinched no prettier neck than hers, and he declared, as the child grew, that her "points" would be best displayed could she go about in the largest and shadiest hat and the most closely fitting tights possible. His house (which, by the way, he had begun to encumber again) was Trant, in Buckinghamshire; but the child was packed off occasionally, to be rid of her, to Mallard Bois, Lord Moone's seat, there to romp with her cousin, Eric Scarisbrick, already preparing for Eton, and such small fry as climbed trees and cheeked the gardeners with him. Here she revelled in the liberty that was denied her at home; and perhaps she already realised instinctively that her mother's relief at having her out of the way was tempered only by the invalid's resentment that the child could be happy out of her own not very cheerful company. Be that as it may, the girl was told, at twelve years of age, that she was getting too big to kick these limbs her stepfather so admired about among growing boys. She was given half-long skirts and French and English governesses: the French one, though she did not yet know it, as a preparation for sending her to a Paris convent.

At fourteen years of age she had not heard of the man whose grey eyes and perfect shapeliness of body she inherited. The Scarisbricks, be sure, had allowed that episode to be hushed up. But the day was bound to come when she should hear of the Honourable Mrs. Causton and identify that lady with her mother. The day did come, no matter how; and, inwardly trembling but outwardly resolved, she sought her mother. Mrs. Chaffinger had just come with a cry out of a doze. Her daughter demanded to be told who the Honourable Mrs. Causton was. She was told that there was no such person.

"Then who was she?" the girl demanded. There were few of her questions to her mother that were not demands.

"Who's been telling you about her?"

That did not seem to Louie to matter. She repeated the question.

"She was a very great fool," Mrs. Chaffinger snapped. "Why aren't you with Mademoiselle?"

"Who was she besides being a very great fool?" the child persisted.

It had to come out.

"Then papa *isn't* my father?" Louie said, pale. All through her life she was pale in her moments of stress.

"I'm your mother, and I tell you to go to your French lesson at once."

But Louie did not move.

"Then who was my father?" she asked.

"Who do you suppose he is, when I was Mrs. Causton?"

"Is? . . . Then he isn't dead?"

Mrs. Chaffinger compressed her lips.

"I was going to tell you all about Mr. Causton all in good time" (her daughter looked coldly unbelieving), "but since you are here I'll tell you now. Sit down on that chair and stop fidgeting—"

And she told the girl the facts, not to be denied, of the divorcing of Buck.

The end of the matter was that Louie now hated, not only her mother, but her father also.

Her stepfather she thenceforward addressed as "Chaff." He liked it.

Three months later she was sent to Paris.

Eight months later still she turned up again, not at Trant, but at the Captain's club in London. She announced that she had run away from the convent and did not intend to return to it. Her arrival, though not unwelcome, was inopportune, for the Captain had a little party that evening and seemed disconcerted. The toyshops, he reflected, were closed, and then he looked at his stepdaughter again. . . It could not, after all, have been one of the more characteristic of the Captain's parties, for he took Louie to it, pigtail and all, and for a whole evening pinched nobody. Then he took her to his chambers, winked at his man in token of something extraordinary, hesitated, and then, with an "Oh, be hanged to it!" expression, gave Louie the key of his own sleeping apartment. Louie examined his prints a little wonderingly, but approved of his ribboned haircurlers and large frilled pincushion, and then went to sleep. The next day the Captain took her down to Trant and left her there.

The next few years were a constant succession of wrangles with her mother. She had flatly refused to return to the convent, and if the Honourable Emily was petulant, her daughter was merciless. She had been put off with the drawing-master version of her mother's marriage, but that was enough; she held it over her mother's head, and Buck, if he had desired revenge, had it. She knew herself to be hybrid, and treated the Scarisbricks and their drawing-masters with equal scorn. Worse, she treated them equally with a contemptuous tolerance. She harped with pride on the baser strain. In a word, there was no doing anything with her.

She reached the age of twenty-one.

At twenty-two she expressed a wish to go on the stage. The Captain, who was genuinely fond of her, stopped that. At twenty-three she declared plainly that "a girl in her position" ought to have a means of earning her own living—not necessarily drawing. The Captain being averse from this also, she took the matter into her own hands by writing to the secretary of a Horticultural College in Somersetshire, paying her fees, and enrolling herself as a student without saying a word to anybody. She packed her boxes, and in the second week of January 1894 presented herself before her mother, dressed for travelling, and announced that she had very little time in which to catch her train.

"Oh, by the way," she said, turning at the door, "if you write, you might address letters to me in my own name—Causton."

Then she left.

"*Was die Mutter träumt, das vollbringt die Tochter.*" Here, with its repetitions of and its departures from that of the Honourable Emily, follows her story.

PART I

RAINHAM PARVA

I

The Horticultural College at Rainham Parva, now defunct, was hardly a college in the modern sense at all. Its technical books were antiquated; it had only one or two old microscopes; and it totally lacked the newer trimmings of specialisation. Its founder, a Bristol seedsman called Chesson, had bought the place cheaply, house and all, a dozen years before, and having five hardy daughters eating their heads off at home, had, as the saying is, economically emancipated them. That meant then (whatever it may mean now) that, realising that the wages of two men and a boy might be saved, he had had them down to Rainham Parva and had set them to work.

The second Miss Chesson, Miss Harriet, had shown a real aptitude for the work. She had won, after three years, a Diploma, and this Diploma, together with the presence in the house as paying boarder of a niece of Chesson's, had put an idea into the seedsman's head—the premium idea. With the Diploma properly advertised, its grantee made Principal, a premium or so forgone (called a Scholarship) and the proper person installed over all as Lady-in-Charge, Chesson had foreseen a good deal of his work being done by young women who would pay for the privilege of being allowed to do it. There is no need to describe the development of the idea. The enterprise had prospered, and when Louie Causton had put her name down on the books and paid her fees the complement of thirty girls was full.

She did not, after all, travel down alone. Her stepfather, hinting that it was not necessary to say anything about this to her mother, made the journey with her. The pair of them shortened the hours by guessing which of the young women in the same train were to be Louie's fellow-students; and when they alighted at Rainham Magna station the Captain put Louie and her traps into one of the nondescript vehicles that only saw the light when the Rainham girls arrived or departed, and drove off with her to the college. There he shook hands with the Lady-in-Charge, Mrs. Lovenant-Smith, and asked her whether she was related to Lovenant-Smith of the 24th. Mrs. Lovenant-Smith's reply did not actually affirm her regret that she was so related, but the Captain's affability dried up suddenly. He was returning to town by the four-o'clock train; before doing so he took a turn round the place with Louie.

"Well," he said, as Louie took her leave of him at the gates, "it's a good growing country, I should say; rum idea of yours though. . . You've heard me speak of Lovenant-Smith, haven't you? Adjutant eight or nine years ago; not a bad chap at all, *I* should have said. She'll be one of the Shropshire lot, I expect. I knew he had people down there. . . Well, mind you don't run away with a gardener. 'Bye, Mops—"

And he was off, tugging at his moustache and inwardly commenting that the whole escapade was "just like Louie."

It was a good growing country. Chesson said that the mildness of the winters was due to the Gulf Stream; Miss Harriet Chesson attributed it to ozone—ozone having been a word to conjure with at the time when she had taken her Diploma. Ozone or Gulf Stream, it provided wild violets in December, lemon-verbena that grew in trees up the sides of the cottages and had to be cut away from the upper windows, and filled the deep lanes with the hart's-tongue fern. It also brought forth rich produce. The dairy business and poultry farm flourished; crates and parcels and returned empties kept the goods clerk at Rainham Magna station busy; and, when the heather bloomed on the hill that rose between Chesson's and the sea, the "Rainham Heather Honey," green as bronze and thick as glue, was at a premium. At the crest of the hill the seedsman's estate ended. Beyond that, dropping abruptly to the west, lay deep wooded coombes, green to the very rocks of the shore.

Louie's age put her at once out of the class of the "new girl" who, in the school tales, sits pathetically on her box and waits for somebody to speak to her. She was twenty-four, and probably only one other student, the copper-haired girl with the long thin neck and the "salt-cellars" showing through her white flannel blouse, who asked her her number and offered to show her the way to her cubicle, was more than twenty-two. Her large black feathered hat (see the first part of the Captain's advice as to how she would make the most of herself), and her expensively simple navy blue coat and skirt down to her toes, further distinguished her among the tweed jackets and ankle-length skirts of the younger girls. No doubt she had her perfect management of these and her numerous other garments from her mother's former interest in the study of Drapery. If the Captain did not think her face pretty, it must be remembered that the Captain had standards of prettiness of his own. Pretty in the professional-beauty sense her irregular mouth and long chin perhaps were not. Her large, clear, pebble-grey eyes at any rate were arresting.

The copper-haired girl, having shown Louie her cubicle, offered to show her the rest of the house also. They began upstairs on the first floor, where the girls slept. The place was an old mansion in the form of a hollow square, and as they came to each latticed embrasure Louie stopped to look at the famous Rainham yew that almost filled the grassgrown inner courtyard. The corridors were dark, and sudden steps where no steps were to have been expected made of the uneven floors a series of booby-traps for those not familiar with them. Memories of the Monmouth Rebellion seemed to linger round the corners and to be shut up in the cupboards of the place. They passed downstairs. Through the doorway of the handsome Restoration façade they saw the yew again, dark beyond the shining flags of the hall. Louie had already been in the reception-room and Mrs. Lovenant-Smith's private apartments on the right of the doorway; on the left, she was told, were the quarters of Miss Harriet (who alone of Chesson's daughters remained there) and the staff. The domestics slept at the top of the house; the four male gardeners (all married) occupied the farm a furlong away at the back.

"But wouldn't you like some tea?" said the copper-haired girl. "It's in the dining-room."

"I was told to report myself to Miss Chesson at five," said Louie, looking at her watch.

"Well, you've just time, if you're quick—"

They sought the room where the housekeeper ran cups of tea from the tap of a large and funereal bronze urn.

It was ten minutes to five when Louie entered the dining-room. Before the clock had struck five she had taken a certain position in the college.

She herself hardly knew how it happened. The room was full of noise and chatter, and near Louie, talking louder and making more noise than anybody else, was a lanky child of sixteen, to be a tall blonde beauty in another three or four years' time, but so far only a mass of unadjusted proportions and movements that lacked co-ordination. She had several distinct voices, and in one of these she was now engaged in unabashed mimicry. Louie, who had got her cup of tea, heard a bell-like "*Os*-trich feathers!" and she was about to put a question to the copper-haired girl when, with a mock reverence and an explosive "Your

Ma-jesty!" the child swept backwards into her. She barely saved her cup of tea. The girl gave a quick turn; her "Clum—" was changed to a "Sorry!" as she saw a new face, and Louie smiled.

"Your feet were all wrong," Louie said.

The blonde child turned eagerly again.

"Can you do it?" she asked.

The next moment, before Louie could get out "A drawing-room curtsy? Yes," the child had cried: "Girls! Girls! Here's somebody who knows how to do it! Do come and show us!"

"Really?" said Louie, smiling, and handing her cup of tea to the copper-haired girl.

"Yes—come here, Rhoda, and watch (that's my sister—she's to be presented, you know)."

Louie laughed. "Quickly then—I have to see Miss Chesson—"

And, pushed unceremoniously forward, and still in her feathered hat and navy blue costume, Louie made her first bow to her fellow-students at Chesson's in the deep and swanlike genuflexion she had practised with her cousin, Cynthia Scarisbrick, a couple of years before. Then she ran out, smiling.

"*How* ripping!" she heard somebody say as she did so. "I expect she's been presented."

Louie sought Miss Harriet.

The Principal, a businesslike, damson-complexioned woman of forty-five, with a deerstalker hat on her close-cropped curly hair, asked her what course of study she proposed to take. Louie replied (in other words) that all courses were the same to her. Miss Harriet had had that kind of student before. She asked a few further questions, and then put Louie down for the elementary course. She dismissed her with a marked syllabus and a copy of the Rules.

Louie read the Rules, nodded, as much as to say, "I thought so!" and then laughed. There was no need to ask who had drawn them up; she remembered the frigid way in which Chaff had been put into his place that afternoon. There was a serenity about them that transcended the ordinary imperative mood. "*Students do not absent themselves from Morning Prayers or Divine Service without Permission.*" "*Students do not give Orders to the Gardeners or Domestics.*" "*Students do not pass beyond the Bounds of the College (Map appended).*" If on occasion students did all of these things, that did not detract from the *largior ether* in which the Rules were conceived.

Nor did mere evidence to the contrary ever in the least degree abate Mrs. Lovenant-Smith's persuasion that the young ladies of Chesson's, being the daughters of gentlefolk, were by that very fact almost to be trusted to do without Rules at all.

On the following morning Louie, with leggings of doe-skin buttoned to her knees (see the second of the Captain's recommendations for the attire that suited her best), and wearing a wide-pocketed jacket not unlike a man's, began the practical study of Horticulture.

II

She was attached to the "posse" of six girls of which the copper-haired student, whose name was Richenda Earle, was the head. This girl, as the holder of the scholarship mentioned a page or two back, was the single non-fee-paying student in the place. Her father was a bookseller in Westbourne Grove, and she had kept his books for him before coming to Chesson's. She had picked up her knowledge of book-keeping at an obscure and ill-appointed Business School in Holborn, but, her health being anything but robust, she had taken up gardening under the impression that it was an out-of-doors pursuit. It was only this at Chesson's to a strictly limited extent. Whatever students did or did not learn, the output for the market had to be maintained, and this necessitated, for days and days together, work in the twelve long glass-houses, from the humid heat of which the girls came out limp and listless and relaxed. Richenda Earle suffered from these depressions more than most of them, and now only remained at the college because Miss Harriet had held out hopes for her of a place on the staff. She was easily head of all the classes of which she was a member, but was hopelessly incapable of making her personality felt. Add to all this that she was avid of popularity, and that her self-consciousness took the form of making her more assertive (without being a bit more effective) than any girl in the college, and you will see why Louie felt a little sorry for her without taking to her very much. She for her part had fastened herself on Louie from the start, and had been the first to put the question that Louie had had to answer a dozen times before she had been at Chesson's two hours.

"No, I haven't been presented," Louie had said, finding herself waylaid almost at the door of Miss Harriet's room as she had come out again. "My cousin has; that's where I learned it. We practised it together."

"I've seen them go in," Richenda had murmured, a little wistfully, a little dully; "the carriages and things, you know. I live in London."

Thereupon she had volunteered some of the information stated above, as if inviting a confidence in return. "I'm glad you're in my posse," she had concluded, as Louie had turned away without giving any information whatever about herself.

The remaining members of "Earle's posse" were the two Burnett sisters ("B Major," the girl who was to be presented, and "B Minor," the sixteen-year-old beauty-to-be), a Scotch girl called Macfarlane, and one other girl, half French, Beatrice Pigou. There were four other posses at the college, and each was told off each day to put itself under the direction of one or other of the four gardeners, to pot, "prick out," water or whatever the task might be. The gardener at present in charge of Louie's posse was a sullen young Apollo called Priddy, whose face and neck and forearms ozone or the Gulf Stream had turned to the hue of some deep and old and mellow violin; and Burnett Minor and the younger girls, talking in terms of the life to which their eyes were yet sealed, discussed Priddy with a freedom perfectly innocent and entirely appalling.

Louie had not been at Rainham Parva two days before she was wondering whether after all she wanted to stay. She didn't know really why she had come. Not one of the three commonest reasons for girls being there—a stepmother, to be able to earn a little pocket-money, or to get over a youthful love-affair—quite fitted her case. And then there were those ridiculous Rules. She supposed that if she stayed she would be on the same footing as the juniors, and she hardly thought she could submit to that. Not that the Rules did not seem to justify themselves; on the contrary, they did. Merely because Mrs. Lovenant-Smith affirmed that students did not do this or that, students as a matter of fact either did not do these things, or else consented to class themselves as transgressors when they did.

But Louie's own attitude in the face of a prohibited thing, inherited from her mother and now made inveterate by her upbringing, was invariably that of a wonder what would happen were the prohibition to be disregarded.

It was just a wonder, nothing more.

Then, on the night of her third day at Chesson's, she made up her mind to forfeit her fees and leave in the morning. The reason for her decision was this:

During the vacation certain digging had been allowed by the gardeners to fall into arrears; and Earle's posse, together with another set of six girls, had been set to do it. Now digging was the hardest work the girls were ever called upon to do, and at the beginning of the term at any rate they were spared it as much as possible. But education or output required that this digging should be done, and accordingly the twelve girls had dug for the whole morning, and in the afternoon had varied the labour by carrying heavy pots from House No. 6 to House No. 10—a distance of perhaps sixty yards. The next morning twelve girls (or rather eleven, for Burnett Minor's unset muscles had suffered but little) were half incapacitated by stiffness, and that night there was an outcry for hot baths and arnica. Louie, clad in dressing-gown and slippers and carrying her soap and sponge and towel, hobbled to the bathrooms, and came, in the box-room, upon an indignation-meeting.

This box-room was the common meeting-ground for students who awaited their turns at the baths. It lay over the back courtyard arch, and the four bathrooms adjoined it, two on either side. It was piled almost to the ceiling with trunks and boxes and dress-baskets, the white initials of which glimmered in the shadows cast by a couple of candles on the floor; but there were isolated boxes enough to make seats for the seven or eight girls already assembled there. They had slippers on their naked feet and single garments on their aching bodies; and on one of Louie's own boxes Burnett Major was peering at the little blue flame of a spirit-kettle and mixing in a row of cups the paste for that beverage of revolt—cocoa. Burnett Minor had traitorously turned the general righteous anger to private account, had "bagged" the hottest bath, and was now carolling at the top of her lungs in the right-hand bathroom.

"——then if Earle won't do it I vote we draw lots!" Macfarlane was exclaiming shrilly as Louie opened the door. "Those lazy louts of gardeners are supposed to have all the digging done before we come up—"

They were not—not if Chesson knew it; but "Of course they are!" cried five voices at once.

"Well, I'm just not going to stand it—there—"

"And I'm not—"

"Nor me—"

"And for two pins I'd tell Priddy so!"

There was a moment's silence, but only because, all having spoken at once, all had to take breath at once.

"It's abominable—"

"Disgusting—"

"Celà m'embête—"

"Here's Causton—what do *you* vote, Causton?" they cried, turning to her.

"What about?" Louie asked.

"Why, everything, of course—this beastly place—and setting us to dig the first week—and Priddy's beastly cheek—"

Then every tongue was unloosed.

"*And* a row every time we want an extra blouse washed—"

"*And* washing two guineas a term extra—"

"*And* only the vuggles for dinner that aren't good enough for the market—" ("Vuggles" were vegetables.)

Another pause for breath.

"Let's what-d'-you-call-it—strike—"

Louie laughed as she sat stiffly down by Burnett Major.

"Oh, I'll vote for anything you like; I don't care," she said.

Then they began anew.

"Earle's head of the posse—*she* ought to do it—"

Richenda Earle's voice broke in in loud complaint.

"How *can* I? You know I would like a shot if it wasn't for my scholarship. But I should just be told that if I didn't like it I could go. Elwell's head of your lot. Elwell ought to go."

"I don't care who goes, but I will *not* be told to do things by Priddy."

"Priddy!—"

(Louie smiled again as there came from the bathroom the joyful voice:

"*Early one mo-o-orning—as the su-un was a-rising!—*")

"And those pots hadn't got to be moved—he was only making work—"

"—gros tyran!—"

"—like they kept us three weeks grading and packing tomatoes last autumn, and called it 'study'—"

"—and the bruised ones for us—"

"—not even fit for ketchup—"

"—Dothegirls Hall *this* establishment ought to be called!—"

Another momentary pause: then:

"—let's all sign a petition—"

"—no, a what-d'you-call-it—an ultimatum—"

"—just telling them straight—"

"Your bath, Earle—"

From the bathroom had come the gurgle of escaping water. Boiled pink, turbaned with her towel, smelling of somebody else's scented soap and radiating unrepentance that Earle's bath must be a tepid one, Burnett Minor bounced in.

"Friends, Romans, countrymen, do lend me a dry towel, just to finish with. Oh, Causton, the curtsy, now that I've something loose on! Crocks! My cocoa, Major, and who said Priddy just now? 'Students do not fall in love with Priddy.' (I sha'n't hush.) Sugar, Mac, and, Causton, I wish you'd do my hair your way, just to see how it looks—"

And, twirling twice in the midst of a corolla of pink cashmere dressing-gown, she sank to the floor and began to nurse a chilblain on her heel.

Louie, her hands behind her head, leaned back and watched the scene with the greatest amusement. A master-rebel herself, she knew that here was no rebellion. The meeting, like other meetings, was merely letting off steam, and the girls who "wouldn't stand it" would be standing it exactly the same on the morrow. Well, on the morrow she herself would be off. Her boxes were only half unpacked; half-an-hour would put the other things back again. Already she saw that this Chesson's was an imposition. In the meantime, the indignation meeting was very amusing. She felt almost motherly towards these tractable revolutionaries. Her indulgence became still greater as they spoke out again.

"Another thing," a girl of Elwell's posse demanded; "why couldn't I go to Rainham yesterday to have my photograph taken?"

("Break the camera," Burnett Minor murmured to the chilblain.)

"And just because somebody'd bagged my boots and I was five minutes late the other day—"

"Je m'en fiche pas mal—" Pigou began.

("Parly Angly, voo affectay feele," from Burnett Minor.)

"I should like to see one of the gardeners at home looking at us the way Priddy does—"

"Or Miss Harriet either for that matter—she's only a sort of forewoman—"

"—applewoman—"

"—tomatoes—"

"—that's all she is really—"

"—nothing else—"

Louie laughed outright. Another gurgle had come from the bathroom, and Earle reappeared. Her announcement that the water was now cold added to the general sense of wrong.

"Not even enough hot water!"

"Scarcely a drop, ever!—"

"Odious!"

"Then will somebody come into my cubicle and rub me—not you, B Minor."

("Just give a squint out of the window, Elwell.")

("It's all right. Her lights are out. Lovey's too.")

"Well, I *won't* have a cold bath, to please Lovey or anybody else!"

Nor did Louie want one. She had risen. She moved to the window that looked out over the courtyard yew—the window from which watch was kept to see when Miss Harriet and Mrs. Lovenant-Smith retired—and yawned. In the middle of her yawn she suddenly laughed again.

"Good gracious!" she thought. It was too amusing.

Suddenly Richenda Earle, who also was standing by the window, spoke to her. Evidently Richenda did not think she had been fairly treated by the meeting.

"Do *you* think they ought to ask me to?" she complained.

Louie turned.

"To ask you to what?"

"To complain to Miss Harriet—me, the only Scholarship girl."

Louie shrugged her shoulders disdainfully. "Oh, they won't complain to Miss Harriet!"

"No—but one doesn't like to refuse things—" Earle said in injured tones.

Before Louie would have had time to reply to this, had she thought of replying to it, a diversion occurred. Nobody had heard steps approaching, but all at once the door opened, and Authority, in the person, not of Miss Harriet, but of Mrs. Lovenant-Smith herself, stood looking in. The hubbub ceased as the boiling of a kettle ceases when cold water is poured in. Several of the conspirators rose to their feet; Burnett Minor, making no bones about it, bolted behind a box. Great is even the look of Authority; it was almost a superfluity when Mrs. Lovenant-Smith asked in measured tones from the doorway: "What is the meaning of this?"

Already the tails of two dressing-gowns had vanished out of the other door.

"What is the meaning of this?" Mrs. Lovenant-Smith asked again.

Then she looked round to see on whom to fasten her displeasure.

Louie saw her look, and instantly fathomed its purpose. She and Richenda Earle stood by the window, as it were the dramatic centre of some Rembrandtesque composition to which all else was merely contributory. The Scholarship girl was going to get into a row. She, Louie, had lived for years among rows; and was leaving anyway on the morrow.

Before the "Miss Earle" had passed Mrs. Lovenant-Smith's lips Louie had stepped forward.

"We've been waiting for our baths," she said.

Perhaps already Mrs. Lovenant-Smith would have preferred Richenda Earle to Louie; there is expediency even in Authority; but the challenge, if it was that, was a public one. Mrs. Lovenant-Smith turned to Louie.

"Do you know what time it is?" she asked freezingly.

It pleased Louie to take Mrs. Lovenant-Smith's question *au pied de la lettre*.

"I'm afraid my watch is in my cubicle. I could tell you in a moment," she said.

This the Lady-in-Charge saw fit to ignore. She drew her own watch from her belt.

"It is ten minutes past eleven," she said. "Students are not out of bed at ten minutes past eleven. Neither are candles burning. Miss Earle—"

But again Louie interposed. After all, it was rough on the Scholarship girl.

"Miss Earle came in only a moment ago to send us to bed," she affirmed, without a tremor.

"Then," said Mrs. Lovenant-Smith, turning to Louie, and perhaps feeling herself once more headed off, "you, Miss Causton, as a new student, are perhaps not yet familiar with the Rules. Be so good as to come to me at ten o'clock tomorrow morning and I will explain them to you."

Mrs. Lovenant-Smith did not make the discomfited rebels file out past her. She herself retired with dignity. Students do not linger in the box-room when it is made known that they are expected to go to bed at once.

But no sooner had the door closed on Mrs. Lovenant-Smith's back than the pent-up general breath escaped again in a fluttering exhalation. In it were awe, delight, homage.

"Oh, Causton!" somebody breathed. "You *are* a brick!"

"*Isn't* she?"

"Wasn't it stunning of her?"

"You'd have caught it, Earle!"

"I saw it in her eye!"

"But I say, Causton, you'll get a wigging!"

"She didn't speak to you, you know!"

"You cut in—"

Louie felt quite confused, so much did they make of so little.

"Good gracious," she said, "what are you all talking about? That's nothing, especially as I was thinking of leaving in any case tomorrow."

There was consternation in the box-room. Had Rebellion found its leader only to lose her again immediately?

"Leaving!"

"Oh, I sha'n't leave till after ten o'clock now, you may be sure," Louie laughed.

"But—oh, I *say*!"

The dismayed voices dropped. There was a blank silence. It was only after half-a-minute that Burnett Minor, who had issued from cover again, begged: "Don't leave, Causton."

"Oh, I shouldn't leave because of anything like this," said Louie, enormously amused at the thought. "The place is a fraud—that's why I should leave."

"Oh, don't leave," another girl begged.

"Well, we'll see what she says tomorrow."

"She can't be *too* down on you—"

"Not the first time—"

Something that can only be described as a pleasant hardening came into Louie's grey eyes. Her laugh dropped a note. She looked at the adoring faces.

"That's just what I mean," she said. "If she *is*—"

"What?—"

"I'll stay."

And that also her stepfather would have described as "just like Louie."

III

Punctually at ten o'clock on the morrow Louie knocked at the door of Mrs. Lovenant-Smith's office or drawing-room—it was both—and entered. Mrs. Lovenant-Smith was writing at an escritoire that was not big enough to accommodate her elbows, and so supported her braceleted wrists only. There was something contradictory about her attitude. Its rectitude as she sat at the inconvenient little desk suggested that she expected Louie, her turn, pause and inquiring "Well?" that she did not. Louie's observant eyes had already noticed a curious inconsistency about the Lady-in-Charge. A great number of things seemed to lie on the tip of her tongue, ready, apparently against her own better judgment, to be detached from it by a perfectly-timed fillip of opposition.

And Louie had only to remember the word or two with which she had dashed Chaff's affability to be fairly sure that though cocoa and candles in the box-room at eleven o'clock at night might seem a good enough reason for the present interview, as like as not another lay behind it. She stood just within the door.

"Well, Miss Causton?"

"I think you told me to come here at ten o'clock."

"Ah, yes. Please to wait a moment."

Louie listened to the squeaking of her quill and the faint jingling at her wrists as she continued to write.

When Mrs. Lovenant-Smith turned again it was almost as if she had thought better of something or other—say of an encounter with this long-chinned, grey-eyed girl who stood, not dressed for gardening, but in a long grey morning frock, looking at her from the door.

"I merely wished to impress on you, Miss Causton, that the Rules must be observed," she said. "I believe there is a copy of them on the smaller bureau by your right hand there. Take it and be so good as to study it. That is all I wished to say."

Louie did not believe the last sentence, but no disbelief showed in her eyes. She inclined her head, but watched Mrs. Lovenant-Smith, waiting for more. She thought that if she waited more would come. It did. Mrs. Lovenant-Smith, having just dismissed Louie, rescinded the decision by speaking again.

"You are older than the others," she said, "and it ought not to be too much to expect of you that you will set a good example."

Louie, perhaps gratuitously, read a meaning into the words. Perhaps you guess what it was. Many of the older people of her world still remembered her mother's first marriage, and Mrs. Lovenant-Smith, though Louie did not like the look of her, was still undeniably of her world. With Louie herself the drawing-master theory of her paternity had long since gone by the board; the girl had not rested until she had discovered that her father was Buck Causton, pugilist and artists' model, none other; and if Mrs. Lovenant-Smith had ever chanced to hear of her as Louise Chaffinger, and identified that person under the name which (whether from pride, spleen, sensitiveness or what not) she had since reassumed, there would probably be something very near the tip of her tongue indeed. And just as Buck had always been a pale fighter, so Louie's own mixed blood, though it might surge at her heart, left her cheeks untinged in moments of stress. She still stood, making no motion to go.

"I don't think I quite follow you," she said slowly. "Why do you say that something 'ought not to be too much to expect'?"

Mrs. Lovenant-Smith stiffened and drew in again.

"It is not necessary to follow me," she said. "You will find all that is necessary in the Rules. You may keep that copy; Rule 6 is the one I wish especially to call your attention to. Would you be so good as to pass me that bell as you go out—the small brass one on the cabinet there?"

She half turned to her writing again.

("Good gracious, what next!" thought Louie.)

The bell was a small Dutch figure in a metal farthingale, and Louie passed it. As she did so she glanced at the hand that took it. Mrs. Lovenant-Smith's face was wrinkled like a dried apple, and the hand, though beautifully kept, was wrinkled too, and had, moreover, rather stumpy nails. Louie's own hands were exquisite. The bell passed from hand to hand.

Whether or not it was the glance at the hands, suddenly the word too much dropped from the tip of Mrs. Lovenant-Smith's tongue. She put the bell down with a little clap.

"The Rules of the college are not called into question," she said. "So far they have proved quite sufficient for the kind of student the college was founded for. By the way, why are you not dressed for the gardens?"

("'Kind of student'—good—gracious!" Louie cried in astonishment to herself. "Very well, madam—")

She spoke calmly, looking modestly down at her long cashmere skirt, but taking in her lovely hands (which toyed with the copy of the Rules) on the way.

"My dress?" she said. "Oh, I wasn't sure whether I should be staying or not."

Louie knew perfectly well that her leaving would make, at any rate until her cubicle should be filled again, a difference of something like sixty pounds a year, with extras, to Chesson's. That is rather a lot of money to hang upon a mere breach of Rule 6. Perhaps Mrs. Lovenant-Smith betrayed herself in the quickness with which she took her up.

"Do you mean you're thinking of leaving?" she asked.

Louie, who had lifted her eyes for a moment, dropped them demurely again.

"I mean," she replied, "that I didn't know whether *you* were going to dismiss *me* or not. You see, you may not want my—kind of student. I'd rather not be in any way considered as an exception," she added.

Had Mrs. Lovenant-Smith known Louie better she would have known that she had now no intention whatever of leaving. As it was, there probably came into her head the thought that after all Louie was a Scarisbrick and a niece of Lord Moone. Ladies-in-charge of horticultural colleges do not fall foul of the Honourable Emily and Lord Moone. All at once her severity relaxed—but she hated Louie thenceforward that it must be so. She smiled a little, but the smile had a twitch in it.

"I don't think we need go quite to that extreme, Miss Causton," she said. "All the same, I'm afraid the Rules are necessary."

"I dare say," said Louie.

"And so long as that is understood, that is the chief thing. In regard to candles in particular, in an old place like this there is always the danger of fire. In fact, I'm not at all sure that a fire drill ought not to be instituted. May I add that I quite appreciated the chivalrous way in which you tried to shield Miss Earle last night? Indeed, I wanted to say that quite as much as the other. I think that is all. Good-morning, Miss Causton."

"Good-morning," said Louie, stalking out.

As she crossed the Restoration hall, "'Kind of student'—good gracious!" she exclaimed again. "To talk to me as if I were Burnett Minor! 'Kind of student!'—I wonder it doesn't occur to her that somebody might have told me all about Miss Hastings and that gardener four years ago!—'Kind of student,' indeed!"

Still without changing her clothes, she walked out past the orchards, up the hill, and sat looking down over the coombes to the sea.

Leave Chesson's, now? Oh no, nothing was farther from her thoughts! She would stay, and why? Not because she had been treated as a junior, but because she had been taken, as it were, at her own word. She herself might be perversely and nonchalantly cynical about her mixed birth, but she did not intend to allow anybody else—Mrs. Lovenant-Smith or anybody—to show as much as a flicker of consciousness of it. "Kind of student"!—Oh no, that amusement was going to be Louie's own private preserve.

For it had been her cynical amusement. Approximately, the mood took her once in five or six months, with or without occasion. Her mother knew its times and seasons, and its passings into abeyance, not into extinction. She did not call her sensitiveness morbid; quite on the contrary, she saw to it that it took the form of a pose of gaiety; she could be pitilessly gay with herself. Meek, harmless Cynthia Scarisbrick, for example, could have told tales about her gaiety when, not knowing whether she herself was eligible for presentation or not (but gathering from the tense silence on the subject that had reigned at Trant that she was not, or at any rate that her mother did not wish it), she had practised the ceremonial curtsy with her cousin. It had been Cynthia, not Louie, who had shed the tears.

But to be agreed with by Mrs. Lovenant-Smith that her origin was open to question (for the Lady-in-Charge had all but said that)—oh no, that was really too much!—

Mrs. Lovenant-Smith, who took a seedsman's salary!

She might have known that Mrs. Lovenant-Smith would know all, all about her—

Then, as she sat, she began to wonder where she had heard the name of Lovenant-Smith before. She had wondered it when first she had received her prospectus at Trant. Of course her stepfather knew these other Lovenant-Smiths, the adjutant's lot, and had probably spoken of them, but she did not think it was that. For a minute or two she sought in her memory. . .

She was ceasing to think when the recollection came of itself. It was only a trifling one after all. One of the boys with whom she had romped at Mallard Bois—Roy she had called him then—had been, she now remembered, a Lovenant-Smith. He would be a connection of the adjutant's. Of course, she had heard the name at Mallard Bois. . .

Then Louie bit her lip. If there had been any doubt at all that Mrs. Lovenant-Smith knew the story of Buck there was none now. The association with Mallard Bois was quite enough. . .

Louie was glad she had looked insolently at those stumpy hands. . . Beast!

The trees below her tossed restlessly, and far out the grey sea was whitecapped as if it had been rasped with a file. No boat had put out for the pollock-fishing or to lift a spiller that morning; only a pilot, a couple of miles out in the Channel, slowly lifted her nose for a moment and then hid it again. Louie felt a little cold, and rose. She made an attractive picture as she did so. Her brown hair was tossed by the wind, and her long grey skirt cracked behind her and clipped her limbs almost as if she had worn the garments of a man.

"Beast!" she muttered again.

Then she thought of another beast—this father of hers whose name she had not needed to take but had taken out of rancour against her mother and despite against herself. (But not for Mrs. Lovenant-Smith to turn up her nose at!) He now (she had this from Chaff) kept a public-house somewhere up the Thames—Lord Moone's cast-off brother-in-law in a public-house!—and any fitful romantic light that might ever have shone about him was now extinguished. Of course the Captain had uttered his usual wistful formula: "Not a bad fellow at all, I should have said"; but that was rather a criticism on the Captain than on Buck. Yes. Buck was simply another beast. But though he were a potman, Mrs. Lovenant-Smith should give him every bit as much deference as if he had been a brewing peer. . .

"And I don't care—if it *is* the pride of the cobbler's dog, I'm going to keep his name," Louie muttered.

Suddenly she turned and climbed the stile that led back to Chesson's land. As she did so she realised that she had been out of bounds. She laughed curtly. Rule 3! Much she cared for their Rules! What about the Rule: "Miss Hastings does not elope with What's-his-Name the gardener"?—but that would keep. In the meantime she would change into her gardening clothes before lunch. She had shown Mrs. Lovenant-Smith that she had garments of freedom. The next time Louie threatened to leave she might be able to add to the force of the threat that she would take half-a-dozen girls with her.

Well, lunch was in half-an-hour; she had just time to change.

But as she descended through the orchards again she came upon Richenda Earle. The copper-haired girl was washing an espaliered plum-tree, and as she turned her head Louie saw that she had been crying. She asked Louie if she was going.

"Leaving here, do you mean? No. What's the matter?"

The girl turned her eyes away.

"Thanks awfully for last night," she grunted. "It was ripping of you. But you see it hasn't made much difference."

"How, not made much difference?"

Richenda glanced at the tree, and from the tree to the syringe in her hand and the pail of disinfectant at her feet. "This," she said. "Anybody can do this job, and I've been sorting out pots over there all the morning," she indicated the yard behind the trees where the flower-pots and debris were kept. "And *I* can't threaten to leave."

"Your scholarship, of course?"

"Yes. And I'm supposed to be working for the medal."

Chesson's wanted a Horticultural Society's medal badly. They had never had one, nor were likely to get one unless Richenda Earle got it for them. Louie, who was quickly fathoming the real economy of the place, looked again at Richenda's red eyes.

"Well, they won't send you away till you've failed," she said.

But Earle made an impatient gesture, and her eyes began to stream again.

"Oh, what's a girl like you know about it!" she broke out. "Yes, I know they'll keep me till then, but you don't know anything at all about it! You would if you'd had my upbringing! You don't know what the struggle is. You think digging and carrying pots is hard work; you wouldn't if you'd seen what I've seen! When you go to London it's just shopping and theatres and suppers and things; but just you try to keep a small bookseller's accounts for him, when they're hardly worth keeping, I mean, and collecting his debts when all his money's tied up in stock and your father's nearly bankrupt—not that he's ever solvent—you'd know what I meant then!"

Then the unexpected outbreak stopped suddenly.

Louie stood silently staring. She disliked seeing anybody cry. Richenda's words had little meaning for her; she supposed they contained a hidden meaning somewhere. Then the copper-haired girl went on, more quietly but no less bitterly:

"I should get a hundred pounds a year on the staff here," she said, "that is, if they won't waste me half-days just out of spite, like they're doing this morning. That's nothing to you. You others are here just for pocket-money, but we live on your pocket-money. I suppose I oughtn't to have come here at all. Not among all you. But I begged father to let me. Father once apologised to me—that was when there was a distraint out against him, if you know what that is—because he wasn't rich. Fathers ought all to be rich, he said. There are seven of us girls at home, and only one married. Oh, I tell you, you don't know!"

Louie wondered why she preferred Richenda Earle loud and striving for the popularity she never got to Richenda Earle unburdening herself thus. She herself went brightly masked, and disliked to see another's mind naked. Richenda's mind was stripped now. It was distasteful. Somehow or other Richenda contrived to miss both the balm of popularity and the solace of private sympathy.

"I'm—I'm awfully sorry," Louie said awkwardly and a little stiffly.

At the tone Richenda drew in instantly.

"It doesn't matter," she said, compressing her lips and beginning to straighten her hair. "I shall just have to buck up, that's all. But girls of your class don't know anything about it, so you needn't think you do. There's the first gong. Come on."

As they passed the dairies a rabble of students raced past the end of the house on their way to the boot-lockers. Louie and Richenda entered by the side door. Richenda plunged at once into the scramble for house-slippers, but Louie, not having put on her garden boots that day, did not need to change. It was too late now to put on another dress. She waited by the inner door.

Suddenly she was spied by Burnett Minor. The child rushed towards her, a book in her hand.

"Are you going, Causton?" she shouted.

There was a loud "Ssssh!" They could be heard from the dining-room. The girls flocked round Louie, and hoarse, excited whispers broke out:

"Are you going?"

"She's dressed!"

"Are you going?"

"Did you see her?"

"Does Causton say she's going?"

"Ssssh—not all at once!—"

"No, I'm not going," said Louie.

Mouths gaped their very widest to make up for the inaudibility of the cheers.

"Hooray!"

"Is she going?"

"No, she's not going—hooray!"

Burnett Minor threw her book joyfully into the book-locker. Ordinarily her reading varied between an adoration of Tennyson and mocking and dramatic declamations either from the "Pansy Library," or from its brother-classics, of which the typical burlesque is "The Blood-stained Putty-knife, or The Plumber's Revenge." But this book was her album.

"I saw you come down dressed, and I did want you to put something in it if you were going," she whispered gleefully; "but you're not going! Hoo—"

Her voiceless mouth gaped wider than them all.

That midday Louie walked demurely up to Mrs. Lovenant-Smith at the head of the table and apologised for not yet having changed. From her tone Mrs. Lovenant-Smith may or may not have inferred that she had spent the hours since their interview in contrite meditation. She inclined her head graciously. But Louie, taking her place for grace between Burnett Minor and Richenda Earle, was murmuring to herself once more:

"'Class of student,' indeed! . . . Good gracious me! . . ."

IV

L ouie quickly became the most popular girl in the college.

HER STUDIES SHE PURSUED VERY much as who should say: "I am Louie Causton—take it or leave it." Neither Miss Harriet nor the gardeners could ever tell when she was interested in a lesson; if she learned, she concealed her processes. Before April was out—(the intervening time may be slipped over; the daily work in the gardens and houses went on as usual, the usual number of crates and parcels was despatched from Rainham Magna station, and already the girls were looking forward to June, which was always a slack month)—before April was out she could "slip" and "bud" as deftly as any when she chose; but few made more mistakes than she, and none accepted correction with her remarkable nonchalance. Afternoon "theory" she had begun to cut almost entirely. A slate hung in the hall, on which students were supposed to write down where they might be found when they left the immediate precincts of the college. One day towards the end of April there appeared on this slate: "Gone to Rainham; L. Causton." Then she awaited events with Mrs. Lovenant-Smith.

There were no events.

She sent to Trant for a bicycle.

Truth to tell, as the spring advanced she needed the air. The glass-houses, with their smell of musk and mould and heated pipes and cherry-pie all mingled, oppressed her; the long forcing-house, where for the time being most of the work for the markets went on, completely took the starch out of her. She felt as if she was being forced herself. She hated the sight of the twelve houses; they merely meant so much ventilation, so much shutting-down for the evenings, so much watering, so much lassitude for the girls, so much money in Chesson's pocket. She was glad she had sent for the bicycle. Somebody else might read thermometers and close down and sprinkle floors and ply the hissing hoses. Louie wanted air.

Yet even the outer air was not sharp enough. It is not an invigorating air in which the lemon-verbena grows in trees up the cottage walls and scented geranium flourishes out-of-doors like a common hedge plant. In the sunken lanes through which she idled on her bicycle the primroses, twice as big as she had ever seen them, and the cowslips, great sub-tropical clusters, were already past; and she expected to see the roses out presently, big as sunflowers. There was something almost rank in the sweet bursting out of the land. She thanked goodness that a daisy was a daisy still, modest and unmagnified. She was not used to hedges of fuchsia. Nature might have been a little more sparing of her myrtle too. Louie always dropped from her bicycle when, coming out of one of the canals of still and scented air, she saw, across a burnt heath-patch or a clump of hardy gorse, a glimpse of the sea. For the sake of a look at the sea she often walked up the hill behind Chesson's and sat on the stile she had crossed on the morning after her interview with Mrs. Lovenant-Smith.

Except by her example, however, she incited nobody else to break the Rules.

It was curious that she should know herself to be popular, and yet at the same time should also be secretly aware that she was a little out of things. All went well enough for the present, but only for the present. She knew quite well what would happen did she, a year or two hence, chance to meet any of her present fellow-pupils. She would not, then, be older than they in quite the same sense that she was now. They would meet; there would be eager recollections of the old days at Chesson's; oh, for that matter she could make it all up now! . . . "Come where we can have a really good talk! Where's Burnett Major now, and her sister? And have you heard from Elwell lately? And I wonder what's become of that red-haired girl—what was her name—Earle—yes, Earle? And of course you know Macfarlane's going to be married. . . Now tell me all about what you're doing!" . . . Oh yes, Louie could make all this up—the bursts, the pauses, the dead stops, and then the falsely bright, perfunctory talk about Chesson's again. For she and her fellow-students would not be doing the same things. They would have taken recognised places, and Louie was not sure that she herself had a place to take. Her father and mother had seen to that. She remained a spectator. If she was liked now, it was not because she went one inch out of her way to be so. She was just as ready to go out of her way to be disliked if she must go out of it at all.

In the meantime, however, here she was at Chesson's, to all intents and purposes her own mistress, and made so much of that she had Mrs. Lovenant-Smith largely at her mercy—for, had she been requested to leave, the two Burnetts, Elwell and others would now have left with her. So, doing exactly as she liked, and adored on every hand,

Louie even wondered sometimes whether she had not been wrong in supposing that restlessness and discontent were bred in the very bones of her.

She was at the very top of her popularity about the time Burnett Major gave the birthday "cocoa" in her cubicle. (That is to say, Burnett Major gave the nucleus of the "cocoa"; the rest of the party happened by a natural process of accretion.) This time the junketing was held by Mrs. Lovenant-Smith's permission; it had been acceded readily. "Lovey's not such a bad old sort when you get used to her," B. Major said. It was in mid-May, on a hot evening, and, though Burnett's window was flung wide open, showing the dark yew outside, not a breath stirred, and the flames of the candles were four inches long in the air. Besides cocoa, Burnett had provided cake and biscuits and candied fruits and an enormous box of "assorted" chocolates; and Burnett's bed was like to break down with the weight of girls upon it.

Louie had had Burnett Major especially in her mind when she had painted her fancy picture of a possible meeting with her fellow-students a year or two hence. The two sisters were the daughters of a Gloucestershire M.F.H., and Louie could forgive B. Major for being a little dazzled by her approaching presentation. There was nothing unfamiliar to Louie, either, in the rest of the things she felt herself, at one and the same time, both "in at" and "out of," for probably Mewley Hall, the Burnetts' home, was not very different from Trant or Mallard Bois. But Burnett Major's position a few years hence was a forgone conclusion; she filled it already in anticipation; and the noisy talk that was in progress as Louie joined the party threw bright lights on it.

They were discussing the coming vacations. These were Chesson's yearly dread. They interrupted his supply of free labour, and there were always fewest girls when he most wanted them. As the vacation arrangements rested after all chiefly with the parents, he could do little except express his preference that as many of the girls as possible should take their holidays in the empty month of June, and his hope that those who did not do so would defer them until as late as they could. Otherwise he was, to that extent, no better off than his trade competitors.

"Here she comes," Burnett Minor was crying as Louie entered the crowded cubicle. "I want to be here when Causton is. It's all right for Major—oh, you needn't think we don't know, Major—if you aren't actually engaged he's always about the place when you're at home—and

I'm going to stalk you both with a camera and then what-d'you-call-it—blackmail him—"

"Shut up, Minor, or I shall send you out," B. Major ordered.

"Then I shall tell everybody who he is and shout his name through the keyhole. It's—" She moved her lips, threatening to pronounce the name there and then.

"Sneak!" said her sister.

B. Minor bridled.

"I *will* tell them if you call me that again! Causton, have you a young man? (That means, Avez-voo un jeune homme, Pig?)"

"Not for you to shout his name through keyholes," Louie replied, smiling.

"No, but do tell us—have you?"

"At my age?" said Louie mockingly, sitting down on the edge of the bed and reaching for candied fruits.

"Go on—you're trying to wriggle out of it—*have* you?"

"Hush, little girl—open your mouth—" She popped a fruit into the mouth that itself resembled an untouched fruit.

Pigou, from the lower deck of the washstand, interposed loudly:

"Elle a vingt-quatr'ans—elle est perdue!"

"Uppé petite chose, avec voter Françay," commented Burnett Minor.

"Cau-ston coiffe déjà Sainte Catherine," said the ruthless Pigou: "à vingt-quatr'ans on est déjà—pff!"

"Non elle isn't pff—rude chose! But she'll tell me when we sleep out, because I'm going to have my mattress next to hers, sha'n't I, Causton?"

"Mais elle vient d'promettre—"

"—and we shall talk about all those things you always say 'Hush' when I come in—sha'n't we, Causton?"

"Prrridd-ee!" taunted the French child: and B. Major spoke.

"But I say, Causton, when do you take your vac.—June or September?"

"And where shall you go?" somebody else demanded.

"I'm going to Ireland—father's taken a house," cried a third.

"Nobody cares where you're going! Causton, will you come home with us?"

"No; come to Ireland with us!"

"Well, can I come home with you? I loved that man who brought you here!" (Burnett Minor was the young woman who had loved Chaff.)

"It wasn't Lord Moone, was it?" Macfarlane asked.

"Or was it your father?"

"Your cocoa, Causton," said B. Major.

Louie had never been so run after before. She curled up among the slippered feet at the foot of the bed (there were four girls stretched upon it), and alternately stroked the hair and tweaked the ears of Burnett Minor, who had defeated Pigou in the scramble to put her head into Louie's lap. "I *can* have the pitch next to yours, can't I?" the child demanded, her eyes turned up and her face (to Louie) upside down. "There, you see, Pig, she says I can—so voo juste pouvez sechey-up, là."

This sleeping out was a summer custom at Chesson's. It began with the warm weather, sometimes in June, sometimes in July. On account of the morning and evening carrying of bedding and mattresses, the "pitches" nearest the house were deemed the most desirable, and weeks ahead there was bickering about the "bagging" of them. They bickered now, and then turned to the vacations again.

Louie listened, saying little. For her, vacations in this sense hardly existed. Vacations lose their value when you study as slackly as Louie did. It might be amusing to go home with one or other of the girls for a week or two, but on the other hand she hardly thought she would. These were the things she was both "in at" and "out of." B. Major was talking about them now. Soon she would be taking her presentation lessons; she was coming out; she had an unofficial admirer; yes, Louie saw quite plainly what B. Major's future would be. What was her own going to be? She had not the least idea. . . No, she did not really want a vacation. More or fewer, there would be girls at Chesson's throughout the summer. Chesson's still amused her; she could leave once for all when it ceased to amuse her. She was learning nothing. She neither wished to start a lavender farm, as Elwell, the daughter of Sir James Elwell of the Treasury, did, nor to grow peaches, as did Macfarlane, nor to add to her pocket-money by selling pot-pourri at extravagant prices to her friends, which was Burnett Major's idea—until she should marry. She could hardly sell pot-pourri to her prize-fighting father. She might (she smiled) sell him hops—she seemed to remember that beer was made of hops. . .

And she certainly did not intend to mug at theory for the sake of a medal, as Earle was doing at this very moment. . .

The party was still discussing this life which was hers and yet not hers when Miss Harriet, going her rounds, tapped at the door and entered.

"Bedtime, young ladies, please," she said. "Mrs. Lovenant-Smith's compliments, and she hopes you have enjoyed yourselves."

Her tone was that of one who might say: "You see, young ladies, what liberty you have *within* the Rules; isn't it much pleasanter all round?"

The party broke up.

The weeks passed. In June a number of the girls went home, Earle among them. Permission to sleep out was given, a little earlier than usual on account of the heavy mildness of the nights; and Louie lay in the orchard, between Burnett Minor and little Pigou. The convolvulus came out, great white trumpets in the hedges; the sea over the hill became of a milky blue; and there floated out to it dense tracts of odours, lilies, and syringa, jasmine and roses and hay. You wearied of the smell of meadow-sweet; in the houses you could hardly take breath. The sun was reflected piercingly from their glass roofs, and the girls spent the afternoons in deck-chairs under the shadow of the courtyard yew.

THE THING THAT (LOUIE SOMETIMES told herself afterwards) made all the difference and yet (as she also sometimes told herself) made no difference at all, began very trivially. It was just such another accident as that which, nine or ten years before, had sent her to her mother with a demand to be told "who the Honourable Mrs. Causton was."

Ordinarily, the girls at Chesson's were a little careless about the dressing of their hair. You cannot move constantly among banks of plants, and pick fruit, and net cherry-trees, and be for ever stooping over beds and frames, and keep your hair fit to be seen. Therefore, once a month or so, the girls might, if they wished, go in parties of four or five to a hairdresser's at Rainham, there to be professionally—whatever the word may be. These parties were made up more with a view to the enjoyment of the half-holiday than to the business strictly in hand; and Louie, had she cared, might have been a member of each detachment that went. On this particular day Louie had had much ado to free herself from Burnett Minor's affectionate clutch.

"Oh, do come with our lot, Causton!" B. Minor had begged. "Oh, you are rotten! You know you went with Elwell before, and with Major before that, and I do want mine properly done like yours, not just punched up the way we do it!"

"What, like Saint Catherine?" Louie laughed.

"Do come."

But Louie had shaken her off.

"He'll remember how mine's done; I was there a week ago. No, I won't come. I'm going to do some theory this afternoon."

"Oh, what a fib! You never do theory!"

"Well, I ought to. No, I won't come."

"Then will you lend me your bicycle?"

"Yes, if you like; but the others are walking, aren't they?"

"Well, I'll wobble with them."

And Louie had watched the party set out, Burnett Minor on the bicycle, "wobbling" and leaving behind her a complicated track in the dust of the drive.

She did not know why she had said she would do theory that afternoon. She supposed it was because she felt slack and bored. Nor did she do very much theory. She went into the classroom, languidly turned over the pages of an old "Balfour," wondered what it mattered to anybody at Chesson's (except perhaps to Earle) that "movements had been observed in the pollen-grains of Cereus Speciosissimus," or that "changes took place in the stamens by suppression and degenerations of various kinds." Then she glanced at a preparation on the stage of the microscope opposite Richenda Earle's empty chair, and yawned. She looked out into the courtyard. Three or four girls dozed in deck-chairs under the dark yew. There was an empty chair—but no; a clatter of washing up was going on in the kitchen under the box-room; she would go up to her cubicle.

She did so, and, pushing off her slippers, lay down on her bed.

Her window was open as far as it would go, but the yew seemed to shut out even what little air there was. All that entered was the faint acrid smell of consuming rubbish; they were slow-burning somewhere at the back. The sounds of the washing up were fainter now; a pigeon alighted on her sill. She had been an idiot, she told herself, to fag herself that morning listening to Hall's demonstration in the forcing-house. She wished there was a pond about the place, with a boat or a punt. She would have bagged the boat to sleep in. It would be jolly to be rocked to sleep in a boat or a punt.

She closed her eyes. The last thing she saw before she did so was the little black-framed miniature of the fourth Lord Moone, the last but three, in his tied wig and ensign's uniform. Louie had tacked it up by her mirror merely because it had been in her room at Trant as long as she could remember and, if one might judge from the youthful face, he was less of an opinionated fool than the other Moones—much less so than Uncle Augustus. . .

She turned over. Then she slept.

Sleep also was deep, too deep, at Rainham Parva. It weighed on the girl like a mulch. At five o'clock Louie could hardly drag herself out of it. She fumbled at her loosened belt and pulled out her watch. Five! The tea-gong must have gone.

Well, perhaps tea would rouse her.

She felt by the side of the bed for her slippers, rose, touched her hair as she passed the glass, and went drowsily downstairs.

As Mrs. Lovenant-Smith and Miss Harriet always took tea in their own or one another's rooms—which, for that matter, the students also were permitted to do if they chose—the meal was a noisier one than either lunch or supper. Louie heard one of Burnett Minor's several voices as she pushed at the door. The child saw Louie's face in the opening and sprang up.

"Here she is—give it to me—I'm going to read it myself—" she cried.

Burnett Minor always wanted to read it herself—"it" usually being one of the sublimer passages from the current number of the "Pansy Library" or an especially choice one from an office-boys' periodical. Louie smiled languidly now as the girl snatched a booklet from Elwell's hand and gave tongue.

"I've punctured your back tyre, Causton, but Mac has some solution and we'll mend it after tea—and I'm always to do my hair like this, Harris says—do look at it, isn't it stunning?—and now—aha!" (somebody had made a grab for her book). "Thought you'd got it, didn't you, Elwell? Now I'll read it first and then show her the picture, and that reminds me, Mac, you've never given me my 'Jack Sheppard' back that I lent you—"

Louie reached for a chair. She yawned again.

"Do give me a cup of tea, somebody. I hope the watering's all done, for I'm not going to do any. What's the child got now? If it's 'Maria Martin' or 'Irene Iddesleigh,' I think I know them by heart."

The child herself answered her question. She jumped on a chair and extended an arm for silence.

"Ready?" she cried. "Now!"

"'The Life and Battles of Buck Causton,'"

she declaimed in her most ringing voice,

"'Being the Full Story and Only Authorised Life of this Famous Pugilist'—

("Causton's uncle, don't forget, girls)—

"'Revised by Himself and now Published for the First Time—including his Historic Encounter with the Great Piker Betteridge'—

("Piker Betteridge—'Piker'—isn't it lovely?)

"'Entered at Stationers' Hall and All Rights Reserved
"'Price One Penny'"

B. Minor drew out every syllable of the linked sweetness, and concluded;

"And lo and behold—on the cover—Buck himself—Uncle Buck, Causton—you needn't say he isn't—as large as life and twice as beautiful—there!"

She held up the booklet in triumph.

But she drew it back again, bubbling with enjoyment. "Wait till I find *the* gem—the one about Piker," she cried.

Her fingers fluttered rapidly through the precious pennyworth in search of the "gem."

Louie's cup of tea had been at her lips, but not a drop spilt as she put it down again. If her colour changed at all it was only as that other pale fighter's had done whose story, Price One Penny, the unconscious Burnett Minor was rapturously searching.

"Here it is!" cried B. Minor, peremptorily extending her hand again. "Listen, everybody!—

"'But the redoubtable Buck refused to allow the wiper to be skied. He recked nothing of his bunged optic and the claret that flowed from his beezer. Game as a buck-ant he advanced for the twenty-eighth round. The Piker, whose bellows were touched—'"

But Louie had risen and walked to the child. She held out her hand.

"Let me look," she said.

B. Minor gave her a suspicious look, as if she feared she might be reft of her treasure. "You will give it me back?"

"Oh yes."

Louie took the book.

She supposed she was awake now, but somehow a curious air of unreality enveiled whatever it was that was happening. She looked at the cover of the "Life" in her hand. The most execrable of woodcuts could hardly disguise what she saw. Traditionally posed, nude above the waist, and clad below only in tights and fighting-shoes—formidably watchful, lightly poised for the blow—in appearance at any rate he was a man and superb. But really he had been cruel, faithless, divorced.

As if she had passed merely from one state of half-wakefulness to another, she did not think of the bomb she was about to drop among the girls. She only wanted to look, and to look, and to look again at this man, who was her father.

"Isn't it just Causton's mouth and chin?" she barely heard Burnett Minor bubbling. "But I can't say she has Uncle Buck's beezer—"

Slowly Louie handed the "Life and Battles" back. At any rate she had now seen him, if only in a wretched woodcut. She looked quietly about her.

"That's my father," she said, perhaps a shade distinctly and loudly.

Then she looked about her again.

Burnett Minor jumped down from her chair. Her eyes shone flattery on Louie. The very audacity of such a lie compelled her admiration.

"O-o-oh—*what* a whopper!" she cried. Louie turned her eyes to Burnett Minor.

"You said uncle. You weren't quite right. That's my father," she said again.

Burnett Minor's life was full of miracles. A miracle more or less made no difference. Her eyes sparkled. She alone of the girls believed.

"Not really?" she gasped.

Louie nodded.

"Qu'est c'qu'elle dit?" Pigou cried excitedly, somewhere at the back.

"Pooh, she didn't—she only nodded—nodding isn't a lie," a casuist scoffed.

"Stupid, don't you see she's joking?"

But Burnett Minor was watching Louie—only to be quite sure.

"Honour?" she cried. "Spit your death?"

"Honour."

"How splen-*diferous*! And you never told us!"

But Burnett Major had already looked at her sister. She was shocked into using her Christian name. "*Genista!*" she reproved her.

"Let me look again," said Louie.

She looked again at the man who had been cruel, faithless, divorced. Again she handed the "Life" back.

"He keeps a public-house up the river," she said.

At that the tension was suddenly relieved. That, of course, was too much. They breathed freely again. The derisive clamour broke out.

"Oh, don't you see? They've made it up between them—frauds!"

"Of course they have! Come and finish tea."

"She'll be saying that was the man who brought her down next!"

"Causton, I'll never, never believe another word you say!"

"Come on—the housekeeper will be here in a minute."

"Pig, you've stolen my piece of cake that I was saving!"

"Hurl the bread and butter, Mac."

And the crowd which had gathered about Louie dispersed to the tables again.

Not until ten minutes later, when she had gone up to her own room again, did Louie begin to wonder what had impelled her to make her surprising declaration. But in an instant her ten-years'-old habit of thought asserted itself again. Why have made it? Rather, why not have made it? She would have made it sooner had occasion offered. Elwell and the Burnetts did not drag their fathers in; she had not dragged her father in either. She had not told them that her mother was Lord Moone's sister—it was known, but she had not told them; why should she have paraded the fact that her father was this redoubtable Buck, from whose beezer the claret had flowed as he had advanced for the twenty-eighth round? They could have known it any time they had wanted! Conceal it? Why, had she not all her life been glorying in that very pride of the cobbler's dog?

And still, deep down in her, she wondered whether it had been even that sort of pride, and not rather that secret hunger of the heart that, while she was "in at" everything, she was also "out of" everything. Had it been that that had caused her to say quietly: "That's my father"?

Or perhaps it was even something deeper still. Perhaps, in a word, it had been her blind groping towards that crude and strong and cruel and joyous life Richenda Earle had said she knew nothing about.

She wondered whether the girls downstairs were talking about her now.

Her eyes fell on the black-framed miniature of the fourth Lord Moone. Then, as if her brain had received a number of disordered impressions all heaped one on the top of the other, she sat down on the edge of her bed, not so much to think as to remember again exactly what had happened.

Gradually the disorder cleared. Phrases and the tones in which they had been uttered began to stand forth more distinctly. Presently she was able to allocate each to its speaker. It was her first attempt to estimate differences in the future her declaration might have made.

Burnett Minor, of course, she could dismiss summarily. To her it had been a high lark, that but endeared Louie to her the more. But Burnett Major? What about her? "*Genista!*" she had exclaimed, shocked at her young sister's apparent belief in the socially impossible. Yes, it would be interesting to see what difference, if any, was to be seen in Burnett Major's attitude now. And Elwell's "*Oh!*" What about that? And Macfarlane's blank look? And what did Richenda Earle think?

Louie did not know yet.

And what about Mrs. Lovenant-Smith? Undoubtedly Mrs. Lovenant-Smith, knowing about it herself, would have preferred Louie to keep silence.

The thought of Mrs. Lovenant-Smith, however, always braced Louie. That curious pleased coldness came into her eyes again. She would see about Mrs. Lovenant-Smith by-and-by. In the meantime, the last thing she intended to do was to absent herself from them all. She would go down to supper.

She took a clean blouse from a drawer, laid it out on her bed, and then, reaching for a towel, started for the bathroom.

Before she reached the bathroom, however, one of her conjectures was already answered. Richenda Earle's cubicle was on the same corridor as hers, four doors lower down, and she met Richenda herself, who had come back from her vacation a week before, by the embrasure of one of the latticed courtyard windows. It was almost dark; in the recess the little reflectored oil lamp had been lighted, and it shone on the Scholarship girl's copper hair and angular shoulders. Louie stopped. She did so deliberately. Let Earle allude if she dared.

"You washed?" she said, on a rising note.

"No, not yet. I—I came up for a book," said Richenda.

"You're not studying tonight, are you?"

"Ye-es—oh yes, I must."

"Classification?"

"Ye-es—yes."

"How far have you got now?"

Louie's mood was on her. It was overdue, but it had come now, and she was challenging Earle. Nevertheless, she was ignorant of what she really challenged when she challenged Earle. Hard knowledge of the true weight of Life will tell, and Earle's knowledge of that weight told now. The girl's head was downhung, so that the nodule of bone at the back of her neck caught the light sharply. Suddenly she looked up.

"But you are Lord Moone's niece, aren't you?" she said, without preface.

Since her vacation, this daughter of a struggling Westbourne Grove bookseller had seemed less assertive than before, and was, somehow, none the worse for it. Louie didn't know what had made the difference, but she momentarily dropped her point.

"Yes," she said. "Why?"

"Then—?" Richenda halted.

"Then what? The other that I told them downstairs is just as true, if that's what you want to know."

"But—but—"

"Well, what?"

Earle evidently mitigated what she had been about to say.

"I only mean that—that you must have thought it queer, my talking as I did—that morning, you know?"

Louie saw the approach of the first attitude for her garner.

"What morning?" she demanded.

"When they punished me—when I was washing the fruit trees."

"I remember. Well, why should I think anything queer?"

Earle's head dropped again. Again the sharp nodule of bone showed.

"Do you mean," Louie said, "that if my father's what I said, no doubt I know as much about what you were saying as you do?"

"Oh no!" Earle said, the more quickly that that probably had been what she had meant.

"Then what do you mean?"

"Only that it's—so odd—"

But suddenly Louie gave her towel a twitch and turned away. She spoke with her chin over her shoulder.

"I don't love my mother," she said, "but for all that she is Lord Moone's sister—Augustus Evelyn Francis Scarisbrick, Lord Moone.

And the other's my father. I wouldn't study too hard about it if I were you. You have your medal to get."

She walked abruptly to the bathroom.

That night, as usual, she sat at supper between Burnett Minor and Richenda Earle. The ordinarily irrepressible child on her left was silent; but others, two or three places removed from Louie, leaned back or forward from time to time to speak to her. She fancied Burnett Minor had been crying; she was sure of this when, giving the child's hand a pat under the table, she felt her own hand impulsively caught and squeezed. Then, in proportion as Burnett Minor cheered up (which she usually did very quickly), the others ceased to talk across to Louie. It was as if, whoever did it, some normal level of chatter must be maintained. Soon supper was as desultorily talkative as it always was. Louie, glancing at the top table, saw that Mrs. Lovenant-Smith knew nothing of what had happened at tea-time. She was, however, quite ready for her the moment she should find out something.

V

One afternoon about three weeks later Louie Causton had occasion to go into the carpenter's shed. This shed lay between the dairies and the boiler-house that was the centre of the hot-water-pipe system, and Priddy had a frame making there. Half this frame, protected by a board with "Wet Paint" chalked upon it, leaned against the outside wall, and, with his back to the sunlit doorway, a young man, whom at first Louie took to be Priddy, was doing something at a bench. Hearing her, he turned. It was not Priddy. Louie did not know him.

There is in the British Museum a small helmeted head very like the young man Louie saw. It is on the upper floor, among the Tanagras, in a case on the left as you walk from the stairs. This young man, of course, was not helmeted. His face was handsome and slightly vacuous; his eyes in particular had something of the blankness of the little terracotta head; and his mouth was full and classically curved, and had the slightest of smudges of dark moustache along the deeply indented upper lip. A pair of rolling muscular shoulders showed through his white sweater; his old trousers were tucked into a pair of wooden-looking boots; and he was filing something. Louie wondered what business he had there.

He told her. He spoke in a slow voice, as if he had got his explanation by rote. He was there by Mrs. Lovenant-Smith's permission, he said.

"We had a smash with the centre-board, you see," he explained. "Crash—just at tea-time. Izzard wanted to send it to Mazzicombe, but I told him they'd charge nearly as much as we gave for the beastly boat. So I'm doing it myself."

Then, as if his presence within the precincts of a horticultural college for young women was quite explained, he bent over his filing again. Louie, who had come for a couple of boards that had been put aside for her, took them and went out. She was twenty yards away when she heard the young man call slowly after her: "I say—I ought to carry those for you, you know—"

The boards were for her bed. This she had removed from the orchard. The new place lay quite beyond the orchard, at the foot of the hill between Chesson's and the sea. There, for the first time on the previous night, she had had the best of what breeze there was.

It had been the attitude of her fellow-students during the past month—or, more fairly, what she had conceived to be their attitude—that had caused her thus to remove herself.

It might be too much to say that she was still not as popular as ever. These things are not demonstrable. Popular she had been; now—well, it depended a little more than it had done. Burnett Minor, of course, would have eaten from the same plate with her by day and shared her bed at night had she been permitted—also had she not left for her vacation a fortnight before; but Burnett Major—Louie was not so sure about Burnett Major. Her attitude had been more than correct; it had been so correct that Louie had been put altogether in the wrong. The words, of course, had never been said, but Louie had imagined Burnett Major's private opinion to be as follows:—

"But why didn't she tell us sooner? What earthly difference does she suppose it would have made? Who cares about things like that? I dare say her father's just as good as anybody else's father; for that matter, mother's grandfather was only a farmer—mother told us so herself; but nobody likes being treated as if they were snobs. It showed a lack of confidence, that's what it showed; and I don't know—now—I mean no girl, unless she *wasn't* quite a lady, would—" Louie could supply that part too.

"I don't care—I *love* Causton!" she had also imagined B. Minor as having sobbed, bold and unconvinced. "He didn't sky the wiper when his beezer was bleeding, anyway!"

Yes: for Burnett Major, presentation and all the rest of it lay ahead.

Matters would probably have stopped at that had Louie herself allowed them to do so; but that would not have been like Louie. Allow them to stop there? Good gracious, no! Her cynicism had become bright indeed. *She* was not the girl to contaminate the innocent Burnett Minor; neither—for she was a Scarisbrick when all was said and done—was she going to be driven willy-nilly into the society of Richenda Earle as company good enough for her. She could look after herself, thank you. Coventry is no unpleasant place provided you have the putting of yourself there, and at any rate her Coventry at the foot of the hill was cooler at night than the other one. It meant carrying her mattress and bedding a little farther, but she had a prizefighter's physique to carry them with, which was more than her nearest neighbour, Elwell, the daughter of the Treasury mandarin, could say.

It is true that she did sometimes wonder (with Burnett Major, perhaps) whether she had not inherited also from the prizefighter something less desirable than his physique—a discontented and ill-conditioned nature. But that did not mend matters. It merely made her, if it did anything at all, distrustful of herself. And as this is the story of Louie, virtues and vices and all, her moods must go down with the rest.

At any rate, rolled in her blanket at the foot of the hill, she could feel the night wind on her face, and see the stars, and in her fancy deride or boast of her parentage to her heart's content.

On the afternoon following that on which she had fetched the boards from the carpenter's shed she went to the shed again, this time for a couple of tent-pegs and a piece of cord for the better securing of her blankets. The vacant young Tanagra was still there. But this time he was not quite so vacant. He had had leisure to think of quite a number of words.

"I say," he said, lifting slow and bashful eyes of the colour of blue porcelain to Louie, "I've been thinking. Haven't I seen you before?"

"Yes. Yesterday," said Louie shortly. He had had the bad luck to catch her at her brooding. But he did not seem to notice her curtness.

"No, but I mean—before—"

"When?"

"Isn't—isn't your name Chaffinger?" He almost blushed.

"No."

"Oh!"

Then she relented a little.

"I was called Chaffinger for a time. My name's Causton. I suppose yours is Chesson, or you'd hardly be here?"

"Chesson? Why Chesson? No. Mine's Lovenant-Smith—Roy Lovenant-Smith."

"Oh!" said Louie. "Then you're right. We have met before, at Mallard Bois."

Roy Lovenant-Smith appeared to be so relieved at being rid of a perplexity that he didn't much care if they never met again.

"I thought we had," he said mildly. "You were Louie Chaffinger then. I knew you were."

"But what," Louie asked, "are you doing here?"

He radiated simplicity.

"That centre-board, didn't I tell you? Izzard would make me go halves in the rotten old thing; just look at her; hardly a shroud on the port side, and the centre-board was hitched up with a piece of old rope instead of a chain and down it came the other tea-time. It's the cabin table as well as the centre-board, you see, and the whole thing shut up—just like that—"

He set the inner edges of his hands together and then closed his palms with a slap.

"All the tea—jam and all the lot," he said.

He amused Louie. "That was a pity," she said demurely.

"Wasn't it? But I say, I shall be catching it. I might use the shed, aunt said, but she told me it was a fixed Rule about men, unless you're a gardener, of course—"

("An obedient nephew," Louie thought.) "Then I must go at once," she added.

"Well, I shouldn't like to get you into a row too," said Roy Lovenant-Smith ingenuously.

"No," Louie agreed, more demurely still. "They have to be strict, you know."

"Rather!" said Roy Lovenant-Smith heartily.

And Louie left him.

She was hardly out of sight before her laughter broke forth. "'All the tea—jam and all the lot!'" she repeated softly, and laughed again. She scarcely remembered this delightful young man. When, as a child of eleven, she had played leapfrog, he could hardly have been more than seven, and she felt herself to be far more than four years his senior now. He was the adjutant's son, she supposed. Well, he would hardly need Chaff's usual extenuation about his being a bad fellow at all: Louie would be very much surprised if he had wit enough to be very bad, or, for the matter of that, very anything else either. Once more she laughed. At any rate she had to thank him for dispelling her megrims for the time being. Still laughing softly, she passed through the orchards, ascended the hill, and sought her favourite place by the stile at the top.

She had not thought very much about young men. She had observed them as so many phenomena, obviously superior to the animals, yet not quite identifiable as beings with inner experiences akin to her own. They looked at her irregular mouth and elongated chin, said the things young men did say, and departed again, taking their various moustaches and their unvarying smell of tobacco to some girl of the kind she knew they accounted "pretty." They were quite different beings from the fairy prince of her childhood; and since her childhood's days she had grown gradually, she did not know how, to a fairly accurate estimate in retrospect of the "little party" to which Chaff had once taken her, pigtails and all. Her views of marriage too were coloured by that mixed parentage that made her, she supposed, not "common" and not "a lady." She would not marry unless this was clearly understood. What else there might be in marriage was shadowy, to be considered after this redoubtable magnanimity was safely out of the way.

With no young man had she ever had "a lark."

She was, however, more in the mood for a lark now—not necessarily with a young man—than she had ever been in her life before. "Cau-ston a vingt-quatr'ans—elle coiffe déjà Sainte Catherine," the remorseless Pigou had said: oh, had she? Did she? Moreover, you cannot put yourself gloomily into Coventry; others must be made to see that you consider your sequestration the most desirable of conditions. Indeed, she had said as much to Richenda Earle only the night before.

Richenda was the only one of the girls who slept indoors, and Louie, carrying her bed-trappings out from the house, had come upon Richenda by the little green door of the espaliered wall that led to the orchards. Richenda had made an advance, willing, apparently, to forget the snub Louie had administered after the "Life and Battles" revelation, and had offered to carry her pillow for her.

"Why do you go so far?" she had asked, as they had left the orchard behind.

"Oh, I hate being disturbed," Louie had replied. "I'd go right down to the shore if it wasn't for the climb up again."

"But suppose you wanted anything during the night?"

"What should I want?"

"Of course, I forgot. You don't have headaches. I have—frightful ones."

"Then why don't you come out too? There's quite a jolly place here. I'd help you to carry your things."

"Oh, I've got to read," Richenda had shaken her head.

"You'd be heaps better for it—"

Louie had not much in common with Richenda—save perhaps (she loved little cuts like this at herself) that both of their fathers were literary. But she had had that rather brutal snub on her conscience. That had come out next.

"You do study too hard," she had said, "and—I say, Earle—I'm sorry for what I said that night—you know—when I snapped at you and said you'd your medal to get. Will you forget that?"

The next moment she had almost wished she hadn't said it, Earle's hungry gratitude had shown so.

"It wasn't your fault a bit," the red-haired girl had broken out impulsively. "It was all mine. I ought to have minded my own business. But I was so—so—"

"Well, try sleeping up here," Louie had cut her short. "It's jolly."

But Richenda had gone on. "I was stupid," she had murmured.

"I don't know that you were. You see how it is."

"Oh, I was, I was—"

"Well, as I tell you, I don't think much of my mother's lot."

"Ah, *you* can say so," Richenda had replied, shaking her head. Then, as Louie had thrown down her mattress, "You don't mean to say you undress here?" she had asked.

"Well, I don't sleep in my clothes."

"But don't your things get wet?"

"I wrap 'em in my waterproof. . . You won't come up, then, and run down to the shore for a bathe before breakfast?"

"Causton, they'll be dropping on you yet!" Earle had said, almost frightened.

"Well, without the bathe?"

"Oh, I should die!"

And Richenda had gone back to sleep where she might find remedies for her headaches within reach of her hand during the night.

Louie sat on the stile. The sea had a soft bloom, and the sky was of the colour of the whites of a baby's eyes. Bees hummed among the scabious, and blue and sulphur butterflies hovered over the patches of wild thyme. A tramp, sullying the air behind her, crept slowly up to Bristol; a single nodding grass-head near at hand shut her out almost completely. Mazzicombe, down under the hill, was hidden. Louie watched it all, thinking of nothing, or, if of anything, of how sweet it was to relax all her muscles to the point of not stumbling off the stile, and all her mind save that she might still be just conscious that she existed and was Louie Causton. . .

"Hallo," said a slow, imperturbable voice behind her; "here we are again."

She started a little. Roy Lovenant-Smith was returning with a baulk of old wood over his shoulder.

"Oh, it's you," she said. She did not know whether she was glad or annoyed to be interrupted.

"Yes, it's me," he replied placidly.

She was silent for a moment; then: "I thought you hadn't to hang about here?" she said.

"Well," he put it to her candidly, "how can I get over the stile when you're sitting on it? How can I, now?"

She laughed. "Well, I must get off on my proper side." She did so. "There," she said.

He climbed over with great deliberateness, walked a few yards with his piece of timber, and then turned again.

"No, you can't see her from here," he said. "She's down under the hill there. I don't think she's worth bothering about, but Izzard says she'll be quite all right with a new stay or two. I suppose I shall have to get 'em."

Louie felt a return of her amusement.

"Who's Izzard?" she asked.

"Izzard?" He looked at her as if she ought to know that. "Izzard's the other chap. Always painting, you know. Painting and mooning about and leaving me to do all the work. He's away there somewhere now." He pointed vaguely across the Channel. "I suppose he'll come back when he's ready. She *is* an old egg-box!—I say, how's your cousin Eric? And that girl—what's her name—Cynthia, wasn't it?"

She didn't know, and told him so; she did not tell him that she didn't care either. He cogitated for a moment, and then said:

"But I say—what do you *do* at this place? Seems funny to me. . . Mind yourself—somebody wants to get over—"

She had not heard anybody approach. It was Priddy, going down to Mazzicombe. Louie stood aside from the stile. Priddy climbed over it and began to descend the hill. Lovenant-Smith looked at Louie in surprise.

"I say," he said, "that's cool! Don't those fellows take their hats off to you?"

"No," said Louie. Then she turned her clear grey eyes on him. She had been fairly caught.

"Don't they? By Jove! . . . What are you looking at me like that for?"

The rippling laugh with which Louie replied dropped a note. "Guess!" she said.

"How can I guess?" he asked, with his innocent and statue-like stare.

For answer, Louie glanced to where Priddy's brown bowler hat was disappearing over the edge of the hill. Roy Lovenant-Smith saw—he really saw—

"What?" he exclaimed. "You don't mean to say that that chap will—?"

She nodded. He stared.

"What, get you into a row for talking to me?"

"He may not."

"No, but really, joking apart?" he said incredulously.

"Perhaps he won't."

"Oh, come, I say! . . . Look here, shall I go back with you and explain?"

The innocent! "I don't think I would," said Louie, smothering her laughter.

"But—hang it all! I say, I *am* sorry!"

"Oh?"

"I mean sorry I've got you into a row, of course," he amended.

"Oh, I thought you meant sorry you stopped and talked to me."

"Of course not. That is, if it doesn't get you into a row."

"And if it did—?"

"Well, a chap doesn't like getting people into rows. Look here—that beggar wants talking to!"

Louie dropped her eyes. "I've been in rows before," she said.

Instantly he cheered up, "Oh, I see! You mean it wouldn't be much?"

"Well, your aunt can't exactly skin me." At the recollection of Mrs. Lovenant-Smith she glanced with satisfaction at her hands.

"Oh, I'll make that all right with her," said Roy Lovenant-Smith hopefully.

She looked at him. He *was* an innocent! "You know what that would mean?" she said.

"What?"

"Well, merely that you wouldn't see me again."

His look too rested on her hands. "Why?" he asked.

She straightened herself. "Oh, never mind about it. I'm going now."

He coloured a little. "But I say—Louie—you don't mind my calling you Louie, do you? I used to, you know.—I should like to see you again."

"Perhaps you'd better not," she said, with great demureness.

"Oh, rot!" he expostulated. "A fellow can't get a girl into a mess and then leave her in the lurch!"

"You'd like to see me just once again, to see whether I'd got into a row or not?"

"That's what I mean."

It wasn't what Louie had meant him to mean, but "Well, once, if you like," she conceded.

"All right. What about here, at this time tomorrow?"

"I'll see if I can get away from my studies."

"Right. And if I see that chap in Mazzicombe, may I say anything to him?"

"Please don't."

"Not about not taking his hat off?"

"Oh, they don't trouble about that sort of thing here."

"Well, they jolly well ought. All right, I won't. Good-bye—"

"Good-bye."

He took his board and followed Priddy; she turned back to the college. She laughed again. At any rate, a lark with a pleasant image was better than a hole-in-corner, Miss Hastings affair with a gardener. She would *not* "coiffe Sainte Catherine."

She duly got her wigging. She was put "on her honour" by Mrs. Lovenant-Smith not to see the young man again who had betrayed the confidence put in him. This struck her as quite richly arrogant. To be put "on your honour" by somebody before whom you stand mute as a fish, and to have it assumed that you accept the bond, was the *largior ether* indeed. Louie did not even feel called upon to say that she declined to consider herself bound. Mrs. Lovenant-Smith might take her "off her honour" again. She met Roy scarcely three hours later. The interview he himself had had with his aunt in the meantime affected the situation but little; his centre-board was now patched up, and the withdrawing of the privilege of the carpenter's shed made no difference.

They met again on the afternoon following that, and again on the one after that. Louie found herself hoping that Izzard, whoever he was, would not return from "over there" just yet. Let somebody else attend to the hair-combing of the Saint.

A SCORE OF DIFFERENT THINGS contributed to her enjoyment of that affair of atmosphere—her "lark." First, the initiative was hers—for her empty-eyed statue accepted everything with as much candour as if he had been born into a virgin world on the eighth day of its creation. Next, the mere disregarding of Mrs. Lovenant-Smith was a pleasure she felt it incumbent upon herself not to forgo. Next, there was the instinctive courage with which she translated her sulks into carelessness and gaiety. Next—but allow what you will for the rest: pique, vanity, her derivation, her upbringing. When, the third time she met Roy by the stile, the half-French girl, Pigou, came upon them, and instantly flew to spread the news among such girls as still remained at Chesson's, Louie's Coventry was the coveted thing she had all along intended it should be.

For she was more than merely popular now; she was romantic, apart, a being to be looked up to with something like awe. Meet a young man! She felt herself to be the channel by which every girl in the place might have access to her own dreams. They gave her longing glances, that mutely implored her to tell them all, all about it; she talked about everything else, but not about that, and hearts and mouths watered. They offered to do things for her—to carry her mattress, to do her Sunday watering, even to clean her bicycle; and Louie let them—but told them nothing. Nay, she even drew Richenda Earle to herself. Richenda actually carried her mattress to the foot of the hill one night and slept out. The two mattresses were placed not six feet apart, and, as the birds settled on the boughs and the stars came out, Richenda set herself wistfully to pump Louie.

Then it appeared why Richenda had seemed changed since her vacation. Speaking in a low voice, she too admitted that there was now—Somebody. Weston, his name was, Louie learned, and he was some sort of a commercial schoolmaster at the same place in Holborn where Richenda herself had studied. So instead of Richenda pumping Louie, Louie pumped Richenda. What was her Mr. Weston like? Well (Richenda said), some might think him an oddity—the Secretary Bird, his nickname was—but he was, oh, a soul so sensitive, so gentle! Was there any prospect of their marrying soon? Richenda sighed; it would be a long time; if she got her post at Chesson's he might apply for a country schoolmastership somewhere near, and then she would get a bicycle; or if he got a "rise" in London she might relinquish her appointment—when she got it. But in any case it could hardly be for years. Louie asked flatly what Weston got, and was told one hundred pounds a year. She looked up in surprise. Her own dress allowance was treble that amount.

"And you'd get a hundred here too?" she asked.

"If I get the place—which means if I get my medal," said Richenda.

Then, Louie thought, that would be two hundred between them—two-thirds of her dress allowance.

"But—but—," she said, "I thought people got paid more than that!"

"I told you you didn't know," said Richenda softly.

"But—but—why, my aunt paid Miss Skrine one hundred and fifty pounds, just to go through her engagements, opening bazaars and charities and so on—just to write down on a slate what she had to do each day!"

"Your aunt's Lady Moone," came from Richenda's couch.

"I *know* she got one hundred and fifty pounds, *and* lived with them. One hundred pounds seems absurd."

"That's what father said when he apologised to me."

"But surely, all—all the people one sees aren't paid at that rate! Why, some cooks get a thousand—I've heard that for a fact—"

"Some don't," came from the other pillow.

"Well, some do, and if you strike an average, or whatever it's called—"

But Richenda interrupted, softly and wearily:

"Oh, you don't, don't, don't know."

Louie asked further questions. She frowned, puzzled, at the answers. Of course Richenda herself wasn't a very effective sort of girl; if anybody had to be downtrodden it would very likely be she; but the things she was telling her now (Richenda had begun to talk again, resignedly rather than bitterly) were preposterous. There must be something wrong with Richenda, probably with her Weston too; she did not look quite right; she was very different from the rosy housemaids at Trant, for example. One hundred pounds a year! . . . She had forgotten all about Roy. When, presently, Richenda came as near to putting a question about him as she dared, she forgot about him again. One hundred pounds a year! . . . She lay on her back, her knees up, her hands behind her head, her sleeves fallen from her wonderful arms, the brows above the grey eyes knitted. She was sure that *she* could do better than that! She even went so far as to say so. Richenda showed no resentment.

"You've got Lord Moone behind you," she said.

"I've got a prizefighter and a public-house behind me," Louie replied.

"Yes—I know you think you know—"

Louie lay awake, still pondering it all, long after Richenda had fallen into an uneasy sleep.

On the following afternoon she met Roy by the stile again. She was restless, unsettled, she knew not what. She spoke almost sharply to him.

"I'm not going to stand here with you," she said; "that's twice I've been seen. Come down the hill."

Roy no longer urged the Rules. They walked together a hundred yards down the hill, and sat down under a gorse-bush. He made her move quite behind it, and even then tucked her skirt a little farther out of the gaze of a possible passer-by.

"Now we're all right," he said. "How's Lovey this morning?"

"I don't know. I haven't seen her."

"Well, don't bite a fellow's head off, Louie."

"Then don't bother me today.—No, I don't want my hand held."

"What's the matter with you?"

"If you don't leave me alone I shall go. I didn't sleep till nearly daylight."

"I didn't sleep for quite an hour, either," he said sympathetically. "I say, isn't it funny, Louie, when you come to think of it, that till a week ago I hadn't thought of you for years?"

"Oh, I wasn't lying awake thinking of you," she said bluntly.

"I was of you." He put out his hand again.

His approach only made her impatient. "Oh, don't!" she snapped. "Really I shall get up and go if you worry me."

He was, as he would have put it, "keen": keen enough to begin to sulk. She let him sulk, and watched the sea, always of a milky bloom, and the sky, still of the hue of an infant's eyeball. After some minutes she turned to him again.

"What *do* people get paid?" she asked abruptly.

"What people?" He spoke over his shoulder.

"Oh, people—you know what I mean!"

"We get dashed little, I know that." (He was going into the army.) "What sort of people? Servants and those?"

"And those—yes."

Roy expounded.

"Jolly good pay, *I* call it; lot of lazy beggars! Why, the fellow down there wanted to charge me two pounds for patching up that centre-board, that I did in about a day. I shouldn't mind getting two pounds a day! . . . Why?"

"I want to know."

"Some of your gardeners been grizzling to you?"

"No."

"A wonder—rotten grousing lot! They ought to have uniforms to buy, and mess-bills and clubs and things; they'd know all about it then! Two pounds for filing a piece of iron and putting a patch on a piece of wood!—I think it will hold all right," he continued naïvely; "we shall make a deuce of a lot of leeway if it doesn't. We're flat-bottomed, you see, with only bilge-keels, and that reminds me; Izzard's coming back on Wednesday; I'd a note from him this morning. But he won't be in the way, dear, if you'll only be friends—"

She could not help laughing. After all, Richenda's "grousing" was a little spoiling her fun. She turned to him again.

"I haven't seen her yet," she said. "Let's go down to her now."

He chuckled mildly. "You do play the dickens with the Rules, Louie."

"Bother the Rules!"

"Well, you don't want to go just this minute; it's jolly here—"

This time she did not withdraw her hand.

But he was very slow, she thought, in kissing her. He had never kissed her yet. What was the good of being caught at—nothing?

Well, statues (she reflected), especially young ones, are slow—

Even as she was thinking it he did that very thing. Perhaps it was to summon up resolution to do so that he had lain awake the previous night. He kissed her cheek.

The result was curious. It was the law of her physique that most moments of perturbation only turned her paler; but at this particular form of perturbation she turned suddenly pink.

In a few moments she was as before. The first sign that she was Louie again was that she forbade him to repeat the offence. He sulked again.

"All right," he said resentfully; "then we may as well go and see the yacht."

"I don't want to see the yacht."

"Well, you needn't be stuffy about it—"

Statues *were* distractingly slow!

Then she looked at him with a faintly mocking smile.

"Aren't you going to say you're sorry?" she challenged him (but she had for a moment a faint return of the unhabitual colour for all that).

He seemed to suspect that he was being mocked; nevertheless it was with a rather tremulous boldness that he answered "No."

"Oh!"

"You see," he explained, "you did let me hold your hand."

She caught her breath. Good gracious! Why, he would be saying presently that she had asked him to kiss her! "You see, you did let me hold your hand!" What next?

"You know you did," he argued simply.

Even so it is written, "Out of the mouths of babes and sucklings—"

Suddenly she laughed. O admirable innocence, that alone can defeat guile! After all, it was too unpardonable not to be pardoned. She turned her face away again.

"You *are* stupid!" she murmured, her face, even her neck, pink once more.

At that quite a new gleam seemed to irradiate his good-looking clay.

"I say," he said slowly, as he struggled with the newness of the idea, "you mean—do you mean?—about my not kissing you—properly?"

Oh, the heaviness! But he should kiss her "properly," as he called it, now!

"Oh," she said briskly, "it's too late now. You can't very well after that, can you?"

But he beamed. "Of course I can!"

"No, Roy!"

"I will—"

This was outrageous. She made as if to rise.

"No, Roy—no—you know very well you don't think I'm pretty—"

"Well, you aren't ugly," said he.

(Great heavens! She "wasn't ugly"!)

"Very well, Mr. Statue," she thought, compressing those irregular lips whose degree of prettiness he estimated so nicely. "I'm going to be pretty in a very few minutes, and you're going to tell me so."

"No, Roy," she said aloud; "just let's sit and talk—sensibly—I don't know what made you behave like this all of a sudden—"

And there was none to say "Provoking hussy!"

AN HOUR LATER THEY ROSE. It was too late to go to the yacht now. They walked together back to the stile. Their shoulders overlapped. The kisses came easily now.

"Then we'll go aboard her tomorrow?" he said.

"Very well."

"'Once aboard the lugger'—ha, ha—but of course she's a cutter, not a lugger. That's just a saying, 'Once aboard the lugger.'"

"Really?"

"Yes, hadn't you heard it? 'Once aboard the lugger and the girl is mine,' it is. And I say, you'd better put some old clothes on if I'm to show you how the centre-board works."

"All right."

"What about Lovey?" he asked once more.

"Oh, we write down on a slate where we're going."

He held her a little away. "I—*say*! . . . You wouldn't tell her where, would you?"

"Why not?"

"What—cheek!"

"She put me 'on my honour'—impudence!" quoth Louie.

"But I say—what frightful cheek!"

"Good-bye—"

"Just a minute—"

"Well—"

Then, "'Bye—"

"Good-bye—"

He called her name after her. "Louie!"

"What?"

"Good-bye—"

"Good-bye, boy—" She waved her hand.

Anyway, she thought with satisfaction, she had made him say—swear—that she was pretty.

THE NEXT AFTERNOON, AS GOOD as her word, Louie wrote on the hall-slate: "Gone to Mazzicombe: L. Causton." Then she walked, whistling, out of the house and up the hill.

VI

This time she fully expected to catch it, and did catch it. No time was lost. A note from Mrs. Lovenant-Smith just before supper ordered her to report herself immediately after that meal. At a quarter past nine she presented herself.

The French window stood wide open, but night was fast falling over the front lawn, and a clipped peacock of box showed against a brownish-green sky. Mrs. Lovenant-Smith stood by the window. It moved as she turned, and there swung slowly across the pane the reflection of the tall, yellow-shaded standard-lamp in one corner. Miss Harriet Chesson had followed Louie in. In her hand was a piece of paper—Louie's "conduct-report."

The beginning of the encounter was no skirmish; its end was positive slaughter. This is no place for a report of it, round by round; it must be summarised, even as the "Life and Battles" summarises the combat between Buck and the terrible Piker. Louie "led," so to speak, by asking whether she might sit down, giving as her reason that she had had a long walk that afternoon; permission was only refused her after she had put her hand on the back of a wheatear chair and said again: "I think you said Yes?" She then placed the chair for Miss Harriet to sit on, as near as possible to that of Mrs. Lovenant-Smith. She herself stood in the middle of the room.

Miss Harriet, evidently wishing she was somewhere else, read aloud the conduct-report. It was longish and detailed. It also, as Louie well knew, did not contain one of the real points at issue. She looked from one to the other of the two women. The Lady-in-Charge wore a discreetly-necked evening frock, with a fichu secured by a mourning brooch; and her fingers kept touching this brooch, and also kept leaving it again, as if Louie's eyes had been capable of a physical plucking of them away. She had had Miss Harriet in, Louie knew, for moral support. The principal's dress, too, was a give-and-take between her gardening costume and conventional evening attire. Her indictment read, she seemed more than ever anxious to depart. Louie, for her part, was rather glad that she had been called in. Buck had always fought better for the eyes upon him.

Mrs. Lovenant-Smith began correctly; her first trace of acerbity showed only when Louie, having listened to her arraignment with downcast eyes, lifted them for a moment to make a modest and quite immaterial correction.

"Have the goodness to cease this exaggerated deference, Miss Causton. It doesn't deceive me. It's only a form of veiled insolence."

Louie heard her indictment out in silence.

First blood was drawn when Louie mentioned the name of Roy Lovenant-Smith. She called him, with aggravating naturalness, "Roy." Mrs. Lovenant-Smith rose nearly an inch in height.

"'Roy!'" she echoed. "'Roy,' indeed!"

"I quite expected Priddy would tell you that first time. Of course he would. The gardeners here don't like outsiders intruding," said Louie.

The point told. There was no need to mention the name of Miss Hastings. Mrs. Lovenant-Smith's face deepened its ochre.

"Go on, Miss Causton," she said; while Miss Harriet timidly interposed: "I think that's all you wanted me for?"

Louie went on. "And anyway, you gave your nephew permission to come on the premises, which seems to me quite as much against the Rules as anything there." She pointed to the charge-sheet.

"Pray go on, Miss Causton," said Mrs. Lovenant-Smith, swallowing her wrath. Piker Betteridge, counting the moral advantage to be more than the pain endured, had formerly been wont to thrust out his undefended jaw in order to prove its invulnerability to attack; Mrs. Lovenant-Smith was doing something of the same kind now.

"Pray go on—" she said.

"And of course that's all bunkum," said Louie, warming, and pointing once more to the paper in Miss Harriet's hand. "That isn't in the least what you mean. What you really hate is my having told the girls what you've had in your mind ever since I came—I mean about my father."

"Pray go on!" The jaw was thrust out once more.

("Perhaps I'd better go?" Miss Harriet still fidgeted. Seedsmen's daughters are not at their ease at these Olympian conflicts.)

"All right, I will go on," said Louie, warming still more. "You would have preferred me to hold my tongue about it, and if you're thinking of asking me to resign I should like to say now that probably at least half-a-dozen others will go with me."

Here, however, Mrs. Lovenant-Smith scored a point.

"That may have been true a little while ago," she said, "but—go on." And Louie remembered certain little incidents and unbendings that had caused it to be indulgently rumoured that "Lovey wasn't such a bad old sort once you got to know her." Louie conceded the point.

"Anyway, that's what she does mean," she said, turning to Miss Harriet—"that she didn't want me to tell them that my father was a prizefighter and kept a public-house!"

"Address yourself to me, if you please," ordered Mrs. Lovenant-Smith.

"Certainly! You've been set against me from the first, for that very reason; and as for your nephew, I've known him for years and years, and you've no business at all to have him here, and it would sound rather well, wouldn't it, if the tale got about that you allowed—"

But at this Mrs. Lovenant-Smith's hardly held composure gave way with a snap. Well-born but necessitous Ladies-in-Charge of horticultural colleges do not submit to being told their duty by the daughters of pugilists. She stamped on the floor.

"Silence!" she cried, shaking. "I was a fool ever to have had you here! You make discipline impossible. You corrupt your fellow-students—you make a boast of your unfortunate parentage—you show no respect for the Rules—you think yourself at liberty to come and go as you please— you carry on a vulgar intrigue—"

"—not with a gardener—"

("Oh, I *really* must go my rounds!" murmured Miss Harriet; but she lingered; the spectacle of Olympians forgetting themselves does not occur every day.)

"—disgracing yourself among younger and more innocent girls—"

"—with a Lovenant-Smith, anyway—"

Again the stamp. "I forbid you to mention his name!"

"Roy—"

"Leave the room!"

("Please, please!" besought Miss Harriet.)

"You will pack your boxes at once!"

"I shall consult Lord Moone's lawyer first. You accepted my fees— your college is an imposition from beginning to end, and I'll see that's known. That will be another scandal—"

"Ah!" choked Mrs. Lovenant-Smith, perhaps with some hazy recollection of the law of slander in her head. "You hear that, Miss Chesson? You hear that? You heard those words?"

"No, I didn't quite catch—ladies—please!"

"If you didn't catch it, I said the whole place was a shameless fraud," said Louie calmly.

"Very good. Ring the bell, Miss Chesson!"

But the servant appeared only in time to see Mrs. Lovenant-Smith's complete collapse. She sank, shaking, into a chair, and gazed unseeingly into a pigeon-hole of her desk, as if she might find some help against this devilish girl there. As she clung (as it were) to the ropes, Louie let her have it (so to speak) on the beezer.

"You oughtn't to be here at all, really, you know," she said. "You ought to be in one of those places—you know—in the Queen's gift, at Kensington or Hampton Court, with the dowagers and maids-of-honour. If you like I'll ask my uncle whether he can't do anything."

And without waiting for an answer she swept out, not by the door, but by the French window. The reflection of the yellow-shaded standard-lamp swung again as she did so.

She entered the courtyard by the side door, passed under the dark yew and the arch beneath the box-room, and made her way through the orchard. She had reached her pitch at the foot of the hill before she remembered that she had forgotten her mattress and blankets. She returned in search of them. Twenty minutes later she was in bed, her knees up, her hands clasped behind her head.

She was white with triumph. That woman! Well, Louie thought she had held her own. She had had the last word, at all events, and an optic-bunging one too. Now should she leave, or stay? It was entirely a question of balance between her desire to see the last of the place and her resolve to go at nobody's pleasure but her own. It might be that she would have to stay another week in order to avoid the suspicion that she was turning tail. The fraud of a place!

She lay, pale and victorious, thinking the matter over.

One thing was certain; she would not return to Trant. She supposed she was vindictive by nature, but that would merely mean at the most a week's gradually increasing strain on her temper and then another series of embroilings with her mother. A philosophic elf somewhere deep within her—it was hardly affection—bade her spare her mother what she had not spared Mrs. Lovenant-Smith. Why seek a known trouble at Trant? If she must take trouble with her wherever she went, she might as well take it to a fresh place.

Before she was aware they had done so, her thoughts had flown to the vouched-for but incredible things Richenda Earle had said about life and London.

Lord Moone had a house, and Captain Chaffinger chambers, in London, and she knew both. For the rest, her knowledge of the place was pretty much what Richenda had guessed it to be—shops, restaurants, theatres. Of her five visits two had been spent at Lord Moone's, two at Cynthia's friends, the Kayes, and one at an hotel—this not counting the night on which, having run away from the convent, she had occupied Chaff's room and had wondered at his large pincushion, his pictures, and ribboned haircurlers that he doubtless kept in memory of his departed youth.

Her father, too, lived in London, or thereby—

She fell to wondering about her father.

There was a full but late-rising moon that night; it had not yet cleared the tree-tops of the eastern end of the orchard below. She watched its silver through the topmost boughs. Already it filled the heavens with a mist of light, dimming the stars; the glister on near leaves was brighter than the Plough over her head. Scents of the distant gardens stole undispersed through the night; that of the night-flowering tobacco-plant was for some minutes almost sicklily oppressive; and behind her she heard the scurrying of the rabbits at play.

It was odd that she thought of her father rather than of Roy. Somehow only Roy's actual presence had the power to colour those now pale cheeks of hers. Certainly it had done so that afternoon. For an hour, aboard the yacht, the rose-peonies in the garden had been paler than she. But her father had her thoughts now, and the sum of them was that she would have given much to be able to think of him as not cruel, not faithless, not a man who had had to be thrust back into the ditch whence he had come. She might have sought him out then.

For she was going to London; that was settled. She had her allowance, more by a half than the income Richenda and her Mr. Weston would gladly have married on, and not one penny more of it would she waste at Chesson's. The next day or two would almost certainly provide her with a "good exit." Then nobody would be able to say she had slunk out.

Oh, if her father had but not been a brute!

The moon cleared the trees, and another too-sweet tract of the night-flowering tobacco enveloped her. A bird or two stirred. Some time before she had thought she had heard the sound of a curlew's whistle, low and not very near, but she had disregarded it. Now it came again. All the effect it had was to turn her thoughts, tardily and almost unnoticed by herself, to Roy.

She knew little about yachts; yachting was no pastime of Lord Moone's; but even her vaunting mood relaxed to a momentary smile as she remembered the yacht down under the hill there. Those two boys must be crazy to risk their lives like that. They had rounded Land's End in her, and in quite good faith evidently expected the miracle to be repeated. The only wonder was that the centre-board had gone before the rest of the crazy fabric. "I told you to put some old clothes on," Roy had apologised for his vessel, "—and I say—I don't think I'd sit on the table if I were you—I'm not *quite* sure about it, you see—may have to send it to Mazzicombe after all—come on the locker." So they had sat on the locker—

She had felt safer when, half-an-hour later, she had clambered down into the little dinghy again. It would be Davy Jones's locker for Master Roy and his friend Mr. Izzard unless some fatherly fisherman took them and their boat in hand.

Then came the thoughts of her unknown father again.

"*Ee-oooo-eee!*"

She sat up. The whistle came from the stile up the hill. And suddenly she knew it was no curlew. It was Roy.

She listened.

"*Ee-oooo-eee!*"

It was Roy.

She knew he would not seek her farther than the stile. Had there not been other sleepers just below the orchard, it would still have been the extreme of his boldness that he had got so far. But—she remembered how from the first she had been the prime mover in their entirely wanton flirtation—was it necessarily the extreme of hers?

Then, as the devil would have it, something brought Mrs. Lovenant-Smith into her head again.

That woman!

All the blood left her cheeks and thronged to her heart again.

Roy would certainly not pass the stile—

She hesitated for a moment longer, and then suddenly got up from her bed.

Her clothes were wrapped in her waterproof; she took the waterproof and put it on. She thrust her feet into a pair of slippers. The waterproof was not so long as the garment beneath it; the moon was now well above the trees; it showed the hurrying white about her heels as she walked quickly up the hill. She drew the under-garment up a little. The waterproof was almost the colour of the scorched grass. The small shadow that preceded her was now the thing most plainly to be seen.

Over the stile she saw the shoulder of his white sweater. Again her caution awoke.

"You might have put a coat on," she said, a little out of breath. "You can be seen half-a-mile away on a night like this."

"I thought you were never going to hear me!" he said.

"Oh! You seem to have been sure I'd come if I did."

"Well, you have come, haven't you?" he answered. "I say, isn't your hair different?"

"Well, it isn't done for a call, if that's what you mean; I always do it like that at night, stupid. But I'm not going to stand here with you as white as a cottage wall."

Thereupon he paid her the only compliment he ever did pay her— and that was unintentional.

"It isn't any whiter than your feet, anyway," he said.

"Well, I'm not going to stop a minute."

"Oh, dash it all!" he protested. She did think him cool!

"Good gracious, how long do you think I *am* going to stay?"

"Hardly worth coming for, I call it," he grumbled.

"*Thank* you!"

"For you, I mean, of course—as if you didn't know I'd walk miles— how you take a fellow up!"

"Well, two minutes."

Two minutes can be a very short time; five minutes had passed when, making a movement to free herself, she said: "Let me go now, Roy—I think we're both as mad as we can be."

"There isn't anybody about," he muttered.

More minutes passed; then:

"Do you really think my feet are white?" she whispered. A slipper had come off.

Then, close against his breast, she made an inconsequential, halting little appeal. "Oh, Roy—don't go in that dreadful boat again! You'll be drowned—I know you will—"

"Should you care?" he whispered.

"Silly boy!"

"No, but should you care?" . . .

"Roy, let me go!" she ordered suddenly. The minutes were passing fatally quickly.

"No—no—"

"Oh—yes—"

"I won't let you go."

"Roy, let me go, I say!"

But it was not a command now. It was a supplication—perhaps not even that.

SHE DID NOT LOVE HIM; in her heart she knew she did not love him. He loved her—years afterwards; only years afterwards. The thought of her left him—but it returned to him, never to leave him again. The moon made the crest of the hill like day, but the shadows of the gorse-bushes lay dark on the short grass and stunted bents and the patches of wild thyme. The moon southed, then rode less high. In the short night a lamb called; and then the birds, reaching the shallows of their sleep, gave a drowsy twittering and went to sleep again. It was the false dawn. The stars grew a little brighter as a deeper darkness possessed the earth; then in the darkness a cock crowed.

THEY MET AGAIN ON THE next night. On the night after that they met once more.

Only after that did she sit down, alone in the box-room, in the twilight, to think.

Her boxes were packed and strapped, and the cart was coming for them from Rainham Magna in the morning.

She wished Burnett Minor had been there. She would have liked to say good-bye to the child. There was nobody else it would break her heart to leave.

Yet Roy was still down there under the hill. The centre-board had gone wrong again. She was to see him at the stile, in the morning, before leaving. It seemed, somehow, superfluous.

But she did meet him. His face was set, and he had forgotten to shave.

"Don't look like that; it wasn't your fault," she said composedly.

"It was—it was—" he muttered, hands clenched.

"Rubbish!" She gave a short laugh. "You've nothing at all to blame yourself for."

"Oh, I have—I have."

Then he turned to her. "Louie, you've got to promise me one thing—"

But she stopped him. She knew what he was going to say.

"That's quite out of the question," she said.

"But look here!" He used the words he had used the second time they had met. "A fellow can't get a girl into a mess and then leave her in the lurch. You must marry me, Louie, if—if—"

At that she had found a touch of her old irony.

"Not unless, of course?"

"Oh yes—yes."

But she turned away. "No. Good-bye."

"Won't you even kiss me?"

"No."

But there was a gentleness in her refusal such as he had never had from her before. Kisses came hardly now.

PART II
SUTHERLAND PLACE

I

Richenda Earle could have told Louie Causton that an allowance of three hundred pounds a year, paid in quarterly instalments, only permits of a sunny little bedroom and a charming sitting-room in Lancaster Gate on certain terms, of which terms a dipping sooner or later into reserves of capital is certainly one. It is true that Louie still had capital of which she knew nothing. She did not yet, for example, count her wardrobe as capital, nor reflect that if its present standard was to be maintained money must be set apart for the purpose of maintaining it. She did not yet count her time as capital, nor write off the days she classed as days of "looking about her" as so many obligations against the time when looking about her would no longer serve her turn. She did not count her health as capital, nor her wild, resilient spirits, nor her "placeableness" at a glance among those whose possession of some capital may be assumed. All she reckoned as capital was the hundred odd pounds she had placed in a small but sound bank of her stepfather's recommendation, and (she had vaguely heard of such things) such additional credit as the Captain's name might command. But perhaps it is enough to say that she had this conception of the potency of the Captain's name.

Nevertheless, her second week's bill at Lancaster Gate was enough to cause her to send for her landlady, and to ask that person whether she had not a single room anywhere empty that might combine the prettiness of her present quarters with the convenience of having all her belongings within a single door. She was conscious of reasonableness, almost of magnanimity, when she remarked that she didn't mind going up another flight of stairs. The landlady had such a room, but pointed out its lack of cupboard-space and the number of Louie's dresses. That, Louie replied, did not matter; she intended to sell a number of the older dresses; and her things were carried upstairs.

Her idea in selling the older dresses was that thereby she might add another thirty pounds or so to her balance; the half-dozen she thought she could spare had cost thrice that amount. The wardrobe dealer who waited upon her offered her five pounds for them. Louie thanked her, told her that she had thoughts of going into a business so lucrative herself, and bade her good-afternoon.

She had come to London at the beginning of September; before that month was out she had decided to leave Lancaster Gate. For some reason or other her quarter's allowance had not arrived, and she wrote to Chaff about it. Chaff promised to look to the matter. She wrote also to Richenda Earle, stating the kind of lodging she required, and asking whether Richenda knew of such an one. To this last letter she had a reply by return of post. Richenda proposed the house of her married sister, which was in Sutherland Place, Bayswater. Without prejudice to her choice, Louie took a walk along Sutherland Place, and received an impression of a quiet street with milk-carts drawn up by the kerb and virginia creeper covering the houses with crimson. As she passed the door Richenda had specified, the door opened, and a squarer and older Richenda came out with a string bag in her hand. That, Louie thought, would be Mrs. Leggat, the wife of the estate-agent's clerk.

A week later Louie moved into Mrs. Leggat's first floor-front-bed-sitting-room. That night she counted her money. The result of her calculations caused her to jump up, as if she had thoughts of seeking some occupation or other that very night. Her quarter's allowance had still not come. Then Mr. Leggat, a lumpy-headed man with rabbit teeth and a Duke of Wellington nose, came in to fix a gas-burner for her, and she fell into talk with him. He wiped his hands ceaselessly on an old rag as he talked. He told her it was a pity that Rich had not stuck to her book-keeping; he himself would have been head clerk by this time had he had her thorough practical grounding instead of having had to knock about the world and fend for himself; and he asked her what sort of a villa-building-site Rainham Parva would, in her opinion, make. He added that it was nice to have "the rooms" (he used the plural) let to somebody they knew something about, and then, having omitted to shake hands with her on coming in, did so before going out, and evidently accounted their introduction complete. He came back presently for a pair of pincers he had forgotten, left her a Carter Paterson card for her window in case she should have need of one, said that one of these Sundays they must all go round to the Earles in Westbourne Grove to tea, made a pun on the words Earle and Lord, and went out again. An hour later Louie heard him tiptoeing discreetly past her door on his way upstairs to bed.

Louie was resolved, however, to put a stop to the "Earle and Lord" business once for all. She was a Causton, not a Scarisbrick, in Sutherland Place.

She felt herself to be already on the verge of a new life that was—let us say amusing—precisely in proportion as it was different from any life she had ever known. She must be—if the word may pass—amused; she told herself so, clinching the argument by adding that it was far better to laugh than to cry. She had promised Richenda that she would call and see her Mr. Weston at his Business School in Holborn; and this might be—well, amusing. She went without loss of time. She took the Oxford Street bus one morning and alighted at the door of the School.

She mounted three floors of narrow, old-fashioned stairs, asked a fair, perky boy, who somehow managed to make a good suit of clothes look cheap, where she should find Mr. Weston, and presently found herself introducing herself to a thin and melancholy-looking man with a sparse and colourless beard, a pair of silver-rimmed spectacles, and a gentle and hopeless voice. This was "the Secretary Bird," then. He shook hands slackly with her, placed a chair for her in one of the bays of a sort of E that was lined with books of reference, and she listened to his soft, dispirited voice and to the clicking of typewriters in an adjoining room. He thanked her for "all her kindnesses" to Richenda, whatever these might have been, and presently a skimpy little woman in green plaid, with eyes that peered quizzically behind spectacles and "destined spinster" written all over her, tiptoed for a moment at the end of the bay of books, uncertain whether to approach. Then the fair, perky boy who made good clothes look cheap also came up. Mr. Weston said: "Excuse me—yes, Miss Windus?" Louie saw that she was interrupting the morning's work. She rose.

"I daresay we shall see one another again," she said. "Good-bye."

And, outside on the Holborn pavement again, she said to herself with decision: "Thanks—but no Business Schools for me!—Poor Richenda!"

Three weeks later she became a student at that very school.

There is no puzzle about it. Some things come no less unexpectedly that they are more than reasonably to be expected. To put this as briefly as it can be put, she had merely discovered that an affair of atmosphere had become an affair of fact. That was all—nothing more, nothing less. But that was no reason why she should not be amused.

The natural thing for young women in such circumstances to do is to seek their mothers. If Louie did this natural thing a little unnaturally—well, she did it unnaturally, that was all. The row, scene, or whatever it was going to be, had better be got over; then she could proceed to amuse herself. She had wired that she was coming; the

Captain had met her at Trant station; but she had had nothing to say to the Captain.

The Captain, however, had had something to say to her. At first his mumbling into his moustache had not penetrated to her intelligence; she had only heard broken repetitions of "Dear old Mops—only for a week or two—knew you weren't without—meant to write, but dashed awkward thing to explain by letter, and was coming up in a week in any case—if she stuck fast he'd see what could be done—"

"Eh?" Louie had said at last. "What's that, Chaff?"

Chaff had repeated his mumblings. At the end of them she had gathered that the needy Captain had borrowed the quarter's allowance that had been entrusted to him for despatch. Louie had merely given a little preoccupied laugh and patted his hand.

"All right, old boy; don't worry," she had said.

A sample or two of her conversation with her mother must answer for the rest. For quite twenty minutes the Honourable Emily's head had been buried in the sofa-cushions, and the Trant coal-and-blanket charitable account had lain where it had fallen from her hand—across her cheek.

"That's all," Louie had ended with hard composure.

"Oh—oh—" the mother had moaned.

"And as I say, I won't marry him."

"Oh—you must—you must!"

"Why? Because Uncle Augustus will say I must?"

"Oh—you must!"

"I'll go and see Uncle Augustus."

"Oh, you mustn't—you mustn't!"

Then, in an interlude, the reasons why everything must at all costs be kept from Lord Moone had been brokenly explained. In another interlude a few minutes later Louie had invented a fictitious name.

"That conveys nothing to me," Mrs. Chaffinger had moaned. "What is he?"

Louie had invented a station in life to fit the name. Her mother's face had disappeared behind the coal-and-blanket account again.

"And this—this!—is your study of horticulture!" she had half faintingly wailed.

"Yes. Yours was art, wasn't it?"

Then Mrs. Chaffinger's querulous despair had shown a weak, vindictive gleam. Both pronouns had been a little emphasised as she had retorted:

OLIVER ONIONS

"I married your father!"

It was only a flicker. Her head had gone into the cushions again.

"That didn't last very long," the devilish girl had commented.

"I married your father, I say—for your sake," had come from the cushions.

"That's one of the differences. There are others. If you're thinking of wiring to Uncle Augustus I'll wait; if you're not, I'll go."

Lord Moone had been wired for. He had wired back: "Impossible"; but a second wire had brought him over post-haste the next morning. The situation had been explained to him; the peer had walked away for a few moments; Louie had thought she had heard something about "our damnable women"; then, coming back, Lord Moone had abruptly convened a Committee of Ways and Means. Words like "Impossible. . . once in a lifetime quite enough. . . secrecy. . . the Continent for a few months. . . institution," had been used; and at one other alternative Louie's eyes had become hard and chill as ice.

"Thank you," she had come harshly in. "As you say, all these things may be possible. I decline them all."

Then Lord Moone, whose habit of ordering masses of men probably misled him into thinking that the ordering of one young woman who says "I won't" was a comparatively simple matter, had made his pronouncement.

"Very well," he had said. "Then as head of the family I order that your allowance shall be stopped till you come to your senses. You hear that, Emily?"

"You mean you'll starve me out?" Louie had said, with dancing eyes. Like her father, she came up to time as long as she could stand.

"I mean what I've said."

"Then ring the bell, please—and don't light that cigar till I've gone. I shall be ill if you do."

And Lord Moone himself had ordered the carriage in which she had turned her back on Trant.

Burnett Minor, when Mrs. Lovenant-Smith had surprised the rebellion in the box-room, had not made herself more inconspicuous than had Captain Chaffinger during this scene. Indeed, probably considering that Lord Moone, his sister and Louie herself formed a quorum, he had presently been discovered to be not there. But it seemed to be the Captain's lot to receive and despatch Louie in her comings and goings, and before the carriage had reached the lodge he had stopped it and climbed in. Ordinarily, the whites of the Captain's eyes had yellowish marblings; the yellow had now deepened to the hue of cayenne. He had blown his nose repeatedly and violently, and Louie, glancing covertly at him, had suddenly had a pang. All at once he had shown his age. Somehow Louie resented his doing so. People and things you have never taken quite seriously have no right to come near the tragic. It was as if some puppet strutting within a proscenium should suddenly bleed.

"Mops," he had said by-and-by, blowing his nose again, "that was a lie you told them, wasn't it?"

Louie had tried to shut her eyes to Chaff's bleeding. Her hand had sought his.

"The name I told them? Of course it was, you clever old Chaff, to see that."

"You don't tell me that, do you, Mops?"

"You?! No, poor old boy, it isn't worth while telling lies to you."

"I'm glad of that, Mops—"

So, for his private comfort, she had invented for Chaff quite a new lie, name, station in life and all.

Then: "Oh, Mops, Mops, Mops!—" he had murmured sorrowfully.

Little parties were one thing, but his Mops quite another.

But her anger had stirred again. She had remembered her uncle's proposals.

"Did you hear what he said—Moone? No; you'd gone out. Listen—"

He had tugged unhappily at his moustache as she had told him, bringing out the words with vehemence and hate.

"Well, but, Mops—" he had demurred wistfully.

"What, are you going to tell me *you* think so too?"

"All right, Mops, all right, all right, old girl—"

"Much I care for him and his family name! He could bully mother into marrying people, but he can't bully me. . . Sorry, Chaff, that was clumsy; we're pals at any rate. Uncle Gus and his Scarisbricks!"

Her exclamations of contempt had occupied the rest of the time to the station. Chaff had put her into her carriage.

"You'll let me know where you are and what you're doing, won't you, dear?" he had pleaded. "I can't let you go like this!"

"I hardly know where I shall be myself yet. Very likely I shall go to a Business School; I shall have to do something, and that's all I know anything about. Anyway, the bank will find me—no, you poor old thing, of course I don't mean the money! Of course I'll ask you for that when I want it. I've quite a lot yet. Good-bye, old thing."

"Good-bye, dear."

And this time he had not warned her not to run away with a student of book-keeping.

SHE WENT TO THE BUSINESS School partly (*bien entendu*) for amusement, and partly because there would be very little sense in sitting all day long in Mrs. Leggat's first-floor bed-sitter in Sutherland Place, Bayswater. Perhaps, too, Lord Moone helped to drive her there. Her very skin crept when she remembered the lengths to which he would have gone—he, the corner-stone of orthodoxy when such subjects came up for (very) full-dress debate—to save that precious thing, the family name of the Scarisbricks. Louie had had vanities of person, scores of them; but she had also the sense of the holiness of the body, and she had had enough of Trants and Mallard Boises and their masters for a time. The Business School would be as amusing as anywhere else; indeed, she knew of nowhere else. Here she was at last in a London that was not the London of shops and dinners and theatres and drives in the Park. She would have the fun—always the fun—of it. She would go with the Leggats to see Richenda's sisters and that father of hers who had apologised to her for having brought her into the world. She would learn these unfamiliar accents that met her ear, breathe this invigorating if dusty air. She would know what life meant to that skimpy woman in the green plaid, would inspect that new specimen, the jaunty boy who made his good clothes look like an ordinary "reach-me-down." And she knew, without knowing how she knew, that before long she would be seeing her father. Sit in Sutherland Place? Oh no, that wasn't amusing. Besides, she would presently have her living to earn. She had thought, when Richenda had told her those dismal tales, that there must be something wrong with Richenda and that she herself would be able to do better. Well, she would very soon know.

II

At Chesson's she had taken her proper place among her fellow-students at once; it was not her fault if here, at the Business School, she did not at first so much make friends as watch a number of amusing phenomena. She watched them with wonder; all was so very, very different. The building itself seemed once to have been some sort of a dwelling-house, for there were cabbagey wall-papers of a bygone fashion on the walls, broken ends of bell-wire stuck out from the mantel-sides and the cornices, and the gas-brackets were old and ornate and grimy. Louie was conscious of something like a shock the first time she approached one of the third-floor bay windows and, looking across the street, saw in the windows opposite men packing things in brown paper, waitresses carrying trays, and gas-jets burning in the dark interiors beyond. They seemed so near. The width of Holborn lay between, but they seemed to crowd on her much more closely than the yew at Rainham Parva had ever crowded on the inner windows of the courtyard. The yew, moreover, was thinned at intervals, but there was no cutting and lopping the forward-thrusting, amusing humanity across the way. They seemed to be caged there expressly for her observation. Well, she was there to observe—to observe, and, of course, to be amused.

Her new companions, too, were unlike anybody she had ever known; they no more resembled them than the sweet heavy airs of Chesson's resembled these diverting smells of dust and damp and bad ventilation and the whiff of the Holborn pavement below. Their accents (amusing, however) struck her sharply; their faces—alert, sophisticated, highly entertaining but without candour—no less sharply. They too, like the buildings across the way, seemed to ignore intervening space and to press intrusively forward to look at her. She was glad that the first thing she had done had been to stop Mr. Weston's mouth on the subject of the Scarisbricks and Lord Moone; half the drollery of her experience would have gone had these people known who she really was. And the things these slovenly voices said had no candour. They struck her as a series of (merry) "scorings-off," a succession of (cheery) "chippings" of one another. If their reticences seemed all in the wrong places, and hand in hand with their defensiveness went an eager volubility about the things Louie would have kept to herself, why, so much the more laughable the whole joke.

She had been only just in time in extorting her promise from Mr. Weston. She was sure of this from his manner of speaking to herself. It was extremely, syllabically distinct. To words that he had been pronouncing correctly and without thought all his life he gave (as if he must find something superior for her, and knowing better all the time) pronunciations marvellously new. He found new words, too; must look 'em up, Louie thought, in the dictionary. Richenda, who had begun by being his sweetheart, became his "intended," and once even his "inamorata." But he was to be trusted. Louie saw that. If he gave away her identity at all it would be only by the portentousness of his secrecy. As a matter of fact he never did so.

It was the skimpy woman in the green plaid, Miss Windus, who answered most of Louie's questions about her new companions. She too was a delightful novelty to Louie. As if to make her own position quite clear at the outset, she had confided to Louie at once that she herself was "partly independent." Seeing Louie's slightly puzzled look, she had gone on to explain that by this she meant that she enjoyed an income of perhaps a pound a week "on her own." With this title to consideration thoroughly understood, she went ahead. When Louie asked a question about the high-heeled little Cockney Jewess, Miss Levey, Miss Windus answered it in terms of her own pound a week. "Miss Levey?" she said. Oh, she'd nothing; she lived at home and had her fees paid for her, of course, and wouldn't stick fast, being a Jewess, not she; but Kitty didn't suppose Miriam Levey had one shilling to rub against another; not, that was, "on her own." Louie, finding other questions answered from this same standpoint, took her cue and framed her questions accordingly. Had the other female student (there were only four women), Miss Soames, anything? Well, Kitty didn't know; she fancied her aunt must have a tidy bit coming in; they lived together in a boarding-house in Woburn Place, and as the aunt did nothing all day perhaps she too was partly independent, or even wholly so. Had Mr. Merridew, the swaggering boy who cheapened his clothes so curiously, a tidy bit coming in? Here Kitty evidently had a tale to tell. Had Archie Merridew a bit coming in, indeed! Why, his father was Mr. Merridew of Merridew and Fry's, the fancy stationers with branches everywhere, so Louie could judge for herself whether that meant a bit or not! Archie a bit? Why, Mr. Merridew Senior had retired, and lived at a big place near Guildford, with a tennis-lawn, if you please. Archie Merridew a bit!—Then what about Mr. Mackie?

(Louie might have been estimating people by what money they had all her life.)—Mr. Mackie? No, Kitty shouldn't think Mr. Mackie had very much, but he had a splendid "permanency" offered him when he had passed his examinations, as an auctioneer's clerk, four pounds a week to start with—to start with, mind you—and a "rise" every year. Yes; Mr. Mackie was all right, and, oh dear! *wasn't* Mr. Mackie funny?

Louie thought this Mr. Mackie more than funny; in her inexperience of the type she could never believe he was quite true. For Mr. Mackie sang songs, imitated music-hall artistes, could "gag" for a whole day on end, and never forget for a moment the immense success he was. He fascinated Louie. "Ladies and bipeds in trousers!" he would begin, with rapid gestures and still more rapid speech, "before the applause I am waiting for has had time to subside—good word, subside—(thank you, Cuthbert, you can take the bouquet round to the stage-door)—as I was saying when Fitzclarence interrupted me, ladies and tripeheads in blouses, whoa, backpedal, never mind—as I was saying, I will now endeavour to give you my celebrated imitation of Roderigo the gasfitter at one o'clock on a Saturday with the thirty bob in his pocket and Hildegarde Ann his wife licking the paint of the lamp-post at the corner to squench her thirst—*heu*, her thirst! . . . Chord on, please, titillate the catgut, Professor, and take firm hold of his hand, girls—"

Then, while the eyes of Lord Moone's niece would grow bigger and bigger, would follow the performance.

"*Isn't* he funny!" Kitty would giggle, faint with laughing; "oh, give us some more, Mr. Mackie!"

And Kitty, like Saint Paul, died daily at yet another trick of Mr. Mackie's—the putting of his handkerchief to his nose, and the drawing of it slowly downwards to the accompaniment of a piercing whistle.

But Louie was only moderately amused by young Merridew. Mr. Mackie had his own perfection; but vulgarity *with* a tennis-lawn! "Good gracious, no," said Louie.

She had entered the School as a day student; but within a week she had put her name down for the evening classes also. Even then she had the evenings of Tuesdays, Thursdays, Saturdays and the whole of Sunday quite unamusingly on her hands. She did not want time on her hands. As much Mr. Mackie as you pleased, but no time on her hands. So she joined the classes that met on the evenings of Mondays, Wednesdays and Fridays.

On her very first evening she saw a student whom she had not seen before.

She had taken a text-book on Elementary Book-keeping from one of the shelves of the E of books in which she had had her first talk with Mr. Weston (who, by the way, had said that he would like to see her for a few minutes before she left that evening), and finding a chair within the recess, had sat down where she was to read it. She had not looked up when somebody had passed the mouth of her little compartment and entered the next one. She had heard a book taken down from a shelf behind her, and, after some minutes, put back again; and had she not chanced to straighten her back at that moment she would probably not have seen the man repass. She had no time to notice more than that he was very big and not very well dressed. She went on with her reading, wondering, in the intervals of her slack attention to her book, what Mr. Weston wanted with her.

She saw the big man again at the close of the class. This time he was standing at the head of the stairs, waiting for young Merridew. He really was immensely big, so big that a too prolonged first look at him seemed unpleasantly like impertinent curiosity. Indeed, he seemed already to feel her eyes upon him, for he moved as if to look back at her in turn; but young Merridew came up at that moment and they went out together. The big man's head and shoulders were to be seen beyond the handrail for quite an appreciable moment of time after young Merridew's had disappeared. But she had been wrong in thinking that he wore a shabby suit. His suit might be shabby also, but it could not be seen. He wore, and had apparently worn in class also, a tawny old ulster of yellow and black check. In spite of its age it seemed somehow a better garment than did the more expensive clothes of his companion. He did not, however, strike her as very amusing.

She turned away to seek the Secretary Bird—Mr. Weston.

For the moment Mr. Weston was engaged. He was standing near the lecture-room blackboard, talking to the girl who lived with her partly independent aunt at the boarding-house in Woburn Place. Louie had already remarked the likeness of this girl, who might have been twenty but looked younger, to Polly Ross, the pretty daughter of the tipsy veterinary surgeon at Trant. Polly too had sported that running of pale blue ribbon beneath the openwork of what Kitty Windus called her "pneumonia blouse," and the clumps of dark hair on her nape too was like Polly's, and she had Polly's dark and sidelong glance, and highly conscious air of unconsciousness when that glance had attracted what it had probably been meant to attract, attention to herself. She had a copy of the Pansy Library in her hand, and Louie smiled as she remembered Burnett Minor and her spoutings. She waited until Weston should be at liberty.

As she waited, Kitty Windus, wearing an Inverness cape and a boat-shaped hat, came up. Miss Windus lived in a street off Tottenham Court Road, and already once or twice Louie had walked with her as far as the Oxford corner. She was waiting for the Polly Ross girl now, whose direction was the same. She asked Louie whether she intended to walk or to "hop on a bus." She always spoke in these rather sprightly terms, just as she always stiffened the line of her back a little the moment a man, any man, entered the room; and she referred, brightly and hopefully, to proposals of marriage as "chances." Louie was already learning when she might expect any given one of Kitty's innumerable *clichés*, and had several times (humorously) given them back to Kitty again with complete success. As they waited for the Polly Ross girl (whose name was Evie Soames) Louie asked Kitty who the big man who had gone out with Mr. Merridew was.

"Oh, the Mandrill!" said Kitty, laughing even before Louie had got out the word "big." "That's Mr. Jeffries. Isn't he a caution? But he only comes in the evenings."

She meant that Mr. Jeffries had not a pound a week on his own. Students who only came in the evenings were of a slightly inferior order to those who came during the day.

"I suppose he had his brown paper parcel with him?" Kitty said, with more mirth in her peering little eyes.

Louie remembered that Mr. Jeffries had carried a brown paper parcel. Kitty twittered.

"Bet you can't guess what was in it—that is, if you haven't heard it?"

She said "it" as if it had been a riddle or some sort of a joke. Louie admitted that she could not guess what had been in Mr. Jeffries' parcel.

"Good old brown paper parcel!" Kitty chuckled. "You'll get to know it by-and-by! You see," she explained, "he goes to Archie's for a bath. Isn't it killing?"

"I—I don't quite see what you mean," said Louie. She honestly did not.

"Why, for a bath—you know, a common or garden bath, with hot water. I peeped into it once (the parcel, I mean; for shame, you dreadful girl!) and it had a clean shirt and a pair of socks in it. I suppose he wraps those he takes off up when he's done."

Louie's eyes had opened very wide indeed. A man to have to ask another man for a bath! Well, that was something learned about London! A bath—a thing so necessary that its existence was assumed—how extremely amusing! She knew that entertaining word, "poor," but what was this other, this new and side-splitting word that meant that a man had to ask another man for a bath? She had never heard of anything so—so—there was no adjective that quite fitted the humour of it.

The next moment she had wasted an irony on Kitty.

"Hasn't he—a tidy bit?" she asked.

But it took far more than this to get through Kitty's hide. She gave another little laugh and drew her gloves more smoothly over her thin hands.

"Him? The Mandrill? (I always call him the Mandrill, my dear.) Not a penny to bless himself with; look at him!"

"Nor a permanency?" Louie asked.

"What, with those clothes? I ask you, now: it isn't a cold night tonight, is it? Well, why does he keep that heavy old coat on all the evening? Enough said, my dear. He works somewhere in the City, I believe—'something in the City'—sounds most prosperous, doesn't it? And Archie's awful kind to him, I think, but of course he is frightfully clever, and does help Archie with his work sometimes, so Archie gives him a bath (I don't mean what you mean, I mean lets him have one). Here's Evie. Are you coming along?"

But Louie, besides being tickled, smarted a little too. To have to beg for a bath—and then to have the gift made a matter of common knowledge and a joke!—

Well, if these people were different, differences, after all, were what she was here to see.

She turned to Mr. Weston.

What Mr. Weston wanted to say to her she could not guess; but he had hardly spoken twenty words before she was smiling at herself for not guessing. The examinations were to be held just before Christmas, and unless Louie could be ready for her Elementary by that time she would have a good many months to wait before she could enter for the examination again. What Mr. Weston had to propose was, in a word, that he should coach her privately.

She knew what that meant. It meant that he would come to Sutherland Place on Sundays and talk about Richenda.

Well, even talk about Richenda would make shorter that *dies non*.

"It really would be a great furtherance of your aims, Miss Causton," Weston said wistfully.

Louie smiled at the periphrasis, and then considered.

"It might be the best thing to do," she said; "but of course I should accept it only on one condition."

"May I venture to inquire what that condition is?" Weston inquired deferentially.

"That you let me pay you for it," said Louie promptly.

But Weston put up a peremptory hand. "Oh no—no, no, no—I should be ashamed after all your kindnesses—"

Louie laughed again. "Good gracious, what kindnesses?"

"Ah, you once shielded an individual very dear to me and took the blame upon yourself, Miss Causton—" His tone was reverential, his eyes did her homage. Louie had forgotten all about the box-room rebellion and Mrs. Lovenant-Smith. She laughed once more.

"Well, just as you like. But no pay, no coaching, that's all."

Weston sighed. No doubt his acquiescence cost him a pang. If he took money for giving lessons, lessons he must give, and the talk about Richenda must go.

"Do you dwell on the point with insistence?" he asked.

"Very much."

"I am far from denying that it would be of some assistance in the furnishing of our future nest, if I may use the expression—"

"Of course it would. So that's agreed?"

"So be it," said Weston.

Louie half expected him to add: "Amen."

She was in the habit of dispensing money a little largely, and for the present she could quite well afford to do this. For Chaff had done more than pay his debt. That very day she had had a letter from him, forwarded by the bank. He had paid one hundred pounds into her account, asking her to regard the extra twenty-five pounds as interest on his unceremonious borrowing. But she did not for a moment believe his cheerful tale that "things were all right again now"; poor old boy, ten to one he had borrowed pretty ruinously elsewhere in order to pay her. At all events, Weston should not give up his Sundays for nothing, and she might, after all, allow him an outpouring about

Richenda and the future nest once in a while. It was only half-a-crown a week.

But as she left Weston she was thinking of something else that half-a-crown a week had power to buy. Half-a-crown a week would have bought this big shabby student a bath almost every day.

To have to carry a change of underclothing in a brown paper parcel to another man's place—

And to have that parcel peeped into—

How damnable—no, how funny, she meant!

In the light of her knowledge of this extraordinary economy Mr. Jeffries had to practise she felt—she didn't know why—almost shy in his presence the next time she saw him. She felt that she possessed something of his—namely, this knowledge—which she ought not to have possessed. She wondered whether he knew how he had been given away. Something about him almost suggested that he might.

Perhaps it was his mouth. It looked, except when he deliberately opened it, as if it might very well not have opened during the whole of the twenty-eight or twenty-nine years Louie guessed him to have had a mouth at all. The rest of his face, which would have been too large for any man less huge, was an unrelenting slab. It was in the mouth if anywhere that sensitiveness must be looked for. Certainly there was none in the eyes. These Louie found (it was on a Wednesday night that she noticed these things; she had seen him first on a Monday) remarkable. They were the eyes of a lion—clear amber, sherry-coloured. They were made more than ever to resemble the eyes of a lion by that tawny ulster he never removed, and she remembered Kitty's sinister and mirthful suggestion. Did his keeping on of that ulster mean something hardly less stark and laughable than the circumstance of the bath itself? (Louie felt that she was learning.) Then she noticed his hands. She always noticed hands. He stopped in passing to pick up a pen for her. The hand that returned it was not only a magnificent engine of sinew and bone and muscle, powerful and heroic; it was also (this was not so funny) exquisitely kept. Her own hand, pale and slender as the leaf of a willow by contrast with his, was not in its different way more perfect. He might cadge for a bath, but his hands he could look after himself for nothing. And that was true of his hair also. It was tawny, close-cut, and took the light as cleanly as a new silk-hat; hair-brushing was evidently cheap also. The man did what he could. She would have liked to hear his voice, but he handed her the pen in silence and passed on.

"Well, he looks forbidding," was her comment on him as the great church-door of his back disappeared into the typewriting-room, "and he has got too big a face and a rather frightening jaw; but he does shave it properly, and I don't see where the 'Mandrill' comes in—wretched little creature with her pound a week! And he is like a lion, with those eyes and that ulster—"

And merely because he seemed to be a person to be scored off and given meanly away, she was already prepared, had she been challenged, to vow that he was handsome—in his heavy and unhumorous way. As a matter of fact, if Roy Lovenant-Smith resembled the little terra-cotta head in the Tanagra Gallery of the Museum, this Mr. Jeffries suggested something from the Assyrian Gallery downstairs—something in black basalt, that might carry the doorway of a temple on its head. In any case, with the ulster, the eyes, and the silky tawny hair, he was as like a lion as needs be.

When she had seen him twice only she took it upon herself to snub young Merridew on his behalf.

She and Kitty were leaving the School at four o'clock on the Thursday afternoon when the son of the fancy stationer joined them, and, taking it quite for granted that his tidy bit and his tennis-lawn made him as desirable to Louie as they evidently exalted him in Kitty's eyes, walked westwards along Holborn with them. He wore a new red waistcoat with brass buttons, and perhaps it was in order to live up to his splendour that he made Louie an offer which she curtly declined. They were passing a confectioner's shop; perhaps he noticed—for he seemed a sharp enough little bounder—Louie's glance at the window; he turned to her.

"Like some chocs?" he said.

Had Louie not already detested him, this would have been quite enough. Priddy would have had less appalling manners. As it happened, she would have liked some chocolates; lately she had craved for chocolates as much as she had hated the smell of tobacco; but she wanted no chocolates of this young man's buying.

"No, thank you," she replied; and presently she contrived to put Kitty (the straight-backed Kitty whom a man accompanied) between Mr. Merridew and herself.

She had the outside berth of the pavement, and she was wondering whether she would not cross the road and hop on a bus, leaving Kitty and the heir to the tennis-lawn together, when something Kitty said detained her. It was something about Mr. Jeffries. Hitherto Louie had hardly been listening.

"—oh, Jeff!" Merridew was saying. "He'll have to go till we come back. Anyway I shall save half-a-cake of soap."

"There's such a lot *of* him," Kitty giggled. "How big's your bath?"

"Well, he's an awfully useful coach for the Method exam., I will say that for him; so we'll call it a fair swap. You know Evie's aunt, don't you?"

"No."

"Thought you did. Good old Aunt Angela! (She always gets ratty when I call her that.) I didn't know she was an old friend of the pater's till we saw 'em at the Zoo that Sunday. So that's why they're coming."

"Oh, perhaps, perhaps not," said Kitty archly. "Perhaps it isn't the aunt they want to see—"

A passer-by elbowed Louie off the pavement; all she caught of what followed was Kitty's laugh.

"So that accounts for the new blouse! You never think of asking *me* down to Guildford, Archie!" she said reproachfully.

"You must get a chaperon," Archie replied gallantly; "can't be did without, Kitt-oh. The mater don't allow running after yours truly."

Then of another light passage Louie heard only the concluding laugh.

"Well, what of it?" Archie was saying knowingly; and Louie heard something else about apron-strings. "Pale blue baby ribbon ones, eh what?" Archie added, with a grin.

"Archie!" Kitty reproved him.

"Oh, come off it!" replied the fancy stationer's son. "As if a fellow hadn't eyes! If you girls *will* wear pneumonia blouses—"

"Archie, you're dreadful!" said Kitty, deliciously shocked.

"Well, it's a tannersworth at the Holborn Public Baths for Jeff next week-end—"

Here Louie interposed. Even amusement can be too rich. "Good-bye," she said, "there's my bus."

She heard Kitty call after her something about the penny stage, but by that time she was half-way across the road.

Brass-buttoned little beast!

She got on her bus.

But a quarter of a mile farther on she descended from it again. She wanted to buy chocolates for herself. She bought them, walked to the Marble Arch, and there turned into the Park. She ate the chocolates as she walked.

Little animal! He appeared to keep the whole School posted about Mr. Jeffries' personal habits. He could not go down to his home for the week-end, taking the Polly Ross girl and her aunt with him apparently, but Mr. Jeffries and half-a-cake of soap must be dragged in. And that pathetic, pathetic care the man took of his hair and hands! For all that, as she strode along, crunching her chocolates, she became almost angry with him too. Was soap so frightfully dear, and was there no water anywhere but at Mr. Merridew's rooms? She could not understand a man who had any sensitiveness at all suffering his mind to be turned over and inspected and thumb-marked by these people in this way.

Still, she must not forget that these things were diverting.

There was no class that night: Louie forced herself to apply herself to her book-keeping until half-past nine, and then went to bed. That, as has been said, was on a Thursday. On the following evening, feeling indisposed to work, she moved about the School, amusing herself to her heart's content. She was getting adept in the sport of it. She bandied back to Kitty Windus, with whom she found herself in talk, half-a-score of her own expressions: "Beg yours," "Granted," "As the poet says," and the like; and she all but openly stalked Mr. Mackie for the sake of the pearls that rippled from his lips. If Mr. Mackie had offered to take her for a walk or to a shilling hop at the Holborn Town Hall on the next blank evening, Lord Moone's niece, who must allow no chance of amusement to slip her, would have let him. Indeed, she was in two minds whether or not to go to this last place of entertainment alone.

It was not for another week that her amusement at the School in general and at Mr. Jeffries in particular became almost painfully ecstatic.

III

On that Friday afternoon she did not go home as usual to Sutherland Place to tea. She went instead to the tea-shop across the street the waitresses of which seemed to crowd upon her as if the width of Holborn did not exist. As she sat down at her little marble table she glanced involuntarily across to the windows of the Business School and for a moment dropped the mask to herself. "Dingy place!" she thought; "well, we're a dingy crew inside it." Then, after a long, long walk down Chancery Lane and along the Embankment almost as far as the ship-breakers' yard at Millbank, she returned to evening class.

It was the evening before the day when Polly Ross—she begged her pardon, Miss Evie Soames—was to go with her aunt to the house with the tennis-lawn at Guildford. Young Merridew was not at the School that evening; indeed, he had only been once in the evening all the week, and then, Louie had thought (dropping the mask for another moment) he had better have stopped away. In a word, she had not been sure that he had been entirely sober. But perhaps in that she had been wrong. It didn't matter. She set a wide difference between the gaieties of the sons of fancy stationers with a tidy bit coming in and such diversions as that to which her stepfather had once taken her, pigtail and all. Besides, if people didn't drink liquor she supposed her father would not be able to sell it.

On two occasions already during the past week that mask of her amusement had not so much fallen off as been twitched off before she herself had been aware. Very remarkably, both times the big leonine student, Mr. Jeffries, had been the twitcher. In both cases the actual incident had been the same—a glance, nothing more. But those two glances had set Louie very curiously indeed waiting to see whether a third surprise of the same funny kind would follow them.

The glances had been given by Mr. Jeffries, and they had been directed towards the Soames girl. There had seemed to Louie to be an extraordinary unfitness about them. Had the red-waistcoated boy stolen those glances Louie would have thought no more about it; he and Polly Ross were pretty much a pair; but they had surprised her coming from the other. Louie had been sure that on the first occasion Mr. Jeffries had fancied himself to be unobserved, for he had looked stealthily round about him, had waited for a moment, and then, moving his eyes only, had given that long, slow, daring, masterful look. This had been on the previous Monday evening, in the general room. A few minutes later Mr. Jeffries had gathered up his papers and had stridden past Evie Soames as if he had been unaware of her existence.

Even had something very similar not occurred again on the Wednesday evening, Louie would hardly have forgotten that look; but it had been repeated. But this time, finding Louie's eyes on him, he had seemed to guard himself, to busy himself quite fussily with his papers, and a little to overdo his sudden affectation of indifference. Louie admitted that it would be at her own risk that she put any interpretation that was not amusing on these trifles; but about the glances, their surreptitiousness and the man's deliberate attempt at concealment, there had been no doubt whatever. Polly herself, Louie had to admit, had been quite unconscious of either look. To all appearances, she had been thinking of nothing but of the new novelette in the Pansy Library, or else wondering whether the new pair of shoes she was to go down to Guildford in would come home in time.

On that Friday evening Louie again found herself a little less inclined for amusement than she knew to be good for her. She supposed she ought to work, for if book-keeping and typewriting and so forth were to be her living they might just as well be taken seriously; but she preferred to work where gossip was going on. So she began the evening in one of the days in the E of reference books, where Miss Windus and the thick-lipped Miss Levey were sitting on the short library-ladder, whispering and tittering. Louie opened one of the windows, for she found the place airless, and then idled towards her two fellow-students.

She had gathered that Miss Levey did not like her. Miriam Levey was far less stupid than Kitty Windus, and it was not safe to hand her *clichés* back to her. Indeed, she had given Louie a far too intelligent look when Louie had gratified this hunger for humour of hers at the unconscious Kitty's expense; and Louie had told herself that it might be as well to be a little more careful. They looked up as Louie joined them, but did not exclude her from their talk.

"I *vill* find out who she is!" Miss Levey was saying—her W's did sometimes become V's. "I shall plague him till I do!"

"He won't tell you, my dear—not if he wouldn't tell Archie."

"But did Archie actually say 'engaged'?"

"Well, a person's either engaged or not, I suppose."

"Oh no, my dear, not by long chalks! Vy, you might as well say that Archie and Evie are either engaged or not!"

"Well, they aren't—yet."

"'Yet'—there you are!"

"Well, I'll bet they aren't, even after this week-end. Why, they're no age! *I* don't believe in getting yourself engaged and done for before you've had a good look round!" Kitty tossed her head.

"Vill you bet they aren't engaged in three months?" said Miriam Levey.

No, Kitty wouldn't bet that. She returned to the original subject, whatever that had been.

"It's all very well to say you'll find out, Miriam, but—how?"

Miss Levey tittered, and then suddenly said: "Ssss—I'll show you now! Just you watch me—"

She slipped noiselessly round to the cords of the window Louie had opened a few moments before.

No doubt her sharp eyes had seen Mr. Jeffries approach. She gave him a helpless look, and he took the cords from her fumbling hands and closed the window for her. It was the more cleverly done that she detained Mr. Jeffries and managed to get closed the window which Louie wanted open at one and the same time. She turned her prominent brown eyes in gratitude to Mr. Jeffries.

"Oh, thank you so much! You see, I've got rather a cold, and I'm going to a dance and don't vant to make it any vorse," she explained. "You don't dance, do you, Mr. Jeffries?"

But Mr. Jeffries merely replied "No," and turned away at once. Miss Levey turned to Kitty again.

"He needn't think he's put me off!" she said. "I *vill* find out! I shall offer him some tickets now, for self and lady. And I bet if she dances I'll make him buy them!"

Kitty tossed her head. "*I* should expect the gentleman *I* was engaged to to take *me* to dances," she said.

"But Archie didn't say 'engaged.' Just after somebody, I should say—and don't I just vish her joy!"

"It's evidently nobody at the School," mused Kitty Windus. "Archie was almost certain about that."

"Vell, it isn't *me*, if you're thinking of suspecting me!" said Miss Levey merrily. "*I* vouldn't touch him with the end of a long pole."

"Chance is a fine thing, my dear," remarked Miss Windus.

"Opportunity's another." (This reply, Louie had noted, was *de rigueur*.)

"I expect she types or something at his place in the City."

"She might be in an A.B.C. shop—no, a Lockhart's."

"Or a barmaid," Kitty hinted.

"Or his vashervoman."

"Oh, I expect he washes his own shirts."

"Perhaps he'll vash her blouses, too, whoever she is."

They both laughed.

Louie, her mask once more a little out of place, turned suddenly away.

Little as she had been inclined to work, she was now, somehow or other, not much more inclined for amusement. She wandered into the shorthand dictation class, but in a few minutes came out again. Then she walked into the lecture-room, where some example or other had been left chalked up on the big blackboard from the last lesson. Thence she went into the typewriting-room, and back to the lecture-room again. Finally she got from the "library"—the little back room where the files and presses and gelatine copiers and a few books were kept—a number of old examination papers, and, finding a chair near the folding door that divided the lecture-room from the general-room, sat down and began to turn them over.

But she thought more of the conversation she had just overheard than she did of the examination papers. It had meant, as far as she had been able to make it out, that Mr. Jeffries had told young Merridew that he was engaged, or hoped to be engaged, to somebody outside the school altogether. That sounded—odd. Of course if Mr. Jeffries said so, Mr. Jeffries ought to know; but it is a difficult matter to disbelieve your own eyes. She supposed she had no choice but to disbelieve them, but—but—there *were* those two glances he had given at the Polly Ross girl—whom, by the way, she must learn to call by her proper name, Miss Evie Soames.

Louie was perfectly certain that she had not been mistaken in the nature of those two glances. Her reason for certitude was quite unassailable. She had known what they meant for the simple reason that she had never received such looks from a man herself.

Suddenly she dropped this mask of fevered amusement entirely. As she had once sat on the stile between Rainham Parva and the sea, so Louie now sat by the folding door—relaxed, thinking of nothing, or, if of anything, certainly neither of her late resolute pose nor yet of study. Her mind was what she had determined it should not be if she could help it—an empty chamber for unknown devils to enter.

Students passed and repassed. Weston had been through several times, and twice Evie Soames had come and gone again. This so-much-talked-of Mr. Jeffries went into the library for a book and walked past with it again. He still wore that concealing ulster; the Soames girl had on a brown tailor-made and a cap of knitted white wool. Louie was hardly conscious that she noticed these things. She still sat, all slack and unbraced, with the examination papers on her knee.

All at once she came to herself. Why she should do so at that particular moment she did not know, but, doing so, she found herself completely awake again. To all intents and purposes she had come out of one of those naps which, lasting perhaps only a minute, have all the effect of a refreshing sleep. She could reassume her mask now. Evie Soames was talking to Weston by the blackboard; opposite her, a pale student called Richardson was copying down an exercise from a sheet on the wall; and she supposed Mr. Jeffries would be bringing his book back presently. Louie was as alive to her surroundings now as she had been oblivious to them a few moments before.

A minute later Mr. Jeffries, returning with his book, passed into the library. A few seconds later still Evie Soames had left Mr. Weston and had followed him.

"Now," thought Louie, "for a little more amusement."

The library had only one communicating door; its other door led only to a small room called the old ledger-room, a dusty cubby-hole, seldom entered, that had no outlet save the small pivoted window, high up, that gave on the head of the stairs. Mr. Jeffries and Miss Soames would have to come out by the same way they had entered, and Louie rather wanted to see them come out. It was no business of hers, but she had remembered those two glances and the conversation between Kitty Windus and Miriam Levey, and she had a perfect right to sit by the folding door and to use her eyes if she wished. She was now almost preternaturally awake. No jot of the jest, whatever it was, should escape her.

Evie came out first, after four or five minutes; but Louie was not interested in Evie. She was merely a dull tale: Louie wanted to see him.

Then, a moment later, he came.

But no amusement came with him. Instead, Louie knew not what sudden private ache stirred deep at her own heart. It was not a question of those two furtive, possessive glances now. Unmistakable enough those had been; you do not mistake the kind of glance for which you yourself have hungered when you see it given to another; but not only had Louie never seen—she had never, not even in her own rapt dreamings as a half-grown girl in her teens, thought it possible that a man's look at a woman could change his face as this man's face was changed now. It was irradiated, transfigured. He took no pains now to hide it. He could see clear down the room before him—could see (or so he evidently thought) any who saw him—

And since he did not see Louie by the folding door, Louie knew that in his former passings and repassings he could not have seen her either.

He disappeared. The Soames girl was waiting by the door, evidently for him. No doubt he was going to see her home. Probably she would have preferred the other, the little cad with the red waistcoat, but she had the lion—

He returned, with his hat on, and they left together.

But what had brought that sudden ache into Louie's breast? Mr. Jeffries was nothing to her. If his face shone, Louie's heart need not therefore ache. What ailed her?

Unmasked, as alive to things within herself now as she had just been to things outside herself, she sat, deeply wondering.

Against the wall at her left hand there stood a tall stationery cupboard. It had glazed doors, and the pale student called Richardson, coming up a moment ago to put his exercise-book back into its place, had left one of the doors open. The door moved on its hinges back into its place. With its motion there swung slowly into Louie's view the reflection of the grimy chandelier with its three naked gas-jets.

Was it this that reminded her of the night when she had swept out of Mrs. Lovenant-Smith's French window with the yellow-shaded standard lamp mirrored in its pane?

It had been on that night—

Suddenly her eyes closed, as if closed eyes could have shut out a mental picture. Her lips trembled—voicelessly they shaped a name.

It was the name of Roy.

HITHERTO SHE HAD HARDLY KNOWN what her feelings towards Roy really were. It had been in order to avoid asking herself that question, among others, that she had amused herself with Kitty Windus and welcomed the buffooneries of Mr. Mackie. But it presented itself to her startlingly now. Her own complete ignorance had just revealed a shining thing to her, the beautiful thing that had transformed Mr. Jeffries' face; now—handy-dandy—that very transformation threw her brutally back on her ignorance again.

She had thought she had sounded a mystery; had she, after all, *not* sounded any mystery, and was she to pay in labour and pain for nothing?

Her thoughts had flown back; they remained where they had flown. Good gracious! What an escapade! Without mercy for herself she examined it. What had really happened? Anything worth what it was about to cost?

The radiant look of another man at another woman answered her: No.

She had courted him—what a conquest! She had made him say she was pretty—what a victory! She had schemed, planned, ensured her kisses—what a triumph! . . . Why, she now asked herself for the first time, had she wanted to triumph? Why had she not seen sooner that what she had really wanted had been to be triumphed over? Triumph?— It came to her with a strange newness that women didn't triumph by triumphing. That man with the back like the church door, for example, who had just gone out with that pretty snippet—

Instantly, and with extraordinary resilience, her mind established a contrast.

No woman would have to cajole this shabby, lion-eyed man into admiration of her beauty. Rather she would have to save herself from his onslaught—and then, in her very flying, she would triumph. Louie had found a fool invincible; but this other, when he loved, would go down with the vehemence of his own assault. When Louie had refused to kiss Roy at their parting she had not known exactly why she had done so: she had obeyed an instinct; a chapter had been closed, and had had to be marked as definitely closed; her heart had known no rancour against him. But now!—she might just as well have kissed him. Now, in this strange place, two strange people—or rather one, for the girl mattered nothing—had in a moment, and infinitely, enlarged her sense of what, at any rate to a man, love might mean. In the light of that enlargement any kiss she could have given to Roy would have meant nothing—nothing, nothing. Poor Roy, whom she had had to woo! This other would do his own wooing. Why, he was doing it now—

Then a startling recollection caused Louie to sit suddenly upright. This lion, who had given those looks at that girl—this shabby giant, whose face she had just seen enheavened out of all knowledge—had told young Merridew, who had told Kitty Windus and Miriam Levey, that his heart was set on somebody outside this poky little Business School altogether!

Involuntarily Louie drew a long breath of amazement.

He had told them that!

Then Louie became matter-of-fact. There was one thing and one thing only to be said. If Mr. Jeffries had told him that, Mr. Jeffries had—lied.

She turned it over again—she found no flaw in it.

Yes, if he had said that, he had lied.

Louie pondered. The result of her pondering was that she said slowly to herself: "Ah—this is going to be more than amusing—unless I'm mistaken it might even become dramatic."

Up to the moment of this astonishing discovery—for Louie knew that she had made a discovery—Mr. Jeffries had been to her a phenomenon, different from Mr. Mackie and Kitty Windus, but not to be observed very differently; now in a twink she placed him in quite another category. Or, if she still lacked a category in which to place him, she certainly removed him for ever from the other. He had called suddenly on her profounder attention, and, as if he had struck upon a rock, the waters of it gushed forth. Apparently to others he was a butt, a jest, a pathetic figure; he was not that to Louie Causton now. They had said, Kitty and the Jewess, that Evie Soames and the red-waistcoated boy, off to Guildford together tomorrow, would before long be engaged to be married; but Mr. Jeffries, the third person in the commonest of dramas, and Mr. Jeffries, the introducer into that drama of a preposterous, impossible fourth actor, whose name Miriam Levey was resolved to know, were not one and the same man. Louie sat astounded again at his lie. It struck her as really in its way stupendous. Others thought he was below his fellows in this shabby little hutch of a Business School; not so Louie now! She saw those clear yellow eyes again. Ruses and machinations lived in them. A butt, with his brown-paper parcel? A pathetic figure, with his cadged baths? No—good gracious, no! The faces of butts and pathetic figures were rather less capable of irradiation. This man's kind made great somethings—great men, great saints, great lovers—if it came to the worst great criminals. Had she, Louie, been that jaunty young man in the red waistcoat, she would have chosen for a rival and enemy anybody she had ever seen

　　　　　　　　　　　　　　　　　　　　　　　　OLIVER ONIONS

rather than this needy, gigantic Mr. Jeffries, who made this barefaced attempt to throw dust into people's eyes by means of apocryphal women he was "after" elsewhere.

And he helped this youngster he must hate with his studies—cadged on his probably-to-be-successful rival for a bath.

He was masked too, then.

Yes, at this dingy School in Holborn Louie had found something even more interesting than amusement.

IV

Louie had not yet allowed herself much time for fear of what was to happen to herself physically; she had amused herself too heartily. She bought chocolates and hated the smell of tobacco; and so far that was all. What hung over her was as inevitable as Death, and for that reason was, like Death, to be kept at arm's-length as long as possible.

But she had already seen enough of Richenda's sister to be aware that in all probability her stay in Sutherland Place would not be a long one. Mrs. Leggat was formally kind, to Lord Moone's niece rather than to herself; but for the rest an armed neutrality seemed to exist between the two women. The Leggats were childless, and for that reason the less likely to be charitable. Louie had, in fact, found the social layer that is bounded on the one hand by the wickedness of pugilists and on the other by the scapes of young gentlemen about to enter the army. Within these limits Virtue reigned—not always harshly, always consciously. Not the wives of the Cæsars (it seemed to Louie) were above suspicion, but the Mrs. Leggats; not the saints, who confessed that they were tempted, but the Westons, who did not know of temptation's existence. It was as if some unseen, august Mrs. Lovenant-Smith had decreed that landladies and teachers in business schools did not do these things. And they did not.

Louie went to the house of Richenda's father, the bookseller—once. She had no wish to go again. As Richenda had described him there had been something tragic about him; to Louie he had appeared merely as a grey-bearded, rheumatic, complaining old man, a picture of pathos without dignity. And those six other Richendas, of various ages, struck her as horribly superfluous. She wanted Life's colour, not its greyness; she greatly preferred the garnish, incredible Mackie.

The weeks passed. Weston came regularly on Sunday mornings, and on Sunday afternoons she took long walks. On the nights when there was no class she rode on buses, along Oxford Street, down Regent Street to the Circus, and back by Park Lane to the Marble Arch and Notting Hill Gate again; or sometimes she went Paddington way, up the Harrow Road and out and back through Kilburn. She began to know something of the streets of London. Her health was far better in London than it had been at Rainham Parva. It was perfect. She still feared nothing.

THE CHRISTMAS EXAMINATIONS DREW WITHIN sight, and hand in hand with the preparation for them another and a more lightsome preoccupation engaged the School. This was the Christmas Social with which the last term of the year always closed. An Executive had been formed; on it Louie's name appeared; and it met frequently at the close of afternoon school. One of the younger students was sent across to the teashop over the way for scones and cake; a kettle was set on the general-room fire; and the social was discussed over tea.

Mr. Mackie was the life and soul of these meetings. He was especially strong on the subject of whether evening-dress was to be obligatory, permissible or debarred. He declared himself at one of the earlier meetings as out and out for fancy dress, but was outvoted.

"See me as a Woodbine, girls, beg pardon, miss-cue, a Columbine, I mean, nearly cold with the kilt, kilt with the cold, I should say, sixpence in the box for the opera-glasses, Gerald, but don't ogle me while mother's in the wings, wishing she was twenty-one again—good old mother—

> *"Here's to the happiest hours of my life,*
> *Spent in the arms of another man's wife—*
> *My Mo-the-rr!"'*

(The shake on the long note produced by a rapid play of Mr. Mackie's fingers on Mr. Mackie's Adam's apple.) "Thought I'd have to backpedal, didn't you, Miss Causton? Nay, fear not, fair damsel, the intentions of Ferdinando are honourable, as long as you watch him, pip-pip, phee-ooo!" (The shrill whistle behind the handkerchief closed the strophe.)

But this was rushing matters. Kitty Windus spoke, no doubt on behalf of the students who hadn't a pound a week on their own.

"Fancy dress would keep a good many away," she said. "I should love it, but it really is an expense, you know."

"Weston can buy a penny bottle of gum and come as a foreign stamp."

"Do be serious, Mr. Mackie, now! We want the social to be for everybody here—"

"*And* their friends," Miss Levey interpolated, with a look of private understanding at Kitty Windus. There was a short interlude between the two women.

"You *won't* find out, Miriam!"

"I *will!*"

"Did you offer him tickets for the Holborn?"

"Yes; but he wouldn't buy them."

"Doesn't Mrs. J. as-is-to-be dance?"

"I don't know. He vouldn't buy the tickets."

"I'll bet you another half-crown you don't get him there, let alone her!"

"Done vith you, Kitty Vindus!" cried Miss Levey excitedly.

Here Mr. Mackie interposed. "Who's that? Jeffries? He can come in his ulster as Boaz—*heu*, how Ruthless! (Beshrew me, but have I not a pretty wit?)"

"He's got that new brown suit to come in—or did he get it second-hand, Archie?" asked Kitty.

"New," quoth Archie authoritatively. "Allworthy's, in Cheapside. Two ten."

"I nearly died when he turned up without that old ulster!"

"Vasn't it screaming?" simpered Miss Levey. "No, don't, Archie!" (Young Merridew was pulling out the frill of her jabot.)

"Do tell us exactly what he said when you congratulated him on his engagement, Evie!" said Kitty Windus, turning to Evie Soames.

The girl coloured a little. In common fairness Louie had to acquit her of full participation in the joke of Mr. Jeffries and his unknown *fiancée*. Louie had learned that it had been in order to congratulate Mr. Jeffries on this supposed engagement that she had followed Mr. Jeffries into the library on that Friday evening before her departure for the week-end to Guildford. She thought little more of her on that account. In being too ready with apologies and congratulations Evie Soames merely showed the vulgarity of the rest of the place.

"No, do let's get on with business," Kitty Windus broke in. "I vote for ordinary dress."

"Yes, ordinary dress," came the chorus.

"Vith vite gloves, of course," said Miss Levey.

"Of course."

"Vot do you say, Miss Causton?"

"White gloves, of course," said Louie, with her demurest look. "And flowers in their buttonholes."

"Some gentlemen don't like to vear flowers," said Miriam Levey suspiciously.

"Aha, doesn't he?" from Mr. Mackie. "*I* saw you at the Holborn, Miss Levey—naughty, naughty—"

"Oh, I don't mean very big ones," said Louie, sipping her tea.

And the discussion went on, and meeting followed meeting; but the examination was to take place before the social.

The only fear Louie had for her Elementary was whether it would be worth very much when she had got it. She supposed that as an earnest preparation for the struggle of life this place was not quite such a fraud as Chesson's, but that struggle could hardly be as fierce as Richenda Earle had said if this Elementary took her very far. Indeed she had wondered more than once lately, especially since she had ceased to amuse herself quite so desperately, whether it was likely that typewriting and book-keeping were to be her destiny after all. She supposed they were, but she couldn't quite realise it. But she was fully prepared, and hoped Mr. Jeffries was as sure of his Honours paper as she was of her simple Pass.

For she had gathered that success in the coming examination was of importance to Mr. Jeffries. She did not know the nature of his studies; later she surmised that those had been only loosely linked to the ordinary school curriculum, and that while for his Certificate's sake he must acquire all that text-books could tell him, his real broodings had been over matters that are antecedent to text-books. That was probably the difference between him and Mr. Weston. Mr. Weston was said to be clever, but his cleverness ended at the point where real inquiry began. More than this Louie did not know. You cannot, after all, ask the pioneer what he goes forth for to see. He goes forth to see whatever there may be to be seen.

The weeks that had intervened since that evening when Louie had seen that wonderful radiance of his face had done nothing to alter her conviction that if there was a dark horse in that Holborn stable at all the name of that horse was Mr. Jeffries.

As it happened, Mr. Jeffries was almost the first person she encountered when, on the Friday morning of the examination, she entered the School at half-past ten. He wore the new brown suit that had been remarked on at the meetings of the Executive of the social, and he was looking with curiosity about him. They had made quite extensive preparations for the examination. The whole place had been divided into compartments with hired yellow-painted screens, and screens also barricaded the E of reference-books near the bay window of the general-room. New pens and new blotting-paper lay on the desks, and the little porcelain inkwells had been newly filled. Then it occurred to Louie that it was more than likely that Mr. Jeffries had never been in the place in the daytime before. He must have got the day off from that "somewhere in the City" that Kitty Windus had said sounded so prosperous. His tawny hair was as flat and silky as ever, and his chin as cleanly shaved. He passed her with a curt bow and continued his inspection of the place. The candidates stood talking in groups, waiting for eleven o'clock.

"Have you discovered your—er—appointed place, Miss Causton?" said Weston, coming up to Louie. "Good, good! I must now take my departure. Members of the Staff are not permitted to remain on the premises during the hours devoted to the examination. I wish you—er—good luck."

He seemed to change his mind about saying "a happy issue from all your afflictions."

By eleven o'clock Louie was seated in her little screen-enclosed compartment. A sort of hired mourner read a formal caution to the candidates. She noticed that it lacked the *largior ether* of the third person indicative, being, indeed, in the second person imperative; and then she drew her paper to her.

Quiet fell on the examination-rooms.

She found her papers no more difficult than she had anticipated. On one point only, a matter of indenting in actual practice, was she a little in doubt, and a minute in the old ledger-room at lunch-time would tell her whether her answer had been right or wrong. She read over again what she had written; it seemed, with the possible exception of that single point, all right; and she tilted her chair, put her hands behind her head, and leaned back. The candidates had been warned that they must bring lunch with them. It was half-an-hour from lunch-time yet.

Her place was by the folding door of the general-room. From it she could see nothing save the stationery cupboard on her left, and, beyond it, the next screen-enclosed compartment. She was wondering who was in it when a foot moved beneath the yellow screen. It was the foot of Mr. Jeffries. Louie hoped that he was getting on well, and then dismissed him from her thoughts. She began to wonder about the practical usefulness of the examination again.

Doubtless it was well enough in its way, but less than ever could she persuade herself that this kind of thing was to be her destiny. There were too many other likelihoods—not to speak of the one certainly so huge that she had sometimes been actually in danger of leaving it out of the account altogether. Idly she counted them. First, there was the certainty. . . Next, she would probably be leaving Sutherland Place soon, to go—where? She did not know. At the price of submission to Uncle Augustus she could go back home; or Chaff would have her looked after; but both these courses were rather out of the question. They were out of the question because lately something else had been more and more in her thoughts—her unknown father. That father might, for all she knew, be the bugbear her mother had always made him out to be; but on the other hand he might not. She knew her mother, and the more she thought of it the more she gave her father the benefit of an increasing number of doubts. Until she should have seen him it was now no more than fair that she should do so. Moreover, she could see him at any time without his being any the wiser of the—inspection. Chaff knew where he was; Chaff, who was always fetching or taking her somewhere, would take her there also. She was resolved to go sooner or later, and later might be—who knew?—too late.

For at last she had admitted a dread.

In any case, her destiny was quite as likely to be determined by a visit to that public-house up the Thames as by writing, in this stuffy Holborn third floor, answers to ridiculous questions about *pro forma* invoices and bills of lading.

She was still turning these things over in her mind when the bell rang for the close of the first part of the examination.

She ate her lunch in the company of Kitty Windus and Miss Levey, and then the three women passed out on to the staircase and sat down half-way down the stairs. But the men had flocked to the staircase for their noxious smoking, and Louie re-entered the general-room again. Then she remembered the doubtful point in her paper and walked to the library. She passed through it into the old ledger-room. Any old ledger would settle the point on which she was not quite sure.

The room was almost dark, but Louie knew where the musty old books were. She put out her hand to the nearest of them. But suddenly she withdrew her hand. The high window that gave on the head of the stairs afforded no more than a glimmer of light, but Louie thought she had seen something move. She peered into the twilight, "Is anybody there?" she said, but she had no answer.

But the room was occupied. The next moment she had seen and fled.

Her irregular lips were pursed as she came out into the light again. There was a confusion, too, in her eyes, probably as much as there had been in the eyes of the two she had come upon in there. They must have seen her come in, and have realised that their only chance of escaping detection lay in keeping perfectly still.

Polly Ross, cheek to cheek with that horrid little bounder!

There was no question now of whom the girl preferred.

Louie, wondering what right she had to do so, felt nevertheless a little sick.

But the next moment her fastidiousness had vanished. The door that led to the stairs had opened; Mr. Mackie's voice sounded loud for a moment on the landing; and then Mr. Jeffries lurched in, stumbled, and almost ran to his compartment between the yellow screens.

How he too knew what was going on in the old ledger-room, Louie could not guess; but she knew that he did know.

She walked slowly to her own place and sat down.

A few minutes later the bell for the second half of the examination rang, and a new paper was put before Louie. But she neither glanced at it nor yet heard the voice of the hired mourner repeating his caution. She sat with her chin in her hands, looking straight before her. She was wondering what was taking place behind the yellow screen beyond the stationery cupboard. Amusement was hardly the word for that.

For she had seen Mr. Jeffries' face as he had stumbled in. She sought words for the expression that had been upon it. Lost—despairing—devilish—

There was not much doubt about who *he* was in love with either.

Devilish, despairing, lost—

"Poor—soul!" she thought compassionately. . .

She wondered why she should be so unaccountably nervous. She was nervous. She even jumped a little when somebody on the other side of the folding door allowed a pen to fall to the floor. She could see the feet beneath the lower edge of the screen in front of her; they did not move; the examination quietness had fallen on the place again, and the very quietness grew on her. Strong drama, if not tragedy outright, was being enacted behind those half-inch yellow boards beyond the stationery cupboard, but the quietness continued. It was such a quietness as she had read of in tales when, somebody's ears being sharpened for an expected scream, their eyes had not at first noticed the little dark rivulet of blood trickling slowly across the floor. Involuntarily her eyes went to the yellow screen.

But rubbish; this was morbid.

Morbid or not, however, her lips almost shaped the words, slowly and deliberately: that boy with the red waistcoat would do well to be careful. He would do especially well to be careful if, after this, after the glare on the other's face, he should still have help offered him with his studies or be asked for a bath. For something would happen then. Eggshells such as he did not come into collision with bronze without something happening. And if anything not easily to be accounted for did happen to that odious little whippersnapper, nothing would ever persuade Louie that she did not know a likely quarter in which to look for the reason.

Blind, devilish despair!

And all for an empty-headed little thing who could have been found in her dozens behind twenty shop counters not a quarter of a mile away! What on earth, what on, or under, or above the earth, could this brooding, clever, gigantic, laughed-at creature want with such a doll? Why could he not leave her in her proper place—cheek by cheek with the little bounder of her choice in that smelly, unlighted old ledger-room? The man must be blind, or a fool.

Then a sort of lethargy took Louie. Suddenly she cared for nothing. Let the fancy-stationer's cub take his risks; let the other eat his heart out if he would; it was no business of hers. Nor was that absurd table of questions before her any business of hers. Kitty Windus might answer that sort of thing; Mackie might answer it; but the Scarisbricks were not Kittys, with her "part-independency," not Mackies, to stuff their heads and ink their fingers like this for their "permanencies." She did not know now why she had ever come to the place, and she wanted no more of it. What she was going to do she did not know. She did know, however, that she was not going to answer that silly paper.

So, by-and-by, she allowed the paper to be collected again, as blank as when it had been placed before her.

She came upon the perverse Mr. Jeffries once more before she left. He almost ran her down bodily as they met in the doorway of the typewriting-room. But this time she did not look at his face. With a swift intaking of her breath she fell back to save herself. She did not hear whether he apologised or not; in one moment, without premeditation, her whole being had become constrained to a new, protective, instinctive attitude.

Slowly and thoughtfully she left the School.

She alone of the students was unsurprised to hear, four or five days later, that Mr. Jeffries, who had passed with distinction in the first part of his paper, had, like herself, failed in the second part.

§*b*

FOR THE EXAMINATION THE ROOMS had been cut up with screens; for the breaking-up social they were cleared of everything that could be stowed away into dark corners. Never was such a hoisting and calling as those with which the hired piano was got up the three flights of stairs. Most of it came from Mr. Mackie, turned for the nonce into a shabash-wallah.

"Mind her funnybone—all together—up with her! Oh, pursue me, wenches, I've got my muscle up, first time since the second housemaid ran away with the dustman! Don't tickle her parson's nose, Archi-bald, or she'll sneeze when I sing, key in the usual place—and mind the stair above the top, it isn't there. This way—excuse my shirt-sleeves, Miss Windus, I'm in mourning."

And so the piano was trundled to its place in the corner by the big blackboard.

Mr. Mackie was of service, too, in the French-chalking of the floor, for the men hauled him about by the arms and legs on a piece of sacking in order to give it its final polish for dancing. Half the students, male and female, helped to wind the blackened old brackets and chandeliers with red and green tissue paper, to set evergreens on the tops of the cupboards, and to affix the trophies of little Christmas tree flags on the cabbagey old walls; and Louie helped with the refreshments. Three women had been got in, one to make coffee and the others to preside in the cloakrooms, and Miss Levey had won half-a-crown from Kitty Windus.

For Mr. Jeffries was coming to the party after all. More, it had been Louie herself who had asked him, though it had been Miss Levey's cunning that had made her do so. On no grounds at all save that it appeared to annoy, the Jewess had once or twice twitted Louie that Mr. Jeffries favoured *her* and, when Mr. Jeffries had declined her own invitation, had nudged Louie. "*You* ask him, and see whether he doesn't come!" the nudge had meant. Louie entered into no contest with Miss Levey. She had turned at once to Mr. Jeffries and repeated the invitation. He had accepted it.

Louie doubted her own wisdom in going to that social at all. Even when she had reached Sutherland Place and spread out her frocks on her bed she still doubted. But suddenly she gave a short laugh. Of course she was going! It was her first "social," and it might be her last; she was going, and she was going to wear the oyster-grey satin that, ever since she had had it, had always seemed to "live" so on her shoulders.

She declined Mrs. Leggat's help in getting into it; if Mrs. Leggat would be so good as to get her a hansom instead——Mrs. Leggat went out. The oyster-grey was one of the oldest of her frocks; Louie knew every stitch of it; and she smiled as she thought that for that very reason she would have chosen it had she deliberately intended to make a conquest. She surveyed herself in it in the tilted glass. Yes, she thought she would do.

"It's your last time on, poor old rag," she muttered.

She heard the pulling up of the hansom; she put on a light shawl and descended; and Mrs. Leggat lingered in the doorway as she drove off.

They had set candles on the floors of the landings of the Holborn stairs, but they guttered in the draughts, and showed little but the feet of those who ascended. Louie followed a pair of orange silk-stockinged ankles and a trammel of orange petticoats (she didn't know whose) up the stairs, and entered the general-room. The library had been converted into a ladies' cloakroom, with the old ledger-room as an annexe; and in this last room Evie Soames, with an elaborate running of pink ribbons beneath the openwork of her cream net blouse, was putting on her slippers. She only showed Louie the top of her dark head; in this and other ways she had displayed reserve since the lunch interval of the examination day. A woman with a pair of very chapped hands and a very clean apron took Louie's shawl; and Louie, first glancing at her hair over the powdered shoulders of the person in orange, went into the double room that had been prepared for dancing.

Students and their friends had turned up in their best bibs and tuckers. Most of the men wore swallow-tailed coats; one of the exceptions was Mr. Jeffries in his brown jacket-suit. He was talking to Miss Levey, or rather Miss Levey was gasping to him; she had just given him, or rather hung upon his wrist, one of the violet-written cards, printed from the gelatine-copier, which served as programmes. Weston wore a tightly fitting old frock-coat, which Mr. Mackie humorously likened to the overcoat of sausage that had spent the night in the coal-hole. Archie Merridew had a white waistcoat. All the men stroked the wrinkles out of their white gloves without ceasing. The women, to the reflective eye, had lost little by the foregoing of out-and-out evening-dress. There was an "I could an' if I would" about their long sleeves and high necks. Kitty Windus, in her blue foulard, with a cutlet-frill about her thin neck, graciously consented to the level of those who had not a pound a week on their own; Miriam Levey, in a maroon pinafore-frock with broad braces over her shoulders, instantly put every simple blouse in the room at its ease. One frock only flouted the modest agreement to which the executive had come; this was the orange satin one which Louie had followed upstairs. It partially clothed a friend of Mr. Mackie's. Louie heard the words in which Mr. Mackie introduced young Merridew to its wearer.

"Mr. Merridew, Miss Dulcie Levine, Miss Levine, Mr. Merridew, two of the best, seasonable weather for the time of the year, ain't it, what? Permit me, Dulcibella, a bit of fluff" (here Mr. Mackie cast aside the bit of fluff, if there was one, which he had taken from Miss Dulcie's shoulder, and represented the noise of its falling by a loud stamp on the floor). "Ought to be dancing soon; what time is it by your clocks, Dulcie? *I* saw them as you got out of the Black Maria, the cab, I mean— *heu*, desist, Mr. Mackie, you wag!" (Mr. Mackie smacked his own wrist in reproof of himself.) "Why am I not in me usual spirits, gin cold, tonight, Dulcinea? 'Tis thy fatal beauty has undone me; what ho, a needle and threat, O fairest of thy socks, sex I should say. . . Ay, she dances, Archibald, but not with thee, base varlet; she dances at the Theatre hight Alcazar, nigh unto ye Square called Leicester."

Louie heard Kitty Windus whisper to Evie Soames that Mr. Mackie was going to be splendid tonight; but her approval did not extend to Mr. Mackie's friend, who was already too splendid. Kitty's head was held so high when Miss Levine passed that she appeared to be looking at her with her nostrils. With her eyes she saw only the orange creature's back. This was a rather handsome **V**, and that did not improve matters. Kitty whispered behind her fan about "some people." Miss Dulcie used Kitty as a quizzing-glass for the inspection of whoever happened to be behind her.

Mr. Jeffries stood with his back against the thrown-back folding door. He did not dance, but he had not at all the air of a wet blanket; on the contrary, his face wore a quite lively smile. He was smiling at the red and green tissue paper that enswathed the central chandelier. Louie saw Evie Soames pass him; his eyes rested on her for a moment, but only as they rested on everybody else, and then went back to the red and green tissue paper of the chandelier again. He had accepted the inevitable, then. Indeed, had he not done so, Louie could hardly imagine that he would have been there. Well, it was the most sensible thing he could do. Louie would go and speak to him presently.

Louie made a tour of the rooms. The E of reference-books had been turned into a place for sitting out, and in the typewriting-room the lids of two or three desks had been wedged up to form card-tables. Into the room beyond, which was the smoking-room, she did not penetrate. Already a fiddle was tuning up, but Louie had told young Merridew, who had magnanimously asked her for her card, that she did not intend to dance. None the less he had taken her card and scrawled something on it. She had tossed the piece of violet-written pasteboard into a corner.

At nine o'clock there was a tapping on the top of the piano, and the music began. Mr. Mackie and the lady in orange glided out over the French-chalked floor. Two minutes later the room was full of waltzing couples.

Louie had sat down on the opposite side of the room to Mr. Jeffries. Through momentarily clear spaces she saw him from time to time. He did not move from his station by the folding door, where, among the hoppers and caperers who sped past him, he seemed to have something of the stability of a monument in some centre of apparently aimless traffic. Still, he seemed to be enjoying himself, and Louie intended to go across to him when the waltz was over.

A word she overheard, however, caused her to change her mind and to rise to her feet at once. Mr. Mackie, passing with his orange partner, had repeated his jape about the Ruthless Boaz.

Without more ado Louie threaded her way through the dancers and stood before Mr. Jeffries.

"Won't you try to dance?" she said.

As he turned the amber eyes on her she had the feeling that she slid all at once into the field of some piece of apparatus with an object-glass. She was the object. For a moment he forgot his smile; he looked attentively at her; and then the smile returned. He answered in an easy, deep voice, the accent of which was neither Cockney nor yet quite of the mode of the men Louie knew.

"Oh, I—I don't dance," he said.

"Won't you let me teach you?"

His eyes were still on hers. He seemed to give the simple question weighty consideration. Then his eyes dropped to his hands.

"Hallo," he said, as if to himself. His programme was where Miss Levey had put it, dangling from his wrist as if from a hook. Apparently he had not noticed it before. Then, looking at Louie again, he said: "I mean, my gloves—I've no gloves."

"Gloves!" she said quietly. "Come."

She took the absurd programme from his wrist, threw it away, and put her gloved hand into his naked one.

She drew Mr. Jeffries into the current.

Louie had danced with ignoramuses before, but never with a man quite so awkward as this. She did her best to steer him, but before they had gone half-way round the room they had collided with Evie Soames, leaning back in the crook of young Merridew's arm—with Kitty Windus, tiptoe and leaning forward over her partner—with Mr. Mackie, who had lighted a cigarette and was singing the refrain of the dance as he passed. Then Mr. Jeffries begged her, out of consideration for herself, to stop. But she had no desire to stop. She wondered why, bumped and trampled so, she should want to go on, but she gave that riddle up. He did not cease to apologise for his ungainliness.

But the riddle of why she did not wish to stop refused to be given up. It renewed itself with each of his apologies. Stumbling ludicrously, she knew that she still wished to go on. What she did not know at that time of her life was that she had secrets that hitherto she had kept even from herself.

Then, all in a moment, the strange thing happened. She felt that colour, that stress and anger never brought there, rise slow and warm into her cheeks. Her glance had merely rested for a moment on that hand of hers that lay slender as a willow leaf in his, but the riddle was a puzzle no longer. Abashed, she *had* surprised a secret.

She had caught herself wishing—half wishing—she did not quite know what—that she too had taken off her glove.

Her colour lasted for half-a-minute; then, perhaps because of the colour, her voice became matter-of-fact. She glanced up at him.

"I'm sorry you failed in your examination," she said.

Louie was tall, but his head was clear and away above hers. He looked down, earnest, anxious, smiling, all three.

"It doesn't matter," he said. "Why should it?" he added.

Louie had thought that it had mattered a great deal, but she was still a little bewildered. Even out of the answer to the riddle another seemed to have sprung already. She laughed a little.

"Oh—only that one doesn't like to be beaten," she said.

This too he seemed to give profound yet (if such a thing may be) absentminded attention.

"Is anybody ever beaten?" he asked slowly. "I mean, unless they deserve to be?"

Archie and Evie Soames had just overtaken them again, laughing together, as, hand in hand, they took a running glide towards the door. His remark came oddly from a doubly beaten man. What then did he call a beating? . . . She looked covertly at the two hands again.

"But—mayn't circumstances be too strong for you?"

This again he considered. "Circumstances are strong," he admitted. "But then, if one's a fool, so are a good many other people. There's always that chance, you see."

He spoke as gently as if he had been speaking to a child, but Louie suddenly found herself wondering whether he had accepted the inevitable after all. This hardly sounded like it. She spoke quietly.

"Nobody thinks you're a fool just because you failed—at least I don't."

"Failed?" he repeated, as if puzzled. . . "Oh, you mean the examination! Of course I ought never to have gone in for it. (Oh dear, another bump—I'm afraid you find me hopeless.)"

"Not have gone in for it? Why?"

The lion's eyes looked at her in surprise.

"Why? Why, because I failed." He seemed to consider it an entirely conclusive answer.

"But you'll surely try again?" said Louie.

"Eh? 'Try,' did you say? . . . Oh, the men who have to try are no good. For that matter it's always the duffers who try the hardest. I admit they pull it off, but then things are arranged so that the duffers can pull them off—have to be, I suppose. But the men who aren't duffers—"

He stopped suddenly.

"What?" she said.

But once more she had the feeling that she had only just swum into the field of his vision. It was singularly disconcerting. His smile, which had disappeared, appeared again. He seemed to remember that he was at a dance.

"I suppose you're coming back after Christmas?" he said.

It was not very likely, but she said: "Very likely. You were saying, about the men who aren't duffers—"

Again he got her focus. "Was I? Well, there aren't so many of them that we need bother about them. So you are coming back?"

Louie found him extraordinary, unclassifiable. She could not say that his answers were not ready; they were instant to the point; but somehow they weren't answers. Of course, they *were* answers if you liked, but they seemed in some way to be private communings as well. She wondered whether he was in the habit of talking much to himself; he spoke rather as if he was—as if, his consciousness of her presence notwithstanding, he considered himself to be as good as alone now.

Louie had heard the expression "second self"—well, this, "second self" or not, was certainly a curious accord. And then he allowed that deliberate, altogether discordant smile (that might just as well have been hooked round his ears like a false beard) to come between, and asked her if she was coming back after Christmas!

Then—this came suddenly—she knew for a certainty what hitherto had hung in doubt—that she would not be coming back after Christmas. She must sit down. Of course, it was to have been expected. She had been unwise to dance.

She spoke faintly. "Please take me to a seat."

Quite automatically he did so. He led her to the **E** of reference-books. The waltz closed. So did Louie's eyes.

"Please leave me alone for a few minutes," she murmured.

He bowed, and retired as automatically as he had come.

In a few minutes she felt better, but she still sat in the little book-lined recess. Her eyes remained closed, but not now altogether from faintness. She heard Mr. Mackie's voice, apparently a long way off, shouting, "Come on—let's get the ice broken!" and partners were being chosen for the Shop-Girl Lancers. More minutes passed. Louie, her eyes still closed, had begun once more to think of that secret she had surprised within herself.

She doubted herself profoundly now. For all she now knew her nature might contain other such secrets as this that had sent the warm blood into her cheeks at a touch—nay, at the thought of a touch. She might have, so to speak, a basic, unsuspected layer of them, needing only to be stirred to provide surprise after surprise. Those surprises might make all she had hitherto known—all—seem stupid and flat and commonplace. If so, why must the discovery come now? Secrets from herself—now? Impossible!

But, as if limned on her closed lids, she saw the two hands again, her own like a lanceolate leaf, lying within that great masculine engine of his.

And all at once she felt unutterably lonely.

It was some time before she opened her eyes again. By that time Mr. Mackie had succeeded in breaking the ice. The floor shook to the fourth figure of the Shop-Girl Lancers, and Louie saw, beyond the reference-books, the Alcazar beauty swung clear off the ground, a goldfish whirling almost horizontally past. Miss Levey's skirts followed, their owner crying, "Help, help!" . . . "*For it ain't the proper way to treat a la-ady!*" Mr. Mackie's jubilant voice sang—and when the figure ended there were shouts and clapping of hands and uproarious cries of "Again, again!"

By-and-by Louie rose. She walked up the room again. At the piano Mr. Mackie, who was to sing, was now confidentially humming the air of his song into the hired pianist's ear. Mr. Jeffries, once more looking as if he needed a niche and a plinth, was standing in his original place, by the folding door. Miss Levine and Archie Merridew were half hidden behind the piano; and Kitty Windus, radiant, was openly flirting with the pale student called Richardson. Evie Soames had just spoken to Mr. Jeffries; she was sulking at Archie's desertion of her. Then Mr. Weston announced, solemnly and distinctly, that Mr. Mackie was about to add to the enjoyment of all present by singing a song entitled "That Gorgonzola Cheese." Applause greeted the announcement, and Mr. Mackie, who had slipped behind the piano for a moment and returned with his coat on the wrong side out, began.

Louie found herself once more by the side of Mr. Jeffries.

"I should like some coffee," she said.

The coffee was in an adjoining room. For the first time since she had been at the School Louie did not want to hear Mr. Mackie.

But the hint was lost on Mr. Jeffries.

"Eh? Certainly," he said, and went away in search of the coffee.

"'Oh—that—Gorgonzola Cheese!'"

Mr. Mackie sang,

> *"It must have been unhealthy, I suppose,*
> *For the old Tom Cat fell dead upon the mat*
> *When the niff got up his nose!"'*

Kitty was laughing almost hysterically.

> *"'Talk about the flavour of the crackling of the pork!*
> *I guess it wasn't half so strong*
> *As the delicate effluvia that filled our house*
> *When the Gorgonzola Cheese went wrong!"'*

Mr. Jeffries had returned with Louie's coffee, but Louie barely touched it. Great stupid fellow!

Then he turned to her with some merely banal remark, and Louie, giving it all the answer it deserved, turned and left him.

That unspeakable loneliness had come upon her again.

Louie made no further attempt to talk to Mr. Jeffries. She watched another dance, heard Mr. Weston recite "The Raven," and then went to the cloakroom for her shawl. There she came upon Kitty Windus, who had found it necessary to do up her hair again.

"You surely aren't going?" Kitty exclaimed. She herself was a-tremble with flirtation and happiness. "Why, you're as bad as Mr. Jeffries! Though I will admit that even *he* came out of his shell for once. I shall begin to think Miriam's right soon!" She gave Louie an arch look.

Louie's opinion was that Mr. Jeffries had never been more completely concealed in his shell than he had been that even, but "Oh, has he gone?" she said indifferently.

"Yes, a few minutes ago. Isn't everything going splendidly! Why, Mr. Mackie's a host in himself!"

"Quite," said Louie, passing her shawl over her head.

"I suppose we shall see you in the morning?" said Kitty. "Everybody's coming to help to clear away."

"Very well," said Louie.

And as the piano broke into the prelude to the waltz cotillion she left.

But she did not leave that dingy Holborn third floor, never to enter it again, without a grateful word to Mr. Mackie. She came upon him on a landing. His trousers were French-chalked almost to the knees with the vigour of his dancing, and for his next song he had put on a false nose with blue whiskers attached to it. He was making sure that the adornment did not interfere with his whistle.

"Good-bye, Mr. Mackie," said Louie, holding out her hand.

Mr. Mackie stopped the whistle. "What, you toddling, Miss Causton?" he said. "Why, we ain't properly warmed up yet!"

"I must go. And"—she smiled almost fondly at him—"I should like to thank you."

Mr. Mackie was quite conscious of desert. "Not at all," he said. "You mean the 'Gorgonzola Cheese,' I suppose? Went all right, didn't it? Never known that song fail yet: it always gets 'em—"

"Oh, for more than that. If you're ever thinking of setting up a cure I daresay I could find you a few patients. You're wonderful. Good-bye."

"Say olive oil, but not good-bye—and Merry Christmas," said Mr. Mackie.

But Louie knew that it was good-bye.

PART III

MORTLAKE ROAD

I

On a sunny morning in mid-January Louie Causton went to see, but not necessarily to be seen by, her father. Captain Cecil Chaffinger accompanied her. As they walked across Richmond Park they talked.

"You're sure the walk isn't too much for you, Mops?" said the Captain solicitously.

She pressed his arm. "No, I'm ever so much better for it."

"We could get a cart or something at the Star and Garter, you know."

"I'd much rather walk, Chaff. We can take the train back."

"All right, little Mops."

They walked for a few minutes in silence; then—

"That woman wasn't—wasn't a beast, was she?" Chaff asked.

"Mrs. Leggat?"

"If that's her name. I mean, there was no row?"

"Not the least in the world."

The Captain tugged at his moustache. "H'm! Not like you. Ever leave anywhere without a row before, Mops?"

Louie laughed a little. "Now you mention it, I don't think I ever did," she admitted. "But there wasn't a word said. She knew, and I knew she knew. So I cleared out. That was all. She made me some beef-tea before I left."

Again they walked in silence.

The daintiest of hoar-frosts lay over the Park; on Putney Heath they had passed skaters. The keen wind had reddened the Captain's nose, and Louie could not help smiling as he took out his handkerchief for the twentieth time. She had remembered Mr. Mackie.

"Ought to have a silk one a day like this," Chaff grunted, blowing hard. "Makes you perfectly raw. . . I say, dear old Mops—"

"What, old boy?"

"Anything *I* could have done, you know—"

She squeezed his arm again. "I shall be giving you plenty to do presently. And you say he's not a bad sort."

"Oh—" said the Captain doubtfully.

"Well, you'll take me in, and then wait outside till I've seen for myself."

But at that Chaff rebelled. "Hanged if I do—dash it all, it's a public-house! You'll find me in the parlour or whatever it is."

"How old is he?"

"Let me see: he'll be fifty. Yes, he'll be fifty. Your mother's fifty-four."

"You'll remember your promise, Chaff?"

"About where you are? Oh, I'll be mum as the grave. Don't you forget yours."

"No. You shall come and see me."

The Captain sighed. His Mops was a strange being. That fool Moone had taken the wrong way with her, but a better way might have been found than this. Well, Chaff would have a word or two with Mr. Buck Causton himself.

They continued their walk.

When Louie had first resolved that she would seek her father, nothing had seemed more natural. In prospect, the thing had been simplicity itself. But it was, somehow, less simple now. Indeed, its difficulties had increased with every step she took. What about Buck? Must he necessarily make her so very welcome? Suppose, when she made her announcement, he should shake hands, ask how her mother was, offer her tea (or whatever publicans did offer ladies), say he had been very glad to see her, and let her go again? How, in the face of that, could she say: "I am your daughter; I really don't know why I have come; I have stayed away a good long time, but here I am, needing friends; why I need friends I will explain to your wife." Was it not likely that Buck had had more than enough of her family?

Had Chaff, as they descended to Kingston, once more urged that she was on a wild-goose chase, as likely as not she would have turned back at the first word.

They reached Buck's public-house—The Molyneux Arms, near the corner of Kingston Bridge.

"Well," said Chaff, stopping, "what do we do now, Mops?"

"We go in, I suppose," said Louie. Without pausing, she moved towards the largest door (there was "Public Bar" written upon it) of an establishment that, if it lacked the garishness of a modern drinking-palace, was yet not quite the red-curtained, lattice-windowed, Christmas-number hostelry of Louie's imaginings. But Chaff, with a "No, not there," drew her round the corner to a quieter door, where small bay-trees stood in green tubs. The step had a brightly polished brass sill and a thick rubber mat perforated with the name "Molyneux Arms." Beyond the little vestibule were double doors with cut-glass panels and a diagonal brass bar on each and a piston for automatic closing at the top.

"Perhaps you'd better wait here," said Chaff.

"All right," said Louie, now heartily wishing she had not left her new abode in Mortlake Road, Putney.

With a soft sigh of the piston, the brass-barred doors closed behind Chaff.

This entrance lay in a short blind alley off the main street, the end of which seemed to be closed by a stableyard. Somebody over a brick wall was walking a horse over cobbles, and a man's voice muttered, "Come up." There was a light clashing of harness, and the same voice began a soft but strong singing, hoisting itself to the higher notes as if the interpolated aspirates had been so many stirrups:

> *"No re-(h)est—but the gra-(h)ave*
> *For the pi-(h)ilgrim of Love!—"*

Then a back door opened, and a woman's voice was heard.

"A gentleman to see you, James."

The song ceased. "A what, Susan?" said the man's voice. "Remember—"

"A gentleman—in a top hat," said the second voice.

"You know that travellers sometimes have top hats, Susan," cautioned the first voice.

"I'm sure it's a gentleman, James—"

"Very well, let us hope you're not mistaken and that you were hooked up behind. Ask the gentleman to wait a minute."

The voices ceased.

Instinctively Louie had walked to a half-open coach door and had looked through. She saw a bright little picture. A horse was being put into a gay yellow trap, and the man who was buckling the harness had begun to sing again:

> *"Oryn—thia, my Belovèd!—"*

All that Louie could see of him was a pair of glossy black boots and a pair of grey check trousers cut close about the knee. The harness twinkled; the horse's coat shone in the sun like Mr. Jeffries' hair; and somebody within the stable was running water into a bucket. Then the man came round the horse, and she saw him—cropped silver hair, long dewlapped chin, and a back and shoulders that might have served

Henson's turn yet. And as Louie watched, with no more emotion than if the scene had been one on a coloured bioscope, he sang again:

"Oryn—thia, my Belovèd!—"

Then, as she watched, it came over her for the first time that she had planned and was performing a suspect thing. She had no right to inspect this man and then to know him or not to know him, as she chose. He had no less right to inspect her. She, not he, stood to gain; cards on the table, then; either she must go away at once, taking Chaff with her, or else take her courage in both hands without further spying.

Which was, perhaps, as much as to say that she had already seen and was willing to risk it.

She passed through the half-open door into the yard.

Yet even as she advanced she had a final cowardice. By a man at any rate, anything would be forgiven her, and she really had had a long walk. . . There was a bench by the stable door. . . But she pulled herself together. No, not that. She was not faint, only very, very pale. She continued to advance.

Then Buck looked up, and their eyes met.

They say of a newly born infant that your first impression of facial resemblance is that to which the child, grown a man, will return. So perhaps it was for one moment with father and daughter. But, if so, it passed instantly. Buck made an upward, deferential gesture of his forefinger.

"Sha'n't be three minutes, m'm," he said. "Now, Judson, the lady's here! He's just ready, m'm. A beautiful day!"

Then something in Louie's look seemed to strike him.

"It *is* for Mrs. Allonby's, m'm, isn't it? For one-fifteen; one-fifteen Allonby, Richards, seven tonight. You needn't have come; he'll be there sharp."

Louie was looking steadily at her father. "You've made a mistake," she said.

"What? Hi, Judson! What's this?"

"I came—I came—with the gentleman who's just asked for you. Don't you—don't you—" she faltered and stopped.

"But aren't you from Mrs. Allonby's?"

Louie was conscious that she was becoming pitifully flurried. She could not believe now that she had ever thought this would be an easy thing to do. And she would have to do it all herself; he had a handsome, slightly pompous face, but it was not the face of a man who apprehends things by intuition. She tried again.

"You are Mr. Causton, aren't you?"

"Beg pardon, m'm? You see, one ear—" The Piker had burst the drum of one of Buck's ears. He inclined his head. "What did you say, m'm?"

Suddenly Louie put one hand on the shaft of the trap and sank half sitting on the step. The trap dipped. Her pallor was now extreme.

"The gentleman who wishes to see you—" she began again.

"Yes, m'm?"

"I—I came with him—"

"Yes, m'm—aren't you well, m'm?"

"Don't you know me?"

"If it isn't Mrs. Allonby's, one-fifteen—" said Buck.

"His name—the gentleman's name—"

Then, as the horse lifted a foot, she slipped a little on the step. She might not have fallen, but his old and instinctive muscular discipline counted for something. Buck had made a remarkably swift movement, and his arm now supported her. Suddenly she surrendered her weight to him.

"Here, m'm," said the astonished Buck, "come and set down on the bench."

Louie turned up entreating eyes. "You can't guess?"

"If it's Richards, seven—"

"The gentleman's name—I came with—is Chaffinger—"

"You said—?"

"Chaffinger."

She was too close to him to notice that he too had suddenly become white. He still held her, but slowly half a cubic foot of air came from his chest. Probably with a purely mechanical movement he set her on her feet. His hand was at his sound ear.

"Will you say it again, m'm?" he said huskily.

Louie did so.

"Cap-Captain Chaffinger, m'm?"

"Oh," Louie choked, "don't call me 'm'm'!"

"You did say Captain Chaffinger?"

Then, leaning limply against the shaft, Louie began to speak low and rapidly.

"Send me away if you like—perhaps I was stupid to come—but I wanted—I wanted—I couldn't bear it any longer—I'm all alone— father! I'm Louie—Louie—"

Only Buck's Maker knows whether even then he fully understood. His grey eyes were stupidly on her grey eyes. Her voice, as she continued to mutter broken phrases, possibly lost itself in his deaf ear; but some other sense informed him that she was telling him that she was his daughter—his daughter—

And then at one of her phrases, he seemed to come sluggishly to life. He repeated the phrase after her.

"Putney, m'm? Did you say Putney?" he said.

"Yes, I live there—"

"You live in Putney? Whereabouts in Putney?"

"Mortlake Road."

Buck made another sluggish effort. A quarter of a century and more before he had said to the Honourable Emily: "*The* Bible, Miss?" Now he said to his daughter:

"*The* Mortlake Road?"

"I suppose so."

"You live there?"

"Yes."

Now Mallard Bois and Trant were more than geographically remote from Buck. They had the immeasurable remoteness of the Scarisbricks. But Putney was near. To keep himself in spring and condition, he frequently walked over to Putney. Putney was a place you could walk to, and it had streets and houses and a green Tillings' bus. And they rowed the boat race there. Therefore, while it outraged all Order that a Scarisbrick should live there, that fact nevertheless brought his daughter into the same world with himself. For the first time he looked seeingly at her, and as he looked, there vanished, more quickly than a finger is snapped, whatever images of her had beguiled his fancy through the years.

This, then, was she, standing against the shaft with head back, lips parted, brows entreatingly drawn, her whole pose an appeal.

"Father," she was saying, smiling crookedly through those rare things, her tears—

Judson came out of the stable. Buck gave him a curt order, and the trap moved away. Its departure left Louie standing by the little bench outside the stable door. Buck had taken a step towards her. He was murmuring something quite ridiculous—something about "strictly for the gentry." Perhaps he remembered that had his little girl been a little boy he would have given her instruction for nothing at the Sparring Academy in Bruton Street.

All in a moment he passed his arm about Louie. Scarisbrick or not, she was going to be a Causton and his for once—just for once. In an hour he might be calling her "m'm" again, but just for once—his face was beautiful.

"That little girl," he said foolishly, holding her with as gentle a fear as if she had been still in her cradle.

Louie's answer was to faint suddenly on his breast.

But of the Molyneux Arms in a moment. A word about Mortlake Road first.

Two houses had been thrown into one to form the establishment at which Louie had now resided for a week. Officially it was a nursing home; actually it accepted declared invalids and quite well but unrobust lodgers alike. Miss Cora Mayville "ran" it; her cousin, Miss Dot Mayville, was "sister," and from four to eight uniformed nurses came and went continually. None of them had theories, moral, social, or of any other description; to them things were as they were. Nurse Meekins made Louie's bed as who should say, "Helpers of people in trouble do not go beyond their proper business"; Nurse Chalmers brought her letters or called her to dinner in the narrowminded spirit of one who leaves the systematics of charity to others. All were reprehensibly incurious and shockingly affectionate, and so far was Louie's case from being peculiar that, in the eyes of the law at any rate, Miss Dot Mayville was herself twice a parent. Twice (when, from reasons Lord Moone could have explained, the real parents had refused to do so) she had signed the birth-certificates of undesired infants. This irregularity the registrar for the district held perpetually over her head. She laughed, and held other things over his head in return. They were engaged to be married.

It was to this retreat that Buck drove Louie back that January evening, cutting "Richards, seven" without compunction. Poor Chaff had been sent off soon after lunch; there was somebody else to fetch and despatch his Mops now. Buck lifted Louie from the trap and rang the bell of one of the two brass-plated doors. A German youth dressed as a waiter appeared, and Buck bade him hold the horse. Then he went with Louie up to her room. He took off her hat and coat for her; he seemed unable to leave her. He had learned how it was with her.

He had hardly turned a hair at the news. He accepted it as part of the Scheme of Things. To him also indiscretions were of two kinds—indiscretions, and the indiscretions of the Scarisbricks. Only a wistful look had crossed his face; he had hoped Louie's somebody was a gentleman otherwise than in the top-hat sense of the word; and Louie had reassured him about that. For the rest, it was not for Buck to inquire into the private affairs of these great ones. He would as soon have allowed the young German who held the horse to inquire into his own.

"That little girl," he said once more, holding her away from him at the side of her bed.

"And you won't call me 'm'm,' daddy?" Louie laughed.

Buck gave it thought; it was not so simple as it looked. "And you really took daddy's name?" he asked. He had asked it twenty times already.

"Of course."

"And told all those young ladies?" (Louie had related the incident of Burnett Minor and the "Life and Battles.") "All about daddy and the Piker?"

"Of course!"

Buck found it too wonderful. He enfolded his little girl again.

"But you must go now," Louie said by-an-by.

"But I can come in the morning?"

"Yes. And, daddy—"

"Little girl?"

"You'll be good to poor old Chaff? He's fond of me too."

Buck promised that he would. Had there been none other, the tantrums of the Honourable Emily were no doubt bond enough between them.

The next morning Buck had to be told that eight o'clock was too early for a visit, and so, on the next morning again, he did not turn up until eleven. After that eleven became his accustomed hour. Wet or fine was the same to him, and he cancelled all afternoon orders for the trap; his little girl must have the trap at her disposal for a daily drive. And because his fidelity to the Social Order and their own professional tolerances amounted in Louie's case to pretty much the same thing, the nurses one and all fell in love with Buck.

And here, once for all, or at any rate for a long time, a cogent matter may be dismissed, even as those pagan nurses dismissed it. It is Louie's conviction of moral guilt as apart from her persuasion of the practical inconveniences of it. Louie Causton would have been poor stuff for the hot gospeller to practise upon. There were things she would have had undone, and that not merely because the consequences pressed upon her; as they could not be undone, she had begun the tune and intended to fiddle it out. What she saw fit to hide her historian hides also. Louie seized what happiness she could, and it served. She was sorrier for Chaff than she was for herself. She would have been less happy had she taken Uncle Augustus's way out.

And whether the days were happy or not, at any rate they were peacefully alike. Breakfast with the nurses, a morning or afternoon drive with Buck or a walk along the river bank or on Putney Heath, tea (if they drove) perhaps at Kingston, supper with the nurses again, and bed—that was the tale of them. She kept her promise to Chaff; several times he came to see her. Twice he met Buck. At these meetings the shade of the Honourable Emily almost visibly presided. . . Chaff tried to talk of "Lives and Battles," Buck of the same—it was not for him to choose topics before his betters. And once, but once only, Buck brought Mrs. Buck, formerly Susan Emmidge, the chemist's servant at Mallard Bois. He hooked her up behind himself before they left Kingston, and Louie did her the same service at the end of the visit. For the rest, if Louie wanted to see her father's second wife she had to go to the Molyneux Arms to do so.

As the singer of "The Pilgrim of Love" Buck was known far and abroad up the Thames. It will be believed that he contrived to get an infinite personal pathos into the song; he also made of it, by means of those gratuitous aspirates, an affective athletic exercise in breathing.

> *"No re-(*h*)est—but the gra-(*h*)ave*
> *For the Pi-(*h*)ilgrim of Love!—"*

As he closed his eyes at each soaring, the effect was as if he inwardly looked back on that remarkable pilgrimage of his own. Bidden to marry, he had married; bidden to unmarry and to marry again, he had done so; and at a word from Louie he would have taken up the pilgrimage once more.

But while Buck exalted the Scarisbricks high above himself, so also he exalted himself high above all beneath him. He ruled the Molyneux Arms with a rod of iron. Only mediately and through him would the two barmaids have dared to address Louie; and his wife's position was altogether anomalous. It was only because Louie would have it so that she sat down to tea with them; and, what with her hooks and eyes and Buck's perpetual admonitions, there was little rest but the grave for her either. Buck subscribed to the *Almanack de Gotha* and *Modern Society*; these were always to hand; but *The Licensed Victuallers' Gazette*, which he took in the way of business, was kept out of Louie's way. Mr. Mackie he would have torn from limb to limb. Far more royalist than the king was Buck; Radicalism was chaos, which word he pronounced "tchayoss." Of pugilism, save to Chaff, he never spoke. "God bless the Squire and his relations."

And (Louie thought) God bless this simple-hearted father of hers also. Buck in the ring had been a better man than Uncle Augustus in the House of Lords, and Henson would not have looked twice at Chaff. Granted he was pompous; with a little more pompousness her mother would have come more creditably out of that old affair. So much for the Scarisbricks. Already, in January, Louie loved her father; by March his daily visit was a necessity of her life. She had been right; her destiny was quite as likely to be bound up with Buck and his beer-pumps as with anything in that dingy old Business School.

Of the Business School she still thought a good deal, however. She could not forget the interesting little drama of which she had seen, as it were, the first act. Somehow, time and distance had simplified some of its details without diminishing her interest in it, and, as she walked along the Putney towpath by day, or lay awake in her white-painted room at night, she wondered that this should be so. By the brutal logic of events, Rainham Parva should have been nearer to her than Holborn; but Rainham Parva seemed now disproportionately remote. Why?

Had the conclusion which persisted in presenting itself not been impossible, perhaps she would not have faced it so frankly. It was impossible—manifestly absurd—that Mr. Jeffries should have any hold on her imagination. Therefore she allowed herself to consider it. No doubt the fancies which filled her head would pass and be forgotten.

Give them a month, then—two months.

She gave them that, and more. They did not pass. But that, no doubt, was due to the curious interrupted story. She felt as if she was reading an interesting serial tale, for the next instalment of which she was suddenly required to wait another month. She wanted to know what was going to happen among the fair, perky boy, the girl who resembled Polly Ross, the lionlike Mr. Jeffries, and that apocryphal fourth actor in the piece. When she had learned that she would close the book. In the meantime she occupied herself, as serial readers do, with guessing.

The spring was advancing towards May when there happened something that suddenly precipitated her guessings. Buck still came daily, but she walked more in the back garden of the nursing home now and less on the heath and on the towpath, and drove, when she did drive, more slowly. Sometimes on her drives a nurse accompanied her. Her doctor found her health excellent.

The thing that happened began with Richenda Earle. Some weeks before, Louie had had a letter from Richenda forwarded from Sutherland Place, which she had neglected to answer; and Richenda had apparently written again, this time to her sister. Louie now gathered that Mrs. Leggat had kept the reason for her disappearance from Mr. Weston, but not from Richenda. By way of Richenda and Mr. Weston it had now reached the Business School. A hastily scrawled letter from Kitty Windus informed Louie of this. Kitty wanted to come and see her.

Well, there was no reason why Kitty should not come. Louie wrote and told her so.

She came on a Saturday afternoon. It was not urgently necessary that Louie should have received her in bed, but the recollection of the spinster's peering eyes held some obscure prompting. Moreover, to receive Kitty in bed would be an intimation that the call must not be a long one, and she had arranged its duration with Miss Dot Mayville.

"Miss Windus," Miss Dot announced, and Kitty entered.

She had brought Louie a bunch of violets; that was the first of several new amenities Louie noticed in her manner. Louie discouraged the second amenity, which was a shy motion as if to embrace her. And the third showed when, after a few minutes in which Kitty's fluttered spirits had become a little calmer (*she* was not the one to turn her back on people in trouble, she had said, let others hold up their heads as they pleased), she wistfully took Louie's hand on the coverlet. She had cried over Louie a little. Her eyes were still wet.

"Of course—but I don't know whether you've heard—I might have been just like everybody else, only something else has made an awful difference too," she said, her eyes downcast.

"Oh? What else?" Louie asked a little offhandedly. She had not wanted to be wept over.

"Oh, then you haven't heard. . . I'm engaged. I've been engaged nearly two months."

"Really? Then I must congratulate you. Is it a secret who to?"

"No," said Kitty. "It's to Mr. Jeffries."

Slowly Louie sat up. She turned, as if, like Buck, she had been deaf on one side. "*Who?*" she asked.

"Yes. To Mr. Jeffries. Since early in March. You remember he told Archie there was somebody?—and," Kitty became suddenly voluble, "I couldn't believe my ears at first. I'd never dreamed—never dreamed. And after I'd been such a beast—I don't mean a beast exactly, but getting at him, you know. I was just as bad as the others—about his baths and all that. Oh, I did feel ashamed—as mean as mean—oh!" She choked a little. "I don't mind saying it now, but I'd—I'd begun to be afraid I should *never* get off!"

"Yes—no, I mean," Louie murmured, dazed.

"Just fancy, it's being me! That night, when he asked me, I thought I should have gone clean off it. Sometimes I can hardly believe it yet. I hadn't a notion—not a notion! And it makes everything perfectly wonderful, knowing a man's so struck on you, though he *is* quiet and don't say much about it. Of course they mean all the more, that sort.

We walk along the streets, but he won't let me stop out late for fear of tiring me, and he always takes me right to the door, and I'm trying hard not to be selfish, but it makes me so sorry for other girls who haven't got off—and perhaps if I sell some of my shares to start us with we can get married next year—if he gets a permanency, that is."

Louie was still thunderstruck. Mr. Jeffries engaged to—Kitty Windus! That unnamed personage was—Kitty Windus! She, Louie, was asked to believe *that*, in the face of all she had seen!

"I am glad," she found herself murmuring again.

"Did *you* guess?" Kitty asked eagerly. She would have given her ears to be told that somebody else had guessed.

"No," Louie replied, and added, seeing Kitty's fallen face: "I should have thought Mr. Merridew. You seemed such great friends."

At that Kitty broke in: "Poor Archie! I said it made one selfish. . . His father's very ill. We were going on Putney Heath today, all four of us, Archie and Evie and Jeff and me; but Archie had a wire to go home this morning, poor Archie, and so I'm going to meet the others by-and-by. But anyway, if anything does happen, he'll be able to get married as soon as he likes—he's an only son."

At this Louie was even more startled. Mr. Jeffries and the Soames girl together at that moment! She remembered those irrevocable looks.

"So Mr. Merridew and Miss Soames are engaged, then?" she said.

"Well," Kitty admitted, "it comes to the same thing. They're as good as. I wish Jeff was coming into a bit, like Archie."

"You say they're here, at Putney, this afternoon?"

"Jeff and Evie? Yes. I'm meeting them at five."

Even as Louie was inwardly predicting that Kitty would not see her Mr. Jeffries at five, Miss Dot Mayville entered. But Louie did not want Kitty to go just yet. She wanted to know more of this extraordinary development of her drama. "May we have some tea?" she asked, and Miss Dot went out again. Louie lay back on her pillow and frowned at the foot of her white-painted bed.

"It's very kind of you to give up your afternoon to me," she said by-and-by.

"Oh, my dear, as if I wouldn't!" Kitty broke out almost reproachfully. "I keep telling myself I mustn't be selfish, when Jeff and I have years before us—I'm just beginning to realise it—years—and, oh dear, here I am, selfish again, talking all about myself and never a word about you."

But Louie did not want words about herself. She wanted to hear all, all, about Kitty and Mr. Jeffries. The thing became more incredible moment by moment.

"I'm sorry about Mr. Merridew's father," she said presently. "I suppose Miss Soames is very much upset?"

"Frightfully," said Kitty. "But Jeff's looking after her. It was he who persuaded her to go out this afternoon. It's better for her than moping indoors."

"Perhaps Mr. Merridew asked him to."

"Oh no. He only got the wire this morning. But it isn't a surprise. Jeff saw him last night—" She checked herself. She had no gibes about brown-paper parcels now.

"Well, you'll be quite a courting quartet," said Louie presently, with a brightness she did not feel.

"Yes; jolly, isn't it? But there, I'm simply *not* going to talk about myself one moment longer. I feel a regular beast. But it's only because I'm so happy. Now let's talk about you. How long are you going to be here? What sort of people are they? Isn't it fearfully expensive? Are you frightened?"

The suppressed inquisitive questions and Louie's preoccupied parries lasted through tea. At a quarter to five Kitty rose. Again Louie found herself wondering whether Kitty would see her Mr. Jeffries that day. Kitty bent over her.

"I should like to kiss you, dear, if you'd let me," she said timidly. "You wouldn't believe what a difference it makes. And I'd love to come again; I love little babies. Now I must run. I won't say a word to Miriam Levey; you know what she is—but I simply must learn not to say those things. Good-bye, dear."

And she was off, waving her skimpy hand from the door.

Louie did not know why her heart should ache already, as at a premonition—for she had no certitude. Indeed, in all that portion of her relation to Mr. Jeffries she had no certitude; but she was only a little less certain on that account. Already she entirely rejected the figment in which Kitty so pathetically believed. Months before she had snapped her fingers at his impudent tale of a shadowy *fiancée*; now she wondered whether he had not been caught in his own trap and found himself compelled, by mere daily exigencies, to give that shadow substance— the substance of Kitty. Impossible—and yet the conceivable alternatives were equally impossible! Incredible that he should have chosen Kitty for his stalking-horse—yet whom else had there been to choose? If this really was a putting-upon the Business School, Mr. Jeffries would see to it that his dupe was as known as his purpose was secret. That left him three candidates from whom to choose indifferently—Kitty, Miriam Levey, and herself.

In her indignation she was unconscious of the pink that crept like a danger signal into her cheeks.

That poor, unconscious, betrayed woman!

Good gracious! It was blackguardly and monstrous! Kitty of all women! To have "predestined spinster" written large all over you was bad enough, without being played upon thus and then cast back into spinsterhood after all! And this new softness of Kitty's, this timid opening of the heart, this new, awkward unselfishness, these pathetic little maxims of conduct! The man must be a cur. Deliberately to waken a heart that was sealed, asleep and not unhappy, and then to leave it to a pain it must keep for ever—good gracious!

Still ignorant of the tell-tale red in her own cheeks, she found Mr. Jeffries vile.

But she must be just to Mr. Jeffries. Perhaps she was wrong. Perhaps there was—nay, there must be—something she didn't know. Why, even if Mr. Jeffries could be so cruel, Kitty herself could hardly be so blind. Struggle with new magnanimities as she would, jealousy was native to Kitty, and jealousy has sharp eyes. No, she, Louie herself, was building a fantastic fabric. It was mere common-sense that Kitty must be supposed to be capable of looking after herself.

But it was one thing to tell herself that she must suspend her judgment and another to do it. That theory of hers seemed to unroll itself brightly and convincingly before her again. She would discard it when she found one that better explained the known facts. Mr. Jeffries was with Evie Soames at that moment. Louie's thoughts flew to Evie Soames.

It was then that she became conscious that her cheeks were hot. It was then also that she told herself angrily that they were not, and found them grow hotter still. The hotter they grew the more she denied their heat. Why should they grow hot? And even granting that they were hot, wasn't this imposture that was being practised on Kitty enough to make anybody's cheek hot? That was it. That discovery made, she admitted the heat—for Kitty's sake. That that great, taciturn, clever man should be infatuated by that pretty fool she resented—for Kitty's sake. That his sleek head, bright as the coat of Buck's horse, should stoop over that empty dark one she found ironically unfit—for Kitty's sake. She told herself all this, forgetting that she had just set Kitty's engagement down also as an absurdity. Her indignation would have been neither more nor less honest had Mr. Jeffries engaged himself (as according to her theory he might quite well have done) to Miriam Levey.

Or to herself.

She lay, the colour coming and going.

At last she roused herself and sat up. "Pretty thoughts for an expectant mother!" she muttered. "I'll go downstairs and talk to Dot."

She dressed, and descended to the nurses' sitting-room in the basement.

Miss Dot and her Registrar were there; they had just come in from a walk. They were telling of a nightingale they had heard sing near Queens Mere. "Oh, and we saw your friend again, the one who came to tea," said Miss Dot, turning to Louie.

Louie pricked up her ears. "Oh? Alone?" she said quickly.

"Yes. Coming down Putney Hill."

"Yes, she said she was going to take a walk," Louie remarked.

But to herself she cried with conviction: "I knew it—I knew it—I knew it!"

For the rest of the evening she was lost in her own thoughts. Miss Cora Mayville worked a hand sewing machine; Miss Dot and her Registrar played bézique at a separate table; other nurses, in print aprons or cloaked and bonneted, came and went; but Louie sat and gazed into the fire. When spoken to she smiled mechanically and then resumed her gazing. There was no more continuity in her thoughts than there was in the shape of the flames that illumined her grey eyes. Roy appeared in them for a moment or two—she had seen Roy's name in *The Gazette* a week before—and then Roy was supplanted by Burnett Minor. Her old French governess at Trant popped up for no particular reason, and then she too gave place to Mr. Mackie. She heard Buck saying again, "That little girl"—and then came a wrangle between Dot and her Registrar. In the adjoining kitchen she heard sounds of frying, and then somebody came in to lay the table for supper. The gas rose and whistled as the stove in the next room was turned off. The three night nurses came down. Louie had her gruel where she sat, and at half-past nine went upstairs again. She got into bed, and dreamed that night that she was dancing with Mr. Jeffries again at the breaking-up party. Her hand lay like a willow leaf in his. "*You* understand," he was saying to her; "it's no good hiding things from *you*; *you've* got the key of it all. It had to be somebody, and you'd left. There was only Kitty for it. You see what an ignominious thing you escape. Don't tell me how degrading it is; I know it; but I'd do it a thousand times for the woman I loved and meant to marry."

Louie knew, in her dream, who that was.

Then she awoke with a start. The street lamp outside, shining through the venetian blinds, made long bars of light on the walls and ceiling. The hot-water bottle at her feet was cold. She heard the creaking of Dot's bed in the little dressing-room adjoining, and the minute ticking of her watch on the table by her bed-head. But what had woke her had been the sound of her own reply, in her dream, to Mr. Jeffries.

"You'll shuffle Kitty off," she had replied, still dancing with him, "but *I* should have found a way to keep you."

Then, with a deep sigh, she turned and went to sleep again.

III

Her boy was born towards the end of June. Her mother did not visit her; instead, she sent a letter the chief characteristic of which was fright that she had dared even so far to disobey her brother. Louie understood, and in her dictated reply made allowances. She wondered whether she should write to Roy also, but in the end did not. The child was born at three o'clock in the morning; he was hardly six hours old when Buck arrived. The old champion stood looking down on his little girl's little boy. It was long before he spoke.

"I wasn't let see you," he said, two big tears rolling down his cheeks.

"You shall teach him to box, daddy," said Louie, smiling up at him.

But Buck shook his head. "No, no," he said gently—"except just to take care of himself—when he's fourteen, perhaps—if I'm here. Swimming, not sparring. They're a queer lot, them in the ring."

"You must go now, Mr. Causton," said Miss Dot.

The boy was thirty hours old when there arrived for him a great case of toys suitable for a child of four. Buck and Chaff had been round the toyshops together. Mrs. Buck, disobeying her husband for the only time in her life, came by stealth with a flannel binder that might have enwrapped a six-pounds' child; Jim (as Louie had decided to call him), weighed ten pounds, beef to the heel.

He throve at once, and continued to thrive.

The pair of them were the pride of that pagan Putney Nursing Home.

The first of the two incidents that may be allowed to close this portion of Louie's story was a second visit by Kitty Windus to Louie.

She came at ten o'clock at night, and only with difficulty obtained admission. She was allowed ten minutes, on the condition that Louie was awake. Louie was awake. Kitty neither lifted her veil nor asked to see the child. There was no trace now of her little maxims of conduct; she spoke agitatedly, and out of a stinging, jealous pain.

"I've come to ask you something, Miss Causton, and you've got to tell me," she announced, without preface. "I've a right to know."

"Speak a little lower," said Louie, glancing at the babe. "Sit down and tell me what it is."

But Kitty would not sit. Incapable of grandeurs of style, she nevertheless attempted them.

"I don't know whether you happen to be aware what people are saying about you," she said. Her boat-shaped hat and Inverness cape gave her a little the appearance of a scanty tree with which some topiary artist had done his best.

Louie could not help smiling a little; she could have that kind of thing out with herself without calling in Kitty.

"My dear! Of course I know they might be saying anything!" She drew her child a little closer to her.

"Suppose we keep the my dears till we've finished talking," said Kitty coldly. "I mean what they're saying at the Business School."

Louie spoke quietly. "I suppose you mean about me and my boy?"

"Yes, I do mean that, and I've come to ask you to your face; *I'm* not the one to beat about the bush! I want to know who—" There was no need for Kitty to complete the sentence.

"You won't know that," said Louie, more quietly still.

"Ah! perhaps you won't tell me because you daren't?"

"I've not told anybody, and I'm not going to tell you. I'd die first. Perhaps before we go any further you'll tell me why you want to know?"

"You don't suppose I'd ask you if it wasn't my business, do you?"

Slowly Louie turned her eyes on her. She spoke slowly too. "We should get on more quickly if you didn't jump so to conclusions," she said. "I don't know what your conclusions are, but you seem to have made your mind up about something. If you'll change your tone I'll talk to you; if you won't, I won't."

At that Kitty began to sob. She had to lift her veil in order to put a wisp of wet handkerchief to her eyes. But she changed her tone.

"I only want to know," she said. "And I don't want to know if it isn't my business. But I *have* seen him look at you, and he *did* dance with you, and when they said—"

"Who said?" Louie interrupted; but she had already made a guess. "And said what?"

"Jeff, of course," Kitty replied. "Miriam Levey noticed him looking at you first, but after that I saw for myself. And you did dance with him. I might forgive him, but I'd never, never forgive *you*."

Louie suddenly put a question. Apparently it was for nothing less preposterous than that question that Kitty was here.

"One moment," she said. "Do you mean there's something about Mr. Jeffries and myself you want to know?"

"Yes; and I mean to know," Kitty snapped.

"And that's all?"

"Enough, *I* should say!"

"Please hear me out. In fact"—Louie paused for a moment and then rapped out sharply—"you want to know whether my lover was Mr. Jeffries?"

"That'll do to be going on with," said Kitty sullenly.

"Then I'll tell you if you'll tell me who said he was."

"I don't see what that's got to do with it, but I'll tell you if you like. Archie Merridew said so. There!"

Archie Merridew!—But Louie restrained her gasp. "Thank you," she said. "May I ask whether you've asked Mr. Jeffries? *He* might be in a position to know, you know."

"No, I haven't."

"But evidently you've seen something in his manner that would make it not quite impossible?"

"I tell you, you've danced with him, and he's looked at you in a sort of way—more than once, Miriam says—and you're trying to shuffle out of the question," said Kitty, her suspicions aflame again.

"Oh, I'll answer the question! If it had been he"—she glanced at the little head under her breast—"I'd tell you in a minute—for my baby's sake, you see. But it was not; and you might have saved yourself a journey if you'd gone to him first. And now please tell me a little more."

Kitty still looked at her suspiciously. "You said you'd die sooner than tell," she cried quaveringly.

"You mean you don't believe me? Well, I can't make you. If I told you the truth you'd just think I'd made up a name."

"It *was* somebody else?" cried Kitty eagerly.

If it wasn't Mr. Jeffries, naturally—there was the child—

"Oh, I *want* to believe you!" Kitty suddenly broke out.

Louie laughed desperately. "Well, my dear, you may. If it was so, I suppose you'd get it out of me. It isn't, that's all. And now I think I've a right to know exactly what this Mr. Merridew has been saying."

Kitty looked hard at her for one moment longer, and then sank on her knees by the side of the bed. She had no choice but to believe. She broke into a torrent of words, low-spoken, not to rouse the child. Louie heard them, amazed. Slowly her incredulity turned into contempt.

The horrid little beast! But, after all, she was not surprised. It was all in his character. Perhaps he had been drunk; perhaps it was merely a fancy-stationery idea of humour. Not that she minded a straw; she laughed; she supposed she was there to have stones thrown at her; it was merely a little annoying that they were not thrown straighter. She could picture the over-pocket-monied little bounder, measuring all pecks out of his own bushel, leaning up against a bar somewhere, probably too fuddled to distinguish his own humorous fancy from a story of life with names given, and believing it himself by the time he had repeated it once or twice.

The little worm!

"But," she said presently, disgustedly smiling, "*you* remember when I came to the School, and that I asked *you* who Mr. Jeffries was—"

"Of course!" said Kitty, suddenly entirely believing. "How absurd! But oh, I do love him so."

Louie mused.

"And he—Mr. Jeffries—knows nothing about this, you say?" she asked presently.

"No. He thinks something's wrong. He's been teaching at the School, you know, and of course he must have wondered what was the matter all this last week."

"It's a week since Mr. Merridew—did me this favour?"

"Yes. But perhaps Jeff thought—" She checked herself.

"What? I think I ought to know what Mr. Jeffries may have thought."

Kitty hesitated, and then, with a little burst, told her. It was curious. It appeared that Mr. Jeffries had been very hard up indeed, so hard up that, quite recently, he had actually had to take a position as a commissionaire. It was known, and possibly he had set any oddities of behaviour towards himself down to that.

A commissionaire! Louie was astounded.

"And aren't you going to tell him?" she managed to get out.

"I must, the very next time I see him."

"You mean tomorrow?"

"I don't know. You see"—Kitty hesitated again—"he's left the School. Practically been dismissed. He's got some work at Bedford now."

"Dismissed on account of this?"

"I expect so."

"And now, of course, you've got to tell him that you believed this?"

Kitty dropped her head on the bed. She gave a little moan. "I don't know how I shall ever do it!" she groaned in the bedclothes.

Louie considered herself entitled to agree that it wouldn't be easy.

Presently Kitty rose. She crossed to Louie's mirror and adjusted the boat-shaped hat. Then she came back to the bedside again and craned her head forward.

"May I see the baby?" she asked.

"Another time, I think," said Louie, her lips compressed.

Kitty left.

Louie's mind was in a whirl. At her request, Kitty had turned out the gas before leaving, and only a nightlight glimmered on the little invalid's table. She gazed at it. So she too had been haled into the drama!

On the young fancy stationer she wasted never a thought, either of indignation or of anything else; but Kitty—Evie Soames—Mr. Jeffries—Roy—herself!—What a nightmare—what a pantomime! What an incredible genius this Mr. Jeffries seemed to have for getting himself into complications and dragging other people after him! It might well have puzzled anybody—anybody who had not the key of the puzzle—to know which among them all he really had honoured with his choice! Only Miss Levey seemed to be immune. Surely, for the sake of completeness, he could have found a way of dragging her in too!

Louie had to hold her key exceedingly firmly in order to retain even that lunatic theory that seemed to be the truth.

By dint of holding fast, however, the theory still stood the strain. Evie Soames and Mr. Jeffries were still the central figures of the piece. Kitty was still the stalking-horse behind which, for whatever reasons, he machinated. She herself was still merely dragged in at the whim of a vicious little scoundrel over whose tongue whisky and calumnies ran indifferently, and this little beast was still engaged, or all but engaged, to Evie Soames. Yes, the triangle re-established itself. Kitty and herself were no more than imported complications. The big man and the red-waistcoated youth were still the protagonists, and they faced one another over the stupid little head of Evie Soames.

And yet Louie, lying with her boy at her breast and blinking at the nightlight, refused to class herself with the superfluous Kitty. She did not see herself in a "walking on" part. Though she made her entry late, something told her that she would have a word to say—or else it was a botched and mangled piece indeed. Of life itself as a botched and mangled piece she had no conception; though she kept her thoughts of Him locked within her own breast, it was still the bed of them that there *was* an Artist over all. But for a false start she would have been on the stage now, and she would have given a voice to that pitiful part of poor Kitty's. Say she had not left that Holborn School when she did—she remembered that breaking-up dance—had one more opportunity like that been given to her—

Then in the darkness she coloured violently. She had realised her own thoughts. This was as much as to say that she would have accepted Kitty's rôle—would have consented to be an understudy—would, like other understudies, have ousted the principal in time—would have topped the bill with a man the latest of whose mysterious activities was that he had been a commissionaire—

She loved, or was on the point of loving, Mr. Jeffries—

"Nonsense!" she ridiculed herself.

But nonsense or not, it was stronger than all her efforts to think about something else. Perhaps it was her own false start that set her wondering, and ever returning to her wonder, whether he had not made one too. He seemed to have set up the figure of Evie Soames in his own imagination, and probably had not looked at Evie Soames as she actually was since. He seemed to have his full share of that masculine vanity which will have nothing to do with the compromise by which the world jogs on; his rapt, lion's eyes might see visions afar off, and he would not as much as know that his shins were black and raw with the bruises of the hard facts among which he stumbled. Little as Louie knew of him, she thought she knew that. Lucky Evie Soames, who might be as stupid as the mud beneath her feet, yet in one man's blind, far-seeing eyes could do no wrong!

But of course it was nonsense that Louie should have to recognise Evie Soames for her rival.

Yet, on one other point, as she lay with the babe at her breast and her eyes fixed on the little flame of the nightlight, she was already prepared to make a wager with herself. Her theory was still only a theory; she could not prove it; but it could prove itself. It would work out or it would not work out; if it worked out—well, Louie was a woman, and no woman hesitates for a single moment to put on the mantle of the prophet. Indeed, she had prophesied long before. "Circumstances are strong," this Mr. Jeffries who had since been a commissionaire had admitted when she had danced with him, "but is anybody ever beaten unless they deserve to be?" And he had taken his failure in the examination as a sign that he ought not to have gone in for it, and had refused to enter again. Yes, the earthenware vessel was on the point of collision with the one of bronze, and which would break the months or the weeks or the days would show. Kitty must not think that it availed a predestined spinster anything that she got engaged; Mr. Jeffries would never marry Kitty.

And if Louie herself had returned to the Business School after Christmas—

Her dream of how she had danced with him, and he had said "*You* understand," and she had replied, "*I* should have found a way to keep you," returned vividly to her—

She would have found a way.

Then she remembered that which even then had stood between.

Excitedly she clutched her boy to her—he woke with the pressure, and gave a little croaking cry.

This, then, was the first of the two things that remained to be told about this part of Louie's story.

For the second of them she had neither years nor months to wait, but a bare fortnight. A very few words will tell it.

One evening after the boy had been put to bed she went down into the nurses' parlour and helped Dot and Nurse Chalmers to overhaul the blouses in which the doctors operated. Besides themselves, only Miss Cora was present; she was reading an evening paper. Louie saw her purse her lips and then throw the paper away. Presently Louie, tossing a patched blouse aside, reached for the paper.

A few minutes later Miss Cora, with a "Why, what's the matter?" started forward and bent over her. Louie had gone deathly white.

"It's nothing—I shall be all right presently," she muttered, her eyes closed.

Miss Cora took the paper. The page at which she herself had last looked was still uppermost. It contained an account of a suicide.

"What is it, dear?" Miss Cora asked again. "Not that?" She pointed to the paragraph. Indeed, there was little else of interest on the page.

"I shall be all right in a minute," Louie murmured again.

There was nothing remarkable about the suicide. A young man had hanged himself behind his bedroom door, and a verdict in accordance with the evidence (which, it was suggested, was largely medical) had been returned. He had left a letter for his mother, precisely like almost every other such letter, and parts of it were quoted. The young man's name was Archie Merridew. He was to have been married on the morrow.

"Is that it?" Miss Cora asked again.

Louie nodded.

"Did you know him?"

Louie made no reply.

They are experienced women at nursing homes; especially about suppressed medical evidence they are able to draw conclusions. The next morning a few rapid guarded words passed between Louie and Miss Cora. The effect of them was to give Louie a sudden feeling of nausea. Miss Cora's whispered explanation seemed only too probable. That also was all in his character.

"That's it, you may be sure," said Miss Cora. "They ought to be lethal-chambered, nasty little sewer-rats; one of'em's saved them the trouble at any rate. Did you know the girl he was going to marry too?"

"Yes," said Louie.

"Well, she's had an escape. But don't think about it. You have your own little boy. Come into the garden till your father comes and then have a nice long drive. Shall we wrap Jimmy up and let him go with you?"

That, then, was the second thing; but already Louie had heard a prophetical whisper in her soul.

PART IV

PILLAR TO POST

I

When, in the October of 1896, Louie Causton left Mortlake Road, with half the nurses of the home waving their handkerchiefs after her, she went to a house near the Parson's Green end of Wandsworth Bridge Road. As she left that house before Christmas, going to another one near the Walham Green Town Hall, there is no need to describe it. Neither need the Walham Green house be described, since from there she went, in February 1897, to yet another house, in a street off the Bishops Road, Fulham. These and other removals did not necessitate the use of a pantechnicon; a four-wheeler sufficed on each occasion. Louie, the boy and the nurse went inside; the top was quite big enough for her belongings. She stuck to the south-western district; at no time did she move farther east than when she took two rooms in Cheyne Walk, over a bicycle shop near the Chelsea suspension bridge—which rooms, by the way, she was forced to leave at an hour's notice, her landlord, a man of straw, being himself ejected and involving his sub-tenant in his own catastrophe. She kept to this district because of its nearness to Kingston and the Molyneux Arms. By the time the boy was nine months old she was living in Tadema Road, not far from where the Chelsea power-station now stands.

The nurse whom she had engaged was a link—save for Chaff the only one—with Trant. She was, indeed, her own old French governess, once Céleste Martin, now Céleste Farnier and a widow. She was a Provençale, from Arles. On the death of her husband, which had taken place while Louie had been still at the home in Mortlake Road, she had sought out Chaff with a sheaf of testimonials, and by-and-by Louie had engaged her. She paid her ten shillings a week, on the distinct understanding that she must not hesitate to accept the first decent post that offered. It was already plain that, even if Céleste could have brought herself to leave the little girl to whom she had taught the order of the personal pronouns in French, her affection for Master Jim would have haled her back again.

Louie changed her abode so frequently for one reason and another. In perhaps a third of the cases the landladies to whom she offered herself as a lodger found reasons for asking her to leave when they saw that her letters were addressed to "Miss Causton." Then, to save cab fares, Louie began to make her position plain at the outset. Sometimes this made a difference, sometimes none. On the whole, London S.W. showed itself charitable or merely indifferent. By May 1897 she was at another house in Wandsworth Bridge Road.

She had not refused to accept, easily and as a loan, a sum of money from Buck; but thrice she had well-nigh quarrelled with Buck because she would accept it only as a loan. Twice, for the same reason, she had had tussles with Chaff. But money, until she should find something settled to do, she must have. No doubt Richenda Earle would have shaken her head and have pointed out that now Louie not only had the Scarisbricks behind her, but a prosperous publican also; but Louie, though she lived as frugally as if she had to earn every penny, did not see why her boy should go short while there was money to be had. She took the sensible view of the matter, and borrowed, while walking her shoes out and answering advertisements for this, that and the other.

Up to the summer of '97 her occupations had been almost as various as her addresses. She very soon discovered that her Holborn training was of little use to her, and she could not (as also she discovered) play the piano well enough to give lessons. What she dreamed of, of course, was a comfortable private secretaryship; no young woman is so ill-trained or so incompetent but she fancies herself good enough for a private secretaryship. Perhaps Uncle Augustus might have helped her to one, but she would have nothing to do with Uncle Augustus; and Chaff was unable to beat up anything of the kind. Buck's proposal, that she should keep his books, had been the cause of their second altercation. Common-sense in the matter of borrowing she was prepared to be; beyond that point she remembered her pride and Richenda's words. So for the present she was spared the worst of the pinch.

So, in the early part of that year, she was in an A.B.C. cash-desk, traveller for a History, and saleswoman at an Earls Court chocolate-stall. Then, in June, she obtained, actually in the face of considerable competition, a place in the showrooms of a Bond Street photographer. Perhaps her dresses, of which several still remained, helped her to this place. She wrote letters, arranged appointments, answered press and other calls on the telephone, and received sitters. No doubt some of these knew Uncle Augustus. Robson, of the Board of Trade (who came one day), would probably know him; so would George Hastie, Robson's friend and colleague, and perhaps Sir Peregrine Campbell and others. Some of them, the more sporting sort, might even know Buck too, for Buck was still a tradition; in short, Louie's own position amused her immensely. By taking her letters home with her and leaving a younger assistant in charge, she was frequently able to leave the showrooms by half-past four and to spend the evenings with Céleste and her boy. Incidentally, Louie improved her French a good deal, for Céleste crooned over the boy in French and English indifferently... "The darleeng—the lo-ove—the précieux—oh, oh, oh, mais il existe—il manifeste, le petiot—"; and she would break off to sing, in a cracked voice, "Le Pont d'Avignon," or some lullaby of Frédéric Mistral. She idolised the infant; when he was put to bed she did not delay long to follow him, for Louie, who had her work to do during the day, must not be roused at night; and so Louie frequently sat alone, writing her letters or wrapped in her own musings. She received thirty-five shillings a week. Her job had the appearance of a "permanency." In July she got a "rise" of three shillings a week. She also got ten days' holiday, the greater part of which she spent in the company of her father. She was beginning to know what holidays meant now.

On one of those days she had an unexpected little meeting in Richmond Park. Céleste and the boy had gone on by train, and she was walking. The meeting was with a girl called Myrtle Morris, who, when Louie had kept the confectionery stall at Earls Court, had sold cigarettes at the stall adjoining. Miss Morris was accompanied by a tall young man; she stopped to greet Louie, and the young man walked slowly on. Myrtle asked Louie what she was doing now. Louie told her. "And you?" she said.

"Oh, I've gone back to my old trade," the girl said, nodding towards her retreating companion. "Artists' model. That's my present employer—Izzard."

"Who?" said Louie. The name seemed familiar.

"Billy Izzard. Know him?"

"No," said Louie. But she remembered now where she had heard the name.

"Jolly clever painter," said the model authoritatively. "Nice fellow too. Shall I call him?"

"Thanks, but I must be getting on," said Louie. "Good-bye."

"So long. Come and look me up some time, won't you? 25 Edith Grove."

"Thank you. Good-bye."

So that was Roy's friend! They had not gone down with the yacht that had lain under the hill at Rainham Parva. But she had only seen

Mr. Izzard's back. For a moment, but only for a moment, she thought of Roy; then the sum-total of a long sequence of reveries returned to her again.

Or rather, the factors that made that total returned. In spite of her broodings late at night, when her letters were written and Jimmy's food prepared for the night, she was still unable to cast them up. Had she been asked to state her relation now to Mr. Jeffries her attempt would have been something like this:

"It's perfectly absurd, of course. There is no relation—nothing that can properly be called a relation. How can there be, with a man I don't see—haven't seen since that queer party? I don't even know where he is or what he's doing; he may be a commissionaire again for all I know."

"Yes, but," she now answered herself, as if it had been some form of a dialogue, "don't forget that other night, at Mortlake Road, after Kitty'd gone."

She did not forget that night. She had told herself that night that it was nonsense that she should love Mr. Jeffries. Again she answered that critical objector within herself.

"But it *is* nonsense after all! How *can* I? I suppose I mean that if things had been different I might have loved him. Moping about a man you never see is all very well for a schoolgirl for a week or two, but not for grown women, and mothers at that."

"Then you mean he's just the same to you as Buck and Chaff?" the dialogue continued, as she walked.

"All I mean is that he might have been more."

"Well, suppose you were to hear now that he'd broken off with Kitty, and—you know—that other were to happen?"

She did know what she meant by "that other." It was the most familiar of her thoughts. It was what in her heart she was stilly waiting for—to learn one day that Mr. Jeffries had broken off with Kitty and had become engaged to Evie Soames. And at that point she always tried to stop the dialogue. Beyond that point lay something that she vaguely apprehended might be horrible.

She had no definite reason for supposing this horrible thing to exist. The horror, indeed, was that it might exist, and to entertain morbid thoughts about something that merely might exist was neither pleasant nor wise. But at times she could not forget the promise she had once made to herself—that if anything unaccountable ever happened to a certain young man she would know in what quarter to look for the likely cause of it. And something had happened. Part of what had happened she had had from Miss Cora; "A lethal chamber—the nasty little sewer-rat!" Miss Cora had said; and it had happened on the eve of his wedding to Evie Soames. To commit suicide had been the only thing to do.

And of course he had committed suicide. . .

Then that second voice within her tried to speak again. "Remember," it said, "that this Mr. Jeffries, of whom you can't help thinking when all's said and done, had suffered innumerable insults from him—you yourself were dragged into one of them—"

"Quiet!" the other self commanded peremptorily.

"—and as far as that girl you hate's concerned—Evie Soames—if the reason was good enough for suicide it was good enough for the other thing."

"What other thing?" Louie, in spite of herself, could not help asking.

"Oh—*you* know!"

"Do you know what you're saying?" This was an attempt to browbeat the other Louie.

"Oh, perfectly well! *I* know myself—you—us—Louie Causton—better than you do! And I know that lion better! Have you forgotten? Don't you remember what you thought of him, that if he set his mind on a thing he'd get it sooner or later, one way or another? Don't you remember what he said—'I wonder if anybody's ever beaten who doesn't deserve to be?' They are dangerous men who believe that! And the way's clear for him now, isn't it? Of course it is! Why, suppose you hear, first, that he's thrown Kitty Windus over; suppose you hear, next, that he's forging ahead in his business, whatever it is—you know he's as ambitious as Satan; then suppose you hear that he's engaged to Evie Soames—married to her. Suppose you hear all this?"

"Oh, anybody can make up an *a priori* tale like that!" the other scoffed.

"Perhaps they can; but what *is* a murder anyway? Whoever sees one committed? Don't they hang men on just such *a priori* tales, as you call it? Suppose that, rather than let him marry that girl—"

"Oh, stop, stop!" Louie positively shrieked within herself.

She was white. This scene always turned her white. She quickened her pace, but her ghastly pallor remained unchanged. A hundred times she had argued it all before, and she knew the conclusion that would presently come.

It came, the conclusion. That portion of herself that always seemed resolved to convict Mr. Jeffries of a hideous thing spoke, as it were, softly, seductively.

"And what then, Louie? What then? Come, don't be afraid of yourself! You know it in your heart all the time! Roy—you remember—*you* had to make the love there; and you want to be *made* love to, not to make love. *You* didn't find Mr. Jeffries a butt and a laughing-stock, you know. You envied that little chit of a milliner's hand—envied her and hated her. And she hates you, and always will, because you caught her in the dark with that other creature. Yes, yes, I know you were overstrung at that time, and didn't see yourself very clearly, but look at the thing now—you're calm now. When you saw his eyes, all full of perils and stratagems and deceits, all for her sake, you know you longed to have a man do all that for *you*! And when he did that mad thing with Kitty Windus, you know you wanted a man who would go even to those lengths for *you*! And you know that when he throws her over—brutally, heartlessly, without conscience—you'll want a man who'll be just as brutal and heartless and conscienceless for *you*! You all want it! You all love a ruthless man! You know it's the men who are the merciful sex when sex comes into the question; you're only merciful when it doesn't—just as those stupid men are merciless about the abstractions you don't care a straw about! . . . So suppose—suppose—"

"Oh, stop!" Louie besought herself faintly.

"—suppose it turns out as I say! Won't you immediately love him a little more when poor Kitty's sent about her business? And won't you love him a little more still when you hear he's engaged to Evie Soames? And won't you, when you learn that he's been willing to go all lengths—all lengths—for love, love him past all mending? You will, you will, you know you will!" The cry rang out almost exultantly.

"But—but—those people—coroners' juries—are supposed to know all about these things."

"Coroners' juries! . . . Do you remember his eyes? . . ."

Beyond that point Louie never got. She usually rose quickly and went out to post the photographer's letters. There, then, were the elements of her sum. Sometimes some of them presented themselves, sometimes others; more and more she shrank from casting the total. And often, to shake off the hideous, fascinating obsession, she did the most trivial thing she could think of—went to a drawer and overhauled her dresses, selecting the one she would wear at the photographer's showroom on the morrow.

It was in her to turn from the thought of a possible murder to the shaking out of a crumpled dress.

But she never wore the oyster-grey at the showrooms in Bond Street. Nevertheless she shook it out frequently, putting it back into the drawer again.

THAT DAY, AT THE MOLYNEUX Arms, Buck was alternately at his fondest and at his most tyrannical. The fondness was for Louie and the boy, the tyranny for everybody else. As Louie entered the little private parlour (she was not allowed to set foot in the rest of the premises) she heard loud crowings; they came from Jimmy, and were for the Pilgrim of Love who held him up at arm's-length in the air; but the next moment Buck was scolding a barmaid who had had the temerity to borrow the current number of *Modern Society* before Louie had seen it. "Not that I don't make 'em all read it," he said, "but at times and seasons, and in their proper places; what with all these Radicals and what not we don't want chayoss coming again! You bring it back this minute, miss!—'Oryn—thia my Belovèd!'"

Buck kept his divided humour through tea; then there was another outburst. This time it was about a letter that had not been given to Louie immediately.

"And how do *you* know that it isn't important?" he broke out on his wife. "Not a word—not a word! I *know* it is important—all letters addressed so are important, mind, for the future! Those letters aren't about the butcher and baker and candlestick-maker, I'll have you know! Give it to her at once, and let Madermoselle hook up the back, or your next dress shall fasten down the front, I promise you! . . . What, little man! A granddad, eh? 'No re-(*h*)-est—but the gra-(*h*)-ave—'"

For all Louie was able to guess from the signature, her letter might have been from butcher, baker and candlestick-maker, all three; the name—"hers to serve, Frank Hickley"—was unknown to her. But the single other name that the letter contained was known. It was that of Kitty Windus. She was laid up somewhere in Vauxhall, and wanted to see her.

The next morning, in a shabby respectable street off the Vauxhall Bridge Road, Louie rang a bell beneath which, punched in a strip of aluminium, was the sign, "F. Hickley, Agent." F. Hickley himself opened the door. Later Louie learned that he was an agent for his wife's shopping, boot-cleaning and potato-peeling. Mrs. Hickley was Kitty's cousin, but the bit she had coming in was not enough to relieve her of the necessity of keeping a lodging-house. That it was a lodging-house Louie guessed from the number and variety of hats and coats that hung in the narrow yellow-painted hall. Mrs. Hickley appeared from somewhere below; Mr. Hickley, descending again, passed her on the stairs.

"Are you Miss Causton?" Mrs. Hickley asked.

"Yes. I've had a letter saying Miss Windus was here."

"Will you come up? Don't take too much notice of her, what she says, especially about tracts; Uncle Arthur's side's liable to it. This way."

"Is she ill?" Louie asked.

"Not to call ill. She'll go to Margate in a week or two, for the air, though Margate's too strong for me; Littlehampton's my favourite. And Bognor. Mind the stair-rod—I must tell Frank to fasten it down."

As Kitty had formerly found Louie, so Louie now found Kitty— in bed. Her muteness as long as Mrs. Hickley remained in the room seemed obstinate, *voulu*; the rapid speech into which she broke without preface when her cousin's step had ceased to sound on the stairs confirmed some vague impression of secretiveness. Louie was uneasy at the change in her.

"You're not to talk about it," Kitty said, the words falling one over the other; "that's what the doctor meant, though of course he didn't know what it was. And Mr. Folliott too—the Reverend Mr. Folliott of St. Peters. He gave me the address in Cliftonville, quite the best end of the town; there's such a lot in a good address, don't you think? You know Margate?"

"How are you, dear?" said Louie gently. "Yes, your cousin told me you were going away for a bit."

"Right away," said Kitty. "I can, you see; I haven't got to work if I don't want to; though I'm not rich, of course. Neither is Annie, but I don't like to see men doing the housework like Cousin Frank for all that. I've told Frank so again and again. '*Be* an agent,' I've said time after time; 'for typewriters, or mangles, or tea, or anything you like, but get out of the house; it isn't a man's place.' And it isn't. . . You've heard?" she broke off suddenly to say.

She blinked at Louie. Her neck above her nightgown was hardly more substantial than that of a chicken; her hands seemed to have become as veined as a skeleton leaf. Louie took one of them.

"Always running errands and setting the table—it isn't a man's life," Kitty continued. "'What does agent *mean*?' I said to him. 'Pull yourself together and *make* it mean something, Frank!' I said. 'You're not very big, but you're strong, and you've got your wits about you,' I said. . . You've heard?" she demanded once more.

"Well, tell me how you are," said Louie, patting the thin hand soothingly.

"But have you heard the news? Glad tidings for all. 'Come unto Me, and I will give you rest'—that's what we all want—rest; though why they should print 'Come' in red and 'unto' in green and 'Me' in purple, and all the letters like twigs, I'm sure I can't tell you, my dear. And always Oxford frames. I must ask Mr. Folliott. 'Though your sins be as crimson—'"

"You haven't asked how my little boy is, Kitty," said Louie.

"'Suffer the little children, and forbid them not'—how is he?"

But she did not wait for an answer. She was off again—the doctor, the Reverend Mr. Folliott, her approaching visit to Margate. And always she returned to the indignity of a man's doing women's work about the house. It was in this connection that she suddenly mentioned, in a way that gave Louie a slight start, the name of Mr. Jeffries.

"I will at least say that for him," she prattled; "I shouldn't have got sick of the sight of him; out of the house at half-past nine he'd have been, and that would have been the end of him till six o'clock; not always bumping into you like Frank. I suppose you know Miss Levey's there too, at his Company? He's getting on there like anything. So's Mr. Mackie; you remember Mr. Mackie? He takes the auction himself now on Mondays and Thursdays; in Oxford Street; everybody stops as they walk past; he's a caution, is Mr. Mackie, I can tell you! But of course Jeff"—here she became mysterious, and nodded once or twice—"Jeff's on the way up—up. It's a different class of work from Mr. Mackie's; better, as you might say; he's in the Confidential Exchange Department, Miriam says—"

"How is Miss Levey?" Louie asked, at a loss what else to say.

"Oh, in the pink—but the soul's the chief thing; what shall it profit a man; and I don't know whether her soul's in the pink. Do you always *hold* with the Church of England, Louie?" she asked earnestly.

There was nothing to be made of her. She ran on weakly, irresponsibly, from trifle to trifle, and it was at Louie's own risk that she gave her talk any significance at all. . . Suddenly she insisted that she herself had broken the engagement, not he. She spoke of his place in the Company—it was the Freight and Ballast Company; it appeared to be a "permanency." He was getting on—on; *he* wouldn't polish brasses and take the lodgers' boots to be mended! . . . As she talked, Louie looked round the poor, neat little bedroom. It had framed texts and a picture of a lady shipwrecked in a nightgown; this was entitled "Simply to Thy Cross I cling." There was a good deal of muslin about, tied back with flyblown bows.

But suddenly Kitty seemed to remember something. Louie was once more gently patting the hand on the counterpane when she gave a quick little clutch and sat up.

"They wrote to you to come, didn't they?" she asked, looking hard at Louie.

"Yes, dear. I'd have come sooner if I'd known. The letter was sent on from Mortlake Road. I came as soon as I got it."

"That's all right," said Kitty, nodding mysteriously again. "I want to talk to you. Is the door shut?"

"Yes; but don't talk. Let me talk to you instead."

"No; there's something I want to say, and I shall forget it if I don't say it now. . . You heard about it, didn't you? I don't mean the glad tidings for all—"

"Lie down, dear." (Kitty was squatting up in bed.) "Tell me the next time I come. I'll come again."

"No, I must tell you now. Though Jeff's sins be as scarlet. Of course you heard about Archie?"

"Hush."

"Of course you'd be down on him; quite right; so was Jeff. Jeff didn't half give him a talking to, I can tell you! 'Oh, I'll give him a dressing down,' he said; he was pretending it wasn't much, so as not to alarm me; but *I* know him! 'Miss Causton and me?' he said. 'What a ridiculous idea!' And he made Archie apologise before the whole school. And now Archie's gone, and they said it was suicide; but what I can't understand is about Jeff's having that black eye, that very day. He'd fallen when he was drunk, he said, but Jeff never got drunk. He said he tripped on the step; but he never *got* drunk, if you understand what I mean. Wine is a mocker, isn't it, Louie? But I'm sure Jeff wasn't drunk. He isn't that kind of man."

Louie herself wondered why she should interpose as quickly and peremptorily as she did. She wondered, too, why she should do so in the words she used and in a voice so thin and harsh.

"Oh—of *course* he was drunk! My father keeps a public-house, so I ought to know. And they often get black eyes when they're drunk. Let's talk about something else."

"Well," said Kitty, with her head on one side, "a public-house is as paying a business as there is, especially in a poor neighbourhood. But I'd rather have my little bit in tramways. People ought to be careful how they invest their money; dividends aren't everything; what shall it profit a man? So you think I needn't worry about Jeff's black eye?"

All at once Louie felt an almost hysterical need to turn Kitty's weak wanderings into another direction—any other direction. Glibly she began to improvise.

"It's horrid," she said, her voice a little raised. "I've seen them at my father's. They get drunk, and fall, and then they get black eyes quite easily. And," she ran on regardlessly, "they knock themselves about fearfully! I saw a man in the Harrow Road one night—"

Feverishly she extemporised. To something she had once seen from the top of a bus she gave colour and circumstance. Kitty was impressed. "Dear me!" she said.

Then, when the danger, whatever it was, seemed to be averted, Louie turned, though not much more calmly, to Margate. Kitty was perfectly docile; Margate or that dangerous other were all the same to her. Louie had never been to Margate, but she compared Margate with other places—Bournemouth, Ilfracombe, Scarboro.

"I should like to go to Scarboro," Kitty mused—"Harrogate too—Harrogate's tremendously toney, isn't it?"

"Very; all hotels and kursaals and pump rooms and things," averred Louie, who had never been to Harrogate either.

Then, ten minutes later, she rose. She said good-bye. But even as she did so she received another start. Kitty had suddenly called in a sharp, loud voice.

"Was that Annie at the door?"

"No," said Louie, her nerves all on edge. "There's nobody."

"Open the door and look!"

Louie did so. There was nobody. She returned to the bed again. Kitty was once more squatting up. She still spoke sharply.

"It's all very well to be so cocksure," she said, "but if Annie was to guess, or Miriam Levey or any of them, it would be all U P, I can tell you! Or Evie Soames either! I only told you because you're different and can hold your tongue! The tongue is a little member, so the best thing people can do is to shut up, you take my tip! And *I* broke it off, mind you! There's as good fish in the sea as ever came out of it, without girls making themselves cheap, and if he ever wants to know I'll tell him straight—no drunks and black eyes for me! Not that I don't forgive my enemies; I'm as good at that as the next one; but when I'm engaged again it'll be to somebody who's Tᴛ absolutely, though he does clean the knives!" Then, dropping her voice again, she said equably: "Good-bye, dear—you will come again, won't you? I sha'n't be going for a fortnight—the rooms aren't at liberty yet—there isn't a sea view, but it isn't a minute from the Ramsgate tram—you must come and stay with me—"

Louie left her. Downstairs in the hall she had a few words with Kitty's cousin. She asked when the engagement with Mr. Jeffries had been broken off, and was told a year ago. Part of the time since then Kitty had spent with another cousin, Alf Windus, who lived in Kilburn and played the first fiddle at the Metropolitan in Edgware Road; part she had spent at Alf's sister-in-law's at Wealdstone; and for the rest of the time she had been at the Hickleys'. She was only a little flighty at times, and Mrs. Hickley was too busy, what with breakfasts at different hours and some liking one thing and some another, to pay much attention to her. She would have taken her for nothing if she could, but life was a struggle and business was business, and Mrs. Hickley had been lucky enough to let her room for the time she would be away at Margate. If Kitty really had anything to keep from her cousin, apparently (Louie concluded) she had kept it. Probably Kitty's condition (Mrs. Hickley added) was a result of the shock of Archie Merridew's suicide, coinciding with her rupture with Mr. Jeffries. Beyond that Mrs. Hickley minded her own business—plenty, too,—

"Thank you for coming," she said, opening the door for Louie.

"I shall come again if I may," Louie replied.

Already she knew that she would go again—must go again—though it was only when she had left the house behind her that she began to ask herself why. Then followed another dialogue. The critical Louie began it.

"Well, what did I tell you? His engagement's off, and he's getting on in his business. I'm right so far, eh?"

"Too right," the other Louie muttered. "Let it rest."

"Will it let you rest—that's the question! Well, what do you want next—his engagement to Evie Soames?"

"I don't want anything. I've got my boy and my living to earn. That fills my life."

"Then why are you going to see Kitty again? Come, don't shirk it. You know why you're going. You're going to—"

"I'm not!"

"You're going to protect him! If that poor creature thinks she guesses, you're going to tell her the notion's perfectly absurd! You're going to lie to her! If she has weak fancies, you're going to see that they're just as wide of the truth as they can be. Do you still deny what the truth is? After whatever the tale is he's been telling about drunkenness and a black eye? *Is* he that kind of man? *Isn't* that just as likely as not to be one of his blinds? A man has to be cunning, you know, to hoodwink a coroner's jury, but somehow he seems to have done it."

"I don't know anything about it."

"You mean you believe he hasn't done it? Then why are you going to see Kitty again? Oh, don't pretend to me! I tell you you're going to protect him. And why are you going to protect him? (Ah, I didn't think of that before, but I see it now!) You'll love him a little more still just for that! You'll love him because you have his safety in your hands. You'll keep it in your hands. Even if you have to take Kitty to live with you, so that you can watch her every spare moment, you'll take care she never, never knows. You're planning it now. You're going to have a right in that man no other woman on earth has, Evie Soames or anybody else. And you're going to take him from Evie Soames too, if you can!"

The other attempted irony. "What, me? With my story?"

"You only regret your story because it stands now in your way of getting him! Would you marry Roy now even if you could gain a kingdom by it? Why, you wouldn't before, let alone now! What are you going to see Kitty again for—tomorrow? We shall see! Your nerves are all a-jump at this moment; you don't feel it safe to leave here even for a few hours! And another thing. Miriam Levey seems to be at his place, wherever it is, and you're positively trembling about *that*! While you're trying to worm things out of Kitty on the one side, she'll be at the other—*you* know what she is! So the first thing you'll do will be to find out exactly what Kitty's got into her head."

But here the normal Louie temporarily triumphed. "What a tale you're making up!" she laughed. "These things simply do not happen. Actually, you're trying to force it on me that I love a man simply because he's committed a—"

"Not simply because—"

"Well, that I'm in love with a man who has committed one. Tell that to the world, and see how you're laughed at! . . . Oh no, it's too much. People don't do it, especially when it's guesswork, pure and simple—"

So she triumphed. The other Louie held her peace.

But for all that she went to see Kitty again on the morrow.

II

It was an error of judgment that caused Louie to leave the photographer's in Bond Street. The money she owed to Buck and Chaff was on her mind; she saw that Richenda Earle had been right; she was not yet out in the open. She sought to diminish her indebtedness by finding a better-paid post.

The opportunity presented itself. She obtained, at a salary of three pounds a week, the coveted secretaryship. Never mind to whom she became secretary; he is now a renowned author; and Louie was with him for just a fortnight. At the end of that time he offered to double her salary. Louie's answer was to walk immediately out of his house. She had now no job at all.

The story of the pinch shall be passed over lightly. The boy did not feel it; it was she who tightened her belt. Promising herself that it was for the last time, she borrowed of Buck, and then removed to Edith Grove, taking two small rooms in the same house as Myrtle Morris, the model. But Myrtle had gone for the Christmas season into pantomime, and as Louie was out all day, and asleep when Myrtle returned at night, she saw little of her. She would have gone into pantomime too, but she was too late, and still hoped for something better. Of necessity Céleste remained with her; Céleste kept the place going with her needle. This was at the beginning of 1898. February found her again in a cash-desk, this time at Slater's. The desk had a mirrored panel in the front of it that extended from the narrow counter to the floor, and at first Louie wondered why clerks and shop-assistants put down their money, stood back from the desk, and grinned. Then one day, when somebody else was inside the box, she noticed the illusion. The head and shoulders of the girl in the cage appeared to be continued downwards by the trousers of a man. As she could not afford to throw up her job, she continued to bear the grins disdainfully. After her day's work she acquired from Céleste the art of crochet. Her mats and table-centres and borders for teacloths went in with Céleste's own work.

Her improved French enabled her to pass, in April, from the cash-desk at Slater's to one at a foreign restaurant in Soho. She still lived in Edith Grove. For several weeks that summer she was again at Earls Court, but with the reopening of the theatres she obtained a place in the ladies' cloakroom at His Majesty's. One night she helped Miss Elwell, the daughter of Sir James Elwell of the Treasury, off with her cloak. She was unrecognised. She wondered how B. Minor was getting on.

She was still at His Majesty's at Christmas 1898; but the New Year saw her at still another place—a Ladies' Turkish Baths, in St. James's. Buck, angry and disapproving of the whole course of her life, liked this least of all; massage somehow brought it home to him. But there was a worse shock still in store for Buck. In the spring of '99 Louie became an artist's model.

Myrtle Morris introduced her to the profession and to Roy's friend, Billy Izzard, at the same time. This also was in Edith Grove. Billy Izzard, whose large, boyish face and loose, shambling figure somehow gave Louie the impression that he had either grown too quickly or else not yet filled out, was telling Miss Morris, with a candour entirely disarming, that for some purpose or other her own form was no good at all; and Miss Morris asked him why he didn't try the Models' Club. He snorted.

"Try it? I have tried it; tried everything. Fact of the matter is, it's like going to a Registry Office for servants; you find the rich people have snapped up all the best before they get there. Old Henson gets 'em. He's got the very girl I want; Miss Gale; but I can't pay what Henson pays. And the rest of you are like that egg—good in parts."

Louie wondered whether Billy had ever heard her name before; she found a way of making sure. The talk turned to holiday-places for the coming summer, and Louie contrived to mention the Somerset coast and the Bristol Channel. The unsuspecting Billy told her that he had once been yachting there with a fellow and had had a smash-up. It was amusing. According to Billy, the other fellow had rather fancied himself as a patcher-up of broken centre-boards and suchlike, had put in at some place or other, and had said he'd made the centre-board all right; and he'd come pretty near drowning the pair of them off a place called Combe Martin. Luckily they'd been spied by the coastguard, and a boat had been put out to them. "Rottenest piece of navigation in England," Billy grumbled on; "there's a place called the Boiling Pot—" He described it. . .

Louie felt a little gush of gratitude towards Roy. He had not chattered. But of course he would not—

She did not offer at once to sit to Billy; it was a fortnight later that she screwed up her courage to do so. During that time she thought the matter out. Perhaps the stark simplicity of the thing attracted her. No acquirement she was ever likely to possess would greatly improve her circumstances; it would probably be the same to the end of the chapter—cash-desk, waitress, Earls Court—Earls Court, mannequin, and a private secretaryship with an offer of double wages. At two colleges she had learned little or nothing; she lacked application; but here was something that quietly brushed acquirements aside—something that went flagrantly by favour. It was femininity reduced to its simplest statement. She had no fear of Billy Izzard. She guessed that to him she would be little more than a more complex whitewashed cube or cone or pyramid.

She did not even colour when she made her proposal to him. . .

"But I expect you'll go off to old Henson or some other swell presently," he sighed, as she stood before him. . .

And of course Chaff, barring her face that was best suited with a large shady hat, had given her her testimonial long before.

Buck was furious. The original, genuine Pilgrim of Love had reason enough to know what happened in studios. Young women of high birth (in Louie's case it would probably be a young man) began to take their lunches there, and one day burst into jealous unhappy tears, and after that the Pilgrimage began. But Louie only laughed at him. She reminded him that she had reason to regard herself as a pilgrim too. At that Buck looked hard at her.

"Little woman," he said slowly, "d'you mean—that there is somebody?"

Louie laughed again, but more consciously.

"Once or twice lately," Buck continued, still looking hard at her, "I've wondered whether there might be—"

"How can there be, daddy?"

"Well, the other isn't befitting," said Buck, shaking his head and returning to the original point.

"My daddy did it."

"Ah, men's different. For high ladies it—it isn't befitting."

"I'm not a young girl, daddy."

"No." Buck sighed. If he had only known her when she was a young girl! But the whims of the Scarisbricks were still the Scarisbricks' whims, and as such above his judgment. "But I want to see this Mr. Izzard," he added grimly.

"That you certainly sha'n't," Louie replied promptly. "Fancy your taking me round everywhere I go!"

"Everywhere?" Buck repeated, alarmed anew.

"Of course. If it's a business it's a business. Why, Mr. Izzard alone would be—dreadful! It's no good, daddy; you can't change my mind."

He saw that he could not, but he still tried. It only delayed a little her carrying of her point. In the end—well, she was her mother's daughter. There was no more to be said.

So she began to make the round of the Chelsea studios, and presently moved, with Céleste and the boy, to more comfortable quarters in Lavender Hill, Clapham Junction. This took her farther from her work in Chelsea, but brought her nearer to the Lambeth and Westminster Schools of Art, where also she obtained sittings, sometimes during the day, sometimes in the evenings also. She sat for Billy when Billy could afford to pay her. "No, no—no tick, Billy," she told him once; "I don't do this for amusement." Of the boy Billy knew nothing. . . Buck, still strongly averse from the whole proceeding, at first refused to hear her gossip of the day's work; but, as his silence did not alter matters, little by little he began to come round. Soon they exchanged experiences quite freely. He told her what Sopley had said about his deltoid, Henson about his thigh. "You vain old daddy!" she said, stroking his cheek, "I believe for two pins you'd do it again!" She took a pleasure in fondly shocking him in the same sort. Sometimes he mused long. You will admit that it was something to muse over. And so—well, so Louie, throwing acquirements aside with her clothes, became, by virtue of her peculiar commodity, economically emancipated. As female models, women are eminently better than men.

She did fairly well at it. So well did she do that from the three rooms in Lavender Hill (the third one Céleste's) piece by piece her landlady's furniture began to disappear. Her own took its place. She intended, when she had enough of her own, to save the difference in rent between furnished and unfurnished quarters by taking a small flat. So her two chests of drawers and her wardrobe were her own; so were much of her cutlery and bed and table linen; and so, of course, were Jimmy's various paraphernalia. But she was not ready to leave yet. The summer of 1900, she thought, would be early enough.

And in one particular at least she was now able to hold up her head. She still owed money both to Buck and Chaff, but she knew as much about the struggle for a livelihood as Richenda Earle herself. And she had not grizzled. Life had not knocked her out. She was her father's daughter after all.

And yet, once more, she felt herself her mother's daughter too. The reason, which was not very far to seek, was this:

The earlier stages of that furtive romance that in the end had left her former husband no Rest but the Grave were known only to Mrs. Chaffinger herself. Henson had not guessed them; Lord Moone had seen only the resultant scandal of them. But Louie understood a little now. She could at least guess what had happened to her mother between her first setting eyes on the splendid Buck and that final petulant, pathetic cry: "Oh, that I should have to beg a man to marry me!" By sympathy she was able now to divine the sighs, the half-acknowledged longings, the half-shamed daydreams, the revulsions, the sinkings back again. For Louie now knew something of these things within herself.

Not that there was not harder stuff in Louie. There was. There was, for example, that sense of proportion which is humour. How could her thoughts of Mr. Jeffries not be rather preposterous? She found it difficult sometimes to remember even his personal appearance; she had well-nigh forgotten his voice; many idle repetitions had dulled the memory of that odd little thrill she had felt when her hand had lain in his. True, she remembered these things in a way. She remembered the tawny bulk of him, the lion's eyes, the gloss of his hair, the modeless fashion of his speech; but these were mere noted facts, no more hers than everybody else's. Yet what (she asked herself) had become of her sense of humour that she should want something of him that nobody else had? What had happened to her sense of proportion that she did not forget him as she had forgotten scores of people of whom she had seen far, far more? And how had it come about that, for one thought she cast on Roy, Mr. Jeffries had twenty? And why this new and curious understanding of her mother?

She asked herself these questions behind the grilles of her cash-desks, behind the counters of her Earls Court stalls, posing or crocheting on her model thrones, riding backwards and forwards to her sittings or what not on the tops of omnibuses. Usually she answered herself more or less like this:

"It looks very much as if I was making of him what he seems to have made of that Soames girl—a sort of *idée fixe*; if I were to fall really in love now, I suppose I shouldn't think any more about him. Luckily it doesn't matter; it's my own affair. Good gracious, suppose he knew! He'd think me as imbecile as I am!—There I go again!" (This probably, some minutes later.) "Suppose I *had* met him earlier, and things *had* been different—what about it? What's the good of remembering all that now? Well, it puts the time on down this beastly Kennington Lane. . . Thank goodness I'm not likely to come across him; I can't help thinking something would happen if I did. . . Poor mother!" she usually ended inconsequentially, "I suppose she'd be about my age. I'm turned thirty—thirty-one in fact—shall have to stop counting soon. Time you stopped counting when it occurs to you that your mother had dreams just as silly as yours—"

And so, whether this Mr. Jeffries meant much or little to her, he did not mean so much but that any trivial near occurrence—a cold of young Jimmy's, a cold of her own that prevented her from sitting for a day or two, or a fall in the crochet-market—put Mr. Jeffries and the wild and tangled ideas that seemed to cloak his image temporarily quite out of her thoughts.

When early in the year 1900 she got regular sittings for a time with an artist who lived in St. John's Wood, she never went up or down Tottenham Court Road in the Victoria bus without half expecting to run across Evie Soames, who lived in Woburn Place. Because she did not meet her, she concluded that very likely she lived there no longer. But, late on a windy afternoon in March, at about the time when the street lamps were being lighted, she did meet her.

It was opposite the Adam and Eve, in Euston Road, and on either of the two women's parts there was a curious momentary hesitation. If Evie Soames still lived in Woburn Place and was going home, the first bus that came would do for her, and Louie had already seen her glance as it approached; but as it happened, that bus was the Victoria bus for which Louie herself was waiting. Louie spoke; it seemed to her that not to speak would be to apologise, by silence, for that episode in her career that had brought Kitty Windus in haste to the Nursing Home in Mortlake Road. A large parcel she was carrying gave her an excuse not to shake hands.

"How do you do?" she said.

Something, she could not have told what, had instantly drawn her eyes to the girl's attire. Evie Soames was wearing a black jacket and black fur cap, but the wind, turning the jacket aside, showed the narrow black and white stripes of the blouse beneath.

"Oh—fancy meeting you!" Evie said, turning her dark eyes as if she had only that moment seen Louie. There was something in her manner that Louie interpreted as meaning, "Very well, if I've got to be cordial I'll *be* cordial!" "Are you going by this bus?" she added.

"Yes."

"Oh! Where are you living now—Putney?"

It may be that Louie met any slight the last word might have conveyed half-way and more. She replied, a little shortly: "No, Lavender Hill; I change at Victoria. After you—"

"Oh no—after you!"

Louie ascended; they couldn't stand on the kerb discussing points of precedence. "Let's go in front," Evie said, "and then men won't smoke on us," and they settled down.

"Well," Evie said, adjusting the apron, "and how are *you*?"

"Thank you," said Louie, "perfectly well."

"There's room for your parcel here. Such ages since we met! Let me see, when was it?"

They discussed when it was, and then, "And have you seen Kitty Windus lately?" Evie asked.

Since her first visit to the Hickleys' Louie had seen Kitty perhaps half-a-dozen times in all, not oftener. Kitty had been to Margate, thence to Whetstone, and after that to Alf Windus the violinist's. Louie had simply not been able to see her oftener; she had had far too much to do. And, after all, nothing (the nothing of Louie's fears and fancies) seemed to have happened. Except to herself (Louie guessed) Kitty made no mysterious allusions to black eyes. She was merely puzzled, pathetic, harmless. She had not that perilous thing, a preconceived theory into which events had a fulfilling way of dropping of themselves. So Louie replied to Evie Soames in a tone as casual as her own:

"Oh yes, I've seen her several times. Of course you heard that her engagement to Mr. Jeffries was broken off?"

"Oh yes," said Evie, looking straight in front of her.

"Have you seen her, then?"

"Oh no. But of course Mr. Jeffries himself would know, wouldn't he?—that is, if you call it breaking off when a person just disappears without saying where she is or anything about it. Don't bother to unbutton; I have some pennies—"

But Louie also had pennies. "Any more fares?" the conductor called, and then went downstairs again. The two women fell into a silence. The early lamplight came and went on their faces as the bus jogged on.

Presently the silence seemed to have taken almost the character of a contest as to who should speak next, with either resolved that it should not be herself. Louie knew perfectly well what was the matter. Miss Soames might speak glancingly of Mortlake Road and offer to pay her bus fares, but really she hated Louie because of Louie's discovery in the old ledger-room on that examination day that now seemed so long ago. The girl seemed to be still in some sort of half mourning—but Louie did not want to think much of that and all that it might mean. Rather desperately, she strove to forget that she had ever had a theory about what might have driven Evie Soames into black and of what might happen when she went into colours again. She must, she told herself sharply, have a hideous mind ever to have thought these things. Indeed, she was so short with herself about it that, relinquishing the contest of silence, she again made the small immediate thing banish the large shadowy one behind.

"Do you ever see Miriam Levey nowadays?" she asked suddenly.

"No," Evie replied. At any rate she had not been the first to speak.

"Oh? But aren't she and Mr. Jeffries at the same place now?"

"Yes, I believe they are—in fact, I know they are. I suppose Kitty told you?"

"Yes."

"Poor Kitty! But let me see: was Miriam at the office when Kitty came to Mortlake Road? I thought it was after that she went."

"I've seen Kitty more than once," said Louie, compressing her lips. The bus was slowing down opposite the Oxford.

"Ah, yes, you said so. Well, remember me to her when you see her again, won't you? I get down here. I hope you'll get your parcel home all right; it's rather a large one, isn't it? Good-bye."

As Evie Soames's figure was lost in the crowd that jostled in the lights of the Horse Shoe Louie did not look round. She was too angry. "Good gracious!" she exclaimed, "the insupportable little creature! Why, I never looked at one of my mother's housemaids so! *De haut en bas*—her to me! But I did catch you that day, Miss Polly Ross, and you know it!"

But as the bus moved southwards again, she was trying once more to forget that white stripe in Evie Soames's dress. She did not want to think that anything had suddenly seemed to come a stride nearer. And she would now rather not have been told, what apparently was the fact, that, whether frequently or not, Evie Soames did see Mr. Jeffries.

The parcel she was taking home contained a dress; she had been sitting in it; but it was not the oyster-grey. The old oyster-grey, too, served to bring her nearer to her mother and that weak flicker of romance long ago in Henson's studio. Not for worlds would she have had Céleste see the idiotic looks she sometimes gave that dress in which she had danced with Mr. Jeffries. And sometimes she would suddenly toss it aside, roughly, anyhow. She was not seventeen (she would tell herself), to moon over a flower a man had given her or a dance programme on which he had scrawled his name. She was a woman of turned thirty-one (she rubbed it in), with her living to earn and an illegitimate son to provide for. . . But sometimes she was very wistful too. She had never (she sighed) really been a girl of seventeen at all; looking back, she saw that she had missed that. She blamed nobody; no doubt she had been unruly, ill-conditioned, unmanageable; still, she had missed that. The thought always sent her off into her reveries again; and then, how differently, how much more admirably, she was able to plan everything to herself! Over and over again she built it all up, unbuilt it again, rearranged it, played with it. Had she, as a girl of seventeen, met Mr. Jeffries—had this circumstance been different, that particular not been the same—had she nursed no grudge against her mother—had it been Mr. Jeffries, not Roy, with whom she had kicked her long legs during the vacations at Mallard Bois—had she, in a word, had the arranging of the world herself and the choosing of the places she and he were to occupy in it—

"Bosh!" she usually cut herself abruptly off. "I shall be afraid of turning a corner soon for fear of walking into the gentleman! What shall I take in for supper?"

SHE DID NOT KNOW YET—INDEED it was only some months later that she learned it, but it is set down here—that already, at a Langham Exhibition, Billy Izzard had one day seen a big stranger standing before one of his sketches, had gone up and spoken to him, and had liked the fellow—had liked his hewn slab of a face with the yellow eyes in it so much that presently, having an old sketch he was never likely to sell, he had given it to him. But Billy would at any time rather give away a sketch to somebody he liked than sell one to somebody he didn't like, and he still set, moreover, less than their real value on those paintings of flowers that he "knocked off" in a couple of keen and nervous hours. One of these sketches, by the way, Louie herself coveted—a straggle of violets, a few white ones among them, in a lustre bowl; and she offered a certain number of sittings in exchange for it—another elementary example of the transaction in kind. But Billy shook his head. He wanted that for a wedding present for a fellow, he said. He'd give Louie another some time—after he'd found another studio. He was sick of Chelsea; when a fellow got to know the cracks in the flagstones it was time he moved. He thought of going up north somewhere, Camden Town or Hampstead or St. John's Wood—better air. So Louie could make up her mind to the bus-rides, or else move too. He wasn't going to let Henson get hold of her.

But Louie still delayed to move from Lavender Hill.

III

L ouie's adventures, as she continued to sit, would fill a book: but not this book. Her sittings were the accidents of her life; her real life she reckoned from Sunday to Sunday. Sundays were the blest days she devoted to Jimmy.

He was now nearly four years old, and (as Céleste continued delightedly to exult) "existed" and "manifested" indeed. Louie herself gave him her bath before she set out of a morning; she did so in a waterproof and little else—why, the splashed condition of the wall-paper in the poky little bathroom explained. It was the same old waterproof she had worn at Rainham Parva. Buck's admiration of the boy's chest and limbs was merely fatuous; he himself was teaching him to swim at the Public Baths. He had announced to Louie, with a great show of harshness, that the money she was fool enough to refuse, the boy would have the benefit of; that at least was something she couldn't prevent, he informed her, and though Louie scolded fondly back, it was a weight off her mind. Chaff, the other grandfather, came occasionally on Sundays; he came, for example, on the Sunday after the opening of the Royal Academy. He brought a catalogue with him, and, taking Louie into a corner, desired her to mark the numbers for which she had sat. Whether the poor old fellow meditated the buying of them all up, or what else, there was no telling. Her sittings, too, were "just like Mops." Perhaps that was more than some of the pictures were.

But it is not true, as has been reported, that for Henson's last picture, "Resurgam," Buck Causton and his daughter posed together. Buck never posed after his first marriage. Louie only posed for Henson once, and that was in wet drapery. She caught a pretty cold in consequence. She exulted in that cold; it gave her three whole days with little Jimmy. They played with tops and balls and soldiers on the floor. The boy wanted an ensign's uniform, like that of the fourth Lord Moone in the miniature, and Chaff bought him a dragoon's helmet and cuirass. Buck laughed because the cuirass was already too small; and then he sighed. Perhaps he remembered the suit of armour of Big Hugo at Mallard Bois.

Well, if a little money was all that was necessary, the boy could be put into the army by-an-by.

And so things might have gone on had they been destined to do so; but into Louie's life of busy sitting and foolish dreaming and Sunday's rompings with her boy, there came a disruptive force. Kitty Windus brought it on a Sunday morning in early June.

Céleste was reading a story to Jimmy when she walked in; Louie was putting the last touches to a piece of crochet; and all three were awaiting Buck's arrival with the trap—he was going to take them to Hampton Court. She entered unannounced, and, to Louie's way of thinking, would have been better in bed. Her face seemed unusually small and thin; she spoke in a high, painful voice.

"Louie, I want to see you—quick—"

It was as if Louie too caught an instant alarm. Hurriedly she dropped her just-finished crochet and rose.

"What's the matter?" she asked quickly. "Come into my bedroom."

In the quite prettily furnished little bedroom Kitty began to walk rapidly to and fro. Once or twice she turned her looks to the brown-papered walls, as if she expected to find texts there; for the rest the blinking little eyes roved ceaselessly at about knee-height from the floor. Then she stopped before Louie.

"They're getting married in a fortnight," she cried harshly, accusingly.

There is no need for Louie to ask who, nor did she know what instinct again, as before, bade her take up a definite attitude without a moment's delay. She only felt in her very bones that delay would be perilous, and that not the shade of an expression must cross her face that was not natural and unsurprised.

"Yes, of course; didn't you know?" she said quietly. "Mr. Jeffries and Evie Soames, you mean?"

Again Kitty made that painful little sound—*à bouche fermée*. "You knew?" she cried.

A simple lie would not have availed; this was so obvious that Louie lied deliberately, circumstantially and at length.

"Yes, of course I knew. Of course I did. Do you mean to say you didn't? I made certain you did; I was going to write to you. In about a fortnight, isn't it? I'm—I'm giving them a wedding present; it's—it's that piece of crochet you saw me doing. It isn't much, but these things don't go by value; it's the intention. What are you going to give them?"

She almost blushed for the lameness of it. As a matter of fact, she had intended that piece of crochet for the new flat, when she should take it; but to soothe Kitty now was of more importance than crochet for new flats. She watched her covertly, anxiously.

"How did you know?" Kitty flashed out, again stopping in her walk.

"Sit down, dear; sit on the edge of my bed; I'm sure you're tired. How did I know? Why, I saw Evie herself. I saw her on a bus one day in Tottenham Court Road. It was near the Adam and Eve. And—I say, Kitty"—dropping her voice confidentially, she made an appeal to Kitty's hunger for gossip—anything for a diversion—"I doubt if they'll have too much to live on—it takes a tidy bit to get married on—and I don't suppose she has any shares to sell."

But Kitty did not seem to hear. She flashed out again.

"Why didn't you tell me?"

"My *dear*! I made sure you'd heard it from Miriam Levey. And I wasn't sure where you were; you move about so, you know. I wonder what Miriam will give them! Something far more expensive than mine, I expect. And you ought to give them something too, Kitty. What's done's done, you know, and after all, lots of engagements are—"

But once more Kitty flashed out. "Oh, *I* shall give him a bottle of arnica, or whatever it is, for black eyes!"

Louie laughed almost hysterically at the joke. The tension was getting almost too much for her. "Oh, come, he isn't a wife-beater yet!" she protested.

"But he will be, that man!" Kitty cried aloud with frightening vehemence. "He'd do anything—anything—much he cares! Did you know I got lost the other night? In Lincolns Inn Fields; policemen coming up to me, if you please, and asking me where I lived! Much he cares! I believe it was her all the time—he never wanted me at all, and as soon as Archie's out of the way he goes and marries her! Miriam Levey herself says she can't help thinking it's funny—and I can't think what *your* game is either, to be going on as if it wasn't! I'll tell you what *I* think, if you want to know—"

"Hush, hush, hush!" came from Louie. She had her arms about Kitty. "Perhaps you're right, dear; he was cruel to you! And"—she rushed into another extemporisation—"I don't know that I would give him a present, after all. If one can't forgive an injury one can't, and it's no good pretending. He did wrong you, and perhaps he oughtn't to be let off, after all. I won't send him one either."

She said it because it was better to confine Kitty to her own wrongs than to allow her to approach a number of frightening unknown possibilities that began with black eyes. And apparently she succeeded. Kitty fell back on her own injury, and became a little calmer.

"Oh," she said cunningly, "but you'd have to send yours, and Miriam Levey'd have to send hers too—then, don't you see, I should be the only one who didn't, and he'd notice it! I just hope he does notice it. Serve him right. I wasn't as hard up for a fellow as all that—I carried on with a fellow at that breaking-up party. I did—you ask Mr. Mackie. . . You *do* think Jeff never intended to marry me at all, don't you, Louie?" She peered curiously at Louie.

Well, better that, Louie thought. "I don't think he meant to for a single moment," she replied.

"Oh, the *rotter*. Come on, let's send your present now. We'll show him! . . ."

She was quite eager about it; but Louie kept her in the bedroom a little longer. Kitty began to speak of texts again. Again she wondered why "Come" was written in green and "Unto" in red and "Me" in purple, and why all texts had Oxford frames. "You haven't any, I see," she said, glancing again round the brown-papered walls. "You ought to have 'Remember thy Creator,' you know, Louie; it always reminds you, you see. What's this?"

It was one of Billy Izzard's etchings. Kitty examined it with her head a little on one side.

"It's very nice, whatever it is," she conceded; "but where's the other one? I always think pictures look better in pairs. But you can get odd ones cheap sometimes; Mr. Mackie had a great sale of Art Engravings one day in one of those Oxford Street places—you can hear his voice right across the street—and *he* said they were cheap because they weren't pairs, but they'd do splendidly for the middle of anywhere, like over a mantelpiece. And what a nice looking-glass! Really, you're quite comfortable here!"

She seemed to have forgotten all about Mr. Jeffries again. She walked round Louie's bedroom, bestowing encomiums and preening herself on her own pound a week.

At midday Buck came, but Louie did not join the party; she sent Céleste and Jimmy, and herself stayed with Kitty. She hoped Kitty would not stay long; she wanted to lie down and think—think. Nor did Kitty stay very long; but before she went she returned to the subject of the crochet. She wanted the article—it was a teacloth—sent immediately; she would run out and post it herself, she said; and *then*, when he got presents from Miriam and Louie and none from herself, *that* would be rather a nasty one for Mr. Jeffries!

"Do pack it up. *I'll* show him I'm not to be trampled on like the dirt under his feet!" she persisted vindictively; and another approach to the subject of black eyes caused Louie to yield hurriedly. She folded the cloth and found a piece of brown paper; Kitty did not notice that she enclosed no message.

But suddenly Louie had an odd little hesitation. She knew it to be ridiculous and a sentimentality, but while she did not want to send a particular message, she yet did not want to send the teacloth entirely without one. The opportunity for the little secret luxury would probably not occur again. . . Kitty was condescendingly appraising her furniture again; on the mantelpiece lay a piece of blank card; it seemed to be there almost for a purpose, and furtively Louie took it. She scrawled an "L" upon it and slipped it into the parcel.

A few minutes later Kitty left, taking the wedding present with her.

Left at last alone, Louie once more went into her bedroom and threw herself on her bed. She lay with her hands clasped behind her head, her gaze now resting on Billy's etching, now straying idly over the brown-papered walls.

So they were to be married. And after that?

Well, she thought that on the whole she was glad. The curtain was about to fall on that drama that had begun at the Business School in Holborn, and so there would be an end of *that*. . . What now? What about those fancy pictures with which she had beguiled herself as she had ridden on buses and trams and worked at her crochet during the rests? What about those half-whispered, nonsensical conversations? What about those drowsy, secret quarters of an hour out of which she had come with slight starts to smile at herself? They were to be married. What next?

The answer came as if for months it had been merely awaiting her pleasure. It was as plain as day that she could now have as much of these as ever she pleased. For what it was worth, the freedom of her cuckoo-cloud-land was about to be definitely made over to her. Because nothing else was hers, that was all the more hers. . . Kitty's tidings brought it so sharply home to her that she forgot that those sweet hours of licence were no new thing. She forgot that it was no new thing to walk, in fancy, the woods of Mallard Bois and the lanes of Rainham Parva with him by her side, no new thing to call his name down the remembered glades—"Jim!" (not, as others called him, "Jeff"). She forgot that it was old and outworn already; she saw in it only newness and liberty and delight. A Jim of sorts was now hers, ineluctably and for ever—a Jim who did not fool predestined spinsters—a Jim who would know better than blunder into a blind and stupid marriage—a Jim whose relentless hand had not—had not—had not—

But here, as she paused, the colour that had made her cheeks rosy ebbed as if a brush loaded with white had been passed over them. His ruthless hand had—had—almost certainly had—

It was as if, in her fancy, a prison bell had tolled and a black flag had been run up in the morning breeze—

He was certainly a murderer; over the threshold of that hideous fact she must step before she could enter her palace of insubstantial delights. Stained she must take even the phantom of his hand, or not at all. Suppose the joy were to leave her, but the horror to remain?

She closed her eyes.

But she opened them again. She faced it. Say he was—that; what then? The joy and the horror were fatally one. A man capable of all—all—even of that—and her lover! Oh, the moment the shudder had passed the worst was over! He had killed; yes, but for a cause! He had been horribly to be feared; yes, but without the dread of him too she would not have had the whole of him, and she wanted the whole of him. *Not* kill, with such a reason? Withhold death, with something approaching that was worse than death? Oh, Louie knew all about that; Miss Cora had told her. . .

A murder? There were things by the side of which a murder, once you had made up your mind to it, was a trifle!

ARE WOMEN SO? IS IT so that they will place their soft hands, like willow-leaves, in those other hands that may be black with dreadful work, red with destruction, yet, seeing less than man and more than man, they care not? Is it so that they will set their lips, as if for a kiss, against the mouth of war itself with its ten thousand deaths? It seems to be so. Their loved ones, when they die, do not do so of fevers and shattered tissues, but of their own clear and trusted heroism. "Go," they say to the next one, even to the little Jimmy, "go—and come back if you may—and, though wooden props keep you together, you shall be beautiful to the mother who bore you—to the wife whose task it must be to take you to pieces and put you together again—to the woman who, because of her own heavenly dreaming, cannot think of the fiend you were in that hour when the call sounded and you dropped the point of your lance to the charge."

BUT ONE THING WAS CLEAR: her dreams must remain dreams. If she would keep what was left her, she must never, never, never see him now!

PART V
THE CONSOLIDATION

I

The habit of sitting for artists leaves its mark on a woman. This mark is the lack of mystery—the "looked at" appearance. But it has its compensations. Chief of these are a physical unconsciousness, an absence of coquetry, and a liberation of the mind so complete that a sudden recall has all the effects of shock. Thus, a model posing for a whole class of men has been known to faint because she has been seen through the skylight by a "man" who mended the roof.

In some such state of liberation Louie, on an afternoon late in the June of 1900, posed for Billy Izzard. It was in Billy's new studio, a large upper room in Camden Town, opposite the Cobden Statue. The place was so light that Billy had actually had to cut some of the light off. The upper part of the far window, that towards which Louie's face was turned, was darkened by a linen blind; the lower part of it was shrouded with tissue paper. The whole corner was enclosed by a screen. It was there that Billy did his etching. Behind another screen was Billy's bed. At present Louie's clothes lay on it.

It was half-past five, but the best light of a changeable day. They had had tea; the tray with the tea-things lay on the floor; and, except that he grunted occasionally, "Raise your hand a bit," or "Head a bit more round," Billy's absorption in his work was complete. He had even worked through the short rests. During these intervals Louie had crocheted. The crochet, only a little whiter than the foot near it, lay on the throne now.

Louie was not thinking; you can hardly call it thought when any trifle on which your eyes rest gives your mind its cue. Louie's eyes, the only parts of her that moved, had rested on the crochet, and that had brought Céleste into her mind. Céleste was leaving her; it had something to do with phylloxera and a brother's vines; Céleste, between two loves, must leave the boy and return to Provence. Then Louie's eyes fell on the chair in which Billy etched, and presently Kitty occupied her—Kitty, who liked her etchings in pairs, but surmised that odd ones came cheaper. Louie had really no choice but to do what she was going to do about Kitty. Jimmy must have somebody during the day, and Louie, moreover, must have ten shillings a week from somewhere. As a matter of fact, Kitty had agreed to pay her fifteen shillings, and, in the intervals of looking after Jimmy, proposed to type. Then, as her eyes moved to the screen round the bed, she remembered that her boots must be resoled. They would carry another sole, and it had been raining off and on during the greater part of the day. And then something else brought little Jimmy into her mind again.

For a wonder, she had not thought of a bigger Jimmy all the afternoon. But on other afternoons she had. Billy sometimes remarked on a passing tender colour; she always had to restrain a smile at that. Her tender colour? There was not a particle of that looked-at superficies of hers that, often and often, did not answer to a secret thought. . . Perhaps Billy, plain common-sense man, could have told her what those secret thoughts really meant. Perhaps Billy, sensitive painter, could have told her how sweet and pale and charming things must shun comparison with the robuster stuff. As, in some delicate pastoral or *fête galante*, art might turn its happy eyes inward on itself, so that the putting on of a slipper and the nymph's hand trembling in a silken fold and the promised favour of a smiling look hardly die because they hardly live, so Louie too turned her eyes inwards. What she found within herself still sufficed her.

"Better rest a bit," said Billy, looking up as he began to scrub in a background.

Louie stepped down from the throne, cast a wrap about her shoulders, and began to crochet again.

Again she hoped she was not doing an unwise thing in having Kitty to come and live with her. But the flat was at last taken. It was a top one in the New King's Road. A Board School now blocks out the pretty view that Louie presently had at night, of the distant cupful of light that was Earls Court, with the illuminated advertisement of the Big Wheel appearing and disappearing as the structure slowly turned. Well, Kitty's fifteen shillings would pay the rent, and the experiment would be a good thing for Kitty also. Louie had furniture enough—in fact, it would be a very good thing—all round.

"Come along—time," Billy grunted. "And I say, can you stop a bit later tonight? I've got to go out, but if I don't finish this thing today I never shall—"

Louie mounted the throne again, and again the silence was broken only by Billy's stepping back from his canvas and forward again.

The light began to fail, and Billy began to work the more furiously. "Give me just another ten minutes," he muttered, a brush between his teeth; "this'll make some of 'em sit up, I think; it's *painting*, this is! . . .

But I don't know, perhaps I'd better let it go as it is; it's a job, anyway. All right, Louie, thanks. . . Right-o, Jeffries; I didn't think it was so late."

The last words were spoken to the man who had knocked at the door and, without waiting for a reply, walked in.

Louie had heard the steps on the stairs; perhaps—she could not tell—she had already thought it unusual that the steps had not stopped at the water-tap on the landing below that was the supply for the two upper floors. Billy used that tap when he washed his brushes; he was looking for his palette-knife now.

But Louie neither saw Billy nor heard his grumblings because the knife was not to hand. She was looking past Billy, past the easel with the study upon it, at the man who had entered. For one moment she was wondering that she had not always known, not only that he would come some day, but that he would come that day; the next moment she had told herself that she had always known that.

Of her whole body, from the foot near the crochet to the last brown hair of her head, her lips were the only portion that did not receive him with a lightsome, quiet, fair, trusting smile.

Absurd ever to have supposed that they would never meet! Wise to have known so perfectly what would happen when they did!

What had happened? Oh, every particle of her seemed to sing to every other particle what had happened! Those pittings of her profession? Oh, there they went, washed out, all out, in the baptism of a look! Her fancies—those idle promises to pay drawn on a non-existent bank? Oh, they had gone, and here was payment itself, the solid, actual cash! She was suddenly rich. As she stood there, rich in seeing him, rich in being seen by him, every one of those worthless bills was honoured in full. She could have laughed at her past poverty. She could have cried aloud: "Jim, I'm here—look at me—no, not my eyes only—"

And he too seemed to be as she had always known he would be—singled out, down to his very manner of wearing his clothes—among men. Stupid, that of all those times she had thought of him she had never once thought of him as in evening-dress! But that, in all this perfection, was only one more reciprocated perfection: she so—he so—

"Oh, Jim—*not* my eyes only!" she well-nigh cried again.

But the lion's eyes never moved from her own grey ones.

"Right, Louie, I've finished," said Billy, looking up from his palette-scraping.

And within herself she wailed: "Oh, *so* soon? Must it be over already? Must I sit for men all these days, and then, when *my* man comes—? Oh, a moment! . . . Well, he shall see me move—and I won't look at him—I'll tell myself—oh, just one more fancy!—that he isn't here."

She descended from the throne and passed behind the screen.

Was it strange that already, as she dressed in Billy's studio, she knew that she would never dress in an artist's studio again, and made of her fastening of hooks and strings a grave little ceremonial?—(There! With that fastening yet another chapter was closed; oh, trust her, there should be no reopening of it!)—Or that she should have a little shiver, at the thought that he might not have come? Suppose he had knocked at the door, and Billy had cried: "Half-a-moment—slide, Louie—come in!" Suppose—but the tremor passed. She had always known he would come; she had known it just as she had known everything else about him. Again every fibre of her was joyous. She was here on the earth—she, Louie Causton, daughter of a pugilist and of a Scarisbrick, gardener, typist, artists' model, and all else she might ever be—that she might know all about this man. To have ever doubted it would have been not to deserve him. And here he was, in the same room with her—he, beyond the screen, she behind it—only the two of them, for Billy had gone down to the tap to wash his brushes.

Now what should she do?

No, she would not go out and join him; not as she now was; not a skirt and blouse, after that fairness. Nor yet would she speak. Surely it was for him to speak now! She had been speaking to him, singing to him, all music to his eyes; there does come a point (she told herself) when the woman ceases to do everything; he must speak now. She knew he would speak. So she stood, upright, close to the screen, waiting.

He did speak, and like smoke another flock of fancies fled for ever. They were the fancies in which she had tried to remember his voice. It came, henceforth unforgettable, pure rest after her strivings. He too seemed to be near the screen; only a screen between them; but the phrases that were breaking their long silence were merely automatic. He was saying something about seeing her presently; she heard him pronounce the word "Piccadilly," and the most familiar image of Piccadilly sprang up in her mind. "Swan and Edgar's," she was whispering back over the screen.

"No, no." This came quickly, protestingly.

"At half-past ten," she whispered.

"Yes."

Then the dialogue was at an end. Billy had returned. Some moments later she heard more words, a laugh, and the closing of a door. She realised that he had gone.

Only then did she come out from behind the screen.

Billy was wriggling into his overcoat and muttering something about being late. "Got to go and keep that chap's wife company," he said. "Regular little Philistine, she is; I suppose that's why I go; can't stand these blessed artists. I say, he'd no idea I'd a model, you know—sorry."

"All right, Billy," said Louie demurely. . . "Sorry!" So was not she!

"And I say, I'm afraid I shall have to pay you next time. I'm cleaned out."

"It doesn't matter. Send me a steak in as you go out; I'll have my dinner here."

"Right. Odd-looking chap that, isn't he? A good sort though. I picked him up at the Langham one night. I took this place from him when he got married."

"He lived here?" (What, another wonder?)

"Yes. Well, I'll send your steak in. Good-bye." Billy bolted.

He had lived there too! How ex—how entirely to have been expected! Louie walked round the room, looking at the walls, the ceiling, out of the windows, anew. He had lived there: read, eaten, slept there; what a coinci—what a perfectly natural circumstance! Then, leaning against the wall, she found Billy's study. Her eyes devoured it. She set it against the throne, and then walked to where he had stood when he had entered. She gave a rich, low laugh; she told herself what a fool she was; but folly so lovely made life. Again she looked at the wet painting. She had looked so to him—

She put the study back against the wall, but in another place. "That study's mine, Billy," she muttered; "mine, not yours or anybody else's, do you understand? You gave him my violets; he's welcome to them; this belongs to me. Jim! Jim!" she murmured.

"Well, I suppose it's crochet now," she went on by-and-by. "Do you realise, Louie Causton, that you've sat your last? And have you any idea of what you're going to do instead? It looks as though Kitty's fifteen shillings would come in useful after all."

As if otherwise she might have forgotten it, she repeated to herself, over and over again, that she was to meet him at Swan and Edgar's at half-past ten. At one of the repetitions—it was as she was cooking her steak over the little gas-ring that, perhaps, had once been his—it occurred to her why he had muttered that quick "No, no," when she had proposed that meeting-place. She glowed, she laughed through a sheen of tender tears. "Dear, dear one! *You* don't think that corner good enough for us, my sweet little outcast and me. Well, we won't thank you; we won't belittle him by thanking him, will we, Jimmy?—"

But she did not promise not to look her thanks when she met him at Swan and Edgar's at half-past ten.

Presently she pushed her plate away; she could not eat. She had felt her bosom rise once more. It had risen as it had never risen for anything or anybody save for the little Jimmy, and it rose, it seemed to her, for a similar reason. For in her hands even his physical safety lay. He was to be mothered too. Her unfelt arms were to be about him, the milk of her protection to be his life. By his strength he had thought to give himself to somebody else, but by his need he was still hers. A gladness richer than she had ever, ever known swelled within her. He, the great weakling—she, the strong one, to cherish and support—

"Jim!" she murmured, smiling, uplifted, lost. It was as if his weary, tawny head was on her breast.

And she was going to hear his voice again, at Swan and Edgar's, at half-past ten.

She feared that her own emotion might have exhausted her ere ever the hour came.

II

"Y our hat will be spoiled if you don't take your share of the umbrella," she said. It was a silk hat, and she supposed that silk hats cost money. A fine, persistent rain was falling.

She thought that he answered that it didn't matter.

"Then you might at least turn your trousers up." Her own shabby old grey coat didn't matter, but his trousers—

He seemed to be on the point of replying that they didn't matter either, but changed his mind. He stooped and turned them up. She held the umbrella while he did so, and then gave it to him again, replacing her right hand where it had been—on his left forearm.

It was on these mere externals of him—his hat, his coat, his trousers, his boots—that she had hardly for a moment ceased to feed her eyes. Anything else might wait; for the present the stuff of his sleeve was more to her than the stuff of his soul. She luxuriated shamelessly in the smallest actualities of his presence; why, even mirth stood but a remove away. His overcoat, for example: it was not that old tawny one that had made him so much like a lion, but it was an old one for all that; was she *never* to see her man in a new overcoat? Jim and his overcoats! But the rest of him was beyond criticism. Certainly he must be making money. She wished she could have called money to him with a wand, conjured it to him, as much as ever he wanted. Had it not been that she would have had to take her hand from his sleeve, she would have liked to step back to look at his great church-door of a back again. Of his face she could see little, but that did not prevent her looking until it would hardly have surprised her had he flushed and said, "Don't gloat over me like that." His hat was tilted down, the large peaks of his overcoat collar projected like wings.

No, she did not want to know what he thought or felt; bother all that part of him! When her thirsty senses had drunk their full, then would be time enough for the other things.

They were walking somewhere behind the Horse Guards. Stretching before them was the long, empty avenue of the Mall. She was looking at the perspective of lamps and trees and drizzle, when suddenly he spoke. Instantly all her faculties seemed to become one overgrown faculty, that of hearing. Not that he was saying anything; he was, as a matter of fact, only asking her whether she was warm; and she replied, "Quite."

She was almost amused that he should ask. His nearness warmed her more than did her garments. Her hand thrilled deliciously on his sleeve again. . .

Oh, the satisfaction of that, just that, after all her past inquisitions into his soul!

But come to speech they must, and that very soon; and perhaps that curious magnification of trifles made it easier. Indeed, half the formidableness of the single question she wanted to ask him had vanished already. To say to him, now or in a few moments: "Did you kill Archie Merridew?" seemed somehow not very much more unusual than asking him the time. Now that she came to think of it, even that question seemed less important than another one: "Can you kill somebody and still be happy?" She hoped in her heart that he could. It would be his justification. Had it been an unrighteous killing, that would have been another matter; as it was, she would have had him unhappy only had he not killed. And, as he showed no sign of breaking silence, she might as well ask him that now.

So, reluctantly turning her eyes from his face and looking ahead into the haze of the rain, she suddenly said: "Are you happy?"

She wasn't surprised that he didn't reply at once. Of course men didn't. They had their usual formalities to go through, of "Why do you ask?" and so forth—a sort of routine before they could answer a plain question. As he began to go through it now she made a little impatient movement. She didn't want all that. Then he deigned to reply to her inferior intelligence. Yes, he was happy.

"You *are*?" she said, with an exultant little leap.

Yes, he was; but again, apparently, he couldn't say a thing and leave it. In the middle of more stupid, logical, masculine things (he seemed to be qualifying his statement with something or other about his conduct to Kitty Windus) she cut him short.

"Tell me," she said, repeating the little impatient gesture, "you killed that boy, didn't you?"

They had been following the railings that divided the Mall from St. James's Park, but she had stopped to ask her question. And she was looking full at him now. But she could not see him very well; a lamp and a plane-tree made all an obscurity of vague shadows and wet reflections. But then he stepped slowly back, taking her umbrella with him, and twice, as he held the umbrella unsteadily, the light came and went on his cheek and chin; and then, as he took a step farther back still, the umbrella bobbed on the railings, from the points of it came little bright slivers of drops, and she found herself searching under a lamplit sector of alpaca for his eyes.

The danger of asking, actually, a question you have asked, but not actually, a hundred times before, is that your own mere familiarity with it throws you out in your calculation. Now she found herself suddenly hoping that what she felt to be working beyond the umbrella edge—for she felt it rather than saw it—was not fear.

For, of course, she had miscalculated a little—had been stupid to think that it was all as old a story to him as it was to her. Obviously it would not at once occur to him that there had been nothing to find out, but that instead the whole thing had been merely enacted before her eyes; he was sure to be thinking that on some point of evidence he had been betrayed. What sort of point that could be, unless it had something to do with the black eyes that seemed to haunt Kitty, he might know, but she could not guess; and all at once she had a purely physical shrinking. She would rather not know. She could string herself up to the thought of murder, but the bestial details—no, not those. Those were his affairs. They were to be taken for granted as things necessarily involved. And already she was on the point of feeling herself a little disappointed in him. For in the shadow of the umbrella her eyes had now found his; his head was a little turned, and she saw the whites of them.

It *was* fear. She, it seemed, could contemplate unafraid a sacrifice that he quaked to have carried out.

But as, with another little falling of drops from the umbrella, he steadied himself and stepped forward from the railings again, additional light came to her. It was fear, but not that fear, that haunted the amber eyes. The fear was of herself. He feared, not the information she possessed, but her whole understanding and condemnation. He feared lest she also should say: "It was murder; you are here to be judged; me too, with all the world, you must account against you; I set my mark too upon your brow."

And as he appeared sorrowfully to acquiesce in that also, nothing could have seemed lonelier nor more touching than the quietly spoken words with which he held the umbrella over her again:

"You're getting wet."

It was as though he told her that though he went outcast she must not get wet.

Her answer was to put her hand under his sleeve again. They walked on.

But he had not answered her question. Perhaps he thought he had: to all intents and purposes he had; but she wanted, not so much the word, as that he should not withhold the word. He was walking slowly, heavily, like a tower by her side; she had the sense of his fearful overweight; she would give him time. They continued to walk, their mingled shadow on the pavement as they passed each lamp creeping away before them as if the beam of some lighthouse had had the sinister property of obscurity.

Then, within a little distance of Buckingham Palace, she stopped again. Again their eyes met under the wet, black mushroom of the umbrella.

"You did kill that boy, didn't you?"

He had a slight start. It seemed to her that he even apologised for having kept her waiting for the answer. Formerly she had seen stratagems in his eyes; now, as he dipped the umbrella for a moment and stood full in the light of another lamp, she looked only into grave, candid depths.

"Yes," he said. "You know I killed him."

"Ah!"

Again her hand slid, as if of itself, back into its place. Again they walked on. The next thing that came to her was another ridiculous yet oddly precious trifle. She wore kid gloves; before, when she had danced with him in an old frock of oyster-grey, she had worn white ones; must she (she wondered) always wear gloves with him, as he always wore old overcoats? She longed to take one glove off; yet she—she, who had met Roy by the stile at night—for very bashfulness dared not. The circumstance struck her; how was that? Gifts of understanding for her he had: had he that gift too, the gift of her own bashfulness back again? Up went her spirit on wings. . .

Yes, it was that—or for a night at least she would have it so. As impossibilities are reconciled in a dream, so he seemed, by his mere towerlike presence, to resolve in one large atonement, her own life as it had been and the sweet and virginal and dear smiling thing that it might have been. In no less a miracle than that she seemed to herself to be walking. He could not only have kissed her; he could have had her first kiss. He could not only have turned, as he did turn, leaning against the pillar-box by the Equerries' entrance of the Palace, to look at her again, but he could have received in return—did receive in return—such a look as she knew he also could hardly have had the like of before. And it made no difference—as in a dream such a thing might make no difference—that he had a wife, she a son. Let him have his wife, she her son; she could find room for wives and sons too. Tomorrow, perhaps, it would not be so; tomorrow might be like yesterday again; but tonight—tonight—oh, the first garden was not less trodden than these rainy streets, the Barracks, Gorringes', and Grosvenor Road! Her hand moving again on his sleeve was telling him even now, if he would but listen, that though man may not know that it is not good for him to be alone, woman knows it, and maybe still remembers it out of her knowledge of the place whence she came later than he.

And he too understood now, for she was not so rapt but that she remembered that he asked her, somewhere between a sandbin and a street lamp, whether she was happy too, and that, looking up at him, she smilingly whispered: "Yes, now." And she was not so rapt but that she remembered telling him, flatly and with another happy and laughing and triumphant look: "You can't prevent it!" But she was so rapt that of much else that he and she said she had no very clear recollection. Words that seemed unforgettable when they came had eluded her almost in their own echo. But she knew that she gave him the liberty of herself with no more reserve than she had claimed that of him. She knew that because, later, but she did not know when, he muttered, in some street or other, she did not know where: "God bless your boy."

Well, if she forgot things now, there would be many days to come in which she would remember them.

Merely because it must be very late—she had no idea what time it was—she grudged the going of the moments almost angrily. Already she was becoming as hungry again as if she had not broken that long, long fast. But she admitted that it was not unnatural that he should think of his own concerns a little too, and want to ask her questions. She began to answer the questions hurriedly, to get them over.—Kitty Windus? Oh (she told him) he might leave Kitty to her; she'd answer for Kitty!—His wife and her complete ignorance? (His wife's ignorance appeared to be complete.)—Miriam Levey? (Oh, why would he not be quick, and she so hungry!)—And then back to his wife again; what about her? (he wanted to know). Louie wondered a little that he should consider her to be his wife's keeper also, but she answered his questions. That, she told him, was his private affair; but, if he really wanted to know what Louie thought about it, Louie could not conceive of a marriage with so huge a secret in it continuing undisclosed. *Voilà*; there he had it; and *now* might she please be permitted to enter into her own happiness again?

She was back into it, bathing in it again, almost before she was aware. A minute before she had not known what street they were in; now she saw the Chelsea Hospital on the other side of the road. On this side was a row of houses; she knew one of them; a painter for whom she had sat lived there; his studio was in the yard at the back. The thought of a studio was all that was needed. She thrilled again.

No more studios! So poignantly did she burn that she could hardly imagine that her glowing did not communicate itself. Studios, after that beautiful, beautiful sketch of Billy's? Good gracious, no! She was going to Billy's to fetch that sketch on the morrow; she would like to see Billy deny it to her! And that poor, poor old oyster-grey! Just because he had seen her in it once she had mooned over it, smiled over it, sighed over it; but it could go now—she had a richer memory! . . . Furtively during the last few minutes she had been working off her right glove; it slipped from her hand to the pavement; but she was afraid to stop. Let it stay; somebody would turn it over with the point of a walking-stick in the morning and perhaps wonder who had lost it. . . She stole another look at him; her hand crept along his sleeve; the tips of her fingers were on his wrist; her lips shaped his name: "Jim!"

Then, unexpectedly, it rushed upon her in full measure. She knew these streets familiarly; they were in Swan Walk now; and the thing happened all in a moment. Again, during those anxious questions of his about Kitty Windus, Miriam Levey, his wife, she had that sense of his terrible overweight: now, passing a doorway, he suddenly reeled. He began to sink. . .

In an instant her arms were about him. Not the unfelt, immaterial arms of her mothering vision in Billy's studio, not that other breast, offered but impressed, sustained him; she held him within her two arms of flesh and blood, upon that firm, warm bosom that changed its shape to his weight upon it—the bosom he had seen yesterday, white hives, all their honey his. . . She bent and kissed the shoulder of his coat. Oh, if he might but faint, quite, that she might carry him somewhere, or, if she could not carry him, stay with him where he was—she cared not—rest by his side through an endless night! Her heart, yes, her lips too, called him; a whisper might not reach him; she called him aloud:

"Oh, come, come! Come, come!"

AFTERWARDS SHE THOUGHT OF IT as a hail from a ship to another ship across a stretch of water so narrow that it was all but a stepping aboard. How could such a hail be a farewell also? They were not passing; as they glided side by side together, either seemed stationary. Other things, the whole offing of Life, were in motion; these slipped past, as it were sky, shore, shipping; but for a space he and she spoke from bridge to bridge. And he heard the hail too, for he opened his eyes. Though they never looked on her again they did so now, relinquishing all to her. Was there anything she had not known? There was nothing she might not know—now—

By-and-by she had helped him to a seat on the Embankment and had made him sit down. She took off his tie and collar; she smiled as he thanked her. "That was absurd," he said.

Then he asked her where she lived.

It was over.

Well, perhaps more would have been more than she could have borne.

But when she sat at last alone in the hansom he had called, conscious that she was wet to the skin and that her boots needed to be resoled, she still had the image of the ships before her eyes, gliding together side by side, with all else in quiet, relentless motion behind them. She held fast to it. She could not have endured to think that of that night's long wandering all that would remain on the morrow would be yet another dream and a wet glove left behind in an empty Chelsea street.

III

L ouie Causton would have been more than human had she not frequently thought, as her life became a moving from pillar to post again, that there was an exasperating proportion of absence in her heart's story. But at first she was not petulant. Some absences are brimful, as other presences are mere vacancy, and, now that she no longer sat, she had other things, plenty of them, to think of.

There was little money in the sale of crochet; there was not much more in sitting in costumes hired from the Models' Club. From both these things she quickly turned. Perhaps she turned from them the more quickly because of Kitty Windus—for Kitty was now with her in the flat in the New Kings Road, and the way in which Kitty, without spoken words, paid over her weekly fifteen shillings, was in itself a spur. Not that Kitty always spared her the words either. Two words at least that she did not always spare her were "rise" and "permanency." Often Louie felt all the amazement, and now quite without any leaven of amusement, that she had felt when first she had entered the Business School in Holborn; but she was not keeping Kitty (or Kitty keeping her) either for love of Kitty or her own mere necessity. To keep Kitty was part and parcel of that absence she was already beginning to resent. It was merely safer to keep Kitty than to have anybody else keep her. Besides, as long as she kept Kitty, she had only to write a note, justifying it afterwards as best she could, and two ships (so to speak) would come together again. She delayed to write the note; none the less it was in her power to do so.

So (to turn for a moment to that moving background of Life in the offing) the September of 1900 found her answering the advertisement of a Bayswater seedsman and discovering the precise market value of her old Rainham Parva training. But by the end of the same month she was temporarily installed at the clerk's table of an exhibition of French paintings at a Mayfair gallery, and glad of the job. Say (the question is hardly worth going into) that it was the influence of the paintings themselves that once more caused a manager to propose that Louie's wages should be substantially increased, for a consideration; it didn't matter; Louie, who did not now throw away jobs for nothing, merely told the man not to be silly—than which, as it happened, she could have done no better thing, for at the close of the exhibition the manager, now looking upon her almost as a dear daughter, found her another place, this time at a gallery academic both artistically and morally, warned her against dangerous young men, and kissed Louie on both her laughing cheeks. After that her French again served her turn, for she entered the office of an illustrated weekly; or if it was not entirely the French that did it, so much the luckier Louie to possess even yet a frock that was a rest to the proprietor's eyes after a succession of applicants in walking skirts and white muslin blouses. This job Louie actually kept till June 1901; then an amalgamation took place that threw her out of work again. Three weeks later, after a severe trial of her temper by Kitty, she was a "carpet designer"—that is to say, she coloured, in an upper room near St. Paul's Churchyard, pieces of paper so minutely chequered that sometimes for an hour or two she could not get the flicker out of her eyes. She made a grace of retiring from this occupation as soon as she saw that if she did not do so her employer would retire from the office of paymaster. After that she was reduced to sitting again, in costume. Nothing else offered. Jimmy must eat, Kitty's fifteen shillings be covered. The female figure in "The Two-stringed Bow," which caused such a (journalistic) sensation in the Academy of the following year, is Louie. Chaff did not recognise it. Billy Izzard, who had seen the costume at the Models' Club, did. He persecuted Louie to sit for him again as before.

Of the Models' Club she was still a member, and she got on well with the girls. Once she took Kitty Windus there, but only once; a black-and-white man, knowing nothing of Kitty's pound a week, asked her to sit to him as Miss Tox, in "Dombey and Son"; and Kitty, presently reading the book, treated Louie for some days with marked superciliousness. That came of making yourself cheap, her manner seemed to say; and she reported Miriam Levey, whom she met near Piccadilly Circus one day, as having said, "Vell, vat do you expect?" Louie did not much like this meeting with Miriam Levey. She remembered the Jewess's pertinacity and curiosity for curiosity's sake. Many such meetings between Kitty and Miriam Levey might easily complicate her own life.

There were two bedrooms in the flat in the New Kings Road. In the larger one, that at the back that Louie shared with Jimmy, there hung at first the sketch she had begged ("stolen" was Billy's word) after she had ceased to sit. When Louie took this down one day and put it out of sight, she told herself that she did so on Jimmy's account; but perhaps those absences that she had to convert into presences as best she could had something to do with it too. Perhaps, if she did not see the thing for a time, its first freshness would return.

Sometimes she thought these absences really too bad; she began to think so with increasing frequency as Kitty's fits of patronage became no rarer. Really it didn't seem fair that she should be asked to bear them. The least Jim could have done, since she bore them for him, would have been to let her know that he still existed. She did not much mind looking after Kitty, but it was a little too much that on his part *all* should be absence!

And that was why, with Kitty always at hand for her excuse, she did not write to him.

In a word, the joy of bearing for him was becoming fainter in proportion as the burden itself increased.

Then a piece of news with which Kitty came home one night added its trifle to her smart. She was alone in the flat that night; Jimmy had been in bed two hours and more, and Louie, after having folded his clothes, cleared up his litter of toys from the floor, and tried to read a newspaper, had turned low the gas, drawn up a chair to one of the three windows that looked down on the New Kings Road, and sat gazing out over the trees and houses and scattered lights that stretched away to Earls Court. It happened that that night the Exhibition was closing for the season; a firework demonstration was in progress; and out of the little pool of orange light rockets rose from time to time, falling again in slow showers of red and green and white. If no cart was passing she could just hear the muffled detonations.

She knew that if an impossibility could have happened, and Jim could have walked into the room, sat down by her, and watched the white and green and red rockets with her, that slight constant smart at her heart would have gone; but now she told herself that it was not as if she was young, with unlimited time before her. She was thirty-two, and too much absence is not sustenance enough for thirty-two. But that, she supposed, meant nothing to a man. Men did not appear to get old in quite the same way. The man who had tried to make love to her at the French picture exhibition was sixty if he was a day; sixty, and still fiery; and apparently he had found her still desirable also. But it was not for much longer. Women died with their beauty. Of course she had her little darling asleep there; men had the comfortable theory that women wanted nothing more than to "live again" (as they called it) in their children; well, all that Louie could say was that she did not agree with them. She knew one woman who wanted more. It might be wicked and unnatural to endow Jimmy, as she had done, with a sort of vicarious father, but Roy was gone out of her life—gone; to have married him would have made more mischief than it would have cured; and Louie saw no reason for not telling herself the truth about herself. But a vicarious father who stayed away was altogether too vicarious. . .

Well, well, she supposed that if a woman would have a man at all she must put up with a selfish one.

He, of course, knew exactly what he wanted, and had got it; nor could she say that he had not earned it—grimly. But now that he had got it, what about somebody else who was helping him to keep it—somebody called Louie Causton, who stepped in when she was wanted, took half the burden off his back, and was presently sent about her business again? (For she had remembered now the quite personal, preoccupied questions, about Kitty and Miriam and his wife, that he had put to her on the night of their long walk.) Oh, no doubt she would be there when she was next wanted, to share with him the thing another woman ought to have shared (but thank goodness the other woman had not!). It had not in the least surprised Louie that his wife knew nothing. It would have surprised her very much indeed if she had known anything. Jim might humbug himself as he liked, but at the bottom of his heart (she now saw) he knew better than to tell her. She was not the kind; it was Louie who was that kind, and he knew it too. But there: she was pretty, and men asked no further; give them hair and eyes and an unlined brow and the rest could go hang. Heart and vision—no; courage and devotion and the strength to bear—no; but twenty years, a curving eyelash, and a bloom more quickly gone than the falling rockets yonder, and ah, how they ran! But they didn't trust them. No, the other sort was sent for then. And it was the business of the other sort to be, always, as strong as they sometimes thought themselves.

The last rocket fell; the lights of the big wheel began to make quicker revolutions; and Louie left the window and turned up the gas again.

As she did so the electric bell in the kitchen rang. It rang again, and then Louie remembered that the street door four floors below would be closed for the night. She passed out on to the landing and descended the stairs. It was Kitty. She had forgotten her key. Kitty panted as they ascended again.

"How long have you been in?" she demanded, as she took off her hat and coat in the little hall.

"All the evening," said Louie. "Have you had supper?"

"No, I haven't," said Kitty shortly, and then came her grumble. Why hadn't Louie had the gas lighted? Fireworks indeed! And there Kitty had been waiting for twenty minutes and more, thinking nobody was in—anybody might forget their key once in a while, mightn't they? Hadn't Louie forgotten hers not a week ago, and that not the only time? Kitty had a right to forget her key sometimes. And there had Louie been in all the time, watching fireworks! Well, what was there for supper? And the fire almost out too; really, if Kitty paid for the coals, Louie might at least keep the fire in!

Louie mended the fire and got Kitty's supper. When Kitty had finished she cleared the little round table again, and by the time Kitty had put on a pair of red bedroom slippers and turned up her skirt to the blaze she deigned to relent a little. She admitted that it wasn't as if Louie had known she was waiting in the street, but all the same it was annoying.

"And now I've got a piece of news for you," she said, warming her hands. "It's a dead secret, but I don't suppose Miriam would mind my telling you. She's in for no end of a good job in a few weeks! But she always gets good jobs. She has determination, Miriam has, you see."

Louie was standing by the end of the mantelpiece, stirring a cup of cocoa. She only said "Oh?" Her own lack of determination was now an old reproach.

"Ra-*ther*! Have you heard me speak of a Mr. Pepper ever? But no, you won't have; you're always a bit sniffy about Miriam, you see, and that doesn't encourage people to talk. Well, she's his confidential clerk at the Freight and Ballast Company, but he's chucking that, and who do you think with?—James Jeffries!"

She paused to see the effect on Louie, and then continued.

"Yes, James Jeffries! What do you think of *that*? They're going to start on their own, in no end of a swell way, and Miriam's going over with them. It's Mr. Pepper's doing, of course, and as Mr. Pepper isn't exactly a nobody even where he is, you may bet your boots he won't change for the worse! Oh, James Jeffries knows the kind of person to hang on to! He's to be a partner, if you please, as good as Mr. Pepper himself; how's that for greasing in? Friends of the mammon of unrighteousness, I *don't* think!"

Kitty had this way now of speaking of her former *fiancé*. Sometimes she so extended his name that it became "Mister James Herbert Jeffries." And however Jim now "got on," his advancement would still be, to Kitty, a magnification of her own superiority in those days when she had had a pound a week and he nothing. She began to take out hairpins and went on.

"Oh dear, I wish my brushes were here!" (Louie fetched them.) "What was I saying? Oh yes, about Miriam. She's to have an office to herself, perhaps, or at any rate she's not going to sit with the other girls; and when I tell you it's in Pall Mall, you can judge for yourself—not just a couple of offices rented, but a whole building—what ho! The stone that the builders rejected if you like! And she'll have her own extending-bracket telephone, the very latest, and arms to her chair to put her elbows on, not like the typists! And Mr. Pepper's most friendly with her—she takes down his conversations with no end of swells! And I say, Evie Jeffries won't be half set up over it all, oh no! Even *his* office—James Herbert's, Miriam says—is going to be perfectly scrumptious!"

Her head was on one side; her short hair, as she brushed it, hardly reached farther than the sharp point of her shoulder; and Louie was thinking of that spurious engagement again. And suddenly—this had happened before, but never before with so keen a stab—the thought set her raging. . . She herself had been so near! . . . Her elbow caught her cup of cocoa; it spilt, and ran in a little stream from the corner of the mantelpiece. . . So near! And once again she cried to herself that *she* would have known how to keep him, Roy or no Roy! . . . Kitty? What could his courtship of Kitty and her bones have been? *She* would have shown him the difference! To have been so near and then—Mortlake Road, Putney!

Suddenly there seemed to her to be a great deal to be said for conventional morality after all.

For a moment her heart was full of hate—hate of Kitty, hate of Evie Jeffries, hate of Roy, hate of herself. To have been so near!

But the sharpness of it died down to a sullen ache. In his affairs he seemed to be going up, up; she had always known he would; and less than ever might she expect to hear from him now. And he would take his common little wife up with him. He might go anywhere, meet anybody; but sourly she wondered what sort of a figure he supposed his Evie would cut up there—would have cut at Trant or Mallard Bois? Oh, Louie would dearly have liked to see her there, to have pointed to her, and to have told Jim to his face that whatever ability he might have seemed to be yoked with an unimaginable stupidity, since he had not known instantly the one woman for him.

Well, there was simply no accounting for these things.

But if he was going up, Louie did not very much like the channel by which she had received the information. She had known that Kitty saw Miriam Levey; now she seemed to hear her thick voice again, "I *vill* find out!" She was aware, too, that there was little love lost between Miriam Levey and herself. She herself had encouraged Kitty in her present attitude of "Mister Jeffries," but it only needed the Jewess to propose the contrary attitude and in all probability there would be a struggle between them for the possession of Kitty. She detested Kitty; yet in order that Evie Jeffries might make an exhibition of herself among the people whose equal Louie was, Louie had to put up with her, bones and chilblains and all! Much he left her, didn't he? Good gracious, yes! And it was about time he was told that flesh and blood women weren't made like that!

Kitty, remarking that it was a shame to leave the now glowing fire, had passed out of the room for a minute; she now returned, in her slippers and nightgown. Her feet, she said, were still cold with waiting on the pavement; she would say her prayers with them turned to the fire. She knelt by a wicker chair, and set the red slippers on the low kerb, their worn soles to the fire. Louie, still from the end of the mantelpiece, watched her. At a slight sound she made Kitty turned her head for a moment; then she put it on the cushion of the chair again.

Yes, certainly Louie must have a wicked heart, or she would not have looked on the kneeling woman as she did. She wondered what, texts apart, Kitty could have to say to God. To pray—with her feet in a warm place! Why, Louie mortified herself more for an absent man than Kitty seemed to do before her Maker! . . . And even when she had stifled the thought she still had no more than a negative compassion for Kitty. She was not unsorry for her and her weakheadedness; beyond that Kitty was not, or ought not to have been, her affair. What was her affair was herself and what little remained of her youth. Kitty was hardly more than a year or two older than she, but she looked a dozen years older; Louie wondered whether her shoulder blades too would soon resemble the set-squares in Billy's studio, whether her waist also would seem a broken thing within empty looking folds. . .

Kitty continued to pray and to warm her feet. Louie, wondering what her next snappishness would be when she rose from her knees again, continued to watch her.

Then Kitty rose. She turned to Louie.

"By the way, did you brush that blue skirt of mine?" she said. "Oh, very well, it doesn't matter now; perhaps I oughtn't to have asked you; thank you; I can do it myself in the morning. Sorry I spoke."

Louie turned away.

These were the times when she could hardly tell what had possessed her ever to have supposed that she would be able to keep watch and ward over Kitty at all. Kitty was perfectly free to meet Miriam Levey or anybody else she had a mind to meet. And why, she asked herself at these times, should she not meet her? Where, hanging and such moonshine apart, was the risk to Jim? Indeed, it seemed to Louie that that story that seemed so to weigh on Jim was quickly becoming altogether beside the mark. The whole venue of his difficulties was rapidly shifting. What he had done had not been discovered and probably never would be discovered; what he wanted now was, not to be protected from remote and shadowy and nonsensical dangers, but to be told how he was to be happy with the wife whom he had seen fit, in the great heap of his wisdom, to keep in ignorance. Of course the remoter danger need not be entirely forgotten, but this, or else Louie was greatly mistaken, was what those scarce-heard questions on the night of that long walk had really meant.

And, in that case, what the devil was she, Louie Causton, doing in this gallery at all, with nothing of Jim but silence and absence, and nothing but peevishness and petty tyranny from Kitty? Roy, it might be, was still ready to marry her; Buck never ceased to importune, sulk and implore; Jimmy, one way or another, would be to provide for; and she knew now how little she could do for him alone. Even her desire to "show" Richenda Earle had now passed. She wanted, desperately wanted, all the things she persisted in rejecting. Why was she becoming morose, disillusioned, devil-may-care? It was a familiar question now, but as she undressed that night she asked herself again what it all meant.

She answered herself that there was no mystery about it. She supposed it happened to every woman. It meant, of course, the passing of her youth.

But, her head on her pillow, she had her compensating hour. No need to re-describe its kind; there was now added again that forced and desperate illusion, of the unity of herself, her boy, and the man she would have had his father. She knew she merely abused her fancy and must suffer for it afterwards, but no matter; if it was a drug it was a sweet one, and that it might stay with her a little longer she chose uncomfortable positions that would keep her awake. She could hear Jimmy's breathing across the dark room. Jim, Jimmy and herself—

It was against her own will that, at two o'clock in the morning, she slept.

IV

It was his voice over the telephone of the Models' Club that broke the long silence. Ten chances to one but the bell had rung in an empty room, for, save for a woman who was washing the hall floor, Louie was alone in the place. She unhooked the receiver. "Hallo!" she called. . . "Yes, this is the Models' Club. . . This is Miss Causton. . ."

At last!

He did not say why he wanted to see her; he only said that he wanted to do so at once. His minimised voice, with its suggestion of distance, seemed to her curiously symbolic of their whole relation. A telephone was supposed to bring voices near, but far more than that the smallness and the distance struck her.

"No, I'm afraid not," she continued to speak into the instrument, "but I can give you dinner here. You know the address? . . . Yes, at seven. . . All right. . ."

Seek him? No, she certainly would not seek him. He must come to her. She could give him tea and chops. As she hung up the receiver again she glanced at the clock over the little service counter. Eleven. Eight hours. . . She had waited for months, now she must wait another eight hours. She could have faced the months again with more composure.

Only to look at the advertisements in the papers had she come to the Club that morning at all. Well, she was not going to answer that clairvoyant's announcement she had seen in *The Telegraph* now. Kitty would ask her that evening whether she had been looking for work, and would hold up Miriam Levey and her determination as an example; let her; Louie couldn't be bothered with clairvoyants and their advertisements today.

And Kitty little dreamed how near Louie had more than once been to showing herself as determined even as Miriam. Miriam was not the only one who might be "taken on" at this new Consolidation of Mr. Pepper's and Jim's, whatever it was. There is such a thing, when a man doesn't come to you, as a miserable, ignoble yielding to the ache to go to him. There is such a thing as the willingness even to keep a door all day for the sake of seeing him go through it just once. After a certain time pride becomes a poor staff, and—but he was coming, in eight hours. That was why she had refused to dine with him. Your pride stiffens again when you have just been on the point of throwing it aside.

She knew that she would be good for nothing for the rest of the day; in that case she might as well go and see her father. She had money enough for her bus fares; half-past one found her at the Molyneux Arms.

Buck was in high feather. His name had been proposed, in the interests of Church and State, as a candidate for the Borough Council; and the chief plank of the platform which Buck occupied during the whole of that afternoon, descending from it with the greatest reluctance only when Louie vowed that she could not stay another moment, was that as long as England had Queensberrys to make her P.R. Rules it didn't matter what Radicals tried to make of her laws. Louie fondled his silver hair; dear old dad! Then she made him drive her back to Chelsea.

(Buck, by the way, was returned at the head of the poll, a few weeks later, amid acclamations that might well have rendered him deaf in his other ear also.)

Back in the Club once more, Louie set aside the best chop, and made a tour of the place in search of the narrowest table. The one she chose was so narrow that the backs of the two chairs she turned up against it almost touched. Lightheartedly she rebuked Myrtle Morris, who asked her whether she was expecting "a boy"; and she laughed as Myrtle went off to tell another girl that "Causton was on the warpath." Her warpaint consisted of a white blouse, low and perfectly plain at the neck, and a navy blue skirt. She was waiting at the window for Jim twenty minutes before he came.

She had schooled herself to a rigorous composure. She opened the door for him and told him to mind the hall lamp, within an inch of which his hat reached; and the hand she gave him was not gloved this time. But she barely touched his hand; had she not two whole hours before her? He put aside a cheap hanging of rustling beads for her to pass, and then followed her into the large room on the left of the hall, empty save for a piano and a few chairs, that was used for parties and tableaux. Myrtle and another girl appeared for a moment in the doorway; the minxes appeared to be waltzing, but they had come to see who "Causton's boy" was; and as they sat down she asked him, as if daring him to find any but the plainer meaning in it, how Billy Izzard was. She exulted that she could say these things and he could not. Then she was told that their chops were ready. They passed into the next room.

The table—it was a flimsy card-table covered with a cheap traycloth stiff with starch—accounted for all awkwardnesses and proximities;

again she found it secretly delicious to murmur a demure apology for its smallness. She lingered over the eating of her chop merely because her plate was edge to edge with his; she would manage badly if she could not keep him at least two hours! Then, when she could linger out her eating no longer, she asked him for a cigarette and a light—for in the studios she had learned to smoke. He gave them to her. Her lids hovered as he held the match; she wondered whether she should look straight into his eyes or keep her lids downcast. In the end she did both, looking at him first, then down. Whether he looked at her at all she did not know; the first at any rate was a miss. She did not ask for a second match (she had, she told herself, some shame); instead, she put her elbows on the table and said, without further delay: "Well, what is it?"

She nodded as he began to tell her; it seemed to be pretty much what she had expected. She listened, or half listened; she would not have sworn, had he challenged her, that her attention did not wander a little. Her thoughts were ahead of his, but a little patience—he would catch up; he would see presently that what his wife might think or what she might not think (for that was what he was talking about) was of less practical importance than he supposed. Naturally his wife must be thinking this and that; marriage that left such a thing as a—call it a private execution—out of the calculation might even turn out to be a little difficult; but she might as well hear what he had to say about it. She waited for the cropping up of the names of Miriam Levey and Kitty Windus; they duly appeared. Mrs. Jeffries, it seemed, wanted to see Kitty, and Miriam Levey wanted her to do so. Why they wanted these things was not very clear, but possibly, if Louie was giving him only half her attention, Jim was not saying all he knew either. He still considered that aspect of the affair to be wholly and solely the problem: but no doubt he would wake up by-and-by.

Suddenly she asked him whether he and his wife had quarrelled. He shook his head that apparently, in spite of its stupidity, she must still love.

"No—oh no."

"Well—"

And on he went again, still quite a number of leagues behind—the complication of his former engagement to Kitty, Evie's sense of unexplained things, Miriam Levey, her voracious curiosity, her presence at this new Consolidation.

But here she interrupted him. "One moment. When do you start—this Consolidation?"

He was toying with a knife; the little reflection passed over his massive face as he turned the blade. "In a few weeks. Why?"

"You don't intend to take Miriam Levey over with you?"

He put the knife down with a little slap. "I do not," he said. Louie had thought as much. So, no doubt, in spite of what she seemed to have said to Kitty, had Miriam Levey.

"Well, go on; I interrupted you," she said.

He went on. It seemed to her that if nothing had actually happened his overcarefulness was the one way likely to bring it to pass. Then, she supposed, he would ring her up on the telephone again.

By this time she was thinking far more of Miriam Levey's empty chair at the new Consolidation than she was of things unaccounted for between her guest and his wife.

And as for those unexplained things (Louie neither knew nor cared what they might be), she could only tell him now what she had told him that night when they had walked together, that wives must either be wives or not, must be told things or else be something less than wives. Perhaps she had not put it quite so plainly to him as that before, but that was what it had amounted to. Men with secrets ought to marry the right women. . . She stole a daring look at him across the table. He was mumbling and twiddling a spoon now. His shoulders, bigger than Buck's, were clothed in an exquisite iron-grey cloth; she wondered whether he knew that she had kissed one of them that night in a Chelsea doorway. . . And then, as he paused and looked up, she spoke. She did so almost curtly. If not telling hadn't answered, she said, she could only suggest, once more, telling. As for Kitty, he might put her entirely on one side; as long as she remained with Louie, Louie would answer for her.

Then, for the first time, he seemed to show a gleam of interest in her affairs. He asked her how she got her living, now. . . Her pulse quickened. Billy had told him, then; by "now" he meant now that she no longer sat; and his eyes avoided hers. He coloured; apparently he thought he was doing her an honour in wiping out all memory of that discovery in Billy's studio. An honour! She could have laughed at him. He little knew how she longed to tell him more—to tell him about the oyster-grey too—to tell him that for her it was as long ago as that. But no, he had seen the pearl—

And it appeared that his talk really had an object now; but, as usual, she had seen the drift of it before he had. He was thinking of Miss Levey's place, if his absurd delicacies would only allow him to get it out.

"Would you accept it?" he managed at last to ask, sounding her earnestly with his eyes.

"Steady, silly woman," she whispered to herself, brightly flushing. . .

But, glancing at him, she suddenly winced. Twice before men had offered her posts, at more than their market value, and there had been no colour in her cheeks as she had refused them; had she coloured now at the quick thought that if *he* had made such an offer she might perhaps. . . ? If so, there was mortification and despite in her colour. Why did he offer her Miss Levey's place? Was it his wife again—always his ninny of a wife? If that was so, so much the worse for him; it was time he learned that if he got into a mess he must make shift to get out of it again. There was a new little twang in her voice as, suddenly looking into his eyes, she said: "You've no right to expect that of me!"

And as soon as the words were spoken, she saw too where she herself stood, and to what point beyond she was prepared to go. She knew now that she would have taken his job, not at added wages, but without wages at all. But to the humiliating thought that he imagined himself to be doing her a kindness was now superadded that of his entire ignorance that she might be making an attack upon his faithfulness at all. Suddenly she saw herself merely wonderful to him—*she* wonderful!— she, who had thought she could spend all her life up in the clouds, be content to be magnanimous for magnanimity's sake, virtuous for the mere love of virtue! Oh, if that was all, he needn't think *that* any longer! Wonderful? . . . What she wanted was not wonderful at all, oh dear, no: merely something common, coarse, filling; nothing more wonderful than that. . . Wise mother, to have known that that was the end of it all, and to have taken, long ago, in Henson's studio, the short cut! She did not even try to check a wild little exclamation. . .

And he evidently saw something too, though what, as he blundered deeper, she did not stop to inquire. He gave a groan. "Poor woman!" he said compassionately.

He might just as well have set a spark to a fuse. There broke from her a peremptory cry.

"Not that, Jim—that's the one thing I will *not* bear—I will *not* be called 'poor woman'—"

And the rest now had to follow. It was the sum of her broodings, resentments, hatreds, dreams, desire, despair. Evie, him, herself—oh, it was not her fault if he didn't see now how the three of them stood. He knew only too well what he wanted: what Louie wanted she also knew only too well. Except to offer her a job that would save him even the trouble of ringing her up on the telephone when her help was required, had he ever, until this moment, looked at the thing from her point of view? He had not. She would help him still; but if their ships must part like this, at least no false tidings should pass from bridge to bridge: he should know exactly what it was he asked, and why she gave it! She began to speak rapidly, uncertainly, but sparing him nothing. Perhaps, after all, she said, his wife would understand; he had only to tell her that her husband made away with her sweetheart; perhaps she could bear it; if she couldn't well—he knew what was his for the holding up of a finger. . .

Then, as suddenly as she had begun, she stopped. Her voice dropped. "I've had no luck," she said, with quiet bitterness. "I'm out of it, and there's no more to say. Give me a match."

And then she rose. He might sit there if he liked.

He rose too, and they walked down the room in silence together. The bead screen of the hall parted and tinkled together again behind the great church-door of his back. Without a word he took down his coat and, under the coloured hall lamp, hoisted himself into it. And then he looked at her.

Already in her heart she knew that that look was the end. Her offer had been rejected. Whatever else might happen, she, Louie Causton, would never come between him and his wife. The woman who had those eyes would keep their looks; had it been Louie's fortune to have them, she would have kept their looks. He was a plotter, but not of amours; a carrier through too, but not of intrigues. So grave an innocence was his that probably he didn't know that his look told her all this; if so, it was final indeed.

So she took her dismissal, and then, with her hand on the letter-box of the door, stood gazing meditatively on the ground. She had wanted to be wooed; failing that, she had once more brought herself to woo; and this Joseph had gravely repelled her.

At last she looked up.

"About what you were saying—I mean that place of Miss Levey's," she said. "I don't think it would do—not now."

The man who could plan a murder but not an affair looked humbly up.

"Why not?" he murmured. It was as if he said: "I don't remember that meetings of ours in Billy's studio; I forget this too. You see how it is. Your taking the job would make no difference."

Slowly she shook her head. "I should be seeing you," she said. "It wouldn't do. Good-night."

She saw that she had missed even more than she had imagined.

And yet, before Christmas came, she was at that self-same Consolidation. In October a lofty refusal; in December a creeping back again with her tail between her legs. Where, she asked herself, was her pride now?

The answer was that that had been in October, and this was December.

When she told Kitty that she was succeeding to Miss Levey's place Kitty had certain things to say about treachery and broken friendships. She said them at some length, and then remarked that after that of course Louie could hardly expect her to stay with her.

"You never liked her," she said, as if not to like Miss Levey was an offence in itself. "And I know you tried to keep me from seeing her. Oh, you think I don't notice things, but you never made a greater mistake; I could tell you things that would surprise you! You and James Jeffries have got some game on; don't tell me he didn't give her the push; Evie and Miriam both say so; oh, you're a deep one, Louie Causton! First you come between me and Miriam; and then that day your father came and I was asking him about black eyes and he told me you could have one *without* having one till you came to blow your nose—oh, *I* watched you! And then to go worming about till you got Miriam fired and then bag her job yourself! Thank goodness, some people have better ideas of friendship than that! I have, for one. Never mind the bit you owe me; you can pay Carter Paterson with it and we'll call it quits. Perhaps it wouldn't be troubling you too much to ask you if you knew where the luggage labels are?"

So Louie let her go. The tract she received by post on the following day: "God's Eye Everywhere, or No Sins Secret," she dropped into the fire. Even if Kitty really was groping blindfold on the track of that stale old private execution, Archie Merridew didn't matter now. The question had already entered the stage of blank fatality.

V

Louie did not succeed to Miss Levey's chair at once. Somebody else got that, who made room for somebody else, who made room for Louie. And her arrival at the Consolidation appeared to be the signal for Jim's almost immediate departure from it—that is to say, she saw him for three weeks, then missed him for some days, asked (in another week or so) a question, and was told that a fall of some sort, supervening on many weeks of concentrated work, had necessitated a trip to Egypt. She hinted that she would like to know what his fall had been, but nobody seemed able to tell her. As a matter of fact, she never knew. It was merely an act of spite on the part of the stars against herself.

The ordeal by absence began again.

This time she was able, somehow, to endure it. She always remembered him when she passed a shipping company's office, with a model of a liner in the window and pictures of palms and pyramids and a sphinx not altogether unlike himself looming up out of the tawny sand; but at other times she well-nigh forgot him for whole days together. She could hardly question her immediate superior, a Mr. Whitlock, about him, and probably Mr. Whitlock could not question Sir Julius Pepper—for Mr. Pepper was made a knight in the new year. Sir Julius had altogether too much *nous* and urbanity to be questioned; he asked, not answered, questions. Such an indiscretion would have stamped Mr. Whitlock himself as a man of a barbarous mind.

The place itself, its plate glass and marble, its gilded lifts and high galleries and lofty central dome, its floes of desks and counters and the tessellated floors over which rubber-tyred trollies ran to the strong-room every night—astonished Louie. What had been consolidated, who the men had been who had reconciled interests so great that the mere overcoming of their mass and inertia must have been accounted a wonder, she never really knew. Perhaps nobody really knew; perhaps not so much men as forces had accomplished that task. In some of its aspects the concern was a huge amalgamation of mercantile companies, mostly railway and shipping; in others it more nearly resembled a Government Department. But she knew that Jim knew all about it. Jim, Mr. Stonor (Mr. Whitlock's junior) told her, and Sir Julius, had planned the whole enterprise. Acting alone, Mr. Stonor said, Jim might have done the work and then have been shouldered out of the rewards by such bustling men as Robson, of the Board of Trade, George Hastie and Sir Peregrine Campbell, and others to whom Louie had lifted up her eyes when she had kept the appointment-books for the photographer in Bond Street; but Sir Julius had seen to that—trust Sir Julius! Sir Julius could cut a throat smiling with the best of them; if Jim was the genius, Sir Julius was the impresario of the enterprise. And by-and-by, from the frequency with which Sir Julius and other potentates said, when puzzled: "What d'you suppose Jeffries would do?" or "Why the deuce isn't Jeffries here?" Louie came to much the same conclusion.

At first she was set to work with twenty other girls who, each sitting under a porcelain-shaded incandescent that burned all day long, tapped typewriters in the back part of the building that looked down on the white-tiled well; and for some weeks it was a question whether she kept her job or not. For she was dreadfully inefficient, and daily expected a reduction to the level of the girls who, with rigid "dolly-caps" clamped round their heads, manipulated the rubber worms of the big telephone switchboard. But again her improved French served her turn. Miss Lingard, who sat in Miss Levey's chair behind a screen twenty yards away, was absent one day; Mr. Stonor haled Louie off to Sir Julius's room; and Louie, following Sir Julius and a Frenchman from one to another of the spring-roller maps with which the room was lined, took down in English short-hand a conversation in French about the boundaries of some concession or other. It was a badly botched job, but it was initialled and passed; and Sir Julius, who did not so much open doors and place chairs as allow it to be discovered that doors were opened and chairs placed exactly when they should have been, looked at Louie, thanked her, and presently sent for her again. One night she had to wait on him after dinner at an hotel, to make notes of certain conversations; and perhaps Sir Julius noted the little dipping of Louie's mouth when she was summoned from the ante-room where she had been kept waiting. She wondered whether he had expected she would turn up in a dolly-cap. A little after that he asked her out to dinner, without any business excuse at all. Presently she was wondering whether she would have to walk out of the Consolidation or else to tell Sir Julius Pepper not to be a fool.

It never came to that; exactly how near it was to doing so, Louie never knew. It was her Uncle Augustus of all people who saved the situation. His name came up; Louie could not restrain a sour little smile; and "Do you know Lord Moone?" Sir Julius asked. "Oh yes," Louie replied. That was all. Sir Julius's charming smile never varied. But the case was altered. Amanuenses of sorts are one thing, ladies with private information about the peerage another. Perhaps Sir Julius was a little of a snob. At any rate, he did not allow his little gallantries to interfere with business.

So Louie became a quite superior writer of Pitman's shorthand. The weeks passed. Jim still remained away.

Nor had she any news of Kitty Windus, of Miriam Levey, nor yet of Evie Jeffries. She still, however, remained good friends with Billy Izzard. It was from Billy that she heard, one night in April, something that filled her with a vague and ineffectual trouble.

She had gone up to his place in Camden Town, intending to spend an hour or so with him; but five minutes was all the time Billy had to spare for her. He was just off to Victoria to meet a fellow, he said; if she was going that way they could go together; and she needn't think he was going to leave her in the studio to steal his sketches. "One of our heroes just come back from South Africa, a fellow called Lovenant-Smith," he said. "Coming?"

"I'll go with you as far as Charing Cross," said Louie.

Before she left Billy at Charing Cross she had learned quite a lot about his friend, Mr. Lovenant-Smith. There was nothing especially heroic about Roy's homecoming; no doubt his work had been useful, but it had not been fighting; for a year and a half he had not left Cape Town. He had now come into money, and was handing in his papers; he would hunt and manage his estate somewhere down in Shropshire. "I shall go and stop with him," said Billy. "I only hope his horses are better than that old yacht he nearly drowned the pair of us in." And at Charing Cross he left Louie.

Roy was back home, then.

Well, it made not one atom of difference. Jim away was all to her, Roy in England nothing. No doubt it was wicked.

So much the worse for Louie.

Then, not a week later, Jim returned from Egypt.

But he returned only to go away once more, this time to Scotland. She saw him, for just one moment, coming out of Sir Julius's room. He was very brown, but much thinner, and he had a new overcoat. He went straight on to Scotland that day. Mr. Stonor said that he intended to stay there for the rest of the summer. "Overwork, of course," said Mr. Stonor.

So yet another absence in her story of absences began.

She filled it chiefly with work. She rarely got home before ten, and, save on Saturdays and Sundays, had to leave Jimmy entirely to the young woman who had succeeded Céleste. Billy had left town, and had probably gone to stay with Roy in Shropshire. Of Councillor Causton she now saw little. She wished she could save more money. Jimmy was now five and a half years old.

Then, in October, Jim returned from Scotland. Louie half expected that it would be she who would have to leave now, but this did not happen. Not that she saw much of him; he did not come until eleven, and went home again for tea. Sometimes, after he had left, she or Mr. Stonor had to ring him up at his house in Well Walk, Hampstead; for the rest, he remained in high seclusion. She was glad it was so. A half absence such as this had not all absence's pangs, nor was his half presence too much perturbation; she could take a command with calmness, and she had nothing but commands to take. She knew by this time that he had a second child, a little girl, and that seemed definitely to close and bar the door against any wild and lawless hopes she might ever have entertained. And so things went on until early in December.

The thing that entirely changed their course may have seemed an accident to Jim, but a little reflection made it plain enough to Louie. She had not seen Evie Jeffries since that afternoon when they had met at the step of the bus opposite the Adam and Eve; and Evie's whole face and manner gave the lie to the story she told when, at a little after three o'clock one afternoon, Louie came upon her in the counting-house of the Consolidation itself. Near the table with the calculating machines Louie heard a clerk whisper: "Mrs. Jeffries!" Forty pairs of eyes were furtively watching her over desk-rails and glass screens. Some of the clerks even made errands in order to get a better view of her. If she wanted her husband she had only to ask to be taken to his room at once, but she stood, a slender figure in new black furs, by a waiting-room door. Then, seeing Louie, she almost ran to her.

"Oh, how are you?" she cried, in an acquired voice, touching Louie's hand then dropping it again. "Really, this place almost terrifies me! I came to fetch my husband home to tea—the car's outside—but of course I know I'm early. I'd such a lot of shopping to do, but I got through it quicker than I thought. Well, how are you?"

It seemed to Louie that she did not do it very well; the manner of the *grande dame* was the last thing she ought to have attempted. As

Evie put up her hand as if it held an invisible quizzing-glass, Louie wondered whether she had come primarily to see her husband at all.

"Really, this is stupendous!" she said. "I wonder if you could show me round—that is, unless I'm interfering with your duties? Do tell me what these things are!"

They were the mechanical calculators; her comment on them was: "How quaint!" Followed by eyes, Louie took her to the lifts; she said they must have one like that put into the new house they had taken in Iddesleigh Gate. "It used to belong to Baron Stillhausen—you've heard of Baron Stillhausen, the famous diplomat?" she said. From the lifts Louie took her to the department where the girls in dolly-caps pulled at the snaky telephone plugs. "Oh," she exclaimed, "so *this* is where you talk to my husband in the evenings from, is it?" . . . Louie had a little start. . . She answered, however, that the private line was in another place, and led the way. No, Evie Jeffries oughtn't to attempt this kind of thing; her touch was too heavy. She told more about herself than she ascertained about anybody else. As they left the private line Louie somehow had the impression that Evie Jeffries was counting the paces from Louie's chair to her husband's room.

She returned to her own place slowly. She wished Evie Jeffries had not come. Her coming seemed all at once to have diminished Louie's composure; it was as if a closed question had been clumsily opened again. "Where do you live? I should like to come and see you," Evie had said, as they had parted at the door of Jim's room; and that was odd, since for quite a number of years Evie Jeffries, had given no sign that she wanted to visit her. Kitty Windus, yes; Miriam Levey, yes; but she had not wanted to see Louie Causton. But she wanted to see Louie now, and had come that afternoon, Louie was now convinced, expressly to see her. Why? Had Jim been talking? Had Kitty and Miriam Levey been talking? Louie did not know. She only knew that she had been settled and at peace and was now so no longer.

And through it all shone an unquenchable recollection—the recollection of how she had once stumbled upon Evie Soames, not in wonderful furs, asking for her lordly husband, but dressed in a skirt and blouse, cheek to cheek in a dark back room with a fancy-stationer's son.

Evie would never forgive her that discovery.

With all the elasticity gone out of her, she resumed the work she had left half-an-hour before.

But as she lay in bed that night in her little flat, Louie ate her heart out again. She hated Evie Jeffries. She had remembered, too, an old, old slander—the slander to know the truth about which Kitty Windus had come to the Nursing Home in Mortlake Road. Was it that that had brought Mrs. Jeffries to the Consolidation now?

Louie tossed and tossed. Oh, she cried vindictively, if it only *had* been so. . . But to have to submit to the indignity of Evie's jealousy and not to be able to give her grounds for it! And Mrs. Jeffries wanted to see her flat! Well, she should be welcome. Louie would hardly be at the trouble to lie about things, but every stick of furniture in this place in which Jim had never set foot might silently lie for her if they would! Would that be to drag Jim in? Well, let him be dragged in; a woman with a husband like Jim, to be jealous! Why, with Louie ready and glad to lose her soul for him, he was the very egotist of faithfulness! He could not be virtuous without damning Louie with his grave and candid looks! She could almost have laughed at him. When all was said, such virtue was a byword, and the story of Joseph a thing for a quiet smile! Then Louie's laugh became a cry aloud, that woke Jimmy. Jimmy went to sleep again, but she was no calmer.

Bitter as spurge was that old story of hers now, and bitterer still the only moral lesson it now appeared to her to have. Oh, no doubt there was a deal to say for their conventional morality, but a pretty moral lesson it was, after all, that you repented of a history with one man only when it forbade a second history with another! And she swore again that that first history should not have stood in her way; more, far more than that was his own headstrong virtue, and perhaps that was not all either. She had been born for him, she knew it; he had had never a secret from her save those large open secrets that scarce a woman shared with a man yet; his hands, that could take life for love, were made to hold her. She knew it in her soul. . . But huge as it was, he didn't see it. He allowed a pretty face to blind him to it all. "Oh, come, come!" she had called to him on the only night, of all those nights, when he and she had walked together; and his answer had been to take himself away. When she had kissed his shoulder she had merely kissed the spot where another woman's head had lain.

Oh, if that slander *could* only have been true!

She looked at, and almost tossed aside unread, a letter that came for her in the morning. Not for a single moment had she slept, and she wanted no letter from Roy—for it was from Roy. Still she might as well read it. She did so.

Billy Izzard was with him; it had come out that Billy knew her, and he wanted to see her. "I've come back for you," the letter said, "and I'm not going to let you go this time. Do write when I can come and see you. Off out now, but do write." She threw it into the fire. Marry Roy? She would far rather commit another sin than such a reparation. The trouble was that she could not commit the sin.

That morning she was sent for by Jim. As she turned the handle of his door she was ready to make a bet with herself about what he wanted her for. She was not mistaken. He wanted to thank her for showing his wife round the day before.

His wife—always and for ever his wife.

"If you feel that you must—" she said, biting her lip with humiliation and passion.

"It's merely—" he rumbled heavily on. . .

As if she needed to be told what it "merely" was! If he cared to hear it *she* could tell *him* what was "merely" the matter with his wife!

"Oh, must you?" she said, quivering under the torture. He was playing nervously with a pen. "Must I what?" he said, not looking up.

"Must you do this?"

He looked up. "Shut the door," he said. "Now—"

She listened to him almost scornfully. Again harping on that informal execution, as if he had been right and not right, and as if it now mattered one straw whether he "told his wife" or not! He was saying something about a doctor; the doctor, Louie gathered, had said she mustn't have another shock; what had Louie—always and for ever Louie—to say to *that*? Louie clutched at her skirt with both hands.

"Don't you know?" she said, clenching the skirt hard.

"I do not."

"Then ask me again and I'll tell you," she threatened him.

"I do ask you."

Well, if he would have it. . . "She's jealous," said Louie.

The smile that stole slowly over his face set her almost beside herself. Even Potiphar's wife was probably not smiled at. Louie cut short the easy words that accompanied the smile.

"Then if she isn't, why does she want to come and see me at my home?" she demanded.

With quite remarkable clumsiness he pretended he had known his wife wanted this, and smiled again. She stamped on the ground.

"My good man—" she broke out wildly. . .

What she said she did not remember very clearly afterwards. It was spoken less to him than to ease her own breast. With nothing to give her, he still could not hold his tongue nor restrain that smile when she told him his wife was jealous. Jealous? . . .

Yes, and with a jealousy that could now never pass away! For, out of absences, silences, refusals, virtues, smiles, everything, Louie had, after all, secured something that all the smiling in the world could not take away. She *had* the secret he had feared to share with his wife. She *had* the answer to every riddle in his riddle-haunted eyes. His wife *had* grounds for her jealousy, after all, had she but wit enough to know where to look for them. But she too was hopelessly behind. She too was smelling at cold scents—telephones and visits to flats. She suspected a gross infidelity, and never dreamed of the existence of one so fatally searching that the other would have been a mere incident by comparison with it. Little dullard, how should she? Her conception even of jealousy was as limited as everything else about her; a call or two on the private wire at night, and she was found asking questions at the Consolidation the next day.

And suddenly Louie saw—fool that she had been not to see it before!—why Evie Jeffries wanted to come to her flat. It was not to see the place and its furniture. It was to see Jimmy.

Oh, if her boy could only have had eyes like a young lion!

VI

When Kitty Windus had come to Mortlake Road and had refused to sit down until Louie had told her the truth about the wanton slander that had linked her name with Jim's, Louie had dismissed the matter with amused contempt. But now there seemed something rather terrible in it. Its author's stamping-out notwithstanding, for Evie Jeffries it appeared still to live. What had brought it up anew Louie could not as much as guess, but there it seemed to be.

"So that's it?" she muttered to herself. "In that case I may certainly expect to see you again soon. You won't say anything to your husband; he'd only smile and disbelieve his eyes and ears if you did—his powers that way are really tremendous; but you'll probably go to Miriam Levey, who's rather a gift for these things, and Kitty'll back her up, and you'll make out your case one way or another. Very well. When the water's troubled there's the best fishing. *I'm* not above certain things now; good gracious, no! I'll find a reason for ringing him up tonight, and if you go to the telephone yourself so much the better. And you'll be round to see me at my flat before very long."

Evie delayed to come, but Louie knew the reason for that. Jim was moving into his great new place in Iddesleigh Gate. That would take a little time. Well, there was no hurry. When she did come Louie would be ready for her.

Did she still hope, if those waters could be sufficiently troubled, for a catch? Was she in her heart now as resolved to wreck the peace of Jim's household as formerly she had been to preserve it? She could hardly have answered the questions herself. It was Evie, not she (she told herself), who was going the right way to make a mess of things; nevertheless, she had only to remember Jim's smile to feel the tigress stretch itself within her. The loved fool! Could he go all lengths for love without thinking that a woman might do the same? Louie could not kill, as he could, smoothly burying the consequences afterwards, but she could do other things; and she was not sure that she couldn't kill too. Ten words, it appeared, would do it. Jim, who did not fear murder, feared those ten words; well, men feared one thing, women another, that was all. She had only to open her mouth where Jim kept his shut.

The only thing was that it did not seem a very sporting thing to do. Jim had taken his risks; she would be taking none. It was not much, perhaps, but it was enough to give her pause.

In the meantime she continued to ring Jim up frequently on the private telephone.

It was on the second Saturday afternoon in April that Evie at last paid her visit. Louie had sent out Rhoda, Jimmy's nurse, for the afternoon, and was herself setting out with the boy for one of their precious jaunts. They were half-way down the four flights of stairs when she heard somebody ascending. She and Evie Jeffries met on the second landing, where the charwoman ceased to whiten the edges of the stairs.

It seemed to Louie that Evie Jeffries must have a sort of lucky-bag of greetings into which to dip. She could hardly have been surprised to meet Louie on Louie's staircase, but she drew a wrong one for all that.

"Well, this is a sur—a pleasure!" she cried. "You see, I promised to come, and here I am! Don't tell me you're just going out!"

"No; we were only going to the South Kensington Museum, and I was in two minds about it. Come up, won't you?" Louie replied.

At first Evie wouldn't hear of it, but even as she spoke she had ascended another step. They went upstairs again, and Louie put her key into the lock. "You'll excuse me a moment, won't you?" she said, as Evie entered. "In there's my sitting-room."

And she herself, turning along the passage, entered her bedroom and took that old study of Billy Izzard's from its paper wrappings. She hung it up on its old nail. If Evie Jeffries wished to see her flat she should see her flat. Then she returned to the front room that looked away over the trees and houses to Earls Court.

"So this," said Evie, as she entered, "is your little boy!"

"Yes, that's Jim. Won't you sit down? I'll put the kettle on and we'll have tea."

She went into the kitchen, filled the tin kettle, and set it on the gas-ring.

Evie was dressed in an exquisite coat and skirt and an expensive and wrong hat; silk linings made whispers whenever she moved; but Louie, who kept her good clothes for the Consolidation, wore the battered old grey felt hat and long grey coat in which she had passed from studio to studio. But she knew that Evie envied her her distinction of motion. Evie's figure was pretty and "stock," charming but with no surprise—

that of a demonstrable beauty. And the acquired tones had come into her voice again.

"How ripping up here!" she approved. "Such a splendid—view! I wish we had a view like it in Iddesleigh Gate; but as I told my husband, even money can't buy a view in London. Delightful! Have you the morning sun?"

"That's in my bedroom," said Louie. "How did you come—by car?"

"No; I felt that I needed the walk. Really people will be forgetting how to walk soon. Well, at all events, he's a beautiful boy!"

Louie saw no reason why she should not say, in the simple French which may more or less be assumed to go with large houses and cars, that she preferred that the boy himself should not be told so; and then she went into the kitchen again to smile. She remembered Burnett Minor: "Voo affectay feele!" she murmured softly. Then she made tea.

"I suppose you're not quite settled yet?" she said, returning with the tray.

"Settled! Why, it will take us months!" Evie purred.

"Of course. It seems very odd to talk over the telephone, though, to a place you've never seen. Sugar? Is this place at all like what you imagined?"

Again came the ready-made answer: "Oh, it's really quite too delightful!" It was a pity, Louie thought, that Mrs. Jeffries had not had the advantage of a few minutes' talk with Mrs. Lovenant-Smith before coming to see her. The Lady-in-Charge at Rainham Parva might have warned her.

But Louie knew that already her very chairs and mats and brown-papered walls were silently whispering to Evie Jeffries. She might talk of Iddesleigh Gate, but she was thinking of nothing less than of Iddesleigh Gate. Perhaps she had been reassured in the matter of Jimmy's eyes, which were as blue as Roy's, but her own eyes were taking in everything for all that. Let them. Louie wondered whether, did she turn her back for a few minutes, her visitor would question the child.

"The Amaranth Room?" she presently interrupted Evie's flow to say. "Have you really a room called that? How lovely it sounds!"

"Nearly fifty feet long, my husband says; why, it has to have three large fireplaces, as well as the radiators, but of course there's steam-heat all through the house. It's delicious, not to walk into cold patches all of a sudden. And all the windows on one side are double, so that the place is perfectly quiet. You must come some time. Of course," she took herself up, "our other house was quite a poky place; my husband never really settled there; but at Iddesleigh Gate, he says, he can really stretch himself."

Louie meditated for a moment. Then: "What's really been the matter with him?" she asked. She knew that Evie would probably not believe she didn't know; for that reason it was better to ask.

But she got no information. It was overstrain, Evie replied lightly, and then on the top of that he'd slipped one night and caught his head on the corner of a fender. He'd slipped because he'd been really fagged out, what with starting the Consolidation and one thing and another. "But he looks all right now, don't you think?" Evie asked.

"Perfectly, I should say, from the little I see of him."

"Of course you mostly do Sir Julius's work, don't you?"

"Mostly."

"It must be great fun for you, being taken out by Sir Julius sometimes. My husband told me that."

"Quite amusing."

"Miss Levey was never taken out like that!"

"No? Have you seen her lately?"

But again Louie got little information. Included in what she did get, however, was a lie. Evie reported that Miss Levey, now at some Women's Emancipation League or other with Kitty Windus, had actually been going to write to Louie to suggest that she, Louie, should apply for her old place. Louie gave a little nod. Of course Miriam Levey, rather than own to defeat, would pretend that she had left the Consolidation of her own accord. Louie rose.

"But perhaps you'd like to see my place?" she said. "Not that I think you'll find it very amusing. But you can see it if you like."

"I should love it! Is Jimmy coming? Do you know, Jimmy, I've got a little boy like you, but not nearly as big?"

"Has he got a helmet like mine?" Jimmy demanded.

"No; but I think I shall have to get him one."

"You stay here, Jimmy," said his mother; and she led the way to the kitchen.

Evie praised the kitchen and its meagre appointments, and was then shown the bathroom. "It hasn't a crystal bath," Louie said, "but it does to wash in." She lingered in the bathroom a little; she was thinking of another bath and certain old jokes about brown-paper parcels. Then, first showing Evie the bedroom that had been Kitty's, she passed to her own room at the back.

Against the wall on the left lay Jimmy's bed; her own was across the room, with its head under the break of the mansard roof. The little built-out window, from the glass sides of which rows of chimney-pots could be seen, faced the door, and over the fireplace on the right, full in the light, hung Billy's study. It was the second thing on which Evie's eyes rested. Louie was careful not to look at it.

For in that place at any rate she was going to strike; the rest might fall out afterwards as it would. As she turned away to pat Jimmy's pillow she was suddenly fighting white; the little creature had come for it and should have it. And she should have it swiftly and without warning. Even as Louie had turned her back her heart had given a leap. . .

For up to that moment it had been always possible that Jim had not spoken of his intrusion into Billy's studio that evening; but there was no doubt now! Jim—or perhaps Billy Izzard—had told her. Probably Billy. Probably Billy first, and then, seeing she already knew, Jim. All at once there rushed upon Louie, as she passed from Jimmy's bed to her own and smoothed the coverlet of that also, what had happened later that same evening, when her arms had supported a collapsing Jim in a Swan Walk doorway and she had passionately called him: "Come, come! Come, come!"

She spoke quietly; quietness was so much more destructive.

"This is where I get the morning sun. But it's very windy. The wind blew that picture you're looking at down the other day." Then, without either pause or change of tone: "By the way, that's what you came to see, isn't it—that and my boy?"

Simultaneously with her blow she was commenting to herself: "That's good-bye to you, Sir Julius; she'll see I don't come back to the Consolidation after that; will you have Miss Levey back again, or will you try her friend Miss Windus? I don't think you'll offer Miss Windus an—er—increase of wages. As for me, I suppose I can sit again; nothing matters now. Or there's a plainer way still—"

The next moment she had called sharply: "Go away, Jimmy, till I call for you! Go and look out of the window for Rhoda!"

Then she turned and faced the woman who had taken two quick, running steps towards her. Insolently she smiled into her eyes.

"That was it, wasn't it?" she said.

Mrs. Jeffries did not fight white. The blood had thronged to her head until her very lips seemed swollen; Miss Levey could hardly have spoken more thickly. She spoke, too, in a passionate ellipsis than which Louie's own five words did not go more straight to the heart of the matter.

"Oh, you would if you could—I've known that a long time!" she cried. "Wouldn't you just—rather! You'd do it if it was only to give *me* one for myself! *I* know you."

Louie thought she rather liked her for making a fight of it. She still smiled. "Then that was it?" she said.

Evie flushed even more deeply. "You didn't suppose I didn't know all about that absurd meeting, did you?" she said, with a still darker flush.

"Dear me, no. I've known for weeks that you 'knew'—if we mean the same thing. Perhaps we don't, though. Anyway, I can quite understand your wanting to see for yourself. Miss Levey can't tell you everything."

Evie's inability to speak for mere fury was so evident that Louie, after watching her for a moment, continued:

"As for that picture, naturally I wanted to keep it. I'm sure you'll see that for yourself."

Here Evie flamed. "'Naturally!'" she broke out. Louie gave an almost humorous shrug.

"Well, surely it's natural?"

"Natural! . . . As if his coming in wasn't the merest accident!"

"Oh, I know that; but what *are* you here for then? And now that you *have* been and seen, what can you possibly do about it?"

Evie's lips seemed as thick as if a bee had stung them. She broke out again.

"'It!'—I like your 'it,' Miss Causton or Mrs. Causton or whatever you call yourself!"

Louie coolly smoothed the folds of her blouse. "By 'it,' I mean, of course, my loving your husband," she said. "As you guessed, I knew that you knew about that picture. But it's really a much older thing than that! I don't quite know how old; while you were still engaged to somebody else—as old as that anyhow. And as it's purely my affair, and even he can't stop it, I wonder what *you* can possibly do!—I'm 'Miss' Causton, by the way."

Louie had almost a genius for these last words that could be taken up; she smiled again as Evie, taking them up, said: "Oh, *are* you!"

"Well, I don't think I need be longer than I like, but that's neither here nor there. The important thing at present is whether you were wise to come today or not. I wonder whether you'd let me give you a piece of advice?"

And that, as Evie still stood speechless with rage, might be described as the end of the first round. There was a long pause during which the two women stood looking at one another. Then the second round began, with a rapid exchange of half sentences.

"Advice! Thanking you very much for your kindness—"

"Oh, please don't raise your voice; they aren't double windows here."

"Advice is cheap."

"Far from it, believe me."

"You common—"

"Sssh, ssh, ssh! Your husband wasn't above asking my advice—"

"I'll take very good care—"

"Please—there are other people in these flats."

"Well, is noise anything new here?" said Evie grossly.

"Oh, you really shouldn't say those things!"

And again they fell back, as it were, for breath. It was Louie who presently resumed.

"I don't in the least know why I should want to advise you," she went on. "I'd no intention of doing so when you came into this room, and to be frank I still half hope you won't take the advice. But you'll please yourself about that. It's this. Don't be a little fool. Go home, and don't tell your husband you've seen me at all. If you do you'll make a sad mistake. You say advice is cheap; well, this isn't; it's fearfully dear. It's not the first time I've tried to help you, and I really haven't strength to do it any more. No, don't try to think of fresh names to call me either; already you've called me common and told me that the tenants here are used to hearing angry wives, and one can have too much of that. So go home, and say nothing to your husband about where you've been. Believe me, it'll be quite the best."

It did in truth cost her more, far more, than she had intended to pay. The greater fool she, she told herself, but—she gave a quick, defiant glance round the bedroom, as if her eyes sought somebody who dared to meddle in her affairs. She would be a fool if she wished; who should stop her? This jealous little scold had fair warning now; let her take it and go while there was yet time. Louie had all but spoken her former *fiancé's* name once; with much more provocation she might forget herself and involve Jim too in a catastrophe of ten little words; and she wanted to do the sporting thing after all. Let Jim's wife take her fill of that canvas of Billy's, then, and go. Her eyes were glued to it now. As she looked Louie exulted; it *had* been so—precisely so; not all Evie Jeffries's looking could alter that fact. . .

But suddenly, as if even in this gratification and triumph lurked a peril best avoided, Louie strode to the canvas, took it from its nail, and set it on the floor by the little fireplace with its face to the wall. She had felt the tigress stretch again. To put that thing out of sight was the safest thing to do. She turned to Evie again.

"Please go," she said. ("Yes, mother's coming in a minute, Jimmy.) You see, he's calling me. Forgive my turning you out like this, but do, do go, and don't tell your husband where you've been. Good-bye."

But Evie Jeffries seemed to suspect that Louie was merely "coming it over her" with something indefinable, essential, not to be acquired. After all it was she, this shabby, grey-eyed woman, who wrote shorthand for a weekly wage, and herself, Mrs. James Herbert Jeffries, who lived in the mansion in Iddesleigh Gate. Perhaps she felt herself challenged; at any rate she plunged her hand into her lucky-bag once more.

"Oh, there's no need for such a hurry," she said frigidly. "For one thing, I'm a little particular about who I take my advice from. You needn't think I don't see you're just shutting me up?"

Louie was almost hushing, soothing. "Then let me shut you up. You've seen all you came to see; if there's anything else you want to know, ask me, quite quickly—"

And Louie, in her eagerness to get rid of her and to remove herself from danger, almost gladly submitted to what Evie said next.

"Oh, of course, if you've—an appointment," she said, with a toss.

"Yes, I've an appointment—you understand," she answered, with a little shepherding movement of her hands.

But the next moment that too had turned into something else.

"Oh, you little fool!" Louie broke out, suddenly seeing. "You don't suppose I'm trying to get you out of the way so that I can meet *him*, do you? Good gracious, woman, he's never set foot in this place in his life, and I'll see he never does! Perhaps I wanted you to think he had—I don't know what I thought—with one and another of you I'm getting almost past thinking—but that's the truth anyway! *Now* are you satisfied? Or have you got the idea so thoroughly into your stupid little head that nothing will shake it? If you're going to spend your Saturday afternoons going round to every place you think might possibly—"

But the denial counted for nothing. Evie turned haughtily.

"Who's making the noise now? And why should I believe you? I knew before I came you'd say that—"

"Oh, how you try me! . . . I *do* say that. There's nothing else to say. Do you think if it was any other way I shouldn't boast of it, to you or anybody else? Why, how *can* you know so little of him—not to speak of myself—"

"You needn't talk as if you hadn't already had the cheek to tell me you loved him!"

"Did I? Upon my soul, I sometimes don't know whether I do or not! Say I don't—say I lied—say I sometimes almost hate him as much as I do you and you me."

"Oh, very likely, the grapes being sour," Evie scoffed.

"Then if they're sour—? What more do you want? Isn't that enough? And isn't it more than enough that I let you stand there and tell me so? Oh, I'm doing my best to warn you—you'll make a great mistake if you make me *try* to get him!" She stamped. "*Won't* you go?"

Evie too stamped. "Oh yes, I'll go, and so will you, I promise you—from Pall Mall—"

"Anything you like—only go—"

But as Evie took a step towards the door a little accident turned Louie suddenly as white as paper. Billy's study leaned against the wall; Evie's skirt or foot caught it as she passed; and the canvas fell. Evie gave a short laugh and pushed it with her shoe.

The dear symbol, nay, the very evidence of so many dreamings, that poor thing of wasted smiles and sighs and tears, the pearl from the heart of the oyster-grey—

A kick of her rival's shoe was treatment good enough for it—

It was as if the hives of her own breasts and the heart beneath them had been trodden on.

Louie stepped slowly forward. "No, stop," she said.

She stood for a moment looking down at the picture; then she spoke slowly.

"You were quite right to come," she said. "You have reason to be jealous."

Evie affected not to hear, but she heard. Louie continued:

"A moment ago I told you not to tell him you'd been here. Now I want you to tell him. He may even be expecting it. You see we have spoken of it, he and I."

Evie Jeffries seemed about to say something, but "Just one moment," said Louie quietly—

She placed the picture against the wall again, face outwards. She did not display it as a taunt now; it had served its turn. As if Evie's looks had cheapened it, she no longer wanted it. She stood looking at it.

"It was the last time I sat," she murmured to herself.

Even that pale shadow of a bridal was to be taken from her.

Well, let it go.

This time it was her own foot that kicked the canvas aside; then like a flash she turned—Louie at her deadliest.

"I suppose you're aware you've lost him, whether he knows it yet or not?" she demanded truculently.

Again she was grateful to Evie that she stiffened up against her. Evie smiled.

"Oh, that way—'whether he knows it or not'—nobody minds *that* kind of losing! *That* wasn't what you were trying to make me believe a few minutes ago. Thank you very much for the tea, not forgetting the advice," she went on, "and if I might return the compliment, I should like to give you a piece of advice too. You say you could get married if you like; I'd jump at that if I were you! You see, there's your boy. Quite a well-behaved little fellow he seems—quite a superior child—and now that I've seen for myself, I'm perfectly satisfied, thank you!"

"Then," said Louie, advancing, "I'm going to spoil your satisfaction. Listen to me." Her eyes were like saucers of ice. "You've lost your husband. I'm not going to tell you how, but I'll tell you how you can find out. You can tell him what he wouldn't believe when I told him—that you're jealous. You've reason; ask him what it is. If he doesn't tell you, he daren't; if he does—ck!—it's all up between you. Do you suppose," she said slowly, "that *you're* the kind of woman men tell things to? You, who can neither trust him nor be trusted by him? You, who spy on him when his back's turned? You, who listen while a miserable little Jewess makes mischief for you—for I guess Miriam Levey sent you here? *You* think you love him? Look at me, I say"—she rapped out the words like a command—"listen, and I'll tell you *my* idea of loving a man! I've messed my life; if you were anything but what you are you'd know that if you wanted to hurt me your way wouldn't be to point at my little boy and look round my bedroom as if you expected to find pipes and overcoats there! Oh, that's not the way!

The way would be to let me see what a perfect marriage could be; there might be tears in my eyes then! But what's this you show me instead? Oh, I know what your marriage is without telling. It would take you and a woman to make a wife for a man! And what would mine have been if I hadn't thrown my chance away? What should I have said if I'd seen what you think you've seen? Listen! I should have said: 'Go, if you like; find a woman if you can whose love's like mine; search the earth for her; I give you leave, and I shall be waiting for you, just the same, when you come back and say there isn't one!' But had *you* thought of that? Not you! At a word you're off, asking whether this and that's true, because you don't trust him; and so he gives his trust to somebody else! That's what you've lost—and you don't even miss it, you know so little of love!"

Evie had fallen back against the wall, a little intimidated by her vehemence. She did not understand, but she seemed to apprehend that there was something she did not understand. Louie broke out anew.

"*You* know love! And when and how did you learn it, pray? As you learned your shorthand and things (oh, you're trying hard to forget you ever knew them!) at that place in Holborn? Why, you failed in your petty little examinations there; do you think love's easier? Something you get out of a text-book and answer a paper on? Your husband might know if you don't! *He* knew just what those other lessons were worth, but he doesn't seem to know that loving has a genius too—that one in a million has it as a gift and the others mimic it as you're mimicking people in your dress and talk now! And you call *me* common—me, who told your husband long ago what his only, only chance was! Oh, I mustn't say any more or I shall say everything! And you toss your head and say: 'Nobody minds that kind of losing!' That's your idea; that's what you really think! Why, your mind wants a window as badly as that little dark back room at your Business College. . . Oh, it maddens me, the sheer waste! A necklace of love—pearls—and good gracious, a bit of cheap glass in the middle of it! Yes, I mean you."

She was walking rapidly up and down; she struck the rail of Jimmy's cot with her hand as she passed. Evie, cowed, watched her from the wall. Louie stopped before her.

"What do you *do* for him?" she said bitterly. "What do you *give* him? What do you *bear* for him, suffer for him? Don't whimper—tell me— you've made pretty free with me—put that handkerchief away and tell me—"

But instead of putting the handkerchief away, Evie burst into loud sobs. Louie watched her remorselessly. Tears, of course—no doubt that was the way she managed Jim—

"That's no good with me," she said harshly. "I want to know what you do for your husband besides following him about and asking questions about him."

Evie's hand moved as if for a chair. There was none. She lifted her head, walked across the room, and fell across Louie's bed. Louie still watched her unmoved.

"Well?" she demanded again, after a quarter of a minute.

Muffled in the bedclothes, Evie's voice came.

"I give him all—all I—have. You talk as if—as if—I'd no right—to be on the earth at all."

"Well?"

"Oh, you do—you do! How—how can I give him more—than I've got? Oh, you think you know, but you don't—you don't know what I've gone through—you've never had that horrible morning—when I was to have been married—and I never expected Jeff to propose, but he did—"

"Oh, for goodness' sake, get up!" Louie cried.

"He did—one day—and I said No at first, but he caught hold of me. . . And even then I was jealous about Kitty—I know I'm jealous—but he told me afterwards that I needn't be jealous of poor Kitty because he'd only done it because he thought he couldn't have me—I know I'm jealous—it hurts sometimes so that I can only cry and cry—"

Louie hadn't wanted this at all. Again she cried: "Oh, get up!" but Evie continued to sob.

"And then when Jeff saw you—that night—at Billy's—it was worse than ever, but I kept it from him. I'm not like you, Louie—it's no good my telling myself I don't mind—even though I knew it was all an accident it was like a knife—"

"Oh, don't lie there like that!" Louie muttered.

"And then Miriam Levey reminded me of that thing Archie had said—but he's dead now—and I know it was absurd, but I did think he liked you. You've—such ways, you see—I expect you've been a governess or something in swell houses—I've got to learn them too, now, but Jeff says I'm really very quick at it—"

Louie was pacing the floor now, but more slowly and with downhung head. This was the very last thing she had wanted. More than ever she hated this unresisting piece of pulp; but strike again she could not; no, not with Evie's soul as it were a naked picture for her to set her foot upon.

And unless she did strike it was now quite, quite final. To take it lying down! Gladly she would have goaded her into a fresh show of resistance; contemptuously she would have told her to stand up and fight; but the child—Louie felt her to be a child, and herself a faded woman—was merely beyond all decency exposed. Louie only wanted to cover her up again as quickly as possible—her confessions, her abjectness, her appalling artlessnesses, her humiliating appeals. She was beginning to sob once more.

"Oh, don't go on like that; do get up and pull yourself together!" Louie snapped.

"I do love him—I haven't anything else to give him—except my life—he could have that—you couldn't give him more than that—"

"I could stop blubbering for him," said Louie curtly, resuming her walk.

Yes, it was final. Evie had overcome; Louie now backed out of the whole affair. If Jim liked to tell her of his own accord, well and good; it still seemed the only way out; but what was the good even then? Evie Jeffries would no more acquire love as Louie understood it than she would ever acquire the *nous* to preside without betrayals at Jim's table at Iddesleigh Gate. And if Evie had lost Jim, so had Louie. By her silence she was relinquishing him now. She saw his image recede, slowly, slowly, as if it had been indeed that ship of her fancy, outward bound, her own vessel already condemned for breaking up. Yes, the ship was drawing away. The eyes of her spirit tired of watching it; surely now she might turn them elsewhere; but no—there it was still, very small, leaning, no doubt, to a brisk breeze, but hardly appearing to move. . . No, it was not gone even yet; that sudden anguished searching for it was but a trick of the eyes; it was still there—a speck—

And it had only needed six words: "James Herbert Jeffries killed Archie Merridew."

Suddenly Louie herself sank to the floor by Jimmy's cot. Evie heard her sinking. She rose from the bed and ran to her. But Louie cried aloud and put up her hand.

"For God's sake don't touch me—go now—and say nothing."

The touch of Evie Jeffries would have been more than she could have borne.

"MOTHER, THERE *IS* A GENTLEMAN!"

It was Jimmy's voice outside the door.

Slowly Louie rose to her feet. "Very well," she called shakily; "talk to him till I come. Please go at once," she added to Evie.

Evie began: "I'm sorry I said—"

"Oh, do you want me to strike you?"

"Can't I—do anything—for you?"

"*Go!*"

She heard the outer door close behind Evie Jeffries. By that time her eyes were straining at a wide and empty horizon. . .

VII

WHAT FOLLOWED WHEN, AFTER A few minutes during which Louie bathed her face in the bathroom, she entered her sitting-room again, fell mercifully flat. Any visit would have been an anti-climax; a visit now from Roy—it was Roy—was even welcome for that reason. If she must see him, best get it over.

He was sitting on a rush-seated chair with Jimmy between his knees. Jimmy was playing with his watch. Save that the rims of his stolid porcelain-blue eyes were pinkish, as if with suppressed tears, he had not greatly changed. He wore a braided morning-coat; his silk hat, stick and gloves lay on another chair. His watch slipped from his boy's hand and dangled by its chain as he rose. His voice carried Louie instantly back to the carpenter's shed at Rainham Parva.

"It's me, you see, Louie; here I am, like a bad penny, always turning up."

Louie spoke listlessly. "How are you? I'll get you some tea."

A minute later, with a "May I come in here?" he had followed her into the kitchen. He merely got in her way, if she could be said, in her complete exhaustion, to have a way at all. She was cutting bread and butter.

"Louie, old girl," he said piteously over the bread-board, "why didn't you—tell a fellow?"

Louie did not answer. Then Roy chirped up a little, as if something might now, past all discussion, be taken for granted.

"Well, this settles it," he said. "Clinches it entirely. You know what I mean."

Louie did know. "Just take the kettle off, will you?" she said.

"So you see that's settled—clinched," said Roy, quite bustling. "Right you are. The only question now is; how soon can you pack up."

"We'll talk about it presently, if there's anything to say. There isn't, though. Will you carry the tray in?"

Jimmy ran straight to his knee again. "May I give him some jam?" said Roy; and then he added to the boy: "Oh, come, don't mess yourself up with it like that!" Louie remembered his account of the accident with the centre-board: "Jam and all the lot!" but she did not smile.

"Rhoda will be here in a few minutes, then I'll have a short walk with you," she said. "I've nothing to say, though."

Presently Rhoda did come in, and Louie put on her hat and old grey coat. They went out and walked slowly across Eelbrook Common towards Walham Green. There she told Roy that his return could make no difference whatever. "Don't talk such stuff, Louie," he said; "sit down." They sat down on a bench on the side of the common past which the District Railway runs and talked.

The air rang with the shouts of poorly clad children at their Saturday afternoon play; the common was a-crawl with urchins. Into Roy's honest, statue-like eyes tears had come; none came into Louie's. She only shook her head.

"You're only lacerating me," she said.

"But, Louie—"

"You want to lacerate me?"

"But—the little chap—" Roy said presently, with a gulp. "Will you tell a fellow how you manage?"

That Louie did not mind doing, more or less. "And now I must go back," she said, rising.

"I'll walk back a bit of the way with you. I'm not going to let you go like this."

At the little drinking-fountain she stopped. "Don't make it harder," she said. He had been indicating the rabble of children.

"But look at 'em, poor little beggars!" he said. "Dash it all, I'm not just blowing off—I *could* do such lots for him—he could ride—and shoot— and fish—and I've a corking little pony at grass now." He mentioned these things one after the other, slowly, as they occurred to him.

Louie groaned inwardly, but aloud she said: "Please don't come any farther. Good-bye."

"But I may come again? You see, I jolly well know I could persuade you."

"N-o—"

"I shall, though—you bet," Roy announced.

She left him, wondering whether it would have made any difference at all had he, in asking her to marry him, told her once, even once, that he loved her.

But she did not return home. Instead, she walked past the block of flats, crossed Putney Bridge, and sought her old Nursing Home in Mortlake Road. As a drunkard might pant for a drink, so now in her extremity she wanted to hear gaiety and laughter and talk. Though she paid for it in prostration afterwards, she felt that without some such intermission she could never get through the night. And tomorrow was that dead day, Sunday. Further than that she did not see; beyond the anodyne of an ordinary human laugh she did not inquire. It seemed to her a matter of the last moment to herself that Miss Dot and Miss Cora should be at home; if they were not, she felt that she must walk straight into a public-house, as a man might, and get herself something to drink.

But Miss Cora and Miss Dot were at home; they had just come in from a matinée. They made an onslaught on Louie. Had she seen the piece? Oh, the funniest thing! They really had had some luck at the theatre at last! The last time it had been a slum piece, all heartstrings and gutter-snipes; and the time before that—would Louie believe it!— just when they had expected to see frocks and dancing and suchlike, the curtain had gone up on a dentist's parlour! Two half-crowns for seats in the pit for that! It was almost like paying money to go and see another Nursing Home!

"But give the poor girl some tea—what are we thinking of!" said Miss Cora.

"No, thanks—I've given two people tea this afternoon already," said Louie. "Tell me about the play."

And, both speaking at once, they told her about the play—*such* a frock as Ellaline Terriss had worn!—an e-*nor*-mous pink hat, pink like a rabbit's ear, and a frock, chiffon over pink satin.

Ah! That was better!

"But where's my bonnie boy?" Miss Cora demanded.

"Oh, let's show her the new one, the little Crowley baby!"

The little Crowley baby was brought in. . .

"May I invite myself to supper?" Louie asked by-and-by.

"Oh, do stop!"

"Then give me some stout or something. I'm not sleeping very well."

"Oh, we'll see that's all right—"

And when, at ten o'clock, Louie left, it was with a sleeping preparation in her pocket. She took it in bed. It did its work. Half Sunday had passed when next she awoke.

On the Sunday afternoon she went with Jimmy and Rhoda to Bishops Park; then, packing them off home, she crossed the bridge again and took the bus to Buck's. At Buck's she again stayed until ten, and she smiled as, on the way home again, she remembered the little party to which Chaff had once taken her, pigtail and all. If Chaff had had a little party that night she would have invited herself to it; it would have been something to do. Although it was half-past eleven when she reached her own door she was not in the least tired; had she not slept until well after midday? She walked back to Putney Bridge again. There a man spoke to her. She wondered what he would have said had she stopped; it would have been amusing to know. She felt that she had not had enough amusement. She wished she could have gone back to the Business School in Holborn again. That had been amusing. Mr. Mackie had been very amusing. One of his songs, he had said, that about the Gorgonzola Cheese, never failed to create merriment.

She hummed as much as she could remember of the air of it as she walked, and took two more of Miss Cora's sleeping-tablets before going to bed.

She found, too, an entirely unexpected amount of amusement at the Consolidation on the Monday morning. Not that everything was not much as usual; the routine was the same; but a quite comic spirit seemed to pervade the whole place. Lacking a Mr. Mackie, Sir Julius, dapper and perfect in his aplomb, who had thought of asking her to be his mistress but had found a more profitable use to put her to, seemed somehow as funny as needs be; she wondered she had not noticed it before. It happened that Mr. Stonor had to rebuke one of the telephone girls that morning; there was diversion in the way in which the girl tossed her dolly-capped head and told him that she would talk to her "boys" if she liked. Quite right; that was the way to take things, as a joke. And Mr. Whitlock was portentously funny over a nought or so that had strayed into a pile of figures; and the glazed screen that marked Louie's superiority to the other girls in the same room seemed inanimately funny, and Jim himself was funny, when you came to think of it, sitting invisible there in his room with people coming and going all the time, as if the earth would have ceased to revolve on her axis or the sun have omitted to rise if Jim had not rung bells and jotted his initials on his bits of paper. And funnier than everything else was the fact that Louie should be there at all. She laughed outright when, at nine o'clock that night (she had been kept on account of some urgent joke or other), she stepped from the upholstered lift and out into Pall Mall.

Again she wished that Chaff had had a little party somewhere. Jim, she understood from Mr. Stonor, was giving a party presently, not a little one, but a large, probably a screamingly funny, one. But its humour would probably be lost on Jim. Jim did not always see jokes; that was where Jim had made the mistake; he needed somebody to point them out to him. His wife, being part of the comedy herself, naturally could not do so; she cried when she should have laughed; she had no "kick," no "buck," in her. It was a pity, for Jim needed these things, and ought to have married a woman who had them. Well, it was rather late, but not too late for Louie to go into a shilling gallery somewhere. Tomorrow, if she could get away early, she would go up to Camden Town and see Billy. Billy was a joke too, spending whole, real days in making artificial coloured shapes on canvases or solemnly scratching his copper plates. One of the best things Billy had ever done a woman had humorously kicked aside with her foot. That showed what these things were worth in the big, big world. Of course a sense of humour was really a sense of proportion. The dreadful lack of it showed when people magnified trifles so. Yes, she would go and see Billy tomorrow. Tonight, the theatre gallery.

She found Billy on the following evening, still etching, the humorous fellow, but amusingly grave too. Perhaps he had heard, or guessed, something from Roy. He was dissolving the ground from a plate; Louie wondered what the curiously sweet-smelling fluid he was using was; and then she remembered. She had smelt that same smell when Jimmy had been born—which event also, by the way, had been the consequence of a lark. She remembered, too, the wonderful, releasing sleep that heavy-smelling stuff had given her. It might be rather a useful thing to know where to find that stuff; it was necessary to Louie's enjoyment of the world and its humour that she should sleep at night. It struck her as a very happy chance that chloroform should be used in the practice of etching. She admitted that it was rather a shame to steal from Billy again, but she felt that she now needed that wonderful, releasing sleep even more than when Jimmy had been born.

An hour later she left Billy's with the ribbed blue bottle in her pocket.

The remainder of the week also was gay; so was the next week, though perhaps with a slightly diminishing gaiety. But the level was restored again when Roy once more turned up at her flat, again on a Saturday afternoon. Really she could have laughed, as they say, fit to split. Roy, who seemed to think that you could ask a woman to marry you without the—formality, call it—of telling her you loved her! It was not for Louie to spoil the sport by pointing out the inessential omission. Not that she hesitated at all now; she had only to think of how it might have read in the paper: "At Saint So-and-So's, on such and such a date, by a Reverend Statue, assisted by another Reverend Effigy, a Tanagra Figure, to a trodden-on Painting by Billy Izzard," etc., etc. Oh no. That wasn't loving—

There was no doubt that Roy loved Jimmy, however; and that was perhaps a little more serious. He had handed in his papers; he could provide for Jimmy; there was riding, and shooting, and fishing, and the corking little pony; but. . . it was impossible, of course. Jimmy was Louie's and nobody else's. If Jimmy must play on Saturday afternoons with the rabble on Eelbrook Common, well, he must; Louie would do all for him that she could. It was a pity—especially about the pony. It disturbed Louie a little. It disturbed her, in fact, so much that that night she remembered something she had forgotten about for ten days and more—the blue ribbed bottle she had stolen from Billy. But as she had left it in her drawer at the Consolidation she had to sleep as best she could without it. Perhaps it was just as well. It was not a good habit. She wondered whether Billy had missed the bottle; she would go up again and see, taking that old painting with her. That would square accounts a little. Certainly it was a shame to loot Billy like that.

She went up to Billy's with the study. Billy received it absently. And she was glad that Billy had a code, for he was grave again, and seemed all but on the point of talking seriously to her, code or none. But it blew over. He asked her whether she'd noticed him with a bottle of chloroform one night; he'd lost one; stupid thing to be careless about; must be somewhere; had Louie seen him with it, cleaning a plate?—

"No," said Louie.

"Well, it may turn up. Thanks for the canvas. To tell you the truth I rather wanted it. Merely as painting it's—*knuk*!" Billy made a delectable little foreign gesture.

"I'm no judge of things as painting," said Louie. "And—I say—Billy—"

"What?"

"I don't know that I haven't changed my mind about not sitting—if you asked me very nicely—"

But Billy looked gravely at her again. "Oh, it doesn't matter. I'd rather you didn't. I think I can manage. You'd do far better—"

He looked hard at her, but the code held.

"To do what?" said Louie.

"Well, not to sit," said Billy, turning away.

Louie felt ridiculously touched; nevertheless, much as she liked his loyalty, she wasn't going to talk about Roy. "Thanks, Bill," she said simply. "You're a good sort." And there the matter dropped. Neither for Billy nor for anybody else did she ever sit again.

It seemed strange that so slight a thing as an indisposition of Mr. Stonor should obscure the mock-sun of Louie's gaiety as if a vapour had crept across it; but so it was. Occasionally urgent messages were taken to Iddesleigh Gate at night; usually Mr. Stonor took them; but one day Mr. Stonor left at lunch-time and did not come back that day. Sir Julius himself, who had had dinner sent in that night from a restaurant, sent for Louie and gave her certain papers and instructions. As soon as she learned the errand she asked whether nobody else could go instead. She invented an improbable engagement.

"I'm sorry," Sir Julius said, "but I want Whitlock—I shall have to wait here myself till you come back. If you could go, and give them to Mr. Jeffries himself—nobody else—" That was as near as Sir Julius ever came to a direct command.

So, as Evie Jeffries had seen Louie's home, Louie was now to see hers.

She went reluctantly, by bus, changing at the bottom of Park Lane. For days she had not seen Jim; she did not want to see him now. Therefore, though go she must, she would not sit down; she would not lift her veil; she would be in and out of his house again as quickly as ever she could. She passed the Marble Arch, and at Lancaster Gate got down and walked. She reached Jim's vast and tomblike house.

At the word "Consolidation" the man who opened the door said: "This way, please," and led her along a low-lighted hall, round a staircase the outspread double wings of which resembled some huge alighting architectural bird, and along a narrower passage to the library. At the touch of a switch the room broke into a softly masked glow of light. "Please to sit down," said the servant; but Louie stood by the great writing-table, looking towards the door. Evie had taken stock of her dwelling; Louie looked only towards the door of Jim's library.

Then, as the door was opened, she pushed up her veil after all. Jim came in.

He placed a chair for her; she still refused to sit. She continued to stand even when it appeared that the papers she had brought would require some examination. As she stood, a bell, not unlike that of a muffled telephone, sounded for a moment and then ceased. It was followed by a tap on the door.

"Come in," said Jim, without looking up.

Evie Jeffries entered, dressed as if for a State ball.

Even had Louie not seen her face, the touch of her hand would have told her what had happened. Evie was back again exactly where she had been; the only difference was that she now hated Louie the more that she had abased herself before her. Many times on that other Saturday afternoon Louie had begged Evie to go; now she longed to fly herself. After another minute Jim put it into her power to do so. He rose and returned the signed papers.

"Thank you," he said, and added, turning to Evie, "I don't know whether Miss Causton's had supper?"

Evie's face lighted up as artificially as if there too a switch had turned up masked lights.

"Yes; won't you let me have them lay a tray for you, 'Miss' Causton? It won't be any trouble," she said.

"No, thank you," said Louie. "Please don't come to the door, Mr. Jeffries."

He came, however.

"Good-night," he said, as the door was held open for her to pass out.

"Good-night," said Louie.

She remembered afterwards that she noticed, out in Oxford Street again, a sandwichman bearing an illuminated board with the announcement of some concert or entertainment upon it. Pasted across the device was a strip of paper with the words "To night" upon it. The date was the sixteenth of May. At midday on the day following, Louie, coming out of Mr. Whitlock's room, saw Jim advancing as if to come in. He saw her, stared hard at her for a moment, paused irresolutely, and then turned abruptly and walked away again. She watched his back, shaped like a church-door, but bowed as if with a load too great for him, disappear in the direction of his own room. He had made no attempt to conceal the deliberate avoidance. She half expected, though she knew not why, that he would send for her presently. He did not. She was infinitely glad. Something, she was perfectly sure, had happened between him and his wife. It was the first time he had not sought her aid. Had he, now that it was too late, told her? Had he realised that it was too late to tell her? Had he, realising this, determined to take his last risk and to tell her nevertheless? Or had something happened that had at last unsealed his eyes so that he now saw with a clearness as merciless as that of Louie herself?

Louie could not tell. She only saw his face again, the face of a man suddenly old as he realised his defeat, and his disappearing back, hunched under a burden that was crushing him at the last.

§*b*

"If I were you, Miss Causton, I should leave early tonight," said Mr. Whitlock that afternoon.

Louie looked up inquiringly from her desk.

"Oh, if you *want* to make it a matter of conscience! But Mr. Jeffries is giving a party tonight, and both Sir Julius and I will be leaving early."

He nodded pleasantly as he dropped his hint, and left her. Louie resumed her work.

It was a report of phosphate deposits, but it had been worked over before and needed little attention; or at all events it got little. At five o'clock Louie gathered the sheets together and put them into the drawer of her table. As she did so some object at the back of the drawer knocked. She thrust in her hand. It was the forgotten bottle of chloroform.

"I'd better throw that down the basin," Louie muttered.

"I think, Mrs. Jeffries, that you and Roy between you put me a little beside myself for a day or two. Much better not to have things like that lying about; to have 'em's sometimes to use 'em. I'll throw it away now."

But as she was rising, one of the telephone girls brought her a cup of tea and a biscuit, and she closed the drawer again. The girl began to talk. She was Ivy Warner, the operator who would talk to her "boys" over the telephone if she wanted. Louie, as a matter of fact, always admired the skill with which she did this. A yard away not a word would be audible, and yet Miss Warner would be carrying on a flirtation in Brighton or Bournemouth under the eye of Mr. Stonor himself.

"Well, how's Harold?" said Louie, smiling over her cup of tea.

"Oh, not at all pleased with himself; backed three winners today, one at thirty to one, a gift; like to see him? He's coming up this evening," Miss Warner replied. "I'd a chin with him a quarter of an hour ago; dinner at seven-thirty, at the Troc; no steak-and-fried and a small dark lager when a thirty-to-one creeps home! He's bringing a friend, too; a dasher, Harold says; he's almost afraid to introduce him; and Daisy says she really must give her steady a show tonight. Know anybody?"

Louie thought for a moment. It was a thing she had never done before. She gave Ivy a sidelong look. Again she had the hunger to go somewhere, to see lights, hear music, smell the cigarettes of men.

"Do you care to take me?" she said.

Ivy was surprised. "You?"

"Oh, not if I should spoil sport—"

"Rather not! Do come! What a lark! I'll get on to Harold again now. You really mean it?"

"Yes."

"Good egg!" cried Ivy, glad to make up her party and to improve her relations with her business superior at the same time. "I didn't really want Daisy, you see. Of course they do talk loud at the Troc, but Daisy's just a *ti*ny bit. . . well, a perfect stranger had the cheek to come up to our table and speak to her the last time—"

Ivy ran jubilantly off to ring up Harold again.

Louie told herself it was a stupid thing to do; she was getting into the habit of loitering about late at night, heedless of Jimmy. But she had promised, and would go. If she didn't she would only be mopishly thinking, and, after all, she would be no more out of place with Harold's dashing friend than Evie Jeffries would be in another place much about the same time. Perhaps the dasher for Evie and Jim's guests for herself would have been more fitting, but no matter. She would be a dasher too. She wondered how Ivy was describing her dashing self to Harold over the telephone.

At seven o'clock she made herself ready and left the Consolidation with Ivy.

She retained no very clear recollection afterwards of the gaieties of that evening, but the little she did remember arrested her a little. She had a confused impression of the lights and tables and pilastered walls of the Trocadero as of a bright beckoning vista, stretching before her as the white road stretches before the knapsacked and stout-booted walker. She knew that many girls went that way. . . The air was heavy with the smell of coffee, smoke, dishes, scent; Harold's friend was a Hebrew "killer," and reminded her of Miss Levey; noisily he claimed the privilege, which Harold noisily disputed, of paying for everything; and the waiter contemptuously accepted a tip of a sovereign from him. Perhaps he was the same cavalier who had resented Daisy's loudness; at all events he appeared to find in Louie's quietness another—or perhaps the same—meaning; and Louie had to move her chair and to change her attitude at the table. Afterwards they went to the Alhambra; it was Ivy who cried out at the sight of two cabs and refused to go unless they all went together. At the Alhambra Louie was afraid she was rather a wet blanket; she declined to "take a walk round" and remained seated in her stall; but Harold's friend was fickle as well as dashing, for by-and-by she had a glimpse of him with another lady, who had not dined with them at the Trocadero. She wondered how Evie Jeffries had got on—or "got off," to use an expression of Kitty Windus's.

Suddenly—perhaps it was this thought of Evie elsewhere that did it—she got up, sought the cloakroom, and walked out of the place. She went home, once more quietly and steadily thinking of that vista of lights and cigar smoke and laughing mouths and gilded pilasters—the way so many girls went.

The row she expected with Ivy in the morning was not a moment delayed. It began in the lift in which they both happened to ascend together.

"Good-morning," said Ivy stiffly. "I hope you got home in good time last night."

Louie waited until the liftman had clashed the doors to behind them; then, "I'd a headache," she said.

"Well, perhaps it's better than having one in the morning," said Ivy, more icily still. "All the same, there is such a thing as playing the game when you go out with people."

"I'm sorry. I oughtn't to have come," said Louie, walking with the angry girl to the telephone exchange, where the lights on the great switchboard came and went like the sparks at the back of a gate. They were coming and going with great rapidity that morning.

"Oh, *much* obliged for your company, I'm sure," Ivy broke out, "but—"

"Sssh!" came from a girl who stretched the rubber worms.

"Sssh yourself, Daisy Dawson—time you knew how to speak into a phone by this time!" snapped Ivy.

But another and a louder "Sssh!" came from another girl, and suddenly Mr. Stonor's head appeared in the doorway.

"Quiet there!" he rapped out, and withdrew his head again.

"Sssh, Ivy—haven't you heard?" Daisy Dawson said softly.

Ivy's own voice dropped. "What?" she asked quickly.

"About Mr. Jeffries."

"No—what?"

Mr. Stonor came in again—but not before Louie had heard Daisy whisper the word "dead."

Suddenly she remembered the face of the liftman. She clutched Mr. Stonor's arm. He looked at her. There was no need to ask.

Dead!

Slowly she walked to her own table behind the screen.

The place was at once busier and more hushed than usual. Presently Mr. Whitlock passed. Mr. Whitlock was thirty-five; he looked fifty. Louie only asked him a single question: "Is it in the papers?" He nodded and passed on. She sought a messenger.

It was on the right-hand middle page. It had happened at one o'clock in the morning; cerebral haemorrhage. That very evening he had given a dinner-party; followed a short interview with Sir Peregrine Campbell, one of the guests; but Mr. Robson, of the Board of Trade, had declined to be seen. There would be no inquest. Heartfelt sympathy was extended to his widow. Half-a-column of "career" closed the announcement. The early edition of the evening paper for which she sent out had it all over again.

Dead!

Another absence!

Slowly she turned the paper and began at the beginning again.

Jim dead!

THAT NIGHT LOUIE FETCHED JIMMY from his cot into her own bed. It was not, she felt, for comfort for herself; she had a strange feeling that she ought to be comforting Jimmy. Jimmy slept, but, her eyes alternately very widely open and very tightly closed in the dark, she whispered to him.

"Well, we've got to look after ourselves now," she whispered to the sleeping child. "I don't think we care to go and see him, do we? I daresay she wouldn't refuse it, but we won't go. That was his wife, who said she'd a little boy like you, and of course we're all very sorry for her. She did give him all she had; she said she'd die for him; but of course that's only a way people have of speaking when they mean they love somebody very much. Nobody wants her to die for him really; that would only be two dead instead of one; and she won't actually die. . . And she'd a sad thing happen once before. Nobody ever knew about that really except me and him; she didn't know; if she did she might die really then. People have to be careful, they say, when they've once had a terrible shock. It's rather funny though, Jimmy, that mother shouldn't feel very much of a shock. Of course I didn't expect it, but as soon as it happened it seemed as if it had been bound to happen. That's queer—and I don't know that I wouldn't have preferred the shock."

She continued her curious consolation of the sleeping boy:

"Poor Jimmy—poor mother! He looked beaten yesterday—done—but I didn't think. . . One never does think till afterwards. . . Ah, but mother did, once, a long time ago! Mother danced with him once, and knew then—and the next time she saw him Jimmy was quite a big boy. If she could only have seen him a few times in between, she doesn't know what she could have done, but she would have done something, and then by-and-by he would have blessed her for it—she's sure, quite sure he would. . . And there she was, with some terrible people at a music hall—"

She choked a little.

Even had it been proposed to her, she did not think she would have gone to see Jim. That was another woman's affair; Louie's part in him had nothing to do with what remained now. Not that she was so absurd as to tell herself she had lost nothing; even when it is only yours to look at, or perhaps to put your arms about just once, a body counts for something; but the other woman had had nothing but that. "Nothing but" was perhaps a queer way of putting it; for that "nothing but" Louie might perhaps have given all the rest; but all the same it was not very much her business now. Her business now, like the other woman's, was to jog on just the same, the one in her empty mansion, the other one it didn't much matter where. Again she whispered to Jimmy.

"How thankful I am that I didn't tell her—something! Oh, I don't think I could bear her to die for him as she said she would! And I do hope he's not been so foolish as to—leave anything about; anything that might tell her, I mean; she can't bear what I can bear. But he wouldn't. He wouldn't cover it all up so cleverly to go and uncover it himself. I always knew it would happen if that insect got in his way; Jim wouldn't think twice about it, except how to make himself safe. . . Was it Kitty Windus who told me that about him—about his father having been an English merchant captain and his mother a Corsican woman he found dancing in a sailors' café in Marseilles? If it wasn't Kitty I dreamed it; mother's done a most foolish lot of dreaming; but it must have been

Kitty. They say they do that kind of thing in Corsica. I shall never know. . . Well, it doesn't matter. . . Poor little Jimmy. . ."

She deliberately tried herself, to see whether she was capable of emotion about him. She seemed to be quite incapable. "I'm simply callous," she thought. . . She tried several days later, on the day of his funeral; the words she repeated to herself had no meaning for her; "gone," was merely a thing of four letters, "never" one of five. The word "absence" she quite failed to understand. She heard that Mrs. Jeffries was prostrated, but quite as well as could be expected in the circumstances. Perhaps Mrs. Jeffries too was repeating the words "gone" and "never." Louie wondered whether she would marry again. It would not surprise her.

Well, if Evie Jeffries could live, Louie could live.

A piece of news, however, which she had from Billy Izzard one night—this was three weeks later, but her stony insensibility had not changed—filled her, she could not have told why, with a quite different disquietude. It appeared that Billy had felt himself permitted to call on Mrs. Jeffries, and had found her (so he told Louie) busy with her husband's private papers. Sir Julius also had been there, to advise if advice was necessary; and Sir Julius had been of opinion that the painful task would be more quickly over if Mrs. Jeffries would have a number of papers that were written in shorthand transcribed by a clerk, if a trustworthy one could be found. "In fact, he mentioned your name," said Billy. But it appeared that Mrs. Jeffries knew some shorthand, had other reasons, and so forth. She had refused to have the papers transcribed. Naturally they had not said much with Billy there, who, indeed, had not stayed many minutes; but he had gathered that the papers formed some sort of a journal.

Louie felt her flesh grow queerly crisp. This, by the way, was in a little restaurant not far from the Palace Theatre. Louie had had three consecutive nights at home, and felt that a fourth would kill her. She and Billy were going to the Palace afterwards.

"A journal?" she said slowly.

"Well, Pepper rather thought a novel of some sort; I'd a talk with him afterwards; but I suppose he only knows what Mrs. Jeffries tells him. It wouldn't surprise me in the least that poor old Jeff dabbled a bit in that sort of thing. I'm quite sure he'd have made a painter. One of the big sort he was, the Titian, Leonardo, Cellini sort—the big men, who can take an art or so in their stride."

"What made Sir Julius think it might be a novel?" Louie hoped that her new agitation did not show.

"My dear girl, you know as much about it as I do."

"And it was in shorthand?" she demanded.

"Yes."

"His own?"

"I'm sure I can't say. It was in his desk though. Why?"

"And you say Mrs. Jeffries is reading it herself?"

"Well, when Pepper suggested you—and a Miss Levey, I remember, whoever she is—"

"Miriam Levey? Yes?" Louie said, with a jerk.

Billy looked hard at her. "What's the matter?" he said abruptly. "You're as queer as Mrs. Jeffries herself was about it."

"She was queer? How, queer?"

"Oh, I don't know. How can one describe things like that—just impressions one gets?"

"Did she strike you as queer because she'd perhaps read some of it?"

"Well, I understand it was private—"

"You mean she *must* have read some of it to find that out?"

"I suppose so."

Again Louie had that curious crawling of her flesh. She hesitated for a moment; then, slowly:

"What sort of terms are you on with Mrs. Jeffries, Billy?"

Billy stared. "Oh, quite all right—I don't understand—"

"Have you any influence over her?"

"What sort of influence?"

Louie hesitated again. After all, it might be only a fear. She went on. "Say influence enough to advise her about reading that journal, or novel, or whatever it is?"

"Lord, no!" said Billy. "I was his friend, hardly hers, you see."

"Well, if it could be put as a matter of friendship with him?" Louie was speaking almost feverishly now.

"I wish I knew exactly what you meant," said Billy.

"Order me another cup of coffee. That's what I can't tell you, because I don't know myself. But let me ask another question. Do you happen to know whether there are any real names in this thing, whatever it is?"

"Really, I—"

"Just a moment. I'll tell you why I asked. If this is a journal, and has names of people in it, the chances are mine's there."

Billy was quick enough. He nodded. "I see; at least I think I see. You mean about his coming in that night and Mrs. Jeffries possibly not liking it? Well, to tell the truth I don't think she did much. I could have bitten my tongue out when I'd told her; but I suppose everybody doesn't look on these things quite as we do. You mean in a word—excuse me for putting it rather stupidly—that she's jealous and thinks she can find out the truth? Supposing there was any 'truth' to find out, I mean?"

"That's the idea. Of course there was no 'truth.'"

"Well? Why not let her discover that and make her happy, poor thing? You see, he was her husband."

Louie winced, but continued. "That's all right as far as it goes; but if there's one name there are probably others."

Billy looked sharply at her. "Other women? Jeffries? Don't you believe it!"

"I didn't say women."

"What then?"

"I can't tell you. And perhaps I'm altogether wrong. But if I'm not wrong, Billy," she said earnestly, "and you've any interest in Mrs. Jeffries at all—say interest enough to want to spare her a shock—she oughtn't to be allowed to read that journal—always supposing it is a journal."

Billy gave a short laugh. "Really, Louie! Is this the Surrey or Sadlers Wells? . . . You're not serious, are you? Of course it's bound to be painful for her at the best, but she's getting on very well—better than we could have hoped."

Louie made a little despairing gesture. "Well, I can't tell you any more."

"Well, if it's as important as all that, why don't *you* tell her?"

"I couldn't do that either. Look here, Billy, couldn't you find out about this for me?"

"Oh, dash it all—how can I?"

The saucer of Louie's coffee cup was full of ashes; she added another butt and reached for Billy's case. She looked Billy full in the eyes as he struck a match for her.

"Do you go much to Iddlesleigh Gate?"

"Well, just at present, you see—"

"I mean, *could* you go? Where does all this take place? In that library? (Yes, I've been once.)"

"Yes. At least that's where we were that night."

Still Louie looked steadily into his eyes. "Now this really *is* Surrey and Sadlers Wells," she said. "Could you get those papers out of her way—anyhow—so that she doesn't read them?"

Billy twinkled a little. "It takes a woman to do these things, Louie."

"Suppose without asking any questions, if you did I'd—marry Roy?" After all, to marry Roy would be no worse than anything else now.

The twinkle disappeared. Billy was grave again.

"I'd like you to marry Roy, Louie."

"Well. . . is it a bet?"

But Billy only shook his head. This was all very well at the Surrey and Sadlers Wells, but—

"It's a physical impossibility," he said. "And if it wasn't, I wouldn't."

"That's final?" said Louie, looking into his eyes for the last time.

"My dear girl—"

Louie rose. "All right. Then we may as well get across to the Palace and see Marie Lloyd."

Could she have said more? She did not see that she could. The chance loomed tremendously large now that Jim *had* been fool enough to write things after all, and perhaps his wife was reading that journal, if it was a journal, even then—

Louie could not stop her—no power on earth could stop her. What Jim had evidently not told her during his life she would read for herself now that he had gone.

He would have done better to tell her.

But there: perhaps it was not a journal—

Envoi

E r—Miss Causton," Sir Julius called—"can you stay for an hour or
so? No, a private affair; I hope it's not inconvenient; thanks."

He was sickly white and tired-looking; Louie's feet dragged, and
her brain was as stupid as clay. She was sorry for Sir Julius; *he* had had
no preparation; as for Louie, it seemed to her now that she had been
passing from preparation to preparation for such things for the whole of
her life. This of the morning paper was only the latest of her fulfilments.
The prophets, she thought dully, must have been very weary men. . .
But on second thoughts perhaps Sir Julius ought to have been sorry for
her. Even shock is better than foreknowledge.

For of course Sir Julius wanted her to stay in connection with this
of Mrs. Jeffries.

She had put on her hat and coat for departure; as if she walked in
her sleep, she passed out of Sir Julius's room and removed them again.
She bathed her face, but felt little fresher; then she returned.

It was about Mrs. Jeffries. It was about them both. Then Louie
seemed to remember that Sir Julius had said something about an
article on his deceased colleague for a Review. She supposed that was
why he wanted her to take down his words in shorthand. Unless it
was for the inquest. Gas-taps turned on, doors and windows sealed, and
so forth usually meant an inquest; and they would not have far to look
for her motive—suicide through natural grief. It was only that morning,
but it seemed an old, old story already.

"'*Tragic Death of a Lady*,'" Sir Julius read out from a newspaper. . .

Well, he wouldn't want that part taken down; indeed, if he had
only known what Louie knew, he would not have asked her to take
anything down at all. But her notebook was on her knee and her pencil
sharpened, and when Sir Julius had finished reading her hand began to
write, purely functionally, of itself. It was no trouble to Louie whatever;
nay, her hand was hardly called upon more than her mind; the pencil
itself did it. After all, foreseeing minds could be put to better uses
than the mere recording of things after the event. . . "Sad business, sad
business," Sir Julius was saying; and "Sad business, sad business," the
obedient pencil wrote. But Louie wondered whether it was so sad after
all. Evie Jeffries had had a sort of foreknowledge too; "I could die for
him; you couldn't do more," Louie remembered she had once said; yet

it was doubtful whether she had died for love of him after all. Call it gas-taps, or the shock of discovering that Jim had been her lover's executioner. . .

Still, she had died, from whatever reason, and she had been quite right in saying that Louie could have done no more.

It was strange the way the pencil wrote of itself. "A page of notes in her husband's shorthand has been found under one of the pillars of the writing-table," it wrote, and it omitted, as if it had been endowed with Louie's own intelligence, Sir Julius's interpolated remark, "I've got that page of notes, by the way." Mr. Whitlock had described to Louie one day a contrivance called a tele-writer; a pen dipped itself into a bottle of ink and wrote, unassisted, a telegraphed message; they were new, and they hadn't got them at the Consolidation yet; but they were putting them into some of the post offices, Mr. Whitlock had said. Her pencil moved like the pen of a tele-writer. She watched it, fascinated. It was writing as Sir Julius talked, about Jim now.

"—lived an intense crowded life too. I should say at a guess there weren't many things he hadn't done at one time and another, short of a murder or a matrimonial infidelity. Don't think he could have been tempted to do that. One woman could do anything she liked with him, but the others wouldn't have much chance—"

Very little chance, Louie thought. That, in a sense, had been the tragedy of it all. Louie knew more about that than Sir Julius; Louie had once said, "Come, come!" to him, in tones that might have brought angels from above and devils from below running for love, but it had not made a ha'p'orth of difference to Jim. Sir Julius seemed to be praising him for it; Louie was not sure that she could exactly do that; she could almost as soon have mocked him for it; but you neither mock nor praise a blind man merely because he is blind. It was funny that Sir Julius, with not very much to boast about himself, should set up an idol of faithfulness; and not just for somebody else to worship either; that was the funny part; men did that kind of thing; sinned, and yet worshipped, and called it "the maintenance of an ideal." They honoured Joseph, and winked when his back was turned. Perhaps they made much of him because of his rarity. Well, it was all the same to Potiphar's wife. . .

But all at once something seemed to have happened to the pencil. It was tele-writing very furiously. Sir Julius was reading from another piece of paper; Louie fancied, somehow, that it might be the piece that had got wafted under the pillar of Jim's desk.

"—show him that red thing on the floor and that curved thing on the door."

But now Archie in his turn seemed to have become divided. He had turned suddenly white. But an habitual pertness still persisted in his tongue. I don't think this had any relation whatever to the physical peril he seemed at last to have realised he was in. I stood over him huge and black as Fate. . . "Spare him if you can," that generous bloodthirsty devil in me muttered quickly. . .

"Merridew," I said heavily, "you'll disappear tomorrow morning—or—"

"Shall I?" he bragged falteringly. . .

He seemed to have hanged him, then; "that curved thing on the door" evidently meant a hook. That was rather revolting; these were the things about murder that Louie had not wanted to know.

"Sort of grim tale he would write," said Sir Julius to the pencil; "and of course—*de mortuis* and so on—but he did marry the wrong woman. I suppose they're together again now."

Suddenly Louie put down her notebook and pencil. Her voice, too, as she spoke, seemed to her a sort of tele-voice.

"Will you excuse me just a moment?" she said. "I'm thirsty."

She went out. When she returned, three or four minutes later, Sir Julius sniffed once or twice and asked her if she had a toothache. She took up the pencil and notebook again. Sir Julius resumed.

"What was I saying? Oh yes, about his marrying the wrong woman. . . But he was a mass of contradictions, and one of 'em was that he merely idealised her. Pretty, of course, but poor Jeffries could have done better for himself than that. She never could bear me. . ."

Louie felt no difference yet; she did not know how long these things took. For a moment she wondered what would happen after. . . and then it struck her as foolish to wonder about a thing she would know so soon. She fastened her eyes on the pencil again. It went on writing, and Louie was thinking of her loved little Jimmy now. . . She could not have done very much for him; he might even have grown up to bear her some sort of a grudge; Roy would adopt him; he would be far, far better with Roy. There was a pony out at grass for him now; he would ride and shoot and fish, and his father would send him into the army; and perhaps there was already a baby girl somewhere in the world who would one day be his wife—the right wife. "Was die Mutter träumt, das vollbringt der Sohn. . ."

It was far, far better. . .

"Well," the pencil wrote, "there's nothing to be said now, poor creatures. . . Funny smell in here, Miss Causton; I'll smoke if you don't mind."

Sir Julius lighted a cigar. Its penetrating odour mingled with that of the sweet, releasing stuff.

Ah! It was coming! The pencil wrote no less quickly, but it looked a little smaller and farther away.

"But sometimes it made me almost angry that he hadn't married the woman he ought. . ."

Louie felt her head sinking. . . Yes, the woman he ought. . .

That had been the real fatality. . .

Her lids dropped for a moment, and then heavily lifted again; but she could still see the pencil—mistily—dreamily—as if endued with a life not her own—flying on.

THE END

A Note About the Author

Oliver Onions (1873–1961) was an English novelist and short story writer. Born in Yorkshire, Onions studied at London's National Arts Training Schools for three years before working as a commercial artist, designing posters and illustrating books and magazines. In 1900, encouraged by poet and literary critic Gelett Burgess, Onions published his first novel. He married Berta Ruck, a popular romance writer, in 1909, and soon had two sons. Throughout his career, he wrote dozens of stories and novels, mainly in the genres of horror, fantasy, and science fiction. *Widdershins* (1911), a collection of ghost stories, is perhaps his best-known work, and continues to be regarded as a masterpiece of supernatural terror. Although less popular, his *Whom God Hath Sundered* trilogy has been recognized as an underappreciated classic of twentieth century literature.

A Note from the Publisher

Spanning many genres, from non-fiction essays to literature classics to children's books and lyric poetry, Mint Edition books showcase the master works of our time in a modern new package. The text is freshly typeset, is clean and easy to read, and features a new note about the author in each volume. Many books also include exclusive new introductory material. Every book boasts a striking new cover, which makes it as appropriate for collecting as it is for gift giving. Mint Edition books are only printed when a reader orders them, so natural resources are not wasted. We're proud that our books are never manufactured in excess and exist only in the exact quantity they need to be read and enjoyed.

Discover more of your favorite classics with Bookfinity™.

- Track your reading with custom book lists.
- Get great book recommendations for your personalized Reader Type.
- Add reviews for your favorite books.
- AND MUCH MORE!

Visit **bookfinity.com** and take the fun Reader Type quiz to get started.

Enjoy our classic and modern companion pairings!